# Wardens of Light and Shadow

## Shadow

### Book One of the Dracus Saga

WARDENS OF LIGHT AND SHADOW: BOOK ONE OF THE
DRACUS SAGA

Copyright © Josh Williamson 2003, 2012

2nd Edition

ISBN -13: 978-0-9885990-8-6

# Acknowledgments

No endeavor is without its high points and low points, and this journey was no exception. My everlasting thanks and this book are dedicated to my family. Without their unwavering support, none of this would have been possible. I love you all.

# Prelude

*Age of Twilight*

*5770 years since the Exodus*

**W**inter is said to be many things. Some say it is a time of cold and mysterious beauty, while others claim that the season is nature's way of culling the excess and the weak while replenishing its life-giving energy. Then there are those whose eyes have seen the greater horrors of life. These people have experienced what the tragedies and hardships of winter truly are. They know that no one can avoid its icy grasp, for it is part of the natural cycle – bringing cold and hardship like spring brings laughter and warmth. These men and women welcome the season with open arms, well aware that what it represents is unavoidable. For all these people, winter is one thing above all else – it is the season of death.

It was winter that had its grip upon the land known as Triclose, and every aspect of the realm reflected the season's bitter influence. From barren trees to terrain garbed in shades of brown and gray, it was easily enough to depress some of the most cheerful of people. Yet, despite the drab atmosphere, there were some parts of Triclose that experienced another color common to the season. In north-central Triclose, where the brunt of winter's wrath had begun to show its true colors, snow covered the land with a blanket of pristine white. For those individuals that viewed winter as the season of death, this strange beauty was a giant contradiction; while it was quite capable of destruction and death like most aspects of the season, the snow also broke the blandness of winter's garb by adding a serene splendor to the landscape that was seemingly at odds with the season's nature.

Amidst this shin-deep white blanket stood three men, the landscape around them devoid of any other visible life except for a grove of leafless oaks a hundred paces to the east. By any measure, the trio's presence in the middle of nowhere would be a curious sight, and would likely attract the eye of any would-be traveler who happened to be in the vicinity. At any other time, these men might appear to be easy prey to brigands hungry for gold and food in the barren heart of winter. Yet, none of the three feared any of this – they knew that there were no travelers or brigands in the area, for neither type would want anything to do with the armies amassed to the west and east. However, even if there wasn't a heavy military presence in the area, the way the men stood tall against the swirling wind and the graveness of their presence would be enough to steer most travelers or would-be assailants clear of them.

If there had been someone passing by, however, and they were willing to brave the cold and wind long enough to observe the trio, they would either mark the men as crazy or dangerous . . . or maybe even both. Attired in only basic clothing and light cloaks, all three were devoid of the typical warm raiments any sane person would wear as protection against the frigid conditions. Yet despite this, they did not appear to be affected by the bitter weather in the least. In fact, if an observer were willing to look closer, they might even note that the light snowfall did not seem to touch any of the three.

The unusual aside, there were signs — both subtle and obvious — that the three were dangerous. From the way they stood to the way they talked, or even the way they made a casual gesture, there seemed to be an inherent and barely contained deadliness in their movements. Yet, one wouldn't have to observe these personal habits to find a clue to the three's lethal nature. After all, their garb and weapons announced their chosen profession like a clarion call.

However, as far as the trio was concerned, speculation over how an observer might perceive their demeanor and appearance mattered little at that moment. Their sole focus was the grim subject at hand.

The snowfall was light that evening, and the glow of the setting sun could just be seen through the heavy gray clouds to the east. For the trio, the dour weather and the isolation of their location was perfect for their mood and situation, for it provided them with a chance to gather their thoughts and discuss the events of the last few months without fretting about prying ears. Wars, plagues, famine and death were rampaging through Triclose like wildfire, leaving destruction and desolation wherever one turned. And while they respectfully understood that such atrocities were worthy of grave concern, they also knew that such events paled in comparison to the bleak nature of their conversation. To their chagrin, their discussion also made them painfully aware that their current seclusion was fleeting — for they wouldn't be alone for long.

As the conversation amongst the three continued, the tallest of the group was all too aware of how little time they had. Known as Doms Luthur Gravit'nas to the inhabitants of Triclose, he stood nearly six and a half feet tall and his golden-blonde hair was pulled back in a horsetail, which left his young, serene features and green eyes free of impediments as he conversed with his companions. Whenever he spoke, his deep voice seemed to reverberate in his chest, and whenever he gestured or moved, his black-as-night leather armor – which, like his black cloak, did little to obscure a frame that was thick with muscle born from years of fighting – would creak softly. However, whether he was talking, or listening to the wisdom of his companions' words, he could feel the weight of the conversation threatening to bow his broad shoulders.

Nothing about the last few months had gone right. Too many were dead or dying, and too many were without the food or shelter needed to survive the winter. Furthermore, events had begun to spiral out of control by the time the rumors of the latest threat had reached his ears. At first, he had not wanted to believe what he heard; and when there seemed to be a lull in the rumors, he had begun to hold out hope that the earlier tales were indeed false. Then, just a few short weeks back, his companions had come to him with more substantial evidence. Evidence that only they could comprehend . . . and fear.

The knowledge of what was out there, and of what was to come, added credence to his words as he addressed the shortest of their trio. Shifting his shoulders beneath the weight of the twin, masterfully crafted katanas that hung in the harness on his back, he asked, "Do you understand your orders, Darius? We can't afford for anything to go wrong – not now, and not with what's at stake. This situation has become too dire, and I'm afraid it will get much worse before there is any chance of it getting better."

The man he had addressed as Darius was the most unremarkable of the three. His black hair was close-cut, and his brown eyes peered keenly from a plain face that sported a broken nose and scores of telltale scars. Contrasting his companions, his fighter's body was attired in gray leather armor and black boots, with a gray cloak hanging from his shoulders. Arms crossed, he had listened attentively to the conversation up to this point, pitching in only when needed or when he felt it necessary to make a point. Of the three, his years were equal to theirs, but his experience did not come close to matching that of his colleagues. However, he knew that, when given, they would listen and value his thoughts and opinions; although at this point, he could do naught but respond to his old friend.

Darius nodded, grim but thoughtful. "Aye. I understand. No matter what happens this eve – whether you do or do not come back – if the weather is with us, the army will attack tomorrow at noon. Should the weather not favor us, we are to pull from the field immediately, drawing them to the north." He hesitated a moment, for once that evening unsure if he should voice the fear in his heart.

Luthur held up a hand, forestalling the question he knew was on Darius' lips. "If I fail here – and let us pray that Corith sees fit that I shall not – arrangements have been made to carry on without me."

Darius stared into Luthur's eyes for a moment, looking for any sign – whether it be one of hope or one of failure. Seeming to find what he was looking for, he nodded his understanding.

"Good. Now get back quickly. I do not want there to be any doubt as to my orders. Travel swiftly, Darius, and may the Light illuminate your path."

Bowing low, fist to heart, Darius then straightened, grabbed the hilt of the simple, two-handed broadsword suspended comfortably at his left hip, and began the trek back toward the oak grove where they had tethered their horses. Unhindered by the snow, he was soon lost in the dark shadows of the trees.

Satisfied that his orders would be carried out, Luthur turned to his remaining companion, who was glaring at him. "Let's hear it, Damion."

Where Luthur could have been easily been perceived as a fighter, or even royalty if one had no notion of his station in life, his companion to his right would be hard-pressed to be mistaken for anything but a dealer of death. Shorter than Luthur by only a few inches, his slender, toned frame was shrouded in black; from his leather armor to his tabard, belt, boots and gloves, other than the steel of buckles and clasps, there wasn't even the tiniest hint of color to be found on his functional attire. Like his clothing, his slightly up-tilted eyes, which peered from a chiseled, hawkish face, were a coal-black and starkly contrasted by snow-white hair that was pulled back in a horsetail.

Throughout the evening, when Damion had spoken, his friends had listened as he added his knowledge to the mix. For Luthur, it was easy to defer to that knowledge. He had known Damion for a very long time, and was well aware that his friend's knowledge and experience not only belied the roughly thirty-five years that seemed to decorate his face, but was – at the very least – equal to his own. Damion was conscious of this, and knew the counsel he offered wouldn't be rebuffed without a valid reason; and if such a reason existed, he knew it would be voiced. In fact, Luthur had done so on numerous occasions that evening, resulting in Damion's current frustrated state.

Throughout the entirety of the discussion, Damion's right hand had continually stroked the artfully carved bone handle of the katana at his left hip; and as Luthur once again requested his opinion, his hand locked tightly around the hilt as a dry smirk cracked the lips of his grim face. "What would you have me say? What you want to hear, or what I think?"

Luthur folded his arms across his chest and grunted. "Don't be sarcastic with me. We both know it's not needed now. I have always valued your opinion – and right now, I need it more than ever, old friend."

The smirk faded from the Velusyian's face, and he gave a casual shrug as he spoke, his irritation began to spill over. "Very well. This is about the most insane idea that you've ever accepted into your skull – and we all know that there have been plenty of those in our lifetimes! In fact, I'm not sure all of the others combined would equal the foolhardiness of this one! What, in Corith's name, could have possibly possessed you to accept his challenge? Up until a few months ago, things have been as peaceful as I can remember in a long time. The only thing that this foolish act will accomplish is the death of one or both of you!"

Luthur chuckled dryly. "That is the most emotion I've seen out of you since Juliana's betrayal all those years ago."

Damion's brow furled in anger, a dark fire igniting in his eyes.

Seeing this, Luthur held up his hands in defense. "Peace. I mean no insult, and you know it. It is good to know that you care about me this much."

Though it took a moment, Luthur's words finally managed to assuage Damion, and he visibly relaxed.

Seeing his friend's rage wane, Luthur offered him a small, sympathetic smile, and stated, "Now listen, my old friend. While it may not be today or tomorrow, or even a hundred years from now, Garith threatens to draw this world back into a war that it cannot survive at this time – you and I both know that. I've also worked too hard to forge Triclose into a unified land, and I will not have it all destroyed just so that bastard can sate his thirst for blood! We scattered the rest of the traitors to the far ends of the world or killed them, so he stands alone and more vulnerable than ever!

"If I face him here and now, with the celums in our favor, we can stop his ambitions! We cannot let him gain a foothold and run the risk of him finding his allies! I have to take this chance, old friend. No matter what the cost – this is an opportunity that cannot be missed."

Damion sighed and rubbed his temples, conceding the point. With a hint of trepidation, he eyed the dragon-inspired collars and leather-wrapped hilts jutting over Luthur's shoulders before saying, "He won't fight fair, you know that? Even with no one to back him up, he wouldn't be so brash as to challenge you without feeling like he has the advantage."

Luthur nodded grimly. "I know, but it's a chance I'll just have to take."

The admission drew a grunt from his friend. "Well then, what about us and, for that matter, Triclose if the cost is your life?"

"The leadership of Triclose will fall to Kluvius Merandith."

The announcement caught Damion off guard. "The younger brother? Duratain will be furious."

Luthur nodded, a slight breeze rustling their cloaks. "I know. But Kluvius is better suited to handle such a large nation. He may be young, but his patience, evenhandedness, and his grasp of diplomacy well outweighs his brother's attributes. Now as for us, leadership will fall to Darkon – as we decided long ago. And should Garith decide to attack in full or seek out the others, I know that you all will stand against him."

Damion stared at him, still disgruntled by the choice of Darkon even after so many years had passed. "Darkon? Why Darkon?" he asked again, as he had done so many times in the past. "He's been less than agreeable about things for a very long time. And let's face facts – his attitude toward you has never been very cordial."

Luthur let out a heavy sigh before reiterating his reasoning, "I know you thought that you would inherit the position, but you can do more if you aren't hampered by the responsibilities that will fall to Darkon. Besides, I want you to keep an eye on him and make sure he remains true to his oaths."

Nodding hesitantly, he looked Luthur in the eye. "I don't like it – and never have – but I shall abide by your wishes as always, old friend. So, is there anything else I should know?"

A small, sad smile crept onto Luthur's lips as he pulled a thick packet of letters from under his breastplate. Bundled together by a lavender ribbon, each letter was sealed with emerald wax that was pressed with the roaring dragon sigil of House Gravit'nas. "Should I not make it back, these letters contain orders for my burial, and information I want only you to know that goes well beyond everything we've discussed." Luthur smirked as surprise crossed his friend's face. "Yes, my old friend, I've still managed to keep some secrets to myself." Damion sighed, to which Luthur chuckled dryly. "In any event, you will know when to open them. Trust no one else with this – not even Darius." Damion took the letters reverently and tucked them under his tabard as Luthur added, "Also – we both know that if things go the way we believe they will, the army will probably see things they won't understand or need to know about. Make sure things are remembered in a more . . . normal light."

Nodding, Damion replied, "Won't be easy anymore, but there are enough of us here to make it happen and hold."

"Good, I–"

Their conversation ceased almost as if a thunderbolt had struck them, a sudden and insistent sensation drawing their vision to the west. Peering intently into the distance, there was nothing visible as far as they could see, but that didn't stop their hackles from rising.

"He's here," whispered Damion, his nerves suddenly on edge.

"I know. His very presence makes my skin crawl," Luthur said with disgust. Shaking his head, he then turned to his friend, his features setting into a sad, serene mask. "I'll see you in a little while," he offered, extending his hand.

Damion grasped Luthur's wrist in a firm warrior's handshake as he stated wistfully, "Come back in one piece, old friend."

For a moment, the two companions stood there in silence, trying to commit to memory what might be the last time they would see each other. Finally, with great reluctance, Luthur broke the hand-shake and turned to the west, walking effortlessly through the snow.

Damion remained there in a silent vigil for a time, watching his old friend vanish into the distance. Even then, he continued to stare at the horizon until he could no longer sense Luthur's presence. Finally, he let out a deep, remorseful sigh. "May Corith and the Light guide you well, my friend," he whispered to the wind, hoping it would carry his wishes to his ancient companion.

With nothing left to do or say, he then turned and made his way to the oak grove to retrieve his mount and inform Darius of the consequences should Luthur fail.

Luthur's long strides carried him smoothly and gracefully forward, the snow parting before him as if it didn't exist. The air was cold, and the wind cut through the sky with vicious intent, assailing exposed flesh as if the breeze were made of a plethora of tiny frozen needles. However, as with the oddity of the falling snow seeming to melt into oblivion just prior to striking him, the winter assault seemed nonexistent to him as he strode forward, his back straight and his eyes on the horizon, each step carrying him closer to an unknown fate. So many thoughts pervaded his thinking, cluttering his mind like a bawdy common room. He couldn't remember the last time his thoughts were so jumbled and so disordered that he couldn't simply banish the unwanted musings and focus on his objective.

Until the rumors of the opposition's new leader had surfaced, neither Luthur nor his companions had lost much sleep fretting over Garith or his lot. The unification of Triclose had taken the better part of twenty years – in what many had come to call the Great War – and no thought had been given to anything but the war effort during that time. The rebellion that had shattered the resulting peace had been thought to be little more than an irritant in the beginning. As the years dragged on, however, it had become apparent that something more was afoot. Three years into the current conflict – now known as the Second Great War – there had arisen a growing sense of worry that someone intimately familiar with Luthur was behind the rebellion. When Luthur's companions finally confirmed Garith's reappearance and his leadership of the opposition, sleepless nights began to amass on their shoulders as old fears crept into their minds. What was Garith up to? Were any of the others with him? Was the Darkness they had fought so long and hard to contain beginning to creep back into the world?

Then, the oddest and least expected action was taken – Garith offered a challenge to Luthur. They were to meet in single combat, which left no doubt in Luthur's mind that the winner would hold a significant advantage over the fate of Triclose and – more importantly – Kylir. Despite the dire implications, Luthur found himself welcoming the challenge with ironic and somewhat morbid amusement. In years past, he had dreamed about being able to settle all their disputes in a fashion similar to what they had agreed upon. This would provide a simple way to end the tension and suspense of always looking over his shoulder and checking every shadow. After all this time, all the suffering, and all the pain and anguish, Garith had appeared from the shadows and provided the perfect opportunity to end it all. Then again, should Garith win, there would be no telling what kind of horrors he would unleash upon the world.

A hard gust of wind blew Luthur's horsetail over his shoulder and into his face as the falling snow grew heavier and thicker. With a flick of his head, he flipped the blonde locks back over his shoulder, a

8

deep sigh escaping his lips as he tried to sort through everything. The thought of what Garith would do to Triclose made him shudder. With all the time and energy he had spent forging the fractured land together, it went without saying that Garith would know that he viewed Triclose as one of his greatest accomplishments. Upon reflection, it suddenly occurred to him that Garith was in all likelihood behind the opposition from the start. That realization made perfect sense. It would have taken a man of Garith's intelligence and dark nature to turn a majority of the major ruling Houses against him. Furthermore, there were many factors that would have made Garith's job deliciously easy. From the fragileness of such a young and vulnerable peace, to the domses that had coveted his throne, Luthur was always painfully aware that all it would take was the proper nudge to send Triclose spiraling back into the dark depths of war – which Garith had apparently provided.

Despite these truths, the amount of malice that resided within the opposition had surprised Luthur. He had born witness to many of the unspeakable acts that Garith's puppets had committed over the years, but he had never expected such ruthlessness and such willingness to do whatever it took to win this war from the Houses that now opposed him. While their armies had met many times over the last two years, the battles since Garith's ascension to leadership had been excessively brutal, and the war had quickly become one of survival. Although the opposition had suffered heavy casualties each time, Garith's forces had also exacted a massive toll on Luthur's army. No captives were taken, and no quarter was ever given. Granted, one could not claim much honor in a fight for survival, but there was no inkling that the opposition cared one wit about such grandiose notions as honor and mercy no matter the situation. For Luthur, such acts were disgusting no matter what Age they occurred in. However, despite his angst with the situation – and much to his chagrin – the current war and all those that had preceded it were beginning to feel pointless; furthermore, in a twisted way, he knew it made perfect sense to Garith's dark mind.

Yes, this threat had to be eliminated now, before things could get any worse. If he was to prevail, then so be it. The world would be without one less villain. If Garith were to win, then there would be nothing Luthur could do about the consequences. He smirked at the ridiculous weight that rested on the outcome of this duel, and then took a deep breath of the icy air to clear his mind. There was no more time to worry about the past. As for the future . . . he firmly believed that was in Corith's hands. Only the battle ahead mattered and, as that was the only thing he could exert some semblance of control over, he turned his attention to it.

Luthur came to a halt and peered intently into the distance. He knew Garith was out there even though he could not yet see him. The question was – where was he? He had forgotten how conflicted and chaotic the ethereal blue currents of fir'gan became around Darkness-touched Gifted, and his inability to locate Garith quickly was a harsh reminder of whom and what he was dealing with. He clenched his fists slowly, the knuckles cracking loudly, and closed his eyes for a moment. When he opened them again, there was a calm about him, as if he was more than ready to accept his fate no matter what. For those like him, their eyes saw the world in a different manner. Where the common person saw merely what was visible to the naked eye, those like Luthur – Gifted as they were known in the annals of history and legend – could see the ebb and flow of the currents of energy that connected all things on Kylir. With a mere thought, he freed his mind to wander the ribbons of energy, his senses expanding into the distance, bringing every sight, sound and smell into sharper focus.

The cold became more intense, and the wind cut sharper than a well-honed blade. The frosty, fresh smell of snow became almost painfully sweet. He even could almost feel every snowflake as it struck the ground. Still, he couldn't find Garith even though it felt like he was standing right next to him. Pushing harder, he expanded his range, his mind racing along the blue ribbons of energy. Nearly a league to the north, he could see, with his mind's eye, a white rabbit franticly running from a leopard, trying in vain to escape from becoming a meal. To the southeast, he could hear the cry of a hawk as it soared in search of a rare winter morsel. In the end, no matter how far or how stringently he searched, Garith was still nothing more than a tingle at the edges of his senses.

Then, with a sneer, it struck him. *"He's masking his presence just enough to annoy me,"* he thought with contempt.

With a deep breath, he changed his tactics. Instead of spreading his mind and senses across a vast distance, he pulled them back close, limiting his focus to the ebb and flow of the currents nearest him. If before his senses had felt sharp, now everything was painfully crisp and clear. The currents of fir'gan became excruciatingly bright. The snow felt and sounded like rocks crashing into one another, and the wind was like red-hot barbs piercing his flesh. For a moment, he began to think even this wasn't going to work; but then he felt something at the edges of his senses, taunting him like a vindictive child. Luthur focused on that feeling, narrowing his senses even further, and it jumped into focus, drawing a shudder of revulsion from him.

Garith's presence enveloped his senses, and he immediately felt like he was being immersed in a fetid lake of rotting corpses and waste. His skin began to crawl as if millions of tiny insects were in a rush to cover and consume him. At the same time, the bright blue light of the currents began to fade and darken as plague-ridden, malicious thoughts began to creep into his mind – unwanted and overwhelming. Realizing what was happening, Luthur pulled his senses back a bit and slammed a mental barrier between him and the macabre aura. It was a child's trick – and he had almost fallen for it. A moment longer, and Garith would have been in his mind, toying with him like a child stomping on ants.

*"Tsk tsk, Luthur. I cannot believe you almost fell for that."*

The thought crashed into Luthur's head like a blacksmith's hammer, drawing a gasp from him. Steadying himself, he glared grimly into the distance at where he sensed Garith, but he still saw nothing but swirling snow. Cautiously, he reached out mentally and replied to Garith, alert for another attack, *"I guess it shouldn't surprise me that you would still try children's tactics. Trying to entertain me, or annoy me?"*

A chuckle entered his mind and he could almost see Garith bowing sarcastically to him. *"Always at your service, Lord Dr–"*

*"Don't say it! You lost every right to address me as such long ago, traitor!"*

*"Why Luthur – temper, temper. It isn't becoming of you,"* chimed Garith with a dry chuckle that echoed about Luthur's skull like a war drum.

*"Out with it, Garith! What are you up to?"* barked Luthur forcefully in his mind, his eyes growing grim.

*"Why Luthur, do you honestly have to ask? I want the same thing I've always wanted. I want . . ."* there was a sudden tug on Luthur's senses and he spun to the right just as a wall of heavy, thick snow blew by, leaving a figure in its wake, "your head," drawled a deep, dry voice.

Garith was without a doubt the most sadistic man, both mentally and physically, Luthur had ever known. His black hair was wildly spiked, and crowned a long, lean, sun-darkened face that was marred with countless scars. Ears lined with simple golden rings flanked his face, and bloodthirsty black eyes glared with malicious intent from under his dark eyebrows. From just beneath his right eye, a red fang was painted down to his jaw line, which served to accent his already imposing presence. Standing as tall as Luthur, two crimson pauldrons rested on his shoulders – black flames like wildfire embossed on them – as if he didn't even notice their weight. The crimson cloak hanging from the pauldrons concealed the rest of his body, but Luthur didn't need to see beneath it to know that Garith was fully armored and armed, which eliminated any hope from his mind of resolving the situation in a nonviolent fashion.

This would be a dangerous fight indeed.

"Flaunting your powers as usual, I see," Luthur said with disdain as he examined Garith's aura with his fir'gan-sensitive eyes.

The snowfall began to pick up, the pristine flakes melting with a sizzle just before landing on Garith. "Ah, Luthur, so good to see you again! It's been so very long, and I've missed you so!" As Garith grinned, revealing a set of perfect teeth and overly large canines, Luthur was reminded that his opponent looked very much the predator when he smiled.

Garith let his gaze wander before it settled on Luthur again. "I see you've been quite busy." He took a few casual steps forward, leaving only a few paces between them. "Actually, I'm quite impressed with what you've done here. I never would have thought it possible to unify this land; and for you of all people to have accomplished it. . . ." He let out a chuckle. "Well – I must applaud you." He clapped his hands mockingly, his cloak parting to reveal hands armored in crimson gauntlets, before shrugging his shoulders suddenly and indifferently. "Not that I couldn't have done it. I just would have done it with . . ." he waved his hand in a lazy circle in the air, "a little more flare."

"You mean total chaos," Luthur stated flatly.

Garith snapped his fingers. "Exactly! Such an observant boy! There's nothing better than a bit of chaos, wouldn't you say? Just think about it! All the blood, violence, carnage and chaos one could ask for!" His voice began to rise in pitch and his eyes grew wide. "We have the power to play these people like puppets! We control who lives or dies! Who suffers or prospers! Just imagine it! A land of pure chaos with us at its helm!" He pumped his hand in the air, his cloak parting wide enough to reveal crimson plate armor that appeared to conform to every muscle and flex with every movement.

"Come now, Luthur, join us. Think about the possibilities! The world and its lifeblood bends to our very will, and the mortals are ants beneath our boots! We're virtually unstoppable now, but with both of our powers combined – we would be gods!" As he said this, his eyes lit up with a wild light and the air around him seemed to glow red for a brief moment.

Luthur scowled in disgust. "Gods, Garith? Now I'm sure there's nothing left in your head. That job belongs to Corith – and I don't think he'd appreciate usurpers."

Waving the comment away, Garith chuckled. "A minor obstacle. Better yet, a lone annoying flea on a giant dog, if you will. Why fear a god that cared so little as to leave flawed stewards to watch over his creations? Join me, and together we will gain the Darkness' favor for us alone! The Darkness will make us gods the likes of which this world has never known! Nothing will stop us! Not the combined armies of the world; not the Darkness; and not even that pitiful old fool of a god you call the Lord of the Light!" There was a burning fanaticism to Garith's eyes as he spit the final words out like rotten food. It pained Luthur to think that Garith could believe such nonsense. Yet, it was plain to see that Garith unconditionally believed what he said – which was a testament to how far he had fallen.

Luthur scoffed at the proposition angrily. "Do you take me for a fool?! You do nothing but stand there and spew mindless drivel from your tainted mouth! Your *beloved* Darkness will not do the things it has promised you! It will continue dangling its promises in front of you and the other traitors like a delicious treat, using you for its own ends! And when it is done with you – it will consume your souls!"

Garith's face contorted with feigned shock. "Why Luthur, your words have cut deep. I do believe you've wounded me worse than anyone ever has. I really thought you had the sense to accept my offer. Just think about it – we could be gods. Gods, Luther! We could be– "

"*ENOUGH!*" screamed Luthur, the currents around him rippling away as thunder sounded ominously in the distance.

Garith glanced toward the storm clouds building to the east and let out a low whistle. Wagging a finger at Luthur, he chided, "Tsk, tsk. You shouldn't get so angry. It's not becoming of someone as righteous as you. Besides," his eyes narrowed and his voice lowered to a hiss, "I don't think you have the stones for it."

Reaching up and releasing the clasp on his cloak, the wind carrying it a short distance away, Luthur stretched his neck, causing the vertebrae to pop loudly. "You are sadly mistaken if you believe I won't fight you, Garith."

A devilish grin spread across Garith's scarred face. "Ah, I see that you do have the stones for it," He replied with zeal as he pushed his cloak behind his shoulders, revealing his crimson armor.

From his breastplate to his greaves, cuisses and gauntlets, every piece of the protective gear – except for his pauldrons – was eerily molded to reflect his musculature. Beneath the wicked armor, and starting just below his chin, a bodysuit of tiny scales – which shone dully in the evening light – enveloped every inch of him like a second skin, the dark coloration of which was complemented by the ebony flames that were embossed not only on his knee plates, but also on the elbow guards that extended from his bracers like bizarre, boney protrusions. Black even found its way to his brown belt in the form of a circular-seal buckle that was molded to look like a pair of obsidian dragons whose paws were locked together as their eyes stared out upon the world.

Glancing at the belt, Luthur saw a katana, which could have been a twin of his blades, suspended from it at Garith's left hip. While the sword would normally be the most obvious danger, Luthur knew that, thankfully, the blade was no longer a threat. It was the unseen, however, that truly worried Luthur.

Noting Luthur's gaze, Garith purred, his eyes flashing with malice and his grin spreading, "Now all I have to do is figure out how I'm going to kill you."

Luthur didn't offer a response. Instead, he locked eyes with Garith, daring him to move.

For a time, the two just stood there staring each other down. To an observer, it might have appeared to be something from a storybook – the gallant hero standing toe-to-toe with the evil villain. And if not for the dire circumstances surrounding the two, the sight might have almost been comical. However, the intensity of their eyes and the deadly promise of their posture could be mistaken for nothing but reality. Still, neither of them appeared to want to make the first move.

As if the land was impatient for them to begin, the wind began to howl about them and another clap of thunder sounded to the east. And then, almost as if on cue, the first move was made. It wasn't a physical move by either man; instead, Luthur saw Garith's aura surge and felt it hammer away at his mental barrier as it grew in strength. It had been so long since Luthur had felt such a flow of power aimed at him that it was awe-inspiring, and even a little overwhelming. However, Luthur maintained his composure and, knowing what was to come, he mentally braced himself for it. The currents of fir'gan began to pulse and swirl violently around Garith as he drew in power, promising destruction untold. Suddenly, before Luthur's eyes, Garith's aura burst to life, sending waves of pulsating crimson power dancing wildly about its master. Like a torrent of blood, the excess power flowed chaotically from Garith's feet toward the sky, sudden flashes of energy bursting to life about him like a thunderbolt, only to fade away the next instant.

As the air between them crackled with the power that the aura held, and the snow at Garith's feet began to melt to nothing from the heat pulsing from him, a resigned sigh escaped Luthur's lips. "I guess we can't settle this like normal men, can we?"

Howling with laughter, Garith slid his sword free of its scabbard and readied it, the polished bluesteel turning blood-red in the light of the crimson aura. "Oh please, Luthur – that would be so boring. This adds a twist and a bit of excitement to it, don't you think?"

Luthur nodded grimly. "Very well, then. So be it."

Focusing his mind inward, he blocked out everything his senses were screaming at him, and searched for the core of power that resided within all of those like him. It took but a moment before he found it, a tiny speck of light he felt pulsing in his heart, and latched on to it as if his life depended on it. As his face contorted with rage, Luthur opened his mind and body to the power. Bringing it forth, his aura exploded into existence, sending oscillating waves of emerald energy dancing about him like barely contained wildfire. Like Garith's aura, bursts of energy flared to life, crackling in the air before fading away. And with both auras putting off enormous amounts of heat and energy, the ground around the combatants was soon clear of snow, leaving only brown grass and quickly thawing turf beneath their feet.

Garith glared at him with a small smile, impressed by the display. "Well done, Luthur. I had no idea you had grown so much in strength, and gained so much control of your fir'gan. I didn't think someone as averse to using their power would be able to accomplish what you have. I do hope you won't disappoint me."

Luthur spit on the ground in disgust. Taking a step forward and removing his katanas from his back, he pointed the bluesteel blade of his left-hand katana at his ancient opponent. "Let's get this over with. I won't tolerate your presence here any longer. This ends now!"

Garith lowered himself into a crouch, his blade held low and pointed behind him, as he let out a chilling laugh. "My sentiments exactly," he hissed, years of animosity dripping from each word.

Frozen earth exploding from under their feet, both men let out bloodcurdling screams and charged forward, bringing their katanas about in vicious arcs that were meant to rend each other open. The trio of blades met with a thunderous crash, bright white light exploding from the contact, and each man's aura flaring with the impact. Luthur broke from the deadlock immediately, dropping low and directing a sweeping kick at Garith's ankles. Anticipating the move, Garith launched himself into a high backflip and landed nimbly, cracks spreading from the impact.

Without breaking his momentum, Garith charged forward, thrusting with all his might at Luthur's stomach. Intercepting the attack, Luthur pushed it wide with his left-hand blade and brought his right-hand katana around for a decapitating blow. Having recovered swiftly from the overextended thrust, Garith caught the descending blade on his bracer, his aura flaring slightly on contact. Grinning, he shoved the blade aside and extended his hand toward Luthur's chest, blasting him squarely with a glowing crimson ball of fir'gan. Caught off guard by the move, Luthur barely managed to gather enough of his power to dampen the blow before he was blasted off his feet and into the air. However, being a veteran of countless battles, he recovered quickly, righted himself, and landed on his feet.

By the time Luthur's feet touched the ground, Garith was charging again. Thinking quickly, Luthur aimed his hand at a patch of snow in his opponent's path and released a fireball at it. The snow vaporized on contact, raising a thick wall of steam. It didn't surprise him when he saw Garith soaring over the top of the vapor barrier with his sword held high – in fact, he had been counting on it. Without a second thought, Luthur let out a scream and slammed a blast of air into his airborne opponent, the hardened currents hammering Garith a good seventy paces backward through the air. Unwilling to relinquish his advantage, Luthur followed the blast with a charge toward where his opponent would land. Garith, on the other hand, had not been fazed by the blast.

Rotating deftly in midflight, he landed hard on his feet, flinging chunks of frozen earth into the air. Nimbly, he sidestepped Luthur's twin upward cuts and brought his own sword around, intent on decapitating his opponent. Sensing the attack, Luthur dropped low and rolled forward just under the blade. As he came to his feet, he turned just in time to sidestep an uncontrolled thrust. Garith stumbled by and felt Luthur ram an elbow viciously into his back, the force of the blow driving him nearly a pace into the ground, chunks of earth exploding from the impact. They both knew the blow would have killed a normal human – but they were far from ordinary. With that thought in mind, Luthur brought his swords up and down quickly, intent on ending the fight. Garith, however, had other plans.

Before the blows could land, he gathered the air around him and shoved it down, angling so that it propelled him up and away from the attack. Luthur's blades bit deeply, but harmlessly, into the ground, shattering the earth around Garith's indentation. Yanking his blades free, Luthur looked up in time to see Garith launching a fireball at him. Bracing himself, he extended his swords as if he was trying to catch the burning projectile. His aura flared brightly as he caught the flaming mass and it exploded against his crossed swords, shoving him backward. The air around him sizzled, and the snow on the ground evaporated as he slid back nearly sixty paces, his feet digging trenches in the frozen earth.

As the blast dissipated, his backward trip came to a halt. Other than a few scorch marks, Luthur appeared unharmed. However, Garith had intended the blast as a distraction, not a fatal blow. Following the fireball with inhuman speed, Garith held his sword high, ready to deliver the killing stroke. Too late, Luthur saw Garith closing in, his blade glinting in the dying sunlight peaking through the clouds. With no time to dodge, Luthur brought his right-hand sword down and caught Garith's blade. Rolling his katana under it, he lifted the locked blades in a futile attempt to force the attack over his shoulder. Time seemed to slow down as he realized that Garith had drawn too close for the parry. Wide-eyed, he watched the swords creep achingly upward until Garith's blade bit hard and deep into his left shoulder, the illusion violently shattered by the blossoming pain. Spinning away, Luthur pressed a fist against the oozing wound, a slight hiss escaping his lips.

Garith chuckled and brought his katana to his mouth. Licking the fresh blood from the blade, he then purred, "Ummmm – sweet. You have no idea how long I've waited for this moment."

Removing his fist from the wound, Luthur saw that the gash had already healed itself. However, something was definitely afoot. While Garith's katana had done no more physical damage than any sword would have, he had felt a subtle flux in the currents within him. It was a mild and weak shift, to be sure, but it was enough to set off alarm bells in his mind. Directing a scowl at Garith, he tested his arm. "Glad you are enjoying it, because that will be the last bit of satisfaction you will ever have from me," he spit, easily hiding his growing trepidation.

"Oh, I think your death will provide me ten lifetimes worth of satisfaction." He glanced at Luthur's shoulder and smirked. "Last chance, Luthur. I'd prefer to have you on my side."

Clearing his mind, Luthur turned sideways, his left-hand katana held high and pointed toward Garith, and his right blade held in a guard position. "Better that no one should have my strength than for it to fall into your hands."

Garith opened his stance as well, and raised his katana to eye level, aiming both its point and his free hand at his opponent. A knowing and menacing smile crept onto his lips. "Oh, trust me – I don't plan to destroy your crystal. I have plans for it."

Luthur's eyes darkened and his face contorted grimly.

"Good," Garith stated with satisfaction. "I see you understand. Now, shall we dispense with the warm-up and do this for real?"

With the pieces of the puzzle beginning to take shape in his mind, Luthur growled and charged in response.

*

Known to all as the Jade Dragons, Luthur's army was camped a full league to the east of the dueling pair. The sea of canvas tents covered a third of a league of frozen earth. Organized into smaller camps by House, tents were arranged in neat and orderly rows, providing easy thoroughfare for both foot and mounted traffic. Guards diligently walked their patrols while other camp hands attended to cookfires or the repair of weapons and armor. However, other than the required duties needed to keep the camp functioning smoothly, it had become a hauntingly silent evening that saw some of the troops sitting in contemplative silence, and others whispering prayers of fortune for their leader as he engaged in honorable combat.

Yet, on the western side of camp, there were some men and women that had ceased their duties and musings to cautiously eye the storm clouds flowing to the west. The dark clouds were building quickly, and the thunder and lightning erupting from them in the distance was haunting. There were some troops that went as far as to make gestures to ward off evil spirits. Few of them, if any, had ever seen a thunderstorm brewing in the middle of snowfall; thus, it was easy to understand how such an anomaly could be construed as a bad omen. For those, however, that knew what the crashes and booms were, the sounds and growing energy behind it brought fear to their hearts.

Damion and Darius, their horses in tow, stood well beyond the hearing of the nearest spectators, their eyes and thoughts fixed on the horizon.

"By Corith, their strength is incredible. To feel it that clearly from here is just. . . ." Darius shook his head in disbelief.

Damion nodded in agreement. "I had not realized their powers had grown so much over the years." He touched the hilt of his katana nervously. "I'm beginning to believe that leaving him to this alone was an even worse idea than I had originally thought."

Darius shook his head in both agreement and disbelief. "I'm not going to argue with you, but they're exerting so much fir'gan that I can barely separate one from the other. It wouldn't surprise me if the currents around them are raging with enough force to rend a person into tiny pieces."

Another thunderous boom rocked the air, drawing Damion's attention. He concentrated for a moment, then smirked. "Well now . . . that is interesting."

Darius eyed him quizzically. "What is it?"

Always the teacher, Damion responded with a request instead of an answer. "Focus your mind, and tell me what you feel."

Darius chuckled and narrowed his focus, trying to separate the two power sources from the swirling mass of fir'gan. Nowhere near as skilled at sensing others of their kind as Damion was, it took him a moment to get a read on the battle. When he finally did separate the two powers, it brought a smile to his face. "Garith is pushing his limits . . . and it appears that Luthur is holding back and wining!"

Patting Darius on the back, he motioned toward the encampment. "Let's find Darkon and see what we can do about making sure this battle is remembered in as much of a normal light as possible."

Though still somewhat worried about the outcome of the duel, they began to make their way back to camp. As they neared the first line of pickets, two men broke from the throng and headed toward them. One man was short, and clad in simple leather armor and a conical helmet. A badge of black embroidered with five golden stars, signifying his allegiance to House Merandith, was sewn onto the left breast of his armor. His face was adorned with a thick black beard, and tired brown eyes that stared from beneath a helm that was failing miserably to protect his nose, which was splayed at an odd angle due to having been broken one too many times. While his grizzled appearance was quite eye-catching even amongst all the veteran soldiers, his companion's exotic appearance managed to make him seem practically normal.

Nearly as tall as Damion, the darlion was a rare sight on Triclose. Umber fur, nearly short enough to be mistaken for skin, covered his entire body, while the long white locks hanging loosely from his head served as his hair. His ears, which swept back from his head to gentle points, were capped with fur that was a match for his hair. Crystalline-blue eyes, with dark vertical slits for pupils, peered at Damion and Darius from astride his broad, flat nose. Befitting his feral appearance, there was a slight hint of elongated canines peeking from between his thin lips. His striking facade was further reinforced by elongated proportions that were reflected in his longer-than-normal strides, which granted him a grace that bespoke of beauty and deadliness. Watching him approach, Damion could only wonder at the mysteries the man was hiding.

When the two groups met just outside the picket lines, Merandith's man bowed to Damion and Darius before saying, "Doms Captains Delverius and Calthis," Damion and Darius nodded in recognition of the respective names they were known by in the army, "Doms Merandith would like a word with you when you have a moment."

Damion, whom the messenger referred to as Delverius, nodded again. "Tell Duratain we will speak with him as soon as Doms Gravit'nas returns from his duel."

The man saluted, fist to chest, and bowed before hurrying off to deliver the message.

Once the messenger was out of earshot, Damion led his two companions away from the picket line and prying ears. "I take it everyone's attention is focused on the show?" he asked as another boom rattled across the air, causing Damion and Darius' horses to snort and paw nervously at the ground.

Darkon hooked his long thumbs behind his belt. "There's some that aren't watching," he replied in his somewhat arrogant, baritone voice. "However, those are either asleep or attending to duties that don't grant them a line of sight." He paused and his eyes became unfocused for a brief moment. "I see Luthur is winning," he said as his eyes regained their focus. "Does he have any orders for us?"

"For right now, he wants everyone to remember this incident as just a normal duel," Damion responded.

Darkon shrugged nonchalantly. "There are enough of us here to accomplish that. Is there anything of real importance?"

Damion eyed him suspiciously for a moment. Was that merely disdain, or arrogantly casual disregard for the complexity of manipulating the minds of this many people? He let the notion go and simply shook his head. "Not right now. We'll know more when—"

A thunderous, earsplitting boom sounded in the distance, drawing everyone's attention and spooking all the animals in the camp. Men and women throughout the encampment either stopped what they were doing to watch or began moving toward the western side of camp as a large dark dome of energy appeared on the horizon, growing rapidly before suddenly vanishing.

"Dear Corith! What was that?!" cried Darius as he fought to settle his horse.

"Weaponized transformation," Damion muttered, his hopes quickly turning to fear as he reached out with his senses, attempting to discern what was happening even as he calmed his mount. At first, it was hard to sort through all the excess fir'gan that had been released. The flood of power almost overwhelmed him even at this distance, but his disciplined mind pushed forward and began to make sense of the currents. To his horror, a cold dread gripped his heart as he began to separate the power sources. Now, instead of two sources, he detected ten distinctly new signatures, two of which seemed almost in harmony with each other. As he had feared, Garith wasn't fighting even remotely fair. Cursing himself, he swung up into the saddle of his nervous mount and signaled for Darius to do the same.

"What is it?" asked Darkon, unable to make sense of the mass of power.

"There's ten new sources out there – and Luthur just released all his fir'gan!"

Darkon's eyes went wide as he cried incredulously, "Impossible! We've been keeping watch ever since we scattered them to the far reaches! We would have known if they moved!"

"I know!" Damion growled in frustration as he swung his horse about violently, drawing angry complaints from her. "Darkon – get the others and alter the army's memories! Don't let anyone follow! Darius – with me!" They then spurred their mounts to a full gallop and were speeding across the snow-covered land with all haste.

Darkon stared at his companions' retreating backs with cold, emotionless eyes as his companions left him to contend with an army of memories.


As soon as they were out of visible range of the camp, they swiftly dismounted. What they felt in the distance was sinking their hearts, and it was becoming obvious that they might not make it in time.

Loosening his katana in its scabbard, Damion stated gravely, "Not too fast. If they sense us, they'll be on us before we can get our guard up."

Darius tossed his cloak onto his saddle and readied his sword before nodding grimly. "I'm ready."

The two eyed each other one last time before they each dug a foot in and seemed to vanish, shattered earth erupting from where they had stood, startling the horses. The land became a blur as they picked up speed. To an outside observer, they would have simply seen a spray of snow and felt the wind from their passing. Still, even as they closed the distance, Damion couldn't help but feel that they would be too late.

*

The snow had melted and the grass had been incinerated, leaving the barren terrain with only smoking, muddy craters as décor. The smoldering carcasses of a few animals unlucky enough to have wandered into the battle dotted the landscape. Just from examining the extent of the damage, one would think that whatever or whoever had caused it could not have survived its own destructive rampage. However, in this case, the two men responsible for the carnage were very much alive.

Luthur parried a downward cut before stepping back and slamming his foot into Garith's face. Bones crunched and Garith stumbled backward, blood trickling from his mouth and nose. When Garith made no move to advance, Luthur took the opportunity to catch his breath. Both men showed obvious and violent signs of their struggle. Luthur's body armor had been shredded and his tattered shirt hung from his belt. Cuts and bruises marred his torso like a second skin, and his right eye was beginning to swell and close up. His aura, however, was still pulsing strongly and the wounds were slowly healing – albeit, much slower than they should have, which added to his unease.

Where most men would be dying from the beating he had taken, the injuries Garith had sustained, on the other hand, would have killed a normal man long ago.

His left pauldron had been shattered, leaving the tattered remains of his cloak hanging from the remaining pauldron. Blood soaked the unprotected shoulder, darkening the conforming black-scaled bodysuit he wore under his armor. Both his greaves had been destroyed and his legs were fractured in numerous spots. His torso armor was rent open from his waist to collarbone, blood trickling from numerous lacerations, and a deep cut in his left side burned with pain. Furthermore, five of his ribs and his nose were broken, and his left eye was swollen shut. Unlike Luthur, however, Garith's wounds gave no indication of healing.

"Give it up, Garith. Your fir'gan is waning and your body can't take much more." Though confident in his assessment, dread that Garith was hiding something was twisting his stomach in knots.

Garith, his breath coming deep and ragged while his aura flickered haphazardly, spit blood at Luthur. "I will not have you pitying me, Luthur! You'll have to kill me to stop me!" he screamed before charging forward, his every injury exploding in blinding pain.

Luthur easily intercepted the arcing blade and pushed it aside. Garith, letting his momentum carry him, delivered a bone-rattling punch to Luthur's face, sending the blonde warrior stumbling backward. The exertion having taken its toll, Garith collapsed to his knees.

Regaining his balance, Luthur reached up and set his broken nose without any visible discomfort. "Give up, Garith. That punch was weak and it has you on your knees." He took a deep breath and stated, despite being unsure of his words, "You're beaten."

Garith looked up at him with a crazed glint in his eyes, and his lips began to twitch before breaking into a giant grin. Luthur glared at him as Garith burst into maniacal laughter despite his broken ribs. Luthur knew that laugh – crazed and deranged, yet sure of himself. Garith only laughed like that when he had his prey cornered and knew he had won.

"*Damn,*" Luthur thought, as suddenly, on the edge of his senses, he felt a tingle of building fir'gan.

Garith's laughter ceased, and he glared at Luthur with deadly intent. Pulling a blue crystal, which was no larger than a man's eye, from his belt, he held it up for Luthur to clearly see. "No, my dear Luthur – you're dead."

The swelling fir'gan reached its peak as Garith casually flung the crystal over his shoulder to land on the shattered terrain. Behind Garith, ten slashes of blue light cut the air just above the ground, rotating open until they were big enough for a human to step through. Initially, nothing could be seen within the rents except pulsating blue energy. Then, as Luthur took a cautious step back and brought his swords up in defense, ten cloaked and hooded figures began to emerge from the rifts.

Luthur let out a growl of frustration. "By Corith, we scattered you all!" he roared in defiance of what his eyes told him to be true.

Garith let out a rasping chuckle and struggled to his feet. "Poor, disillusioned Luthur. Did you honestly think you could keep us apart all this time without destroying us? For that matter – did you really think I'd fight fair?"

The implications of it all struck Luthur fully. He had always tried to avoid killing his former friends and fellow Wardens in the hope that one day they could be brought back to the Light. Damion had called the notion childish and dangerous. Darkon had simply scoffed at him. Yet, he had held as close to his nonviolent beliefs as he could. He almost laughed at himself then. *"This is what we get for putting a monk in charge, I suppose,"* he thought.

With his heart breaking, Luthur knew what he would have to do.

Let his arms fall to his sides, his swords slipping from his grasp, he said, "You win, Garith."

The joy in Garith's grin was almost too much to bear, and Luthur dropped his gaze. "Good boy, Luthur. That's smart of you. This way, your death won't be too painful." He waved his free hand toward Luthur. "Kill him."

The newcomers, nine with swords drawn and one with a giant axe, started forward, their fir'gan auras bursting to life in a myriad of colors.

Luthur looked up and met the eyes of each assailant deep within the shadows of their hoods, easily identifying the individuals and their threat to him. Then, as the snow turned to rain, he looked skyward and whispered, "Corith, forgive me." He squeezed his eyes shut for a moment as the rain ran down his face like tears. When he finally returned his gaze to the situation at hand, there was death in his eyes.

For the first time in centuries, as he gazed deep into those eyes seething with rage and promises of death, Garith felt true, undeniable fear. Like every engagement in the past, Garith had counted on Luthur's abhorrence of violence to temper his actions. There was no reason, in his mind, to think Luthur would dare go this far. Yet, despite that reasoning, this was exactly what Garith desired. Still, it did little to quell the fear that suddenly gripped his heart. Before anyone had gotten within twenty paces of Luthur, what he feared and his goal were jointly realized.

Luthur's aura suddenly winked out as his face contorted with rage, and the two katanas lying at his feet began to dissolve, wisps of energy rising into the air from the vanishing weapons before fading to nothing. Visible streaks of energy began to crackle in the air, flashing in and out of existence, while rivulets of midnight-purple energy began to crawl over his body. All around him, eyes widened in fear and awe as the ground beneath them began to shake and break apart, chunks of frozen turf rising into the air only to explode upon contact with flashing bolts of energy. Then, from around Luthur's feet, veins of the same midnight-purple energy began to creep across the ground, forming an intricate circular array around him. They all knew what the array that resembled two dragons – their paws locked together and eyes staring blankly out upon the world – was for, and that the buildup of power was a clear indication that Luthur planned to use it as a weapon, yet it took them all a moment to react.

Garith's mind was suddenly racing. He had accomplished what he wanted – forcing Luthur to unleash his full power. Now, as the results of his goading stared him in the face, he realized that he had expended too much strength and allowed himself to take too much of a beating to survive what was brewing before him.

Shaking off his shock, Garith screamed, "PROTECT ME!"

The fighter nearest Garith, wielding a slender and elegant longsword, jumped in front of him. Arms raised and crossed protectively, the cloak opened to reveal a leather-clad, feminine figure. In an instant, her emerald aura flared brightly and grew to encompass Garith.

It was then that Luthur let out a scream full of rage and anguish that had been building within him over the centuries. He was tired of the fighting and killing. He was tired of the destruction. He was tired of it all. Now was his chance to end it for good – and he would take that chance.

The array exploded, launching a midnight-purple dome of energy skyward and outward, chewing up the ground and enveloping all the combatants. A few of the fighters' auras flared brightly in an attempt to strengthen their defenses as the wall of power washed over them. When the dome reached seventy paces in diameter, it flared out of existence with a bang, revealing the results of Luthur's outburst.

All of the new arrivals, except for Garith and the woman protecting him, were sprawled about the six-foot-deep crater left by the explosion of fir'gan, their clothing singed and bodies battered. One assailant was unconscious and sprawled on the far side of the crater, alive for the moment despite a missing arm and the generous amount of blood pumping from the wound – which was quickly closing. Other than that man, no one else appeared fatally wounded. After what seemed like an eternity, the survivors began to stir and make their way slowly to their feet.

As for Garith, he was on his knees atop an island of partially frozen, muddy earth, his eyes locked on Luthur from behind his guardian. His protector, her cloak burnt away, was slender and noticeably beautiful despite the dangerous situation. When she was sure it was safe, she looked up. Short-cropped emerald hair adorned a perfectly sculpted face that was fitted with up-tilted eyes that were a match for her hair color. Those eyes found Luthur, and her ruby-red lips parted in awe at what had entrapped Garith's gaze.

His midnight-purple aura flowing and crackling about him, Luthur stood across from Garith on the same island, looking like a new man. His blonde hair had turned a deep blue and was pulled back from his grim face in a horsetail. Running from underneath each dark eye to his chin, almost as if he was weeping blood, a fang-shaped portion of his flesh had turned blood-red. A similar streak of red also ran from cheekbone to cheekbone, across the bridge of his nose, as if the skin had been sliced open by a keen blade. On top of a black bodysuit of tiny scales, which started just beneath his chin, he now wore a suit of jade-colored, conforming armor — each piece eerily mimicking his musculature. Black flames adorned each pauldron, knee and elbow plate, as well as the back of his gauntlets. Cuisses embossed with black flames protected his legs, and a round belt buckle held a simple brown belt in place about his waist. The buckle was a circular seal that mimicked Garith's buckle with the only difference being that the top dragon was red and the bottom black. All that seemed to be missing from Luthur's new attire was a weapon.

With that in mind, Garith's gaze slipped to the orb of midnight-purple energy held in Luthur's hand, and he feared what it was for.

A long, agonizing moment passed in which no one dared to move for fear of provoking an attack from Luthur. Finally, the emerald-haired woman helped Garith to his feet as the others began to spread out around the island. Garith's face was frozen in shock. He couldn't believe what Luthur had done. In all the years he had known him, Luthur had always held a complete revulsion for both summoning his armor, and using his powers to their fullest. He also knew that such restraint was born from his ancient rival's fear of being tempted by so much power, which meant that Luthur felt he had no other options left. Despite getting exactly what he wanted, Garith's breath caught in his throat. If Luthur feared his chances of survival had grown that slim — as Garith had intended — and he wasn't afraid of summoning his armor, then that ball of energy in his hand was. . . .

He quickly scanned the terrain for Luthur's discarded swords. When he didn't see them, he knew he needed time to gather himself if his plan was to succeed. Panicking, he screamed, "Attack now, you fools!"

The order froze the others in their tracks for but an instant. Suddenly, except for the woman guarding Garith, they all charged with inhuman speed. One of the figures, carrying a large claymore and surrounded by an orange aura, suddenly vanished.

Luthur was aware that none of the arrivals had summoned their armor, giving him a significant advantage if he acted quickly. So with a smile, he let the orb wink out, and then launched himself skyward, drawing two others behind him. Luthur spotted the man who had vanished diving toward him, claymore readied for a killing blow. Luthur slid to the side in his ascent, the force of his passing blowing the hood from the attacker's head, revealing a bald, whirling-tattooed head crowned with a long red topknot. Lashing out, Luthur latched on to the topknot with both hands, nearly wrenching the man's skull from his neck.

Pivoting hard in the air, Luthur swung the man around hard and launched him back toward the ground. The man whistled through the air, barreling through the yellow- and green-auraed trailing duo before crashing deep into the ground. Luthur pursued quickly, the air screaming about him. The yellow-auraed assailant tried to reach out to grab him, and had his arm sheered from his torso for his effort.

Vomiting blood, the man with the topknot pushed himself to all fours as the air about him began to shriek. Looking up, he had only a moment to register what was happening before Luthur's fist blasted into his skull as the violently descending warrior landed with a massive impact. The man's body snapped up in the air as his skull was driven into the ground, the impact causing his head to explode and extinguishing his aura. A soup of rainwater, blood, and bits of brain and skull showered Luthur as he swiftly stood, spun and landed a bone-shattering kick to his remaining pursuer, launching the attacker into the distance. The man's shattered body skipped across the ground like a pebble on a lake before landing in an eruption of earth and snow.

Luthur didn't pause to savor the moment; instead, he ducked low as a giant axe sailed over his head. Spinning, he stepped into his red-auraed attacker and landed an uppercut to the massive figure's jaw. The jawbone shattered, blood and teeth spurting into the air as the hulking figure was launched airborne. Flipping over backward, the axe-wielder landed in a muddy puddle with a sickening thud as his aura winked out. Knowing the man was at least incapacitated, Luthur quickly glanced around and saw the remaining four closing swiftly.

Quickstepping backward, he brought the orb back to life and clenched his left hand around it. The orb began to expand away from his hand just as a blue-auraed attacker darted to the right and vanished. Luthur snarled and began to spin to his left, the orb expanding and solidifying into a bluesteel sword with a simple crossguard, the blade of which was a foot and a half in width and nearly nine feet in length. Runes, glowing midnight-purple, were etched up the center of the blade, leaving a glowing trail in the massive sword's wake.

Luthur took a two-handed grip on the simple hilt as it solidified, and continued his spin toward his target. The attacker had appeared to his right, airborne, with his large broadsword held high. Luthur could see his assailant's eyes go wide as he brought his giant slab of steel around with astonishing ease and speed. The enormous blade bit hard into the attacker's side, cutting through the torso and exploding out the other side, bathing the area in blood. The two halves of the man hit the ground a few paces apart with a sick thud, spilling organs and fluids onto the earth.

Two of the three remaining attackers halted their advance at the sight, no longer wishing to test their luck. The third, however, closed with a howl from Luthur's left. Luthur sidestepped the wild, one-handed thrust, and brought his colossal sword down in an overhead chop, severing the purple-auraed attacker's arm at the elbow. The assailant went down in a gush of blood, screaming loudly. A second scream echoed from behind Luthur, and he turned to see another figure – surrounded by an identical purple aura – on the ground, clutching at the same type of wound.

The remaining assailant, his violet aura winking out, began to back away from Luthur, giving every indication that he wanted no part of the fight.

Luthur smiled and turned his attention to Garith. However, when he looked to where Garith and the emerald-haired woman had been, neither were to be seen. Suddenly, his vision exploded as a fist hammered into the back of his skull. He stumbled forward a few steps before spinning around with a snarl, expecting to see Garith's broken body standing there. Instead, the emerald-haired woman stared at him smugly, her green eyes aglow with power and her emerald aura raging fiercely.

"Not too bad of a punch for you, Juliana. However, you and I both know you're no match for me."

Juliana let out a seductive, throaty laugh. "Presumptuous of you, Luthur. I was simply buying a little time."

He blinked at her and thought, *"Buying time for what?"*

She laughed at the look on his face and stepped aside. Garith stood directly behind her, breathing heavily from his wounds. Luthur was still a bit confused until he saw the grin on Garith's face. Then, to his horror, the sword in Garith's hand began to dissolve as crimson energy flowed from the blade and into its wielder.

"Dear Corith, no . . ." Luthur breathed with apprehension as the flux in power he'd felt with every sword slash, and his slow healing suddenly made dreadful sense.

As the energy washed over him, Garith's wounds began to heal, rents in his armor began to mend, and shattered armor began to rebuild itself. In mere moments, Garith looked as he had at the beginning of the fight. Yet, the changes didn't stop there. Rivulets of pure-black energy began to crackle about him as horrific, pain-filled moaning filled the air, and the color began to drain from Garith's skin until he was a pure, pale white. However, Luthur barely paid heed to any of the changes as he was ensnared by Garith's eyes. His sclera had turned black, and his irises were now a bright yellow that seemed to glow with chaotic energy.

They were the eyes of the damned.

Luthur had only seen the eyes once, long ago, and their meaning tied his stomach in knots. "Shadow Touched," he whispered as it dawned on him that the other fighters had been brought in to buy Garith time to gather his strength for the transformation.

His crimson aura now tinted black about its edges, Garith cackled, his raspy voice echoing in on itself. "Oh Luthur, such a display. I'm sure you thought you might actually win if you went all out." Garith let his yellow eyes wander about the battlefield. Above the remains of the man Luthur had cut in half and the headless corpse floated a blue and orange crystal, respectively. Each was no bigger than a man's fist and pulsed dully. Garith chuckled to himself. Killing a Warden without a crusader required tremendous strength, and Garith found himself slightly impressed. "Juliana, be a dear and collect Bastion and Tyreal's crystals for me."

Both Garith and Luthur watched with growing tension as Juliana vanished, only to reappear next to the blue crystal and collect it before doing the same with the orange one. Satisfied, Garith turned his attention back to Luthur and grinned devilishly. "Tell me, Luthur – is the mighty Warden of Light, in all his glory, scared of a Shadow Touched like me?"

Luthur snarled and brought his sword to the ready. "Shadow Touched or not, you have no crusader – and without it, your powers are incomplete," he stated in defiance of what his heart and eyes told him to be true.

Garith shook his head in mock disdain. "Tsk, tsk, Luthur. Have you learned nothing? Not everything is as you believe."

Garith's crimson cloak parted and he held up his right hand, which held a black orb of energy. He clenched his fist with a maniacal laugh, and the orb burst forth into a sword befitting its wielder. As long and as wide as Luthur's, the blade was notched like a key on one edge, and black runes that crackled with energy ran the length of it.

Luthur could only stare in disbelief. It shouldn't have been possible, yet somehow, someway, a new crusader had been forged.

Pointing the macabre sword at Luthur, he laughed again. "You should have accepted my offer. We could have been gods."

Luthur shook himself from his stupor and snarled at Garith. "I already told you–"

He didn't get to finish his sentence as Garith vanished in a blur and Luthur felt the massive, key-notched blade rip into his chest – just to the right of his heart – and explode from his back. Lifted off the ground and over Garith's head, he was spun about and driven into the ground, the massive sword pinning him there. Luthur's body convulsed and blood poured forth from both the massive wound and his mouth to mix with the water and churned mud beneath him. He could feel his fir'gan trying desperately to keep him alive and heal the horrifying wound. Luthur wanted to laugh cynically, but couldn't. Instilled with the power to sever the connection between wielder and the fir'gan that kept them alive, crusaders were made to kill beasts that were much stronger than a Warden – as such, there was no surviving a crusader-inflicted, fatal wounding.

Luthur stared past Garith's victorious visage and into the storm clouds above, feeling the raindrops fall upon him as if the heavens were weeping. He could feel his connection to the currents beginning to slip. No more fighting. No more pain. He could simply let go and slip into Corith's embrace.

Garith leaned hard on his sword, staring at Luthur with unabashed glee. After all these centuries, he had won! He slowly twisted his crusader in an attempt to elicit a scream from his fallen foe, but there was nothing . . . not even a whimper. Dismayed that he wouldn't be able to physically torture his longtime foe, he then noticed that Luthur was staring past him, the light slowly fading from his eyes, and he knew it wouldn't be long. Elation once again flooded through him as he examined Luthur for any other signs of demise. Luthur's fir'gan was fading fast, and his armor and crusader were beginning to lose their substance. Suddenly, Luthur's crusader flared and began to dissolve, orbs of midnight-purple energy floating away from the massive sword and vanishing into the air.

His raspy voice echoing loudly, Garith roared with laughter as Luthur's matching katanas reappeared where the massive crusader had once been. Oh yes, now was the time! His rival and enemy was dying, giving him the chance to claim Luthur's crystal and move one step closer to becoming unstoppable.

He let go of his crusader and crouched down over Luthur, trailing a finger through the blood oozing from the ghastly wound. "Oh yes, Luthur – *so* valiant and *so* honorable. At one time, you might have beaten me. Your nobility and sense of honor held you in check, didn't it? You see – I wanted you to fight me with your all. I wanted you to die knowing that *I* was more powerful, and that the Darkness is no longer a shadow on the edge of your senses. We are becoming stronger, and soon – oh so soon – we will have the knowledge we seek. I'll use the Darkness to grow stronger, as I have with your death. And when the time is right, I will cast the Darkness down and claim Kylir for myself!" Garith's yellow eyes burned with madness as the last of the words slithered from his lips.

Breaking from his reflections, he smiled at Luthur. "A shame for you, really. I was willing to share it with you." He shrugged and laughed. "A boon for me, though. With your crystal, I'll be just a bit closer to everything I desire!"

Luthur blinked at the mention of his crystal and seemed to come back to his senses for a moment. He knew what Garith was after, and letting him have the crystal was not an option. Dying or not, he could not allow this. Letting his armor fully fade, he pull what remained of his fir'gan within himself, building it and focusing it. He did not know if he had the strength left for an attack, but he could not let Garith have his crystal.

Garith's grin faded as he noticed the building fir'gan within Luthur. Suddenly, Luthur's hand latched on to the back of his neck, pulling him close enough that their noses touched. Juliana moved to help, but was emphatically waved away. "Get back! You know what he's doing as well as me! Protect yourself!"

As Juliana backed away, her emerald aura flaring protectively, Garith began to struggle against the death grip Luthur had on him. Unable to speak, and barely able to see or hear, Luthur held on with everything he had left as he continued to accumulate fir'gan within him. Terrified at the sheer volume of power he sensed growing within Luthur, and with his aura flaring and whipping about wildly, Garith pawed vehemently at the restraining hand. To his dismay, his struggles only served to tighten Luthur's grip. It was then, as Luthur's fingers sank into his neck, that Luthur managed to smile.

Stunned, Garith froze at the sad, simple smile. It was a smile he had seen many times when they had been friends.

He had never expected to see it again.

The explosion rocked the air as midnight-purple energy burst from Luthur's body and punched through the middle of Garith's torso with enough force to lift him high into the air. As the violent, short-lived blast faded, Garith landed unceremoniously on the soupy terrain at Juliana's feet. Writhing on the ground, a keening howl erupted from Garith's mouth as dark energy crackled around the gaping hole in his torso. Wide-eyed, Juliana fell to her knees and pinned down his body as the Darkness-spawned energy worked feverishly to close the wound.

As Garith howled, she noticed that his giant, key-notched blade had vanished, its power needed to heal Garith, and his katana had reappeared in the mud at its injured master's side. Knowing it was only a matter of time before Garith was fully healed, she slipped a glance at Luthur's corpse. There was no indication of life left in Luthur's body, leaving only that sad smile as the only hint to Luthur's final thoughts. What caught her eye, however, was the multifaceted emerald crystal hovering in the air just over where Luthur's heart would have been. Round in shape and about the size of a large man's fist, it pulsed dully in the dim light like a beating heart as the rain tapped a melancholy melody upon its crystalline surface. She knew it was what Garith wanted, but if she didn't hold him still, the healing process would likely kill him; and if that happened, the uncontrolled power might rage loose, destroying her in the process.

She refocused on the rain- and sweat-drenched Garith as he howled again. The hole in his torso was almost closed, and that meant he would soon be fully healed; after which, he could claim his prize.

Suddenly, on the edge of her senses, she felt a familiar presence. As it dawned on her who it was, her breath caught in her throat and panic took root. They couldn't afford to be caught in this condition. Healed or not, the amount of power Garith was using up would leave them vulnerable.

Reaching behind her belt, Juliana quickly pulled out a simple, round disk set with a small blue crystal and threw it against the ground a few paces away. The disk and crystal shattered, pouring forth blue energy that spun and twisted into a portal like the one she had arrived through. She then collected Garith's sword before hefting him to his feet – the hole in his torso now fully closed – and guiding him toward the portal.

By this time, Garith had noticed the crystal hovering over Luthur, and he was struggling against her to get to it. "What are you doing, you bitch?! It's right there! I must have it!"

She scowled and continued to steer them toward their escape route. "Don't be a fool!" she hissed. "Can't you feel him coming?"

Garith blinked and stared at Juliana before he reached out with his senses. She was right of course, he could feel the two men approaching, and he was in no condition to face them. He growled as he released his Shadow-Touched form and returned to normal. "Get us away from here," he ordered weakly. "Too many old friends have come out to play today."

They limped over to the portal where he stopped her and turned them back for one last look. What they saw froze them in place. Neither of them had felt him arrive, and that terrified them. They could still feel that his companion was a ways off, but that didn't concern them. If the man who was obviously ignoring them decided to attack, their odds of survival were slim.

Garith's fingers sunk into her shoulder, bringing her out of her dazed state. "Move!" Garith hissed into her ear.

She nodded slowly before shooting one last awe- and hate-filled glare at the man standing over Luthur. Then, with great reluctance, they stepped through the portal.

The portal closed behind them with a bang and crackle of energy, but Damion, his hair matted to his head from the downpour, ignored it as he had the two that had stepped through. If he had wished it, he could have killed them and the others that were unconscious on the ground about him. There was a slim chance that some of them might die from their wounds, but it was likely they would all survive. At this point, he simply did not care. Luthur's broken body lay at his feet, his crystal hovering above the massive rent in his chest where his heart should have been – and Damion's heart was broken. So many of their kind had died over the years. So many friends and loved ones wiped from all but a select few individuals' memories. However, nothing could have prepared him for the loss of Luthur. If crying were still an option to him, he would have wept. Instead, he could only let the rain serve as his tears.

He felt Darius arrive behind him, and could only imagine the horror and pain he was feeling. Darius, like himself, had been very close to Luthur, and as slow strides brought Darius to Damion's side, neither one of them could find the words to express their sorrow.

Therefore, beneath a shroud of heavenly tears, they found what comfort they could in each other's presence as they stood in silent vigil over Luthur's broken body.

Finally, Damion knelt down and retrieved Luthur's katanas. Sliding them beneath his belt, he then reverently reached out and collected Luthur's crystal. With a broken sigh, he tucked the pulsing emerald crystal into his tabard and stood back up. Even through the horror of their loss, concern and suspicion were beginning to creep into his mind. The size of the rent in Luthur's chest could only have been made by a crusader, yet he knew the betrayers' crusaders had been destroyed – he had personally seen to that. That such a wound had been inflicted on Luthur terrified him and summoned up dark thoughts and suspicions for which he had no answers.

With his mind already working through the implications of the wound, he turned to Darius and said in a voice that was barely above a whisper, "You'll have to deliver the body to the army . . . and then inform the Merandiths of their new role. Also . . . let Darkon know of his new position – I'm sure he will be thrilled."

Darius, blinking back tears, nodded slowly. "I . . . I can make the body look more presentable. . . . What are you going to do? For that matter, what about the survivors?"

Damion eyed the bodies strewn about dully. "Leave them. I haven't the heart for it now. If they die from their wounds, so be it. As for me . . . Luthur gave me my orders, and I intend to see them through."

Darius stared at Damion thoughtfully before his bloodshot, brown eyes widened with comprehension. "You're leaving us, aren't you?"

Damion nodded. "For a time. I wish I could explain, but to do so would place more souls than necessary in jeopardy. Just accept my word that I will be back as soon as I can." He grasped Darius firmly by the shoulders and gave him a small, sad smile. "Take care of yourself, old friend."

Darius nodded as Damion turned his back to him and began to stride way. It suddenly occurred to Darius that he might never see his friend again. He thought about all he could say, yet all he could manage to do was find concern for himself and the others. With his own tears beginning to mix with the rain trickling down his face, and his voice thick with emotion, he shouted, "What should we do in your absence? I don't trust Darkon!"

As the heavens continued to weep, Damion halted in his tracks and, without looking back, stated, "My friend – prepare for war."

# Chapter One

*Age of Twilight*

*5972 years since the Exodus*

*F*or each day, there is a beginning and an end. From darkness to light and from light to darkness is the pattern each day has followed since the dawn of time. It was as if these primordial elements were locked in a never-ending cycle of pacifistic warfare for dominance over each other – each having its moment of supremacy, but always unable to destroy the other and attain absolute power. For many, this unceasing battle seemed an allusion to the greater picture and power at play.

In an era known as the Age of Power, there arose a great evil that threatened to engulf all life and vanquish the Light from the world. Of all the races, only the dragons sensed the growing plight. These majestic and noble beasts opposed this evil with all their might, seeking to eliminate it before it could destroy all that was good in the world. Despite their best efforts, this entity – which came to be known as the Darkness – defeated them at every turn. In their despair, the dragons retreated against the growing corruption, escaping to lands untouched by the evil. There, they licked their wounds and asked Corith, Lord of the Light, for guidance. With Corith's guidance, along with the help of the races of the land, the dragons began to fight back.

In the end, it was not enough.

The Darkness' corruption spread through the forces arrayed against it, killing many and turning more to its cause. The dragons were slowly killed off or turned, weakening the forces of Light's ability to oppose it. Soon, the Darkness' followers threatened to consume the world.

Then, from the ashes of destruction, there arose those who had resisted the Darkness' taint. They stood against the Darkness when and where no one else could. Through their determination and sacrifice, the Darkness was pushed from the land. The people of the world – a world known as Kylir – celebrated the destruction of the Darkness. Those that had stood against the malicious entity, however, knew better.

The Darkness had not been destroyed. . . .

On the far western side of the Galerad Ocean, shielded to the east from the Stormsea by the land of Solarson and to the west by the Sea of Twilight, is the continent of Triclose – the land of eternal war. It has been nearly two-hundred years since the Second Great War, and the ruling throne of Triclose remains vacant. Many Houses have risen up to take the throne and failed. The people of this land of perpetual war have only seen two generations of relative peace in the last two centuries, leading many to believe that there will never be true peace on Triclose until the ruling throne is filled. War has become life and life has become war for the inhabitants of Triclose, the cycle perpetuated by the stories of noble battles and heroic ancestors that parents feed their children from the moment they are born. Thus, with each new generation, loyalties are sworn, hatreds are renewed and the wars begin anew.

From far off the Southern shores of Triclose, a muggy wind began its journey north. Passing over the tropical coast, it ushered clouds and rain onto exotic and lush forests full of vibrant creatures and denizens that cared little for what went on outside their secluded world. Bereft of its moist cargo, the current swept north over verdant plains, growing hot and violent as it breached the deserts of the South. The sun- and wind-hardened people of this sea of sand paid little heed to it, nor cursed the wind for the lack of rain as their minds concentrated on survival and battle.

Unabated, the wind progressed northward into the Dragonspine Mountains, growing cooler and once again building up precious, life-giving rain to deliver upon south-central Triclose. As the chilled wind passed through the towering peaks, delivering snow to its caps, a large black mountain hawk soared on the late-season thermals, casually hunting for small game unwise enough to scamper into the open. A pain-filled roar caught its attention, and the hawk banked to the east to sate its curiosity. The hawk soon spotted the cause of the commotion and, upon seeing there wouldn't be a free meal, gave a cry of acknowledgment to its fellow predator before returning to its regular course.

The giant beast the bird-of-prey had acknowledged finished off its quarry. Snapping the neck of its smaller mountain cousin, the beast glanced skyward with eyes of molten ember, sniffing at the wind. Its journey had been long, and there was still farther to go, but the passing wind told the beast that it was moving in the right direction. Though it was urgent that the creature reach its destination, it was satisfied with its progress and understood that there was still time to enjoy a meal before venturing into strange lands.

Ignoring the beast as it did all things, the wind continued its northward journey, delivering rain upon the foothills. Once again relieved of its cumbersome burden, the wind then hastened further north, toward the plains of Central Triclose, where the scent of carrion and decay alighted on its ethereal existence.

Upon these plains, two armies met beneath the northbound wind. It was not the first time they had met – nor would it be the last. Throughout the morning, amongst the chaos of ringing steel and spilt blood and organs, men and women danced with death to the screams of the dying.

They did so because their domses commanded it.

They did so for the belief that their doms was the one to claim the Jade Throne.

They did so for peace.


Craigan Murandi Suldamik, Doms of House Suldamik and the realm of Surandia, sat upon his painted destrider in full, ornate platemail that was unmarred by the day's fighting. His blue eyes, weary from attesting to the deaths of his people, gazed into the distance where he knew his enemy was encamped. Like all the others in league with House Suldamik, he despised and loathed House Merandith with enough malice to last uncountable lifetimes. Seventeen years of near-unceasing war had plagued Triclose, resulting in innumerable casualties. If any of the other Houses had been in control, the length of the war and the number of dead would have been enough to force them to surrender or sue for a truce. However, Craigan believed with all his heart, and what was left of his soul, that House Merandith cared very little about the fodder they tossed to their deaths. Such a man could not be allowed to sit on the throne – no matter the cost.

A hot breeze from the east rose up unexpectedly, casting his white-flecked, brown hair about his chiseled and scarred face. The nauseating smell of carrion assaulted his nostrils, compelling his nose to twitch with each breath of the sinful air as he scanned the corpse- and carcass-covered battlefield. His mailed hands tightened about the reins of his powerful steed as he watched both the crows hopping amongst the bodies, and the bloated, black-beaked and -feathered mud crows that were worming their way through the carnage. The carrion feeders pecked and tore at exposed flesh even as priests in their black-cowled robes, along with the aid of camp followers, worked to extract the dead, loading them into carts before hauling them to the funeral pyres in each camp.

He almost laughed at the irony of it all. Both sides worked so hard to kill each other only to have the priests work peacefully alongside one another to bring the bodies back to their respectful factions. In the end, death was the third foe in the war – bringing a final, unbiased equality to all.

*"Maybe in the end, the priests and the dead have it figured out,"* he thought to himself.

Tearing his eyes from the blood-painted field of death and mutilation, he focused his icy gaze on the rise to the east that he presumed sheltered the opposing army from sight. Four figures could be seen atop the rise. There were no discernible details at this distance, but Craigan knew deep in his soul that it was the Doms of House Merandith. He knew that the young doms was waiting for him to make the next move, and that simple reminder of his current situation made Craigan scowl with unabashed disgust. The young Merandith had proven a hardier foe than his father, pushing him back and surprising him on numerous occasions. Yet, he knew that all he wanted to achieve could be accomplished if he could find a way to force his opponent off balance or catch him off-guard. If he could manage that, then House Merandith would eventually falter and stumble into a predicament from which it could not gain deliverance.

The sun slowly crept its way from west to east and was soon directly overhead, bringing warmth that was unusual this close to winter. The battlefield was nearly clear of bodies and Craigan's priests had fully withdrawn from the field. With his demeanor worsening with each agonizing moment, Craigan continued to watch Merandith's priests extract bodies from the field, piling them on carts swarming with flies. Behind his rigid back, he could hear the chaotic symphony of his mobile army's rear guard preparing to relocate to better fortifications. Prayers for the dead carried over the clamor as the priests unloaded bodies from the carts and piled them on one of five large funeral pyres. At the rate preparations were progressing, it wouldn't be long until the fires were lit and the living moved on.

Although House Merandith's loses had been substantial, Craigan's had been worse, and he had no desire to tempt fate more than once in the same day by remaining anywhere near the enemy. Early estimates indicated that three hundred of his men had perished, and another two hundred had been injured in the early morning melee, including friends, relatives and nobles. He knew that death came to everyone – it was a fact of life the people of Triclose tended to learn at an early age – but the manners in which most had died in this war were not the most honorable or respectable ways to pass from this life. For each man, he had mourned. For each, he had memorized their names until they were etched so deep into his mind that he would never forget. He would make sure that not one person, not one soul, would be forgotten or lost to time like so many others. Deo willing, he would live to record the dead's names for all to remember.

Reining his painted warhorse about, Craigan focused his attention on the southern base of the hill where his remaining forces were preparing to move.

Once, he had led the most awe-inspiring army to ever campaign across Triclose, attracting more to his banner at every village and city. From a formidable force of fifty thousand – which he had inherited from his father – his army had blossomed to one-hundred-thousand strong by the start of his second year in command, which was the largest force Triclose had ever seen. Full of confidence, Craigan had put his numerical advantage to work, pushing House Merandith hard. The toll it took on House Merandith was devastating as they lost territory after territory over the next year. In the end, after only two years of his leadership, House Merandith's doms and doma were slain, and Craigan had every reason to believe victory was in his grasp. However, it wasn't meant to be.

The young son of the late Doms Merandith reorganized the military and began a slow and methodical campaign that recaptured most of the lost territories and, despite his smaller army, began to reduce Craigan's numbers through a series of brutal battles and ambushes. As a result of senseless violence and dissension in his ranks, Craigan lost two-hundred men at the Battle of Corthas; all the while, he was forced to stand by and watch as House Merandith sundered his men limb-from-limb. Four hundred more fell at Hagan Pass in an ambush that was executed with ruthless and meticulous efficiency. That day, the pass ran red with blood as Merandith archers picked off troops from niches along the treacherous pass walls. Once again, having made it through ahead of the main army, he was forced to watch helplessly as the stragglers perished. Sadly, the worst was yet to come.

At the Battle of Sparros, he was forced into a running confrontation that lasted for almost a week. Merandith's forces, using ambush tactics, expertly carved small portions of his army away from the main body before slaughtering the cutoff men. By the end of the battle, Craigan had lost two-thousand souls, and neither army had been able to retrieve their dead. To this day, he still wondered if the crows were still feasting on the carnage.

Nevertheless, House Merandith did not get off lightly even in victory. Reports estimated that Merandith lost close to one-hundred-and-fifty men at Corthas. Hagan Pass left Merandith with only a handful of dead, while the slaughter at Sparros had cost House Merandith six hundred more souls. However, Merandith's losses did little to offset House Suldamik's significant personnel losses and demoralizing defeats. Yet, even beneath the crushing weight of the defeats, Craigan did not fold. He had fought back with similar tactics over the last year, inspiring his men and exacting vengeance many times over. The brutality and ferocity of the battles had taken its toll on Merandith's army. But was it enough?

Including the battle this morning, Craigan's entire military still numbered around sixty thousand, while reports estimated House Merandith's forces to be around fifty thousand. Arrayed before Craigan at the base of the hill, was a small portion of his nearly twelve-thousand-strong mobile army. Depending on the reports, Kale had just shy of ten thousand resting somewhere to the northeast. Not the greatest odds, but as long as Craigan held the numerical advantage, he felt he still had the upper hand. Yet, despite his feelings, or how much he might convince himself the reality of the situation wasn't as bad as it was, he found himself retreating before the enemy with his nose bloodied again. He knew he needed to rethink his strategy and find a way to take advantage of his numbers. Be it luck or fate, winter was nearly here, and would provide a break in the fighting that would grant him the time to do just that. Very few people were foolhardy enough to engage in a campaign during Triclose's brutal winter. The few times any doms had gotten overzealous and attempted a winter campaign, the consequences had been disastrous and fatal. Craigan was not that foolish. He would pull back to secure, defensible positions and wait out the winter.

The remaining tents in the encampment came down with disciplined efficiency and, once disassembled, were loaded onto one of the thirty wagons located on the southwestern side of the camp. Soldiers and camp followers alike moved about dousing fires, loading packs and wagons, and readying mounts. It took about an hour more to complete the preparations, leaving only the pyres burdened with the dead, and the priests who continued to deposit more bodies upon them as the only traces of their encampment. Five-hundred troops had remained behind while the main body had marched ahead. Now, two-hundred light cavalry and three-hundred infantry were arranged on the field in neat, orderly columns of fifty deep, draping the area in a cloak of steel and cloth. The wagon crews, four to each wagon, were making one last check of their wagons to ensure everything was secure and in good shape before climbing aboard.

A group of officers gathered about an armored man at the rear of the column began to disperse, each officer mounting up and joining their respective units. The armored man began to look about, and upon noticing Craigan, made his way up the hill. Even in full platemail and with his back burdened by a kite shield displaying his family crest – a roaring lion against a black- and yellow-checkered field – he made the ascent easily. As he approached, Craigan could see that the visor of his devilish helmet was down, which hid his features completely from sight, and that his left hand rested on the hilt of the simplistic broadsword at his hip.

Upon reaching Craigan's position, the man saluted. Even without his sword drawn, he was quite the imposing sight. Standing nearly six feet in height, the man was thick and powerfully built beneath his practical armor. Raising the snarling, demonic visor to expose hard black eyes astride a broad nose, the man reported in a deep, throaty voice, "All is ready, Doms Suldamik. Your word is all we await."

Craigan's response was long in coming as the reality of the march set in. At least three days of grueling and pitiless, full-blown marching lay ahead, foreshadowing an increase in malady and death within the injured ranks. As it was, he could only imagine the current situation in the medical wagons. "How far do you think the men can travel before we lose the light?" he asked, his own deep voice nowhere near a match for his subordinate's timbre.

"Possibly six leagues," the man promptly replied. "We'll catch up with the main body quickly enough, but with as burdened down as they currently are with wounded, it would be difficult to make better time without leaving them behind."

"Do be truthful, Dromick – the men are more than capable of ten," stated Craigan in his baritone voice.

"Aye, Doms, and many will perish – both wounded and healthy. Your men have just fought bravely and honorably for you, and are already beyond exhaustion. It would be self-slaughter to try to make ten leagues today."

Craigan stared sternly at Dromick. "Are you afraid of losing men in this most noble of causes?"

Doms General Dromick de'Suldamik Leonbane of House Suldamik pulled himself up proudly, offended at such a slanderous remark. "No, Doms Suldamik – I am not afraid of losing men or giving my life in battle. However, if more men are lost on the march than necessary, we may find ourselves at a great disadvantage when next we face House Merandith. There is no honor to be found dying of fatigue while on the march."

Craigan shifted his weight in the saddle as he evaluated Dromick's words with court-like efficiency. He valued Dromick's council greatly and, given what they had gone through recently, it certainly made more sense to move slowly and allow his men to rest. However, the idea of a hard-and-fast march to their destination, which would result in more time to recuperate in secure surroundings at the sacrifice of a few more men who weren't guaranteed to survive, was a more alluring choice for Craigan. Granted, he hated the idea of losing more souls to something as mundane as a march, but the longer they remained exposed on the open plains, the greater the chance that they could be attacked in their current weakened state. Besides the obvious, they needed the secure surroundings of a keep to prepare and plan.

Committing himself to a decision, Craigan resolutely ordered, "You have your orders, Doms General – ten leagues by nightfall."

"But the men—"

Craigan edged his horse forward. "Ten leagues, Dromick – no less. Tisss, yaw!" Craigan declared before digging his heels into his horse's flanks. Galloping down the hill, he proceeded to the front of the amassed troops, leaving his general with no chance to argue further.

Dromick remained where he was for a time, fuming at the callous command. Then, as the priests' prayers dropped off and the pyres were lit, he muttered in disgust, "Bloody Hills of Sparros! The man will be his own undoing," before, with a sharp about-face, he snapped his visor closed and made his way down the hill

*

His dented and blood-spattered armor reflected his mood as aptly as the blood-covered longsword standing erect in the ground before him reflected his deeds during the fog-cloaked morn'. Short-cropped blonde hair swayed restlessly in the mundane breeze as his ever-vigilant green eyes gazed thoughtfully – betraying no emotion – over the grisly field. With the fruits of the morning melee spread unapologetically before him, Kale Jorbic Merandith, Doms of House Merandith and the realm of Tiliea, couldn't help but reaffirm his belief that Craigan and his execrated family were unequivocally responsible for the life-altering tragedy known as the Third Great War.

Behind him, mounted on armored steeds of war and girded in platemail that was as functional and as unadorned as what he wore, his three remaining bodyguards gazed protectively over their tired and troubled doms. In a matter of mere moments, they had seen their eight companions fall in ways none of them would wish upon anyone. None of them had grown completely callous to the death and chaos they witnessed and partook of every day, but rather cold-hearted enough to keep a singular train of thought during battle – kill. Now that the fighting was over, the reality of their deeds and what they had witnessed was sinking in, leaving them to mourn their lost friends and loved ones. They knew, though, that none took it harder than their doms. For most of his life, Kale had viewed violence as a measure of last resort, and the deaths of those that died serving and protecting him left a bitter taste in his mouth.

Nothing, however, could have prepared them for Kale's reaction to the death of his bodyguards. Even the eldest of the three bodyguards, a grizzled and deadly Sword Master, had given way to Kale's vengeful blade when the others had been slain. Eight men had been horribly butchered by Kale before his remaining bodyguards had been forced to pull him back, preventing him from being lost to the seething mass of chaotic combat. During the extraction, another twelve of Suldamik's men had fallen to the bodyguard known as Mathis, which bought enough time for reinforcements to arrive and break Suldamik's ranks. However, it was the sight of the horribly mangled and maimed bodies as a result of their doms' rage that stuck in their minds; without question, it was an experience they were wholeheartedly averse to reliving. Even now, the sight of Kale's six-foot frame encased in bloody armor and standing vigil over the battlefield was haunting. It was as if an ancient god of war had descended from the heavens to bask in the results of the bloody offering that had been made.

As he gazed upon his Doms with concern, the Sword Master scratched at the irritated skin just below the eye-patch covering the empty socket of his left eye. Six months had gone by since he'd lost the eye defending Kale, and the socket still got horribly enflamed when he exerted himself or fought. He chided himself for scratching at it and forced himself to stop. It had taken him weeks to adapt to fighting with one eye and, while his skills and reactions had diminished some with the years and the missing eye, he was still a formidable foe.

Realizing that if no one said anything, they might be on this hill the rest of the day, he cleared his throat and said, "Doms Merandith, we should be returning to camp soon. The contingent from Sur'datha should be arriving within the hour."

Kale remained motionless, apparently oblivious to the comment. The minute breeze died down for a moment before returning in greater strength. Kale's gaze swept over the carnage, barely taking notice of the busy priests as they moved through the butchery like black-robed specters of death. "Tell me – does it seem like this will ever end?" His monotone voiced question was not expressed to anyone in particular, leaving his bodyguards to wonder if they should respond.

The Sword Master shifted in his saddle, endeavoring to get blood flowing down to his legs and feet. His roan mare destrider shifted and snorted in reaction, earning a calming pat from her rider. He had already spent the majority of the morning battle in the saddle, and he still had a tremendous amount of work ahead of him before he would receive a chance to refresh his battered and sleep-deprived body. Deciding that responding to the question might help to expedite their return to camp, and therefore a chance to rest both themselves and their mounts, he spoke up. "Aye, Doms Merandith, it will end – and we will prove to be House Suldamik's betters."

Kale nodded at the expected answer and wished he could fully believe in it. To say that he would forfeit all claims to his lands and titles for the chance to live a life where this war – this feud – did not exist would be an understatement. For each man and woman who died, he had wept. For each life he threw away without a thought, he had mourned. For each, he had died their deaths alongside them a hundred times over. No one had ever suggested war was going to be entertaining or, for that matter, easy; however, he saw it as a necessary evil to be used against an even greater abomination. House Suldamik could not be allowed to claim the Jade Throne. If that meant that people had to lay down their lives, then so be it.

In Kale's memories, however, peace still reigned at times. He could still remember the days of his irrepressible youth, when the sun shone bright and all things were in harmony. He could see with his mind's eye his living and loving mother and father, both of them smiling and laughing with not a thought toward House Suldamik. For them, their innocent child mattered more than politics. However, his eyes darkening with each memory, then the cataclysmic flames of war had erupted, consuming all that stood in its way. Fathers, mothers, children, young and old – there was neither discrimination nor concern for the lives it destroyed, for death was all it sought, and it was relentless in its pursuit.

He had watched his father die in battle against Craigan, the elder Merandith's head split like a ripe melon. Kale was only sixteen that day, his sword skills and battle prowess barely hinting at his potential, and he had been helpless to aid his father that day. Two years later, his mother had been murdered while observing a battle, an assassin's crossbow bolt through her heart. Kale ascended the throne of House Merandith that very day, tears flowing down his grim visage as the crown was placed upon his head. His thirst for vengeance gave birth to a campaign of bloodshed and slaughter, reclaiming territories at the cost of countless lives. Yet vengeance never came, and the war dragged on. Eventually, his lust for retribution began to fade with the birth of his daughter; as a result, rational thought returned and he shifted his focus from his own selfish endeavors to the good of his people – like his parents would have truly wanted of him.

Movement from behind pulled him from his melancholy reflections. Shorter than him by a few inches and nearly fifty-five summers old, the Sword Master had dismounted. Handing the reins of his and Kale's mounts to the other men, he strolled up beside his doms, curious as to what had held Kale's attention for so long. Unable to spot anything, he grasped the hilt of the broadsword sheathed at his left hip and continued to survey the battlefield with his remaining brown eye. Movement in the distance caught his attention as two armored figures disappeared from sight, descending the rise they had been observing from. The Sword Master snorted and scratched at his four-days growth of beard. Like his short-cut hair, it was more gray than black. However, it was coming in nicely, but was bloody irritating when soaked with sweat like it was now.

"They'll be on the move soon," he rumbled.

"I know."

"Where do you think they'll go?"

Kale shrugged. "Someplace where they can lick their wounds and feel secure as winter sets in."

"They'll grow in numbers, Doms Merandith."

"As will we. Besides, I believe you said reinforcements will be arriving soon." Kale pulled his longsword from the ground and wiped off what little moist blood there was before returning it to the harness on his back. He then turned to face the Sword Master. "I don't intend to give Craigan much room to feel comfortable, Jerom. We cannot afford to lose our advantage just because the season is not favorable for a campaign."

Jerom snorted. "So that's what this harebrained scheme of yours is about." Not wanting to foster another debate, he decided to change the subject. Eyeing Kale's sword and armor with a grunt, he stated, "Let's get you cleaned up. We can't have your kit rusting, and we certainly can't have you greeting the Sur'dathans looking like death's keeper."

Kale smiled at that and clapped Jerom on the back. "Thank you, Uncle. Shall we?"

"Aye, Doms Merandith. As you wish."

The two mounted bodyguards handed the reins of the riderless horses to their respective owners before reining their own mounts about and descending the rise at a slow walk, leaving Kale and Jerom to mount up and follow.

Once on level ground, Kale and his bodyguards quickly found themselves amongst the solemn procession of priests and their wagons toward the six pyres that were already piled high with bodies. As they approached the pyres, the mere sight of all the lifeless bodies made Kale want to scream at the heavens and weep at the same time. Sightless eyes seemed to stare accusingly at him, while gaping mouths seem to be frozen in silent wails for help. Kale reined in his gray destrider stallion in front of the first of the massive pyres, forcing himself to pause and accept the accusatory cries and stares. In the end, no matter who had dealt the killing blow, the blood of these soldiers was on his hands. The muscles of Kale's jaw flexed and drew taunt as he reaffirmed his goal to make sure none of these deaths were meaningless. Kale bowed his head and said a silent prayer before thanking the priests for their efforts. Then with a deep sigh, he tugged on his reins and continued on toward the camp in the distance.

The Five Stars – what the army affectionately called themselves in honor of House Merandith's banner – was encamped on a relatively flat stretch of grassy land to the northeast, nearly half a league from the battlefield. While this provided the army some sense of security from being attacked during the battle, it made the journey back to camp for the troops – both wounded and healthy – arduous. The camp proper was organized into five large squares – one central block flanked on each side by the other blocks, which in turn were subdivided into smaller blocks based on the troops' respective Houses and units. Latrine pits and the corrals were stationed outside the perimeter picket lines well downwind of the main camp. And surrounding it all, was an outer perimeter of patrols that provided both protection and an early warning against attack.

The four guards stationed at the entrance to the camp, all from House Merandith per the usual post-battle duty assignments, saluted sharply as the small party approached. Kale acknowledged them with a smile and a nod as they passed through the picket line and into the din of noise and activity of the bustling mobile city. The main avenue, which was wide enough to permit two supply wagons abreast of each other, was alive with men and women attending to work. No matter what their task, troops paused to salute Kale as his party ventured through camp. Not only did Kale respond in kind, but along the way, he would call for a halt at random cookfires and spend time talking with the throng awaiting food. It brought a smile to his face to see the joy and respect they felt as he inquired about their families, their health, and even shared a joke or two. In the end, however, the smile on his face would vanish each time as he remounted and continued on.

The rhythmic pounding of hammer on steel began to ring louder and the smoke hanging in the air grew thicker as they moved deeper into the camp and neared the small army of forges. Kale eyed the bustling blacksmiths through the rows of tents with fondness. He had spent much of his free time as a youth learning about metalworking and the forging of the tools of war. The familiar sights and sounds usually made him smile, but after the bloodshed of the morning, he couldn't find that grin. Shaking his head, Kale nudged his mount onward.

Eventually, they reached one of the guard posts in the picket line that separated the inner block from the rest of the camp. All six men stationed there wore black tabards – which were embroidered with the five gold stars of House Merandith on their chests – over their leather armor. With Kale's arrival, they snapped to attention and saluted their doms before waving him and his party through.

The inner block was made up of strictly House Merandith's forces – which amounted to nearly four thousand strong. The men and women of House Merandith prided themselves on their attention to detail and organization as much as their fighting prowess, and it showed. Black tents – flying pennants that were just as black and embroidered with five golden stars – were arranged in an orderly fashion along walkways that were clear of obstacles. Though it had been but a short while since the morning battle, troops were already busily attending to chores that ranged from keeping the common areas neatly organized to mending clothing and equipment, or even cooking meals. To Kale's eye, so many of them looked tired and haggard, yet they went about their tasks with a determination that made his heart swell with pride.

They finally reached the center of the central block where Kale's command pavilion was located. Coming to a halt in front of Doms Merandith's quarters, all four men dismounted as the two men guarding the tent's entrance saluted crisply and a pair of young stablehands rushed forward to collect the party's destriders. As the warhorses were led away for a well-earned rub down and feeding, Kale's two remaining bodyguards consulted with Jerom before taking their leave and making their way to their tents, which were stationed to the right of the pavilion. With their departure, Kale couldn't help but glance at the now ownerless bodyguard tents that were erected to the rear and left of Kale's quarters.

Catching Kale's eye, Jerom nodded to let him know he was ready to proceed. As they approached the pavilion's entrance, the guard on the right pulled aside the entry flap while the one on the left said, "Doms Merandith, Amroth awaits you inside."

Kale nodded to the guard and then proceeded inside. It took a moment for his eyes to adjust to the dim illumination before he could make out his surroundings. The interior of the pavilion would have been considered spacious if not for the heavy, hanging cloth dividers that separated the larger space into three smaller rooms. His bedroom was setup to the left of the main room, and his study to the right, while the main room served as a war room. A large, simple oak table occupied the center of the room with five unremarkable chairs surrounding it. Maps depicting Triclose and the occupying realms in detail littered the tabletop; some were very general in their illustration, while others showed specific locations in great detail, escalating Kale's capacity to plan for distinctive terrain. Fresh reports, notes on supply routes and quantities, along with letters bound for home were stacked neatly on the far side of the table. Kale eyed the reports reluctantly. He had a feeling that by the end of the day, he would be inclined to personally end the lives of a few select domses over their endless requests, many of which he found trivial and superficial. Fortunately, he wasn't commonly prone to such violent thoughts or actions away from battle. Still . . . the urge was a bit too enticing at times.

All thoughts of violence were scrubbed from his mind as his gaze came to rest on the man lounging in one of the chairs behind the table. Though Kale was a head taller and five years older, the man in the chair was, by far, much more imposing than he. His black hair was tied back at the nape of his thick neck, and eyes of a darkness to match scanned the maps on the table while a strong, callused hand toyed with a half-empty goblet. Corded muscles rippled as he shifted position and glanced up at the arrivals, his clean-shaven and solemn face breaking into a smile. Putting down the goblet, he then wiped his hands on his sleeveless, simple linen shirt before standing. Soot stains marred his shirt and the leather pants and boots that completed his attire.

Kale laughed for the first time that day and shook his head. "Straight from the forges again, I see. Would it hurt for you to bathe before paying me a visit?"

A smile cracked the stoic features of the visitor's face as he stood and moved around the table to embrace Kale, seemingly oblivious to the dried blood on Kale's armor. "I managed to wash my hands and face. Isn't that enough?"

Kale pulled away and chuckled. "If you're going to be visiting your doms – I should say not." He clapped the man on the shoulders before moving past him and unbuckling his sword-harness. "What brings you here, Amroth?"

Removing the harness, Kale leaned it against the table before working at the system of buckles that held his armor in place. When it became obvious that he was having a difficult time, Jerom let out a snort and moved to his aid. "Stop it, lad, and let me help. You'll end up breaking a strap or hurting yourself at the rate you're going."

Kale nodded his consent with a welcoming smile.

Amroth chuckled at the two as he picked up Kale's sword and unsheathed it, examining the blade with a practiced eye. "Well, Barniban wanted to make sure you were alright . . . and he also figured your kit would be in need of repairs. Judging from what I see here, he was right." Resuming his place in the chair, he pulled a whetstone, polish and cloth from his belt pouch and began to work on the blade. "Honestly, Kale – would it kill you to be more careful with this? It looks like a drakuma hammered it into a boulder all-day."

Jerom snorted as he removed Kale's breastplate and placed it on the table next to the matching pauldrons. "The lad needs to figure out that staying out of the fight would do us all a lot of good – less work for you smithies, and less of a strain on my heart."

Kale laughed and smiled softly as he began to remove his armor-harness and padding, the tension of the morning slowly draining away. "You both know that will never happen. So quit your bellyaching and get used to it." He dumped the harness and padding on the table before occupying the seat opposite Amroth and propping his feet upon the tabletop so Jerom could remove his greaves.

Jerom removed the armor quickly and shoved Kale's booted feet off the table – which Kale promptly returned to the tabletop. Snorting, Jerom playfully chided, "You've too much of your father in you – reckless and ill-mannered. If you were still a child, I'd cuff you a good one for putting your feet up on the table."

Amroth chuckled, drawing a glare from Jerom. "As for you, lad, I'd suggest being on your best behavior 'fore I decide to find you something to do that isn't as pleasant as polishing a sword."

Amroth stifled his laugh and sat up straight in his chair. "Yes, sir!" he barked sarcastically while offering a crisp, mocking salute.

Jerom grumbled under his breath, scratched at his beard, and dropped the greaves at Amroth's feet. "I've got better things to do than cater to you two pups," he declared with mock indignation before grumbling to Kale, "I'm going to go and see if the arrangements for the Sur'dathans' arrival are in order. Deo only knows what put you up to this idea." Leaving no room for a reply, Jerom strode aggressively toward the tent entrance where he paused and turned back to face Kale. "As for you – Doms Merandith – I suggest a change of attire. Dirt and blood do not make a good impression." Kale gave a firm nod as his acknowledgment before Jerom, barely containing a smile, exited the tent.

"You do know you're asking a lot of the men?" Amroth stated seriously after the tent flaps had settled behind Jerom.

Kale sighed. "Not you too. We've been over these plans for months. Besides, it will do the men some good in the end, as well as provide a bit of a morale boost."

Amroth shrugged. "If you say so. All I know is that I see a lot of very tired and strung-out soldiers about camp."

Moving his feet from the table, Kale stood up and let out a sigh. "All that aside, I guess he's right about one thing – tattered war gear is not the way to greet someone." He plucked at his stained shirt. "If you'll excuse me for a moment. . . ."

Amroth nodded and flipped Kale's sword over, turning his attention to the other side of the blade. Kale let out a bemused laugh in response to Amroth's focus before stepping through the divider and into what served as his sleeping quarters.

Small and sparsely furnished, Kale's sleeping quarters were – outside of the rugs underfoot – rather simplistic compared to other nobles. Along the left-hand wall was a washstand that was occupied by a warm pitcher of water, washcloth, towel, and mirror. Situated on the opposite side of the room from the washstand was a simple chair at the foot of a soldier's cot. The cot, which was only a little larger than the standard issue, was cushioned with a feather mattress that was currently home to a set of neatly folded blankets atop a pillow, and, of more importance to Kale, a fresh set of clothing and polished leather knee-boots.

Kale grinned at the preparations before he stripped off his soiled clothing and tossed it all on the chair. Scars from a lifetime of battles and training painted a violent picture across his body. Muscles, toned and hardened from rigorous training, rippled as he stretched and made his way to the washbasin. "You two can't stop looking after me for one moment, can you?" he called to Amroth.

"Someone has to – otherwise, you'd be a mess, and your wife would rain all hells upon us."

"Hummm. That might be true. However, if you two are going to act like my caretakers, you could have at least found me some soap."

There was a snort from the other room. "Good luck with that – we ran out of soap almost three weeks ago. If there is any to be found, it's either been hidden carefully or become a valuable trade item amongst the troops at this point."

"Oh well – I guess smelling like an overworked blacksmith won't be too bad," he replied sarcastically.

Amroth chuckled. "You could do worse. I hear the stable-hands smell nearly as bad as the latrines."

Kale smiled and poured the pitcher of water into the washbasin. Soaking the washcloth in the water, he placed it on the side of the bowl before proceeding to wash his face and hands, which quickly turned the liquid a ruddy brown. Picking up the washcloth, he then rubbed every inch of himself down, the warm water soothing his aching muscles as he washed the grime of the day away. Finally, he leaned over the basin and emptied the water remaining in the pitcher over his head before scrubbing his hair and scalp vigorously.

Once finished, he dried off before the brisk air made him uncomfortable, and proceeded to don the fresh clothes. Quickly pulling on the brown pants, he tossed on the dark-blue linen shirt and tucked it into his pants before binding the sleeves at the wrists with a pair of simple leather bracers. The knee-boots were a bit difficult to maneuver, but he managed to slide them on and buckled them in place with minimal effort. A simple sword belt followed, which he settled comfortably about his waist, completing his uncomplicated attire. While nowhere near as regal or flamboyant as some domses' apparel, it still felt opulent compared to the blood- and gore-spattered armor he had worn throughout the morning.

Feeling mildly refreshed, Kale returned to the main room to find that Amroth had finished with his sword, which now rested in its harness against the table, and was now working on his greaves.

Flashing Kale a quick, admonishing glare, Amroth returned his attention to the greave in his hands, and with a sigh, stated, "I'll be busy, again, tonight. The beating your armor took today is simply amazing – I'm surprised the sword and greaves are in as good of shape as they are."

Kale rolled his eyes. "I'll be sure to tell Suldamik's men to take it easy next time," he stated sarcastically.

Amroth nodded. "I'd appreciate that."

"Would you like me to invite them to dinner as well?" Kale added with a dry smirk.

Amroth held the greave up in the dim light, examining a spot near the knee closely. "If you think that would help." He muttered something under his breath. "Alright – I can't do any more for this mess here."

Kale bowed mockingly. "My apologies, good Blacksmith. Shall I lend you a hand in returning the armor to your forge?"

Amroth rolled his eyes and stood up. "Oh, enough of that! Although – now that I think about it – you did make the mess, so you might as well be the one to lug all this metal back to the forges."

Kale snapped his heals together and saluted sharply, fist to heart. "As you command, Master Blacksmith," he teased.

Amroth rolled his eyes and simply laughed.

# Chapter Two

**D**rake Elifis was old and very much feeling his age. His long, braided hair was more white than brown, and while his black eyes still shone with intelligence and a quick wit under thick eyebrows, he certainly didn't see as well as he used to. Sweat-drenched wrinkled, sun-baked skin that was haphazardly decorated with a host of scars garnered from a lifetime of combat. Beneath his leathery hide were muscles, which looked more like they belonged on a man half his age, that ached from the day's events. The life of a soldier was never dull for long, but with it came a host of injuries that took their toll, and he had lived long enough to begin to wonder if the old wounds were asking a price of him that he wouldn't be able to pay in the years to come.

He had served his House, and by extension House Merandith, since he was just a boy. The youngest son of a minor shi'doms, the family lands and titles had fallen to his older brother. As a youth, this reality had left him with the choice of living a life of luxury at the feet of his brother, or striking out on his own. He found he had no mind for mathematics, nor was he blessed with the tongue of a poet. While smart in his own right, he was no scholar either. However, constant fights with his brother while growing up had shown him a talent for combat. So, when it came time to make a choice, he began his tutelage under the House's Weapon Master. Forty years and countless campaigns later, he found himself a captain in Doms Merandith's army – proud of his accomplishments and well respected within his own House. Yet, none of that could improve his current mood.

"No, ye dogs! I said move the horses, not make them comfortable! We've got guests coming in, and I don't think they want these damn creatures wandering around where they're supposed to be bedding down!"

The northern side of the camp was bustling with activity as troops broke camp and relocated in preparation for the arrival of the Sur'dathan contingent. Scouts had already reported that the reinforcements were behind schedule, though the way Drake pushed his subordinates gave no indication that he cared. There were also nervous grumblings as to just what was going on. With more than enough room for the new arrivals to make a camp, it was odd that a full quarter of the mobile forces was being uprooted and moved with orders to make a minimal camp. The general consensus was that it all pointed to a move. The when and where is what had the soldiers nervous. Some speculated that they were being force-marched after Suldamik's forces, while other rumors suggested a more clandestine objective. Whatever the reason, these kinds of orders when everyone was tired did more to encourage tongues to wag instead of motivating the troops to accomplish their tasks.

Shouting and cursing confirmed that the soldiers' minds were anywhere but focused on the task-at-hand. Support lines for one of the pavilions had snapped, catching one man full in the face and collapsing the structure on two others that were inside. Blood oozing from the gash caused by the snapped line, the injured soldier was escorted away as other troops moved to help extract their trapped brethren. Drake rubbed his temples and cursed under his breath. Despite the numerous scars that littered his body arguing to the contrary, he felt it would be incompetence that killed him, not an opponent's blade.

He spotted three soldiers standing idly by, bantering amongst themselves. "You three! Yes! Ye sods! Get over there and lend them a hand with that tent! Be quick about it lads – or I'll have ye up to your hips in shite, cleaning out the latrines with your hands!"

As if a fire had been lit under their feet, the three soldiers scrambled to the accident site, eager to avoid drawing the captain's ire further.

"Problems, good Captain?"

Drake turned quickly, his chain armor rattling, startled by the voice from behind. He cursed softly under his breath and removed his gloved hand from the hilt of the broadsword at his left hip. "Don't sneak up on me like that! I got too few years ahead of me, and I don't need ye scaring them away!"

Still wearing his blood-stained armor, Jerom chuckled and scratched at his beard. "Sorry about that, old friend – seems to me that you're just tired and a bit cranky." He stopped next to Drake, taking in the scene before them. The men had finished extracting the trapped soldiers – neither of them badly injured – and were clearing the collapsed pavilion away.

Drake eyed Jerom's armor and grunted. "Aye, we're all a bit of that. Too much fighting and not enough rest. Doms Merandith is asking a bit much to have this area cleared so quickly after the battle this morning. Given how I feel, I can only imagine how the others are doing." He grunted again. "And I can't believe we've gotten this much done."

"Sore or not, these men aren't nearly as old as you. . . ." Jerom smirked before adding knowingly, "Or as anxious to find a bed and something hard to drink, I would guess."

Drake grunted. "Aye lad, I'll give ye that. I'm feeling every blow, ache and pain more and more every day." He cleared his throat and spit on the ground. "Won't be long before I have to think about take'n Doms Merandith up on the Academy commission."

Jerom barked a laugh. "Deo be good – we don't need to do that to all the young ones!"

A snort of disgust greeted Jerom's friendly quip. "Bah! Enough of yer jabs! What brings ye away from yer baby-sitting duties? Amroth decided yer old bones need a break?"

Jerom had to smile at the imagery. "Something along those lines. I'm afraid, however, my visit is of a serious nature."

Drake perked up, his aged and stern visage turning serious. "What's wrong? Doesn't have to do with the Highlanders be'n late?"

Jerom shook his head in the negative as the two friends stepped to the side of the path, allowing a column of troops to pass that was carrying supplies from the dismantled camp to a staging ground for redistribution amongst the ranks. Once Jerom was satisfied there were no prying ears within range, he said, "Our losses were heavier than expected this morning. While this wouldn't normally leave me nervous, we took a large hit amongst Doms Merandith's bodyguards."

"How bad?"

"Only myself, Tazrim and Mathis remain."

Letting out a low, concerned whistle, Drake breathed, "Deo be good."

"Aye – so we're in a bit of a bind. Given my nephew's adventurous spirit, three of us simply won't be enough to keep him safe," Jerom stated with a mix of concern and consternation.

Drake laughed dryly. "Don't tell me ye be wanting me to join up? We may be about the same age, but I don't have the energy to keep up with younglings like yer nephew."

Jerom shook his head. "Won't say the thought didn't cross my mind. But, Kale had an idea that seems good. It will provide a distraction and possibly boost morale. Aside from that, it's more traditional than just tossing troops to the wolves like we've been doing."

Drake's black eyes lit up with comprehension. "A tournament, eh? Hasn't been one of them in nearly ten years. It would help the spirits of the men. Hells – explaining what all this mess," he waved a hand in the direction of the disassembled camp, "is about would help too."

Jerom nodded. "All in good time. Kale will let us know when he's ready."

Drake snorted, knowing Jerom was holding back on him. "So what do ye need from me?"

Jerom scratched at his chin. "Suggestions and thoughts on viable candidates. You're amongst the men more than I, and, quite frankly, I would rather we pick from veterans than the fresh blood from the Academy."

Drake scratched his head. While it was true that he was more aware of the activity within the rank-and-file, coming up with someone trustworthy enough to guard Doms Merandith's life was a difficult task. Most soldiers would not want such a responsibility. Sure, the pay and accommodations would be better, but being shouldered with Doms Merandith's life was not something that many would stomach well. The few possibilities that came to mind were of noble blood, and it would not do to have personal ambition get in the way.

Just as he was about to respond in the negative, it occurred to him whom he could suggest. Smiling slyly, he told Jerom, "Oh aye, there's one man I can think of that would fit the bill."

Jerom arched an eyebrow at him, the broad smile suddenly putting him on guard. "Am I going to like this?"

Drake laughed and draped a meaty arm around Jerom's shoulders. "Aye, ye'll like him – strong lad, fierce fighter and full of fire."

Rolling his lone brown eye, Jerom said, "Why do I get the feeling I'm not going to like this, despite your assurances?"

Drake spotted one of his lieutenants. "Lieutenant! I'll be stepping away for a bit. Make sure these pig-trough dwellers keep at it!"

The soldier snapped off a crisp salute and began shouting at the workers.

"Ah, now where was I. . . ." He turned and began leading them toward the main camp. "You'll like the lad, Jerom. Never seen one like him."

Jerom stepped out from under his friend's arm. "Oh really?"

"Aye, aye. Yer favorite kind of fighter. Uses an odd weapon, though. Terrifies the men."

Jerom came to an abrupt halt as it struck him where the conversation was going. "Wait – you're not serious?"

Drake turned and grinned at his old friend. "Aye, I am. Nothing better to protect our young doms than a Roselian clansman."

Jerom groaned.


They could hear the cheers and shouts before they could see the cause of the commotion. Drake had led Jerom almost clear across camp to where House Trivant's forces were stationed. The orange and black tents of House Trivant were orderly arranged in groups of six tents surrounding a common area. The common areas were normally occupied by a large cookfire along with men and women that were either socializing or taking care of tasks. However, Jerom and Drake soon saw that the common area of one of the tent clusters deep within the camp was filled with a throng of cheering soldiers.

Standing across the path from the gathering, Jerom muttered under his breath, drawing a chuckle from Drake. "What's wrong, lad?"

"What's wrong? Being led around by the nose to find a Roselian clansman that you think would be a good option – that's what," he declared with a scowled. "What makes you think one of those muscle-brained oxen would meet with my approval?"

Drake smiled and nodded to a fully armored squad that passed them on their way to take over guard duty. "Come now, don't ye be judging them all by the one or two that made yer life miserable at the Academy. Besides, yer standing in a camp that prized fighting force is part of. Don't want one to overhear ye and swear a Blood Oath against ye."

Jerom scowled. "One or two? I have the unfortunate privilege of their presence too often, as Trivant seems to love them as his personal guards. Hells, he's distantly part clansman himself. They're noisy, hot-tempered, and honor-bound to a fault. There's no telling what has that group cheering like that – as likely to be some Blood Oath come to a conclusion, as it is a drinking contest. They drive me mad! And don't be worrying about if they hear me or not! I'm too old to be fretting over some pup wanting a piece of me over some imagined slight!"

Laughing, Drake responded, "Aye, they are that. Just give this one a chance." He shot his friend a toothy grin. He knew Jerom too well. While his words implied a hatred for Roselians, Drake knew the elder Merandith had grown to respect the nation and its fearsome fighters over the years.

Jerom shook his head with a sigh. "Lead on, then."

Drake led them across the crowded path and forced their way through the cheering mass to a position where they could see what the crowd was focused on. In the center of the common area, two Roselian clansmen of imposing stature fought. While one was noticeably shorter than the other, each man shared the visible traits of a clansman. Both were bronze skinned and their naked and scarred torsos decorated with clan tattoos; furthermore, each had their raven-black hair pulled back from their faces and braided into a long horse-tail.

It appeared that the two had been engaged in their brawl for some time, as their fists and faces were blood-spattered, and numerous bruises littered their bodies. Although neither man was currently in great condition, the shorter of the two seemed to be in the worst shape. Not only was he bleeding from fresh cuts under his eyes and on his lips, but there was blood seeping from freshly bandaged wounds on his arms and lower torso. However, despite his bandages and the sheen of blood and sweat that covered his body, the serpent tattoos that decorated his body were still easily identifiable.

As for the tall Roselian, his body was covered in wolf tattoos, and his nose had been flattened earlier in the fight. Although he appeared to be in better shape than his opponent to the spectators, his vision was severely hindered by a swollen right eye and the blood that was oozing from a cut above it. Like his opponent, not only did he seem oblivious to his wounds as they circled each other slowly, but his grim face declared that he was just as unwilling to concede the fight as his foe.

Jerom leaned closer to Drake and asked, "I take it one of these two is who you had in mind?" Drake nodded, drawing a snort from his friend. "Not going to be much good to me if he's nothing but a walking injury."

Drake smiled. "Oh quit yer bellyaching and watch! If I'd been here at the beginning, I'd have a few coins on the short one."

"The short one, eh? A bit scrawny by Roselian standards."

"Aye. His name is Dakan Holdreth – a corporal in House Trivant's Regulars. Fought beside and drank with the lad on a few occasions. He may be short, but the lad's full of piss and fire. Just ye watch – he'll topple the giant!"

The crowd roared as the giant stepped forward and began raining vicious blows to his opponent's head and torso. Arms raised to absorb the blows, his opponent slowly sank toward the ground in an attempt to gather his legs under him. Seeing the toll his punches were exacting, the large Roselian grinned.

Suddenly, his shorter foe lunged forward, driving a fist hard into the tall Roselian's stomach. He followed that punch with another one, and then another, driving the air from the massive fighter's lungs, each punch granting him more room to stand up. Gaining solid footing and the opening he needed, the short Roselian's body coiled before he exploded upward, hammering an uppercut to his opponent's jaw. There was a sickening crunch as the large Roselian's jaw broke. Stunned, the man's eyes then rolled back in his head and he collapsed to the ground like a rag doll.

Cheers and curses filled the air as the crowd showed where their bets had been. A medic, who had been asked to observe and tend to the fighters afterward, rushed forward to check on the fallen combatant even as two men moved in to collect bets and make payouts. It was a difficult challenge for the small, white-robed woman to push through the milling mass of onlookers as they surged about the victorious Roselian, offering their praises and congratulations. Once she was able to reach the downed fighter and confirm that he was in no immediate danger, she enlisted two of the spectators to carry the defeated combatant to the medical tents. The two soldiers, disappointed that their celebration would have to wait, carefully lifted the man from the ground and made their way through the throng. The medic then went to check on the bleeding victor, but he waved her off, motioning for her to attend to his opponent. She eyed him skeptically, but nodded her acknowledgment and moved to follow her charge.

Jerom and Drake stood clear of the celebrating crowd, observing it all. Jerom grunted his begrudging approval of the selfless act. "Alright then – he's strong and durable, as well as selfless. Not too many people would be able to fight all-day and then take that kind of punishment." He grunted again. "Deo only knows what led to the spat," he muttered before adding, "So, if you can separate your proposed choice from that mess and get him cleaned up a bit, I'll speak with him."

Drake clapped Jerom on the shoulder and grinned. "Glad ye see it my way. Wouldn't want to have to beat some sense into ye like the old days."

Jerom snorted. "Would you just get on with it? I've got more important things to do than keep your company all-day."

Drake laughed and smiled. "Aye, aye. I'll collect the lad and see that he gets fixed up, then bring him to ye."

Jerom scratched at his chin. "Good. I've got a few other matters to attend to. I'll also need to visit Trivant's clerk and look into the corporal's record. Bring him to my tent in an hour, and I'll have my measure of him."

Drake nodded and began to make his way through the crowd. Jerom observed the victorious clansman a moment longer before shaking his head in amusement and setting off to attend to the rest of his duties.

Despite serving as one of Doms Merandith's bodyguards, Jerom had been issued a tent befitting his status as Shi'doms of House Merandith and Doms General of the Five Stars. He had long ago abandoned any thoughts of House Merandith's throne being his; his brother had been a better leader than he, and the son was proving to be more than his father before him. Instead, Jerom had settled for guarding his brother and his nephew, as well as assisting with running the Merandith household. While at home, this entailed managing business affairs, helping to settle disputes, or even just baby-sitting Kale's daughter. In the field, he not only defended Kale, but also served as a doms general of the army; in this capacity, he helped oversee the day-to-day affairs of the military, thus removing some of the load from his nephew's shoulders.

Even amongst House Merandith, there were some that believed he did too much for his nephew, but with no children of his own and his wife having passed away decades ago, Kale and his family were all that he had left; anything he could do to reduce the burden on them was a small price to pay to promote their happiness and wellbeing. As a result, he found himself seated behind his large oak desk, poring over a large portion of the reports that would have normally been Kale's responsibility. It wasn't what he wanted to be doing, but with the Sur'dathan reinforcements behind schedule, he had found himself gifted with some unexpected downtime until Drake brought the clansman to see him. With nothing else to do until then, he had decided that eliminating some of the reports would be a good use of the time.

Preferring a measure of comfort while toiling over the dull reports, he had changed into clean attire upon returning to his tent. Though he still retained the boots he'd worn all morning, he now wore a loose white shirt tucked into brown leather breeches. As for his armor, all but his sword had been taken by his squire to the blacksmiths for repairs. He was never without his sword if he could avoid it, and he took great pride in maintaining the blade himself; therefore, the beloved, simple and functional broadsword sat in its freshly oiled scabbard, which currently hung from the back of his chair.

Jerom occupied the heavily carved chair with an arm draped over its back, his fingers tapping on the sheathed blade as he read over the reports. Candlelight, along with the natural light seeping in through the tent walls, shone off the polished, heavily and elegantly carved desk that was neatly organized to help make his life a bit easier. Incoming reports and requests were stacked neatly on the left side of the desktop, while both those that he was done with and those that required a response were orderly piled on the right. This helped to make sure that not only was there room for a writing kit, paper, and wax for his seal, but that there was space enough for him to compose any responses or orders that were needed.

Tossing the report he was reading on the desk, he leaned back in his chair and rubbed his lone eye. The reports had become repetitive over the last few months as supplies dwindled. Too few rations; not enough leather and thread to make repairs; the need for more grain to feed the horses or to make bread – the requests seemed endless and he could almost recite them before opening them. It had gotten so bad that the items in need were either being hoarded or used for bartering; he had even seen ration tokens and bowstrings being exchanged in the aftermath of the morning melee. There was, unfortunately, very little he could do to appease his subordinates. Fresh supplies were still a few days out according to the last word they had received nearly a fortnight ago. All he could do was redistribute as possible and ask that everyone be patient.

With an exasperated sigh, he leaned forward and penned a quick response to the report, sealed it with his seal, and added it to the outgoing pile. Leaning back in his chair, he let his vision wander about the spacious tent.

His tent was large by bodyguard standards, but empty compared to most royals. Aside from his desk and chair, the main room of the pavilion was occupied by two extra chairs for guests, an empty brazier for the cooler nights, and a smaller table upon which rested two simple goblets and a pitcher of warm red wine. Behind his desk was his bedroom, which was separated from the rest of the tent by hanging dividers. Like his brother and his nephew, opulence wasn't in his blood. He preferred things simple and efficient – though he did tend to splurge on good drink, comfortable clothing, and good steel. While that might seem opulent to many of the soldiers and commoners, it was practically pauper status amongst the vast majority of the nobility.

Standing, he moved to the wine pitcher and filled one of the goblets halfway. As he sipped on the rich red liquid, he chuckled to himself. A noble pauper – practically a contradiction in terms. He shut his eye and sighed as the alcohol slowly relaxed his muscles and dulled some of his aches. He found it sad and nearly pitiful that many nobles saw the Merandiths as weak because of that. There were domes and domas amongst Suldamik's ranks that saw the Merandith tendency to shun opulence and take a more everyday approach to things as a weakness to be burned out like a plague.

Jerom snorted. Greed and opulence were two of the many factors that had brought Triclose to its current situation; and as far as he was concerned, those factors and a lust for power were what drove House Suldamik. The stories commoners brought with them when fleeing lands controlled by House Suldamik and its allies were horrible. Starvation, inhuman work conditions, whole families burnt as heretics and dissidents – these were crimes against the people that shouldn't be tolerated by anyone. Granted, not everyone in support of House Suldamik were callous and cold-hearted individuals, but their support of Craigan made them just as guilty of the crimes as he was. It was curious, however, how Craigan seemed surprised and ignorant of such charges when confronted by them. Jerom wasn't sure if he was a good actor and liar, or if he was truly in the dark about what was going on in his and his supporters' lands.

He was brought from his reflections by the rustle of his tent flaps being pulled back. Turning, he saw that his squire – whose lean, twenty-summer-old features were sadly showing the tolls of war – had stuck his shaven head inside, his green eyes focused on his shi'doms. "Shi'doms Merandith – Captain Elifis is here to see you with the man you requested."

Jerom finished off the wine in his goblet. "Send them in, Tavid, and then go see how the repairs on my armor are going."

Tavid nodded and stepped out of the entryway, allowing Drake and his charge to enter. Drake eased into the tent, one hand resting on the hilt of his broadsword and his black eyes glinting in amusement. Cleaned up from the fight, his clansman charge followed in tow. Dressed in a black leather vest, loose-fitting wool pants, and black boots, he appeared unbothered by his host of injuries as he positioned himself next to Drake at attention.

Jerom returned to his place behind his desk and settled into his chair as both men saluted, fist to heart. Drake then stated, "Shi'doms Merandith – I present to ye, Corporal Dakan Holdreth of the Northern Clans, currently in the service of House Trivant."

Jerom nodded. "Captain – if you would be so kind as to wait outside, I'll join you as soon as we're done here."

Nodding, Drake then saluted again and exited the pavilion.

Once Jerom was sure the tent flaps were secure, he turned his attention back to the corporal. "Have a seat. It seems you've had a busy day today."

Dakan eased himself into one of the guest chairs with no indication of pain or discomfort from his wounds. In fact, Jerom felt like he was looking at a coiled trap ready to spring. Everything about the man spoke of a fighter bred – there was a measured coolness in the dark eyes set astride his broken and reset nose, and his posture and movements were shrouded in readiness.

"Thank you, Shi'doms," Dakan replied in a deep, rich voice that held just a hint of the violence coiled in his muscles.

"I notice you don't have your weapon on you. From what I know of the Clans, one's weapon is nearly as important as one's family."

Dakan nodded. "It is. Mine was confiscated by my lieutenant before the dispute was settled."

"I saw that. An impressive display. Mind telling me what it was all about?"

Dakan cocked his head to the side. "It was . . . personal."

Jerom sat back and nodded. He knew that personal disputes amongst Roselian clansmen took on a whole new meaning. Sharing the object of or reason for a dispute outside of a trusted few was tantamount to adultery. Those that broke Clan law had been known to be found dead or beaten severely. "Fair enough. As Doms Trivant and Merandith respect Clan law, so shall I."

"Thank you, Shi'doms."

"Down to business then." Jerom pulled a piece of paper from under his writing kit and began to read from it. "Corporal Dakan Holdreth of the Northern Clans, under the protection of the Clan of the Wolf. Ten years service to House Trivant in the Regulars. Commendations for bravery and valor on multiple occasions. Recommended for promotion on three occasions – which you declined each time. Multiple minor infractions, mostly involving clan affairs. Hard labor for the deaths of two other clansmen as a result of clan disputes." Jerom returned the paper to his desk and eyed Dakan curiously. "From what I can see here, you've got quite a reputation. On one hand, you've shown yourself to be trustworthy and a survivor. On the other hand, you've shown an adherence to Clan law that has

64

not only interfered in your service to Doms Trivant, but has also resulted in the deaths of your brothers-in-arms. So I'm wondering – what kind of man sits across from me now?"

Dakan folded his arms across his chest and looked Jerom directly in the eye. "I am who I am. I am of the Northern Clans, and Clan law applies in nearly all situations – no matter who I serve. As I serve House Trivant, then House Trivant is part of my clan until my service is over. So, I think the better question is – why am I here?"

Jerom leaned forward, resting his forearms on his desk. "Well, Corporal, I have a bit of a situation on my hands. We suffered significant losses amongst Doms Merandith's bodyguards this morning; as such, it falls to me to return us to our proper numbers. You have been recommended to me by Captain Elifis – which is high praise – and I don't take his word lightly. So, what I have to determine is if you are truly worth my time."

"If my record and my following of Clan law is concerning to you, why make such an offer to me? You present a position of status and honor that a clansman would rarely have the chance to reach."

Jerom laughed, drawing a raised eyebrow from Dakan. "Present? No lad – this position is not offered, it is earned. We handed out the position too often to men and women with impressive training but lacking in real fighting experience, and this situation is the result. No – we won't be handing out the position this time. Instead, it will be earned through trial-by-combat – a tournament, so to speak. So what I'm offering you is a potential spot in said tournament. Skill and prowess will be the determining factors, not verbal praise and promise."

Dakan leaned back in his chair, deep in thought. He had come to know Captain Elifis as a good friend and drinking partner over the years. They had fought side-by-side in many battles and saved each other's skins on many occasions. For Captain Elifis to make such a recommendation was a stunning admission of the high regard he held for Dakan's skills and character. While his ego was elevated by such a prospect, leaving his current post was not so simple. He was Roselian to the core – and that meant serving his clan and doms to his dying breath. To change his allegiance, even if it was to the supreme leader of the army, would require the blessing of his doms and the clans' High Elder.

He almost smiled at the thought. The current Elders would probably be glad to be rid of him. Including the High Elder, many amongst the Northern Clan Council saw Dakan as too brash and quick to anger – which was saying a lot about a clansman. The two deaths on his hands were considered pointless, as the issues were viewed as petty. Dakan didn't see it that way and held to his convictions firmly, which had led to countless conflicts between him and the Council. As far as he was concerned, age had softened most of the Council members, and this would be an opportunity to prove his ability and prowess to the clans.

"I won't lie – your offer is tempting. The decision isn't a simple one, though. I would need both Doms Trivant and the Council's blessing to even attempt what you offer."

Jerom nodded. He had already anticipated a similar complication with many of the possible candidates, and had composed a number of post transfers just waiting for the proper names to be filled in. "Aye, I'm familiar with the proceedings. I can see to the post transfer from Doms Trivant's service. But I believe the issue of asking permission from the Council would be up to you?"

Dakan nodded. "It would be. Can I ask what would be asked of me?"

"Simply put – you'd be mine until the tournament and beyond unless you drop out or lose. You would have to learn House Merandith's procedures, our training, and be available to Doms Merandith or myself at all times. You will, in every sense, be a trainee again; if that offends your sense of honor and pride, and you can't swallow that, then we're done right now."

Jerom noticed Dakan's jaw clench and the muscles flex as he digested what would be expected of him. "I could . . . follow such rules, though it does go against everything I believe. I have earned my position, and to sacrifice it like it never existed is . . . sickening."

Jerom laughed. "Honest – even if it cost you your shot right here and now. Honesty is something both Doms Merandith and I appreciate and expect from those around us, even if it is blunt."

He noticed the tent flap stir, and Drake stuck his head inside. "What is it, Captain?" Jerom asked.

"Shi'doms – there's a runner here to see you."

Nodding, Jerom said, "Send him in."

Drake nodded and stood aside, holding the tent flap open to admit a dirt-stained and exhausted runner. The runner was one of the few youths traveling with the army. Like many of those that were too young to serve in combat, the boy had been brought along to fill one of the many noncombat roles. Jerom couldn't recall when, but somewhere in the last two years, the boy had become not only Kale's personal messenger, but had also been brought into service as his squire. The boy, who was around thirteen summers old, was breathing heavily and his shaved head was glistening with sweat as he entered the tent. From his nearly threadbare wool attire, to his worn but well-maintained boots, the youth's ragged appearance was an apt complement to the exhaustion expressed in his blue eyes.

"Catch your breath, Gammon," Jerom bade. "I take it you bring word from Doms Merandith?"

Taking a few deep breaths, Gammon then nodded and replied, "Yes, Shi'doms. He sends word that the Sur'dathans have arrived, and he wishes your presence to receive them."

"About bloody time," Jerom muttered as he stood – Dakan following suit – removed his sword belt from the chair and buckled it on. "Thank you, Gammon. Why don't you go and help Tavid retrieve my armor from the smiths. After that, take the rest of the day off. You've earned it, and I'm sure Doms Merandith would agree with me."

Gammon bowed. "Thank you, Shi'doms. Doms Merandith wants you to also know that he has already gone ahead."

Jerom arched an inquisitive eyebrow. "Was anyone with him?"

"Just Amroth, Shi'doms."

Jerom rolled his eye before digging around on his desk and coming up with two ration tokens. He tossed them to Gammon, who caught them deftly. "Get going, and get yourself and Tavid an extra ration on me. My nephew has run you ragged today, and Tavid has suffered no less from me."

"Yes, Shi'doms." Smiling gleefully at the unexpected reward, Gammon bowed once again before quickly leaving the tent.

Jerom snorted in mild amusement and moved to the tent entrance. Pulling the flap aside, he turned to address Dakan. "Well lad, I don't have the time to keep this conversation going. If you do choose to accept this offer, I'll expect you to present yourself to me by noon tomorrow."

Dakan nodded as the two of them exited the tent. "I will let you know by then."

Drake, pacing back and forth just a few paces away, made his way over to them upon noticing their appearance. "What's the word?"

Jerom settled his sword at his hip and gave the tents around his a once-over. Kale's pavilion was definitely empty, as his guards were seated at a low-burning fire set just outside his tent. The tents of his two remaining bodyguards also appeared inactive. Given the stress of the morning's battle, it wouldn't have surprised Jerom if both men were sound asleep. Whether or not that was truly the situation, the mere fact that Gammon had delivered word of Kale's departure was evidence enough that Doms Merandith had not been near his tent upon heading out to receive the Sur'dathans, which meant it was likely that Amroth was his only protection.

"The word, Drake," mild irritation at his nephew's rashness creeping into his voice, "is that the Sur'dathans have arrived, and my nephew has already headed out to greet them."

"Alone?" Drake asked skeptically.

Jerom shook his head. "No. He has Amroth with him."

Drake snorted. "Hells, that's not enough to guard his hide."

Jerom grunted in agreement. "I know, but Kale simply won't listen at times."

"Seems very foolish from a man that doesn't appear like that the rest of the time," interjected Dakan.

Both Jerom and Drake stared at him incredulously, neither man accustom to such blunt observations about royalty from a common solider in the presence of said royalty. Drake finally barked a laugh and grinned, while Jerom could only shake his head. "See, Jerom, I told ye the lad had some fire in him!"

"Aye. And you're right, Dakan – it was foolish of him to do this. However, with as much as we hover over him, it's no surprise he likes to try and ditch us from time-to-time. Quite frankly, I think he likes to make a game of it."

"So what do we do now?" asked Drake.

Jerom turned his lone eye back to his old friend. "I am going to go and greet our Sur'dathan visitors, and possibly give my nephew a severe tongue-lashing. I want you to go and make sure their camp-site is clear. Oh, and take Dakan with you. I'm sure you could use another hand. Gentlemen." Jerom nodded to the two men before spinning on his heel and hustling off in the direction of the horse corrals.

Dakan and Drake watched him vanish behind a row of tents before Dakan let out a, "*Humph!*"

Drake glanced at him sideways. "What's that for, laddie? Not up to helping an old soldier with some manual labor?"

"No," he shook his head, "I was just a little disgusted that I would be asked to guard such a thoughtless man, even if it did get me out of the clans' hair."

Drake cuffed him on the back of the head, drawing a baleful glare. "Watch yer tongue, lad! Hells, ye'll end up in the stocks with such baseless remarks! Doms Merandith is anything but thoughtless. Young? Aye. A bit rash at times? Aye – but ye'll never find a more noble and worthy soul to follow. He's a better man than most of us'll ever come close to being. If Jerom really did offer ye a place in Kale's Guard – think real hard on it, laddie. The guards remain'n are some of the finest swordsmen alive, and ye'll get to learn from them, serve beside a great man, and have a chance to be something more than just a mere clan footman."

Dakan's glare turned thoughtful as he digested Drake's words.

Drake grunted in approval. "Now that I see yer brain is working, Corporal, let's get to the task at hand. I have me a bed and a hot meal awaiting, and I intend to enjoy it."


The sun was well into its decent in the eastern sky as Jerom exited the camp to the northwest, where the camp guards indicated Doms Merandith had gone. The northern side of the camp was nearly ready to receive its new occupants by the time Jerom galloped by on his refreshed roan destrider mare, anxious to catch up with his nephew and find out what had taken the Sur'dathans so long. With as helpful as Drake had been today, he was glad to know that he had very little left to do this day. Dakan was an unusual find. Rarely did a clansman show any interest in leaving their clan or changing loyalties – their upbringing just didn't include those teachings. This also meant there were problems between the clans and Dakan. What those issues were, Jerom had no idea, but there was always a possibility that those issues could become a problem down the road. Jerom shrugged mentally. If Dakan decided to join the tournament, the training up to it would not only prove whether or not he was right for the job, but it would also provide him time to find out more about Dakan's past.

Half an hour later, Jerom encountered one of their outer perimeter patrols. The three light cavalrymen informed him that Kale had ridden by only a few moments before and had taken half of their patrol with him. They pointed Jerom to the north before he thanked them and continued on. It did his heart some good to know that Kale had acquired extra protection, but it still didn't excuse him from running off without his bodyguards. Even though their scouts had confirmed that Craigan had pulled fully from the field, venturing outside the perimeter with so few men was dangerous; compounding the reckless decision was the fact that Jerom also trusted Mathis and Tazrim's abilities significantly more than a dozen common soldiers – let alone a paltry trio of cavalrymen.

It wasn't long before he saw Kale and his escort in the distance. As the gap closed, he eventually could make out a party of four armored riders nearly a hundred yards beyond Kale and his group. Flying the snow-toped-mountain standard of House Hagail from their devastating saber-lances, the quartet of armored heavy cavaliers was an impressive sight in the dying sunlight. To Jerom's relief, he saw that their destriders were devoid of armor, which was a clear indication that they felt the area was secure. The cavalrymen's ease with the situation, however, did nothing to dispel his displeasure with his nephew's careless actions.

Kale's party finally noticed his approach, and the three patrolmen that had accompanied him turned and readied to charge. Thankfully, Kale recognized Jerom and ordered them to stand down. Upon reaching his nephew's party, Jerom reined in his destrider and walked her around them while glaring at his nephew. He noticed, in passing, that Amroth had brought his broadsword with him for once. He wasn't sure how much of a fight the lad would put up in a real battle, but at least it gave the impression that Kale had some protection.

Pulling alongside his nephew, he stated angrily, "We'll discuss this later. Those men are the Sur'dathans, I take it?"

Kale chuckled. "Hello to you as well, Uncle. And yes, those are their representatives. I was just about to ride out and meet them when you came galloping up."

Jerom snorted. "Then let's be done with this. The day is getting long."

Kale chuckled. "Alright then. Amroth and Jerom – you're with me." He nudged his horse forward while Jerom and Amroth fell in on opposite sides of him. Noting Kale's advance, the Sur'dathans spurred their horses forward at a casual pace.

After only about a minute of riding, the two groups came to a halt within six feet of each other. Though each of the cavalrymen had an imposing Sur'dathan claymore sheathed within easy reach along the length of their mounts, Jerom's eye was immediately drawn to the horrific lances the Sur'dathans carried.

The ghastly weapon was originally created by the Roselian clans as a heavy spear to hunt the large and dangerous torgen. Years later, the Sur'dathans had adapted the spear to hunt the cats and mon-

70

strous kyrams of the mountains before admirably modifying the weapon into a lance for mercilessly killing people. In its current incarnation, the shaft was made of northern ironwood, the upper quarter of which was fitted with a sturdy steel mount that supported a four-winged lance head that was designed to do catastrophic damage when thrust into a target. Once firmly implanted in a target, the viciously hooked ends of each wing made removing the weapon more dangerous than being speared by the weapon.

The Sur'dathans drove the butts of their saber-lances into the ground – which snapped Jerom's attention back to the riders – before raising the grilled visors on their matching half-helms. Each man was adorned with an identical suit of functional heavy plate, the breastplates of which were emblazoned with a burnished-silver two-headed hammer. Unfortunately, to Jerom's chagrin, their armor also sported a few scratches and dents that looked all too fresh to him.

The lead Sur'dathan rider, whose helm was crested by a charging kyram, nudged his mount forward a bit, drawing everyone's attention to him. His keen green eyes focused on Kale and his party from astride the crooked nose that graced his aged, sun-darkened face. A neatly trimmed, rust-colored beard, which was showing a generous amount of white, concealed a portion of the jagged scar that spanned from his cheek to his chin, marring the right side of his lips. Raising his hand in greeting, he smiled slightly – which was ruined by the jagged scar – and said, "Gregor Netwyn of House Hagail, Doms Captain-Commander of the 3rd Heavy Armor – known as Hagan's Hammer – at yer service. Doms Hagail sends 'is greetings to Doms Merandith and the Army of Five Stars." His thick Highland accent was a bit hard to understand, but not nearly as indecipherable as some of the Highlanders the Merandiths had met over the years.

Jerom nodded to Gregor in acknowledgment. "Well met. I'm Shi'doms Jerom Merandith, Captain of Doms Merandith's Personal Guard and Doms General of the Five Stars." He gestured to Kale. "And this is Doms Merandith."

Gregor saluted, fist to heart. "A pleasure to see ye two again, Doms. Doms Hagail sends 'is regards and apologizes fer our late arrival. Also – our condolences on tha passing of yer mother and father. They were good friends and vital in keepin' Cravon from take'n control o' Sur'datha."

Kale smiled softly. "No apologies needed. And I thank you for the thought. I hope your delay wasn't caused by anything bad?"

"Just a minor scuffle with a few of Suldamik's raiding parties." Jerom and Kale stared at each other in concern, drawing a baffled look from Gregor. "Ye didn't know about tha raiders in tha North?"

Jerom shook his head and scratched at his beard. "We'd heard rumors, but hadn't been able to confirm their existence."

Gregor gave a firm, sincere nod. "Aye, they're real. Had ah few scraps with them all the way south. Been harass'n all tha North fer a good three months. Not ta worry, though. They've been nothing but an annoyance. In fact, we saved one of yer supply trains from ah nasty situation tha other day. Suldamik's men had been harass'n them day and night for nearly a fortnight."

Kale's visage darkened. While it was good to know why their supply lines were behind schedule, the fact that Suldamik had managed to get raiders behind his lines for this long without his knowledge was concerning at best. "My thanks for saving my men. We hadn't had word from them for days, and were beginning to wonder."

Gregor inclined his head. "I know it's not good news, but tha supplies ar' intact, an only a few fatalities. As fer the goin' ons in tha North – Doms Hagail has reports, and I believe there was a messenger with tha supply train bringin' word from yer lands."

Kale's hands tightened on his reins as anticipation immediately took root in the pit of his stomach. He hadn't heard from home in nearly a month and, good or bad, it would do his heart good to hear from his wife. "Very good," he said, masking his anxiousness easily. "We've prepared a site for your men to set up camp. Please give my regards to Doms Hagail and extend my thanks for his help so far. If you and he would also be so kind as to be my guests at dinner, I would very much like to hear what you both have to say on the situation in the North."

Gregor gave a firm, affirmative nod. "Aye, I'll pass on yer invitation, Doms Merandith."

Kale nodded. "Very good then. Gentlemen." Kale, followed by Jerom and Amroth, wheeled their horses about and moved off at a swift canter.

The Sur'dathans remained in place until Kale had rejoined the remaining members of his party, at which point – unable to contain himself any longer – the younger of the two other heavy cavalrymen shook his head and exclaimed, "Bloody hells, Gregor! Did ye be see'n tha young lad with Doms Merandith?"

Gregor spared the black-eyed young man a sideways glance. "Aye, I did. What of it, Donald?"

"Just ah wee bit amazed, sir. I didna think there'd been any survivors of that horror."

"Aye, lad, there were a few. Kale's father found tha wee lad hidden away by his mum. Took tha lad in and raised him as one o' his own." He shook his head. "Deo bless his soul, that lad be tha last remainin' member of a dead clan. Doubt tha lad even knows what was stolen from him."

"Think he be know'n his heritage?" Donald asked, unable to contain his amazement.

"Does it matter? Tha Lowlands were absorbed years ago, and most o' that is still not fertile; nothin' can live there. If Kale's father told him more than his family name, I'd be surprised." He snorted. "Let tha dead be rest'n as far as I'm concerned." He paused and gave both men a stern glare. "I dunna have ta remind ye two that ye shouldna' be speak'n a word about tha lad to anyone, do I?"

"No, sir!" both men barked assertively.

Gregor eyed the two a moment longer before he gave a grunt, pulled his lance from the ground and nudged his horse into motion. "'Nough of that now, lads. We've got to get back and report in. Don't know about ye two, but I'm a wee bit peckish."

# Chapter Three

The man known as Gregor Netwyn was by far one of the most outstanding examples of Sur'dathan chivalry and honor that existed within the army, which had garnered him respect and admiration that he might otherwise never have known. For years, his ability to adhere to his ideals had helped him to attain respect within the army and the attention of Doms Loridak Hagail. Hagail had come to hold Gregor in the highest esteem for his honorable actions and bravery in combat throughout the years. This, along with his knack for tactics and command, earned him the privilege of being promoted to command the highly feared and admired heavy cavalry company known as Hagan's Hammer. While the horrible events surrounding the promotion were nothing to be proud of, Gregor would use the horrifying tragedies, as well as the loss and razing of much of the Lowlands, as motivation to strive for a better Sur'datha. As commander of Hagan's Hammer, he would be integral in the three campaigns that would see an end to the Cravon Uprising and the official annexation of the Lowlands into Sur'datha during the early years of the Third Great War.

Gregor and Doms Hagail had been eager to join Kale's father, Bordin Merandith, against Doms Suldamik after learning the Suldamiks had funded the Cravon Uprising. However, like many of the Northwestern realms, there was the constant threat of invasion from House Suldamik's allies to consider, as well as the weakened state of the army after the Cravon Uprising. Both factors would make it difficult for Hagail to protect his own borders, so instead of marching alongside Bordin when he left Sur'datha, Hagail remained behind to fortify his fully united realm against any further attempt by House Suldamik to invade. To that end, he set Gregor with the difficult and important task of defending the southern border in one of the few areas of Triclose that the Contested Territories did not provide a constant buffer. Granted, there was still the northern reaches of the Dragonspine to contend with, but invasion wasn't impossible; as a result, Gregor found himself successfully defending the border with ruthless efficiency from numerous small incursions.

Indecision seemingly plagued Hagail night and day for the next nine years. In that time, his army swelled from nearly five-hundred to one-thousand strong. Yet, Hagail could not sit completely still; given Gregor's success defending the border, Hagail decided on two things – he promoted Gregor to the rank of doms captain-commander for his outstanding service, and placed upon Gregor's already burdened shoulders the responsibility of organizing raids to harass any and all House Suldamik forces beyond Sur'datha's southern border. While the task was daunting, Gregor welcomed the challenge as a means to be more proactive.

It was at this time that Hagail received word of Bordin Merandith's death, which devastated him completely. To add insult to injury, House Suldamik used the mourning period to drive hard into the heart of Five Stars controlled territory. Using surprise to his advantage, one of the first places Craigan captured was the Utherian Valley – the longtime resting place of all of Triclose's domses and domas. This prevented Bordin from being laid to rest in his rightful place. Had Hagail known about it at the time, he might have made a move to avenge such sacrilege, but winter had fully enveloped the Highlands, preventing word of the Utherian Valley's capture from reaching him until the summer. Hagail had felt that Bordin was the only chance of the first peaceful, fully united Triclose in over a century. With Kale only sixteen summers of age and newly married, his mother, Doma Missia Merandith, was forced to preside as Doma General of the Army of Five Stars. While Hagail didn't disregard the cunning and battle prowess women could possess, Missia was one of the gentlest people he knew. Hagail assumed – and hoped – that Jerom would assume command, but Missia put her heart and soul into seeking revenge for Bordin's death and Craigan's refusal to let her husband be buried in the Utherian Valley. Her actions after taking command laid his fears to rest.

Not only did she assume command with authority, but she began a march that would reclaim much of the territory lost in the mourning period for Bordin. In the two years that Missia ruled over House Merandith, she united the people under her banner with her friendly, outgoing personality and strong leadership. In the end, if Craigan had hoped to end the war with Bordin's death, he was gravely mistaken. However, he never gave Missia the satisfaction of reclaiming the Utherian Valley. By the end of Missia's second year of rule, House Merandith and the Army of Five Stars had become a formidable adversary, forcing Craigan to accept the very real reality that House Suldamik could lose the war. In an effort to fortify his position and to deal House Merandith a staggering blow, Craigan committed what many viewed as his most dishonorable act – he sent the assassin Kazenti Bloodblade for Missia. It was a sad day for the Merandiths when, surrounded by her own army on all sides, Kazenti's signature black bolt found its way into Missia's breast, piercing her heart and killing her instantly. No one saw where the shot came from, and the assassin was nowhere to be found.

Kale, only eighteen, had been handed a devastating blow with the loss of his mother, dumping the weight of ruling House Merandith squarely on his young shoulders. Turning to Jerom and his wife, Marie, for counsel, they decided that a month of mourning would be observed as per tradition. The risks were obvious, given what Craigan had done after Bordin's death, but the love and esteem the people held for Missia could not be ignored. As they feared, Craigan once again took full advantage of the Merandith's weakened state. He pushed hard during the time of mourning, reclaiming most of the territories he had lost during Missia's campaign. Villages and cities fell, women were raped and killed alongside the elderly and children as Craigan's Jade Talons cut a vicious path through the small outposts and token forces still in the field. Outraged at such vile and horrendous acts, Hagail could no longer wait. Putting his army into motion, he used hit-and-run tactics developed and refined by the men under Gregor's command while defending the borders to great effect, drawing Craigan's attention and purchasing Kale the time he needed to finish the mourning period and to prepare his army for war.

Upon ascending to the throne, Kale had informed Hagail of his forthcoming campaign. He would march south toward Gravail before turning southwest to reclaim territories and drive Craigan toward his original borders. Hagail was to bide his time and continue to harass Craigan in the Northwest until such time as Kale sent for him to begin the second phase of his plan. For Hagail, the next five years would be an emotional ride unlike any other. Not only was he not sure Kale could prevail against a superior and confident fighting force, but he was stunned by how Kale began his campaign. The acts of violence Kale committed were akin to those perpetrated by Craigan. Hagail was horrified that the child of such loving and compassionate parents could be responsible for such travesties. Yet, Hagail refused to rescind his oath of loyalty. Despite how much he was dismayed by the acts, he couldn't be sure he wouldn't have done the same given the situation. To lose both parents to the same House in the same war would be too much for anyone no matter how much good was in their heart. The violence also served as a way for the army to vent their frustration and anger. In the end, the acts proved cathartic – solidifying the loyalty of the men and women under Kale's command.

Hagail's respect for Kale grew through the latter portion of the campaign as Kale's anger waned and the kind, loving person Hagail remember reemerged. Kale reined in the rage and violent lust of his men – ending the pillaging, and the rape and killing of prisoners that had heralded the start of his campaign. By the time Hagail received the order to join Kale in the field near the end of the five-year campaign, Craigan was on his heels. A large portion of north-central Triclose was completely in Kale's control, and if the current streak of good fortune continued, eventually they would control all of Central Triclose, and more importantly the Utherian Valley; furthermore, Craigan's reach would be returned to its original borders. However, with the oncoming winter, it looked as if that would have to wait for the spring.

So, with curiosity driving him, Hagail and the pride of the Sur'dathan military pushed hard to the south and east, determined to arrive before winter could fully envelop Triclose. It was by mere coincidence that they had stumbled upon one of Kale's supply trains. Raiders that Craigan had moved behind Kale's lines – amazingly braving the Contested Territories – without notice had been harassing the North for some time. If they had succeeded in destroying or capturing the supply train, it would have left Kale in a weakened state.

Therefore, with pride and the supply train in tow, Hagail and Gregor arrived at the Army of Five Stars' camp ready to do whatever was necessary to keep Craigan on his heels.


Aside from the victory that morning, the arrival of the supply train was reason to celebrate. And by the time the stars began to pierce the clear sky, the whole camp was doing just that. Food had grown so scarce over the last two months that with the infusion of fresh supplies, the men and women of the Five Stars were making up for lost time. Blazing cookfires were surrounded by the men and women of the army as they helped themselves to their first full meal in what seemed like a lifetime to most. The drinks and food flowed, people laughed and danced, and for the first time in a long time, it seemed like the war was far, far away.

Kale's pavilion was no exception to the joy that a hearty meal brought. The central room of Kale's tent had been cleared out to make room for a large, rectangular table and four simple chairs. The sturdy oak table was burdened with ample food and drink fresh off the supply wagon. Kale sat at the head of the table with a generous portion of food and a stack of signed and sealed documents before him. Jerom and Gregor sat opposite each other on the table's flanks, indulging in the venison, fruits, spiced bread and wine that were arranged before them. Hagail sat on the opposite end of the table from Kale, a pitcher of wine and a plate full of food garnering his attention. All four men talked and laughed while consuming the fare like famished bears and enjoying the warmth of the brazier setup at the back of the room. It was a pleasant aside from all the violence of the times. However, work and duty were always lurking at the edge of their thoughts and, as their plates emptied and bellies filled, the real reason they were all gathered quickly became unavoidable.

Adorned in chainmail beneath a loose-fitting House tabard of red and blue, Doms Loridak Hagail was a burly man of short stature. Nearly sixty summers old, the wear and hard living of a fighting Highlander was carved into the wrinkles of his leathery, wind-darkened skin. His receding hair and braided beard were white with a peppering of black, and his green eyes glowed with flames born of the toughness and sternness required to rule in the Highlands of Sur'datha. In his younger years, he would have cut a strong and terrifying figure. Though age and time had bowed his back some, there was still an air of power about him that was intimidating and awe-inspiring at the same time. Through the entirety of the meal, he ate like a man forty summers younger, and conversed with a mind and tongue that was still sharp and quick.

Kale had had very few encounters with the Doms of Sur'datha over the years, so what he knew of him came mostly from his father and uncle. They painted a picture of a man cut from the land he had been born in – stubborn and unmoving. He was a man that treated his friends with respect and loyalty, while his enemies received his scorn and destructive wrath. To a young Kale, his father and uncle's stories made Hagail seem like some terrifying titan. While the man seated before him now was no mythological titan, Kale could sense the intensity and strength behind his green eyes that had led to such tales.

Hagail reached a meaty and callused paw out, his wrists bound in studded leather bracers, and enveloped his tankard, bringing the simple mug to his lips for a sip of the blood-red spiced wine contained within. Though he had only spent a few hours with the young Doms, Kale already reminded him of the late Doms Merandith. Both father and son carried themselves and spoke in a similar fashion, and there was even a family familiarity in the way they held a utensil or a goblet. With both men having been Academy trained, he could well imagine that there was a ghostly echo of the father's combat prowess in the son. Hagail, however, wasn't going to let that fool him. Just because there were similarities between the father and son, it didn't mean they were the same. Kale's brutal response to the death of his mother was something he did not believe the elder Merandith would have been capable of nor approve of. If not for the way Kale had conducted himself of late, Hagail knew he would not have marched in such force. It had taken him months to sneak his forces passed Craigan's scouts and small patrols. By the time they had reorganized and begun their march in full, Hagail had a thousand men at his back, leaving Sur'datha more vulnerable than he would have liked. He could only hope it would be enough for what he believed Kale had planned.

Hagail returned the tankard to its place on the table. "I haven't had much time ta be learn'n the complete situation, Doms Merandith, but I heard about yer losses and the deaths of so many of yer Personal Guard. A terrible loss of life. I believe many of yer Personal Guard also held tha same position fer yer father and mother?"

Kale nodded, his eyes somewhat sad. "Aye, they did . . . and our losses were larger than I would have hoped for." Shaking his head, he flashed a soft smile. "And let's not be so formal. Away from the public's eye, we are just common men who, by some bit of luck or curse, happen to have been given a title that grants us power over others. My father and mother were a doms and doma I can only hope to come close to equaling. I'm only in this role because of my blood. Do not confuse me with those that love to sit on their thrones and have their people mewling and kissing their feet. I do only what I can. So please – call me Kale."

Hagail shifted in his seat, somewhat taken aback by the gentle admonishment. "As ye wish, Doms Mer– err . . . Kale." Hagail took another sip form his mug, smiling to himself. *"Aye, he is his father's son. It be not a wonder that his people love him as much as they did his parents,"* he mused inwardly. "So," he said aloud, "See'n as Suldamik left the field – and that ye be given no chase – I have ta be wonder'n what ye have in mind."

Jerom snorted and scratched around his eyepatch. "Chasing them might have been a bit too foolhardy at the moment; losses on both sides were heavy. Besides, I'm not so sure any of us had the heart or," he gestured to the remains of the feast before them, "the stomach for it."

Kale put down his cup and smiled slightly. "That's one way of putting it, Uncle. But, yes – chasing him would have been foolhardy. As a whole, we are worn down and tired. Our push south was hard and fast to keep Craigan from gaining any sort of a foothold. However, the last few years of this were probably more than I could have hoped for . . ." he chuckled dryly, "and more than I probably had any right to ask for."

Hagail nodded. "Aye, that be ask'n a lot of yer men. I'd say they responded well." Kale picked up the stack of letters, held together with twine, and handed it to Jerom who then passed it to Hagail. Doms Hagail accepted the letters, each sealed with black wax pressed with the five-star seal of House Merandith, and eyed Kale curiously. "What are these?"

Kale picked up his goblet and sipped from it while examining Hagail over the rim of the cup. He wasn't sure how his idea would be greeted by Hagail. Jerom and his commanders were torn between it being a blessing in disguise or just short of insanity. Either way, he was determined to push forward – those that fought for him deserved it. "I'm not going to play you or Gregor for fools, so I'll give it to you straight – I want you, Doms Loridak Hagail, to assume command of the Army of Five Stars."

Silence and shock greeted his statement as if he had just announced he was Deo given flesh. Hagail and Gregor seemed to sink into their seats, shock and bewilderment plainly displayed on their faces. Both men had firmly believed they'd had some idea of what Kale wanted of them. Winter was coming – and if there was anyone that could be considered an expert in winter warfare, then House Hagail was it. The long and brutal winters in the Sur'dathan Highlands had forced the inhabitants to adapt to fighting in extreme conditions in the early years before all the clans had been united. So it wasn't a stretch to be ready to assist and advise House Merandith in dealing with a war in the heart of the frigid season. But to be handed control of the entire army? Nothing could have prepared either of them for that commission.

Flustered, Hagail emptied his tankard in one gulp and quickly refilled it. "I don't know what ta be say'n. Ye honor me with this offer. I. . . ." he shook his head and sipped from his goblet. "I honestly don't be know'n what ta be say'n."

Jerom folded his arms across his chest. "You could tell my nephew that he's a bit daft to see this plan through."

Hagail blinked and drank from his tankard, still not sure he'd heard Kale right.

Gregor, dressed in attire that matched Hagail's, had heard it quite clearly. Although the statement had stunned him, his mind was already racing with ways to organize and train the army. Running a hand over his hair, which was pulled back and bound by a red and blue strip of cloth, "Yer offer is quite gracious and generous. This kind of honor doesn't come lightly, and I be think'n ye have somethin' in mind other than lettin' us run wild. . . . Nor do I think ye be up and run'n away from yer cause without good reason."

Hagail nodded slowly, his mind gradually beginning to wrap itself around the offer. "Aye Gregor, my think'n as well." He settled back into his chair. "So tell me, laddie – just what is crawl'n around yer head?"

Kale leaned forward and picked up the pitcher of wine. "Can I refill anyone's cup?" Jerom and Gregor readily accepted the offer. Once the cups were filled, Kale returned the pitcher to the table and leaned back in his chair, his green eyes alight with thought. "I believe, after all these years of fighting, we're in need of a break. We have pushed very hard since my mother's death, and I believe the constant strain of battle is wearing us thin. My men have fought with more vigor than I could have hoped for, and many of them have been fighting since Craigan's father moved to ascend the Jade Throne and my father to stop him. That makes what . . .? Sixteen? Seventeen years of near-constant war? They need a brief respite. To be honest, I have selfish reasons as well. I haven't seen my family in some time now, and we could use the time to accelerate the training of the young pups that continue to trickle into the Academy. After reading the missives from home, I also now believe that Craigan needs to be sent a message. I won't tolerate raiders behind my lines – and I intend to see that they are taken care of."

Hagail nodded slowly and scratched at his beard. This wasn't exactly what he had expected; however, he now fully believed that he knew where this was going. Kale's motives were honorable and showed his continued change from the young doms that had entered the war with a taste for blood. Compassion sometimes won you more hearts than an iron fist and a sharp blade. Kale was learning – and humble about it. This settled the situation in his mind, but he wanted Kale to put it all before him before he made a commitment. "Aye lad, I can be see'n where yer go'n and why ye'd want to be do'n this. Tell me though – what's ta be stop'n Craigan from ruining all that ye gained while yer gone? He's done it twice before. Nothin' ta say he won't be do'n it again."

Kale nodded, sympathizing with Hagail's concerns. "Aside from winter and the fact he's hurting bad from his losses? You'll be why he won't try to invade. This isn't a mourning period, and I won't be caught with my pants down . . . so to speak. You'll be in charge of harassing his borders and returning the favor with raiding parties – which, I might add, should be significantly easier to accomplish without the Contested Territories to deal with. I won't ask you to continue to push, that would be asking too much given the season, and a siege in winter is lunacy for everyone involved. I want you to keep him off balance and make his winter a nightmare. I'll take the majority of both mine and Trivant's forces, along with a few of the minor Northern Houses, with me. The rest of the army will remain here with you. Weather permitting, we will cycle relief to you after three months from Haltho. Other than my orders, which are in the letters I gave you, the army will be yours to do as you see fit. If things go well,

I'll rejoin you no later than mid-spring with another round of relief troops and we'll drive a dagger through Craigan's heart."

Kale leaned forward, an insistent glint in his eyes. "Accept, Hagail! Do this for me! Consider it a favor to be paid back in full or an act of honor – but don't back out on me, whatever you do! I'm giving you a chance to play a huge part in this war and help rid Triclose of House Suldamik's cursed manipulations. I'll need you here, though. Please, Hagail, do this for me!"

Hagail studied the reactions of the other two men in the room as he absorbed Kale's words. Gregor was oblivious to the conversation, his mind already at work planning for a winter campaign. Jerom was toying with a piece of meat on his plate with his knife, his somewhat sour expression and previous comments showing a certain level of concern with the plan. "And what 'bout ye, Jerom? Yer look'n a wee bit bothered by this plan."

Jerom let his knife fall to the table and planted his elbows on the tabletop, his fingers interlocked before him. "Aye – I am bothered by it. We've got Craigan on the run and hurting. His border forts are within reach, and beyond that – Chalin and the Utherian Valley. With a hard, concentrated push, we could at the very least take down the border forts before winter hits in full and let him stew with us on his doorstep." He paused and sighed. "But, I'm not a terribly stubborn man. I see the merits of this plan as well. While Craigan may be able to bring in reinforcements over the winter, it will still be a stressful time for him. Hit and runs will keep him guessing and, hopefully, jumping at shadows. Come spring, we could find him so fatigued that reclaiming the Utherian Valley might not be near as costly as it would be now. Throw in the fact that these raids near home rub me the wrong way, and I'm willing to go along with the plan and give it my blessing."

Kale chuckled, an amused smirk on his face. "I'm so glad you agree, Uncle."

Jerom shot him a glare and waved a dismissive hand at him. "Bah! You'd do it without my blessing, I know. Just be glad your officers and I support you like we do."

Hagail shook his head in amusement at the exchange. "That be remind'n me – what are the other domses and generals think'n 'bout this?"

"They're more or less on board. Some think as my uncle does, while others are jumping at the chance for a rest." Kale took a sip from his goblet. "Quite frankly, I had quite a few Northern troops jumping at the chance to remain south this winter, even if it meant continued fighting. So, everyone remaining behind is more than willing to be here and under your command."

Hagail nodded. "Just one more thing, lad. What should I be do'n if things don't be go'n accord'n to yer plan?"

Kale shrugged nonchalantly. "Well, I do expect you to keep me routinely informed, but should things start to go sideways . . . improvise."

Hagail snorted. While he'd already decided to accept his role before hearing these details, he suddenly felt like he'd been handed just enough rope to hang himself. "Alright, lad, I'm yer man. Deo only knows what we're walk'n into with this."

Kale smiled pleasantly and nodded. "Good. Well then," he raised his goblet and the others followed suit, "a toast to our future and the end of the war."

Hagail nodded. "Aye, lad! May our enemies be quak'n in fear at the sound of our hoofbeats and the roar of our soldiers!"

The men downed their drinks to the sound of Gregor's enthusiastic cheer of, "Huzzah!"

*

The star-filled night sky was clear save for a dusting of wispy clouds. The full moon had passed its peak, its bluish-silver glow bathing the land in soothing light. Long after the last of the cookfires died and the men and women of the Army of Five Stars took to their blankets, small signs of life could still be seen. Sur'dathan men and women attended to the last details of settling in, while guards patrolled through and around the encampment. Across the entirety of the Five Stars, candlelight softly illuminated the walls of a few tents as their inhabitants remained awake into the late hours, and the occasional bark from one of the many hounds that traveled with the army broke the night's blanket of silence. Fires still burned and hammers still rang out as a few of the blacksmiths plied their trade. For those that were blessed with sleep that night after the horrors and torments of the morning, it was a peaceful rest on a full stomach.

On the south side of the Five Stars' encampment sat the orange and black tents of House Trivant, their groupings of six tents were orderly arranged so that the two-thousand-plus soldiers could traverse without impediment. These brightly dyed tents housed the main bulk of House Trivant's army, which was composed of men and women that either had enlisted or were career military. Hardy people, they hailed from the coastal regions of Triclose and were predominantly descendants of the plains clans that dwelled further inland.

The uneducated would have thought, given the amount of coastline in House Trivant's holdings, that the inhabitants of Roselia would have taken more to seafaring trades. While it was true that Roselia sported an impressive trading fleet and a modest but capable navy, Roselians were still men and women of the soil. Throughout their history, House Trivant was known for its footmen, and the prowess of its light cavalry and mounted bowmen from the plains. This mix of cultures was also the reason for House Trivant's uniqueness within the Five Stars. Where each doms or doma maintained uniformity in their ranks and the way they setup camp, House Trivant was divided between the main army and the small contingent of men and women from clans.

The clans had erected their tents along the eastern flank of House Trivant's forces. Their tents were as distinctively different as their lifestyle was to that of the common Roselian. Made of deer and torgen hide, their tents were erected over thick and sturdy poles. The hides of the tents were adorned with tattoos and clan wards to both protect and bless those within. Intricately weaved talismans of protection, made of grass and wood, were hung above each tent's entrance. The only similarity between the encampments was that they shared the same layout; however, where Trivant's tents were centered around Doms Trivant's pavilion, the clansmen's tents were centered on a larger version of their hide domiciles. This large pavilion served as a place of assembly for the Clan Elders and was where they oversaw the affairs of the clans. The tent was called Vorta'hal – meaning 'Hall of Wisdom'.

It was at this late hour, and in this all too familiar tent, that Dakan found himself standing before the Clan Elders.

The Vorta'hal was round in shape with a domed roof, its walls made of thick torgen hide painted with a vista of wards and blessings in rich blues and violent reds. Its supporting poles were made of thick ironwood from the Alderian Forest, which separated the plains from the coast. The supports were carved and gilded with animals, wards and blessings sacred to all the clans. Smoke drifted out of the Vorta'hal via a hole in the ceiling, informing all that the Clan Elders were present. Two burly guards, their raven-black hair adorned with fetishes and their skin tattooed with hawks, flanked the tent's entrance with their heavy, short stabbing spears firmly in hand. Their job was to make sure the Elders remained undisturbed, and woe betide anyone who dared test the guards' resolve.

The interior of the tent was lit only by a large fire, the smoke from which dulled the light before escaping through the hole in the roof. Arranged around the fire in a semi-circle facing the Vorta'hal's entrance were thirteen backless chairs made of hide stretched between four crisscrossing legs. The sigil of each of the twelve clans hung from the totems erected behind the seat of each Clan Elder. This night found only the central five seats occupied, signifying that the matter before the Council pertained strictly to the Northern Clans. Wolf, Bear, Elk, and Hawk – the Elders of each clan stared intently at Dakan as if trying to pierce into his soul and learn anything and everything about him. Even the elderly gaze of the High Elder, who was seated in the center of the group of Elders, seemed more intense and harsher than usual. The stares didn't bother Dakan – he was used to their accusing gazes – but the tense silence that permeated the tent was beginning to gnaw at his nerves.

With the fire between him and the stoic visages of the Clan Elders, Dakan stood with feet spread and hands clasped behind his back. Sweat not only glistened on his shirtless, tattooed torso, but had also soaked through the bandages covering his wounds, and drenched his braided black hair. Even in his injured state, Dakan had stood before the Elders with pride – and some might say arrogance – as questions and accusations were flung at him earlier. He bore the long silence that followed with barely contained rage at the insult it was. Even now, he could see the disdain on their aged faces and feel it in their stares as they looked upon the serpentine tattoos of a long-dead clan that adorned his body.

He was kasteri – clanless. When he was just a child, his entire clan had been wiped out during an uprising. As one of the only survivors, he had been taken in by the Northern Clans and raised by all as per their customs. For deeds not his own, Dakan became the target of relentless persecution that followed him even after his adoption into the Clan of the Wolf. When he decided to add the serpent tattoos to his body partly from spite and partly from pride – and continued to do so despite warnings not to – he only further served to isolate himself. When House Trivant came seeking the aid of the clans for the war, the Elders had refused to allow Dakan to join them on the march. As he was kasteri, he had no right or obligation to join the War Host. In an act of kindness, however, the Elders had granted him permission to serve House Trivant directly. Dakan had no idea why he had been given permission. Some even viewed it as the Elders trying to cast him out and cut ties with him. Yet, despite the whispers and rumors, he continued to answer to the Clan Elders and those that had raised him. Though he wondered, as he stared back at the Elders with his own dark eyes, how much his current request made them weep or cheer.

The Elders, ranging in age from thirty-two to the nearly ninety summers of the High Elder, were adorned in nothing but deerskin kilts and bone and bronze torques. The sigil of their respective clans was stitched into the kilts and worked in silver into the center of each torque. Like Dakan, sweat glistened on their naked torsos and soaked their hair. If the situation hadn't been so tense, the bare and wolf-tattooed breasts of the young Wolf Clan Elder would have been a distraction. As it was, Dakan's focus was on the situation and not carnal wants.

Sitting to Dakan's right, in the last occupied seat, was the only female Clan Elder. Back erect and breasts thrust out, the thirty-two summers old Wolf Clan Elder's gray eyes were a match for her etched and handsome features, which often made men forget her short stature either from intimidation or lust – depending on what she wanted them to see. Her salt-and-pepper hair was matted to her head and neck, beads of sweat dripping off her normally thick locks and sliding down her torso. Like the men of the clans, she was muscled and toned from a lifetime of hard work and fighting. While it was rare for a woman to ascend to Elder status, she had proven her worth time and again. Yet, it was likely that she meant more to Dakan than all the clans combined. For the entirety of Dakan's life as a kasteri, she had been many things to him. In his early years, she had served as a mother figure and then as a mentor. As he entered adulthood, she had evolved into his friend and lover. So it came as no real surprise when she spoke on his behalf.

"My fellow Elders – we all agree that Dakan has his flaws and, at times, has been an embarrassment to the clans. But does he deserve our venom? I certainly think not. He is here at our graces, and his request is intriguing. To have one of the clans so close to one such as Doms Merandith would be a great honor."

Seated opposite of the Wolf Clan Elder, the dour visage of the grizzled Bear Clan Elder broke into a sarcastic laugh, the fetishes in his white hair clinking together gently. "You would think and say such a thing, Beliza. You'd say anything to keep the kasteri licking your boots and warming your bed. The man is a curse and a blight! We were too generous in allowing him to live!" He waved a callused hand in Dakan's direction and declared with a heavy amount of disdain, "See how he paints his skin with the markings of a forsaken clan like they still exist – he does this to insult us and make a mockery of all the clans stand for! Keep the kasteri as your toy, but I won't be responsible for casting such a curse upon the Merandiths."

Beliza bared her teeth in a vicious smile. "Who I bed is none of your concern, Bear. Just because you wouldn't know what end of a woman to stick it in doesn't mean you can take out your failings on Dakan . . . or me." The Bear Clan Elder's round, creased face turned bright red with indignation and rage, widening Beliza's smile. "You are a wicked, stoneless shame of a man. I'm surprised your clan still lets you lead, much less that son of yours remain your heir. Oh, wait. . . I mean wife's bastard. Can't very well father a child with no stones."

Dakan fought hard to suppress a grin as the barrage of insults brought the Bear Clan Elder to his feet, his entire muscled, towering frame trembling with rage.

The infuriated Elder pointed a thick finger at Beliza, his brown eyes burning with anger. "You vile, gutless, whore-mongering—"

Beliza laughed. "Oh please, Vagain, stop with trying to fight with big words. You'll hurt yourself. I know you're too afraid to Challenge me. Losing to a woman who is more man than you would just—"

As Vagain took a threatening step forward at the continued goading, the Hawk Elder seated next to him put out an arm to restrain him before shooting a warning glare at Beliza. "Sheathe your tongue, woman! You're barbs have no place here!" He turned a stern glare on Vagain. "And you, Vagain – sit down and control yourself! This is neither the time nor place for personal quarrels!"

Vagain shot Beliza one more hate-filled, baleful glare before easing himself back into his chair.

Once the Hawk Elder was sure neither Vagain nor Beliza would reignite their feud, he turned his attention back to Dakan. Meeting Dakan's gaze with his own black eyes from beneath his heavy brow, he said, "As for you, Kasteri, I think we would be better off if you were gone. I have no love for you, nor did I care for your clan while it still existed. If it had been up to me, you would have been executed with the rest of your clan." He let out a sigh as he ran an aged and gnarled hand through his long white hair, his rough voice softening as he continued. "But you live – and I will not begrudge you that. I do not know your motives in this, just as all your actions are puzzling. If this is what you want, I think we should allow this and be done with you once and for all."

Dakan inclined his head slightly in thanks for the backhanded support. "Thank you, Elder. I firmly believe this would be best, and would bring honor and glory to the Northern Clans." The Elder sitting next to Beliza snorted in cynical disdain, drawing Dakan's gaze and an arched eyebrow. "Do my words amuse you, Elder? I assure you my intentions were not to be funny."

The large, elderly Elk Clan Elder shifted his muscular bulk forward, sweat rolling off his shaven head and down his wrinkled body. Holding Dakan's gaze with his small, sharp brown eyes, he replied, "Oh aye, Dakan – ye amuse me and sicken me. Elder Valcor's words ring true, and I whole-heartily agree with Elder Vagain. Yer a black mark on the clans! I for one would be glad to gut you here and now and rid us of ye and yer clan's cursed existence!"

A small smile cracked Dakan's lips as he replied, sarcasm dripping from his words, "Then it is good we are such close friends – I would hate for you to stain your hands with my blood."

All the Elders except Beliza glared hard at Dakan as the Elk Elder replied, "You're spiteful and sarcastic words are wasted on me, lad. I won't be goaded into stupidity, and I'm not an empty-headed woman to be swayed by a youth's touch. Yer an eyesore, and I mean to see it removed. . . . But I think giving him over to the Merandiths would be even worse. Dakan is our problem, and there's no honor in passing off our burdens to another."

Beliza eyed the Elk Elder in amusement. "Well said, Durak. I didn't think honor and malice could be so artfully mixed." She turned her attention to the aged High Elder before Durak could retort. "High Elder – I think we are beyond the point of arguing. Our words have been spoken, and the decision is yours. Let's end this over-exaggerated debate over such a simple request."

Grudgingly the other Elders nodded their agreement.

The High Elder, a man of nearly ninety summers, was still stout and strong for his age. The scars of his youth were as much a sign of his life and origins as the myriad of torgen tattoos representing his original clan, as well as those that represented all of the clans, that were inked into his leathery skin. Sweat rolled down his shaven head, soaking his bushy white eyebrows and the whiskers of his chest-length white beard. Though clouded by failing vision, his black eyes still glowed with an inner strength. He was a man that was well respected by the clans, and, despite the ill will the High Elder had shown toward him in the past, Dakan feelings were no different. No matter his decision, Dakan was determined to live and die by it.

Gnarled hands moving slowly, the High Elder held up one hand for continued silence. His voice, rough and weakened by age, sounded with authority, "I have heard the words of the Elders of the North and, in spite of the venom many of them hold, hear the truth in their words. Now I will hear what Dakan has to say. Speak plainly Kasteri, and know that even though my feelings toward you echo my fellow Elders, I will do my best to listen with pure ears."

Dakan mentally sighed with relief. He had been waiting these long hours to speak without interruption, though he knew no matter what he said, it would be met with suspicion and disdain. Save for Beliza, he was trying to plead with enemies, and that never worked. However, protocol and honor demanded that he follow the traditions, and Dakan was not about to spit on Clan law no matter how much and how often the others thought he did.

Focusing his attention squarely on the High Elder, Dakan took a deep breath and let his deep-timbered voice ring out with confidence. "Thank you, High Elder. As I stated earlier, I am requesting permission to transfer my service from House Trivant and the Northern Clans to the service of House Merandith. I firmly believe that if I can become one of Doms Merandith's Personal Guard, I can bring great honor to the Northern Clans. I also believe that the Spirits have brought this opportunity to me so that I may reclaim my honor and that of my clan." The last statement drew a scorn-filled snort from Vagain. Dakan ignored it and continued, his jaw muscles clenching as he fought down his anger at prostrating himself before the Council like this. "If my service, and possibly my death, can redeem the Clan of the Fang and return our name to its rightful place, then I am prepared to do whatever it takes. Grant me this opportunity, and I will either restore my clan's honor or come home on my shield!"

The oath caught the Elders off guard. None of them would have expected such a weighty oath to be taken, especially from someone they considered irresponsible. The mix of emotions and thoughts racing through the Elders' minds played out on their faces. Vagain's face was screwed up incredulously, his eyes bulging and his cheeks burning red with rage. Valcor looked like he simply wanted to gut him on the spot and end the nonsense once and for all, while Durak had the appearance of a man tired of hearing the same thing over and over again. Only Beliza seemed to approve of his request. Her eyes glowed with something that appeared somewhere between lust for Dakan and pride in him. Only the High Elder remained unreadable. It was almost as if he had not heard a word of what Dakan had said.

Silence persisted for a few long and agonizing moments. Just when it looked like no one would say anything, the Elders came to their feet and the tent erupted with angry shouts and accusations. Insults were hurled at Dakan like spears. Venom-filled accusations of collusion between Dakan and Beliza to bring back a fallen clan rang loudly. Beliza defended herself and Dakan with retorts and insults meant to cut as deep as a well-honed dagger. As the shouting persisted, the subject at hand was soon forgotten as heated tempers and long-standing tensions got the better of the Elders and enflamed their verbal sparring. Old feuds and hatreds flared, and the barbs being flung about turned personal and violent. It was becoming readily apparent that if something wasn't done soon to defuse the situation, blood would be spilt.

Through it all, Dakan and the High Elder remained mute, their eyes locked on one another as each man took their measure of the other. After what felt like a lifetime to Dakan, the High Elder gave a slight nod, apparently finding whatever he had sought in the depths of Dakan's eyes.

"Silence!" The authority in the High Elder's voice clipped the heated words of the other Elders short. Each Elder stared at the High Elder in disbelief, amazed that the aged Roselian could still project such power with his words. The High Elder met the gaze of each Clan Elder as he commanded, "Sit down and be silent! Be still! Save your anger for those that deserve it."

"Yes, High Elder," murmured the Clan Elders as they returned to their seats like chastised children. Their egos were bruised by the High Elder's words, but the heat of their arguments still burned in their eyes. No matter what the High Elder said to calm them or how he chastised them, there were some wounds that would never close, and this situation had reopened some and caused others to fester.

Once the High Elder was sure there would be no more outbursts, he returned his strong gaze to Dakan. Once again, the aged High Elder's voice rang out with strength and authority that was out of place with his age. "Dakan Holdreth of the Northern Clans – your words have been heard, and so have those of the Elders you see before you. You are kasteri. We have suffered your presence and those of your ilk because we cannot hold the child responsible for the errors of the adult. Of all that survived, your blood is the most tainted. Despite that, you have at times shown the strength of heart to overcome such a failing. Yet, you also continually show the traits that led to your clan's fall. You openly flaunt the markings of a clan that is dead – this is a clear sign that your father's blood burns strongly in you. You push and prod this Council like a toy with your repeated requests to restore the honor of your clan, to which you receive the same answer. We are aware of this as acutely as we are of your involvement with the Wolf Elder."

The High Elder let out a tired sigh even as the other Elders eyed one another cautiously, unsure of where the High Elder was going with his speech.

"I am old," the High Elder continued, his tone softer than before. "I have seen the tragedies and triumphs of life. I have seen

90

our clans survive harsh conditions and face extinction. I gave the word to execute your clan for their betrayal so that others might survive. I do not fall victim to the words of the Wolf Elder at your expense, nor do I fall prey to the venom in the requests of the other Elders or the hate that lies within my own heart. I am not without compassion, as your very presence here shows. Despite the venom in the Elder's words, they also are not without their . . . merits." He paused for a brief moment and then, taking a deep breath, said, "Dakan Holdreth – you have spoken and I have listened. Clan Elders – you have spoken and I have listened. This then is my decision."

Dakan's back went ridged with anticipation, and he noted the hopeful gleam in Beliza's eyes, as well as the scorn being directed his way from the other Elders.

"Dakan Holdreth – you are granted permission to join House Merandith's forces and to serve him as you would the clans." Smug looks of satisfaction graced the faces of the three Elders who had long wanted to be rid of him. "However – let it be known amongst all the clans that should you be seen to redeem your clan through deed or through your death, the Clan of the Fang shall be reborn and acknowledged by all! Until then, when you leave us to serve House Merandith, you will no longer be one of us! Come back to us in honor or on your shield!"

"But, High Elder – this is outrageous!" exclaimed Vagain, rage making his body shake and his eyes look like they were going to pop out of their sockets.

The High Elder turned his clouded gaze to the Clan of the Bear Elder and stared him down. "Do you dare to challenge my decision? It is within his right to ask, and it is mine – and only mine – to give! If my leadership displeases you – " he looked at everyone in turn, "any of you – you may claim your right to Challenge and a moot will be convened!"

Vagain lowered his gaze, though his body still trembled and his rage was still evident in his voice. "No, High Elder, I do not challenge your judgment."

"Good." The High Elder swung his attention back to Dakan. "You have heard our terms. What do you have to say?"

Dakan could barely contain his excitement. While the terms were not exactly what he had been hoping for, it was a huge victory for him in its own right. He would get the chance to restore his clan's honor – something he had been striving for, for a very long time. "Yes High Elder, I hear your words and agree to them."

The High Elder nodded. "Very good. You have until night-fall tomorrow to remove yourself from this camp. This Council is now over!"

"That was brilliantly done, Dakan! I cannot believe how successful we were!" Beliza intoned with a gleeful laugh as she sauntered into her tent. Stepping around the fire that her handmaidens had already lit for her arrival, she hung her wolf-skin cloak from a hook embedded in one of the support poles.

Dakan slipped in behind her, his eyes adjusting to the firelight. Having spent many nights in it, he was very familiar with the spacious and somewhat unremarkable tent. Beliza's bed of blankets laid on the far side of the fire, and her clothing was stored in a large pack that rested against the tent wall. Charms and fetishes hung from the support poles like rain frozen in mid-fall. A simple table of birch and deer antler occupied a small portion of the tent, warm mugs of spiced wine and a plate of bread and dried beef sitting on its surface. Her assortment of bows, swords and axes rested on the ground to his right, deerskin wrappings protecting them from the elements.

"I agree, we were successful," he said as she weaved her way back to him, picking up the mugs of wine and handing him one. "But there is a long and hard road before us. I don't think we should celebrate too much."

She sipped from her mug as she slipped an arm around his neck and pressed her body close to him. "Oh, foolish Dakan – you still can't enjoy the successes you have. Always looking forward to the next challenge." She leaned in and kissed him full on his resistant mouth. Pulling away, she stared at him and laughed, her gray eyes sparkling with unabashed amusement. "Resistant tonight are we? Come now, we should celebrate!"

Dakan disengaged himself, walked over to the table and placed the mug back on it, the intoxicating liquid untouched. "Be serious, Beliza. I have too much to do now. I won't be welcome in the clan camps much longer."

Beliza took a long draw from her mug, emptying it, and made her way over to the table with a pout painted on her face. She let her full breasts graze Dakan's muscled torso as she placed her mug on the table. "Very well then, Dakan. If you're determined to be so somber, then I have two things for you." She made her way over to the weapon's pile, her hips swaying seductively.

Dakan almost laughed. She was determined to bed him tonight no matter how much he protested. Even the way she crouched

92

at the weapon's pile – presenting her backside to him – was in an enticing manner. Seeing her positioned that way, he had to admit it was certainly working, as arousal stirred in him.

Beliza carefully sorted through the pile of weapons, reverently picking up and placing the armaments to the side until she came to the one she wanted. With effort, she wrapped her hands around the haft of the giant axe and stood up. Turning to face Dakan, she made her way back over to him and presented the weapon to him. "This is yours," she purred.

Dakan's dark eyes lit up and his breath caught in his throat as he took hold of the large weapon and examined it. Where Beliza had strained to carry it, the axe was light as a feather in his hands, almost as if it was a part of him. The axe was five feet in length, its shaft made of dark, polished ironwood. Its butt was capped with a short spike, and its shaft was inlaid with twin silver dragons. Originating from the pommel spike, the dragons intertwined their way to the top portion of the shaft where their heads sprung from the steel cap in opposite directions. The vicious two-and-a-half foot long, and just over a foot wide, winged axe blade sprouted from one dragon's mouth while an equally deadly and nontraditional counter spike flared from the other mouth. Clan charms and wards were etched into the blade, and every inch of the axe was polished and well cared for. It was, and always had been, the most beautiful lochabre axe he'd ever seen.

"Where did you get this?" he croaked in awe.

Beliza placed her hands on the axe, running a finger along its haft as she admired the craftsmanship. "Your father gave it to me before your clan marched. He knew how they would be viewed, and knew that such signs of the clan would be destroyed if not kept safe. He . . . hoped that the Clan Elders would be merciful on the young left behind and that one day the axe could find its way into your hands. The Wolves have done all we can to support the Fang from the shadows, and this is my last major debt to them paid in full. The axe is yours, Fang, carry it with the pride your father did."

Dakan ignored her as she slipped away and made her way over to her bed of blankets. "I simply don't have the words to thank you," he breathed, his mind full of swirling emotions.

Her laughter drew his attention away from the axe. Beliza stood before her blankets, her legs spread and her fingers working at her kilt's ties. "To thank me . . . you simply have to claim your second reward," she purred as she let her kilt fall to the ground. Lowering herself to her blankets, she presented her toned, naked form to Dakan.

His mind afire with ideas for the future, and his arousal burning hungrily, he reverently leaned the axe against the table and moved over to Beliza. Lowering himself into her embrace, he whispered to her, "As you wish, my lovely Wolf."

The early risers found that a blanket of fog had settled on the camp overnight. Gray skies and dim lighting brought a sour look to some of the inhabitants of the Five Stars camp, while others felt the overriding urge to return to their blankets. For some of those who had yet to see their blankets, the bland weather was the perfect companion to accompany them to their much-needed slumber. The morning, however, found one person that was immune to its dreary influence.

Slipping from his lover's tent with his new lochabre axe firmly slung across his back, Dakan no longer showed any signs of his wounds from the day before as the quick healing blood of the clans once again proved its usefulness. There was also a renewed sense of vigor and righteousness about him that had very little to do with his healed physical wounds. The previous night's victories, as well as the passionate celebration that followed, were what had his spirits high. With a small, satisfied smile on his lips, he set out immediately for the Merandith encampment, determined to keep the good chain of events moving. The previous night's proceedings had left him more fulfilled than he had been in years. There would be no more looking over his shoulder or suffering the barbs of the other clans. He was his own man with his own destiny now. Nothing could spoil his mood.

As he strolled through the maze of tents, movement caught his attention out of the corner of his eye. He stopped in the middle of the aisle and peered to his left through the fog. Three cloaked and hooded figures were moving quickly through the camp, doing their best to remain inconspicuous. Dakan snorted to himself. If stealth was what they were looking to achieve, they were failing miserably. While it would be easier to go unnoticed through the camp at this early hour, their assassin-styled attire would immediately set off warning bells for anyone that saw them. The muscles of his bare arms flexed and his jaw muscles clenched. His instincts were screaming that something was definitely wrong. Appearances aside, such clandestine actions in friendly territory was suspicious enough to warrant investigation.

Tying his hair back from his face, Dakan moved off in the direction the three men were headed, carefully keeping his distance as their route took them northwest through the camp toward the blacksmiths. Three times the men stopped and hid from guards walking their patrol routes, each stop further enforcing the feeling within Dakan that something was afoot. Just before the darkly dressed trio reached the Blacksmith Enclave, they swung east toward the Merandith encampment, their pace quickening. Suddenly, the three stopped and one gestured urgently to his right. Moving in the indicated direction, they quickstepped between the tents, Dakan matching them step-for-step and with significantly less noise. When they emerged onto a main thoroughfare, Dakan saw them slip in behind a lone, large man that was lazily making his way toward the Merandith camp. His eyes growing grim, Dakan removed his axe from his back and quickened his pace.

For a bleary-eyed Amroth, sleep was a welcome respite that was long overdue.

Strong shoulders sagging and exhaustion permeating his every feature and movement, Amroth trudged through the maze of tents at a slow and deliberate pace. The previous night had been one of many filled with backbreaking labor, as there was more work than the smiths could handle. Between the repairs, the melting down of irreparably broken items, and the forging of new equipment from the repurposed metal, Amroth was beginning to think the work would never end. As it was, the corded muscles of his thick frame ached, his black hair was disheveled, his dark eyes were dull with exhaustion, and his body and clothing were marred with a layer of soot and sweat. At that moment, even his boots felt restrictive and highly uncomfortable. And while those discomforts were individually annoying, when combined, their demand was clear – he needed sleep. He would have loved to have ceded to that demand hours earlier, but he had been involved in the one task he took immense pride in – the care and maintenance of Kale's kit. However, even if he had been free to do as he pleased, the arrival of the Sur'dathans had troubled him enough to keep his mind racing.

He wasn't as ignorant about his past as many thought him to be. When he was nine summers of age, Doms Bordin Merandith had deemed it time to inform Amroth of his past in general terms. Amroth had always suspected he wasn't a true child of House Merandith. While he had been raised and treated as one of their own, his features didn't match, and when visitors from Sur'dathan or even clansmen and women from Roselia visited, he was generally kept out of sight and under guard as much as possible. So when Doms Bordin had informed him that he was the last surviving member of a condemned and executed Sur'dathan clan that had dared to rebel, he was only mildly surprised. It was more like he was being told the sky was different across the ocean when he had suspected it all along. He had been aware for so long that something was different, that the news wasn't outrageous – just a confirmation of his suspicions about being different. To the Merandiths' relief, instead of rebelling with the news, Amroth embraced it as he would a history lesson and pursued it as such. With Bordin's permission, he studied up on his forsaken clan and the laws of the Sur'dathans, finding out as much as he could – from a distance – about the civil war and the unification of Sur'datha.

His studies revealed a troubling past for his clan and the realm of Sur'datha. Constant war, infighting and blood feuds made it a vulnerable target any time the war for the Jade Throne flared up. By uniting the clans, House Hagail put an end to the realm's vulnerability. However, Amroth never discovered who was responsible for his birth clan's rebellion, nor why they received help from the distantly related clans of Roselia.

What he did learn, to his horror, was that the rebellious clans had been dealt with in a ruthless manner that left very few survivors; as such, the knowledge brought with it an understanding of not only what the Merandiths had risked in taking him in, but why there were those amongst their allies that would just as soon see him dead. No one wanted a reminder of such an ugly stain on their past roaming about where it could be seen. Thankfully, to this day, he had never had any issues with the Roselian clans. And from what he could tell, the majority of Sur'datha either seemed to consider the matter closed or had no idea about the truth of his past. However, his exposure to Sur'datha had been sparse since his dealings with them had been restricted to Doms Hagail and his family and trusted friends. He had never visited Sur'datha, and had very little knowledge of how the common folk viewed him. So it was ignorance of who he truly was, not fear, that made him nervous when the Sur'dathan contingent arrived.

Despite his casual approach to the situation, Amroth was glad his exposure to the recently arrived Sur'dathans had been limited so far. His work in the forge had kept him there the rest of the day and all-night. A few of their footmen had paid a visit to the smithies to have some repairs done since it would take a day to get their own blacksmiths settled in and set up. None of the footmen had spared more than a glance his way while they had talked with Barniban the Forge Master. Sensing no threat, Amroth had continued his hard work and ignored the Sur'dathan visitors that had trickled in throughout the day and into the evening.

Even as he trudged through the early morning fog, he didn't feel the need to be on guard. After all, he was in friendly territory and fairly well-known throughout the camp for his excellent craftsmanship. Fearing for his life was not something he was used to, nor was it something he felt was needed amongst the Army of Five Stars. And so it was that he found himself nearing the Merandith portion of the camp, oblivious to the three men who slipped out of the fog behind him.

Solid steel collided with the back of his skull, sending him sprawling face-first into the churned turf. A myriad of brightly colored stars danced across his darkened vision as he gasped for air and tried to ward off fainting. Forcing his muscles to respond, Amroth had just managed to gather himself and push up to all fours when a hobnailed boot smashed into his ribs. His breath driven from him, he collapsed to the ground again, pain lancing through him from cracked ribs. A series of kicks to his torso had him scrambling the best he could to protect himself. Blow after blow made solid contact, driving the air from his lungs and leaving him with violent bruises that were already beginning to show. Suddenly the blows stopped and, with his vision swimming, he slowly rolled over to his back to the amused laughs of his assailants. Though his vision was impaired, he was able to discern that his assailants' faces and bodies were veiled in heavy cloaks and cowls, making it impossible to identify them.

One of the men, who was carrying a simple shortsword with a bloodied pommel, stepped forward and placed his hobnailed boot on Amroth's throat, applying just enough pressure to draw blood and make breathing extremely difficult. Amroth clawed at the boot, his face turning red and his breath coming in ragged gasps. His frantic movements only drew more laughter from his assailants.

"Well, well, lads – what do we be hav'n 'ere?" the man stepping on his neck drawled, his voice deep and muffled, but full of malice. "Looks like we be hav'n a wee bit o luck. Found us a Theirigaldian rat that somehow escaped justice. What do ye be say'n to that, lads?" The two other assassins nodded, and the man removed his foot from Amroth's throat, allowing him to take deep breaths between ragged coughs. "Pick 'em up and hold 'em still, lads."

The two men hauled Amroth to his feet. Not only was Amroth's vision swimming and his throat bruised and raw, but blood caked the back of his head and trickled from his nose, mouth and the tiny pricks on his neck. He knew he should try to fight back, but his body was exhausted and beaten to the point where it wouldn't respond. Finally, he worked up the breath to speak, his voice hoarse and croaking as the breath forced its way past his raw throat. "Afraid . . . you've got me mixed up with . . . someone else. I'm a . . ." he gasped, "Merandith."

The man with the sword laughed before backhanding him with a hand encased in a steel-plated glove. Stars burst to life before Amroth's vision as blood spewed from his mouth and the cut on his cheek from the blow. His head started to droop forward, but the man grabbed a fistful of hair and wretched his head back so he could look Amroth in the eyes. Peering from the shadows of his hood, the assailant's dark eyes were full of bloodlust and violence. It was then that Amroth knew there would be no reasoning with him and that his fate was sealed.

"Oh aye, lad, we be know'n yer parad'n about like one of tha Merandiths, but it don't change the fact that yer still a Theirigaldian – and the Theirigaldis Clan was ordered executed. Now, we wouldn't be do'n our duty if'n we let ye run free. We're stand-up citizens and proud Sur'dathans. Can't be havn' a stain like ye marr'n our honor." He let Amroth's head drop and patted him on the head like a man comforting his dog before stepping back. "Hold 'em still, boys." Amroth felt the other two men's grip tighten about his upper arms. "Sorry, lad. Noth'n personal."

"Indeed," replied a deep voice from the fog behind the swordsman.

The eyes of the two men restraining Amroth went wide with shock as their leader pitched forward violently, a large axe buried in his back. They hesitated only for a moment, prepared for their assailant to come charging in, but when they saw only fog, they dropped Amroth and turned to run, choosing to abandon their assassination attempt if it meant living. Before they'd made it more than a few steps, Dakan came rushing out of the fog, his eyes cold and deadly. Startled, the two men froze, giving Dakan all the time he needed.

Stepping forward smoothly, Dakan's left hand darted out at the nearest attacker. His stiff fingers connected solidly with one of the hooded men's throat, crushing his windpipe and sending him sprawling to the earth. The second attacker, seeing his remaining compatriot go down, cursed loudly and drew a shortsword from under his cloak. Screaming loudly, he rushed Dakan, sword held high in his right hand. Dakan darted in close and lashed out with his muscled and serpent-tattooed arms, his strong hands locking on the attacker's chin and the wrist of his sword arm. With deft movements, Dakan brought the man up short and swung himself behind him. Releasing the assailant's sword arm, he latched firmly on to the attacker's forehead and, with a violent jerk, he snapped the man's neck before letting the body crumple to the ground like a child's rag doll.

Dakan stood over the bodies of the fallen, his breathing calm despite his muscles trembling with violent rage. He could already hear alarms being raised because of the commotion, and he knew it wouldn't be long before someone arrived on the scene. Still, he took a moment to calm himself. He had heard a name mentioned before his intervention, and wanted to confirm what he'd heard before any guards arrived. Once calm, he made his way over to his axe and wrenched it from the man's back before striding over to Amroth.

By this point, Amroth had managed to collect himself and sit up. When Dakan stopped in front of him, he looked up into his grim visage and nearly froze. There was a dark violence about the man looming over him that took his breath away. Yet he had rescued him, and he didn't feel that it was right to fear his savior.

"Those men called you a Theirigaldian. Is that true?" growled Dakan.

The man's tone took Amroth aback, and suddenly he wasn't so sure he shouldn't fear the man. However, if this large man wanted him dead, there was little he could do about it. Figuring the truth was as good as anything at this point, Amroth replied, "Aye, I am. My birth name was Amroth Drakoni of Clan Theirigaldis."

Dakan's knees almost went weak, and only his axe kept him standing when he heard the name again. A Theirigaldian right under his nose – and a Drakoni no less. He never thought he would hear that name again, much less find a living member of a dead clan. So much of his parents' teachings and those of Beliza came rushing back to him. Lying before him was the living embodiment of everything that had brought both clans to their knees.

Before him was family.

The long pause since he had uttered his birth name left Amroth wondering if here was another who would hold a name that held little meaning to him against him. Finally, Dakan nodded slightly and extended his hand to him, which Amroth readily accepted.

Hauling Amroth to his feet, he pronounced, "I am Dakan Holdreth of the Clan of the Fang. Well met, Brother."

# Chapter Four

"**B**loody hells," remarked Jerom as he and Kale emerged from the crowd of curious onlookers that had gathered around the scene.

A ring of House Merandith guards surrounded the incident scene, keeping the crowd back. The three assailants had been moved from where they'd fallen, their bodies orderly lain out in the center of the path. Their masks had been removed, revealing the faces of three aged and grizzled men. Doms Hagail and Gregor stood over the bodies, deep in discussion, their chainmail-clad forms rigid with tension. Amroth and Dakan sat on stools off to the right, conversing while a camp medic attended to Amroth's wounds. Dakan's lochabre was slung on his back, cleaned of the blood from his early morning melee. Between the axe and the array of clan tattoos decorating his body, he still seemed a danger just sitting down.

Kale, clad in dark pants and a white long-sleeve shirt beneath a purple-trimmed tabard in Merandith black, clenched his gloved hand tightly about the hilt of his sheathed sword. The cold, quiet morning had been brutally shattered by horns sounding the alarm and Jerom bursting into his tent already belting on his sword. Kale had been in the middle of enjoying a simple breakfast of cheese and hot cereal while composing a letter to his wife. The simple statement that Amroth had been assaulted in the middle of the camp shattered his good mood and sent him scrambling to throw on his boots and belt on his sword. They had rushed to the scene with very little knowledge of what had happened beyond the fact that the victim was Amroth. For all they knew, he was face down in the dirt. Both Merandiths, however, had their fears over who would have done such a thing. While it wasn't beyond their imaginations that Craigan might pull something, they both felt that the arrival of the Sur'dathans and this assault was more than coincidence.

As soon as Kale saw that Amroth was alive, he let out a deep, relieved breath and closed his eyes to offer up a quick prayer to Deo. Just as he was about to walk over and see about his childhood friend and adopted brother, Jerom held out a restraining arm.

Scratching around his eyepatch and at his salt-and-pepper beard, Jerom said, "Hold up, lad. Here comes Hagail. This ought to be good."

Kale steadied himself as he watched Hagail and Gregor walk quickly over to them. It was painted on both men's faces just how much this incident angered and horrified them. Gregor's sun-darkened visage was grim, and he looked like he was very much ready to find an outlet for the anger growing inside him. Doms Loridak Hagail's face was a match for his second's. There was genuine anger in his green eyes, and it seemed like the only thing keeping him from exploding was the tight grip his meaty hand had on his sword hilt.

"Doms Merandith," Hagail intoned as both men bowed slightly to him, the chainmail beneath their red and blue tabards rustling gently. "I can be only offer'n ye my humble apologies– "

"Are those your men?" barked Kale in a low, demanding tone as he fought to keep his voice under control so that the surrounding onlookers couldn't hear their conversation.

Hagail cleared his throat at the interruption and met Kale's hard stare before responding in a similarly hushed tone, "Aye, that they are – though I'm think'n their quick deaths were a wee bit less than they be deserv'n." Kale's jaw muscles tightened as his fears were confirmed, prompting Hagail to quickly continue. "They be from the Vanmulik Clan; they're Lowlanders that stood against Cravon and had been recive'n tha worst of it dur'n the Uprisings. I dunno how they be recogniz'n the lad for what he is, though. Few even saw tha lad as a babe."

"And you didn't think something like this might happen?" asked Jerom.

Hagail nodded slowly. "Aye, it was a possibility. But I could na' be leav'n men behind just because of what clan they be in fer fear of someth'n like this happen'n. That'd do more damage than this 'ere incident."

Kale's eyes bulged in anger. "Worse than this?! My brother is assaulted and nearly killed, and you have three dead men! How, in Deo's name, could it be any worse?!"

Gregor cleared his throat. "If I may, Doms Merandith, there be few that be know'n of tha lad's existence. If'n we left people behind out of fear for tha lad's life, we'd just raise suspicions. I dunna not think any of us be want'n vengeful clans come'n after him. Sad as it may be, these men being dead is a good thing. It's no less the fate they would be recive'n if'n they'd survived and met our justice. It's also three less that be known'n tha lad's face."

Jerom nodded, conceding the point. "He's right, Kale. It was always going to be a risk having Amroth here with so many

Sur'dathans around. We probably should have anticipated this. Although, I'm not as sure about their deaths being a good thing."

Hagail shook his head. "If ye be know'n who rescued tha lad, it is a good thing. Honestly, I'm shocked and a wee bit amused at tha fickled fates that brought this together."

Kale, his anger dissipating, asked, "Who might that be? All I see is one of Trivant's Roselians."

Jerom nodded. "I know the lad. Dakan Holdreth is his name – he's one of Trivant's Regulars. Offered him a spot in the tournament just yesterday."

Hagail smirked. "Got a thing about pick'n up strays now, don't cha?"

Jerom arched an eyebrow at him. "Why's that?"

"The tattoos on the lad mark him as Clan of the Fang. That's the same clan that be com'n ta the aid of Cravon. It also means tha two of them are blood." Kale and Jerom's blank, shocked stares were confirmation enough for Hagail that neither of them were aware of the connection. "Aye, however ye may view it, tha Roselian clans aren't as . . . strict as we were. Tha Clan of the Fang was stripped of its lands and position amongst the clans. As I be understandn' it, the older members were either executed or left to fend fer themselves, and tha young were taken in by the other clans n' raised by them. Tha lad be too young ta not have been raised by tha others. It's amazin' that he was allowed ta wear those tattoos."

Jerom nodded. Dakan's somewhat independent and rebellious nature seemed in line with Hagail's assessment of clan society amongst the Roselians. "What do we do now? This is a very ugly mess. Last thing we need is some ancient clan blood feud starting a war amongst our ranks."

Hagail grunted is agreement. "As soon as we be leav'n here, Gregor's gonna be mak'n sure that we don't have any more rogue Vanmulik about. I'd be suggest'n that ye keep an eye on yer lad till ye depart."

Kale's green eyes were already alight with his racing thoughts. "Agreed. I have something in mind for Amroth, and I'll be speaking with Trivant myself. Jerom – I want you to see to it that arrangements to march are expedited." He eyed everyone sternly and added, "I want this situation taken care of and any such actions discouraged. Is that understood?"

"Aye, Doms Merandith," echoed each man.

"Good. Well then, gentlemen, I believe we all have work to attend to." Kale nodded curtly to Hagail and Gregor before stepping past them and making his way to Amroth with Jerom in tow.

Hagail and Gregor turned and watched as the Merandiths walked away. Neither Sur'dathan was happy with the events of this morning. Not only had House Hagail and the Sur'dathan name been dishonored this day, but more importantly, the petty vengeance of the dead men could have cost Sur'datha and the war effort. Kale would have been justified in changing his plans and putting someone else in charge of the army. Even worse, he could have simply sent them home. It was even more sickening to them that a member of the Clan of the Fang had been the one to rescue Amroth. They watched as Dakan stood to greet Kale and the two men shook hands, further twisting the Sur'dathans' stomachs. It felt like Deo was playing some sort of perverse joke on them.

"Gregor," growled Hagail, "I be want'n ye ta find who be talk'n and ta send a message. If'n it's a Vanmulik – send um ta an early grave, then round up the rest and be mak'n sure they're sent home."

Gregor nodded grimly. "If'n it's not a Vanmulik?"

"Use yer discretion. I just want ta be mak'n sure a strong message is sent. There won't be anyone or any clan's petty feuds ruin this fer everyone."

Gregor nodded his acknowledgment as they turned and pushed their way through the crowd, both men eager to see their work done.


Dakan watched as the two Sur'dathans vanished into the crowd. Both men had seemed visibly disturbed by what had happened, and from what Kale had just told them, they were dead set on making sure it never happened again. The only reason he was inclined to believe so was because it was Kale that said it. He had no love for the Sur'dathans. What they had done to Clan Theirigaldis was only slightly more unforgivable than what had been done to his clan. The violent, honor-driven side of him practically demanded that the instigators of the genocide be executed in retribution for their appalling acts. However, his practical side saw just how useful clan fighters were in this war. More often than not, a clansman was worth five of any of the other Houses' fighters, which made the death of the three assailants only slightly regrettable.

"Are you okay, Dakan?"

Kale's question drew him from his thoughts. Nodding, he answered, "I am. I caught them off guard and the fog gave me the same advantage that they had over Amroth. I'm simply glad I was where I was, when I was. Such underhanded actions are . . . disgusting," he finished with a sneer.

Kale crouched down and placed a comforting hand on Amroth's shoulder, his green eyes filled with concern. "What about you? It seems your thick head was good for something after all."

His brother smiled softly and tried to laugh, the pain in his ribs and throat pulling him up short. "I'll live," he croaked with a wince. "If Dakan hadn't happened along when he did, a few inches of steel would be telling a different story."

Kale turned and eyed the sword lying in the dirt beside one of the attackers. Two threadbare-dressed men had arrived with a large handcart and were loading the bodies into the cart. "Jerom, collect the sword for me, would you?"

Jerom nodded and moved off to retrieve it. He got there just as one of the men was about to toss it in the cart, and the man turned the sword over to Jerom with a bow. As Jerom stepped away from the cart and it started to roll away, the onlookers saw its departure as their signal to return to their day and began to dissipate. Returning to the others, Jerom noticed the pleasantly plump, white-clad medic hovering behind Amroth, her homely features fixed in consternation at being kept from her patient. Nodding his thanks for her patience, he handed the blade over to his nephew. "What do you plan to do with it?"

Kale stood and accepted the blade. "Well, I'd offer it to Dakan as reward for his actions, but a lochabre of that quality tells me that a sword of this make would be an insult. So, if no one minds, I think I'll have Barniban melt it down and make it into something useful."

Jerom snorted. "Just a blade . . . no sense in wasting it. Might do someone some good in its current state."

"True," Kale said as he slid the blade through his belt. "But it will certainly make me feel better to see it melted down." He signaled for the medic to approach.

She gave one frustrated tug on her braided red hair, stepped forward, and curtsied. "Yes, Doms Merandith?" she asked in a strong, firm voice.

Kale almost smirked at her. It was obvious she didn't like being interrupted in the middle of her duties to indulge someone in a chat with her charge, but she was doing a good job of holding her tongue. "Your name?"

"Liza Nolandrith, Doms Merandith," she replied quickly.

"My thanks for indulging me, Liza. Amroth here is a bit thick-headed and tends to try to act tough. So while I'd love to believe he's just fine, how bad are his injuries?"

Amroth rolled his eyes at the jab even as the medic listed off his injuries. "He has three broken ribs, numerous bruises, a nasty gash on the back of his head, small punctures to his throat, numerous cuts, and possible head-fog. It also appears that he's bitten his tongue. I can tell better when we get him to the medical tents, but there doesn't appear to be any internal injuries and he seems to have all his senses about him. He'll hurt for a while and breathing might be a bit of a problem. I would say all that muscle saved him from a worse fate."

Kale nodded and smiled. "Well then, I don't think we should keep the lady waiting any longer. See to it that Amroth is well taken care of, Liza."

"I will, Doms Merandith," she replied with a curt nod.

"Good. As well – given this morning's nasty circumstances – I'm sending Jerom along to look out for him."

"I'd like to accompany them as well, Doms Merandith," interjected Dakan.

Kale looked at Dakan curiously as he asked, "Jerom?"

"Aye, I'd welcome him, Kale. Besides, we have some business to finish from the other day."

Kale looked to his uncle and nodded. "Very well." He then turned his attention back to the medic. "Jerom and Dakan will accompany you to provide protection should anyone else decide to do something foolish."

Liza's soft, middle-aged features screwed up in consternation and her brown eyes took on a frustrated edge. She wanted to protest the presence of two men who, in her opinion, would be a distraction from her duties. However, she was in no position to deny the request of a doms. "As you wish, Doms Merandith." Gesturing to Amroth, she ordered with a hint of frustration, "Someone give him a hand. The trip is short to the medical tents, but I don't want him straining himself too much, and he's not hurt enough to bother with a stretcher."

Dakan leaned over and helped Amroth to his feet, providing support with a strong arm around his waist.

"What about you, Kale? Don't want to be at my side through this trying time?" quipped Amroth hoarsely.

Kale let out an amused laugh. "Sorry I can't be your nurse-maid. Thankfully, I have a date with a blacksmith that I simply cannot miss."

"If we're done joking, could we please get going? The longer we delay, the longer his wounds remain unattended to," interjected the medic as she gave each man a pensive glare.

Jerom smirked and motioned for them to get underway. "Go ahead. I'll be along in a moment."

Liza nodded. "Very well. Good day to you, Doms Merandith." She curtsied to Kale before straightening, turning on her heel – the split skirt of her practical white dress swirling about her feet – and leading Dakan and Amroth south through the tents toward the medical facilities.

As soon as they were out of earshot, Jerom turned to Kale, his bearded face taking on a serious edge. "I have to ask – what do you want to do with Amroth? I know we're leaving soon, but that may not be fast enough if there are more would-be murderers about."

Kale nodded and ran a hand through his short-cropped blonde hair. "I know . . . and I think I have an idea. Missives will need to be sent ahead of us so that people can prepare for our return and, with the news of fighting behind our lines, I'd feel better with one or two more bodies watching over my wife."

Jerom snorted. "You can't be serious? That's a long journey for an injured man."

"I know. But he *is* clan, Uncle. And while he might not be healthy enough to ride immediately, he'll heal up quick enough. Besides, it will also be safer for him on the road than lurking about camp. Furthermore, it's about time that he gets over his aversion to fighting and learns to put what skills he has to use. He needs to be ready and willing to use a sword instead of just wearing one for show. Hells, if he'd been wearing one and willing to use it, this might not have happened."

Jerom scratched at the irritated skin around his eyepatch. He knew Kale was right. Amroth's pacifistic nature was fine if all he was doing was working at a forge. However, if he now had a target on his back, it would be better that he learn more about using a blade and was willing to use it. "I can't argue with that," he finally said after the brief moment of reflection. "But I hope you have some idea of how to get him to come around, because Barniban's training and his time at the Academy couldn't convince him to do so."

Kale nodded. "I didn't until now. I think sending Amroth north along with Mathis would do the trick."

Jerom blinked in amazement, not quite sure he'd heard his nephew right. "You can't be serious? Mathis is the best bodyguard you've got, and a damn fierce fighter. I don't want to lose him with as shorthanded as we are."

"Don't act like I don't know that. The fact of the matter is, Amroth needs him more than me right now. Mathis is skilled in all weapons and was an excellent teacher before the war. He can do more for Amroth than either of us. As for being shorthanded – you're pulling together the men for the tournament, which will supply us with extra help until we get home." He smirked. "Besides that, Dakan has already proven himself today, and the mere sight of a Roselian carrying a lochabre will cause many to piss their pants."

Jerom couldn't hold back a laugh at the imagery. Roselians were feared for their tenacity – especially if they were from the clans. However, a Roselian carrying a lochabre, specifically one that knew how to use it, was truly a terrifying sight to behold. "Very well. . . . I don't have to like it, but I have to agree that it would be best for Amroth."

Kale smiled, "I knew you'd see it my way, Uncle."

Snorting, Jerom barked, "Bah! I don't have time to mess with you, and I'm too old to have to deal with your sassiness! Get going before I decide to turn you over my knee and give you a whipping like your mother used to!" Kale smiled and gave his uncle a mocking salute before turning on his heel and moving off at a quick pace. Jerom could only shake his head at Kale's retreating back and smile as he muttered, "Kids."


Kale's pace was quick and deliberate as he made his way through the maze of tents toward the Blacksmith Enclave. Dark smoke and the rhythmic ringing of hammers on steel served as an unerring guide for his steps. Men and women stood aside for him, bowing and saluting as he passed. Kale gave them a cursory acknowledgment in return, his mind focused on the morning's events and the task before him.

To say the news of the assault on Amroth was a surprise would be an understatement. Amroth was a friendly and congenial man when he wanted to be. He did have some difficulties making friends as he tended to be somewhat reserved, but he also rarely made enemies. So, when word of the attack reached Kale's ears, he could only assume Amroth's dark past had caught up with him. It didn't matter that Amroth was just a babe when the Cravon Uprisings were put down, there would seemingly always be those that viewed anyone of Cravon's blood as a glaring reminder of Clan Theirigaldis' betrayal. The Merandiths, along with the full support of House Hagail, had done an excellent job of shielding him from would-be assailants up until this point. They had even run the risk of Amroth's resentment by telling him of his past and letting him explore it.

Kale's fears had come true with this assault. Someone had recognized Amroth's features as Theirigaldian and believed he should be eliminated. It was somewhat amusingly ironic that a Roselian clansman was Amroth's rescuer. He could only imagine what was going through Dakan's mind. The Roselian clans had been more lenient with those that had ridden to the Theirigaldian call, choosing to seize their lands and strike their clan name from existence. Only those that they viewed as having committed the most heinous crimes had been executed – which, in their view, was the vast majority of the adults. The adults that had been spared were left to their own devices; however, no one held any illusion about what that meant – on the plains, such punishment was tantamount to a death sentence. Therefore, while Kale never feared violent actions from Trivant's men, he also didn't fully expect any of them to lift a finger if Amroth was in danger. Whether Dakan regretted his actions or not, Kale was glad he had been there. He had very little family left, and Amroth was his last link to his father and mother. Amroth was a brother to him, and losing him would be as devastating as the loss of his parents.

The problem now was protecting him. Kale and his father had always found Amroth's pacifism to be a commendable but dangerous flaw in these trying times. Amroth had been more than willing to learn basic swordsmanship for the dual purpose of appeasing Kale and Bordin, and obtaining a better understanding of the items he would be asked to make and repair as a blacksmith. Furthermore, even his choice of professions had kept him out of the melee and well-protected until now. This incident, however, had brought Amroth's nature squarely into Kale's sights. He wasn't about to leave Amroth vulnerable to attack, but neither could he spare men to guard him day and night. So it fell to Kale to find a way to not only persuade him to further his skills as a swordsman, but to also convince him to fight – if only in an emergency.

Kale had been mulling this for a long time and had concocted a few ideas on how to proceed, but the attack this morning had quickly limited his options and provided a motivating factor that even Amroth could not ignore. It was simple courtesy and an old friendship that brought him to the blacksmiths so that he could inform Barniban of his decision. Ignoring the fact that he would be taking one of Barniban's best smiths from him, all Kale had to do was send a missive informing Barniban of his decision. However, it wasn't in Kale's nature to treat friends that way, even if he did receive a scolding from his old Forge Master.

"Ho! Doms Merandith! Watch yourself!"

The warning jerked him from his musings. One of the veteran blacksmiths, his body still muscled despite his age, was looming over Kale, a load of swords wrapped in a leather cover supported firmly on his right shoulder by meaty hands. The man's eyes sparkled with amusement as Kale's head jerked at the warning and he sidestepped quickly out of the smith's path before he could violently bounce off the large man.

Looking around, it dawned on Kale that he had wandered into the Blacksmith Enclave without realizing it. Looking back at the blacksmith, he smiled sheepishly and replied, "Thanks for the warning."

The man nodded, his gray-bearded cheeks swelling with an amused smile. "My pleasure, Doms. You looked a mite bit preoccupied; didn't want to run you over." He shifted the load on his shoulder to get a better grip. "Got a delivery for some of Trivant's men and didn't want it spilling all over the place and giving you unsightly injuries."

Kale shook his head. "The fault is all mine. Should have been paying attention to where I was going." He looked at the man in puzzlement, trying to recall the smith's name. "Grathorn . . . isn't it?"

The aged giant nodded. "Aye – served your father and Barniban for nigh on thirty years. I even remember giving you a lesson or two when you were just a lad. If I might be asking, what brings you here all by yourself? Normally have a few tin cans hovering over you like panicked nursemaids."

Kale laughed at the imagery. "A bit of business with the Forge Master. Is Barniban about?"

"Oh, aye. He's at the main forge. In a bit of a mood as well. He was giving a few of the young pups a tongue-lashing over some shoddy work. Though I think a visit from you might make his day a bit brighter. Well, I best be moving on. Good day to you, Doms Merandith."

Kale nodded to him as the large blacksmith stepped past and continued on his way, leaving the path clear to the Blacksmith Enclave.

Surrounded on all sides by the men and women of the Army of Five Stars, the Enclave was situated near the center of the main camp. In total, sixty blacksmiths and nearly two-hundred assistants and students provided the muscle needed to maintain the equipment of the marching army. It was a daunting task, to say the least. Arranged in rows of six smithies per row flanking the large, open-sided pavilion of the main forge on both sides, each smithy burned nearly day and night to meet the demands of the army. The small army of blacksmiths was comprised of men and women from all the Houses, but they answered to the Forge Master, Barniban Vormat – Master Blacksmith and the personal smithy of House Merandith. To the chagrin of some of the more nonchalant workers, the grizzled blacksmith ran the Enclave with a ruthless efficiency that kept the work flowing in and out of the forges in an effort to keep the army equipped properly and in better shape than their enemies. To that end, the smiths worked in rotating shifts that accounted for most of the day and night. Except for a few hours in the deep of night, the fires of the forges burned bright and the hammers sang their soaring song as a constant reminder to the troops of their presence.

Kale's path took him parallel to the shops, all of which were busy. Even from ten paces away, he could feel the heat of the roaring fires in each shop. A few of the workers noticed his passing and offered a small salute or bow in acknowledgment, but their unending work kept them from doing more. While it wasn't proper decorum, Kale was glad no one was making a fuss over his visit. They had their work to do, and he didn't need to be weighed down by protocol. Although very little was being made of his presence, it couldn't keep word of his arrival from spreading. A few of the workers popped their heads out from their stations to catch a glimpse of him, reminding Kale a bit of curious prairie dogs popping up from their burrows. As he turned onto the wide avenue leading to the main pavilion, he saw Barniban standing before the open-air pavilion, wiping his hands on his heavy leather apron and grinning broadly.

Stocky and bald, Barniban made for an imposing figure despite his sixty summers. Constant work at the forge kept his muscles hard and toned. Small burns – some healed and some fresh – marred his bare arms and hands, telling the story of his lifetime of labor. A leather apron protected his torso from below his neck, over his modestly round belly and down to his feet – though many thought his skin thick enough to protect him from stray sparks. Gray eyes that reflected his years sparkled with mirth as Kale neared and raised a hand in greeting.

"Hail, Barniban!" greeted Kale as he halted in front of his old teacher and offered him a hand in greeting.

Barniban's thick and callused hand wrapped tightly on to Kale's wrist in a firm handshake before he pulled him into a sweaty and strong hug. "Deo be good! I hav'n seen ye in a long time, lad! Been months since more than ah scribbled note or word passed on through Amroth served as conversation!" He let Kale out of the musty hug and held him at arm's length. "How are ye, lad?" he inquired in his deep, throaty voice.

Kale patted Barniban on the shoulder. "Tired and worn out of late, my friend. We've had a lot going on over the last couple of days. How have you been, old man?"

The Forge Master snorted. "I'm not that old."

Kale chuckled. "My apologies."

Barniban looked past Kale, noting the number of growing spectators and the diminished sound of hammer on metal. "Back to work, ye dogs! That steel ain't gonna be fix'n itself!" he roared.

The workers scrambled back to their stations and the sound of ringing steel once again sang out at a furious pace. None of them wanted to cross their boss. Those that had gone against him in the past had suffered humiliation enough to scare the others.

Once satisfied that their audience was back to work, Barniban grinned at Kale again. "So what brings ye here?"

Kale pulled the sword used in the assault from his belt and presented it to Barniban. "Was hoping you could melt this down and make use of the metal."

Barniban accepted the weapon with a curious look on his face. It didn't take him long to notice the dried blood on the pommel. "Do I want ta know, lad?" Kale nodded, drawing a grunt from Barniban. "Just a moment then."

Rubbing the pommel down with his apron, Barniban went back into the pavilion and pulled one of the younger workers aside. He then handed the sword over and sent the lad running off. Barniban then returned quickly to Kale's side, his face a bit more serious than before. "There now, tha blade's on its way to one of the smelters. Come on in and let's get ah bit o' privacy. Don't be need'n these young'ns getting distracted, and I suspect ye'll want it fer what ye've got to say."

Kale chuckled at his teacher's astuteness. "Lead the way."

The central pavilion was sectioned into four workstations surrounding a massive, central furnace equipped with large bellows to keep the fire burning bright. A sturdy steel chimney funneled the generous amount of smoke from the furnace through a hole in the shelter's roof. Two of the four stations were in use, as Barniban's apprentices busily repairing armor. The third station belonged to Barniban, and was occupied by a young man that was watching over the beginnings of a blade that was buried deep in the coals of the furnace. As for the remaining station, it belonged to Amroth. Quiet and a bit messy, the station showed the signs of heavy, long-term use with little thought to cleanliness by the overworked blacksmith.

Barniban led him to his tent at the back of the pavilion, giving directions to each of his apprentices and assistants as they went by. Kale received polite bows from them, but like the other workers, they went back to work as soon as the last words left Barniban's lips. Once Barniban was sure everything wouldn't collapse into chaos while he was absent, he led Kale into his tent.

Unlike many of the other blacksmiths, Barniban made his home where his work was. The tent was small and without unnecessary luxuries. A cot for sleeping was at the back, and his belongings were scattered about the circumference of the tent. At the foot of his cot sat a small table that was home to a clay jug of water and an unmarked, dark bottle of alcohol. There was an assortment of weapons piled on the right side of the tent, and on the left, Kale's armor was neatly lain out on a threadbare blanket. It appeared all the repairs were done and Barniban was just polishing the protective steel before returning it to him.

Barniban took a swig from the water pitcher before lowering himself to his cot, which creaked in protest under his weight. "Aye, yer armor is almost ready," Barniban confirmed when he saw where Kale's attention was fixed. "Just a bit of polish and a few straps to replace, and it'll be good as new. Amroth's work'n his arse off, so I thought I'd give tha lad a hand so he could be focus'n on other tasks." He chuckled a bit. "Honestly, I think the lad takes a bit too much pride in work'n on yer gear."

Kale absently ran a hand through his short-cropped blonde hair, his green eyes reflecting some of the anger and fear he felt at the events of the morning. "He does, doesn't he?" he said softly.

Barniban noted the reflective tone. "What's the matter, lad? I dunna think ye came all this way just ta be chatt'n with me – and that blood on tha sword is ominous."

Kale nodded and pulled his attention from the armor. "Aye, there's more to this visit than just friendly banter. You would have heard about it sooner rather than later – Amroth was assaulted this morning on his way back to his tent."

Barniban's eyes widened in shock, and he slumped back against the tent wall. "Deo be good," he breathed. "So that's why ye wanted that sword destroyed – and I can't blame ye! Is the lad alright?"

"He is . . . though a bit worse for the wear. Jerom is with him and getting his wounds tended to."

Hagail shook his head in disbelief. "The lad's ah tough one and he'll heal fast enough," he stated confidently. "Any idea who did it?"

Kale chuckled dryly. "I can't go into too much detail, but his attackers are dead."

The Forge Master ran a large hand over his face, trying to gather his thoughts. "That's good ta know. And I'm glad ye brought word 'fore rumors got ta me, but I know ye better. With Amroth do'n okay, ye wouldn't be delivering the news in person unless there was something more. I'd bet a month's wages that it's not a coincidence that this happen just when them Sur'dathans showed up."

Kale smiled softly. "Still sharp as ever, I see." The smile faded quickly as he added, "But yes, I'm afraid that his past might be catching up with him; unfortunately, that means I'll be taking your prized student away for a while. Though we'll be leaving soon, I don't feel like I can protect him adequately in this environment if a few malcontents within the Sur'dathan ranks get determined to kill him for some damned grudge that isn't of Amroth's doing. So I'm going to send him on ahead of us with someone to protect him and teach him."

Barniban snorted. "Well, I can't say I'm happy or surprised. Them Highlanders can hold a grudge better than most. Hells, the only thing worse is a Roselian with a pole up 'is arse 'bout something." He scratched his head and sighed. "I'll have ye know, ye'll be put'n a dent in our output, but noth'n we can't handle." Barniban scratched at his chin. "Can I ask what ye plan on teach'n tha lad? Not much about run'n a forge one can learn on the road."

Kale folded his arms across his chest and gave Barniban a firm stare. "Swordsmanship."

The large Forge Master gave a scoff of disbelief and shook his head skeptically. "Swordsmanship? That lad? He's not got the personality for it. Deo be good, if it wasn't for the lesson I give me students, I'd be afraid he'd stick himself! Yer ask'n a lot if yer gonna get him ta fight. Fer that matter, who's gonna be willing ta try and teach an ambidextrous person? They're few and far between, 'n most teachers just get frustrated and either quit or make'um somethin' they're not. Tha lad don't deserve that, and he don't need it shoved down his throat either."

"I know. But I'm hoping this incident will change his mind. At the very least, he needs to be ready and willing to defend himself. We've been foolish to think that someone wouldn't eventually come after him – and that foolishness led to a lax in vigilance that almost cost him his life. Teaching him to protect himself is the least I can do. If, along the way, it gets him to fight alongside me, it would just be an added bonus." He shrugged, seemingly indifferent to what Amroth did with the training just as long as he learned to defend himself. "As for the job of enlightening Amroth. . . . I think Mathis will do."

Barniban barked a laugh. "Mathis, eh? Figures as much. That man has been trying ta get him ta be a respectable fighter fer longer than ye. In fact, he once came by ta ask me ta let him use my forge ta make the lad a pair of swords. 'Course I refused, know'n tha lad's peaceful nature, and not want'n just anyone ta be use'n my tools."

Kale blinked in surprise at the bit of information on his enigmatic bodyguard. "You're telling me Mathis can work a forge? I never knew that."

"Aye. It surprised me too." He shrugged his powerful shoulders. "Like I was say'n, I did na know that and told him no. Thought that would be the end of it, but he wouldn't let up. Came by once ah year on the lad's birthday ta make the same request and met the same end. Did this fer five years, then he started do'n it twice a month till the lad was nine. When I still refused him, he started up once a week till he caught me drunk 'nough to agree just ta get him off my back."

Barniban pushed himself to his feet and knelt down next to his cot. He rummaged around for a bit before pulling an unremarkable wooden case from under the cot. Leveraging himself up, he placed the case on the cot and released the brass latches before laying it open and stepping back for Kale to see. "He was always insistent on what he wanted. I managed to get him to tell me ah bit about what he wanted, and I'd think him ah bit daft if'n I hadn't seen what he could do with his sword. So, in tha end, I let him work tha forge. He and yer father even had tha gall ta have me locked out of me own smithy till he was done. Took him a month! One month of be'n locked out of me own forge and hav'n ta use the smaller ones!" He snorted before continuing. "Then when he was done, he had me hang on to 'um till Amroth was ready for 'um. Dunno why he did na just hang on to them himself."

There was a tinge of jealousy to Barniban's comments that didn't make sense to Kale until he set eyes on the swords. Standing over the case with his eyes wide with awe, Kale understood why Barniban would be jealous. Inside the case were two long, slender swords resting in padded backs. Identical in every way, each sword was four feet in length with blades featuring a gradual, elegantly sloping curve and only one cutting edge. Rippling waves defined the cutting surfaces from the rest of the bluish steel blades, and a simple, square collar separated the blade from a two-handed hilt wrapped in simple brown leather and capped by a steel pommel.

"Amazing," Kale breathed, astonished that a man like Mathis was capable of such a stunning feat.

"Aye. . . . And made from tha Velusyian bluesteel. They're even lighter than they look, and tha edge on 'um would skin ye without drawn' blood. I'll be damned if I could ever figure ah way ta work metal like that, and I have no idea where he learned ta' work bluesteel. Never 'eard or known a Velusyian to be spill'n their prized secrets." Barniban picked up the bottle of alcohol and took a long draw from it.

Kale raised a bemused eyebrow at him. "A bit early to be drinking, don't you think?"

"Bah! It's me stomach! Look'n at that work makes me sick!" he stated, unable to hide his jealousy.

Kale reverently closed the case and secured the latches before picking it up and tucking it under his arm, amazed at how light it was with two swords in it. "In that case, my dear Barniban, I'll just have to take them off your hands. Wouldn't want you drinking yourself under the table."

Barniban waved a dismissive hand, scowled, and took another swallow. "Bah! Go on and get outta here. Ye've got more ta be worry'n 'bout than an old codger like me. Know'n Amroth, he'll be ready ta ride some by the morn'n, so ye've got some work ahead of you. Damn clansmen and their quick heal'n." His face suddenly softened. "Just do one thing fer me, would ye?"

"What's that?"

"Give tha lad me best. Ye know I can't be go'n with ye, and I dunna know when I'll get ta see tha lad again. Winters 'er long, and war's a bit too fickled for my taste."

Kale nodded and patted his old teacher on the shoulder. "I will." He adjusted his grip on the case and walked out of the tent with Barniban in tow.

Their emergence from the tent was noticed by the smiths in the pavilion, but it didn't stop their work. Turning to Barniban, Kale offered his hand and the Forge Master gripped his wrist in a good-bye handshake. "Wish I could stay and visit longer. Maybe lend a hand with all this work."

Barniban snorted. "Bah! Ye'd do more damage than good! Yer better at use'n what we make than mak'n it yerself." He shook his head, recalling Kale's unremarkable years studying at the forge, before offering a soft, friendly smile to his doms. "I'll have yer armor sent over as soon as we're done. Ye just make sure those get ta Amroth and that ye take care of yerself; I'm sure we'll all have a chance ta sit 'round a fire exchanging stories like some sickly happy family."

Kale smiled. "You as well. Oh, and try not to work your apprentices so hard – they're human too."

Barniban slapped Kale on the shoulder and waved a hand in the direction of the main camp. "Would ye get go'n? Yer just keep'n me from the real and important work! Don't need ta be coddling royalty all-day!"

Kale laughed, adjusted his grip on the case once more, turned and made his way from the pavilion toward the Merandith portion of camp. Barniban's vocal instructions followed him on the air, ushering his apprentices to work harder and providing Kale with a reminder of fond memories of a better time. Each swift step Kale took made Barniban's words a bit harder to understand until the rhythmic pounding of hammer on steel drowned his words out and washed away the memories, leaving only a symphony of steel ringing in his ears.

\*

The sun was high overhead by the time Gregor found his mark. He had spent the better part of the morning subtly inquiring about the incident in an attempt to get a feel for it within the ranks and confirm where he believed the information had come from. Between his investigation and attending to his regular duties, it had turned into an arduous task. While he firmly believed where the indiscretion had come from, he didn't want to jump to that conclusion

116

without proof. Thus, it came as no surprise when answer after answer pointed to the same man and a tongue loosened by alcohol.

He found himself standing in front of a familiar tent amongst the kyram-hide shelters of his own men – one of the few that had been erected before nightfall the previous day – his gloves creaking at his sides as his fists clenched and unclenched. The muscles of his jaw flexed under his rust- and white-colored beard, and his green eyes glowed with rage below his furrowed brow as he worked to control his anger. He held no illusions that Donald's loose tongue was responsible for the attack. Donald was renowned for his drinking and womanizing during his downtime – two indulgent activities that were well known for addling wits and loosening tongues. Gregor was veteran enough not to let his anger with Donald get to him too much, but as a precaution, he left his sword in his tent before seeking his subordinate out. However, that didn't mean he wasn't going to teach the lad a lesson.

Pushing the tent flaps aside, he strode inside and was greeted by surprised cries and a litany of curses. As his eyes adjusted to the dim lighting, he could see that the five-man tent was littered with clothes, armor and personal effects. His focus, however, was drawn to the frantic movements of the two naked women and the lone man as they scrambled to cover up their nude forms. Normally, it wouldn't have bothered him that the tent's other occupants had given Donald the tent for the night, but given the situation, such generous behavior had him seething.

With his eyes fully adjusted to the muted illumination, Gregor recognized the women as two of the prostitutes that traveled with the Sur'dathan army. Though somewhat plain, both voluptuous women sported auburn hair and green eyes – just the way Donald liked his women. In fact, he was pretty sure he'd walked in on them with Donald before. If the situation was any different, Gregor might have thought about seeking them out later for his own amusement, but his anger kept him from the carnal thoughts. After all, there was punishment to dispense.

Blankets held over their torsos, the two tousled and hung-over women hid behind the toned body of Donald as he adjusted his blanket to cover his lap. Gregor eyed the two hung-over camp prostitutes and growled angrily, "Out! Now!"

The young women, sensing the growing tension, let the blankets drop and quickly collected their clothes. Sparing a moment to blow quick kisses to Donald, they exited the tent as they slipped on simple tunics.

117

Donald, his mouth agape, ran a hand through his messy, short brown hair as he stared at his commander with bloodshot black eyes. "Captain what—"

Gregor stepped forward and slammed his fist into Donald's face, cutting his sentence short. Donald sprawled backward from the blow, blood trickling from his nose. Before he had a chance to recover, Gregor hauled him up from his cot and hammered two more punches to his face before backhanding him and letting him collapse onto his cot.

Face red with rage, and his eyes staring daggers at Donald, Gregor barked, "Ye bloody bastard! Don't know how ta be keep'n yer trap shut! This time yer loose tongue nearly cost all of us horribly!"

Donald shook his head to clear the cobwebs and sat up slowly. His face was bleeding from cuts on his cheeks, and his right eye was already darkening into an impressive black-eye. He spit blood on the ground before asking, "What are ye on about?" The question earned him a stinging, open-hand slap from Gregor. Donald rubbed his jaw as Gregor began pacing the width of the tent. "What'd I do, Captain? Dunna see anythin' wrong with a littl' drink'n and play'n with tha lassies – 'less we've got some new rule."

Gregor, stalking back and forth, kicked Donald's breastplate across the tent before turning to face him with a dark scowl. "Aye, no rule against that – though yer loins could use some protect'n. But ye done gone and blabbed 'bout see'n the Theirigaldis lad, and it nearly cost him 'is life this morn'n!"

Donald blinked at his captain like he'd been punched again. "I dunna think that—"

Gregor jammed an accusing finger at him. "That's right! Ye dunna think! Yer too busy drink'n and chas'n women's arses ta use yer brain fer once! Now ye better start remember'n and talk'n, lad. I need ta be know'n who ye talked with that would be want'n the lad dead!"

Donald winced from the pain in his face and dabbed at the blood trickling down his cheeks with his blanket while he thought about it. It had been a long night of drinking and gambling, and he had talked to many people about a variety of subjects. "I dunna know, Captain. I spent me time talk'n and game'n with a lot of the men last night after we set up camp. Threw dice with some of our men, then spent a bit o' tha night drink'n with them lassies and some of tha infantry. We talked for a bit and then tha lassies came back 'ere with me."

Gregor, his hands planted firmly on his hips to keep from hitting Donald again, scowled. "Think, damn ye! What were ye all gabbing about? Someth'n must've been said."

Donald glared at his captain. "Why 'er ye go'n on about this at me? Calvin was with us too. Might've been him who talked."

Gregor snarled at Donald's attempted to divert the blame. "Weren't Calvin! That lad's smart enough ta not talk 'bout things he's not supposed to talk about! Besides, tha lad was help'n me get settled in last night! So 'nough with tha excuses and start use'n yer brain! What'd ye say to them, and who are they?! Be quick 'bout it, fer I decide it's all yer fault and put yer head on ah pike ta decorate me tent!"

Donald's eyes went wide and he held up his hands as if to ward off a blow. He knew his captain well and, in Gregor's current mood, he wasn't about to take the threat lightly. "Alright! Alright! Le' me think! Ye know as well as I do that Bruman Ale'll knock ye fer a loop!" Donald dabbed at the fresh blood that was oozing up from all the talking before continuing. "Let's see now. . . . We gathered where tha infantry had set up camp, and gamed and drank all tha night away. I remember that we were talk'n 'bout the upcomin' campaign and what ta expect. A few of the older fellas started on 'bout tha good ol' days, say'n how this'll be easier than putt'n down tha Cravon Uprising." Donald paused, his brow furrowing as he tried to recall the previous night. "I . . . I think some o' tha Lowlander infantry started talk'n 'bout how they'd seen ghosts of tha dead Theirigaldis clan roam'n the plains and . . . and . . ." Donald's face sunk as the evening came back to him.

Gregor noticed Donald's reaction and stared at him sternly. "What?" he demanded.

Donald looked at him with apologetic eyes and took a deep breath before continuing. "Ye gotta believe me – I didna know. I joked that I'd seen a lad that eerily looked like ah Theirigaldis. Most o' tha lads just laughed it off, but 'ere was one man that seemed ah wee bit more interested than tha others. Kept ask'n questions 'bout tha lad. I could na' tell him much other than describe tha lad, but that seemed 'nough. Honest, Captain, I did na think I was do'n harm!"

Gregor snarled in disgust. "Focus lad – who was this man?"

Donald stared to speak then stopped, his face screwing up in confusion.

"What is it, lad?"

"Honest, Captain, I'm try'n ta remember, but . . . but he seems foggy."

Gregor raised his eyebrows in surprise. "Foggy?"

Donald nodded. "Aye. I can 'na remember his features."

Gregor stepped forward and bent over, placing his hands firmly on Donald's shoulders. "Think, lad. Anything will help. Eyes, beard, scars – anything ta help identify him."

Donald shook his head and sighed. "Honestly, it's all. . . . Wait. . . There was one thing that stood out 'bout tha man. He had a dragon tattoo on 'is wrist."

Gregor stood up and shook his head in disgust. "A dragon tattoo? That's tha best ye can do? Deo be good, Donald! That'd be half tha Lowlanders with us, and who knows how many others in tha other camps! Can ye be more specific? I can 'na be go'n person ta person check'n their wrists!"

Donald shrugged. "I know Captain, but I canna recall it clearly. It feels like a miracle that I can be remember'n that."

Gregor could only shake his head in disgust as he walked over to a pile of clothes belonging to Donald and picked up a shirt. He knew he wouldn't be getting any more from his subordinate at this point. Maybe after he sobered up some more, he'd be able to recall in better detail. At that moment, however, his memory was fairly useless. Turning, he tossed the shirt to Donald and ordered, "Get cleaned up and dressed. I want ye out help'n with dig'n tha latrines, then ready for maneuvers before dinner."

"Aye, Captain," Donald muttered.

Gregor made his way to the tent entrance. Just before he exited, he turned to Donald and declared in a deadly serious tone, "Oh, and Donald – if'n I ever catch ye or find out ye have jeopardized our stand'n with tha others or our efforts against tha Suldamiks, I'll personally ride one of tha horses used ta draw and quarter ye."

Donald – bruised, bloodied and shirt in hand – sat in stunned horror long after Gregor had left his tent, knowing that his captain meant every word of the threat.

*

*Sssut! Ssssut! Ssssut! Sssssut!*

The rasp of the whetstone filled the tent with each pass as it slid down the blade with the care of a lover's caress. Oil ran away from the stone, causing the two-toned ripple that delineated the cutting edge from the rest of the blade to sheen in the light that poured in from the tent entrance. The man's hand – callused, and with long and nimble fingers – guided the whetstone with precision, each stroke removing small imperfections and honing the edge to lethal perfection.

Seated on his cot, back straight and katana across his lap, Mathis was a picture of calm and control. He held the blade steady while his other hand worked the length of the gently tapering blade with steady and graceful movements, his coal-black eyes keenly focused on the honed blade edge. Calm, middle-aged features betrayed little of what he might be thinking, nor what he was looking for in the sword. Even his attire reflected an organized and calculating person. His hair, which was still black despite his fifty summers, was cropped short and pulled back into a short horsetail, freeing his clean-shaven face from vision-impairing hair. The clothing adorning his athletic frame was as simple as his surroundings; his white shirt was cuffed at the wrists with dark leather bracers and belted at the waist with a utilitarian belt, while his functional pants were tucked into polished black knee-boots.

His small tent was neat and orderly like his person. To his left was a washstand with a pitcher of water and a simple mirror on it. To his right was a wooden stand that was adorned with his polished armor. His clothing and personal effects were stored in a simple chest beneath his cot, and his pack, bedroll and saddle sat at the foot of his cot. There was no waste with him, each thing in its place and in harmony with his needs.

Standing in the tent's entrance, Kale once again found himself wondering how such a clean, organized and graceful man could be such a lethal force on the battlefield. Aside from Jerom, Mathis was the eldest of his bodyguards – having served through the entirety of his father's reign – and the most lethal. While Kale regretted parting with him, he felt that Amroth needed Mathis' protection and wisdom more than he did at this moment.

"Come in or leave; either way, you're blocking my light," Mathis said with little concern for whom was filling his tent's entrance.

His purple-trimmed, black tabard rustling with his movements, Kale stepped into the tent and to the side, allowing the light to pour in fully. With an amused smirk, Kale leaned the wooden sword case against his leg before quipping, "Is that any way to speak to your doms?"

Still focused on his work, Mathis replied, "Rudeness is inexcusable – even from a doms; and I would say loitering in a man's entryway is quite rude. Wouldn't you agree, Kale?"

Kale chuckled and gave a small bow of apology. "My apologies, Mathis. I was simply admiring how you care for your sword. There are men that don't treat their wives with as much tenderness and love as you show toward that blade."

Mathis grunted as he held the katana up to the sunlight and examined the edge on both sides of the blade. "Fools, the lot of them."

Kale smiled in amusement. "I couldn't agree more – but one would think you care more for cold steel than the warmth of a woman."

Mathis grunted and wiped the blade down reverently one last time before picking up its black-lacquered wooden scabbard and gently sliding the sword home. "Think what they will, it matters little to me. This sword keeps you and I alive on the battlefield. I can't say the same about a woman's bosom."

Kale laughed, his eyes twinkling with mirth. "Very true. But a woman's bosom does give many a man something to live for."

Mathis grunted again as he placed his sword next to him on the cot. Standing up, he eyed the wooden case leaning against Kale's leg with a bit of surprise. Gesturing to the case, he said, "Either you've been rummaging through other people's belongings, or someone has been talking about things they had no right to be."

Kale shrugged slyly. "Something like that. You never told me you could work a forge with such skill."

"What I do with my free time isn't much of anyone's concern. Besides, you never asked." Mathis paused and eyed Kale knowingly. "I suppose you already know who those swords are intended for?" Kale nodded in confirmation. "Well . . . then I can only assume this has something to do with Amroth. I would even go so far as to say the assault this morning was directed against him."

Smirking, Kale quipped, "Always astute, aren't we?"

Mathis shrugged. "It's not too hard to connect the circumstances. There's an assault within the camp this morning, very soon after the arrival of the Sur'dathans. Then you show up here with a set of swords I was keeping secret. Now, throw in the fact that you've been trying to get Amroth to learn swordsmanship for quite a while, and I would imagine you're here to get me to teach him."

Kale's eyes gleamed as he laughed with genuine amusement. "Will you ever cease to amaze me, Mathis?"

"Possibly."

Kale laughed again and shook his head. "Well, you're mostly right."

Mathis arched an eyebrow. "Mostly?"

Kale nodded. "Aye. It's true that Amroth was assaulted this morning – he's doing fine, I might add – and that I want you to . . . encourage him to actually learn to defend himself. I also want to get him out of camp and away from any other possible attempts on his life."

Mathis thought about it and nodded slowly. "I can see where you are coming from. What would you have me do?"

"We're leaving in a few days, and I need someone to ride ahead to make sure supplies are setup for us and to inform my wife and others of our return so they can prepare. I want that person to be you, and I want you to take Amroth with you. I want you to protect him and get him to come around to learning to protect himself. When he does, then teach him."

"Presumptuous, aren't we?"

Kale smirked. "A bit. But I'm sure you can figure it out." He patted the sword case. "Besides, it seems like you've been planning this for a while."

Mathis nodded. "Indeed. It's not too often you find someone with his particular . . . talents."

"You mean because he's ambidextrous and no one has ever tried to *fix* him?"

"Indeed. He's a rare gem. Given his background, I thought it wise to nurture and put that gift to use instead of repressing or changing it. Amroth, however, has always been very . . . stubborn when it comes to learning how to fight."

Kale nodded. "I cannot argue with that. If not for Barniban's mandatory training, I don't think he would have touched a sword other than to make one after leaving the Academy."

"Probably so." Mathis ran a hand through his black hair. "This could prove to be quite interesting."

"You'll do it then?"

Mathis smirked. "Do I have a choice?"

Kale laughed, his green eyes twinkling. "Not really, no. Then again, you and Jerom seemed to like arguing with my orders."

He shrugged. "We have to find our amusement somehow. Besides, if we just blindly followed orders, we'd be no better than those following Craigan." Standing, he fell just short of being as tall as Kale. "What are your orders?"

Picking up the case and handing it to Mathis, Kale smiled. "I knew you'd see it my way. I want you and Amroth to ride ahead of us starting tomorrow. You'll have a writ from me to cover your expenses. Make sure to collect reports on the current local situations and inform the proper parties of our return home. Starting tonight, I want you guarding Amroth."

Accepting the case, Mathis nodded and placed the sword case on his cot. "Have you informed Amroth of your decision?"

Kale grimaced and shook his head. "Not yet. Jerom is watching over him while the medics attend to him, so I'll inform him tonight. Given how quickly he heals, I think he should be ready for a little saddle time in the morning."

Mathis nodded. "What about you? Simply having Jerom and Tazrim isn't much to watch your back."

Kale laughed and waved a dismissive hand. "Nothing to worry about. Jerom is gathering possible replacements for a tournament, so I'm sure we'll be giving them their chance to spend time with me. Besides, I'll have Trivant with me."

Mathis looked at him skeptically. "That's not the same."

Kale shrugged. "True. But we make-do with what we have. Amroth needs you more at this moment. Besides, the man who saved Amroth is one of the possible candidates. A fierce Roselian clansman with a lochabre axe." Kale laughed. "The mere sight of him should be enough to discourage an attack on my person."

Mathis folded his arms across his chest, his eyes growing serious. "A Roselian clansman? What is going through that head of yours? They're temperamental at best. You'll have to keep him from gutting someone just for sneezing in your presence."

Kale laughed again and shook his head. "I thank you for your concern, but I seriously doubt it will be as bad as that. I met the man already today, and he struck me as dependable and capable . . . though he did seem to take himself a bit too seriously."

"A trait all too well known amongst the Roselian clans. Speaking of which – did you find out which clan he belongs to?" Kale seemed to withdraw for the briefest of moments, but Mathis didn't miss it. "What have you gotten yourself into this time?" Mathis demanded sternly.

Deciding he wouldn't be able to keep it from Mathis for long, Kale figured it would be best to be straightforward. Taking a deep breath he said, "Clan of the Fang."

Mathis' eyebrows shot up in surprise and amazement. "Clan of the Fang? Are you sure? There's so few of them left, and it'd be easy enough for someone to mistake a dragon or snake tattoo for clan markings if they weren't well-versed in clan traditions."

Kale nodded his head. "I'm sure. Doms Hagail was the one who marked him. He would know better than anyone, other than the Roselians themselves, how to identify a clan marking."

Mathis lowered his head and let out a deep breath while running his hands over his head. Giving his horsetail a small yank, he then looked back up at Kale and shook his head. "Your family has a strange habit of attracting unusual people to your banner."

Kale chuckled. "You just noticed? I would have thought that obvious when you and Allanian showed up in Merset. Besides, I believe you were the one who found Amroth."

Placing his hands on his hips, Mathis said, "Point taken. But it doesn't mean I like it. You're walking a fine line by collecting so many outcasts – especially those from families involved in such a bloody mess like the Cravon Uprising. If you decide to keep this Roselian close by . . ." he shook his head and sighed. "Just be careful."

Kale gave Mathis a dry look. "Thank you, Father. Would it make you feel better if you met him before I ask permission to keep him around?"

Mathis cracked a smile and shook his head. "A smart mouth isn't going to get you anywhere with me. However, yes, I wouldn't mind meeting the man who saved Amroth's life."

Still giving him the same dry look, Kale answered, "Well Mathis, it just so happens I was planning on having him to dinner to thank him for his actions. I was also planning to have you join us so you could be there when I tell Amroth the good news that you'll be guarding him. I think it's a wonderful coincidence that our wants line up. Don't you agree?"

Mathis tossed his hands in the air and shook his head in defeat. "Very well. I'll be there."

Kale smiled and clapped his hands. "Excellent! I'll make sure to have an extra place set. We'll dine just after sunset. Now," he made his way to the tent's opening, "if you'll excuse me, I have to make sure everything is proceeding smoothly with our preparations for departure. The mess this morning has already put me behind as it is. I'll see you tonight."

Mathis dipped his head in acknowledgment. "Indeed. Tonight then, Doms Merandith."

Kale slipped out of the tent with a half grin on his lips.

Mathis stared at the tent entrance for a moment before taking a seat on his cot next to the case, a stoic mask overcoming his face. Reaching under his pillow, he pulled a single-page letter from where he'd hidden it and read it over again. Chin cupped in his right hand and forefinger tapping his upper lip, he began trying to piece together what Kale had just told him with the contents of the letter. There was more going on here than anyone was letting on or knew, and it was raising the hairs on the back of his neck. Eyes narrowing, he realized there was planning to be done, and there might be very little time for it.

# Chapter Five

ightfall descended upon the Army of Five Stars heralded by a cornucopia of orange, red and pink hues painted upon the eastern sky as the sun set. With all there was to attend to within the camp, very few paused to admire the majestically painted heavens before the colors were swallowed by the dark of night and replaced by pinpricks of light and a glowing full moon seated in a clear sky. Although the day's activities had been overshadowed by the assault on Amroth and the rumors that followed, business within the camp had proceeded at a good pace. Gregor and Doms Hagail had seen to it that their forces had finished setting up camp before nightfall despite their efforts to quietly hunt for the man with the dragon tattoo. Though it had occurred to them that Donald's drunken haze might be leading them on a wild and altogether fruitless chase, they continued with their efforts knowing that to do nothing would be viewed poorly.

To the east and north of the Sur'dathans, the temporary camp for those that would soon be returning home had grown drastically throughout the day. The excitement within the ranks of those camped there was palpable. For many of them, it had been years since they'd seen home, and their daily life-and-death apprehension now gave way to joy and anxiousness. They knew they'd be leaving within the next few days and only awaited the Merandiths and Trivants to strike their camps; once that was done, they could begin the journey home and enjoy a winter of much-needed rest. Though neither camp had made great strides in packing for the trip home, there was one man who was already relocating.

The day had been long for Dakan. He had spent the better part of the morning by Amroth and Jerom's side in the medical tent. While Amroth had his wounds attended to, Jerom had questioned the clansman about the fight, trying to gather as much information as he could so that they could determine if the dead soldiers were alone in their actions. Dakan had been noticeably irritated by the inquiry, though it wasn't because of the actual questions. The questions – and lack of answers – only served to drive home that he had no idea who had been behind the assault on someone that was a blood relative of his. True to his Roselian heritage, an assault on blood was tantamount to an assault on the whole family and he wanted nothing better than to find those responsible and choke the life from them with his bare hands. Jerom had assured him that they would do everything they could to protect Amroth and find out who was behind the attack, but that did little to placate him. However, he did not allow his rage to dictate his actions. Dakan decided that swallowing his anger at this time would serve himself and Amroth better, allowing him a clear line of thought and a better capacity to focus on his tasks. He was now serving Doms Merandith with the potential to become one of his bodyguards, so going off on a rage-filled hunt at this point in time would not only reflect badly on him, but would also dishonor the Merandiths.

Past the noon hour, the medics had declared Amroth fit to be released from their care. Dakan and Jerom then escorted their charge back to the Merandith encampment, where they saw to it that Amroth was provided with a bed in Kale's tent. Doms Merandith's only available bodyguard, Tazrim, was then assigned as protection. While Dakan would have preferred the task, he was in no position to argue and Jerom had assured him that Tazrim was more than capable of defending Amroth. Though it stung that he wouldn't have the opportunity to get to know Amroth better, his service to the Merandiths had begun and he wasn't about to disobey orders. After being given a chance to retrieve his sleeveless deerskin tunic in order to make himself more presentable, he spent the rest of the day following Jerom as his shadow, serving as an extra pair of hands for the veteran Sword Master while receiving his first taste of how things were done within the Merandith household.

It was an afternoon full of amusement and surprises for Dakan. He found Jerom to be a very direct and sometimes abrasively blunt man. Yet, despite his sometimes brutish behavior, there was a respect and love the men and women of House Merandith showed for Jerom that seemed to go beyond his status as the brother of the late Doms Bordin Merandith and uncle to Kale. He didn't throw his weight about like other nobles tended to do; instead, his orders, though direct and occasionally leaving very little room for argument, carried the air of a request made of an equal. It was something Dakan was more accustomed to seeing from clan life than from those of the ruling Houses, and it was quite refreshing.

By nightfall, they had managed to complete all their tasks for the day and had confirmed the recruitment of nine other potential bodyguards for the tournament. Those interviews left Dakan more amazed with House Merandith than he thought he could be. Of the nine they interviewed, five of them were not from Tiliea. To make matters even more shocking, two of those weren't even originally from Triclose! Dakan couldn't even fathom why someone would travel across the ocean, much less serve a doms not of their own land if they had a choice.

As the sun set and they were making their way back to the Merandith camp after collecting reports from the other Houses, he finally had to voice his curiosity. "I have to ask, Doms Captain – why are so many people that aren't from Tiliea so willing to serve Doms Merandith? They seem almost proud of it."

Jerom stopped in the middle of the path and turned to face his charge, an amused smile cracking his bearded face. "Lad – we Merandiths have a different view on things. Aye, we rule from a place of power and wealth. But if all the people that make it possible resent us, what good is it? No matter what you believe, a doms rules because of his people, not over them. Those that fight with us believe that to varying degrees. On the other hand, Craigan would have you believe that we rule by divine right and that the people are meant to serve us at our whim." He scoffed and scratched at the skin around the eyepatch covering his missing left eye. "Bloody fools, the lot of them! Any person with half a brain knows that a life of blind, unquestioning servitude is no life at all! Those that live in Tiliea do because they want to. Those that serve in the military do because they want to – not because we put a sword to their throats and conscript them."

Dakan blinked and folded his serpent-tattooed arms across his chest, eyeing Jerom skeptically. "You're telling me that every one of the soldiers serving your House is a volunteer?"

Jerom laughed and hooked his thumbs behind his worn sword belt, his lone brown eye twinkling with mirth. "Oh, aye, that they are. It's why we've survived this long, and why House Suldamik will never win." The mirth in his eye and voice was replaced by solemn, unequivocal conviction in his words as he said, "Those fighting for House Suldamik do so out of obligation or at the point of a sword. Our men fight because they want to. They fight because they want to defend their land and their homes from a fate they view as worse than death. They fight so they won't become slaves of some mad and power-hungry doms." Jerom's strong gaze bore into Dakan as he asked of the clansman, "What about you, lad? Why do you fight? Is it because you were told to, or because you want to?"

Dakan was taken aback by the introspective question. It was something he had never really thought about. He, like all clansmen and women, had been raised to hunt and fight – their sole purpose firmly entrenched in the prosperity and survival of the clan. It had never occurred to him that he might actually have a choice. The mere thought that he could have done something with his life other than what he had was almost unnerving. "I . . . I don't know," he replied hesitantly. "I'm a clansman. We're raised to fight. If we don't, then the clan could fall. I'm not sure we could imagine having a choice other than that."

Jerom nodded, understanding the dilemma. "Clan life is a bit different, eh? Everyone contributes or else everyone suffers. It's a fairly black-and-white lifestyle, isn't it?" He shrugged and looked up into Dakan's dark eyes. "I know your life can't have been easy, nor has it given you many choices. Think on it, though, as your time with us goes on. Are you here with me now because you want to, or is it something else?"

Dakan stared back at him and nodded, his eyes reflecting a new-found and somewhat troubled introspection as his mind chewed on Jerom's words.

Jerom smiled sympathetically and patted him on the shoulder. "Let's get moving, lad; we've got a few more things to do before you can move your belongings to your new home, and I do believe Kale will want a word with you tonight."


Jerom had been right – Kale did extend an invitation to dine with him and a few others that night. As a result, he was left with very little time to return to his tent in the Roselian camp and retrieve his belongings. Like many within the clans, Dakan carried only what he need to survive. The interior of his tent was practical and devoid of unnecessary decoration. Having anticipated his move, he had already begun to pack, leaving his tent looking almost as if it was abandoned. With his belongings consisting mainly of clothing, armor, and tools to maintain his equipment, it didn't take him long to gather his remaining possessions and neatly stow them in a large pack before securing his tightly rolled bedroll to the top of the pack. Since the portable domicile would soon be given over to another clan member, he felt no desire to spare a fond glance for his tent as he shouldered his pack and exited. Nothing was wasted; when one clan member no longer had use for something or passed on, the items that were not claimed by family would be handed down to someone in need. Dakan had made good use of what little had been given to him and was more than happy to see it go to someone else. In fact, as his steps carried him through the camp, he was beginning to feel like his transfer into House Merandith's service was going to be very good for him.

The cold night air felt good on his bare arms, clearing his head and adding a bounce to his step. Like all clansmen, he healed at an unusually fast rate, and, that morning, he had been able to remove his bandages from the brawl and battle the previous day. Fast-fading scars and minor bruising were all that was left from the fight. He

130

suspected that if Amroth was as true to his clan blood as he, then the wounds from the assault that morning would already be quickly mending.

He already was of a mind to teach Amroth to better defend himself. Jerom had informed him that Amroth was a bit of a pacifist. The news that someone of clan blood could detest fighting was appalling to him and nearly inconceivable. Fighting was in their blood, and their gift of swift healing was the Spirits' way of letting the clans spend their time in glorious battle instead of recuperating in a bed – or so the clans believed. A clansman should spend his time bettering the clan, or in battle where his spirit could soar. To be of clan blood and reject fighting was practically an insult to the Spirits – or Deo if that was one's chosen focus of worship – and one's forbearers. As one of Amroth's few remaining blood relatives, distant as it was, he felt it was his obligation to ignite the fire of Amroth's clan blood and show him the thrill of combat.

A grin suddenly broke out on his face. Although it wasn't as if he never smiled, it came as no surprise that a few of the men and women gathered about the campfires he passed stared at him. Some stared in shock at the smile, while others looked on with unabashed hatred. He knew there were many that wanted him dead and others that would be glad to see him gone. However, the smile on his face announced to them that he didn't care, for he had found something in a few short days that he'd spent most of his adult life searching for. He had found a purpose beyond the scheming of clan members and clan leaders.

He had found a purpose that was his own.

"Well, well. . . . You weren't planning on leaving without saying good-bye? Were you?" purred a voice from the shadows to his right.

Dakan came to a halt with a start and turned, his right hand shooting up to the haft of his axe. He let out a curse and relaxed as Beliza sauntered out of the deep shadows. "Damn it, woman! You could have gotten your head cut off startling me like that!" He glanced around to make sure no one could see them together before grabbing her wrist, stepping past her and pulling her back into the shadows of the tents.

Clad in a mid-thigh length tunic, that revealed more of her ample wolf-tattooed breasts than it hid, and knee-length boots of deerskin, Beliza laughed and pressed in close to Dakan. Salt-and-pepper hair hanging loosely about her shoulders, she purred, "My dear Dakan – I didn't think you were one to rut in public." She grinned devilishly, her gray eyes twinkling with amusement.

131

Scowling, Dakan growled, "Damn it, Beliza! You know very well that it does neither of us any good to be seen too often in public together!"

Beliza stuck her lower lip out in a pout even as she traced a finger across Dakan's chest. "What's this now? Am I not your beloved Wolf? Are you so ashamed to be seen in public with me? You have the High Elder's blessing now; there's no more shame or dishonor to be heaped at your feet. And we certainly shouldn't worry about how the Wolf and Fang Clans' friendship is viewed."

Dakan's face softened at the chastisement. "Very well, Beliza. You're right . . . to a point. Things could still go wrong for me; and if our involvement is made too public, the Wolf Clan stands to lose the most."

"Ah, but there's so much to gain!" She hooked her left arm around his neck lovingly while the forefinger of her right hand trailed down his chest, stopping at his belt buckle. "Imagine a union between our clans and what it could mean for us all!"

Dakan blinked, blindsided and stunned by the statement. "A union? What are you after, Beliza?"

She leaned up and kissed him. "Why you, my dear. You, your love, your seed, and your clan. What else do you think this is all about? Our fathers planned this union long ago. They saw that a union of the Wolf and Fang would strengthen us all and give birth to a bright future for the clans."

Dakan's dark eyes grew bewildered at the statement. "What are you talking about? Have you been drinking? There was never such talk. A union between our clans could have been viewed as treasonous."

Beliza laughed. "My dear Dakan – who do you think your brother was to marry?"

Dakan's brow furrowed as it all began to sink in. He had been but a child when his older brother had been betrothed, and he'd had never known to whom it was, but if what Beliza was implying was true. . . .

She laughed as she saw the realization dawn on Dakan's face. "I see you put it all together."

He pushed her to arm's length. "So all I've been to you this whole time is a means to an end?"

Beliza folded her arms under her breasts. "Don't be cross with me. A means to an end you ask? Bluntly? Yes – though it isn't without love. Aye, Dakan, I do love you and have for a long time. Is

132

it lessened because I have a vision for our clans? I don't think so. You have a chance to bring your clan back into good standing. If you do that, then we can wed and bring about the dawn of a new age for the clans."

Dakan scowled. "You assume much and reach for even more. What makes you think I love you and would marry you?"

Shaking her head knowingly, Beliza said, "Come now, Dakan, you're as tired as I am of our clandestine unions. I know you burn for me as much as I do for you."

Dakan stared hard at her before replying. "Aye, Beliza, I do love you; and the honor of having a Wolf as my bride would burn as hot jealousy in the pits of many a man's stomach. But we talk of flights of fancy. I go to serve House Merandith. If all goes well, then honor will be restored and your ideas will stand a chance of coming to fruition." He shook his head to clear it of what he currently viewed as far-fetched ambitions. "That's a long way down the road, however. I could die or fail these trials. What then? Run away together and bring dishonor and ruination to your clan?" He shook his head sternly. "I will not be responsible for bringing low another clan."

Beliza grinned happily. "Oh, I have no doubt that you will succeed. If not," she shrugged, "I believe you've been referred to often enough as my pet that they wouldn't mind if I kept you as such." Dakan scoffed and shook his head. "However, I don't think it will come to that. I believe I have found a way to restore your clan's honor no matter the outcome of your little stint in House Merandith's service."

Dakan chuckled skeptically. "And what magical means have you discovered that didn't exist before?"

She grinned at him and gave him a sideways look. "I have it on good authority that you rescued quite the notorious person today?"

"Notorious? Beliza, I have no idea what you are . . ." Dakan trailed off as he realized whom she was talking about. "You mean Amroth?" he asked cautiously, his voice growing guarded.

"Aye. That's the one."

Disturbed by what he was hearing, Dakan shook his head and asked, "What has he got to do with this?"

"Think, my dear Dakan," she purred. "What clan is he?"

"Theirigaldis – which makes him blood."

She arched an inquisitive eyebrow. "I know. But what family? What name does he carry as secretively as you brazenly wear your serpent tattoos?"

Dakan's face sank. "Drakoni," he stated bluntly, his heart sinking.

She nodded, her smile growing. "And that makes him . . .?"

He closed his eyes and sighed. "Cravon's son."

Beliza clapped her hands joyfully. "Indeed it does! Cravon dishonored his clan with his actions, and dishonored his blood by bringing your clan into the fight. While the Theirigaldis Clan answered to the barbarisms of Sur'dathan justice, they never answered to us. Your clan suffered because of this. If you were to bring him before the Elders to answer for his clan's crimes. . . ."

Dakan opened his eyes and stared hard at his lover. "Honor could be restored to the Fang for turning over those responsible for the dishonor."

"Now you see, my love," she stated with pride.

Dakan's face hardened. "I won't do it. He is blood and was just a babe when it happened. He is no more responsible for his father's actions than– "

"You were for your father's actions," she finished for him, and his face sank. "You see, Dakan, some things are greater than the individual. The return of your clan's honor and the strengthening of our clans as a whole outweigh the life of the lone remaining Theirigaldis."

Dakan scowled at her, his heart and soul desperately wanting to reject her suggestion. "It won't come to that – I swear it. My actions will restore my clan's honor, not the death of an innocent."

Beliza stepped in close and patted his cheek lovingly. "Of course you will, my love." She leaned in and kissed him deeply.

Dakan tried to resist, but he eventually gave in and returned the passionate kiss.

Beliza pulled away with a devilish smile and took a step back. "Just keep the option in mind. Now, I had best be getting back to my clan before people begin to wonder." She kissed him one more time, trailing a finger down his chest, before stepping back and walking off into the shadows.

Dakan remained where he was for a long time, his mind and emotions a turbulent mess. His love for Beliza and honor as a clansman warred with his own personal sense of honor and the respect he felt should be given to family and blood. As his thoughts and emotions waged war in his mind, he suddenly realized that his sense of purpose had just been shattered.

As he cleared the last row of tents and entered the clearing surrounding Kale's pavilion, it was easy to spot the illuminated structure. The tents of Kale's bodyguards, which were arrayed to the left and right of the pavilion, were all dark, creating a shadowy backdrop for the interior-lit walls of Kale's quarters. Dakan suspected that Jerom was already within the pavilion, and he wasn't surprised to see Tazrim standing guard along with another Merandith soldier just outside the entrance to the tent. A blazing fire and evenly spaced torches illuminated the majority of the makeshift courtyard Dakan had entered, making it virtually impossible for anyone to approach unobserved. Adjusting his pack on his shoulder, Dakan walked from the shadows with confident strides that hid his brewing inner conflict.

Clad in studded leather armor and heavy black boots, Tazrim was a short, grizzled veteran of forty summers with a shaved head and stoic blue eyes. The hilt of a bastard sword jutted over his armored right shoulder, and one of his thick, callused hands held a simple pike before him. Dakan had recognized him as a dangerous fighter the first time he had met him earlier in the day. Although the clansman was a head taller than him, Tazrim's muscular bulk made him seem as thick as an oak tree and as immovable as a boulder. Scars crisscrossed his square-jawed face like war paint, and his nose appeared to have been broken on numerous occasions. It was a wonder that he still possessed both eyes given the extent of the damage done to his face. Combine his macabre mask of injuries with the knowing, deadly glint to his eyes, and a lesser man would turn to mush before the veteran fighter. And while Dakan found the veteran to be formidable, Tazrim was no clansman. Outward appearances did only so much to intimidate clansmen who were accustomed to using tattoos, piercings and scarring to terrorize their foes; therefore, Dakan wasn't even remotely fazed by the bodyguard and felt fully capable of defeating the man should he need to.

Ever vigilant, Tazrim immediately noticed Dakan's approach from the shadows, and both he and the other guard slid their pike across the entrance to the pavilion. Once Dakan entered the heart of the light provided by the torches and fire, Tazrim was able to identify the clansman and he relaxed his posture; pulling his pike back, the other guard followed his lead and did the same.

Dakan halted a few paces before the pavilion and eyed the other guard before turning his attention to Tazrim. Giving him a slight nod of respect, Dakan said, "Well met, Tazrim. Doms Meran-dith should be expecting me."

Tazrim grunted. "Well met indeed, young Dakan," he replied in his deep, rumbling voice. "Kale is indeed expecting you – and you're late."

Dakan cringed a bit at the accusatory tone. "My apologies. A few of my clansmen decided to give me a proper farewell and I'm afraid we lost track of time."

Another grunt, this one sounding skeptical, greeted the excuse before Tazrim replied, "Right. Well, go on in. Kale's expect-ing you." He then pulled back the pavilion flap and motioned Dakan through.

Dakan nodded and stepped through, his entrance silencing the pavilion's occupants.

The larger central room of Kale's quarters had been cleaned and rearranged to accommodate the dinner being held within. Kale's large oak table still occupied the center of the room and an assort-ment of mismatched chairs had been brought in to accommodate the extra dinner guests. The maps and reports that would have normally covered the tabletop had been removed, and there was no indication of where they had been relocated to. A delectable spread had been laid out on the table instead, the aromas of which caused Dakan's mouth to water as soon as he entered the tent. Fresh loaves of bread, dried fruits, wine and ale accented what appeared to be a fresh side of deer meat that was neatly carved and sitting in the center of the table. There was even a cast-iron pot of stew on the table. Over the last month, the sight of stew would have led to speculation about the ori-gins of the meat contained within, but between the deer meat on the table and the fresh supplies, Dakan doubted it was dog or horse.

Clad in a casual long-sleeve white shirt, black pants and boots, Kale stood up from the head of the table to greet him, his blonde hair framing his face from which his green eyes glowed with mirth and a broad smile beamed forth. "Welcome, Dakan! We were beginning to wonder where you were."

Dakan let his gaze take in the occupants of the tent as he nodded. Jerom was seated to Kale's right, a tired visage painted on his face. An empty seat was to Jerom's right, while Amroth and a man Dakan didn't recognize sat on the opposite side of the table from him, both of which had turned in their seats to see who had entered. Dakan nodded to Amroth in greeting before his eyes met the stern, intense gaze of the stranger and he felt his stomach twist with trepida-tion. He had been the target of his fair share of intimidating glares, but there was no doubt in his mind that these were the eyes of a cold-blooded killer.

All kinds of thoughts began to race through his mind before regained his composure and reminded himself that Kale was awaiting his response. "My apologizes, Doms Merandith," he finally said. "I'm afraid a few of my friends within the clans felt a sending-off was in order, and the time got away from me."

Kale chuckled in amusement. "No worries. We were just chatting about the day, and the food and drink are still fresh. We simply awaited you before partaking of this enticing spread." He motioned to the seat next to Jerom. "Come, put your pack down and join us. A couple of our scouts managed to luck into a deer, so we have fresh meat for our meal tonight. Not as much as any of us would have liked, but it wouldn't have done to deny the scouts the spoils of their kill." Kale smirked. "I would imagine there's a few jealous troops salivating over that campfire about now."

Dakan couldn't help but let a small smile creep across his face as he dumped his pack and lochabre next to the pavilion entrance and made his way over to his chair and took his seat. Other than horse or dog, fresh meat had been hard to come by for a while. Even the salted meats that the supply train brought in were no replacement for fresh-off-the-spit meat. As he settled into his chair, Dakan could feel the eyes of the stranger sizing him up. There was little doubt in his mind that the stranger was a man who took very little for granted and missed even less. However, he wasn't about to be intimidated, so he returned the man's inquisitive gaze with one of his own.

As Kale returned to his seat, he noticed the silent exchange and the potential for tension between the two if he didn't step in. "I don't believe you've met the hero of the day, Mathis. This is Dakan Holdreth of the Roselian clans. He's the one that saved Amroth's life."

Mathis nodded, his coal-black eyes losing some of their intensity and his plain features relaxed somewhat. "Well met, indeed," he declared, his voice possessing a sternness that commanded attention. "As I'm sure the others here did before me, let me offer my thanks for your intervention. Amroth is family to us. It would have been...tragic if anything had happened to him. Though I must admit, it was a bit brazen of you to kill the attackers. Much could have been learned from them had they lived."

Dakan nodded and relaxed somewhat. Although he felt the tension between himself and Mathis had lessened slightly, there was something unnerving about the simply clothed and astute veteran. He couldn't help but think back to his conversation with Jerom earlier when gazing upon Mathis' unfamiliar features. To the best of his knowledge, he didn't recognize Mathis as a native of Triclose, leading him once again to be somewhat amazed at the collection of foreign blood gathered about his new doms. "I suppose so. My intention had been to simply disable them, but when they made to strike a killing blow," he shrugged, "I couldn't let that happen. They were about to commit murder within our camp – and that made them enemies. Their deaths, at the time, seemed a proper end."

There was a moment of uneasy silence at Dakan's admission. Mathis continued to stare at Dakan while Kale looked on cautiously, and Amroth feigned interest in his empty plate.

Finally, Jerom let out a snort of dismissal. "You two are likely to start a fight over nothing! What's done is done! They would have ended up mud crow fodder either way. For now, it's Hagail's mess to deal with. Amroth is alive – and that's what matters. I'm thinking any of us would have done the same in Dakan's position – and that includes you, Mathis. You're more cold-blooded than a snake at times. Don't tell me you wouldn't have diced them up nice and neat had you been there."

As a small smile broke his lips, Mathis turned his gaze away from Dakan and settled it on Jerom. "Astute as ever, Jerom. I will, however, stand by my statement that we would be better off to have had them alive for questioning. I detest loose ends."

Jerom snorted again and scratched at his salt-and-pepper beard. "Aye, I know. And I detest sitting about and chatting on an empty stomach when there's good food to be had." To punctuate his point, he picked up his knife, skewered a chunk of loose meat from the deer platter, and dropped it on his pewter plate with a thud. "Deo be good – a man could die of old age before you two stop talking long enough to eat!"

Kale smiled, doing his best to ease the tension. "As usual, Uncle, your unique perspective keeps us grounded on what's important. Eat up, everyone!"

"Damn right!" muttered Jerom as he began piling food onto his plate.

Everyone took the opportunity to fill their plates as a diversion from the conversation. Even as they ate and polite conversation was joined, Dakan already had the feeling that this dinner was more of an assessment of him as a person than a thank you for saving Amroth's life. Although there were polite inquires into how he was doing, the morale of House Trivant's forces, or even talk about the weather and their status in preparing to march, Dakan couldn't help but feel their eyes upon him, judging without remorse.

Through it all, Amroth remained relatively quiet. He responded to questions when asked and even contributed his thoughts at times, but he seemed quite withdrawn and occupied with his own thoughts. Dakan could sympathize with him. After his run-in with Beliza and her suggestion that eliminating Amroth would be in his and his clan's best interest, he was more than ready to be alone with his own inner turmoil. As it was, between his own inner conflict and the constant feeling that he was being judged, Dakan decided to try to steer the conversation in another direction as they were finishing their meals.

Taking a sip from his nearly empty tankard of ale, Dakan asked of Amroth, "Why so glum, Amroth? You look like you're already recovering from your wounds."

Toying with a leftover dried grape on his plate, Amroth was caught off guard by the question. Looking up at Dakan in surprise, he sat back in his chair and gave a small shrug. "I didn't mean to give that impression. It's been a long day, to say the least." His voice was still mildly hoarse, though there was no longer any indication of injury on his throat, and the exhaustion in it confirmed what his posture was showing. "I still feel like I got trampled by horses, but my wounds are healing nicely, and that awful brew the healers provided seem to help some with the pain."

An amused smile cracked Dakan's face. "I sometimes think healers of all kinds purposely make their medicines taste foul either out of vengeance for making them tend to us, or out of some perverse form of amusement." The others chuckled at the jest as Dakan downed the last of his ale and placed the tankard back on the table. "Don't worry, your wounds will heal fast enough. After all, you're clan."

Amroth leaned forward and rested his forearms on the table, a slight wince the only indication that his ribs were bothering him. "So I've been told. That does remind me – when you rescued me, you called me brother? Why did you call me that?"

An awkward silence descended on the group like a heavy fog. Dakan looked like he wanted to answer, but was unsure if it was his place to do so. Amroth looked at each person at the table with puzzlement etched on his face. It was apparent to Amroth that his question had touched on a sensitive subject that the others were reluctant to address. Jerom and Kale were eyeing each other as if they were looking for permission from the other to speak. Mathis simply looked at Dakan with an unreadable glare.

Amroth shook his head and sat back, running a hand through his black hair, he gave his short horsetail a tug of frustration before turning his curious dark eyes to Kale and Jerom. "What could be so awful as to keep you all so quiet? I know my clan was responsible for the Cravon Uprisings. So why so silent?"

Kale finally broke the tense silence. "It's not that, Amroth," he stated in a soft, reassuring voice. "We never wanted you to feel responsible for actions beyond your control or understanding. That's why we never encouraged you to study your past, but it's also why we never stopped you from learning about it." Cringing, he added, "And to be honest, none of us were aware of the connection until today."

Amroth's brow furrowed in puzzlement. "I don't understand."

Kale sighed. "Amroth – the clan you descend from is related by blood to Dakan's."

Amroth blinked in amazement, caught completely off guard by the admission. He looked at each man in turn for confirmation and found it in their eyes. Still, he needed to hear it spoken. So with trepidation, he asked of Dakan, "Is this true?"

In answer, Dakan presented his tattooed arms, the inked serpents winding their way about his corded arms, and met Amroth's gaze squarely. "These tattoos mark me as Clan of the Fang. My forefathers were originally of Clan Theirigaldis and part of the many that migrated from the Highlands during the Long Winter to escape what they saw as certain death. We never forgot our blood; and when we were called to the side of Clan Theirigaldis, we answered . . . and paid a hefty price for standing at their side. What remained of us were scattered or absorbed by the other clans." He put his arms down and sat back in his chair. "I am one of the last of my clan . . . as you are the last of yours."

Shock painted plainly on his face, Amroth sat in his chair dumbfounded, trying to absorb all he had just heard. Even in all his studies, he'd never found mention that there was a relation between his roots and the Roselian clans. Granted, he was no scholar and had not thought to question those in the Merandith household that were educated in such matters. He had simply been content with knowing where he had come from. To learn that he had living blood relatives – however distant they might be – was a shock to the system. He had long ago come to think of himself as a Merandith in both name and spirit, but now he knew he had actual family related to him by blood. It was as if someone had just hurled a boulder into the peaceful lake that was his life, creating disruptive waves. Concerned looks from Jerom and Kale told him they were waiting for him to respond in

140

some fashion, but he simply could not find the words to express the chaos of the thoughts in his mind.

He was saved from having to speak by Mathis, who chose that moment to break his silence. "You say you're Clan of the Fang, and your tattoos mark you as such, but isn't it a bit . . . conceited to wear the markings of a dead clan?"

Dakan turned a cold, hard glare on Mathis. "Unlike the others that chose to renounce their blood or hide and waste away in shame, I take pride in my past. No matter what it costs me to wear these markings, I bear them proudly and without regret."

Mathis smirked, drawing a dark glare from Dakan, and glanced at Jerom. "You'll have your hands full with this one."

Jerom snorted in reply.

Kale, sensing that the conversation was on the brink of heating up beyond control, cleared his throat to catch everyone's attention. "Peace, all of you. We're all friends here; there's no need for unfounded hostilities. It has been a long day for all of us, and I fear that the stress of the day's events," he chuckled and gestured to the empty pitcher on the table, "and possibly the alcohol, are making us a bit . . . touchy. I think we should call it an evening and get some rest."

There was a moment of tense silence before Jerom pushed back his chair and stood. "Well, I'm too old to be getting involved with some late-night, half-assed drunken argument. I think Kale's right – we should all get some sleep."

Kale smiled at his uncle. "Afraid I need you to hang around just a bit longer if your old bones can handle it."

Jerom scoffed and sat back down, folding his arms across his chest in mock anger. "As you wish, Kale. Just warning you that it's on your head if I wake up with a hangover."

Kale smirked slightly before turning his attention to the others. "Mathis – if you'll show Amroth to where he'll spend the night, I would appreciate it. His things have already been moved and I've seen to it that he's packed for the morning. When do you plan on leaving?"

"I plan on being on our way just after sunup. With Amroth's wounds, I'd like to cover as much ground as possible without pushing him too hard."

Dakan – who had withdrawn a bit at Kale's gentle chastisement in order to better control his tongue and temper – perked up at the mention of Amroth's departure from camp. It now made sense to him why Amroth had been so glum during dinner. In one day, he'd been assaulted and was being sent away from his friends and work. Most people wouldn't take very kindly to being uprooted so suddenly, and Amroth was no exception. "You're leaving camp tomorrow, Amroth?"

Amroth nodded silently, but it was Kale who answered. "Yes, he is. We still don't know who was behind the assault on him. There may be no one else out there, or the culprit could still be lurking about camp. I simply won't take the chance that there's still someone within our ranks that wishes him harm; so, he'll be headed home ahead of us."

Dakan flinched inwardly when Kale said he wouldn't take a chance on someone wishing Amroth harm. His conversation with Beliza already had his emotions pertaining to Amroth in a jumbled conflict. House Merandith trusted him enough to invite him to participate in a tournament that could result in him becoming one of Kale's bodyguards, yet he had Beliza whispering words to him that would result in harm to his blood and to those showing trust in him. However, he was profoundly relieved when Kale confirmed that Amroth would be leaving camp for a time. With Amroth gone, Dakan wouldn't have to worry about the prospects of whether or not to eliminate him. Granted, he planned on winning the tournament and never having to set foot on that dark path, but he was uncomfortably aware that the possibility could not be completely banished until he succeeded.

Dakan nodded to Kale. "As much as I'd like to have the time to get to know Amroth better, I would rather see him safe." He gave a friendly smile to Amroth. "I guess we will have to get to know each other better at another time, Brother. It seems fate wants to keep us apart a little longer."

Amroth nodded, a bit uncomfortable with the moniker being used by anyone other than Kale. "It would seem so. I look forward to hearing more of our mutual past, Dakan."

Kale smiled at them all. "See – being friendly is so much better than the animosity you all were trying to brew earlier." Jerom rolled his lone eye at the veiled chastisement. "Now get some sleep. We've got a long day ahead for each of us."

Mathis, Amroth and Dakan all stood, each bowing to Kale and excusing themselves. Mathis and Amroth led the way out while Dakan stopped to collect his things. As Dakan shouldered his pack and hefted his axe, Kale called out to him, "A moment, if you would, Dakan?"

Turning to face Kale, he asked, "Yes, Doms Merandith?"

"I apologize for Mathis' behavior. He has no real love for any of the clans – both Sur'dathan and Roselian – after the way they dealt with those involved with the Cravon Uprising. I respect your loyalty to your clan and your choice to continue to represent them. Just remember – you're now part of House Merandith, and your duties and loyalty to us come first for as long as you remain with us. Is that clear?" Though the words had been spoken softly, there was no doubting their veracity and the hidden threat lurking beneath them.

Dakan nodded sternly. "Understood, Doms Merandith."

Kale smiled and leaned back in his chair. "Good. Tazrim will show you to where you'll be staying. Sleep well."

Dakan nodded and said, before stepping into the night, "You as well."

Kale and Jerom sat in silence for a moment after Dakan left. The remaining guard eventually stuck his head in to see if anything was needed. Kale dismissed him for the night with orders to send his replacements.

Once the remaining guard was gone, Jerom let out a deep, loud snort of dismissal. "Well, that was nearly a fantastic disaster. There's too much pride flowing in those two's veins. They'll come to blows sooner rather than later."

Kale laughed and leaned back in his chair, his face growing thoughtful. "I suppose you're right. They'll have to learn to at least pretend to get along eventually. A friendly fight between the two might just put Dakan in his place. For now, though, what do you make of Dakan? You've had him for a day and you've seen how he reacted tonight. I'd rather eliminate a problem now and send him back to Trivant than keep him on and end up with Deo only knows how much trouble."

Jerom settled back in his chair and, nursing what remained of his drink, snorted. "Trouble? Oh, aye, he'll be a bit of trouble. What clansman wouldn't? However, he does seem to want to be here, and he seems to take pride in doing his duties properly. Besides that, as long as Amroth's around, he'll view it as protecting family. That should keep him in line long enough for us to break that prideful, stubborn streak in him."

Kale nodded. "That's what concerns me. That kind of devotion to blood could become a burden. Amroth hardly considers himself clan, but that won't affect Dakan's view if I had to guess." His brow furled thoughtfully. "Be careful with him, Jerom. He could be extremely useful to us if he makes it through the tournament, but we'll have to watch him closely. We both know that clansmen can be unpredictable."

Jerom nodded. "Aye, that they are." Looking into his tankard, he lost himself in the dark liquid within for a moment. Shaking his head, he snorted and set the tankard on the table. "Now, be a good lad and fetch your uncle that bottle of Velusyian Blue you've been saving. Deo only knows we could both use it."

*

"You're a curious one."

Just nodding off to sleep, the words were like a slap to the face, startling him awake. Sitting upright quickly, Dakan reached for his lochabre, his eyes immediately drawn to the silhouette framed by the moonlight in the tent's entrance.

The man held up a hand just as Dakan took hold of the axe on the ground next to his cot. "Don't bother. Believe me when I say – if I'd wanted you dead, we wouldn't be having this conversation."

Dakan's eyes narrowed and he cautiously withdrew his hand from the axe. The tent was empty except for himself and the man in the entrance. There was room for three more soldiers, but for the time being, he had it all to himself. With no one else present and the ease with which the man had gotten this close without him noticing, Dakan was ready to believe the man was speaking the truth. Still, it angered him that someone could sneak up on him. Shooting the man a scowl that was more meant for himself, Dakan asked, "What do you want?"

Mathis slipped into the tent and closed to within a couple of paces of Dakan with deadly grace. "To talk," he stated simply.

Dakan arched an eyebrow. "Talk? I thought there'd been enough of that at dinner." Dakan eased back on his cot as he casually slipped a foot beneath the haft of his axe. He didn't feel safe around Mathis, and he wasn't about to be caught napping again.

Mathis shook his head. "Don't be foolish – I only want to talk."

Dakan nodded and folded his arms across his chest, but left his foot where it was. "Then say what you have to say. I'm sure we both have better things to be doing this late at night than chatting like gossiping women," he replied bluntly.

Hands behind his back at his waist, Mathis nodded. "To the point. Fine by me. I'll keep this simple. I don't know what your intentions here are, and I honestly don't care. Kale and Jerom say you

144

are worth having around, so I'll trust them . . . *for now*. Slip-up, and you'll answer to me. Do we have an understanding?"

Dakan stared at him hard, trying to fathom why he'd deliver this message in the middle of the night. Mathis came across as cold and ruthless to him, so maybe this was just his way of intimidating him or sending a message. Either way, while he was wary of Mathis, it angered him more than it intimidated him. "We have an understanding," he stated, hoping it would move the man along and let him get back to sleep.

"Good." Mathis stepped toward the tent's entrance, stopped, and turned back to face Dakan, his hand resting casually on the hilt of his slender sword. "Oh, and one more thing – no one can stop you from talking to Amroth, but watch your tongue. His blood may be clan, but he isn't. I won't suffer any attempts to bring him around to a clan lifestyle or way of thinking."

Perturbed, Dakan glared at him and asked, "What did the clans do to make you hate them so much?"

Mathis ignored the question and continued on, staring daggers at Dakan. "You want to play at being the last of the Clan of the Fang? Fine. But don't drag Amroth into your little schemes. He means too much to us, and we won't risk him to some petty infighting or scheming. Amroth is a Merandith – no matter his name or blood. Harm him or the Merandiths in any way, and you'll answer to me."

Dakan might have taken the threat as nothing but bluster from any other man, but, though the light was dim, the hard eyes that seemed to bore into his skull promised more than the words implied. There was something in his gaze and tone that suddenly made the pit of Dakan's stomach turn cold. It was as if Mathis knew of the conversation with Beliza and was searching his soul for the truth of the matter. Looking into Mathis' piercing gaze, he suddenly knew that this man was an executioner with death ridding at his shoulder.

Knowing there was nothing he could say, Dakan simply nodded.

Apparently, Mathis could see the nod, for he returned it and simply said, "Good." He let his gaze linger for a moment before striding out of the tent, letting the flap close behind him.

Dakan sat in stunned silence, his gaze focused on nothing while his mind did its best to deal with the situation. He had fought, killed, brawled and argued, and was familiar with fear. Yet, nothing matched what he had felt during that conversation. It was as if death had walked into the tent, sucking the heat from the air and toying with his soul. There was no doubt that Mathis would make good on his promise, and that left Dakan feeling cornered. If he failed to win the tournament, he would be left in a horrible predicament. Should he fail and refuse to bring Amroth to the clans for judgment, Beliza would more than likely kill him for ruining whatever her plans were and staining her honor. If he did follow through with taking Amroth to the clans, Mathis would hunt him down. Death awaited him no matter what if he failed.

His mind racing, he lowered himself back onto the cot and held his hands up before him. He thought, for a moment, that his vision was blurry or weak in the dim light. Then, to his profound amazement, he realize that his hands were shaking.


Dawn crept slowly across the western horizon, warm red hues burning away the gray of the false dawn. Sunlight glistened on the frost that blanketed the ground and gently coated everything within the Army of Five Stars' camp that was exposed to the elements. Aside from those that had business this early in the morning, the camp was slow to rise, leaving it devoid of the cacophony of noise that blanketed it all-day.

Bundled within a thick cloak against the morning chill, Amroth sat his roan mare with slumped shoulders, his face fallen from a mixture of pain, exhaustion, confusion, and just a bit of anger at his situation. He hadn't slept well that night. While the drink the healers had given him dulled the pain so that it didn't cloud his senses, his broken ribs still caused enough discomfort to make sleeping near impossible. As if that wasn't enough, both the conversation at dinner last night and Kale's orders for him to return to Merset had left him emotionally confused and with more questions than answers.

He wasn't in the habit of touting his clan heritage. Far from it. While he had chosen to learn his family name as a sign of respect to his ancestry, he had been officially adopted into the Merandith family as a child and unequivocally viewed himself as such. Kale treated him like a brother and Doms Bordin, Deo rest his soul, had treated him like a son without hesitation or regret. Despite being orphaned as a babe by the Cravon Uprising, he had always had a family and never once felt like he didn't belong. His brush with death, however, was threatening to change all of that in his mind. Suddenly he had a distant blood relative trying to muscle in and claim him as family, and Kale was sending him away for his own good. He knew what Kale was doing was in the best interest of everyone involved. If he stayed with the army until they marched, he would remain a target and a distraction. Kale would then be forced to spend time guarding him while both conducting an investigation and prepping an army to move. Amroth knew that would just result in a delay that could see the soldiers dreaming of home stranded where they were, their return foiled by the onset of winter. No matter the hurt to his emotions, Amroth wasn't about to have that on his conscious.

Still, it rubbed him wrong that he had no say in the matter. Worse yet, he was being sent off with Mathis as his bodyguard. The irony wasn't lost on him. While Mathis was the one to stay the blow that would have ended his life as a babe, he had always distanced himself from Amroth as a possible close friend. Normally his dealings with him were with others present or the result of Mathis and Kale's attempts to get him to fight, or at the very least, learn to protect himself. Where Kale's urgings were normally friendly and growingly half-hearted – mostly due to trying to respect Amroth's pacifistic views – Mathis was cold and sometimes harsh in his approach. Amroth had even been beaten bloody in his early years in an attempt to get him to appreciate the value of learning to fight and defend himself. While Mathis had received a severe admonishment and a temporary suspension from Bordin's service for the beating, it had done little to curb Mathis' earnest approach to the subject. Amroth could appreciate that Kale was parting with someone who was probably the best swordsman in his forces, but it did little to curb the anxiety gnawing at Amroth. Weeks on the road with Mathis as his only company didn't strike him as a good way to heal, and he fully expected a very uncomfortable journey.

Muted conversation from behind interrupted his melancholy reflections. Wincing from the sting of his injured ribs, he turned in his saddle and saw Kale and Mathis approaching. Garbed against the chill of the morning with thick clothing and heavy cloaks, both men were deep in conversation. Kale carried a leather satchel, which Amroth could only assume carried the letters they were to deliver, in his gloved hands and was doing most of the talking. Mathis, his riding leathers peaking from beneath his cloak, guided his large black destrider behind him as they approached, his attention fixed on Kale.

Pulling alongside Amroth, the conversation ceased as Amroth's roan snorted and stepped away from the large beast that served as Mathis' warhorse. The large black horse seemed to almost sneer in contempt at Amroth's roan. It was as if the destrider was offended to be in the presence of a lesser beast. Mathis stroked a soothing hand along his mount's nose, forestalling any further protests.

Kale grinned as he turned the satchel over to Mathis – who then tucked it underneath a large wooden case he had secured beneath his bedroll and pack behind his saddle – and quipped, "A bit grumpy this morning, isn't she?"

Mathis grunted as he double-checked his saddle straps. "Your father bred them to be a bit grumpy. Said it made them more aggressive when the fighting started." He scratched his mount behind the ears, drawing a content snort from her. "Personally, I don't see it. Slate is quite calm and even-tempered."

Kale rolled his eyes. "For you maybe. I'd say that stablehand that lost a finger to her would beg to differ."

Shrugging, Mathis pulled his sheathed katana from underneath his belt and strapped it to his saddle so it could be easily drawn while riding. "It was his fault. He should have given Slate time to cool down after that battle. She was still chomping at the bit for a good fight."

Kale's eyebrows shot up in feigned shock, and Amroth just shook his head. "Why Mathis – was that an attempt at humor?" asked Kale.

Mathis gave him a flat stare. "Not at all." There was no hint of sarcasm in his tone, which drew amused smiles from the others.

"On that note," stated Kale, "I think you two should get going. Any more of Mathis' jokes and I might die of laughter."

Mathis grunted as he swung himself into the saddled, his mount quickstepping a bit as she adjusted to the added weight.

"You'll be heading for Haltho first, I take it?" Kale inquired.

Mathis nodded in confirmation. "Seems to me to be the best place. It puts us well away from the Contested Territories and any chance of accidentally crossing into them. Besides that, we can be in Haltho in under a week. We can deliver yours and Doms Trivant's dispatches personally and take on full supplies before moving up the coast toward Merset. Depending on how Amroth heals up, we could be in Merset within five weeks . . . weather permitting."

Smiling, Kale walked up to Amroth and patted him on the leg. He noted that Amroth's broadsword was strapped to his saddle, which granted him a measure of relief. Whether he chose to use the sword or not, at least having it provided an option. "How are you feeling? Think you can handle that pace?"

"Don't sound so concerned," Amroth replied dryly. "Sounds like we're going to be setting a very casual pace. You know good and well if you started your march now, you'd be there in almost the same amount of time."

Kale held up his hands in defense. "I know, I know. I'm sure Mathis will adjust his pace accordingly." He eyed Mathis. "Won't you?"

"Indeed," replied Mathis sternly.

Kale gave Amroth another friendly pat on the leg before moving away from the two to give them some room. "I know I don't have to repeat myself, but I'm going to anyway. Be careful. We don't know if what happened here was an isolated incident or not. On top of that, word from the North is that Craigan has raiders ghosting about trying to stir up as much havoc as they can before the snows. Whatever you do, just keep moving. No need for heroics if you should spot anything suspicious."

Both men nodded their agreement.

"What about you?" Amroth asked before Kale could send them on their way. "When will you start home?"

Kale chuckled a bit and shook his head. "Not as soon as we thought, according to Barniban. The repairs I asked for are behind. Says losing you is the cause of it." Amroth smiled softly for the first time that morning, drawing a small laugh from Kale. "I know. I think he just wants to keep me around a little longer as punishment. We should start moving within a week. I imagine we'll take it slow for a bit to let the men rest and enjoy themselves some, but travel should speed up as we shed numbers, which means we'll be home about two months after we leave if the weather holds, more if it doesn't. Either way, I intend to be home for my child's birth – even if I have to ride on ahead."

Amroth nodded. "Take care of yourself."

Kale smiled and nodded. "Don't worry about me. You just concentrate on staying safe, and promise not to give Marie too much trouble. She's already probably doing more than a pregnant woman should."

"I will," Amroth promised.

Ready to get started, Mathis nudged his horse forward and stopped before turning in his saddle to say, "Let's get going, Amroth. We've got a long road ahead."

With a last look at Kale, Amroth urged his roan forward with a wince as she moved under him. Mathis nodded to Kale and started out to the north with Amroth in tow.

Kale watched the two ride off for a time, his thoughts a jumble at seeing his friend and brother ride off under these circumstances. He knew Amroth was hurt both physically and emotionally, and probably resented him a bit for it. As he had to do with so many hard choices since the war fell to him from his parents, he could live with Amroth's resentment. With Amroth gone, his mind felt a bit more at ease. However, there was still the issue of whom was behind the attack on Amroth. He didn't know if he could find out who it was before they left, but the extra few days Barniban's delay had bought him would provide some time to hunt the mastermind down.

From a large grove of evergreens to the northeast, which was being used by the Army of Five Stars as fuel for fires and repairs, Beliza watched the two riders depart from the comfort and concealment of the shadows. She was wrapped in a thick woolen cloak against the morning chill, the edge of which was balled tightly in her fist in frustration. Her gray eyes stared daggers at the departing duo as she watched one of her options depart from her immediate grasp.

*"Ah, the best-laid plans . . ."* she thought to herself in frustration.

Never one to approach her goals from one direction or to be deterred from her ambitions, the surprise departure of the Theirigaldian still managed to vex her. She had no doubt that her careful guidance of Dakan would give her the results she wanted, but he was stubborn and prideful. No amount of prodding – be it emotional or sexual – would force him into a rash decision. She'd known that even as she planted the seed in his mind for him to bring Amroth before the Council as a means to her goals. She wasn't even sure Dakan would ever follow through with such an action. However, no matter which option she pursued, Dakan was a vital tool that was proving somewhat difficult to manipulate. He was focused so intently on his quest to restore his family name that the thought of guiding the clans to their ultimate destiny still seemed a flight of fancy to him. Her frustration with bringing him around to her point of view was growing, as was her Master's. She feared little in this life, but her Master's displeasure was one thing she did fear.

She owed everything to her Master. She and her clan still existed because of her Master's intervention. Where Dakan was her unknowing toy, she gave herself wholly to her Master – her body, mind and soul devoted entirely to her Master's whim. She wanted nothing more than to rule at her Master's side as High Elder of the clans and warm her Master's bed at night as a willing lover. All that was in jeopardy now that Dakan had been slow to come around. Heaped upon that conundrum was her Master's decision to order the death of Amroth. While she trusted in her Master's judgment, she felt the order was quite impulsive given that less volatile options were still available. Though in hindsight, delegating the task to another was probably not the best way to show her displeasure with the decision. The failure was, no matter her feelings on the matter, bitter bile in her mouth and wholly her fault. To her chagrin, she had no doubt that her Master would view it in the same light.

However, the failure had one unintended benefit, though it was overshadowed by Amroth's departure – suspicion was now cast upon the Sur'dathans. She would never be able to forgive them for their treatment of Clan Theirigaldis, and she did her best over the years to nettle them when and where she could. Unfortunately, the joy it brought her to see the barbarous clansmen under such a heady cloud of suspicion did little to curb the sourness of failure. The small bit of vengeance against them would have to satisfy her until she could resolve her current situation and see her Master's plans come to fruition. Then, and only then, could she turn her focus and wrath on Sur'datha.

The right side of her scalp beneath her silver-streaked hair began to tingle and then burn. She closed her eyes and sighed in ecstasy from the burning pain that announced her Master's arrival. She had never seen her Master, and did not know whether she served a man or woman. However, her Master's gender did not matter. What her Master promised always came to fruition. There was power and authority in the person she served, and that aroused her in ways no man's touch could.

She could feel the shadows behind her thicken into the presence of a person, but she could not get a feel for the person's size or shape. A moment later, her Master's strength and power reach out and wash over her, drawing an aroused shudder from her.

A powerful voice, neither male nor female, seemed to emanate from the shadows, vibrating along the invisible strands of power that embraced her and seemed to penetrate every part of her being. "My sweet, dear Beliza – what have you been up to? I ordered the Theirigaldian dead, yet I see the opportunity slipping through your fingers. That's not like you."

Where there'd once been arousal, a spark of pain surged through her to emphasize her Master's displeasure. "I know, my Master," she said with shuddering breath. "The . . . attack– *huhuuuhaaa* . . . was interrupted and–" she moaned in pleasure and pain at the same time, ". . . and the Merandiths grew overly cautious. But not to– *haaah* . . . worry, my Master. Killing the Theirigaldian now would waste the opportunit– *huhuuuha* . . . he presents. I've planted the seeds in Dakan's mind to accomplish all your goals. It just needs–" she groaned again, " . . . a chance to bear fruit."

"And if it doesn't? The Theirigaldian could prove to be an impediment if our other options fail."

Pain lanced through her again, ripping a whimpering yelp from her. "I– " she gasped, "will see to it that the Theirigaldian is dead should it come to that."

A short wave of pleasure made her gasp as her Master purred to her, "Goood, my sweet." She felt his power caressing her body, eliciting sighs of pleasure as it washed over her breasts and groin. "Now, what about the man you sent to kill him?"

Eyes rolling back in her head, she managed to gather herself for a response. "He– He," she whimpered, "is gone – sent away. I thought to kill him," she gasped, "but he is yours to punish or reward, not mine." She moaned and cupped her right breast as if her Master was doing so. "The Merandiths," she purred, "will be chasing a ghost. We will rule the clans, Master, and then all of Triclose. No one can stand before you."

Suddenly, she felt her Master's power begin to withdraw as the shadows behind her began to lose their cohesiveness. She collapsed to the ground with a heartbreaking sob as she felt the pleasure and pain that her Master delivered to her begin to ebb away. Faintly, ever so faintly, she heard her Master whisper on the winds as she lay curled on the ground, her body twitching from the afterglow of pleasure, "Good, my dearest sweet. Events have been set in motion, and you must not fail. If your pet cannot do as he's told, then see to it that the Theirigaldian is dead so that we can rule the clans and guide Triclose to glory it hasn't seen in ages."

Lying in a heap of fading ecstasy, Beliza wept as visions of the glory to come danced in her head.

# Chapter Six

*T*he song of clashing steel is one of the most glorious anthems a warrior could ever want to hear. The song owes allegiance to neither country nor combatant; instead, it only sounds wherever battle is joined and weapons clash in a struggle between life and death. It is the song that heralds all-mighty and ever-elusive glory, singing loudly and proudly for its one and only master. For no matter who wields the weapon or the motive, the haunting melody rings out for death and death alone.

Craigan Murandi Suldamik danced away from his opponent, his white-flecked, brown hair flinging sweat into the cool air. The muscles of his bare torso and arms flexed and pulled taunt as he brought his large full-moon axe to bear. His blue eyes burned with pent-up hatred and frustration – desires that could never be quenched, only sedated by combat.

Gathered on the eastern edge of the camp, the circle of soldiers surrounded Craigan and his opponent, a burly, dark-skinned Pelasian. Cheering and jeering the two on, each of the twenty-five men had a similar axe in hand and were very versed in its usage. They were Craigan's personal unit, answering only to him. Everyone was Academy trained and honed, their talents and skills pushing them above and beyond the average army fodder. Though many had fought and died over the years, new blood kept their ranks full. They were eager to serve and even more eager to draw Merandith blood for their doms. In victory, they were praised; and in defeat, they were dishonored. And though they cheered the fighters on, they all knew that this was about their failure.

The Pelasian growled and charged toward Craigan, his shaved head and amber eyes glinting in the sunlight. When he saw his opponent drop his axe low, Craigan smiled and let his top hand slide up the shaft of his axe a hand's width. The Pelasian brought his axe around hard in an upward slash at the last moment, but instead of finding Craigan, he found only empty air. Before he could recover, the flat of Craigan's axe slammed hard into the Pelasian's back, sending him sprawling forward. The sun-darkened man hit the ground with a thud, his breath driven from him and his axe sliding out of reach. Shaking his head to clear his vision, he scrambled to his feet and lunged for his weapon. His massive hands curled around its shaft and he rolled over in time to intercept a killing blow from Craigan's axe. The soldier shoved the weapon to the side and kicked Craigan squarely in the stomach. Doubled over from the blow, Craigan stumbled backward while the Pelasian scrambled to his feet. Knowing he had a momentary advantage, the soldier charged his stunned doms.

The dark-skinned combatant brought his axe around from the left, angling it upward toward Craigan's groin. Though partially stunned from the blow to his gut, Craigan saw the move coming and brought his axe down to intercept the attack, pushing the Pelasian's axe out wide before stepping in and hammering his fist into the man's nose. Nose bleeding and off balance, the soldier fell backward, landing hard on his seat. When his vision cleared, he found Craigan's axe blade resting under his chin.

"Do you yield?" huffed Craigan.

The Pelasian nodded as best he could, conceding the match.

A sudden cheer went up for Doms Suldamik as he withdrew his axe and helped the man to his feet. Craigan patted the man on his back and motioned him toward the circle of soldiers. The Pelasian stumbled toward the others, doing his best to keep his balance and stem the flow of blood from his nose. One of the soldiers, who had been holding the combatant's shirt, tossed the worn garment to him. As the defeated Pelasian took his place amongst his fellow soldiers, receiving a few pats on the back and conciliatory congratulations for a good fight, he ripped two small strips from his shirt and stuffed his bleeding nostrils with them.

Standing in the center of the ring of soldiers, Doms Suldamik rested his axe against his right leg and wiped the sweat from his brow. The fight had been a strain and closer than it had appeared. *'I'm getting old,'* he thought to himself as he let his gaze sweep the crowd. He was easily ten summers older than the oldest amongst their ranks. Many of the veterans had either moved on to posts as trusted officers or died on the battlefield, leaving him with predominantly raw, young talent. Many were faster and stronger than him; however, at least for now, that did little to counter his years of experience.

The chatter amongst the men died off as his intense gaze fell on them. Though none of them knew what thoughts were going through Craigan's mind, each man felt as if their doms' blue eyes were boring deep into their souls, searching for something that only he would know to look for.

"So . . . this is what I've been sending against Merandith all this time," Craigan drawled in disgust, the venom in his voice causing some of the men to glance at one another nervously. They knew all too well that their doms had a temper that sometimes spilt over into violence that was occasionally fatal for its target. "You fight like a bunch of untrained desert barbarians! Your axe control is beyond horrible, and your balance is pathetic! A *baby* could beat you down with a twig!"

Craigan began to pace, his axe hanging limply from his right hand. "Just three days ago, I sent this very squad against Merandith himself and his paltry group of bodyguards. Eight of them fell before you! Eight! Their small numbers should have been nothing against your might! Then what happened?" Craigan spread his arms wide and turned a slow circle. "Those of you who were not worthy of this post were cut down by Doms Merandith and that infernal Mathis! Twenty-eight of you died there! Twenty-eight! Two men effectively bought enough time for reinforcements to arrive and brake your ranks! You had Merandith in your grasp and let him slip away! I have *never* been so disappointed in my soldiers!"

The men began to shuffle and glance at one another nervously. None of them had ever been chastised like this, especially by their doms. Their failure sickened them like a slow-acting poison, but, for many of them, they could live with that. Their doms' displeasure, on the other hand, hurt worse than any battlefield wound.

Craigan stopped his slow turn, shouldered his axe and sighed. "But I am a forgiving man. You are all young and still have much to learn. I don't need to do anything here to make an example of you all. The shame of failure is enough." A few of the men sighed or closed their eyes in relief. "However," he barked, "You all will receive no reprieve during the rest of the march! You will continue to train on top of your regular duties until we reach Chalin! There, you will work with an Academy representative until I say you are fit to stand beside me on the battlefield once again!"

As he expected, there were some muted grumblings from the men. He wasn't even surprised when a voice from one of the men behind him blurted out, "What would our other option be?"

Craigan turned and faced the young soldier, grinning devilishly. "An option? You're a soldier, lad – which means you have no other option but to follow my orders. However, if you're looking for another way of doing things, step forward, and you can train under me and most likely die under my axe." The young man's eyes widened and the color seemed to drain from his face, drawing an amused smile from Craigan. "However, you're not here to die in training. Instead, I expect you to kill House Merandith's forces and, Deo willing, die from old age." A nervous chuckle greeted the statement. "Well, now that the entertainment is over, how about some refreshment?" A cheer went up and a smiling Craigan whistled loudly.

Two men, carrying a large keg each, entered the circle and placed them down next to Craigan. A third man followed with a crate full of wooded mugs and set it next to the kegs. The three then bowed respectfully and retreated from the circle.

"Let's drink!" shouted Craigan as he hefted his axe and busted the lids with it.

The men quickly collapsed on the kegs, their exuberance for the drink causing them to carelessly splash ale about as they filled and distributed the mugs. Using the distraction to slip from the crowd, Craigan retrieve his white wool shirt and put it on before entering the maze of hastily erected tents.

The Jade Talons' camp was sprawled out over nearly half a league of the Chalin Sea – the wide-open grassy plain that served as the final stretch before reaching the city of Chalin and the prize it guarded. They had marched near nonstop in the three days since their departure from their last encounter with House Merandith, putting a firm sixteen leagues between them and the Merandiths each day after the first. During the hard march, many of the wounded had healed enough to leave the medical wagons and join the other troops. However, as Dromick had predicted, they lost over a score to the grueling pace. None of his commanders had been happy with what they viewed as unnecessary loses, but Craigan saw the cost as more than worth it to retreat to a safe harbor where he could think clearly and ride out the winter from behind strong walls. Still, he continued to keep a watch on the morale of his soldiers. Irritated officers were one thing, but if the men and women of the army began to lose faith or view his decisions in a poor light, he could end up with worse things to deal with than training soldiers. The last thing he need was another Battle of Corthas on his hands.

As he made his way through the camp, he received greetings and bows from the men and women of the army. The camp was alive with activity during this day of rest. More tents had been erected than normal and the camp followers were taking the time to bend their energies to repairing armor, weapons, tents and clothing. From what he knew, the tailors and leatherworkers had been overwhelmed with repairs to clothing and boots. There had been requests for extra hands to handle the workload, and he'd received the same requests from the blacksmiths; however, if he provided help to one group, he'd have to pull more troops away from their rest and duties to help the others. Everyone would simply have to make-do with the re-sources already available to them.

A unit of footmen, adorned in an eclectic ensemble of mis-matched armor, marched by under the banner of the army – a green talon on a black field – as he neared the center of camp and his own pavilion. The mounted sergeant, adorned in chainmail and a green and white surcoat, saluted as they passed. Craigan nodded in acknowledgment as he stood to the side and waited for the column to pass by. Continuing down the main thoroughfare after the column passed, it didn't take long for him to reach the center of camp. His pavilion – a large green and white, waterproofed canvas tent – was set amongst those of his generals. Unlike the Merandiths, he didn't feel the need for bodyguards. In fact, he saw such a need as weakness. As far as Craigan was concerned, anyone who felt they needed someone else to protect them from their enemies was weak and unfit to rule. Instead, he kept two guards outside his tent at all times and his generals close at hand. If any would-be assassin made its way passed his guards and managed to slay him, then – as far as he was concerned – it was Deo's will that he should fall.

The two halberd-wielding guards – girded in white and green tabards over full suits of chainmail – stationed outside his tent snapped to attention at his approach and saluted, fist to chest, as he entered his quarters. The inside of the pavilion was spacious and sectioned off by hanging curtains into a bedroom to his left, council room to his right, and the foyer he occupied; furthermore, each room was fully lit by candelabrum. Unlike many of the domses and domas he knew, his tent was devoid of rugs or carpets to cushion his feet. He saw such luxury as frivolous and completely obscene to carry with an army on the march. However, as he would do at home, the foyer did contain two simple high-back chairs flanking a table that had two wooden tankards and an empty pitcher on it. Normally the pitcher would be full of drink for those that were awaiting an audience with him, but it was empty at this time. Yawning and stretching, his cramped back popping loudly, Craigan leaned his axe against the pitcher-bearing table before walking into the council room.

As well as being lit by simple wood and bronze candelabra, the council room was spacious and occupied by a large, plain mahogany table in the center of the room with four matching chairs. A large map, topped by painted wooden miniatures representing the respective armies, occupied the top of the table. Craigan planted his battle-worn hands on the tabletop and leaned over the map, studying it with a trained eye. Triclose had been painstakingly inked on the map. From the deserts beyond the Dragonspine Mountains in the southwest to the shores of Tiliea in the Northeast, every realm was carefully drawn in detail. Miniature towers of bright green, representing the Jade Talons, occupied the southern and western parts of the map while black miniatures, signifying the Five Stars' forces, occupied the northern and eastern regions. A generous portion of Central Triclose – which spanned nearly the breath of the land – had once been barren of towers, but now hosted an appalling number of black towers. The once eerily empty expanse represented the Contested Territories – realms that had played host to the majority of battles and changed hands so many times that they were practically abandoned, their rulers and people now residing in other realms depending on whom they had sided with in the war. To Craigan's chagrin, the Contested Territories' borders had moved an inexcusable distance south and west. However, the majority of the map barely played into Craigan's thoughts at that moment.

For the first time in years, a black tower now occupied territory on the very edge of the southeastern border of Central Triclose. It was a black scar reminding him of his recent defeat. If it held, House Trivant would extend its borders to its historical boundaries for the first time in five years. More importantly, the loss was undeniable proof that he was on his heels. Did this mean defeat had become a genuine possibility? Only if one accepted being pushed to one's original borders as defeat. That definition of defeat, given the way wars worked on Triclose, was viewed more as a setback than anything else – House Merandith's response to their drastic territorial losses was proof enough of that.

He snorted in disgust as he eyed the city of Haltho. Failure to take significant portions of House Trivant's holdings, in particular the capital city of Haltho, rankled him to this day. The war could conceivably be over if Haltho had fallen. Controlling the vital port would have possibly dealt a fatal blow to Merandith's operations in the south. It had been quite the unforeseen gambit to bypass the Contested Territories in an attempt to catch House Merandith off guard. While he had managed to capture a portion of the relatively uninhabited southern region of Roselia, the tenacity of the Roselian clans and Kale's thrust southward had made any further advancement impossible. To his dismay, he had found himself facing the same problem he faced with the Contested Territories – an inability to maintain control. Even more unnerving was just how close the Merandiths were to Chalin. Shaking his head again, Craigan turned his attention to other portions of the map.

Neither army had to worry about their rear. For Kale, the Ice Fields made any thoughts of attacking the Merandiths from the north suicidal at best, and even then, Craigan would have to take Sur'datha to consider such a move. Then there was Kale's eastern flank, which consisted wholly of the Galerad Ocean; no one had a naval force strong enough or large enough to sail around Southern Triclose and mount a seaborne assault.

Craigan was as equally well-guarded. His rear was protected by the Sea of Twilight to the west, granting him the same defensive boon as the Galerad Ocean did for Kale, and his southern flank was guarded by the daunting Dragonspine Mountains and the untamed wilds of the Scorchlands. Craigan smirked as he eyed the Scorchlands, home to the desert-dwelling Pelasians. The Pelasians were a wildcard in this war. They and their doma had supported him only loosely ever since the disaster that had claimed his father and Doms Ithikia's lives. Though part of Triclose, the Dragonspine Mountains cut the lands beyond it off from the day-to-day politics of the rest of the continent. The Pelasians seemed to prefer it that way, as they typically remained withdrawn outside of a small amount of trade. Consequently, Craigan felt that the trickle of support he received was more about maintaining the status quo than about whom ascended the Jade Throne. Although, knowing Doma Ithikia, there was always more to her actions than she let on. He snorted. Hells, he knew their fathers had wanted more out of their alliance, but the depth of their goals – beyond a possible union of Houses – was lost on him.

Craigan turned his blue eyes to the central plains and the mountains of Triclose where crudely carved forts spanned the breadth of the land, most notably along the borders of the Contested Territories. There was a time when the forts had changed hands as readily and as often as talons on a game of dice. Now, however, the forts remained relatively stagnant. Very few had fallen or changed hands in the last few years with the bulk of the fighting falling on the shoulders of the mobile forces as Kale had advanced along the eastern edge of the Contested Territories. He had reclaimed a few of the realms that made up the Northeastern Contested Territories, but he had skirted the border for the most part until nearing Roselia. Kale's recent victories had seen the map once again redrawn, technically pushing the Contested Territories' eastern border to the west with the reclamation of the small realm of Lerilia. While it would take time to reinstate order to the small realm, reclaiming Lerilia and southern Roselia had punched a hole in Craigan's eastern flank, which was reason for concern. Granted, Kale would have to come through Chalin to accomplish anything from that position, but Kale's victory a few days ago had been viewed as a bad omen. Something would have to be done sooner rather than later to stymie Kale's momentum.

Anger still gnawed at Craigan's stomach when he looked at the new tower and reflected on the damage being inflicted on both sides. Though he held himself responsible for what he viewed as his fair share of deaths, he still saw Kale as the pestilence killing the land and himself as the cure. The deaths and carnage needed to stop in order for Triclose to heal, but to do that, he would have to find a way to thoroughly defeat Kale and crush any thought of rebellion beyond that. He would need to continue to operate from a position of power to do so; unfortunately, the recent defeats were severely eroding such a position. To his chagrin, he was beginning to feel like his back was to the proverbial wall. It was one thing to lose battles and territories in this seemingly never-ending chess match, but should Chalin fall. . . .

He rubbed his eyes and yawned. The number of black towers that occupied the map had grown at an alarming rate, adding to his quandary over how to end the war for good. There were so many situations to consider, and he could see how one could go mad if they tried to prepare for every possibility; however, being a cautious man, Craigan didn't like making a move without being as informed as possible. To that end, when they had pulled from the field, he had left scouts to observe Kale's movements. He not only hoped to hear from them within the next day or two, but that their news would help him to see the situation more clearly. He needed answers . . . and soon. With a frustrated shake of his head, Craigan stood up and turned to leave, only to find Dromick had slipped in without being noticed.

Sheathed broadsword in hand, his thick and powerfully built frame clad in padded leathers and a white linen undershirt, Dromick sported a layer of dirt from the training grounds where he had been putting squads through their paces. Sweat glistened on his baldhead like tiny crystals, and his strong-willed black eyes carried an edge of exhaustion.

Craigan smirked dryly at his friend and second-in-command. "What brings you away from your fun?"

Dromick snorted and rubbed at his broad nose before he responded in his deep timbre voice, "I grew tired of kicking the pups around, so I turned them over to Captain Sargeth." He eyed the map on the table and then Craigan. "Hovering over these maps day after day isn't going to do you any good. I don't think paper and wooden miniatures are going to magically give you the answers you're looking for. All you're going to do is give yourself an ulcer."

Craigan chortled as he ran a hand through his white-flecked, brown hair. "I suppose so. We need answers, though. Kale has been too successful for my tastes. Winter will give us some relief but . . ." he trailed off and shook his head.

"Peace, Doms Suldamik. This is just a phase like many we've experienced before," Dromick stated confidently. "If Doma Ithikia holds true to her promises, we'll have an advantage come spring that the Merandiths won't be able to counter."

Craigan turned a skeptical eye to his friend. "Do you honestly believe her? True, we'll have an influx of much-needed manpower. But this talk of magic is a bit hard to swallow."

Dromick nodded, conceding the point. "I'm not sure I totally believe her, but the Utherian Valley is proof that magic existed at one point in our history."

Rubbing his eyes, Craigan said, "That kind of mysticism died out with whoever built that tomb. Despite the Pelasian's long isolation from the rest of us, I cannot imagine that magic – *if* it did exist – didn't suffer there as it did everywhere else." He smirked and chuckled at himself. "Listen to us – babbling on about children's stories and flights of fancy. If anyone heard us, they'd think we were going senile." He motioned to the foyer. "Come, let's sit and have a drink. At least then we can blame the alcohol for any nonsense we utter."

Dromick gladly followed his doms back into the foyer where Craigan had one of his guards send for a fresh pitcher of mulled wine before they seated themselves. It wasn't long before a servant in green and white livery was admitted with the requested beverage. Craigan took the pitcher from the young boy, thanking him before dismissing him. After the servant departed, Craigan filled the two tankards and offered one to Dromick. Dromick accepted with a nod of his head and the two friends sat back in their chairs, sipping at the warm red wine. Though it wasn't quite cold enough for such a warm drink, the fruity warmth soothed both mind and body as it trickled down their throats.

The two conversed as they sipped on the florid beverage, discussing recent events and the possibilities for the future. They even dared to entertain thoughts of what Triclose would be like under Suldamik rule. It would be a bright future, they both agreed. Strong and fair rule for all is what they envisioned. It would be a land devoid of the rebellion and treachery that had so plagued it since Doms Gravit'nas' death. Not one negative word was spoken, as both men viewed such pessimism as an affront to their goals and the respect they had for Doms Gravit'nas' memory. The optimistic atmosphere was a far cry from what Craigan had been battling with earlier, providing a temporary reprieve from such dour reflections. Soon, the hours had trickled away like the wine, leaving the sun well below the eastern horizon, the pitcher empty and both men asleep in their chairs with tankards hanging from limp hands.

As darkness took hold and the candles burned down to nubs before flickering out, a solitary man in worn riding leathers was admitted to the pavilion. His dark-blue eyes scanned the room before landing on the slumbering figures. With his vision already adjusted to the dark, he could easily make out the two men and was able to identify Craigan. Carrying him quickly and cautiously as his job required, his footfalls were silent and carefully measured as he approached Craigan's slumped form. Crouching before his slumbering doms, he placed a gloved hand on Craigan's knee. "Doms Suldamik?" he queried in a soft voice.

Craigan groaned but did not move.

Giving Craigan's knee a firm squeeze, he tried to rouse him again, "Doms Suldamik, I– "

Without warning, Craigan bolted awake in a rush of movement. His instincts taking over, Craigan delivered a solid punch squarely to the man's face, sending him sprawling onto the ground. The man didn't know how long he had lain there with stars filling his vision, but when his vision did clear, he found Craigan offering him a hand with an apologetic look etched into his face. Blushing in embarrassment, the man accepted the hand and was hauled to his feet. Dromick, looking quite amused despite his groggy state, watched the scene for a moment before he stood and moved off to replace the old candles.

"What's your name?" asked Craigan.

The short man, his black hair cut short, straightened his leathers and adjusted his sword belt before replying, "Scout Hirok Tsumasta, Doms Suldamik."

Craigan nodded, recognizing the golden-skinned Shalusyian scout. Hirok was a slim man with a deceptive build. His eyes were tilted up slightly and, oddly enough, they were dark-blue, hinting at a mixed heritage. Craigan settled himself into his chair as warm light began to fill the room from the fresh candles. "My apologies for striking you. Your presence was unexpected."

Hirok bowed slightly. "The fault is mine, Doms. I should have announced my presence before entering."

Craigan shook his head. "It was the guard's duty to announce you. However, I'm assuming your presence here was kept quiet to avoid unwanted prying ears, so I think we can overlook it. By the look of it, you've ridden hard to deliver your news; so tell me, what's so important?"

By this point, Dromick had finished lighting the candles and had returned to Craigan's side. "Aye. Your party wasn't due to rejoin us until after we reached Chalin."

Hirok nodded to Dromick. "That's true. However, the sergeant felt you need to receive the news now instead of later."

Craigan leaned forward, but Dromick beat him to the question. "Were you seen?"

With a shake of his head, Hirok replied, "No, but we lost one man when his horse was spooked and kicked him in the head."

Ignoring the unfortunate death of the scout, Craigan asked with an edge of anxiousness in his voice, "What of Merandith's forces?"

"It would be best if the sergeant told you. I didn't believe it when I saw it and, no offense intended Doms Suldamik, I don't think you'll believe it from me."

Nodding, Craigan eagerly stood and gestured to the exit. "Lead the way."

The night watch had done a good job of keeping the Hirok's arrival a secret. The camp was quiet except for the snores of the sleeping soldiers and the clink of armor from the night watch. The three men moved toward the eastern edge of the camp as discreetly as possible as Hirok led them to the site of Craigan's training session from earlier in the day. There, three of the seven scouts Craigan had left behind awaited them. Four dark, lean horses were lathered in sweat, and blood flecked their muzzles, giving every indication that they had been ridden hard. Layers of dirt and mud caked the scouts, and heavy-lidded eyes attested to their sacrifice of sleep in the name of speed. It was important or dire news indeed to make these men push themselves and their prized mounts so hard.

The sergeant, Kirk de'Suldamik Galanti by name, was a tall and lanky man of fifty summers. His shaved hair was white, and his body and leathery skin showed the wear and tear of years on the road. Although his age and appearance told the story of a worn-down, grizzled veteran, his eyes were sharper than many of those younger than him, and his skill with a bow was unmatched within the Jade Talons.

Upon seeing Craigan, the three scouts quickly knelt. Craigan hastily motioned for them to rise, eager to hear their report. "Report, Sergeant."

The three men stood, tired eyes fixed on their doms. The sergeant met Craigan's gaze before replying in a sandpaper voice, "Doms Suldamik – we've news of importance that I didn't feel could wait for us to complete our assignment."

"So I've been told," Craigan responded with anxious irritation. "Out with it then."

Kirk nodded. "Soon after your departure, the Merandiths began reorganizing their camp. It took us a day to find out just what they were up to, but every indication is that House Merandith and at least two others are preparing to retreat for the winter."

Craigan arched an inquisitive eyebrow. "News to be sure, but not unexpected. Winter won't allow for much this far north of the Dragonspine. Did you see any other banners to indicate who was going with him?"

Shaking his head in the negative, the sergeant replied, "Nothing that we could confirm before we left, but it looked like House Grevorian and Trivant were just as active as House Merandith."

Astonishment tickled Craigan's mind and set alarm bells ringing through his thoughts. "Just those two? Are you sure?"

"As sure as we could be at the time, Doms Suldamik. Even if one or two of the minor House were going, that's – as you pointed out – to be expected. What brought us back is of more importance. We spotted them soon after your departure and followed them for a few hours to confirm their direction. The next day confirmed it." Kirk caught Craigan's gaze and held it. "Doms – House Sur'datha and a fresh supply train arrived the evening of the day you left."

Craigan's throat tighten as the unexpected development fell on his ears. Retreat for the winter was one thing, but the arrival of the Highlanders and the departure of so few could only mean that Kale was preparing for a winter campaign. As to what extreme he'd go to, Craigan had no idea, but his mind was already racing with the implications. It took him a moment to realize that everyone was staring at him, awaiting a response. Giving an emotionless smile, he said, "Thank you, Sergeant. You and your men may retire. See that your mounts are attended to."

Kirk bowed. "Thank you, Doms Suldamik. One last thing before we go – I left two of my men to monitor the situation and finish the assignment. We should have more answers then, but I thought this news was of importance. We're ready and willing to ride out again in the morning if you wish it."

Craigan shook his head. "That won't be necessary. I commend you on your forethought to leave eyes behind so you could bring this news to me. Take your rest."

"Thank you, Doms Suldamik."

The four scouts gathered their respective reins and vanished into the dark camp in search of the corral.

As soon as they were out of earshot, Dromick turned to Craigan and found a dark expression had crept on to his doms' face. "Sir, I–"

"Summon the others, now!" Craigan growled as he pushed passed Dromick forcefully and marched into the darkness.


"Damn it!" Craigan barked as drove his fist into the table, causing the miniatures to bounce on the map. "I should have seen this coming when Janson failed with Cravon! Those bastard Highlanders would be wanting blood!"

Craigan's council room was well-lit and crowded, the tension palpable. An enraged Craigan stood at the head of the table, fists planted on its surface, with a concerned and equally troubled Dromick at his side. Three very tired royals had been roused and quickly ushered to Craigan's tent – Doms Thakian of Terial, Doms Astica of Faridin, and Doma Ithikia of Pelasia.

Seated to Craigan's left was Doms Astica. Short and burly, Doms Astica had hastily thrown on trousers underneath the loose sleeping shirt that covered his bulk. A gimpy leg from an old war injury in his younger years had seen the end to his fighting days, but as gray slowly replaced black in his long hair, his mind had sharpened like his sword had once been. This night, however, exhaustion clouded his normally bright-blue eyes and his sharp mind. Yawning and waving a dismissive hand he said, "Tis' nothing to get so upset about. We expected a winter retreat. Kale is simply trying to act clever."

Craigan shook his head and gave a disgusted chortle. "Idiot! He *is* being clever! None of us saw this coming! Winter should have kept those forsaken mountain men locked in till nearly summer! For them to come down now. . . . Oh yes – Kale has something up his sleeve!" he spit.

The venom in Craigan's voice seemed to rouse a bit of fire in Doms Astica, but with it came a clearer line of reasoning and he thought better of retorting.

"Domses," chimed the throaty, musical voice of the lone woman in the tent, "I believe we are overreacting to a situation that we still do not have full details on. As I see it, the situation still favors us in the long run."

In contrast to the men in the room, Doma Ithikia's presence was as refreshing as it was distracting when she wanted it to be. Seated at the far end of the table, her nearly transparent silken gown

165

seemed to cling to every curve of her slender, toned brown-skinned figure. The low-cut neck on her gown plunged so deep that more of her ample breasts were on display than was hidden. Long white hair framed a red-lipped face with up-turned amber eyes that suggested everything pleasurable yet promised nothing. Her beauty, however, was a misleading guise for the sharp mind that it hid. Many were the unfortunate men that saw only her beauty and gave into lust. The rumors of the number of dead and financially broken men in her wake were numerous and outlandish. Never the less, none of the men in the room were foolish enough to be taken in by her charms, but they were smart enough to listen when she spoke.

"Nonsense, Alestra," barked Doms Astica, turning his frustration with Craigan on her. "We all know what Hagail and his Hammer did to Janson and Cravon's forces. As much as I respect your opinion," there was a tone to his voice that seemed to suggest contempt instead of the professed respect, "you know that you are here by invitation only. The few Pelasians you've brought and your promises only garner you so much."

Seated opposite Astica was Doms Thakian, a frail yet devilish man of nearly seventy summers. His limbs seemed too long, his baldhead too big, and his hawkish green eyes stared intensely from astride a beak of a nose. However, at the moment, a stranger would find it hard to take the man seriously since the thick wool robe he wore seemed like it was trying to swallow him whole.

He had remained silent until now, but he finally spoke up in support of his fellow Doms, the same hint of contempt in Astica's words tinting his. "I am reluctant to agree with Astica, Doma," Doms Thakian's passive, elderly voice interjected, "but I must. Hagail is an opponent that is not to be underestimated no matter how many men are under his banner. Besides, we have yet to see much more than words from the great Pelasia. The majority of the men you brought with you leech off of Chalin's teat while the rest of us get bloodied."

The elderly doms' final barb was intended to get Alestra's ire up; instead, she pushed a lock of hair behind her ear and smiled slightly. "Old and tired do not make for a good combination on this night, I see. Dimwittedness seems to be infectious between you two." Her barbed remark drew angry looks from her two counterparts and seemed to almost pull an amused smile from Craigan. "If Kale does retreat – as it looks like and as we expected – we have very little to worry about. Supposing that Kale leaves Hagail in charge of a winter campaign, I doubt Kale would loosen his grip completely on him; furthermore, honor will prevent Hagail from doing anything too . . .

166

rash. He would not dare take a victory away from Kale that wasn't sanctioned by him."

She picked up one of the black miniatures and toyed with it between long fingers with black-enameled fingernails. "Additionally, we drastically outnumber anything Hagail could bring against us in open combat. Any concerted move into our territory would be crushed. On top of that, you've already dispatched orders to begin the second phase of raids. Kale will have his hands full no matter what he does or doesn't do."

Craigan leaned forward and looked intently at Alestra. "What would you suggest I do?"

She placed the miniature back in its place and waved a dismissive hand in the air. "We wait and gather more information. Move back to Chalin, as the original plan called for, and resupply and rest from a secure location. If we keep this pace up, we'll be within sight of the city before nightfall tomorrow. Once there, we can gather the information we need and then reconsider our situation. If there's need for us to fight an all-out winter campaign, then so be it. If not, however, then let Hagail and Kale run their armies ragged. Either way, we still hold the position of power. Be it winter or summer, if they attempt to take Chalin, not only will we see them coming, but we can make the cost in lives so drastic that they'll eventually decide it simply isn't worth it."

The room remained silent for a time, each man weighting Alestra's words carefully. Finally, Doms Astica nodded, conceding the point. "She's right. Hagail's not going anywhere for the moment."

Craigan looked to Doms Thakian. "Sevarius?"

Doms Thakian had his fingers steepled before him, his eyes staring into space. After a moment of introspection, he nodded as well. "I agree, but urge caution. It appears that Kale still isn't fully aware of just how large our operations in the North are – which will alter his thinking eventually – and that still plays to our advantage. However, we are all very aware of how good Kale is at turning a disadvantage into an advantage, and we all know that he excels at disguising his actions. I fear there is more to this than we can see."

With a forceful nod, Craigan stood. "Very well. It's settled then. On the morn' we will continue to Chalin. I want fresh scouts sent out and our border forts notified to keep a watchful eye about. Your counsel tonight has been invaluable and I thank you. Please, return to your beds with my apologies for pulling you from your sleep."

Chairs were pushed back and the doma and sleepy domses stood to leave. Dromick was the first to file out and was quickly followed by the two domses. Doma Ithikia, however, remained where she was, her amber eyes staring intently at Craigan.

Once he was sure the others had departed, he gave her a confused frown as he asked, "Is there something else, Alestra? I sincerely hope you're not waiting around for an apology for the others' jabs at you tonight – because you won't get it. A few men and outlandish promises won't buy you the respect you think you deserve."

She tilted her head back and gave a throaty laugh. "Oh my! Trying to be funny are we? You know that I neither need nor want their respect. Their opinions of me are of little consequence."

Craigan gave her a stern glare. "Careful that you do not alienate your allies, Alestra. We do not need to make enemies amongst ourselves."

"So you've told me before. However, that is not why I've remained."

Craigan folded his arms across his chest. "What is it then?"

She smiled broadly at him, her intentions clearly stated in her eyes before she spoke. "I am concerned about you." She slipped around the table and approached him, picking at the ties to her gown. "The defeat troubles you, and now you are jumping at shadows. While it is true I have brought few men with me and made my share of promises, I do believe I can provide you with services to help you . . . relax." Looking up at Craigan slyly, she slid her gown from her shoulders and let it drop to the floor, the garment pooling at her feet.

Craigan could feel his anxiety swept away in a rush of lust at the sight of her naked body on display for his pleasure. With thoughts of the war momentarily washed away, he let out a lustful growl, picked her up and carried her to the bedroom.

He awoke early the next morning to the harsh symphony of a camp preparing to march. A probing hand found the blankets next to him were cold, and a weight on his feet told him fresh clothing had been laid out by his servants at the foot of his cot. Alestra had returned to her tent sometime during the night as she always did after sleeping with him. It was no secret that she frequented his bed; in fact, many believed that was the only reason she was allowed to remain. There were even those amongst his own House who bantered about the hope that he would follow his late father's wishes and marry her, which always made him laugh when he caught wind of such chatter. He had his reasons for never marrying, and no amount of prodding would change his mind. Granted, there was a need for an heir – and Deo only knows he probably had fathered his share of bastards – but there was a time and a place for everything. War was not a time for marriage and a family. For him, it was a time for solitude so that one could make the hard decisions needed to win a war. Let the people enjoy their flights of fancy if it amused them or brought them happiness, he had too many things to think about right now, and he enjoyed his solitude. Ridiculous notions of marriage to someone like Alestra, or anyone for that matter, would just be a distraction.

The news the scouts had brought disturbed him greatly, just as Alestra had observed. The move was unorthodox for Kale and had caught him off guard. He couldn't put his finger on what Kale was trying to accomplish by these actions. It wasn't retreat, Craigan was sure of that. However, if it wasn't retreat, then what was it? Would Kale have the audacity to eventually try to fight the war on more than one front? Or was Kale trying to lure him into making a rash move or mistake? More disturbing was the notion that Kale was truly preparing for a winter campaign. Craigan shook his head and pulled on a fresh shirt before slipping from the warmth of the blankets. None of the notions sat well with him. Craigan fully believed that Kale's Academy training would discourage fighting the war on more than one front if possible. If proof of the disastrous consequences of such a folly was needed, then Craigan's own attempts to establish a second front would more than adequately serve as evidence; his two-front venture had been thoroughly crushed with horrific losses. Therefore, he couldn't fathom a situation where Kale would make the same mistake. As for it being a trap? Well, he felt it was too obvious for Kale.

He did smile as he pulled on his warm breeches, riding leathers, and boots. If this little maneuver of Kale's was frustrating him, then the raids he had started behind Kale's lines would bring House Merandith their fair share of headaches. Right now, however, the only thing that Craigan could do about his situation would be to follow Alestra's advice – go about business as normal until there was information to alert them to Kale's intentions. With that thought in mind, Craigan secured his weapon-harness on his chest and slung his axe on his back before striding from his tent to prepare his army to move.

# Chapter Seven

C halin, the City of Dreams. When first conceived by Doms Gravit'nas centuries ago, it had been heralded as the city that would unite Triclose under one banner, bringing hope and prosperity to all. The stories told of towering spires, immaculate living conditions, and streets aglow in the warm embrace of lights that were fueled by magic. Indeed, if one believed the tales, the citizens of Triclose did prosper under the gleaming beacon that was Chalin. Poverty was all but driven from the land, food was plentiful and life was good. Then came the betrayal and the beginning of the Second Great War. Historians, to this day, argue over what drove Triclose to tear this near utopia apart. However, it was agreed upon that, even as the war waged on, those under House Gravit'nas' banner continued to thrive. It wasn't until Gravit'nas' passing, without an heir to take up the throne, that darkness truly descended on Triclose. The cost of the war saw cities stripped of their valuables and anything else that could fuel the war effort. Chalin wasn't excluded from this. It was said that at some point in the war, after every last ounce of gold and steel was stripped from the city, even the great spires were demolished for raw materials. By the end of the Second Great War, the City of Dreams was no more – an empty shadow of broken promises.

Though the history books are fuzzy on the details, it wasn't until years after the Second Great War and the establishment of Doms Gravit'nas' tomb that Chalin began to come back to life. As part of the cession of hostilities, it was agreed that a new tomb for Doms Gravit'nas would be built in the vicinity of Chalin – though historians agree that it was unfathomable that any person or group of people could have created the Utherian Valley. The city would be rebuilt as a place for all with good intent – no matter whom they bent knee to – to visit and live. Though a shadow of its former glory, the citizens of Chalin held their heads high as they served as a bastion of tranquillity in a stormy sea even as the Houses continued to war for the Jade Throne on and off through the decades. Domses of every House were crowned in the shadow of Doms Gravit'nas' glorious tomb and, in death, buried in Valley. Citizens throughout the land were granted the privilege of visiting the tomb of Triclose's greatest doms. Not once was a weapon drawn within the confines of Chalin or the Valley in relation to the ongoing battles throughout the rest of the land.

That all changed with Craigan.

In an act of defiance or self-delusion, depending on whom one asked, Craigan made the bold move to capture Chalin, bringing it and the tomb it guarded under his control. At the time, the city was nestled comfortably inside Jade Talon territory and the war remained a distant thought; however, that didn't prevent the fury his actions brought about from costing him many of the minor Houses allied with him, nor the resulting explosion of House Merandith propaganda. Many of the citizens of Chalin, horrified that their peaceful existence had been shattered, fled wherever they could simply to try to find a place away from the war. For those that could not or would not flee, Chalin surprisingly remained relatively the same despite the citizens' fears. While the city's walls were militarized and Doms Gravit'nas' tomb was cut off from anyone that wasn't allied with Craigan, life went on as usual.

As Craigan sat his horse, gazing thoughtfully at the city set against the horizon in the slowly fading light of day, he still felt right in capturing the city. As far as he was concerned, those that sided with the Merandiths were traitors and their presence inside the city or at the tomb was a blight on Doms Gravit'nas' honor and intentions. Yes, the city no longer resembled the glorious images carefully depicted in the ancient texts, but its purpose and meaning were still the same. From its heart, Craigan ruled and intended to see that message spread to all corners of Triclose.

Even at this distance, Craigan could not only make out the wall towers, but he could also see the spires of the keep. Though they weren't the soaring architecture of old, they were still inspiring and impressive even at this distance. In his mind's eye, he could see the careful craftsmanship that had gone into its rebuilding. Every stone had been measured, cut, and fitted with care. Cobblestone roads were kept clear of debris and trash, and the buildings of the city were arranged in an orderly fashion along Chalin's meticulously laid out streets, providing the citizens with ease and freedom of movement. He could even see the myriad of colors in the keep's halls, cast by the sun illuminating the numerous stained-glass windows. How he loved the city and all it stood for. Nothing would separate him from his home and what he viewed as his destiny.

Tearing his eyes from the jewel on the horizon, he turned his attention to his left where his army marched passed his position; a swirling cloud of dust and dirt kicked up by their heavy and tired feet hung about them like a foggy haze. As the army slithered into the distance, the dying sunlight glinted off armor as if the protective steel were the scales on a snake. The first of the troops would reach Chalin's gates within the hour. Riders had been sent ahead to prepare the city for their arrival, and Craigan could well imagine the relief and joy the sight of the city's walls was bringing to the men at the front of the column. Chalin was an end to a grueling march and a chance for much-needed rest.

Craigan almost smiled as he thought about the chaotic task that awaited his officers. Maintaining discipline was going to be difficult tonight as they set about making camp and arranging leave for the men. Turning in his saddle, Craigan could just make out the end of the column. If they kept marching at their current pace, it would be well past nightfall before they reached the city. Those at the rear would be too tired to venture into the city this night, but he knew the joy they felt with their objective in sight would not be diminished in the slightest by the prospect of being unable to partake of the city's bounty for a little while longer. Yes, things would be difficult for the officers tonight, but for the first time in months, Chalin would have new life breathed into it. The troops would be paid over the next few days and coin would flow like the drink it would eventually purchase.

A cry from behind caught his attention. Twisting around in his saddle, Craigan spotted Dromick galloping toward him with a hand raised in greeting. Always one to be prepared, Dromick was dressed in his chainmail and his sword was strapped to his saddle where he could easily draw it. As he drew closer, Craigan could see that sweat glistened on his baldhead despite the chill in the air, and that his posture and black eyes radiated excitement and joy.

Reining in as he drew near, Dromick circled his horse around Craigan before pulling alongside of him. Leaning on the pommel of his saddle, he smiled at Craigan. "Doms Suldamik," he said in greeting.

"Dromick," he replied dryly. "What has you so excited?"

"Chalin, Doms! It's always a sight to behold! Besides, I'll get to see my family! Haven't seen them in nearly two years!"

Craigan glanced at Dromick, unable to hide the surprise. "Have I really kept you away from them that long?"

Dromick shrugged. "More or less. We write to each other, but it's never quite the same as spending quality time with them."

Craigan chuckled. "Indeed. Your son ought to be what now? Ten?"

Dromick nodded, a beaming smile painted on his face. "Aye. And our daughter'll be turning three soon. Deo be good, it feels like it's been ages since I've seen them!"

172

Craigan gave a heartfelt laugh. "Indeed it has been. I hope you'll give my regards and my apologies to Verana for keeping her husband away for so long."

Dromick laughed. "Aye, I'll do that."

Craigan glanced back toward the city, his own enthusiasm to be home growing in him. "Any word from the city?"

Dromick gave a curt nod. "Aye, they're ready to receive us. They even sent hunters into the Valley for some deer and fruit. That Valley is a miracle, to say the least. These men won't know what to do with a fresh meal."

Squinting, Craigan could just make out the fertile green hills that stood as natural guardians around the Utherian Valley. Though the city held little of the glamour it once boasted, the Valley still flourished – for no matter the season, the Utherian Valley was a thriving bastion of spring at its peak. The powers that enabled such a beautiful and miraculous oddity to exist were enough to convince even the deepest skeptic that there really was magic beyond the sleight of hand used by the con artists on the streets or the entertainers at a carnival.

"Indeed they won't," he replied as he stared longingly at the city and Valley. All the talk of home – and with it in sight no less – was beginning to gnaw at Craigan. Nodding to himself, he stated to Dromick, "Spread the word – I'm riding ahead. Keep everyone marching till we're all camped in the shadow of the walls. You're in charge until I get back."

Dromick smiled and nodded, knowing all too well what was on his doms' mind. "Aye, Doms Suldamik, as you wish."

Craigan nodded to Dromick once more before spurring his horse forward as Dromick peeled off to deliver the orders.

A cool breeze buffeted Craigan's face, whipping his white-flecked, brown hair wildly behind him as he spurred his painted de-strider forward. Men passed by in a blur as he pushed his horse even harder, the horse's ears flattening against her skull as she strained against the reins and Craigan leaned over her neck. After a few more minutes of riding, he adjusted his course to the north. He knew that if he hadn't already been spotted by the lookouts on Chalin's sturdy walls, then he would be soon; word would then be sent ahead via raven-wing pigeon to notify the guards at his destination of a rider's approach. Until then, he had the open plains to himself.

He cherished this rare opportunity to be away from the constant hum of the army. The noise could be deafening, addling one's wits. When alone like this, he could be at ease and allow his mind to wander. However, Dromick's talk of family had struck a nerve, though he would never show it, and his thoughts began to drift toward marriage. It was something many wanted for him, and, in a small hidden corner of his mind, something he secretly wanted for himself – though not in the arranged fashion his father had intended nearly nine years ago. Long before the marriage-alliance was even a glimmer in his father's mind, he had come to the realization that a marriage without love was something he wanted to avoid; and when his and Alestra's fathers had gone to their final rest, he and Alestra had agreed to put the matter aside until a later date.

In the years that followed, Craigan somewhat convinced himself that his lifestyle and current goals made the comfort and passion that a marriage could possibly grant him unrealistic. As a result of that halfhearted self-delusion, he relegated himself to purchasing his pleasure or, in the case of Alestra, claiming it from the willing. In his mind, he tried to believe that it was safer that way; turn over a little money for a night of ecstasy and leave after it was over, forming no emotional attachments – clean and simple. Yet, he knew it was by no means that simple. More often than not, Alestra was a willing visitor to his bed, and he to her's, which often left him wondering if some part of them sought a union of Houses.

Adjusting his course to follow the hills of the Utherian Valley, he reminded himself of the main reason – though he would never express it aloud – why he had never married and why he might never take that path. While his outward reasons held a modicum of validity, it boiled down to one simple fact – she would die. Sure, it might not be right after the wedding, but old age or an assassin's dagger could end it in an instant. For all that he put on a gruff exterior in his everyday dealings, Craigan was a bit of a romantic at heart. He wasn't sure he could handle such a loss – and he even secretly regretted delivering such a tragedy upon House Merandith. While killing Doms Bordin Merandith hadn't cost him any sleep, signing the death warrant for Kale's mother had actually been the hardest thing he had done in the war. She had been a loving mother and was beloved by her people, but she was a danger to the stability of Triclose and had to be removed for the greater good. Though he loathed his actions, it was the right choice; and given the chance to do it all over again, he would not hesitate to sign the order.

Still, assassination made him sick to his stomach and he had secretly sworn to never to tread that path again. Kale's lovely wife was too delicate a flower to be harmed – even though she was with her second child. Heirs to a throne were always dangerous, but in this instance, Craigan was willing to look the other way for now. He had once loved her as much as Kale did now, but with Haltho seemingly

174

out of reach, his father had chosen to make other plans for Craigan, forcing him to let her go into the embrace of his enemy. While he didn't regret the decision to let Kale's wife live, he did realize that he would have to do something about her and her children once he ascended the Jade Throne. He couldn't afford to leave a banner for his opponents to rally behind. It would be a sad day indeed when he finally had to come face-to-face with that decision.

The hills of the Utherian Valley had drawn closer, and Craigan could just make out deer darting in and out of the densely forested hilltops. If anyone thought they could simply ascend the hills and find themselves in the Valley, they would discover a nasty surprise on the other side. A sheer drop-off surrounded the interior of the Valley on all sides, allowing for entry from only one of two points. The first access point was heavily protected within the city itself, while the second entry existed within the hills of the Valley and served as private access for the domses and domas of Triclose.

While access was severely restricted, anyone could observe that the wildlife living on the hilltops remained there year-round, benefiting from the boon of the Valley. Though few had witnessed it firsthand, perpetual spring invigorated the Valley, allowing it to provide food, fresh water, and lumber year-round to the citizens of Chalin. To Chalin's citizens, the Valley was more than a tomb – it was a holy place blessed by Deo. It was viewed as the most extreme sacrilege to try to profit from the Valley; and on the rare occasion that profiteers did try to take advantage of the Valley's bounty, their efforts had been met with severe punishment no matter who ruled over Chalin. As a result, only the animals of the vale were free to roam it without fear of suspicion or persecution.

Craigan smiled as he watched the deer flittered in and out of the trees. It was a blessing to see that such freedom and innocence still existed in this war-torn land where death, rape and violence had become all too common. Peace seemed like a concept that the people no longer knew how to comprehend, much less live with, but it was a standard he was intent upon reinstating. How to do it was the problem that continued to hound Craigan. He knew all too well how extensive Kale's Academy training was, and he knew blind luck alone wouldn't be enough to back the Merandiths into a corner. Something more would be needed. He grinned wryly. He almost envied the creatures of the Valley. Sure, they might end up on the plate of one of Chalin's people, but they lived a carefree life devoid of what they would probably consider petty human stupidity – assuming they had any comprehension of human behavior.

Easing his destrider to a halt, he swung from the saddle and led his warhorse along at a leisurely pace, giving his legs a much-needed stretch and his steed a chance to catch her breath before he covered the final distance to the Valley's private entrance. Alestra was right – Chalin, and by extension, the Utherian Valley, would be the perfect place to rest and plan his next move. It would be foolish for Kale to try to assault Craigan while he was protected by the city's imposing ramparts. Winter's onset aside, he would have to first deal with a border fort before contending with the city itself. Bolstering Craigan's confidence further was the fact that, for the entirety of its existence, the city had fallen to a conqueror but once – and that was to Craigan. Even then, Craigan's capture of Chalin had been a peaceful transition of power. Though he had bluffed his way through most of the terse confrontation, he had been willing, in an extreme situation, to break the long-held taboo of violence upon both Valley and Chalin soil. For as long as anyone could remember, desecrating Chalin – and by extension, the Utherian Valley – with war-related violence was punishable by death. While he hadn't feared such punishment, Craigan was, without a doubt, glad he hadn't been forced into making that decision.

Coming to a halt, Craigan looked back the way he came and could make out the large black mass that was his army. At their pace, it would still take hours for them to fully reach Chalin. Looking ahead, though it was obscured by the Valley's hills, he knew the garrison he had erected to protect the private entrance into the Valley awaited. He had maybe another half-hour ride ahead of him to reach it. A grin crept onto his face as he swung back into the saddle. Although he still had a ways to go, it always made him giddy with anticipation when he ventured to the Valley. As he urged his mount into motion, he couldn't help but laugh with joy.

Ever since its discovery decades after the Valley's completion, the secreted-away entrance to the Utherian Valley had been used as the private entrance for all domses and domas. Like its larger sister entrance within the city, the heavy, ornate doors could only be opened by a key attuned to each Houses' bloodline. Unlike the city entrance, however, a more direct path was provided to the treasures the Valley housed, allowing domses and domas alike to come and go without notice. One of Craigan's first acts upon seizing Chalin and the Valley had been to commission the construction of fortifications around the private entrance to the Valley. While it was commonly viewed as impossible to bring a large enough force capable of taking the city close enough to use the second entrance as a means of assault without notice, Craigan wasn't one to take chances. He feared that a small and determined force could easily overcome the lone squad that was traditionally stationed there in the past. Better to be over-prepared than to be caught off guard, his father had always taught him.

As the sun neared the eastern horizon, Craigan closed on the new fortifications and was pleased to see that the primary construc-tion was done. From a distance, he could clearly see thick stone ram-parts surrounding the hillside that housed the entrance. Crenelated towers were stationed at each corner of the walls, and two others flanked the lone gate. The granite rock face – and by extension, the Utherian Valley – jutting from the hillside completed the fort's de-fenses, making the fort unassailable from behind.

As he drew near the fort, he could see guards patrolling the battlements and lookouts on top of the towers. Though he couldn't hear anything at this distance, he knew he had been spotted when he saw – per his standing orders to consider all that approach as possible hostiles – men scrambling to make ready. Within moments, the bat-tlements were filled with soldiers, the dying sunlight glinting off of armor and spear tips. He could just make out archers readying their bows in case he somehow presented a threat or was the precursor to something greater. Craigan smiled as he drew nearer, pleased that his men were not only doing as he commanded, but doing so with speed and efficiency.

Even before he drew within the shadow of the walls, he had been recognized by the men on the battlements. Welcoming cries and cheers of praise were rained down upon him as the men relaxed upon seeing their doms. Craigan waved a hand in greeting as he skirted the spike-filled moat that surrounded the walls. It was delightful to hear his men were in good spirits. He spent so much time surrounded by the pain and suffering of the battlefield that he had forgotten how good such heartfelt cheers could feel. By the time he reached the fort's entrance, the cheers had died down and the thick wooden gates had opened to permit the lowering of the drawbridge. Craigan reined in his mount just in front of the drawbridge as it thudded to the ground.

Waiting on the other side of the bridge was a somewhat port-ly officer dressed in a split, full-length chain hauberk beneath a green and white surcoat secured by a thick sword belt. Shoulder-length white hair was neatly tied back at the nape of his neck, keeping his lined visage free of obstruction. Striding across the bridge, the officer moved like a man half his age as his powerful strides carried him for-ward. Even from across the span, Craigan could make out the worst of the scars marring the man's stoic face, but as he neared, it was impossible to ignore the eyepatch over his right eye nor the mauled right ear that made his ragged features and near-red left eye seem positively demonic. A long, jagged scar ran from the top of the man's scalp down over his left eye to his lip. No hair would grow on in the damaged area, leaving a bald patch on the edge of his scalp and in the middle of his left eyebrow. Craigan felt that this was a man whose outward appearance reflected the plight of Triclose – scarred, wartorn and tired, but pushing forward with grim determination.

The officer stopped in front of Craigan, hand on the hilt of his simple broadsword, saluted and bowed. "A pleasure to see you, Doms Suldamik. We were informed there was a rider headed our way – although, I suspected it would be you. There aren't many that would dare to come this way alone."

Craigan grinned at the man. "Many, Captain? I didn't think anyone came this way but me."

The captain nodded. "My point exactly, Doms Suldamik," he replied in a dry tone.

Craigan laughed. "Well met, Cathis! It truly is good to see you again!"

"You as well, Doms. Though I would be remiss if I did not mention that I would prefer to be with you on the march instead of playing shepherd for these pups."

"I know, my friend – but there are very few I'd even consider trusting with this command. Besides, you've earned it. If I had you out in the field, you'd come back so scarred up that the women wouldn't dare touch you and children would scream in terror." Craigan grinned mischievously.

Cathis grunted at the friendly jab before spinning on his heel. "This way, Doms. The longer I keep this gate open, the draftier this fort gets."

As soon as the two of them crossed the drawbridge, it began to close, the sturdy chains rattling and grinding as they were reeled in by men within the protective confines of the gatehouse. Craigan could feel the eyes of his soldiers watching him through murder-holes as they passed through the gatehouse and into the fort's courtyard. The fort's main building and barracks stood against the rock face of the hill. A gatehouse had been erected around the tunnel that led to the Valley's entrance, and its iron portcullis, which served as a final defense before reaching the Valley entrance proper, was already being raised. A small smithy, standing cold at the moment, had been erected against the Eastern Wall, and stables had been built along the Western Wall. Thirty of the fort's complement of seventy-five sol-

178

diers were assembled in the center of the courtyard in three rows of ten, all at attention. The remaining men, all manning the ramparts and towers, looked down from their positions. The soldiers were clad in an array of armor, each with a green and white tabard belted at the waist. These were all men from Craigan's home realm of Surandia, many of which had served his father before him. They were loyal to him to a fault – for which Craigan was immensely thankful. He didn't trust anyone but his own men with the task of guarding the gate.

Cathis and Craigan halted before the assembled men, receiving crisp salutes from the soldiers. Both captain and doms returned the salute and the men returned to attention. Cathis then eyed his doms and asked, "We're at your disposal, Doms Suldamik. Would you care to inspect the men?"

While he normally would have taken the opportunity to inspect the fort and men as a matter of decorum, he was eager to be on his way. "Not this evening, Cathis. I have other things to attend to. I think I should be able to pay a visit to see how things are going later in the week. However, you might be able to convince me to join you for dinner when I'm done in the Valley . . . if you still have a few bottles of Velusyian Blue about?"

Cathis grunted. "As you wish, Doms. The gate is open and you may proceed at your leisure. I'll see if I can dig up a fresh bottle and have a warm meal waiting for your return."

"Deal." Craigan nodded to the men before guiding his horse around the assembly and making his way toward the tunnel at a slow trot.

The captain watched his doms vanish into the darkness of the cave mouth before grunting again. Turning to the men, he barked, "Dismissed!"

Though dark for a few paces beyond the passage's threshold, torches held in sconces that were mounted on the stone walls soon appeared at regular intervals, providing eerie, flickering light that danced hypnotically upon the rough-hewn walls. Craigan dismounted and led his horse forward, whispering soothing words to calm the nervous breathing of his painted destrider. He couldn't blame her for being anxious, given the history of the tunnel. The discovery of the passageway had been an exciting occasion as it eventually gave the domses and domas of Triclose private and direct access to the Valley. However, what they had uncovered after excavating the tunnel had horrified workers and historians alike. It was said that hundreds of partially preserved corpses had been found piled throughout the passageway, all the way to the Valley's gate. Claw marks had been found on the walls, and many of the corpses were either twisted in the horrible throws of death-by-suffocation, or showed signs of a violent struggle. In the end, it was concluded that they were the remains of the workers who had helped to build the entrance and the Valley itself. Many believed they had been sealed in the tunnel in order to preserve the entrance's secrecy. Others argued the validity of that theory; they countered with the fact that the Valley was a public place with nothing to hide, thus making such a draconian measure pointless. No matter the reason for such barbarous methods, those that both guarded and used the private entrance to the Valley always felt unnerved by the passageway.

Even now, Craigan felt like the shadows dancing on the walls were reaching out for him in anger and desperation. Adding to the disturbing atmosphere was the constant sensation of a breeze that was not there, as if a giant creature was breathing on him, carrying with it damp and oppressive air that clung to his person. As he ventured further along the tunnel, he could swear that he could make out sections of the walls and floors that were permanently stained with the blood of the executed workers. Though he didn't believe in curses or restless spirits, the atmosphere in the passage was nearly enough to make him change his beliefs. Was it enough to dissuade him from ever venturing into the Valley? Simply put – no. While the city-side entrance was a viable option, the more direct access to Doms Gravit'nas' tomb and the wonders of the Valley that the underground entrance provided were worth a bit of discomfort.

After ten minutes of traversing the winding tunnel at a steady descent, Craigan emerged into a vast, oval chamber. If the chamber had been solely lit by the torches on the walls, not only would the ceiling have been lost in shadow, but the majority of the chamber would have followed suit. To combat the difficulty in lighting the chamber, sconces mounted on iron stands had been arranged in a circle at the center of the cavern. However, while the torches certainly provided enough illumination to see by, they still fell well short of dispersing the shadows that sheathed the ceiling.

The portions of the cavern that were illuminated, however, were intriguing enough to vanquish the unseen parts from thought as effectively as the shadows hid the ceiling from sight. It was debatable which of the two objects within the chamber was the most fascinating, but the one that the torch-bearing stands surrounded was certainly one of the Valley's most unusual features despite its simplicity. Set in the ground was a marble disk that was surmounted at its center by a flawless pure-blue crystal that never seemed to dull or show the wear of time. No one had any idea what it was or what purpose it

180

served, which only added to the mystery surrounding its odd placement and lack of identifying marks; this, in turn, was what made it one of the most intriguing, if not most baffling, features of the vale.

Guiding his mount around the central torches, Craigan's attention was drawn to the other feature of interest in the cave that towered above him on the far wall. Standing nearly as tall as five average men balanced on each other's shoulders, the forged-steel doors were recessed within a relief-carved marble arch. Torchlight shimmered over the perfectly polished doors and danced over the arch's relief carvings, painting both in red and orange hues. The peak of the archway displayed the roaring dragon sigil of House Gravit'nas with grandeur, the awe-inspiring badge serving as the origination point for the finely carved and amazingly detailed dragons that twisted and turned about the length of the archway. Some of them appeared to be playing, others flying, while still others were locked in mortal combat. Despite the beauty of the craftsmanship, every doms and doma that had ever passed through the doors had been unnerved by the way the eyes of the dragons seemed to follow their every movement. Craigan felt that the long-dead artists were imparting the message that the gaze of House Gravit'nas was always on them – even in death. Whether or not that was true, for Craigan, it was inspiring to believe Doms Gravit'nas could still influence Triclose in some fashion so many years after his passing.

Craigan came to a halt and gave his nervous steed a reassuring pat on the neck before continuing to the doors alone. Even from a distance, it was easy to see and be drawn in by the etchings at eye level where the doors met. Halting in front of the etchings, Craigan reached out and trailed his fingers over them reverently. Consisting of two concentric rings surrounding a central carving, the outer ring was filled with writing in a language lost to modern-day Triclose. The strokes were intricate, beautiful, and possessed a fluid grace that was breathtaking. As for the central carving, it had been carefully crafted to represent two dragons circling each other with their gazes focused out upon the world even as their taloned feet grasped at each other in what some thought was battle. Like the archway, the detail was exquisite; furthermore, the technique used to create it was unmatched and as lost to time as the language was.

It was the inner ring, however, that was the focus of Craigan's attention. Fourteen circular recessions, each one representing one of the original Houses of Triclose, flowed around the central carving. Each circle was evenly spaced and about half-a-finger deep. At the back of each recession, there was a medallion-like imprint that varied slightly from circle to circle. As Craigan's fingers hovered over the top left circle, his jaw locked with anger. The recession belonged to House Merandith. He had tried to have it removed at one point, but nothing had been able to scar the surface. Even attempts at filling the circle had been rebuffed – molten metal refused to harden, and patches simply fell away.

Swallowing his anger, Craigan moved back to his saddlebags and rummaged around before pulling out a thick black hood. Whispering soothing words to his mount, he then slipped the hood over her eyes. Once he was sure his horse was calm and couldn't see, he returned to his saddlebags and plucked out a round amulet made of silver that matched the imprint in the top-right recession. A leather thong was threaded through a small circular gap in the top of the amulet, allowing him to wear it around his neck when he chose to.

Turning the amulet over in his hand, he examined the precise cuts that worked together to form the lone rune in the center of the amulet. The amulet had been handed down from generation to generation, never once needing polish or showing signs of wear and tear. Each of the original Houses owned a similar amulet that matched one of the fourteen circles on the door. With no practical way to acquire the amulets of the traitorous Houses, and no known way to fill the holes in the door, the garrison that now guarded the entrance also served as Craigan's answer to denying the traitorous Houses potential access to the Valley. Stealing the amulets had been suggested to him at some point, but he had dismissed the notion, figuring the chance of success was extremely slim. He had even briefly considered assassination to remove the Houses' rulers, but the amulets were attuned to the blood of each House, which meant he'd have to kill every last blood relative of the offending domses and domas to ensure the amulets could not be used. The task would have been daunting, and the results couldn't be guaranteed given the number of bastard children that were possibly lurking about. As for destroying the amulets . . . his was the only one he could test such measures on, and he was not about to risk his prized possession.

With a reverence that was reserved for the amulet alone, Craigan returned to the door and placed the amulet within its parent receptacle. For the briefest of moments, nothing happened. Then, as Craigan took a couple of steps back, the amulet began to glow with a glorious golden halo. Just as suddenly as it started to glow, the golden light winked out and the amulet appeared to have merged with the door. The first time he had witnessed the process, he had been overcome with the fear that he had forever lost a relic that was sacred to his House; thankfully, he quickly had his fears alleviated.

Suddenly, the thin sliver that delineated one door from the other began to radiate a dim white light. The light crept up the tiny gap between the mammoth doors and began to spread across their surfaces like water on a well-oiled table. As the glow progressed, it grew in intensity and illuminated the surrounding area as if he were standing beneath the noonday sun. Finally, without even the slightest creak or groan of protest, the ancient doors swung inward, and a blinding light spilt forth.

When the light finally vanished and the colors stopped dancing in front of his eyes, Craigan was able to make out what laid beyond the gate. The view that greeted his eyes was as removed from the current season as it was from the landscape surrounding Chalin. Before him, the vibrant-green grass of a small glade swayed in a breeze that only blew within the Valley. Where it had been sunset with cloudy skies outside the Valley, the inside of the vale was bathed with pristine bluish-silver moonlight from an unidentifiable source, and bright pinpricks of starlight glittered like diamonds in the clear night sky. Thick forest was visible in the distance, delineating the edge of the clearing. Hovering in the air at the edge of the forest, glowing orbs marked the start of a path and flanked it as it disappeared into the depths of the woods.

Grinning ear to ear, Craigan returned to his mount and removed the hood before leading her through the gate. Whispering reassuring words to her, he let go of the reins, allowing her to roam the glade and feed on the tall, luscious grass. Returning to the gate, he touched his amulet and closed his eyes, bidding it to return to him. There was a small flare of light and an audible click as the amulet came loose and fell into Craigan's hand. As the doors slowly began to swing closed, Craigan slid the amulet over his head and tucked it under his tunic before turning and striding toward the path.

The Utherian Valley was not only the final resting place of the only man to hold the Jade Throne and to rule over the entirety of Triclose, but it also hosted the tombs of every doms and doma to pass since Gravit'nas' death. If one believed the fables surrounding its construction, then the Valley was truly a miracle. Though none could agree on the exact location of Doms Gravit'nas' seat of power before Chalin's construction, it was rumored that he had always ruled from the same site and the Valley had simply been built upon the bones of an older city. Supposedly, great powers had been called upon to alter the gently rolling plains of the Chalin Sea, raising the mountainous hills and sinking the land beyond them. Some stories even said it had taken mere hours to create. The skeptics scoffed at such notions, contending that only Deo himself was capable of such actions, and that no single man was important enough for a god to faun over in such a manner. As Craigan strolled along the path, it was clear to him that the Valley was Deo touch, if only because he scoffed at the notion that the entire Valley had been constructed by men in mere hours. Origins aside, those that had visited or relied on the Valley for sustenance found it impossible to deny the majesty and magical aura about the place.

The Valley was considered one of the most tranquil places in the land – out of touch with reality and frozen in perpetual spring. A bubbling stream, originating from a lake at the base of a glorious waterfall, coursed through the landscape, its offshoots providing nourishment to the green grasses and luscious forests that covered the hills and valley floor like a cozy blanket. Those same forests played host to a variety of animals. The upper hills of the Valley were inhabited by deer and a few wolves, all of which had grown wary of people due to steady hunting. In contrast, the animals that occupied the dense woods of the valley floor coexisted peacefully with the occasional visitor, paying little or no heed to the few humans that visited; in fact, it was as if the animals had no real idea that the visitors were there as long as the people stayed along the paths and within the areas they were intended to be. Like the tombs, these wonders had once been shared by all of Triclose, but they now solely helped to sustain Chalin. Of only slightly more importance to Craigan, it served as his private escape – a place that would always provide seclusion from the evils of the real world.

As the path took him deeper into the Valley, it eventually split – one path winding its way north toward the tombs of Triclose's departed domses and domas, and the other path falling in line with the stream. He took the path along the stream without pause and was soon greeted by the soothing melody of the crickets' nightly performance. A gentle breeze swept through the forest like a mother's loving caress, the stream's own melody dancing playfully in the air. Craigan stopped and crouched next to the stream, watching the reflections of the blue and white wisps frolicking in the air above him, their glow bathing the area in soothing, colorful light. The Valley was truly a completely different world – nowhere else could wisps be found other than in children's tales, and nowhere else could such tranquility exist.

A small smile touched his lips. Why it did, he didn't know – but it felt good to smile.

Leaning over, Craigan dunked his head into the stream and pulled it out after a moment. Gasping for breath, he laid back in the lush grass and gazed up into the star-filled sky. Feeling refreshed by the cool water, he let his gaze alight on the wisps dancing hypnotically through the air. He felt like he could just lie there and let all his cares simply slip away. A lesser man might even have given in to such temptations; however, he knew he couldn't shirk his responsibilities for long. He indulged himself for a few more moments before climbing back to his feet with a soft, reluctant sigh and continuing on his way. For the next fifteen minutes, he slowly walked alongside the stream, following every twist and turn, the wisps dancing merrily alongside him. Then, as if by magic, he emerged from the woods and came to a halt, his breath stolen by the sight before him.

Bluish-silver moonlight slid across the mirrored surface of the large, pristine lake, whose waters lapped gently at the shore. A myriad of wisps danced and darted over the surface of the rippling waters, providing a light show unlike anything he'd ever seen. In the distance, shrouded from sight by the night, a tumbling waterfall roared as it emptied into the lake. Before him, an elegantly crafted stone bridge arched from his side of the shore out to the island in the center of the lake, the white stone of the bridge seemingly aglow with moonlight. All that was enough to enrapture a person no matter their status, but, as Craigan reverently strode forward, it was the object floating over the island that captured his full attention.

The Sky Tomb – the final resting place of Doms Luthur Gravit'nas. To most, it was just a legend that they would only know of in word, but never see. Majestic in all aspects, no other creation on Triclose came close to matching its haunting beauty. Suspended in the air a few feet off the ground, it was inclined slightly to face the bridge. A frame of solid gold, glowing softly in the moonlight, supported the six-sided coffin's clear crystal panels. The panels caught the myriad of light from both the heavens and the wisps before casting it about in a cornucopia of color. As Craigan crossed the bridge, his footsteps echoing off the stonework, he could see the runes that were etched into the crystal radiating a soft light. There also seemed to be a gentle, warm hum emanating from the casket.

Halting a few paces from the casket, Craigan bowed reverently to the man entombed within. Preserved by the magic of the Tomb, Doms Luthur Gravit'nas' body was clearly visible through the panels. Though long dead, he look as he had before he had passed on – his skin and blonde hair untouched by the ravages of time. Though his eyes were shut, it appeared that he was sleeping rather than a soulless vessel. Adding to the grandeur of the Tomb, Luthur's body was encased in finely crafted, gold-plated platemail that had been meticulously etched with filigree by the finest of craftsmen. The gem-studded hilt of a ceremonial longsword was clutched in his hands over his heart, the polished blade of which extended to just past his feet. Craigan stood speechless before his hero, awe stealing his faculties. Though he had stood in this spot time and again, its grandeur never seemed to lose its power over him.

Unable to speak, Craigan's eyes slowly drifted downward to where a marble pillar had been erected. Standing waist high, runes were carved around the perimeter of the top face of the pillar, framing two phrases —

*'By blood, by honor and by deed, this I swear. . .'*

*'Hope'*

Not one scholar knew what the first phrase meant or even what it might stand for, though many believed it might have been the motto of House Gravit'nas. It was the second, simple statement that resonated with Craigan the most. *Hope.* Such a simple word, yet it implied much and carried a weight few were willing to bare. It was easy enough to understand why such a potent word was carved into the plaque. Luthur had been the hope of the land — a shining beacon in dark times. Craigan liked to think he shared that place with his idol, though he had no delusion that he could truly equal such a historic man. Where Luthur had been the hope of his generation, Craigan could only aspire to be that for his.

Time slipped by as Craigan stood in the light cast by the Tomb, seeking to absorb all that such a simple phrase meant. Finally, with a heartfelt sigh, he cast his gaze upon Luthur's entombed form. "*'Hope'*, your plaque says. Your final, lasting message to us. I'm afraid that time has not seen that message embraced. It still puzzles those that care to think on it as to why you never married and produced an heir, or why you never spoke of a successor. Our histories tell us little, and our stories are flights of fancy. What is without question or debate, however, is that we have been fighting over your throne for more years than any one of us dare to remember.

"Hope," he chuckled softly. "I'm afraid many are beginning to lose it. I even find myself wondering why I still fight at times. Kale is an opponent similar to his father, but seems impossible to kill. Whatever we throw at him, he rebuffs. He's a snake in the grass, striking when we least expect and with efficiency I can only envy. Even though I do believe that Kale has grown wearier of the fighting than I, there is a tenacity in him that reminds me of the stories of your glory days." Craigan sighed deeply.

"The stress has begun to show in my forces . . . as well as in me. We've fought for so long that we have begun to grow complacent, and we are losing battles that we shouldn't. Just the other day, we lost a battle because we failed to notice a missing cavalry unit until it was too late. Given the way things have gone . . . if I were a lesser man, I would consider a peaceful surrender." Craigan's fists clenched at his sides. "That isn't an option, however. What is owed to your memory will not allow for such weakness! Triclose needs strength and an unwavering resolve to unite it! Kale might be an excellent general, but he is not fit to sit on the Jade Throne! Please, if you are out there somewhere listening, give me the strength to carry your message of hope forward! Give me the courage to finish what you started and bring lasting peace to all of Triclose!"

Glancing skyward, he unclenched his fists and sighed again, letting the tension drain from his body. He said nothing for a time, his eyes staring wistfully at the stars above almost as if he would receive an answer to his pleas. He knew there would be no answer; after all, the dead had no power to answer prayers. Still . . . it didn't hurt to hope.

Finally, he returned his gaze to the Tomb and said, "It looks as if my time here draws to a close . . . and I must once again leave the peace of your Tomb. I know your heart would weep for what has happened to your land, and I swear to you – I will find a way to restore Triclose to its former glory." He let the oath linger in the air for a moment before adding, "Rest in peace, my doms."

Bowing reverently, Craigan took two steps back before straightening and pivoting on his heel. Jaw locked in grim, renewed determination, he strode back toward the woods, every fiber of his being rededicated to his mission. He would bring hope to the land – and no one would stand in his way.

# Chapter Eight

**T**all and proud, the nearly thirty-three-summers-old man walked the battlements deep in thought. A slender face with brown eyes and short red hair was a picture of deep contemplation. His green and white tabard was faded and showed signs of heavy, long-term usage; the meticulous maintenance that had sustained the tabard, now obvious to even the untrained eye due to the sheer volume of repairs, was a tribute to the skilled seamstresses that had mended the garment over the years. Chainmail glinting in the afternoon sunlight, he paused in his trip around the battlements and leaned against the top of the western wall before turning his gaze to the open expanse around the fort.

The landscape was relatively flat and boring, the vastness disrupted by the occasional rise or copse of trees that sprung up like a pimple on the oily face of an adolescent. The fort occupied one of the largest of the rises, granting it a fairly unobstructed view in all directions. Four sturdy oak walls of robust pylons – sharpened at their peak and standing nearly forty feet tall and three paces thick – protected the fort on all sides. Two gates, one in the east wall and one in the west, provided egress to and from the fort, each portal flanked by towers. Battlements, which were sturdy enough to support iron cauldrons of burning pitch when needed, ran the length of each wall. A one-story command building and barracks for two-hundred men occupied the main courtyard along with stables and the facilities to handle repairs and the day-to-day needs of the men. Like many of the border forts, its job was to serve as a staging ground and to slow any large enemy troop movements. Granted, a siege of substantial force would easily overrun the garrison, but the shear fact that the fortification would have to be dealt with would waste enemy time and men.

A dry, weary smile crept onto his thin lips. He had quite thoroughly enjoyed his command at this particular fort. Not only did he like the view, but the fort had rarely seen combat. In fact, the closest battle had ever drawn to them under his command was when he had received word that Doms Suldamik appeared to be pulling back to Chalin. He had put the men on alert as soon as he received the report. If Kale chose to pursue, then his beloved command would have to be dealt with. Thankfully, it hadn't come to that. Not that he was opposed to fighting – especially against House Merandith – he just didn't like all the senseless deaths in the last few years; the betrayals and apathy that seemed to be plaguing House Suldamik had been costly and left a sour taste in his mouth. What bothered him the most, however, was that with the reclamation of the eastern edge of the Contested Territories by House Merandith, his border fort now stood as the only significant defense between the Five Stars' current position and Chalin. He had no doubt that unless something changed drastically over the winter, the wonderful blessing of peace that sheltered his command would be shattered come spring or summer.

Turning around, he leaned against the wall and watched the activity within the sturdy fortifications. All about the grounds, the proud men of the Jade Talons went about their business with efficiency. The forge was afire with activity, and two squads drilled in the courtyard. He had doubled the patrols both abroad and on the wall ever since Doms Suldamik had retreated, and he was remiss to slacken the vigil until winter set in fully; thus, the privacy to be found on the wall was mostly limited to his inner thoughts as the battlements were crowded with chainmail-armored soldiers making their rounds. Each and everyone were loyal to House Suldamik and their doms captain, and ready and willing to die for the cause – or so he liked to believe. Even as the guards offered him salutes and greetings as they walked past him, he knew that their willingness to sacrifice their lives for the Suldamik cause could never be fully tested until the moment was upon them. Most of the men under his command had been through the crucible of battle more than enough to harden their resolve and prove their merit. However, there would always be the few that would turn and run when confronted by the horrors of war. Strip away all the stories of overblown honor and glory, and soldiers soon found that war was nothing but a macabre butcher shop.

Satisfied that everything was moving smoothly within the fort, he turned his attention back to the landscape, his eyes searching the horizon. Two weeks ago, Doms Suldamik had sent him orders, along with two-hundred light cavalry and footmen, to begin preparing for raids within Roselia and Tiliea. As there wasn't enough room within the walls to house the large influx of soldiers, the newest arrivals had been forced to camp outside the western gate. Thankfully, there had been only a few halfhearted complaints about the lack of accommodations in the beginning. However, as the days dragged on, the grumblings were growing louder, and he honestly couldn't blame them. They were all eager to get underway and had expected to have received orders by now to do so. He knew it wasn't like Craigan to wait so long to give the execution order on something so important to his long-term goals.

That morning, he had begun to seriously contemplate initiating the raids simply to avoid the risk of the unrest amongst the raiders becoming a problem. To his instant and profound relief, one of his scouts had returned late in the morning with word of an approaching rider bearing Suldamik colors. Once the scout's report was confirmed upon his partner's return, orders had been dispatched to the raiders' commander, Fulin Castin of House Ithikia, to begin preparing for departure. It had made the doms captain grin inwardly at how quickly the commander jumped into action. House Ithikia had contributed very little to the war effort so far, and the crispness with which they went about their business was refreshing. Though he didn't know how well the desert-dwelling Pelasians would handle a northern winter, the fact that they were ready and willing to take on this task brought hope to his heart. For now, though, all he could do was watch from the ramparts for what he believed were the orders to begin the raids.

From off to his right, he heard the approach of heavy footfalls. Looking away from the empty horizon, he saw his second-in-command approaching. Simply known as Shinks, he was one of the rare desert dwellers to have made his home north of the Dragonspine, though none knew why he had abandoned his home. Unlike many of his fellow Pelasians, he stood well over six feet, was built like a mountain in contrast to their leaner build, and his scarred face was wide and square-jawed. If not for the hints of white hair on his shaved pate and his amber eyes, he could have easily been mistaken for a Highlander who'd spent too much time in the sun. Skin the color of mud was decorated with tribal tattoos and an array of scars, and part of his upper lip had been torn away in some small skirmish in the early years of the war. Studded leather armor and spiked gauntlets added to his imposing presence.

However, the full-moon axe strapped to his back was what terrified most men. Wickedly curved and honed to a razor-fine edge, the twin blades were mounted on a thick ironwood shaft that was reinforced with leather and steel, while two long hawk feathers hung from leather straps strung through the axe's spiked pommel. Any normal man would struggle to wield it with two hands. Shinks, however, swung it about with one hand as if it were nothing.

For years, the man's skill with an axe had earned him the right to serve as an Academy instructor, but his brutal teaching methods had been frowned upon for so long that when a student finally died under his tutelage, he had been expelled. Craigan's father had recruited Shinks, despite his disgraceful exit from the Academy, and put him in charge of training his son. Craigan had been brutally beaten under Shinks' uncompromising tutelage, but many firmly believed the drive and stubbornness that Craigan showed as a man was thanks to such draconian teaching methods. No matter Shinks' past and origins, the doms captain was glad to have such a hardened veteran under his command.

The giant of a man stopped next to him. "Doms Captain Jeinis," rumbled Shinks' deep voice in greeting.

Jeinis nodded. "Well met, Shinks. What brings you up here?" He laughed in his mind at the absurdity of the contrast between the two of them. He sounded almost feminine when compared with the bass voice of Shinks.

"I caught wind of a rumor that we're expecting a messenger today," Shinks said, to which Jeinis nodded in the affirmative. "Do you think he'll have the orders?"

Offering a casual shrug, he replied, "In all likelihood. This has been an exceptionally long waiting period for Craigan. I can't believe he'd want to push these raids off any more than he already has."

Shinks nodded slightly, the muscles in his neck and jaw flexing. "I agree. Patience was never his strong suit. He used to wear bruises like a woman's face paint because of his rashness." Jeinis laughed at the imagery. Shinks glanced at him dryly, the faintest hint of a smile on his lips. "Laughing at one's doms could be viewed as dishonorable or even treasonous."

Jeinis snorted. "You stopped scaring me long ago, Shinks. Besides, I think you've had your fair share of laughs at our doms' expense."

Shinks conceded the point with a slight nod of his head. "True. But I'm not the one that was considering action without orders. Does impatientness run in the Suldamik blood?"

A soft laugh escaped Jeinis' thin lips. "You have me there. If those men have to sit around too much longer, I'm sure we'll have quite a bit of trouble on our hands. As for impatience, the Corandit's are so far removed from the main bloodline that I hardly think we could be considered even distant family."

Shinks grinned. "Indeed. So, when do you expect the rider?"

Jeinis looked out into the distance for a moment before suddenly grinning. Pointing at a dark speck on the horizon that was moving steadily in their direction, he said, "I'd say that's him right there. At that pace, I'd say he'll be here in about an hour, maybe two, depending on how hard he's pushed his horse."

"Good," Shinks said with satisfaction. "Why don't you join me for some lunch? We can meet with the messenger afterward. I hear the kitchen has prepared a passable meal for once."

Jeinis clapped Shinks on a muscular shoulder and laughed. "That would be a first, wouldn't it?"

The two men made their way to the nearest staircase and descended from the battlements. Jeinis left orders with the western gate's guards to retrieve the raider's commander and himself upon the messenger's arrival, and to also bring the messenger directly to the war room. He and Shinks then made their way toward the northern wall where the simple command building, barracks and mess hall were located.

There was nothing about any of the buildings that screamed opulence or luxury, for function and durability were preeminent in their design. Each building was walled with robust, well-fitted timbers, while narrow windows that could be shuttered against the night and inclement weather provided additional light during the day. Furthermore, the buildings were fitted with clay-shingled roofs that would not only insulate the fort's occupants from the weather better than traditional roofing, but would also significantly reduce the chances of the structures catching fire during a siege – which meant one less thing to worry about in such nightmarish circumstances.

The mess hall, located between the command building and the barracks, was the smallest of the three structures and only able to hold fifty men at best. As the two officers entered, and their eyes adjusted to the dimmer light, they saw that only about ten soldiers sat on the benches of the crude longtables that were arranged in two orderly columns of three within the single-room mess. Along the left-hand wall, there were three small tables that were reserved for officers, none of which were occupied at that moment. The candles at each table remained unlit since there was enough natural light spilling through the simple windows to see by. Fresh straw and sawdust covered the wooden floor, the boards of which creaked as the two men made their way to the back of the hall where pleasant aromas were seeping from the kitchen door. A long, simple, food-laden table separated the dining area from the kitchen that was secluded in the rear of the building. Arranged along the length of the table was a spread of food that consisted of a large iron cauldron of soup, platters of meat, a few loaves of bread, and cups of water. The smells of what appeared to be fresh fare made Jeinis' stomach growl with anticipation.

The fort cook stood behind the table, wiping his hands on his apron as if he'd just come from the kitchen. Scrawny and aging, the veteran was dressed in richly stained clothing beneath an apron that

192

was too big for him. Smiling a mostly toothless grin at the two, his dark eyes glowed with mirth as he said, "Good day ta ye, Captain and Commander. What can I be doing for ye?"

Jeinis smiled broadly. "Well met, Drudger. I guess it all depends on if what you've got qualifies as food."

The old man cursed and scratched at what remained of his white hair. "I'm hurt, sir. I be providing ye all with tha finest eats in these parts, and all I get is complaining. . . . Begging yer pardon, Captain," he added at the end, dipping his head.

Shinks grunted in amusement. "Your food is *the* only thing we can attempt to eat around these parts, cook."

Drudger pointed a bony finger at Shinks and winked at him. "Exactly! Complaining ain't gonna get ye nothing! Ye all need to learn to treat an old man better and appreciate what little he can offer!" He clapped his boney hands together and rubbed them. "Now, what can I get ye? We've got potato soup with a few spare vegetables I found lying around. There's even some fresh-off-the-skewer rahken, as well as some day-old bread – still soft, mind you."

Jeinis chuckled. "It sounds delicious, Drudger. I'm just glad it's not dog or horse this time."

Drudger scowled as he spooned soup into two bowls. "Bah! Fix it right and no one's tha wiser! Horse meat is better than most of ye deserve!"

Smiling, Jeinis handed a platter of rahken and half a loaf of bread to Shinks before filling his own platter. "So, I guess that means that having rahken should be like basking in Deo's presence then?"

Drudger muttered something under his breath and slid the two bowls toward them, the murky brown liquid sloshing over the edges. Cleaning his hands on his already-stained apron, he barked, "Bah! Go on ye two. I've got enough problems without ye look'n down yer noses at this fine cook'n!"

Nodding his thanks to Drudger, Jeinis picked up his bowl and platter. Shinks, however, paused for a moment and sniffed at the bowl. Arching an eyebrow, he said, "I know an excellent recipe for adding some bite to a soup. Ask me sometime, and I'll show you how to prepare the scorpions."

Drudger blanched and cursed loudly before storming off through the back door into the kitchen, drawing a throaty laugh from Shinks.

Winding their way between the longtables toward one of the officer's tables setup in a corner, they acknowledged the nods and greetings from the other soldiers. After setting his food down, Shinks returned to the bar and retrieved two mugs before settling in. Though the hall was mostly empty, word of the impending arrival of the messenger appeared to have spread and was the main topic of conversation. Given what they could overhear, and the tone of the conversations, it seemed most of the men agreed that the raids would begin soon. Jeinis knew that as far as most of the fort's regulars were concerned, this couldn't happen soon enough. The raiders were an extra drain on resources, making an already structured and rationed setting even more uncomfortable.

Jeinis noticed a couple of fairly raw recruits talking amongst themselves at a table just behind them. Their words were those of youthful exuberance, giving voice to their hopes that the men of the garrison might be called into action as well. This drew amused smiles from Jeinis and Shinks as they ate and listened. They knew the inexperienced amongst them craved action and adventure, and eagerly awaited their shot at House Merandith. Though Shinks and Jeinis applauded such enthusiasm, they were all too aware of the horrors of war; once the killing began, they knew that many of those that longed for battle would quickly find their world shaken – their views irrevocably and horrifyingly changed.

The rest of lunch saw the two officers fritter away their time as they talked about family and reminisced. Shinks, despite his gruff exterior, had a huge heart when it came to his wife and five-year-old daughter. They owned a small farm far to the south, nestled within the foothills of the Dragonspine Mountains. Their distance from the war always left Shinks with a peaceful heart and allowed him to commit to his duty without reservation. However, like many of the other soldiers who had families awaiting their return, he longed to be home with his wife and daughter.

Jeinis could sympathize with his second-in-command. He had a lovely wife of his own awaiting him at their modest estate in Chalin. Craigan had bestowed the magnificent house and its lands upon him for services rendered. The gift had significantly elevated their standing in life, but neither he nor his wife knew how to manage such a large house. He hated that she had to deal with it, and everything that came with their new position and riches, on her own. While he hoped that she had found trustworthy help to manage the estate, he desperately wanted to be there for her. However, his loyalty and duty to House Suldamik came first. If he ever found himself regretting his commitment to his job and position, he simply reminded himself that if House Merandith won the war, then they stood to lose everything. Thus, he pushed aside such thoughts except for times like this.

An hour passed, and their conversation lasted much longer than their food. Though they teased Drudger about his cooking, not a morsel was left on their table. Since their arrival, the mess hall had filled up with off-duty men trickling in for lunch, filling the small hall with a rising din of voices. Without interrupting their conversation, Shinks and Jeinis acknowledge the salutations of the new arrivals and soon found that they could barely hear themselves over the increased racket. Just as they were getting ready to relinquish their seats, a young man adorned with chainmail slipped in the door and made directly for them.

The brown-haired lad, barely able to shave from the looks of him, stopped at their table and snapped a quick salute. "Doms Captain Corandit and Commander Shinks. A messenger has just arrived and is being shown to the war room. A runner has been dispatched to inform Commander Castin that you wish his presence as well."

Jeinis nodded. "Good. Take a moment and get yourself some lunch. Afterward, take some food to the other gate guards – no sense in making them settle for the dregs of Drudger's cooking."

The young man smiled broadly. "Yes, sir!" He saluted and quickly moved to the long meal line.

Jeinis smiled as he turned to Shinks. "Well, shall we find out what Doms Suldamik has to say?"

Shinks nodded as he stood. "Lead the way."


The war room was located in the center of the command building, adjacent to Jeinis' office. It was a modest-sized, square room with little in the way of excessive décor. Candelabra in the four corners of the room and two lanterns on the central table bathed the interior in warm light. Large bookshelves stood against the rear wall, filled with books on military strategy and an assortment of maps and notes. The large table, which was made of oak, was surmounted by an equally large map of Triclose that was anchored at opposite corners by the two tabletop lanterns. Eight chairs of simple fashion surrounded the table. A door on the right wall offered access to Jeinis' office, and another door on the front wall provided admittance to the room proper.

Hinges squeaking from lack of proper maintenance, the main door opened to admit Jeinis and Shinks. Having arrived ahead of time, the messenger and Fulin were seated opposite each other at the table. Both stood and saluted upon Jeinis' arrival. The captain waved them back to their seats before he sat himself at the head of the table and Shinks took up the seat to his right.

Commander Fulin Castin of House Ithikia, when standing, was nearly six feet in height – tall for a Pelasian. Middle-aged, he was a whipcord-strong man who had the look and air of a caviler. Clad in a thin gray tunic and black breeches, his highly polished boots were only surpassed by the sheen of his spurs. Leather bracers, with a rearing stallion stitched into their backs, encased his forearms. His white hair was cut close to his bronzed scalp, and his square jaw sported a neatly trimmed beard. Piercing amber eyes, which always seemed to demand attention and respect, were gleaming with the possibility of receiving the orders he had been anxiously awaiting.

The messenger, having collapsed back into his chair, was Fulin's opposite. Short and lanky, the boy was no older than twenty summers and showed the signs of a forced ride – his riding leathers and face were caked in dust and mud, his hair was windblown, and his skin was burnt from the sun and wind. Dull green eyes showed his exhaustion better than his slouched posture; however, despite his fatigue, his grimy hands clung resolutely to a weather-beaten satchel.

Jeinis eyed the satchel with anticipation as he said, "Good afternoon, gentlemen. I hope that our small gathering will prove beneficial to all." Switching his gaze to the messenger, he added, "I believe you carry orders for us?"

The boy sat up a little straighter and nodded. "Yes, Doms Captain Corandit." Undoing the satchels straps, he reached in and pulled forth a letter sealed with green wax that was pressed with the talon seal of House Suldamik. Handing the letter to Jeinis, he said, "With Doms Suldamik's compliments and best wishes. He also says to tell you that should you have anything to report, I can carry it to him. Also, he says to inform you that in order to rest his men and replenish supplies for the winter, he is returning to Chalin until further notice."

Jeinis nodded, fighting to keep his brown eyes from wandering to the letter in his hand. "Very good. You're dismissed for now. Have the guard outside escort you to the mess hall for food and then find you a bed for the evening. I'll call upon you in the morning."

The messenger stood and bowed. "Thank you, Doms Captain." Tired strides took the boy to the door where he exited quietly.

As soon as the door groaned shut, Jeinis broke the wax seal on the letter and eagerly read it over. A broad smile spread over his face as his eyes skimmed the elegantly penned dispatch. Placing the missive before him, he looked at the other two men with satisfaction. "Well gentlemen – these are the orders we have been waiting for." Relieved and excited expressions greeted the news. Standing, Jeinis leaned over the map and pointed to spots along Roselia's Southwestern border as he said, "Fulin – you and your men are to depart before dawn and cross into Roselia here, here, here, and here. Once safely within Roselia's borders, half your men are to then proceed into Tiliea. You are to cause as much damage and confusion as possible. There are to be no prolonged engagements. I would advise staying close to the Roselia-Lerilia border. While the Merandiths have technically reclaimed it, I highly doubt they've been able to establish law and order this quickly. It should still provide an unobserved corridor for the men you send to Tiliea should they need it.

"Doms Suldamik has given you free rein over the operation once you are within enemy territory, but your top priority is to draw attention to yourselves without getting caught. He wants Merandith's attention split and confused. If at all possible, discover supply routes and disrupt them. The mission's length is at your discretion, but he urges caution. He would rather you withdraw if the situation gets too dangerous than to lose men unnecessarily." Jeinis took his seat again, awaiting Fulin's response.

Stroking his bearded chin, Fulin stood to examine the map. He agreed with Craigan's orders, and had even expected them to be along those lines. Hit-and-run warfare was a specialty of the dessert tribes, which made his charge that much more important. His would be the first real action any of House Ithikia had seen; more importantly, it would prove their worth to Doms Suldamik and Doma Ithikia. However, his knowledge of Roselia's terrain was limited even with the firsthand reports he received from locals under his command. He also had his fears of how the winter snows, which he'd heard so much about, would affect their ability to move and fight. Snow and sand were hard to maneuver in, but that was where the similarity ended. The majority of the men under his command were dessert dwellers, and while the desert nights could get extremely cold, he had no real idea how they would respond to the frigid conditions. However, orders were orders, and he wasn't going to disgrace his doma.

Fears aside, the chosen border crossings appeared to be excellent – the terrain appeared to be mostly flat, which would expedite their progress, and there was dense forest that they could use to hide their movements. This would go a long way to both getting everyone in position with very little chance of being observed, and commencing with their mission before the snows got heavy.

Finally, he nodded his agreement. "Doms Suldamik has my compliments on this plan. We'll push hard to get into position, and the weather looks to remain good at least for another week. Assuming the weather holds, and with these crossing points, I can have my men into Roselia in two days. Reaching Tiliea's borders will take longer – I figure six weeks after entering Roselia . . . faster if we're lucky."

Jeinis nodded. "Good. The quicker you're in place, the sooner House Merandith will have to deal with the war on another front. Just be careful – the further north you go, the more patrols you will encounter." He paused, and then hesitantly asked, "I mean no disrespect, but are you sure your men can handle the snow?"

Fulin grunted. "None taken. I have my fears as well, but the desert teaches one to adapt to survive, or die. The cold may sting us, but we *will* adapt. We'll be operating in small, independent groups to keep Merandith guessing. We'll sting them hard and often, giving them no choice but to deal with us." He grinned slyly, revealing teeth chipped by the pommel of an enemy sword. "Of course, he'll have to find me first."

Jeinis returned the confident smile. Shinks, on the other hand, eyed Fulin carefully. He had no desire to dampen the cheerful prospects of this venture, but the practical side of him felt it necessary to mention what was causing his stomach to churn with unease. "Let's not get ahead of ourselves. If the situation within both nations is the same as it has been for the past year, then your job will not be even the least bit easy."

The smile slowly vanished from Fulin's face and he asked skeptically, "What does he mean, Jeinis?"

Jeinis ran his hand over his short red hair and sighed. He knew where Shinks was going with this, and he was perturbed that it hadn't occurred to him as well. "Not that a man of your talents can't handle it. Shinks was just urging caution since you'll more or less be operating on hearsay."

Fulin's brow furrowed in consternation. "What in Deo's name are you two so afraid to mention?"

Jeinis shook his head. "We're not afraid – it's just that the mere mention of him makes my skin crawl." He shook his head to clear the shiver that was running up his spine. "We're telling you to be careful of Kale's Deo-forsaken cat demon."

Fulin raised an eyebrow. "Cat demon? Surely you jest? That sounds more like some drunken tavern banter."

Shinks shook his head adamantly. "We do not. The creature is real enough – I saw him with my own eyes years ago. His skin is near the color of snow, with two chunks of blue ice for eyes, and long, pointed ears. He moved like silk and struck like lightning. He also carried the largest bow I've ever seen, and I'd swear he could shoot a man in the eye from three hundred yards."

Fulin paled. "You jest. . . ."

Face grim, Shinks stated, "I do not. There is no doubt about his existence . . . or the carnage he can reap."

Fulin cleared his throat as color seeped back into his cheeks. "Does this creature have a name by which I can call it before I kill it?" he asked with feigned self-confidence.

Meeting Fulin's gaze, Shinks saw through his fellow Pelasian's façade as he replied emphatically, "His name is Allanian – remember it well."

"Allanian," whispered Fulin before smiling brightly in another vain attempt to hide his unease. "Yes, well, I thank you for this warning, and I shall keep it in the forefront of my mind. Now, if you'll excuse me, I'll see to readying my men for our departure. Gentlemen."

Jeinis nodded in dismissal and Fulin bowed before taking his leave.

"Well . . . what do you think?" asked Jeinis when the door shut firmly behind Fulin.

"About what? His reaction to Allanian?"

"No – Craigan pulling back to Chalin."

Shinks drummed his fingers on the table. "I believe the reasons Craigan put forth, but I'd bet my farm Merandith bloodied his nose."

Jeinis sighed. "I'd come to the same conclusion."

His second-in-command grinned. "Cheer up. I'd also bet my farm that Merandith came away bloodied too. Besides," his deep voice rumbled on, "with winter coming, it is a good time to do this. The raiding parties will be able to do more than the mobile army."

Jeinis conceded the point after a moment of thought. "You're right. Craigan knows what he's doing." A sudden chuckle escaped him as Fulin's reaction to Shinks' story crept to mind. "Did you see the look on Fulin's face when you told that story? I'd have sworn he was going to faint. The Ithikiains can be a bit superstitious, and the mention of a cat demon . . ." he shook his head and chuckled in amusement. The chortle died just as quickly as it arrived when he saw the haunted look in Shinks' eyes. "Look – I've heard the rumors too. But you can't be serious? No one moves that fast, and no bow can shoot that far, that accurately."

Shinks nodded his head slowly. "I'm very serious, Jeinis. I bore witness to the horror he can bestow." He pointed to his right shoulder and, despite the fact Jeinis could see nothing but clothing, declared, "There is a scar under here that he gave me. I tried to get between him and Craigan's father. The arrow went clean through and struck Doms Suldamik in the heart."

Jeinis simply stared at Shinks in amazed disbelief. There was nothing he knew of that could do such a thing. The amount of force needed to send an arrow through an armored man and into another was inconceivable outside of a ballista. Yet, he knew Shinks wasn't one to exaggerate. Instead of challenging the statement, he simply inquired in awe, "You were at the first Battle of Sparros? I never knew that."

"I was." Shinks clamped his hands together tightly. "Pray you never encounter that demon. Most battles you worry about what's in front of you, but with that creature . . ." Shinks trailed off, shutting his eyes in an attempt to block out the memories of the horrible screams and the elusive killing machine that haunted his dreams. Opening his eyes, he found his captain's gaze and held it. "Just pray you never encounter him. If you do – and if at all possible – run the other way. . . . Run as hard as you can."

# Chapter Nine

**N**ight's cold hand held the traveler in its grip, yet the bitter air appeared to have little effect. Frigid wind, originating from the snowy Northlands leagues to the north, cut across the traveler's path, howling as it sliced through the grove of trees in the distance as if it was warning visitors away. Beneath a star-filled night sky that was blotched with heavy clouds, long, lithe strides carried the traveler along the dried bed of what had once been a raging river; now, however, only rubble and aged waterlines gave any indication that one of nature's most potent forces had flowed there.

Following it for a time, the traveler eventually left the shelter of the riverbed and emerged into the open. As the traveler did so, a sudden gust of wind set the traveler's cloak flapping about wildly, exposing a feminine figured clad in dark leather armor. Securing her cloak and hood about her, she paused at the edge of the grove and eyed the towering oaks and ironwoods warily. An owl hooted in the distance and the woman's eyes narrowed within her cowl; concealed within her cloak, the glove on her right hand creaked softly as she fingered the hilt of the slender, gently curving blade at her right hip. After an extended moment of tense silence, she cautiously entered the grove.

Save for the slivers of moonlight that managed to filter through the thick branches of the barren canopy, darkness ruled inside the grove. Soft earth, still damp from the rain two days previous, muffled her light footfalls to the point of near silence, but she knew that did little to hide her presence from the nocturnal creatures of the grove. Oddly enough, though they were active, they seemed unusually hesitant and suspicious as their bright eyes peered intently at her from within the deep shadows. Their demeanor aside, she knew the animals of the grove were no threat to her, and, more importantly, she was glad for their presence. There was an aura about the night that had her on edge, and she welcomed anything that would give her an advantage on such an evening.

The wind suddenly picked up, rattling the treetops and moaning like a wounded animal, causing the hairs on the back of her neck to stand up. The symphony of the grove slowed to a stop and she came to a halt, her hand tightening about her sword hilt. Letting her cloak hang loosely about her frame, she opened her mind and reached out with her senses. Carried on ribbons of ethereal blue energy, a torrent of information about her surroundings flooded her senses. She could hear the insects scuttling about in the underbrush, and she could feel the eyes of a pair of owls watching her from the treetops. In the distance, she could sense a pack of wolves loping through the woods to her right. Suddenly, she felt the wolves pause and look her direction, their fangs bared in a snarl.

*With movements so fluid that they seemed unnatural, she spun and drew her katana in one motion, the gently curved blade biting deeply into the stomach of the tall creature that had crept up behind her. Her assailant fell to the ground with a muted howl as it tried to catch its guts and stuff them back inside. Two other humanoid figures rushed at her from her left in a vain attempt to flank her. With deft motions, she danced into them, her katana becoming a blur of movement as she forced the second attacker's sword high, spun low and slit open the third attacker's belly. Black blood streaking her blade and dampening the earth, she rolled to the side to avoid the second attacker's vicious overhand chop. As she came to her feet, her right hand darted upward, launching a tanto skyward. Her second assailant had recovered by then. Turning to face her, the body of a fourth attacker tumbled from the tree branches and landed with a thud on the ground between them, the tanto buried in its right eye. The second assailant had just enough time to stare at the body in dumbfounded surprise before her sword licked across its neck, removing its head from its shoulders.*

*Breathing softly, she stood in the center of the carnage with her katana at the ready. Though it took only a few seconds, it seemed like minutes crept by as she searched her surroundings with her senses, probing for other assailants. Now that the presence responsible for the tension in the air had been removed, the woodland natives were beginning to once again move about fearlessly. Satisfied that she was safe for the moment, she bent over the creature with her tanto buried in its eye and retrieved the short blade. She had gleaned an idea of what had attacked her right before the fight started, but a closer inspection of the corpse confirmed her suspicions and made her stomach twist with cold dread.*

*Dark, molted skin was stretched tightly over a high-cheekbone face that was fitted with pure-black, almond-shaped eyes that now stared off into oblivion. The creature's long, pointed ears were heavily scarred as if they'd been chewed on endlessly. Greasy black hair and a large, hooked nose were accented by enlarged upper and lower canines. The attackers' bodies were elongated and somewhat out of proportion, as their arms and legs were too long for their slender torsos. No identifying marks could be found on their black leather armor — but she didn't need any to know what they were.*

*With a disgusted scowl, she meticulously cleaned the black blood from her katana and tanto with her assailants' clothes. Once she was positive the blades were clean, she checked herself for wounds and any trace of the black blood. Finding nothing but a few specks on her pants, she gently took hold of the currents and summoned small, controlled flames over each spot. The tiny flames burned hot and bright for an instant, burning tiny holes through her pants. As she let go of the currents and the flames winked out, she could see the extent of the damage to her pants and cringed with a bit of regret; while the holes were small and hardly something to be embarrassed about, the pants were ruined. However, it was a small price to pay to ensure none of the blood came in contact with her skin.*

*Standing, she sheathed her blades and eyed the bodies as her mind chewed on what the corpses implied. She didn't like what such a brazen attack could mean. She had known something was wrong well before she'd entered the grove, but she hadn't been able to detect what was causing the sensation. The fact that her attackers had gotten the drop on her was appalling; such a thing shouldn't have been possible, but the bodies at her feet told a different story. Even in death, the disgusting corpses seemed to either consume or repel the blue ribbons of energy that were visible to people like her, creating hard-to-detect dead spots within the currents. Normally, she would incinerate the corpses to cleanse the land of their taint, but she had no desire to announce her presence to any other would-be assailants that could be in the area; she could easily return and dispose of the infectious bodies once she had finished with her current task.*

*Shredding one of her attacker's cloaks, she carefully wrapped up the severed head and secured it before continuing on. Caution now weighing her steps down, she moved deeper into the grove, her path carrying her toward the center of the woods. The head she now carried was proof that events were growing significantly more serious than she had believed.*

*The flickering, bluish-silver moonlight was soon joined in its dance by an orange glow that reflected off the naturally polished bark of the ironwoods. Someone had lit a fire at or near her destination. While she knew her compatriots awaited her there, the attack had left her nerves rattled just enough that she continued to proceed with caution. The orange radiance began to glow more vibrantly and welcome waves of heat began to reach her, which told her that a large bonfire burned in the clearing near the center of the grove. As she drew closer, she could just make out two voices over the roar of the bonfire. Halting within the shadows at the edge of the clearing, she carefully examined the area.*

*Bathed in dancing orange light, the clearing was nearly sixty paces in diameter and surrounded by trees on all sides. There were two men standing on the far side of the bonfire, their attention focused on their conversation. One was a human of short stature, whose thickly muscled frame combined with his lack of height to make him seem unmovable. Black hair, with the slightest hint of purple in its highlights, was cut short and framed a handsome, masculine face and black eyes. A blue wool shirt, black leather pants and calf-boots fit his body loosely, allowing him freedom of movement. There was a broad grin on his face that was shattered as he belted out a rich laugh, possibly at a joke she couldn't hear from her position.*

*Turning her gaze to the other man, her attitude began to sour.*

*The taller of the two was a darlion. His hair was more akin to a long white mane, and the rest of his body was covered in short umber fur that looked astonishingly like skin from a distance. Long, pointed ears swept back from his head and were capped with tuffs of white fur. His lean-muscled frame was clad in a plain black doublet over a gray shirt, and his long, deceptively powerful legs were encased in wool stockings and black knee-high boots. To his credit, it helped* make his sharp, feral features and crystal-blue eyes, which were set slightly wide astride a broad and rather flat nose, seem more devilish than they already were. Like his companion, there wasn't a visible weapon on him, but she knew better than to underestimate the two — which further soured her mood. Both the knowledge that they should have sensed her assailants and the casual way they went about their conversation rubbed her raw.

Undoing the knot on her makeshift sack, she strode forcefully into the glade, bringing the conversation to an abrupt halt. With a flick of her wrist, she sent the head rolling along the ground before anyone could react to her arrival, the macabre trophy coming to rest near the fire. "Either of you want to tell me what in the hells this was doing here, and why neither of you noticed?!" her normally soothing, beautiful voice rang out with angry accusation.

As the darlion moved around the fire and crouched down to examine the head, the human glanced at the holes in her pants with curious suspicion before he too moved to the other side of the bonfire. In the firelight, the head was even more grotesque than in the dark — boils that looked ready to burst dotted the head generously, and bulging veins scoured the dark flesh like aged parchment.

The darlion stood up quickly, hissing violently at the head. "Where did you get that!?" he demanded, his baritone voice rife with shock.

"You tell me!" she retorted as she tossed back her hood. Thick hair, the color of a radiant blue sky, tumbled down her back as she freed her hip-length ponytail. Her slightly up-tilted eyes were narrowed, their sky-blue hue burning with anger. The full lips of her tanned, heart-shaped face were pressed together firmly — only slightly ruining her plain, yet lovely features — below her high cheekbones and slender nose. She crossed her arms beneath her modest, but full breasts in anger. Digging her fingers into her upper arms in an attempt to fight her building rage, she glared at the darlion and barked, "I was ambushed in the forest by four of them! What, in Corith's name, is going on?!"

The darlion snarled. "I don't know! We wiped them out!"

She scoffed in disgust. "I know that! I was there when we destroyed the last of their nests! There shouldn't be any way for them to still exist!"

The darlion scowled darkly. "Well — apparently we missed something!" He nudged the head with a boot. "This also makes me rethink the reports I received from Darius."

Her eyes narrowed further and she planted her hands on her hips. "What reports?"

The darlion met her gaze before stating, "He said his scouts reported seeing elfin-like creatures skulking about the forests and mountains of late. Furthermore, he reported that the remains of the units that had engaged and been slaughtered by the creatures looked twisted and bloated as if suffering from a virulent poison. He even asserted that Cat fell victim to them."

"Damn you, Darkon!" she roared, her eyes flashing and hands clenched at her sides. "And you didn't think to inform the rest of us?! It sounds like we've got a serious problem on our hands – not a few stray blackhearts or an army of mundanes to deal with! What were you thinking!?"

"The same thing you would have, Kara!" he spit back. "Rumors and hearsay! I was there too! And as far as I was concerned – we wiped those abominations from the face of Kylir! We all know Warrick is in the north, and it was easy to assume he killed Cat, not a long-dead abomination! But this," he gestured to the head, "has sinister implications when added to the reports." He gave Kara a grim, determined stare. "I won't take it lightly, Kara. I swear – I'll deal with it personally."

By this point she had moved closer to the bonfire and was warming her hands; it was a pointless gesture as the cold did not bother her, but it was an old habit that made her feel just a bit better. Darkon's promise had assuaged her anger with him somewhat, but it did nothing to relieve the dread gnawing at her gut. "And what about Darius? This changes the situation there drastically."

Darkon nodded. "I agree. Since I now have to look into the reappearance of blackhearts, and you two have other duties, this leaves only Greatjon. I'll have him leave immediately."

Kara stared at him in disbelief. "Greatjon . . .? Are you serious . . .? You'll only be adding fuel to the fire!"

Up to this point, their companion had remained silent during the exchange, but he finally felt the need to lend his voice to the conversation. "I agree with Kara, Darkon," he declared in his smooth, somewhat cocky voice. "We all know Greatjon's feelings toward the Vale. He's likely to do something foolish and make the situation worse."

Darkon shook his white-maned head. "It can't be helped. If Darius is under siege by these abominations, then I need Greatjon there. Your task is too important to delay, so Greatjon will have to do for now. Besides, Cat's replacement is in Darius' care – and we cannot afford to lose her."

Kara remained silent for a moment before muttering, "I don't like it one bit. . . . But it shall be as you say, Darkon."

Darkon eyed the other man, "And you, Mat? Do you object?"

Mat shook his head and grinned. "None whatsoever. Greatjon might make a mess of things, but he'll do the job. Besides, it's what his Order was created for, and I'm anxious to hear what you have for us. It should be a great deal more entertaining than keeping watch on King Drugal day after day."

Darkon gave a succinct nod. "Good. Then I won't waste any more of our time. Let me be blunt with you both – as of last month, the darlion High Council voted unanimously to end all military aid. Their memories are long, and they want nothing to do with our conflict anymore. I fear, before we see an end to

205

*this, they will withdraw from the world as the elves did before them."* The unhappy news fell on Kara and Mat like a stone wall, leaving them with dismay splayed clearly on their faces. Darkon noted their worried expressions and shook his head. *"I'm afraid that isn't the worst of the news, given Kara's 'gift' to us. We're all aware of the large force that has been cutting a swath of carnage through the mountains for the last few months. Cat should have been enough to secure the mountains, but with her death and with this,"* he waved a hand in disgust at the blackheart head, *"as evidence, I am forced to assume that blackhearts make up a portion of the army."*

*"Any estimates on what Darius is facing?"* asked Mat.

*"Roughly eight-hundred strong were accounted for, according to the report. However, if there are blackhearts lurking about . . . then that means something far worse is marching with this force. At this point, it should be roughly a week before the army reaches Castle Blackstone, but I fear the worse. Even if Greatjon were to leave tonight, with Portculim travel suspended, I fear he may get there too late."*

A glum silence threatened to enshroud them as the weight of Darkon's words set in. Given the rumors and evidence they had to work with, it wasn't a stretch to presume that Warrick was at the head of the army. They all understood the implications of such an assumption – especially Kara and Darkon.

With a wave of his hand, Darkon seemed to dismiss the thoughts. *"But that's not your concern right now. You two have a very important task ahead of you. There have been disturbances in the flow of fir'gan that would indicate there are Gifted beginning to come into their own unlike any the world has seen in . . ."* he chuckled. *"Well, a very long time. Yorien and Trina's crystals have shown signs of resonating to the disturbances, but I dare not risk a Search by Warden or Seeker at this great of a distance. Therefore, I have made arrangements for the two of you to travel to Triclose. Once there, find them and protect them."*

*"Us?"* asked Kara with an upraised eyebrow. *"You want Wardens to Search? Are you mad? If there are any others on Triclose, we'll stand out like a blazing beacon! We could easily send Seekers instead!"*

Darkon nodded. *"I know Kara – but it is the fear that our enemies are gaining an unbeatable advantage that drives me to send the two of you. I know that Seekers could easily fine the Gifted, but they would be no match for a Warden in a battle. I need two of my best there – we cannot afford to lose these two."*

Mat scoffed. *"Great,"* he muttered sarcastically, his enthusiasm for the task slipping away. *"So you want to send us off on a task someone else could do, when we could be put to better use achieving our goals by helping Darius."*

Kara thought Darkon's words over with a heavy heart before replying, *"As much as I hate to admit it, Mat, Darkon is right. We're short on manpower – and with only interim Preceptors leading the Uthariyan and Osterias Orders, they're practically of no use to us."*

206

"I know," protested Mat. "But isn't the overall goal more important? If we can save Darius and find Luthur's crystal, won't that make everything else meaningless?"

Kara sighed and gave him a small, reassuring smile. "I know it seems that way, but if we're outmatched, we won't stand a chance of finding it as we battle for our lives." Her eyes dropped to the fire and her voice softened. "Besides, it's what Damion would—"

"Don't speak his name!" bellowed Darkon with a hiss. "Don't you dare invoke that traitor's name!"

Kara looked up, her blue eyes glinting with fury. "He's not a traitor, Darkon! And you know it!"

Darkon held his hands wide and scowled at Kara. "Then what is he, Preceptor? Tell me that! What do you call a man who vanishes without a trace and abandons his friends and responsibilities?"

"That's not true! Darius said—"

Darkon cut her off again with a scowl and a dismissive wave of his hand. "Darius said! Bah! The man is too old-fashioned, and Damion was like a brother to him! He said whatever he could to save face! No — Damion took Luthur's crystal and abandoned us, of this there can be no doubt! He is a traitor, plain and simple! If he ever grows the stones to show his face, I'll be there to cut off his cowardly head!" he hissed violently.

Mat took a step back as Kara and Darkon stared daggers at each other. He'd born witness to many of their arguments over the years regarding Damion, but never did he sense fir'gan stirring like it was. Fearing that this time it would come to blows, he forced a pleasant grin and said, "Come now, let ghosts lie in the past. Neither of you will convince the other of your viewpoint — and you both know it. We have real enemies to battle in the now. Infighting will just do us harm, agreed?" For just a moment longer it looked like violence might ensue, when — finally — the tension went out of their bodies and the flow of fir'gan in the clearing settled down. "Good," he stated as Kara and Darkon continued to glare at each other. "Now, where are we to leave from?"

Darkon gave Kara one last glare and turned to Mat. "Your ship, the Blue Trident, will sail from Durathan at noon two days from now and put in at Haltho. Good luck to you both, and may Corith guide you well." Reaching into a pouch on the back of his belt, he removed a coffer and held it before him for all to see. He spared one last glance at Kara before tossing it to her. As she caught the coffer, he kicked the blackheart head into the fire, a foul stench quickly filling the air as the flesh burst into flames, and spun on his heel before marching off into the shadows.

Mat watched Darkon's hasty retreat with a dour look while Kara reverently examined the container in her hands, each of them ignoring the stench filling their nostrils. Finally, Mat shook his head and returned to the other side of the fire. Crouching down, he retrieved his sword belt and then stood. As he belted it on and settled the sheathed, matching broad-bladed shortswords at his hips, he smiled ruefully.

Kara caught his expression out of the corner of her eye and looked up. "What are you grinning about?" she barked.

"You've got to be more careful around Darkon, Kara," he chided. "You push him like that, and he's eventually going to bite. Take me for example," he pointed to his swords. "I'm one of the few that actually disarms in his presence as he likes. Simple things like that could go a long way toward easing the tension."

Kara ran a hand lovingly over the bone coffer, her eyes enthralled by the opalescent colors that danced across the ironwood-bound bone surface. Her heart and mind suddenly heavy with the weight of the crystals that resided in the specially made and very rare coffer, she sighed and tucked it into a pouch on her belt before she folded her arms under her breasts and hugged herself. Realizing that Mat was expecting a reply, she said, "I know, but," she growled in frustration, "he's infuriating. I don't know what he has against Damion – but there is no way Darius lied to us. Damion would never betray us. . . . He just wouldn't." She waved a hand in the direction Darkon had vanished. "Hells, he didn't even inquire if I'd gotten blood on me!"

He recognized the firm conviction in her voice, and knew there was no way he could convince her otherwise; therefore, seeking to lighten the mood, he quipped, "So . . . that explains the holes in your pants. And here I thought you were trying to set a new fashion trend." The glare Kara shot him told him that his attempt at humor was ill-conceived. Shrugging as if to say he tried, he then said, "That may be, Kara, but I'm sure it just slipped his mind." Kara snorted, but Mat ignored it and added, "As for Damion . . . I'll just have to take your word on it. Besides, I care that you're okay. I don't want to ever witness that kind of death." He laughed then, looking up at the stars as he suddenly realized something. "Corith be good! I wasn't even born when that mess went down, and I've got to listen to you argue like two old fools!"

A smile broke through Kara's sour mood at the comment. "You're what now? Ninety? Don't worry – in a few centuries, you'll start sounding just like us," she quipped dryly.

Mat barked a jolly laugh. "Corith forbid!" Shaking his head in amusement, he then added, "Well, let's get going, you old crone. I haven't been to Durathan in a while, and I do miss it so much."

Kara shook her head with equal amusement. Waving her hand toward the bonfire, the flames went out with a hiss as a wave of fir'gan smothered it, casting the clearing in sudden darkness. "You just miss the women," she stated knowingly.

*Mat grinned at her as the light quickly faded from the dying embers. "I do indeed. I do indeed."*

She awoke from her attempt at mediation slowly, the memories of that night slowly fading away. Her sky-blue locks hanging loosely about her like a veil, she sat cross-legged in the center of the gently rocking cabin that she shared with Mat. Despite the cold temperatures, her naked body was covered in a sheet of sweat, the light from the two lanterns secured on the walls reflecting off her tanned skin. Her blue eyes were slightly glazed as she opened them and tried to focus on her surroundings. She had been trying to meditate and purge her excess rage as she had been taught centuries ago, but the memory of that night kept popping up and ruining her efforts. Her anger with Darkon had grown over the years since Damion's disappearance, and Darius' seclusion within Blackstone had left her as the only significant voice of opposition to Darkon's views. However, Mat was right when he had said that she needed to back off. At the rate they were going, it would definitely come to blows sooner rather than later.

Remaining seated for a moment longer, she took a couple of slow, deep breaths to steady herself as she let the currents of fir'gan wash over her. She then climbed to her feet and padded past the small anchored table and its pair of anchored chairs. Reaching the far wall where her hammock and clothes were, she retrieved her pack and began to dig through it. Though the temperature and weather didn't affect her or Mat in the slightest, they always maintained their charade with a normal outward appearance. Given the frigid temperatures onboard the *Blue Trident*, moving about the boat without winter garb would draw unwanted attention and raise questions they were in no position to answer.

Finding a spare shirt, she quickly toweled off with it before dressing. She slid on thick wool stockings before pulling on a matching long-sleeve tunic, both of which were dyed a dark-blue. Fur-lined boots fit snugly about her feet, and heavy leather gloves, that were the envy of some of the sailors, fit her hands as if they'd been perfectly tailored for her. Gathering her thick hair at the nape of her neck, she tied it off with a purple leather thong before securing her thick black cloak about her. Once she was sure she looked like freezing was a concern, she exited the cabin.

The *Blue Trident* was a large cargo vessel, nearly two hundred and fifty feet from bow to stern. Three thick masts supported large white sails that eagerly swallowed up the wind to propel them on their journey. She was crewed by thirty men, most of questionable rapport.

Her captain was a grizzled old sailor who claimed to run an honest business transporting cargo. Kara knew better, though. Aside from taking on the occasional passengers, the *Blue Trident* served as a smuggler's vessel, her captain ready and willing to transport nearly anything without question . . . for a small fee, of course. The captain also served willingly at Darkon's beck and call, which was why he'd been so willing and able to leave port without taking on full cargo. Kara chuckled to herself as she made her way from the bowels of the ship and up onto the deck. She had a sneaking suspicion that before they had left port, the captain had somehow managed to stuff the ship's hidden holds full of goods that either had been banned or were becoming harder to acquire on Triclose. After all, where there's war, there's coin to be made.

Sunlight and bitter winds greeted her as she set foot on deck. They had been at sea for a week, each passing day that they moved north and west brought colder temperatures, and with it, freezing rain and spray. The ship's crew was already busy with their routine for the day by the time she made her appearance. Though the crew of the *Blue Trident* was garbed against the cold and used to these conditions, it did little to reduce the difficulty of their tasks nor the pain that came with it. Some of the crew were on their knees scrubbing the salt and wash from the deck, their body heat preventing the water soaking their pants from turning to frost, while others were high on the masts and rigging, attending to routine repairs and checking for any damage the weather may have wrought. A handful of sailors were busy breaking ice off the boat that had formed overnight, their mallets, daggers and picks chipping away at the dangerous buildup. There was a constant battle with the ice this time of year, and the sailors always had to be diligent with it, else the ship could become too heavy and capsize.

Looking about, Kara saw no sign of the aging captain as she made her way to the aft of the ship and ascended the stairs of the wheelhouse to the accompaniment of hammers and picks chewing away at the ice. She nodded in greeting to the bundled-up helmsman, a short burly sailor with more hair on his head than teeth in his mouth, as she walked past the sheltered wheelhouse to the railing of the quarterdeck.

Dressed in a loose white wool tunic and snug black wool breeches, Mat was leaning against the rail, his dark cloak and boots displaying a smattering of frost. He turned at her approach and grinned, showing off his pearly teeth. "Well, well. Decided to join the waking world?"

Kara smirked at him as she ducked beneath the boom of the mizzen mast and came alongside him. Leaning on the railing, watching the wake behind the boat, she informed him, "Darkon ruined my mediations again, so I thought I'd get some fresh air and clear my head."

Mat gave her a friendly pat on the back and leaned his back against the rail, his vision focused off in the distance before the ship. "Don't let him get to you – he's too old and too cranky for his own good. Besides, once we're on Triclose, the distance will keep him from bothering you too much."

Kara nodded and took in a deep breath of the clean, salty air. "It can't come soon enough." Sighing, she eyed Mat. "I heard from him last night."

Mat arched an eyebrow. "Oh? What did our glorious leader have to say?"

Kara rubbed her hands together, remembering the short, terse communication. "It's not good. It's been a week since Greatjon was sent to Blackstone, and he hasn't received any word from him."

Mat shrugged and tried to give her a comforting smile, though his own mood and thoughts reflected hers regarding Darius and Greatjon's situation. "Come now, I would think no news would be good news. Maybe they've just got their hands full."

Kara shook her head, her blue hair gently riding the breeze about her. "I wish I had your enthusiasm, Mat. But I've been at it too long," she said dejectedly. "If one of us fails to report in a situation like that, then nothing good can come of it." She sighed deeply. "Blackhearts, moving armies, dying Wardens . . . and not a single overt sign of the Darkness 'intent. I can't help but think we're missing something. I feel like we're flailing about like children. I. . . ." She shook her head, then continued softly, "I miss the old days. . . . I miss Damion and Luthur's leadership . . ." she trailed off into a somber silence.

Mat looked at her with concern before turning and placing a comforting arm about her shoulders. "Don't get all glum on me. This is my first trip to Triclose, and I don't need you turning it all gloom and doom on me. We'll do our job there – enjoy a few of the sights of course – and get home so we can put an end to all this suffering."

She gave him a weak smile. "The enthusiasm of youth, eh?"

He laughed and rubbed her shoulder. "I do my part to keep you all from feeling your age."

Kara smiled brightly at him. "I really hope you can keep that outlook, Mat. I truly do. Anyways, I'll contact Darkon one more time before we make port. Hopefully he'll have good news for us then."

Mat smiled reassuringly. "I'm sure he will."

She nodded and turned her vision back to the rolling sea as she thought to herself, *"With the way things are going, I hope you live long enough for age to become a problem, dear friend."*

*

Snow. Pure and untainted, it falls without bias upon the land and the creatures that roam it. Animals are not safe from the beautiful white powder, nor are the families that huddle about the fire that provides a false sense of security. For if the fates deemed it, snow could change from a beautiful creation to a deadly mistress. Yet, not all are affected by the white chill. Far to the north, where winter's grip had already tightened upon Solarson, the denizens of the land had long since grown hardened to winter's deadly harbinger. Embracing winter like one would a lover, they faced the trials of winter head on, determined to survive the worst the season has to offer.

Deep within the treacherous White Fang Mountains resides a fortress of immaculate and haunting design. A sixty foot stone wall – its vertical surface encased in a thick sheet of ice, which only added to its sturdiness and beauty – stands as a silent, impassive guardian over a flowing, cathedral-style keep. Two round towers flanked both the gatehouse and the lone wall as the barrier crawled across the open valley between the towering mountains that protected the fortress' flanks and rear. Battlements, manned by the heartiest of men and women, surmount the proud wall like a glorious, ice-sheathed crown. Across the exterior surface of the stone barrier were cunningly cut arrow-slits, their artistic design equaled by the murder-holes lining the interior of the gatehouse tunnel; each feature was cleverly designed to appear ornamental while providing a nearly unassailable venue from which to defend. However, it was the building that the mountains and wall stood guard over that was the main work of art.

Extending deep into the mountain, many wondered how such a beautiful piece of architecture could end up secluded deep in the seemingly impassable mountains. Ice-covered towers of black stone leapt skyward, their roofs protected by blue clay shingles and trimmed with gargoyles. Balconies adorned the towers and the keep alike, their heavy doors shut tight against the cold. Massive buttresses, whose sweeping arches were home to majestic icicles, provided support to the towering structures, while stained-glass windows lined the walls of the main building's lower floors, delivering an array of vibrant color to the drab gray of both the mountains and keep. Yet, amongst the majesty of the fortress, it was the simplest of the windows that caught one's eye without fail. Set above two reinforced bronze doors on the building's main face, the large, round window was made of eye-catching, bright-red glass. There was nothing artistically remarkable about the portal, yet its ability to enrapture was undeniable.

It was safe to assume that the architects of the fortress would have considered the windows lavish enough for a fortress that wanted to balance the martial with the artistic, but upon closer inspection, the keep still held a few surprises. The entirety of the lower third of the keep's walls was adorned with the most intricate of carvings that ranged from powerful dragons to the simplest of flowers, leaving the upper reaches of the keep as the only surfaces untouched by an artisan's hands. Even more surprising than the carved walls, the interior of the keep was more palatial than martial. Brightly lit, the rooms within the keep were designed with comfort in mind; many of the walls were plastered or wood-paneled, and hardwood or lush carpet were the predominant floorings of choice. Where the rooms or halls were left raw, thick rugs and tapestries were used to enliven the atmosphere. Yet, while the keep was draped in luxurious trappings, it was still a military structure, making what was arguably the most surprising feature of the keep very ironic – the halls of the keep were home to grand works of art and libraries full of tomes that most scholars could only imagine studying.

However, before it was possible for anyone to enter this sanctum of art and knowledge, much less venture close enough to observe the wall carvings or view the eye of red glass over the keep's doors, guests and residents alike would have to pass through the massive gate set in the frozen wall. The lone, towering gatehouse harbored two massive steel doors that were nearly two feet thick and etched with breathtaking scrollwork by artists long forgotten. Be it winter or summer, the gate guardians were not only nigh impenetrable when sealed, but they swung on impossibly silent hinges, the secret of which was known only to the keep's master.

Once through the gate, people were then greeted by the one feature of the keep that might be more enthralling than the red stain-glass window. Ten feet in diameter, and positioned in the center of the courtyard so as to be the first thing one would see upon entering the grounds, was an elegant white marble fountain. In vivid contrast to the fountain, the ground beneath it was paved with expertly-fitted black stone in the shape of a thirty-foot circular disk. When flowing, pure mountain water would rain from the mouth of the majestic dragon rearing skyward at the center of the filigree-carved basin, the bubbling liquid providing ample water for the keep's residents. During the winter —as it was now — the water would be allowed to freeze, creating a breathtaking ice sculpture.

There was an awe-inspiring beauty to the keep people called Castle Blackstone, and its residents took pride in their home. Normally, they maintained it with care in the summer or the harshest of winters, keeping the castle in pristine condition and alive with activity. Yet now, in these dark days, the bailey was oppressively quiet, and it seemed as if only soldiers and refugees roamed its snow- and mud-covered grounds. The keep's smithy was silent, and the protective wall was eerily somber. Within Blackstone Village, which occupied the far side of the small woodland that separated it from the castle, very few of the villagers ventured outside; those that did, moved quickly and with purpose. Despite their hardy constitutions, tensions were high and spirits low for the people of Castle Blackstone. For while the trials and tribulations of winter could be viewed as disheartening and possibly deadly, the denizens of Blackstone and the vale it occupied knew only one enemy was truly fatal and worthy of such soul-sucking apprehension —

Man.

From the southeast the armies came, snaking their way through treacherous passes and canyons, up dangerous inclines and down slippery slopes packed thick with snow and ice. Led by both men whose souls were darker than a moonless night, and creatures born of the most twisted of imaginations, they moved through the winter-locked mountains with methodical efficiency — plundering, raping and killing their way to their destination. They took their time in their macabre journey, basking in the debauchery and leaving no soul alive. They lived by a doctrine that was a twisted parody of a code of honor that was older than any living creature could imagine. Forged in a time that most considered myth, when honor was a man's life and the Darkness was just a fleeting shadow, the code had been corrupted to the point that only those that lived by it could be deluded into thinking it meant anything. Their perversion was of such a reprehensible nature that it could be viewed as none other than pure, unequivocal evil.

However, for every evil there is a good. Maybe not the purest good one could want or imagine, but a good never the less.

Within the castle that was the army's target, resided one of the few that had tried to withstand the growing night. Simply known as Darius to his subjects, he had once been a priest of the strictest vows before his dark past and search for redemption ushered him down a path very few were capable of surviving. When the armies arrived on their wave of destruction and debauchery, the populace turned to him for protection. With open arms and a foreboding edge to his eyes, he welcomed the people within the gate. For weeks, people fled to Castle Blackstone in search of shelter and protection, bringing with them tales that bore the weight of horrors beyond comparison. Each successive story further hardened Darius' resolve and darkened his soul until it seemed like it would absorb all the light and warmth within him.

The gate remained open night and day until the army that had massacred its way across the mountains reached the vale Blackstone occupied. On the afternoon that the army arrived in the Vale, Darius, with a voice as cold and hard as the ice coating the wall, ordered the massive gate closed, cutting off hundreds of stragglers from sanctuary. Caught between the defenseless village and the towering wall of Blackstone, some of the refuges decided to take their chances within the woods, while others returned to the village with vain hopes of defending it. With revolting zeal, the invaders hunted down and slaughtered every man, woman and child that remained outside the wall regardless of their age or gender. As the army went about its macabre mission, buildings were put to the torch, and agonizing wails climbed into the air, ripping the depths of one's soul asunder.

Through it all, Darius stood atop the protective battlements, bearing silent witness to the horrors. Opening his senses to the currents, he seemingly could feel the pain of the tortured, the stark terror of the imprisoned, and the agony and wails of the raped as the currents were thrown into chaos by the carnage. To his enhanced senses, the howls of glee from the invaders were crystal clear, sickening him and making it ever-so tempting to withdraw his senses – but he did not. Instead, he forced himself to bear witness to the tragedy that played out unapologetically before him, for it was the least he could do for the fallen. He would have wept, but instead, he kept his face impassive. Strength was what his people needed now, and he would be that for them.

Suddenly, with his enhanced senses bringing the macabre scene into focus, his eyes found a target for the rage building in his stomach and the reason for which he had proceeded with callous caution. Hard faced and bald, a raven-wing tattoo covered the left side of his target's head like a badge of honor. Crimson-enameled armor encased the giant of a man that strode among the invaders, urging them on in their depraved celebrations while shoving his massive axe in the air to their cries of victory. Darius could see the fir'gan swirl about the man like wildfire. He knew there were only a handful of people on the wall that could see the ebb and flow of fir'gan as he could, and he was glad for that minor blessing. Even he was terrified by how the ethereal blue ribbons of power responded to the bald man's presence. But what truly rattled his soul, was the mind-numbing realization that the crimson barbarian was only tapping a small portion of his power.

The man suddenly stopped and turned his vision toward Blackstone's wall, his red eyes immediately focusing on Darius. He could see Darius just as clearly as Darius could see him; knowing this, he flashed Darius a broad, sadistic grin and reached out along the currents, probing for Blackstone's master. Their minds touched for the briefest of moments, but it was enough for a single thought to be shared between them –

It was a good time to die.

Darius desperately wanted to unleash his rage upon the man and bring the same type of carnage to the invaders' ranks that they had bestowed upon the terrified refugees huddled behind Blackstone's wall. However, aside from the terrifying power residing within the crimson-armored man, there was a necrotic presence slithering its way through the attackers' forces that made Darius' very core go cold with dread. The miasma he sensed would mean a painful and agonizing death for even one as powerful as he. To his chagrin, he had already seen one friend felled by the miasma, and he knew that to risk the same fate would surely doom everyone within the keep – and that was a risk he was not prepared to take. Yes, he would bide his time and await the help he knew would eventually come. He could only pray that it would not come too late.

Not far to the west, nearly a week after Darius and the crimson-armored man locked eyes, a lone figure ran through ankle-deep snow as if it was merely an illusion. A thick, plain brown cloak and hood concealed his features, and provided protection from the weather even though he had no need for it. The hilt of his large claymore jutted over his right shoulder, its claw-shaped steel pommel gleaming dully in the moonlight, while his dark-brown eyes stared intently from the shadows of his cowl. The eyes seemed empty of joyful light, hinting at vile and dark deeds that would give most people nightmares for the rest of their lives . . . and possibly even after death. Peering into the distance, his eyes observed the slick rock surfaces that lined the pass he was traveling through, alert for any sign of activity. He did not fear the deadly animals that roamed the mountains – his companion had seen to it that no such creature would bother him – nor did he fear attack, for his nearly six and a half feet tall, thickly muscled body would deter most men. However, he knew there were enemies ahead that would not be so easily dissuaded.

His conscious told him to be cautious. His dark dreams elected for retreat. But his soul saw things differently. His soul – one that teeters on the fine edge between good and evil – demanded that he move forward, seeing in his objective a release for years of torment and anger. It was a simple choice for most people – listen to their dreams and flee in the face of what could be certain death.

He, however, was not most people.

He chose, instead, to listen to his soul, the one thing he believed he could unequivocally trust. Despite caution having tempered his pace of travel to this point, he decided he could risk a bit more speed. Quickening his pace slightly, he plunged forward with the reassuring weight of his claymore on his back and his soul howling like a wolf in anticipation.

Hours later, night fell and he continued on tirelessly. His mind told him that food and rest was needed, but he knew he could march on for days without such necessities. However, he gave in to common sense for a moment and, without losing stride, he lowered his cowl. Rust-orange hair, which was gathered in a horsetail at the nape of his neck, bounced about his handsome, solemn face as he pulled a biscuit from the pouch at his waist with a gloved hand and brought it up to his wide mouth. The biscuit was cold, hard and tasteless in his mouth, but he knew the nutritional value it held far outweighed how tasteless it was. Finishing his meal, he pulled his cowl back into place and hurried onward.

Bright, twinkling stars and bluish-silver moonlight set the snow aglow, illuminating the path before him. Soon, the pass he was following ended, and he found himself ascending treacherous and impossibly sheer mountainsides. Not once did he have to pause to search for proper handholds or footing. Instead, his hands and feet sank into the frozen rock face as if it was a soft cake, steam rising into the air each time his fingers and feet dug through the ice and into the stone. With as cold as it was, the holes froze over as soon as he removed his large hands and feet. Hour after hour slid away before he realized he had climbed most of the night away. Eventually, he came upon an outcropping that provided him a view for miles around and offered him an opportunity to rest and stretch.

Scrambling atop the outcropping, he stood up and turned away from the mountain, letting his eyes take in all before him. Endless open sky and howling winds greeted him, threatening to take his breath away. For as long as he could remember, he had always liked such nights. The cold reminded him that he was alive, and the vastness of the starlit sky reminded him of just how insignificant he truly was. At any other time, he would have let the humbling awe that the vista inspired wash over him, but he couldn't afford to do so now. With the knowledge that there was no time to truly enjoy it, he allowed himself to bask in the vista for a moment longer, the biting wind revitalizing him. As a deep, heartfelt sigh escaped his lips, he finally turned away from the breathtaking view and continued his climb.

By the time he pulled himself onto the relatively flat surface of the mountaintop, the sky to the west was beginning to brighten and a light snow had begun to fall. All about him, patches of ice and snow dotted the unyielding stone, potentially making footing dangerous. While he didn't fear injury, falling upon the unyielding stone would still hurt; therefore, with quick, cautious strides, he picked his way across the mile-wide mountaintop. Even with his guarded pace, it was a quick trip and he soon found himself standing motionless at the edge of the mountaintop. With the sun at his back, he let his eyes drink in the sight before him.

Flowing out into the unending expanse below him was a view to rival the one of a few hours past. Beneath the gentle snowfall, snow-capped mountains sprawled out in all directions as far as the eye could see, their peaks glistening dully in the new day. Hardy mountain birds dotted the sky like specks of ash as they searched for a meal. Except for the occasional bird cry or gust of icy wind howling through the pitiless peaks, everything was silent and at peace. Letting his eyes drift over the mountain range, they eventually came to rest on the towering peaks that he knew guarded his destination. Eyes widening with dread, the details of the once beautiful scenery suddenly took on a new meaning.

Where once the snow-capped peaks were just that, now they were mourners. The birds that were simply in search of a meal, now were carrion crows hungrily circling a battlefield. As for the wind that once howled through the peaks as nature intended, it was a now a mournful dirge for the dead. This transformation of perception seared itself into his mind as his eyes drank in the orange glow emanating from the north side of the Vale. Letting his eyes drift upward from the glow, cold dread gripped his heart as he followed the columns of sinister black smoke that rose toward the heavens like snakes slithering from a burrow. It was clear that the situation had grown far worse than his original information had indicated, and he could feel his throat constricting with rising anger. He had hoped to find that the situation wasn't anywhere near as bad as reported. He was even prepared to walk into a dangerous and possibly dire situation that he could potentially rectify – but he had not been prepared for this.

The Vale was burning.

# Chapter Ten

*T*he sun began to dip below the eastern horizon as the bitterly cold wind of the White Fang Mountains blew in from the north, cutting deep and adding to the misery of the survivors huddled within the protective confines of Castle Blackstone. Yet, there was one man that stood unaffected by the cold. Hidden within the shadows of a copse of trees on the northern side of the Vale, his brown eyes – rage simmering in their depths – drank in the devastation that had befallen Blackstone Village. With the shadows providing a measure of safety, he watched the invaders moving through the village as if they owned the place. Soldiers drunk with victory and booze stolen from the village tavern stumbled about, their loud bluster and bawdy songs easily reaching his ears. His nose twitched as he caught the scent of a miasmic presence amongst the soldiers. He had yet to see or locate the source, but he recognized the scent and it raised his hackles.

Screams broke the air near endlessly in a horrifying symphony of pain and agony as the soldiers tortured and raped their captives for entertainment, drawing a dark scowl from him. The depraved acts he had witnessed in the last few hours reminded him of a time so far gone that the memories almost seemed false – if not for the fact he had lived through it all. The ghastly sights had been enough to tempt him to rush headlong into the ruins of the village, unleashing his rage in a wave of destructive retribution. However, the foul smell filling his nostrils and the presence lurking just on the edge of his senses held him in check, reminding him that there was more at stake than rage-filled revenge.

A sudden but gentle nudge at his hip drew him from his dark thoughts. Reaching down, he patted the large, muscled neck of the direwolf. "Too much like old times, eh girl?" he whispered in his deep voice.

The massive black- and gray-splotched direwolf gave a low growl in response before wheeling and padding quietly into the woods. It still amazed him that his childhood friend and companion could move with such stealth while weighing as much as three men. Moving to follow with the silent toe-heel stride of a darlion, he caught up to the direwolf and trotted silently alongside her. Even without the help of wet pine needles and soft ground, no one would have noticed their movements.

Stars began to punch holes in the sky and fires sprang to life in the invaders' camp as night fell. As the ruins began to glow brighter with the added firelight, it forced the two travelers to slow their pace as they moved from copse to copse, skirting westward around the village in search of the unbroken woods standing between the Blackstone Village and the keep. Soon, night had taken complete control of the sky, and the volume of bawdy songs and torturous screams increased as the invaders' camp broke into a haphazard celebration. He frowned at the antics, his stomach twisting with anger at the grim source of the revelry. The brief surge of fury pushed him to move faster. The direwolf, sensing his urgency, ran ahead to make sure their path was clear.

Their roundabout journey was agonizingly slow and done in complete silence, the sounds of celebration and rape accompanying them like an unwanted overture. During one close pass to the ruins, he came to a halt in an uncomfortably small thicket, his attention caught by a scream of such terror and agony that it felt like a fist had hammered into his heart. Sending his companion ahead, he crouched amongst the shadows, his eyes seeking the source of the cry.

Just on the edge of town, framed by the dancing glow of firelight, was a young girl – barely a woman – being viciously raped by a trio of soldiers drunk with booze and power. Red welts, teeth marks, bruises, and numerous bleeding cuts covered her naked body like a second skin. Blood tricked down her garishly bruised inner thighs in what seemed like an impossibly constant flow. The three soldiers had her bent over a pile of crates as they took turns abusing and violating her in every way they could imagine with enthusiastic zeal. Where many would have succumbed to shock long before this or accepted their fate, her constant screams and sobs of painful and heart-wrenching agony showed that some part of her still fought to endure and survive the horror. He didn't know if he should respect her inner strength or pity her. It was clear that some part of her believed she would and could survive, but he knew better – she was as good as dead once they were done with her. Unfortunately, until that moment arrived, she was the bastards' toy and pain would be her eager friend. Impulse and his code demanded that he interfere with the repulsive act, but common sense held him in check. Despite the many horrible acts being committed and how it angered him, rushing headlong in there would be a costly mistake.

Suddenly, she screamed in agony as her head was jerked back violently by the thug having his way with her. One of the other soldiers emptied the bottle of alcohol he'd been drinking all over her back, setting her wounds afire and ripping a throat-shredding scream from her. The soldiers laughed gleefully, truly finding pleasure in the

220

girl's terror. That final act of depravity settled it for the traveler. While he couldn't brazenly assault the invaders and risk failing his mission, he could do something for the girl.

Setting his jaw, the traveler reached out along the currents of fir'gan he could see swirling before his eyes and built up the air around the girl's throat. With a slight growl, he hardened the air and squeezed it violently, snapping the girl's neck. Her tormentors' laughter stopped as they realized her screams had ceased and her body had gone limp. If they were surprised or disappointed, they didn't show it. With a few laughs and shrugs of the shoulders, they hitched up their pants and moved on, leaving her desecrated body slumped over the pile of crates.

The traveler paid little heed to the soldiers as the moved off, his gaze enthralled by that of the girl. Already bereft of life, her empty eyes were focused on him in a way that made his breath catch in his throat – it was almost as if she was thanking him from beyond the grave.

*"Sir, the castle wall is ahead,"* a deep, feminine voice stated in his head.

The telepathic communication hammered into his skull with more force than a blacksmith's hammer, shattering the illusion and drawing a hiss and cringe of pain from him. "Not so loud, Lina," he growled softly.

*"Sorry, sir. I–"* she started to respond with the same intensity before catching herself. *"That was a noble thing you did for that girl,"* she finished with less aggressiveness.

He shook his head to clear the cobwebs before responding. *"It was nothing,"* he thought softly, sadness caressing his words. Shaking his head again, he asked more firmly, *"Now, what have you found?"*

*"I made it to the edge of the woods. There's a minimal guard on the wall – I'd say about twenty or so sentries. There's also no sign of the enemy between us and the castle, though it smells like there was a clash recently. You can enter the woods and approach without worry."*

*"Thanks,"* he thought as he started off at a trot, his connection to Lina guiding him in a southwesterly direction, and was soon clear of the village.

As he entered the woods and quickened his pace, Lina's voice entered his head again. *"By the way, sir?"*

*"Yes?"*

*"The humans inside the wall smell worse than you do."*

He smiled briefly at Lina's attempt to cheer him up. *"Thanks for that. You're not being fair, though. They've been trapped in there for days and hardly have the means to do anything about it."*

When he finally caught up to the direwolf, she was looking back at him with an amused glint in her yellow eyes. "What are you looking at, Deralina?" he chided playfully in a whisper.

Deralina cocked her head in amusement before turning and trotting out of the woods and into the clearing that served as the final stretch to Blackstone's wall, leaving the man to catch up.

Before either of them had gone more than a few paces into the expanse of open ground, their presence was noted and the sentries along the wall began to stir. Though they were still a good two hundred yards from the wall, they could just make out the voice of a sentry as he shouted, "Halt! If you move any farther, you'll be shot!" As if to emphasize his point, the battlements began to fill with archers and footmen. A few torches were even lit in anticipation of a full-scale attack.

Deralina's sharp ears could hear the creak of the bowstrings as the archers readied their bows. *"They're serious, sir,"* was the message that seeped into the man's mind.

*"You don't think I know that?"* he retorted.

*"I just thought—"*

*"Kill the chatter, Lina. We need to get inside before our friends in the village grow curious as to what is causing the commotion."* He glanced around even as he finished the thought, gauging the distance to the wall. Even with elevation on their side, the archer's bows would begin to lose accuracy at this range. However, he would bet good coin that Darius had enchanted the bows to bring the woods into range, and he had no desire to test that theory by moving forward and creating an incident.

Before he could decide on a course of action, the sentry shouted again, "Who goes there?"

The man cringed again. Without his enhanced senses, he would have had a hard time hearing the man at this distance, but that wasn't his main concern. While he did not believe the invaders could hear the commotion, the increase in noise and light was eventually going to draw unwanted attention – and that was unacceptable. Gathering fir'gan to him, he used it to project his voice so the sentries on the wall would hear him as if he was standing next to them, eliminating the need to shout and further decreasing the odds that the invaders would notice the commotion. "Tell your master that the Knight of the Bestyne Order is here to speak with him."

He could see that his declaration immediately sent a wave of excitement through the men on the battlements. It was safe to assume that hopeful thinking had spread rumors of rescue through the masses gathered behind the wall, and his arrival would only lend credence to such hopes – much to his chagrin.

Fifteen tedious minutes of nerve-racking silence followed before another sentry appeared on the battlements accompanying a frail figure. The direwolf and her master perked up when they saw the new arrivals. It didn't take either of them long to realize whom it was and just how dire the situation they had walked into was.

*"Can you feel it?"* came Deralina's sorrowful thoughts.

*"Aye,"* he replied softly, his face sinking. *"He's dying."*

He could see the fir'gan gathering about the frail figure, sputtering like a fire gasping for air, and suddenly a question was voiced by a hoarse voice as if it was right next to his ear, "Who approaches Castle Blackstone?"

The tall, powerfully built man took a step forward and lowered his cowl so the frail man on the wall could see his face clearly with his fir'gan-enhanced vision. Touching his fist to his chest in solemn salute, the rust-orange-haired man replied, "Greatjon Durmont of the Bestyne Order."

A brief moment of silence preceded a hoarse, despondent reply. "Approach the gate, Sir Greatjon. Be welcomed to Castle Blackstone, and bear witness to our final hours."


The small study was dark except for the roaring fire in the hearth built into the left-hand wall. In recent days, the room had been cleared of all furniture except two plush high-back chairs. A simple table had been brought in and now sat between the occupied chairs, two full crystal glasses and a decanter of dark liquid sitting on it. At one time, the room had served as Darius' study. Greatjon could remember the days of his youth when he would sit in this very room receiving his schooling from the wise man that had raised him. Sadly, the study now felt like a mausoleum – dark and depressing, it somehow felt like it too was fading like its master. The stench of death permeated the room as it did the entire castle. The smell was enough to make Greatjon want to vomit, but he fought down the urge for the sake of his old friend.

Leaning back in his chair, Greatjon's brown eyes gazed thoughtfully into the fire. Deralina was curled up at his feet, feigning sleep. Darius' condition was a heartbreaking shock for them both. They had expected to find him healthy, albeit stressed from the current situation, but neither of them had been prepared for what they had found. Pale and skeletally gaunt, Darius' black hair hung limp and oily about his shoulders, and from the depths of sunken sockets, his brown eyes appeared dull and listless. A thick bearskin robe was wrapped about his frail frame despite the presence of the roaring fire. He had become so shrunken that both the robe wrapped about him, and the chair he was sitting in, seemed to be trying to swallow him whole. More disturbing to Greatjon was how the currents of fir'gan behaved around his friend; instead of flowing through and around him freely, they seemed to be avoiding him like a high-class parade sidestepping a leper.

Outwardly, Greatjon face was impassive, showing no signs of the remorse and sadness he felt. In his heart, however, he wept for his old friend and mentor. No man deserved such an agonizing death – especially one as noble and as cherished as Darius. However, the world was not fair; it was a cold and dangerous mistress, bereft of concern for the labels and status of people. This lesson was learned – and learned early -- if any of their kind had any hope of living for a long time.

With the finality of their conversation weighing heavily on his mind, Greatjon glanced over at his shriveled mentor and asked softly, "Are you sure you want it this way? I can have you out of here this very night."

Darius shook his head weakly and coughed slightly, dark blood staining his lips. "I'm sure," he answered hoarsely. "I'm too far gone at this point. The blackheart's poison is a death sentence . . ." he tried to chuckle as he eyed Greatjon, but it only resulted in a dry cough, "for all but a few. At best, I have one more day." He smiled weakly. "It's the perfect case of irony – you think you've got till the end of time . . . and then a small cut dooms you."

A small, sad smiled touched Greatjon's lips. "I'm sorry."

Darius waved his apology off weakly. "Don't be. It's not your fault that Darkon gutted your Order after Damion and Valisiana vanished. Besides, even if there was still a full-blooded Bestyne Preceptor, I'm too far gone to be cured."

Greatjon nodded, knowing Darius spoke the truth. "Then is there anything I can do for you?"

"Ay–" he started to say before a violent coughing fit ripped from his lungs, causing Deralina to perk up and Greatjon to lean over to aid him. Waving him off, he let the fit subside before resuming. "Aye. Don't worry about me. What you should be concerned with, is keeping mine and Cat's crystals out of Warrick's hands."

Darius had mentioned this once already, and the weight and implication of the words once again crashed squarely on Greatjon's broad shoulders, weighing his spirit down. "I can do that," he said solemnly. "But what about your people?"

Another coughing fit racked Darius' body, but he seemed oblivious to it as he stared into the fire. Finally, when the spasms passed, he spoke with a great sadness filling his words. "I first came to these mountains when I was only seventeen. I was a young monk full of visions of piety and purity, with designs on bringing Corith's word to the masses. I even was further blessed to be the founder of the Simoria Order and establish this castle. I have watched the people of the Vale grow, marry and die for longer than I can remember." He paused for a moment, sinking into silence. When he did continue, there was a calmness to his words that seemed to reflect his acceptance of his fate. "When the first Blackstone was destroyed all those years ago, I feared that all the villagers had been wiped out. The thanks I offered to Corith when I found survivors – and when I found you – was great. Despite my failings, I have been blessed, Greatjon. I have known great men and evil men. . . . I have seen the best and worst that life can offer. . . . I have no regrets. . . ." A mournful sigh turned to violent coughs as he trailed off.

When the fit passed, he continued. "Now, I have two favors to ask of you. First, is this," he reached a skeletal hand into his robe and pulled forth a gray crystal and then a purple crystal. Light pulsing dimly within each one like a slow heartbeat, each crystal was about the size of a man's fist, and both appeared to be missing a pair of tiny slivers.

Greatjon couldn't hide the shock and horror he felt upon seeing the crystals. "You've already severed your ties to your crystal? Corith be good, Darius! How– "

Darius shook his head weakly. "Strength of will. Besides, I couldn't risk my crystal becoming tainted – such a loss would be unacceptable." He coughed violently and had to take a few deep, phlegm-filled breaths before continuing. "Now then, I want you to take these and protect them. I have no Seeker amongst my men now, so someone else will have to do it. If you would – I wish that Caldain Forsandi be given the task."

Greatjon's heart broke as he stared at the crystals, the finality of Darius' act striking home. "Caldain?" he asked softly. "Damion's man? This is rather . . . odd. Besides, Darkon will be furious that you would entrust a traitor's man with such a task."

Darius shook his head as he handed the crystals over. As Greatjon reverently accepted the crystals and placed them within a pouch at his hip, Darius said, "I've taught you better than that. Damion is no traitor and you know it." He sighed and softly beseeched, "Please – see that Caldain gets that crystal. He is the best there is."

Greatjon nodded slowly, knowing Darius would not deceive him. "Very well. What about yours and Cat's crusaders?"

Darius paused for a moment as if to gather himself, then stated bluntly, "Both destroyed. The corruption had run too deep before I thought to separate myself from my crystal, and its strength was needed to keep me alive." He shook his head. "Too much of the blade's fir'gan has been used for it to re-form. I believe that Cat's crusader fell victim to this as well." He coughed roughly. "I had to take precautions, so I had the vessels destroyed. I simply had to, Greatjon. I didn't know. . . ."

He nodded, understanding Darius' dilemma. *So that's what's been keeping him going,* Greatjon thought before asking aloud, "And your other favor?"

Darius' pain-filled eyes stared lazily into the roaring fire. "My men know how to get the survivors out, but there is one I wish you to find and protect. This is possibly more important than protecting the crystals."

"Couldn't this person get out with the others?" Greatjon asked in puzzlement.

Darius coughed and replied hoarsely, "Possibly. But she is .. . special."

Greatjon perked up. "She?"

"Aye – she. I've been observing her for a while; I noticed her potential long ago, and I've seen her connection to fir'gan grow over the years. She is a Gifted, Greatjon. When Cat died, I knew Corith had blessed me by bringing her to me."

"She's Cat's replacement," Greatjon stated with absolute certainty.

Darius nodded. "That she is. It didn't take a Seeker to see just how strongly Cat's crystal reacted in her presence." Darius reached out a skeletal hand and grasped Greatjon's forearm tightly. Looking directly into his eyes, Darius spoke with the unflinching au-
226

thority Greatjon had come to know and respect. "You will find her and protect her. Tell Darkon nothing of this – keep her existence quiet and train her in secret."

Greatjon stared at Darius in confusion. "Are you feeling alright? None of us may find Darkon's presence appealing, but to deceive one of our own in such a way is treasonous."

The intensity in Darius' eyes grew and his grip tightened. "You will be responsible for her, Greatjon – no one else! Damion vanished for a reason, and Valisiana said she feared for her life before she disappeared! I have never trusted Darkon, and nothing has been right with the world since Luthur's passing! Darkon may be our leader, but I fear we are treading down a path where the reward may not be worth the danger! Swear to me you will do as I ask, Greatjon!"

Greatjon continued to stare at Darius, wondering if the fire burning in his eyes was intensity or fever. Finally, he nodded slowly. "I swear."

"Damn you, Greatjon – swear it!"

Taken aback by the outburst, Greatjon could only believe that Darius was deathly serious. While he didn't find Darkon as obnoxious as the others did, he had long ago learned to trust Darius. Nodding sternly, he consented to Darius' request. "By blood, by honor and by deed, this I swear – I will protect her with my life, and do hear-by take full control of her training. My life will be hers."

Darius nodded and fell back in his chair, a chain of violent coughs stealing his intensity and energy. "Ask the captain," he coughed again, "where Aseria Mitsurea is." A stronger coughing fit struck, forcing him to double-over as blood flecks burst from his mouth with each chest-rattling convulsion. Greatjon bolted upright, startling Deralina as he moved to aid his friend. Darius held up a hand, forestalling the offered help. "Go!" he cried weakly. "Find her and get everyone to safety! My time is nearing its end and yours is just beginning! We must not fail!" He sank back into his chair, exhaustion weighing him down.

"I'll keep her safe, my friend," Greatjon said remorsefully before he stood and gathered his cloak and claymore from next to the hearth. "Rest well. Lina – come."

Greatjon and Deralina made their way to the study's door, but before they could leave, Darius' weak voice called out, "Remember – protect her and protect the crystals. If . . . if you ever encounter Damion, tell him I'm sorry it had to end this way. Tell him that I . . . that I always appreciated everything he did for me."

Greatjon leaned his head against the doorframe and closed his eyes, his heart aching for his friend. "I will, Darius," he replied sorrowfully, "I will. May the Light illuminate your path." With solemn silence, he and Deralina exited the room, the door closing with a profound click of finality.

Darius sat there for a time, his thoughts lost as he stared into the fire. Finally, he whispered a reply . . . though there was no one there to hear it. "May Corith guide you as well . . ." the corner of his lips tugged upward for a moment, "my friend."

Greatjon slung his heavy brown cloak on over his padded leathers and slid his claymore home over his right shoulder as they moved through the barren and cold halls of Blackstone, his mood matching the chill. Every one of the main hallways of Blackstone sported vaulted ceilings that consumed the light of the lamps hanging at even intervals along the walls. At one time, art and furniture had adorned the halls; now, however, every resource had been deemed expendable and the luxuries had been removed to help fuel the fires keeping the refugees warm. It was just another depressing detail that made Greatjon's heart feel like his happiness was being devoured in the same fashion that the vaulted ceilings consumed the lamplight.

As they strode through the upper halls, barren walls were soon broken-up by leaded-glass windows that were taller than two men standing upon each other's shoulders. Moonlight spilt through the portals, adding its airy bluish-silver glow to the warm lamplight. Normally the sight of a full moon and a star-filled sky would cheer Greatjon up, but on this night, it seemed more like the moon and stars were keeping a mournful vigil. His mood must have been palpable, as two guards making their rounds quickly made way for the fierce direwolf and dour man. Neither Greatjon nor Deralina paid the two men any heed as they continued past them and stepped upon a winding staircase of blue marble that would take them from the upper floors directly to the main floor.

As empty as the other floors – the refugees having been restricted to the courtyard in an attempt to prevent prying eyes from discovering Darius' fatal condition – the main floor maintained the eerie, sorrowful atmosphere of the rest of the castle. Making their way in and out of the muted pools of color cast by the stained-glass windows, Greatjon and Deralina remained mournfully quiet.

Eventually, feeling that the woeful silence had gone on for too long, Deralina broke the dour hush between them. *"It won't be the same without him,"* came the mournful, telepathic condolence.

"No it won't," was his flat, vocal reply.

*"I'm truly sorry, Master. He was a great man,"* Lina added, emotion making her normally bright, telepathic voice seem fraught with deep heartache and loss.

Greatjon nodded numbly in response.

They finally reached the large double doors that served as the main entrance to the castle. The sturdy bronze panels were pulled open by two chainmail-adorned guards, granting them passage into the cold, star-filled night. Neither Greatjon nor Deralina felt the cold like the residents of the Vale, but the cloak and thick clothing kept up appearances. As they moved across the courtyard toward the barracks at a solemn pace, it was impossible to ignore the despair permeating the air. All about the courtyard, refugees were packed into every available space. Some of the people moved about their makeshift camps lethargically, some slept, and others were huddled about the numerous fires that burned brightly, trying to absorb what warmth they could.

Whatever their activity, for the greater portion of the refugees, coming to terms with the events of the past few weeks was proving difficult, if not impossible; one only had to see the empty, bleak eyes of those that sat staring into oblivion to grasp the depth of their trauma. The sights and sounds they'd born witness to were more horrific than any of them had ever imagined possible. Nearly everyone had lost a loved one or friend in the attacks or on the harsh trek to Blackstone, but death was something they understood and accepted as inevitable. It was the extent that the invaders had gone to that had rocked them to the very core of their being. No matter how dangerous, deadly or twisted they thought humanity could be, none of them had thought anyone or anything capable of such malevolence. Darius had done his best to help them contend with the tragedies; however, once he fell ill, the villagers lost their one bit of solace and had once again been left to cope on their own.

Deralina sniffed at the air as she glanced about, smelling the fear and anxiety on the air. *"Do they have to be sacrificed?"*

"Have to? No," he muttered. "But it may come to that."

*"Is it the same as last time?"*

"Unfortunately." He sighed deeply. "Let's go see the captain and find out where our new charge is."

Finding the captain was the easiest thing they had done all-night. Greatjon's first instinct was to check the captain's office, which he recalled being in the main barracks; however, on the off-chance that he happened to be somewhere else, Greatjon inquired of one of the many soldiers roaming the grounds about the captain's whereabouts. Not surprisingly, they eventually found themselves standing in the entrance to the captain's office, their objective seated at his desk and deeply engrossed in mapping strategy. A lone candelabra lit the room, exposing it to be a very plain and barren space except for a paper-laden desk, a chair for guests, and the simple chair that the captain occupied.

The bald and grizzled captain, a thickset man of fifty summers with jolly bright-green eyes, looked up when the two entered. A broad, gap-toothed grin spread across his visage when he saw their familiar faces. Standing, his chainmail hauberk rattling, he said with enthusiasm, "Well I'll be a— Greatjon! I'd heard you came sneaking in! How have you been? Please, have a seat! Have a seat!" The two men clasped wrists before Greatjon sat in the lone extra chair. Eyeing Deralina as he returned to his seat, the captain quipped, "How ya been, Deralina? Eh? Still hanging around with this old looser?" Deralina barked a gruff reply, drawing a laugh from the captain as he replied, "Thought so."

The smile quickly vanished and he sighed, his tone turning serious. "So what brings you two back home? I trust you've already seen Darius?"

Greatjon nodded grimly. "Tell me what happened."

Grant sighed. "As stupid as it sounds, it was a damn accident. They were simply pelting the walls with arrows; wasn't anything more than harassment, and only those foolish enough to stick their heads above the wall got wounded. From what I gather, Darius was mad and wanted to vent his rage in some fashion." Shaking his head, Grant rubbed his face. "Long story short, he scythed down most of the archers, but managed to get himself nicked by a damn arrow in the process. Just our luck that it was a Corith-be-damned blackheart arrow. Had to be the only one, too; none of the other wounded fell ill."

Shaking his head at the absurdity of it all, Greatjon pulled out the gray crystal for the captain to see. "Well, as you can see, Grant . . . the situation is not good."

Captain Grant shook his head and swore. "Never thought I'd live to see that, but I guess it was to be expected. I guess this means we don't have much time left, eh?"

Greatjon nodded, returning the crystal to his pouch. "Indeed."

Grant ran a hand over his baldhead before scratching at his chin. "Not good. . . . Did he leave any final orders?"

"Aye," Greatjon nodded again. "He asks that we holdout long enough to get as many of the villagers out as possible."

Nodding thoughtfully, Grant replied, "Oh, aye, I was expecting that. We've been clearing the tunnels beneath the castle since Darius was wounded, just in case it came to this." He laughed cynically. "Morbid that we'd already be prepared for the worst, eh?"

Greatjon shrugged indifferently. "It was always Darius' way. Prepare for the worst and hope for the best."

Grant snorted. "Well, hoping didn't do us much good – those damnable blackheart abominations saw to that." He snorted again in disgust. "Two dead Wardens and an army of nightmares beyond our wall. I'm glad you're here, Greatjon – but alone, I don't think you can do all that much. Maybe if Darius hadn't sent Lan on a fool's hunt for Damion we might stand a chance with you two." Sighing and shaking his head, he added, "Well . . . what's done is done. No sense in bemoaning the past, eh? So, is there anything else that I should be aware of?"

Greatjon couldn't help but grind his teeth both at the mention of Darius' long missing Knight, and at once again hearing Damion's name spoken aloud. It seemed to him that tragedy after tragedy could be laid at that man's feet. Taking Grant's advice, he cast the line of thought aside and turned his focus to the present, saying, "You'll be in charge of the wall. Darius wants me to see to the refugees' safety. Also, there's one person, in particular, he wanted me to find."

The captain barked a sarcasm-laden laugh. "Well – that shouldn't prove *too* difficult. As you've seen, we have just a *few* people crammed in here," he drawled.

Greatjon stared at him gravely. "This is important, Grant. Darius deemed her survival more important than anything else."

Grant nodded apologetically. "Aye. Aye. Well then, lad, who's this prize of yours, then?"

Greatjon leaned forward. "Her name is Aseria Mitsurea. Darius said you could point me to her."

The captain smiled dryly and shook his head. "Figures as much. She won't be hard to find at all. You see – she's a darlion." Greatjon blinked, taken aback by the statement, drawing an amused smirk from Grant. "Oh, aye, I see Darius didn't mention that. Aye, she's a darlion, and a bit of an odd one at that. When all the others left, she decided to stay. Honestly, never seemed to get along with her own kind very well. Quite a looker, I might add . . . if you've got a thing for the exotic."

Greatjon shook off his shock and pressed forward. "Where is she?"

Grant motioned outside. "She's on the battlements. Scares the men to death, the way she perches on the merlons like its nothing." Grant paused, gauging Greatjon before asking, "Tell me something – why's she so important?"

Greatjon stood and moved to the doorway. "She's Cat's replacement."

Grant nodded and sat back in his chair. "Ah, I see. Well then, the best of luck to you and her. Now get out of here. I've preparations to make, and I suspect very little time left to do it in."

Greatjon smirked. "Thanks," he said as he turned to leave.

"Greatjon," stated Grant.

"Yeah?" he replied, looking back over his shoulder.

"Sorry we had to meet again under such circumstances. I would've liked to share that bottle of ale you promised me all those years ago."

Greatjon smiled sadly. "Me too." With those parting words, he and Deralina left Grant to his work and made their way back into the cold night.


The battlements were crowned with thick crenels and merlons, and a twenty-foot wide ironwood wall walk providing sturdy footing. Twelve unlucky watchmen patrolled sixty-foot sections of the wall, each of them bundled against the cold and bitter wind that blew about the top of the towering fortification. Fires burned in braziers in each of the towers, warming those lucky enough to have a moment to escape the wind-battered wall. The guards inside the West Tower, warmed by the brazier and tired from a long day, paid little heed to the rust-orange-haired man and the gray- and black-splotched direwolf as the two ascended the tower and made their way onto the battlements.

The cold wind cut mercilessly into anyone taller than the nearly six-foot-tall merlons, which Greatjon was. Closing his eyes, he smiled, allowing the wind to relax and refresh him. He needed time to think and to make a report to Darkon – though he had no idea what he would say. However, the night was not quite over. Relaxing his mind, he told Deralina, *"Let's go find her."*

The three guards they passed as they trekked across the battlements acknowledged them with two slight nods, which Greatjon returned curtly. After a short jaunt, he finally spotted his target and slipped a hand into the pouch where the two crystals now resided. By touch alone, he could distinguish between the two; as a result, his hand quickly settled on the one that had formerly belonged to Cat and he felt for its pulse. To those like him, the extent to which they could feel a crystal's pulse was a gift unto itself. However, no matter how skilled one was, a crystal's owner could be found simply by measuring its beat. The closer a crystal was to its owner, the faster the beat. Seekers were so skilled at reading a crystal's pulse that they could find an owner from leagues away with no assistance, whereas a Warden or Knight would need to amplify the ability with fir'gan, exposing their presence to would-be enemies. However, on this night, Greatjon had little need to enhance the reading – the crystal hummed with life, beating strongly as it neared its would-be host.

Crouched on her haunches, the darlion balanced on her toes atop a merlon near the gate tower like a living gargoyle. The strong wind whipping across the top of the wall buffeted her long yellow-blonde hair about her, but there was no indication that the wind gusts disturb her balance.

Greatjon stopped before they reached her and held a hand down in front of Deralina's nose to halt the direwolf. *"Why don't you go and find something to eat,"* he suggested.

What he could only interoperate as a laugh came back to his thoughts. *"I was about to suggest the same. You know how much darlions smell like cats to me,"* she replied playfully before turning and loping back the way they had come.

Greatjon continued on slowly, trying to think of what to say. The responsibility that would soon be placed on her shoulders could not simply be dumped on her. He needed to get her out of the castle and somehow convince her of the truth about her existence and the world itself. Most people went about their lives oblivious to what was actually happening around them in the shadows, which made it difficult to bring them around to the truth. He sighed to himself. No one ever took life-altering news well – especially when it asked you to abandon everything you had ever known. His thoughts continued to mull on this until he drew close enough to make out her features.

Her face was slender and attractive in the cat-like way of the darlions. Lightly accentuated cheekbones and a slender, flat nose graced her face with exotic and alluring angles. Long ears, their tips capped with tuffs of white fur, swept back from her head, adding to the feline grace of her face. Her long yellow-blonde hair – which was in actuality fur – would have hung to her waist when at rest, and her bangs would have just reached eye level. Her face was covered in fur short enough to be mistaken for skin if not for the white color and small accent stripes of yellow. Though she appeared to be slender underneath her fur cloak and leather armor, Greatjon was sure she was blessed with the whipcord muscles of her people that would give her strength and grace that belied her slender build.

As she turned her head in his direction to scan the horizon, it was her eyes that demanded his attention. Large and almond-shaped, her blue-lavender eyes were like brightly lit, warm pools as they gazed out toward the glow of the burning fires in Blackstone Village. Though darlions rarely stirred lustful desires within him, Greatjon felt that a man could drown in those eyes.

*"Is that a sense of lust or passion coming from your cold heart?"* came the telepathic taunt from Deralina.

*"Awe at a beautiful sight in dark times."*

*"It will stain."*

*"That's the sad part."*

Greatjon shook his head and steeled himself before approaching and stopping next to her. She was short for a darlion; had she been standing on even footing with him, she would have only come up to Greatjon's chin. For a moment, he just stood there, waiting to see if she would notice him. When it became apparent that she was either oblivious to his presence or ignoring him, he decided to speak. "What do you see?" he asked suddenly.

Though startled, she kept her balance as her head whipped around to focus her bright eyes on Greatjon. "Excuse me?" her musical voice chimed.

"What do you see?" he asked again.

She gave him a quizzical look, baffled by both the sudden arrival of a complete stranger and the odd question. "Why should I answer?"

"Because I asked."

She looked him over, her ears twitching. "You're the Bestyne? Right?"

He nodded. "I am. And a friend of Darius as well. Greatjon Durmont is the name."

She nodded. "Well then, Greatjon, I would suggest being watchful. The last friend of his to visit lost her life to that crazed, red-armored man's demon-spawned creatures."

Greatjon flinched visibly at the narrative.

Raising an inquisitive eyebrow, she asked, "Did you know her?"

He nodded solemnly.

"Ah. . . . Well, I was friends with her while she was still alive. A beautiful brunette and an animal with a blade. Cat certainly carved her fair share of the enemy to pieces before she went to Corith's embrace."

Greatjon smiled sadly. "Aye, that sounds like her."

The darlion stood and stretched, her back arching gracefully, before nimbly hoping from the merlon to the walkway. Looking up at him with her bright eyes, she nodded in sympathy. "I'm truly sorry you lost your friend, but if you'll excuse me, I need to be getting some rest while I can. Corith only knows when they will decide to attack in full." She started to go around him, but quickly found her path blocked as he stepped in her way. Impatient, she hissed her irritation and motioned for him to move with her gloved and armored hand. "Would you please move? I've got better things to do than play games!"

Greatjon reached out and grabbed her firmly by the shoulders. "Sorry – but my business with you hasn't ended."

"Look," a fierce light began to burn in her eyes, "I don't have time for this! I need to rest and– " she tried to shake his hands off, but found them to be as immovable as a mountain. She gave a violent shake but could barely budge the grip. "What the hells?" she exclaimed looking up into Greatjon's eyes, surprise and confusion written clearly on her face. "Who in the hells are you?"

"I told you," he said sternly, "Greatjon Durmont. I'm a friend of Darius."

"If you're really a friend of his, then you'll let me go!"

Two guards from the gate tower peaked out to see what the commotion was about, but a firm look from Greatjon sent them back to their fire. Turning his attention back to the darlion, he said, "I can't do that – Darius has put me in charge of you."

She stared at him in amazement. "He did what? I don't think so. I am his charge! He wouldn't do that! Now let me go! I want to speak to Darius about this treatment!" She tried to wiggle free again — to no avail.

"Darius is dead," Greatjon stated bluntly, bringing an abrupt end to her struggles.

Sagging in his grip, her eyes grew wide with a mix of horror and sadness as she whispered, "What did you say?"

"Darius is dead," he repeated firmly, his words softened by remorse. "His final orders were to place you under my protection."

She blinked in disbelief and shook her head. "I knew he was sick, but. . ." she shook her head again before looking back up at Greatjon with sad eyes, tears welling in the corners of them. "You're telling the truth, aren't you?"

Greatjon nodded and slowly released his grip on her shoulders. "I'm sorry, but it's true."

She shook her head again as she struggled with the news. "I'd heard whispers that his condition was fatal, but I never thought. . . ." She suddenly shuddered and sighed before finishing weakly, "He was always so strong." Closing her eyes, she gathered herself before looking Greatjon in the eyes. "You say that he placed me in your charge?"

Nodding, he answered softly, "Aye."

"Darius had always taken a special interest in me. He was even responsible for me meeting Cat. They'd made mention of special training for me, citing my work ethic and skills, but I never would have thought their interest would run so deep as to assign me a protector." Her brow furrowed. "Why would he do that?"

Greatjon leaned against the wall. "The fact that you know of my Order leads me to believe he's told you some about who we are. Correct?"

She nodded. "He did, but he always seemed a bit elusive. When his friend died, his interest in me grew; he started to tell me more, but then . . ." her throat clenched as her train of thought led her thoughts to Darius' death, "then . . . he fell ill . . ." she finished and shrugged weakly, tears slipping from her eyes. "That was that. I haven't spoken with him since then . . ." she trailed off. "Guess I never will," she whispered as Darius' death continued to sink in.

Greatjon nodded. "Then let me give you the short of it. Each of our Orders has a hierarchy, and when one of those positions is left vacant, it is left to the rest to fill it. When Cat died, her position of Preceptor and Warden was left vacant. You, Aseria Mitsurea, have been chosen to fill her position."

All thoughts of Darius' death vanished as Greatjon's declaration cut through the fog of loss threatening to engulf her mind. She stared at him blankly, not quite sure she'd heard him right. "Me? An Order Preceptor?" she asked slowly. "I know you are joking now. A position of such importance should always go to the next in line, not some outsider."

Greatjon stared at her firmly. "It doesn't work that way. Our ranks are determined by our skills and our destiny – if you want to call it that." He sighed and folded his arms across his chest as she smirked in disbelief and shook her head. "You are what we call a Gifted."

"Gifted?" her brow furrowed in puzzlement as she wiped her eyes clear, her tears quickly drying up as her focus shifted. "I'm good with a bow, sure, but I wouldn't call it something so grandiose."

Greatjon shook his head. "That's not what I mean. Have you ever heard the term fir'gan?"

"Fir'gan? Now you're bantering about terms normally heard in sermons," she said with a bemused chuckle. "It's nothing more than a youngling's tale."

Greatjon pushed away from the wall. "No, it's not. Fir'gan is the lifeblood of all things – and it is very, very real." Before she could retort, Greatjon held up his hand, palm upward, and brought to life a small fireball with barely a thought.

Aseria yelped as it burst into existence, the young flame hissing and spitting as the strong wind fought to extinguish it.

Overcoming her surprise, she leaned forward to investigate it, awe and amazement written all over her face. "How did you do that?" she breathed, her melancholy thoughts completely banished by the display and replaced with disbelief.

Greatjon closed his fist, extinguishing the flame with a hiss. "Fir'gan. I am like you, Aseria. I can see and control fir'gan – I am a Gifted," he stated bluntly.

She stared back at him, still mired in disbelief. "I'm not sure I can swallow all this. Why me? Why now?"

Greatjon turned to face the glow of the fires burning in the village and pointed into the distance. "What do you see?" he asked in answer to her question.

She looked at him quizzically. "If you're asking me if I can see fir'gan – I don't. What I do see, however, is an army of invaders who have attacked and raped this land and its people for no other

reason than to indulge their blood lust as humans seem to always do."
She hesitated just a moment and then asked, "What do you see?"

Greatjon's brown eyes stared in the direction of Blackstone
Village coldly. "I see a man who's done this before. I see an army
that kills every man no matter his age and rapes every mature woman
– including those who have barely begun to show signs of woman-
hood. I see depravity on a tremendous scale, and I see everything
that is wrong with humanity and a mockery of Corith's will."

Despite similar assertions, she stared at him, aghast at what
she had just heard. "How can you speak with such coldness about
such horrid things?" she hissed with a mix of disbelief and anger. He
turned his gaze on her, and she could see the pain of countless years
gazing back at her. She'd seen that look before in Darius' eyes, and
had never fully come to terms with how one could carry such a burden.

Words spoken with a calmness that belied the rage burning
behind them, he said, "Because I've seen it happen before, and I
know the army and the man you face. None of us stands a chance
against a man like him in our current situation. If you choose to believe me and trust me, then one day you might be strong enough to
face such a demon."

"Who is he?" she inquired.

Greatjon turned away from her, ignoring the question. The
currents, both within the keep and toward the village, were beginning
to behave in a foreboding manner. Fighting down a growl of anger,
he said, "This castle will not see another night. If you wish to live and
truly make a difference against atrocities such as what has befallen this
Vale, then meet me in the courtyard in five hours – there are things
about you that you need to know."

Before she could respond, his long strides had carried him
down the battlements, leaving her to digest his cryptic words.


The fire had burned down to glowing embers, casting the
study into deep shadow. Darius sat silently in the shadows of his
chair, watching the fire slowly die as if it was a mirror of his own life
force. Ever since the blackheart's arrow had nicked him, he'd been
slowly dying. If he had been normal like those he had fought to protect for so long, he would have suffered a horrible but quick death.
Instead, because of the small amount of poison in his system, his gifts
had kept him alive for much longer than he had any right to be.
However, his choice to break the bond with his crystal had seen his
illness accelerate, drawing him closer to death's embrace. He didn't

regret the choice in the least. By severing the connection, he had saved his crystal from the corruption that would have consumed it had he died while still bonded. A violent cough disturbed his motionless body, forcing black blood onto his lips, the despoiled liquid sliding down his chin. He didn't bother to wipe it away; he no longer had the energy or the care to do so.

A bright blue light burst forth from the shadows at the back of the room, illuminating the study for moment before quickly fading. There was a moment of silence before a soft, mournful woman's voice gently said, "You should have called me."

For a moment, Darius' eyes lit up and a smile tried unsuccessfully to creep onto his face. "I know," was all he managed.

The shadows in the back of the room shifted and a long, strong feminine figure separated from the inky depths. Moving in front of Darius with silken, animal-like grace, she crouched on her haunches so she could peer into his eyes. Placing a graceful, four-fingered hand on his lovingly, she said mournfully, "I am so deeply sorry, my beloved."

Though it was difficult to smile, his eyes did for him what his lips were struggling to do as he tried to make out her features. The shadow's hid much, but he could see her sharp bronze-colored features and long, swept-back ears. Golden eyes, with their vertical pupils, glowed in the dying firelight as they met Darius' lovingly. "Not your fault, Love."

Her sleek head shook resolutely, her thick black hair shining dully in the dim firelight. "It is – I should have been here with you! I never should have–"

Darius reached a hand forward and weakly stroked her high cheekbone along one of the white stripes he could make out on her tanned skin, relishing the feel of her soft, almost fur-like flesh. She leaned into the gesture and closed her eyes, tears beginning to stream down her cheeks. "Shhhhhhhhuuush. It's all right. None of this is your fault," he whispered consolingly.

She sniffed and opened her eyes. "No! It is! I ran when I should have fought! I left you alone in all this!"

Darius forced a smile, draining his energy even more. "My dear, sweet Valisiana – you have a heart too big for your own good. If you hadn't run, you would be dead and so would our child. Darkon would have seen to it that our . . . violation of protocol was fixed. Because of what you did, you lived – as did our child."

239

She smiled and tried to laugh with joy, tears streaming down her cheeks, but failed completely. "You are the brave one, my dearest. You helped keep me and our child secret and safe. For that, I will be eternally grateful. . . . And your son would be too, if he knew of our sacrifice."

Darius gave the briefest hint of a smirk and nodded slightly. "You have watched over him, yes?"

"I have, from a distance," she said, reassuring him despite knowing that he was well aware that she always had. She smiled again, white teeth and elongated canines visible. "He's like us all too much. He . . . he even has a wife of his own, and she is with child! We're going to be grandparents, my love!"

The news forced another weak smile from his battered body and a tear of joy escaped his eye. "Thank you for that news, my love. I am at peace knowing that our future is in good hands." He gave her cheek one last loving stroke before dropping his hand to his lap, his strength slowly fading. "I have one last thing to ask of you, my dearest."

Valisiana nodded enthusiastically. "Anything."

Darius gestured weakly to the shadows to his right. "There is a hidden coffer in the wall over there. Mine and Cat's crusaders reside within. Take them and guard them until such a time that new and trustworthy masters are found." He coughed violently. "I will not risk more crusaders falling under Darkon's will." Valisiana nodded, squeezing Darius' hand firmly to let him know she understood. "Go now," he whispered. "If you remain too long, you may draw unwanted attention. Keep our child and his family safe. Don't let them become a target of his unwarranted rage."

Darius could feel tears dripping onto his hand as she cupped it in both of her hands and brought it to her soft lips, kissing it with a passion that conveyed the profound sense of loss she felt. "I will miss you, my love. Kylir will be a darker place without you." She kissed the skeletal hand deeply one last time, no longer bothering to fight back the tears.

With movements that were extremely tentative despite their grace, she stood up and walked back into the shadows. Darius could hear the familiar click as the hidden coffer was opened. There was a brief rustle and a suppressed yelp of sadness as his beloved retrieved the swords. A moment of silence followed, and then the flare of blue light returned for a brief period before it winked out and she was gone.

Darius turned his gaze back to the dying fire, tears of joy running down his cheeks. He could pass in peace now, without fear for his family or retribution for their transgressions. His son lived and was to be a father soon – he couldn't ask for more. As the fire slowly died, he offered a silent prayer that his son could be the father that he had never been. Slowly, ever so slowly, his breathing slowed and his eyes grew heavy. Then, as the last of the embers in the hearth died, he could almost hear the castle moan with loss as the last of his breath passed from his body.

With the gentlest of smiles upon his withered lips, he slipped into Corith's gentle embrace.

# Chapter Eleven

**C**old can be described as many things. Some say that it is a feeling that only animals and people experience when life-sustaining warmth is leached from the body. Others say it is simply a part of nature that accompanies the onset of winter. Then there are those who say it is a state of mind achieved when someone either loses touch with their emotions, or detaches themselves from the consequences of their actions.

Greatjon stood in the courtyard as an example of detachment. His brown cloak concealed his body all the way to the tops of his black boots, the heavy fabric rustling lazily in the bitter breeze. The bangs of his rust-orange hair framed his face like a cowl as his brown eyes followed the movements of the guards pacing their sections of the towering wall. It was with cold detachment that Greatjon realized those men, though they might be prepared for it, were unaware of the fate that would befall them this day.

Deralina nuzzled his hand through his cloak, drawing a half-hearted pat on the head. *"Thanks,"* she said with dry sarcasm.

Looking down at her, he cracked a half-smile. "Sorry, Lina," he spoke aloud.

*"She'll show up."*

*"I hope you're right,"* he replied as he shifted his shoulders, adjusting the weight of the claymore on his back.

For half an hour, they had been waiting in the deathly silent courtyard, hoping that Aseria wouldn't lose her nerve and decide not to show. So it was with the greatest relief that they saw her making her way toward them from the barracks – ten minutes late.

Fur cloak swaying with her fluid movements, she picked her way through the makeshift camp. A heavy traveling pack was slung over one shoulder and a slender longsword was strapped across her back, its leather-wrapped hilt easily accessible over her right shoulder.

When she finally reached them, she let the pack drop next to her feet as she stared directly into Greatjon's eyes, her bright blue-lavender eyes glowing with intensity. "Before you say anything," she stated firmly, "I want you to know that your . . . *our* cowardice is unprovoked. They'll break on our wall. I don't believe this castle will fall."

Greatjon folded his arms across his chest and cocked his head to the side curiously. "Then why – if you're so confident – did you show?"

She shrugged with cat-like cuteness and indifference. "Curiosity, I suppose."

He nodded, not believing her indifference in the least, but more than willing to accept her reason if it meant getting her out of the keep. "Very well then – follow Deralina, here." He patted the direwolf's thick neck. "She'll take you to our escape route."

Aseria eyed Deralina skeptically and asked, "What about you?"

Prior to Aseria's arrival, Greatjon had been using his senses to get a feel for the state of the castle structure, and the results had further solidified his belief that they had little time left. With Darius' death, the fir'gan that helped support and reinforce Blackstone had begun to crumble and fade. The centuries-old structure would soon succumb to its advanced age, making it more fragile than any building of that magnitude had any right to be. The wall would fall easily and the rest of Blackstone would follow. He also knew that if he could sense this, then the bastard leading the forces in Blackstone Village was well aware of it as well – and that realization was gnawing at him. Grant had yet to begin moving the refugees in-mass to the tunnels, and he was beginning to think that the delay was going to exact a massive toll in innocent blood.

Instead of telling her the truth, he banished the dark thoughts for a moment and forced a smirk. "Don't worry about me. I have something to take care of before I can leave; I made a promise to Darius that I would see to it that as many as possible escape, and I intend to make good on that promise."

She stared at him for a moment, gauging the weight of his words, and nodded. "Good. Then I won't. On the other hand – can I trust a direwolf to guide me?"

Greatjon smirked in true amusement this time. "Of course you can. Direwolves *love* cats." Leaving no chance for a retort, Greatjon then turned and headed for the main gate and the sight that he knew awaited him.


Even from the battlements, the sun was not yet visible; however, when Greatjon turned his gaze skyward and to the west, he could not only see the darkness of night beginning to fade to gray, but he could also see an ever-so-subtle hint of red silhouetting the peaks on the horizon. He wished with all his heart that the sunrise signified a new and great beginning. Instead, he knew that it heralded an end. Like the red hue that was slowly creeping across the sky, he knew that the castle grounds would soon run red with blood.

Shaking his head in sadness, he turned his gaze to the north, his fir'gan-enhanced vision showing him things that the others along the wall would not be able to see. The field that he and Deralina had crossed the previous night was dew covered and quiet. There was no sound except the howling of the wind, which was odd. Suspicion growing within him, he narrowed his focus upon the forest that stood between the castle and village. Within moments, he knew they were in trouble. Hidden by the howling wind was the thudding and clanking of an army on the march. The ominous sound reverberated in his ears like a mourning bell, drawing a glower from him. It didn't take him long to make out the strengthening glow of torches beneath the canopy as the army slowly made its way along the main path. Aware that he was the only one that knew of the advancing force, he realized that he needed to sound the alarm. Though they stood no chance of winning, he still thought they deserved a fighting chance.

Glancing to his right, he barked at the soldier leaning against the wall, "You there!"

Startled, the tired soldier in thick furs jumped and stared at Greatjon as if surprised to learn someone was on the wall with him. "Ye– Yes, sir?" the guard managed to stutter.

"Go fetch Captain Tarmir," he ordered bluntly.

Though he appeared groggy, the sentry didn't hesitate at the chance to escape the wind and cold. He scurried around Greatjon and into the tower. Although he returned surprisingly fast with Grant in tow, Greatjon felt like a lifetime had passed as he monitored the advancing force.

Clad in chainmail and a gray tabard slashed with purple, Grant looked like he had been expecting the summons. Just below the buckler strapped to his forearm, his left hand gripped the hilt of his broadsword with nervous tension. Grant placed himself next to Greatjon and dismissed the guard before turning his grim gaze on the orange-haired warrior. "What's up? Did you find Aseria?"

Greatjon nodded. "That we did. She's waiting for me with Deralina."

Grant sighed with relief. "That's good. At least she'll get out of here alive."

"You felt it then?"

His grip tightening on his sword hilt, Grant nodded grimly. "Aye. I may not be as old as the lot of you, and nowhere near as gifted, but I've been here long enough to know Blackstone. The castle wept for its master and now it's following him into the great beyond. We won't make it past the morning, will we?"

Greatjon knew the question was rhetorical, but he answered anyway. "Aye – Blackstone has nothing left to give." He took a deep breath as Grant shook his head. He could see in the old captain's eyes that he had already resigned himself to the fate that awaited them all. "You had better get your men ready and get the refugees moving into the tunnels with a sense of urgency. He's in the woods already."

Grant's head shot up and his eyes showing just a hint of fear. "Warrick?"

"Warrick," he stated simply.

A sharp intake of breath by the captain was followed by a string of curses. "Guess he's tired of toying with us, eh?" He sighed and shook his head. "I've been gifted with a hundred and fifty years, lad. Too old for any human, and I don't see how the lot of you manage it. With Darius gone and Blackstone to follow . . ." he shook his head again and put on a false smile. "Well, I guess my time is up too. When this place goes, I'll go with it. We'll see to it that you get the time you need to get Aseria and the others out of here."

Greatjon nodded softly and started to reply, when suddenly he froze and turned to face the woods, his face hardening into a grim mask.

Grant stared at him in curiosity. "Are you alright, lad? Can I–"

Greatjon held up a hand, cutting him off and forestalling any further comments.

*"Well, well. . . . It looks like I'll get more than I bargained for."*

The slime-filled, grating words hammered into Greatjon's head, drawing a scowl from him. *"Hello Warrick,"* he retorted mentally. *"I see that this game hasn't gotten old for you."*

*"Of course not, old boy! Destroying this vale and making your lives miserable is my favorite pastime. Besides – no one's really ever stopped me yet, have they?"* There was a momentary pause before Warrick continued, his sarcastic words dripping with glee. *"By the way – how is Darius? I'm concerned about the old bugger's health."*

Greatjon's scowl deepened, causing Grant to take an involuntary step back. *"He's dead,"* he growled in reply.

"*Ah, such a shame. I truly was hoping to gut him myself. Blackheart poison is so . . . impersonal. Oh well, I'll just have to settle for you.*"

"*You sick bastard!*" Greatjon barked violently.

An echoing chuckle rattled in his head. "*Oh, such compliments from an animal like you. I'm honored. Granted, you're just a pup, but just imagine how my standing will improve if I bag not only Darius and Cat, but your miserable carcass too? I'll have the others groveling at my feet.*"

"*Rot in hells!*" Greatjon retorted in rage.

Another glee-filled laugh greeted the statement. "*Been there, done that – got bored. You really should–*"

Greatjon cut the connection, shutting his mind off to Warrick. Refocusing his thoughts he said, "*Lina – did you hear all that?*"

"*I did.*"

"*Get Aseria out of here now. I'm going to stay and buy as much time as I can.*"

"*You're not going to fight him?*" came the worried question.

"*No. This is neither the time nor place to die. We're already down too many Wardens, and foolish deaths will serve no purpose at all. However, I do think I can stall him and thin his ranks a bit.*"

"*You're not going to use your fir'gan in that fashion? Excessive use of fir'gan has been expressly forbidden for centuries . . . and Darkon won't like it one bit.*"

"*Darkon and ancient orders can rot in hells,*" he growled. "*He's not here getting his hands dirty, now is he? I'll do what I see fit to make sure this mission gets accomplished.*"

An amused chuckle greeted his statement. "*Very well. You're too much like you're mother, you know that?*"

"*So you keep telling me.*"

"*Take care of yourself,*" Lina offered solemnly.

"*I will.*" Greatjon turned to Grant, his brown eyes firm and unrelenting. "Get your men ready. Warrick is almost here, and he's hells bent on turning this place to rubble."

"Will you be leaving now?" The question was voiced in such a way that Greatjon wasn't sure if Grant would feel better with his presence or with him gone.

Greatjon shook his head. "Not yet. I'll buy everyone as much time as possible. Now get ready – he's coming."

Grant gripped Greatjon's shoulder tightly and they shared one last solemn glance before the captain hurried off, his deep voice calling archers to the wall and soldiers to the ready. The castle burst to life as the alarm was raised; voices began to fill the air along with footsteps and the rattle of armor as Blackstone's forces readied for one last stand – one last sacrifice. Confused questions and voices soon joined the symphony of noise as the refugees were gathered together and slowly herded into the castle despite desperate urgings to move faster.

As the battlements filled with soldiers whose faces – both young and old – were masked with solemn acceptance of their fate, Greatjon purposefully avoided making eye contact, keeping his gaze focused on the woods. He had no desire to see the depth of their acceptance of what they thought would be an honorable and worthy death. With Cat and Darius' passing, he alone understood what was marching on them. There was no honor in what was to come – only unimaginable pain and suffering awaited them.

It wasn't long before the sound of marching soldiers and the glare of torches became evident to the defenders on the wall. As the invaders spilled forth from the woods – nearly eight hundred strong – in orderly ranks, guttural chants arose from the long, lean forms of the blackhearts that made up half the attackers, their sinister ranks arranged just behind their general.

Clad in armor the color of blood, their general stood out like a blazing beacon against the shadows of the early morning, drawing Greatjon's gaze like a moth to a flame. Greatjon's mind began to haze over with anger as he watched Warrick march steadily forward, an axe nearly twice as large as a lochabre held aloft over his head, the dark steel blades glinting in the early morning dawn. While the armor was just regular steel and the axe was nothing but an imitation of the crusader Warrick had once wielded, it did nothing to diminish how much of a threat Warrick presented to the defenders – and that included Greatjon. A raven-wing tattoo darkened the left side of Warrick's face and shaven head, making his deranged, bloodlust-filled cries seem all the more disturbing. Somewhere over the years, he had used the currents to alter his eye color to a violent red, ever eager to make himself appear more imposing. As the gap closed, Greatjon could see Warrick gathering fir'gan to himself. Though only visible to Greatjon, Warrick's aura suddenly flared with power, energizing the blood-red waves of energy that pulsed about his body. Fir'gan continued to flow into Warrick at a hectic pace as the ethereal blue currents bowed to his will. Suddenly, his pulsating aura flared and became visible for all to see. Warrick's own forces cheered even as the soldiers lining the wall recoiled in fearful shock.

Realizing what was to come, Greatjon turned and leapt from the wall, his own green aura flaring to life, visible for all to see. Like an emerald star, he crashed to the ground next to one of the catapults that had been wheeled into the courtyard, startling the men around it. With a snarl, he bolted for the western portion of the wall even as he heard the call for both the archers on the wall and the catapults in the courtyard to make ready. A wave of refugees and soldiers making for the castle hampered Greatjon for just a moment – but that was all it took.

Even as the command to fire was issued, and the air filled with the hum of bowstrings and the thud of catapults launching their flaming balls of pitch, Greatjon felt a great wave of air pressure build and release from Warrick. A horrifying, wind-born scream preceded a deafening thud and explosion as the wave of air crashed into the western wall. Agonizing screams filled the air as the western portion of the wall exploded, sending chunks of stone, dust and bodies soaring through the air like carelessly thrown grain. Shrapnel and shredded granite tore into the refugees even as the shockwave shoved them to the ground, littering the area with debris and mangled bodies. Greatjon had barely managed to brace himself, erecting a barrier of fir'gan around himself and a few others, but he had known it would be nowhere near enough to protect everyone. When the air cleared, he and the few he'd managed to protect found themselves surrounded by mutilated and crushed bodies. Screams of agony tore the air even as the stench of death flared into existence.

The horrifying scene sent a wave of anger surging through Greatjon, forcing him into motion. Letting his shield fade, he bolted for the gaping hole in the wall. Displaying the excellent training provided by Darius, soldiers were already clearing the area and massing behind the sixty-foot gap. A shield wall quickly formed, but the grim look on the soldiers' faces told all there was to tell – they knew they were going to die, and they were ready to pay that price.

Greatjon halted in front of their ranks and saw the horror that was charging toward the fatally wounded wall. The field outside the broken defenses was littered with corpses; some were dotted with arrows, others crushed under boulders, while some burned from the pitch that had crashed into their ranks. To his horror, nearly every corpse he could see belonged to a blackheart. And with that simple observation, Greatjon learned everything he needed to know. Warrick did not care about his losses – which meant that the blackhearts were expendable. Such a callous misuse of force could only mean that there were fully functional nests somewhere, and the supply of the foul creatures was ample.

The front rank of blackhearts suddenly stopped and dropped to one knee as the rank behind them raised bows that appeared to be made from gnarled, rotting wood and let fly. Caught by surprise, Greatjon gathered fir'gan to himself and erected a barrier to fill the gap in the wall as the air filled with dark arrows. Neither as skilled nor as fast as a Warden, he was a moment too slow and the vast majority of the arrows made it through. While a few did bounce off the shield of air, the rest slammed into himself and the ranks around him. Greatjon's ears screamed in pain as horrified howls erupted around him. Men and women squirmed on the ground as the virulent poison spread through their bodies – skin molted and boiled, turning black and spewing pus, while limbs twisted and cracked as the poison sheered bone and mauled muscle.

Greatjon took it all in even as he pried the arrows from his body; six had hit him in total – three in the chest, two in his right leg and one in his left arm. His body felt like it was afire as the poison tried to take root, and as he removed the arrows, dark blood pumped forth from wounds framed with necrotic flesh. However, mere seconds after the last arrow fell to the ground, the burning subsided and the blood oozing from him cleared up before the dead skin flaked off and the wounds were sealed by healthy pink flesh. With his wounds healed, he roared in rage, his soul lit ablaze by the call of battle and his order's purpose – the destruction of the blackheart pestilence.

His focus narrowed by rage, Greatjon lashed out with his fir'gan, scything down the front rank of blackhearts. Even as the first wave of blackhearts fell to pieces, Greatjon used the currents to collect burning pitch from the field and gather it above the heads of the rear ranks of the foul creatures. Just as the blackhearts started to charge, apparently unfazed by the gruesome deaths of their comrades, Greatjon fed a sudden surge of air into the airborne pitch as he dropped the flaming mass amongst their ranks. A bone-shattering explosion thundered through the air as the pitch made contact with the blackhearts, detonating violently and tearing their bodies asunder. The survivors around Greatjon cheered as they watch flaming chunks of flesh thud into the ground to the accompaniment of the blackhearts' high-pitched death howls; however, only one sound reached Greatjon's ears – Warrick was laughing.

Momentarily stunned by the cackle, his concentration was broken and the fires in the field flared brightly before winking out as Warrick overpowered him and smothered the flames. Before Greatjon could recover and respond, a blast of pure fir'gan, tinted slightly purple from Warrick's handling, slammed into his barrier and shattered it, leaving the gap wide open for the enemy soldiers charging through the smoke of the extinguished fires.

Snarling, Greatjon used the currents to cut down the front ranks of the attackers in a bid to buy a bit of time for the defenders. He then drew his claymore and raised it high with a rage-filled scream that was echoed by the soldiers around him, bolstering their spirits and granting them the courage to make the sacrifice they knew was needed to buy the time for the others to escape. Even as the defiant roars reached the first of the soldiers to reach the breech in the wall, another flight of the dark arrows went up and crashed amongst the defenders scattered atop the wall. Bodies, blood, and arrows rained down on the courtyard as the forces met on the courtyard side of the breech, screams of mind-numbing agony becoming the chorus for the slaughter.

History would record the ensuing battle as the beginning of the end. Within the hour, the mighty wall of Blackstone crumbled before Warrick's power, forcing the defenders to withdraw to the keep. Blackstone's defenders gave ground as slowly as they could, knowing that the longer they held, the more time the civilians had to escape. Their bravery and the tenacity with which they fought was commendable, but with every blackheart they cut down, they ran the risk of dying themselves. Countless defenders fell to the creatures' corrupted blood; whether it spurted from a wounded blackheart, entered their bodies via a cut inflicted with the blackhearts' blood-coated weapons, or simply ran down a defender's weapon and made contact with exposed flesh, the agonizing screams of the poisoned defenders heavily outweighed those of the attackers. It was a constant, indisputable reminder that Blackstone would fall, yet the defenders fought on with grim resolve. Death was inevitable, but they were determined to exact a heavy toll.

Before long, the courtyard was bathed in blood, and in the center of it all were two whirling maelstroms of death and violence that greatly exceeded the grizzly devastation caused by the blackhearts. Greatjon and Warrick cut separate but equal paths of destruction through the battlefield, each man lashing out with their powers – fires erupted and were doused, scythes of air rent men into tiny pieces, and chunks of the shattered wall were hurled about as if they were lighter than air, the massive stone projectiles crushing friend and foe alike as they bounced and crashed through the throng. Through it all, somehow Blackstone's forces managed to hold the courtyard for longer than Greatjon thought possible – however, he knew they couldn't hold for much longer. He was growing tired at a significantly faster rate than Warrick. He was no Warden, and his relatively limited power was being strained as he tried to defend and attack while his body was constantly healing and fending off the blackheart's poison.

Inevitably, their defenses bulged and they were forced back onto the steps of the keep. Greatjon, standing at the base of the stairs, cut down a pair of blackhearts with his claymore – their corpses quickly incinerated by him to prevent accidental exposure to their blood – before he detonated a blast of air in front of him to clear some space. Bodies torn asunder by the blast dropped to the ground instead of catapulting into the air, demonstrating just how weak he had grown.

Off to Greatjon's left, Warrick grinned with zeal when he saw the feeble attack. With his massive blood-covered axe, he lopped off the head of the man he had been toying with. Extending his free hand, he directed a fireball into the ranks before him – their bodies incinerated before any of them could utter a scream – blazing an open path to Greatjon. Howling with glee, Warrick's aura flared as he gathered his fir'gan in front of his outstretched hand, readying the killing blow.

Hobbled by an arrow in his right leg and the loss of his left hand, Grant was still standing and fighting. He never qualified himself as a Gifted; his long life was attributed to a heightened sensitivity to the currents of power, but he had no ability to manipulate them. He held no delusions that he could even think of crossing blades with Warrick, and luckily had not crossed the madman's path. He had also counted himself blessed during the fight – none of the foul blood had touched his skin, and his wounds had been inflicted by weapons free of the blackheart taint. Even Greatjon's quick thinking had saved his life earlier; by cauterizing his wrist shut, Greatjon had postponed death briefly, allowing him to remain in the battle. He now fought in the middle of the stairway, bodies piled about him, knowing full well the end was drawing near.

Another blast from Greatjon cleared the front of the steps, buying a small breather for the front ranks. Grant smiled in appreciation of his friend's tenacity, but he knew it was time for Greatjon to be gone from this slaughter. Before he could move to his friend's side, the ranks to his left – both friend and foe alike – burst into flames as Warrick cut a fiery swath through the bodies. The smell of burnt flesh tearing at the back of his throat, he coughed to clear his lungs as he tried to peer through the smoke. He could just see the red-armored man grinning devilishly as he extended his hand, aiming clear and true at Greatjon. Though his affinity for fir'gan was extremely limited by Gifted standards, Grant was a lifetime soldier and knew a killing blow when he saw one. The pain in his leg be damned, he leapt the bodies and steps, bellowing a warning.

Everything seemed to suddenly move in slow motion as Greatjon turned to look at Grant. Wide-eyed, he swung to the left, following Grant's outstretched arm. There was a sudden howl of glee from Warrick and everything seemed to return to normal speed as he released the massive surge of power. Scythe-like, the blast tore toward its target, slicing through the few unlucky soldiers that wandered into its path. Greatjon extended his hands to erect a barrier to deflect the attack, but he knew he was too slow. Even as the barrier lethargically formed, he could feel the power from the blow singeing his flesh. And then, suddenly, Grant was there, his armored body between the blast and Greatjon. Grant's body took the brunt of the blow, blood bursting from his mouth and his eyes. Excess energy seeped past Grant's rigid form and deflected off the small shield Greatjon had managed to erect, slashing open his face from his brow down to his chin. Blood pumped from the wound, spilling into and blinding his right eye, but he ignored it. All he could see was Grant's rigid form before him – a small, contented smile on his haggard face.

Time seemed to freeze for Greatjon for a moment as shock sunk its claws into his brain. Grant gave a slight nod and mouthed, *"Go,"* before he seemed to finally realize that he was dead. His body suddenly convulsed, and a red line of blood oozed forth from his head to his crotch before the two halves of his body slid apart and thudded wetly on the steps.

Greatjon blinked, staring at the body. It wasn't supposed to be like this. He was suppose to be saving them, not the other way around. Rage burning in his eyes, he looked up and directed a howl ripped from the depths of his soul at Warrick's laughing face. Before Greatjon could throw himself recklessly into the fray, the soldiers around him latched on to his gore-covered frame and dragged him into the keep. He fought them step for step, unwilling to leave the battle. To his chagrin, Warrick's maddening, self-satisfied grin followed him until the keep's entryway broke their line of sight.

Almost as if losing sight of Warrick broke the dam on his energy, it seemed to flood out of him as the soldiers released him and he slumped to the floor. As his escort raced back to the doors, wounded soldier after wounded soldier stumbled into the keep and made their way past Greatjon as quickly as they could manage. The soldiers at the doors waited as long as they safely could before finally shoving the doors closed – likely dooming many of their brethren to certain death – and braced them with sturdy, three foot thick ironwood pylons. Collapsed on his knees, Greatjon watched dully as the doors slammed home and the braces were secured. Suddenly, there was a flare of light as runes appeared around the doorframe and bright blue energy began to flood across the doors. When the energy reached the center of the doors, there was a flash of blinding light that left everyone scrambling to recover. When their vision cleared, they were greeted by a baffling sight. Where once there had been doors, there was only solid, uninterrupted wall covered in glowing blue runes. Some of the men stood around mystified by the sight, while others began tending to the wounded crowding the entry hall. It wasn't long, however, before a few of the soldiers began escorting the more able-bodied deeper into the keep, making for the stairs that would lead to the escape tunnels.

For what seemed like an eternity to him, Greatjon merely remained where he was, staring blankly at the wall and its glowing runes. As he stared vacantly at the runes, his emotions a jumble and rage threatening to consume him, his mind finally began to work again and the purpose behind the runes sunk in. Climbing slowly to his feet, his eye grew wide as he read them again to make sure he understood them. Smiling sadly to himself, he offered a silent prayer of thanks to Darius for his forethought before shouting, "Everyone to the tunnels, now! We don't have much time!"

A few of the men nodded numbly and began to stumble deeper into the keep while a handful of the others, shock disconnecting them from reality, remained where they were. Greatjon moved through the remaining few, doing his best to shake them from their stupor. However, when he saw the runes flare again and veins of power begin to creep out from them, crawling onto every internal structural surface of the keep and illuminating other sets of previously invisible runes, he knew he was out of time.

The castle groaned as the blue spider web of power filled every surface of the castle, drawing the attention of some of the remaining soldiers and spurring them into motion. Urgency filling his words, Greatjon pointed into the keep and barked, "Go! Now!"

As soon as those few were past him, Greatjon gave the entry hall once last glance. Five people remained, their minds firmly shielded from reality by shock, and another seventy were dead from their wounds. With no time to rescue the living, he let out a growl as he turned and hustled deep into the keep. Navigating the twists and turns of Blackstone's halls, he quickly caught up to the wounded soldiers and urged them onward.

Within minutes, they reached the vast, treasured library of Castle Blackstone. At one time, three magnificent golden chandeliers had provided warm light by which scholars could enjoy the cherished volumes that had once filled the shelves; now, however, the chandeliers were as dark as a moonless night, and the shelves sat as depressingly empty as the castle. On the far wall of the vast, one room library, the shelves had been moved aside to reveal the once skillfully concealed entrance to the Underhalls. As Greatjon and the last of the soldiers hustled across the red-carpeted floor to what seemed like the painfully distant escape portal, the castle suddenly groaned loudly and violently. A loud crash in the distance and an eruption of dust and debris through the library doors urged the stragglers along and announced Darius' final gift to his people – time.

Barking loudly at the last of the soldiers to hurry along, Greatjon knew, with grim satisfaction, that no one would have Darius' home to ravage and desecrate ever again.

Castle Blackstone was collapsing.


Soon after entering the raw, hand-cut tunnels, Greatjon saw to it the entrance was collapsed behind them before he took the time to take stock of things. His own wounds had closed up and the blood had cleared from his right eye. As an honor to those that had fallen, and to remind himself of what was lost that day, he chose to keep the wound from healing completely, allowing a jagged and discolored scar to remain. Aware that now was not the time to grieve, he went about organizing what was left of Blackstone's forces and the refugees.

Sixty of the castle's garrison had survived and were already distributing amongst the survivors lit torches and supplies from heavily laden handcarts – which now contained the remnants of Blackstone's prized possessions – that had been moved to the tunnels in preparation for just such an evacuation. Of the nine-hundred refugees that had made it to Blackstone, only one hundred and fifty had survived the massacre. Greatjon had the soldiers double-check the counts before making his way to the front of the column. He could see the pain in each persons' eyes as he made the solemn journey to the front of the mismatched column, each survivor either suffering from shock or doing their best to deal with the flood of emotions at hand; there were a few that wept openly and others that either stood or sat staring into nothingness. There were no words Greatjon could offer to assuage the survivors of their overwhelming despair, so he said nothing and continued on his way, eventually making it to the head of the column where a worried Aseria and Deralina awaited him.

As Deralina came up to him and nuzzled his leg with a slight whimper, Aseria stood from where she had been crouched next to the direwolf, her sorrow-filled blue-lavender gaze peering into his pain-filled eyes. "I'm sorry," she whispered.

*"Sorry for what?"* he thought cynically.

*"Does it matter, Master? This whole tragedy is something to be sorry for,"* chided Deralina softly.

Afraid of what he might say, Greatjon simply nodded to Aseria. There was nothing he could say or do that would be of any worth or meaning now.

A cough from behind brought him around to find a young man of maybe only eighteen years standing before him. Clad in blood-drenched leather armor, he was missing his right ear and, with the way his amber iris stood out against the blood-fill sclera, it looked like he might lose the vision in his right eye to the same cut that had claimed his ear. His nose was broken and bloody, and his blonde hair was caked with dried blood. Of more concern was the blood oozing from his numerous nicks and wounds, making him pale from the blood loss. At one point, the boy might have been considered attractive, but not anymore. Greatjon was sure the boy was in pain and was amazed he was still standing.

"Sir," he said weakly, "we're ready to go."

Aseria gasped and covered her mouth as she recognized the boy. "Baris? Is that you? Corith be good!"

Baris looked past Greatjon and tried to smile at Aseria. "Aye, it's me, lass. Afraid I'm not in very good shape. Don't guess the ladies will be calling on me anymore."

Tears slipping down her cheeks, Aseria whispered, "Oh, Baris. . . ."

Greatjon, placed a hand gently on the boy's shoulder and asked, "Baris, are you the highest ranking soldier left?"

He shook his head weakly. "No sir, but Lieutenant Rican is in shock and isn't responsive. He's bled out badly from a missing arm and I do not think he'll last, to be honest." He sighed with exhaustion, "That makes me the highest ranking man here."

"Your rank, son?" Greatjon inquired gently.

"Corporal, sir," Baris replied weakly.

"Well then, Corporal, you're my man until Rican recovers . . . if he survives."

Baris straightened up, trying to hold himself with pride. "Yes, sir."

Greatjon smiled gently. "Now then, I can't have you dying on me from blood loss, can I?"

"No sir, but there's others that need the thread for stitches more than me."

"I know," said Greatjon as he held his hand up to the gash. "I want you to close your eyes – this is going to hurt."

Baris swallowed hard and nodded as he closed his eyes. As soon as Greatjon was sure Baris' eyes were shut, a controlled gout of flame erupted from his palm, searing the wound shut. The smell of singed flesh drifted through the tunnels, drawing the attention of a few people. When they were sure there was no new threat, they withdrew into their own thoughts. Unaware of the refugees' brief gazes, Greatjon proceeded to cauterize the worst of Baris' remaining wounds. Through it all, Baris whimpered and ground his teeth, valiantly choking off the screams of agony that so desperately wanted to escape.

Letting the final flame dissipate, Greatjon said gently, "You can open your eyes, now."

Baris opened his eyes painfully and nearly dropped to the ground from weakness.

Greatjon caught him and held him up by the shoulders. "Are you alright?"

"It hurts like all holy hells," he breathed through clenched teeth, "but I'll live. Thank you, sir."

Greatjon nodded. "Thank me when we're out of the tunnels. If you're okay to travel, then let's get moving."

Baris nodded and weakly made his way back down the column to relay the order.


The five days that followed were ones of torturous silence. Each and every one of the broken survivors was left alone with their thoughts, speaking only when spoken to or needed. It was a sorrowful journey that played nursemaid to the shattered hearts and tattered souls of a people whose lives had been irreparably changed.

Like everyone else in the woeful column, the long and dark journey through the tunnels provided time for Greatjon to cope with what had transpired. For someone that was at times considered coldhearted, he seethed with rage and pent-up fury. For the second time in his life, he had borne witnessed to the destruction of his childhood home. He had long ago come to accept the first incident. Being only a young boy at the time, there had been very little he could do about it; however, now that he held the power and strength to stop such atrocities, it angered him beyond counsel that he had not been able to

256

avert the slaughter. Every part of his heart and soul screamed at him to do something to avenge the fallen, but his promise to Darius held him in check. Without it, he would have abandoned the others to their fate and tried to put an end to Warrick – though he knew his chances of surviving such a battle, even if he was lucky enough to face him one-on-one, were slim at best. It even occurred to him that Darius might have foreseen such rash actions and forced the promise to see to the survival of Aseria and the refugees from him to keep him from said actions.

Either way, Greatjon was disgusted with himself and he let his thoughts turn inward, ignoring the outside world except when he was needed. He ignored Aseria's concerned inquires and even closed his mind off to Deralina's attempts at a conversation. He wanted to be alone with his anger and resentment; in his present state of mind, they were his best friends, companions and lovers. In them, he found refuge for his broken heart and fuel for the vengeance taking root in his soul.

Even the nights spent in the tunnels failed to provide respite for the refugees. Where the soldiers and villagers struggled to find sleep despite soul-sucking fatigue, Greatjon's slumber was dominated by nightmares. In his dreams, he could see the first time his beloved home was razed. His mother and father had been butchered, and his sister mercilessly raped and then beheaded. In his rage, he had tried to kill those responsible, but it had been to no avail. In the end, the only thing that had stood between him and death was Darius and Deralina. Then there were the dreams about the recent attacks; more vivid than the others, and a jarring reminder of his perceived failure, he would bolt awake with a blind rage in the pit of his belly. Sleep would escape him after that, leaving him even more withdrawn the next day.

For Aseria, being one of the more hale amongst their group, she spent the journey doing her best to assist Baris with whatever he needed. Her young, injured friend was overwhelmed with the burden dumped on him, and she felt it was the least she could do to make the trip a little more bearable. There were wounds to stitch and clean, broken bones to splint, and minds to assuage. At times, she simply provided a friendly ear for those that needed it. The work not only kept her busy, but it also kept her mind off the life-altering information she'd been fed and the horrible events that followed. However, while she did the best she could to tend to the needs of the column, she knew it wasn't enough. Without proper medical care, they would inevitably lose more to infections and illness. She could only hope the journey would end sooner rather than later, but until then, her meager ministrations would have to do.

As for Deralina, the massive direwolf never strayed from Greatjon's side. She did her best to comfort her master, but with his mind closed to her, there was little more she could do than be a reassuring presence for him. Ironically, her thoughts were nearly as dark and as vengeance focused as those of her master – though for her, the target of such musing included more than Warrick. The fall of Blackstone had cast a harsh light on old, anger-filled memories that she had long fought to suppress. Like her master, the journey provided the perfect haven to nurse her anger and to think. There was atonement to be paid for past actions and the fall of Blackstone; the when and where, however, were a matter for debate. While the temptation to collect was intoxicating, she was old and wise enough to realize that patience was as important to this as it was to stalking prey – wait for an opening to present itself and be ready to strike without hesitation. In the end, no matter when it was paid, she was sure of one thing – it would be paid in blood.

And so it went day after day and night after night, until on the afternoon of the fifth day, they emerged from the dark tunnels into the bright light of a snowy day. They had lost ten more people on the journey, including Lieutenant Rican and two other soldiers, their corpses interned within the tunnels. Everyone was caked with dirt and grime on top of the blood and gore from the battle. The arrival of fresh air was a welcome blessing to lungs heavy with smoke and dust, putting a bounce back in some of their steps and making the task of hauling their heavily laden handcarts just a bit easier. They were nearly twenty leagues from Castle Blackstone in another of the many valleys that could be found within the White Fang Mountains. The snow-covered landscape was broken up by hills, a few small crevices, and the occasional stand of evergreens. However, the survivors of Castle Blackstone were more concerned with being free of the tunnels and the horrors of the past than the surrounding landscape. Many of the soldiers and villagers fell to their knees and began to offer thanks to Corith for their deliverance, while others embraced family and friends or wept openly.

Greatjon sneered at the display. *"Damn them for being happy when so many are dead!"* he thought to himself before he shook the thought from his head. What a rash and unthinkable thing for him to even contemplate! He knew they had every right to be happy! They had survived the macabre! They were alive!

With another shake of his head, he stalked away from the group and signaled for Deralina to follow. *"I'm sorry for the way I acted in the tunnels,"* he thought as he dropped the barriers between him and his lifetime companion.

*"Don't apologize. Remember – I was there the first time too."*

*"How can I forget?"*

*"You can't,"* she replied in a matter-of-fact tone.

He reached down and patted her on the head. *"I need you to run on ahead and see how far we are from the Portculim, and make sure the way ahead is clear. I doubt Warrick is watching the Portculims, but I don't want to take any chances."*

Deralina nuzzled his leg and ran off.

As the minutes slid by in agonizing slowness, Greatjon remained motionless, isolated from the others and staring off into the snow-covered distance. Eventually, Aseria quietly approached him from behind and joined his vigil. He glanced at her quickly out of the corner of his eye, but said nothing. Though she was just as dirt-caked as the rest, it did little to mar her beauty or dull her bright eyes.

Unaware of his cursory glance, she respectfully allowed the silence to drag on for what seemed like endless minutes as she waited for him to acknowledge her. When it seemed that Greatjon was content to ignore her, she finally spoke, her musical voice soft and gentle. "The village and castle were important to you, weren't they?"

He contemplated not responding, but decided against it. "It was the closest thing to a true home I'd ever known," he said softly.

She nodded sympathetically. "It was, for a time, like home for me. I'm so sorry for your loss."

Greatjon didn't know why the sympathetic condolence irritated him, but something in him snapped at the soft-spoken words, and before he could stop himself, he turned and barked, "Don't ever be sorry! Don't *EVER* be sorry!" She blenched at the harshness in his tone even as he leaned in close, a snarl painted angrily on his face. "You know why you can never be sorry? Because if you ever let that emotion cloud your judgment for even an instant, you will fail! And where your destiny is taking you, failure will only be met with one punishment – death!"

He growled at her and spun away, almost tripping over Deralina. "What?!" he roared.

By this point, his outburst had drawn the attention of the refugees. Curious about the commotion, Baris made his way over as Deralina backed away from Greatjon, hurt painted on her face.

Greatjon shook his head and sighed as he rubbed his temples. *"I'm sorry, Lina. I shouldn't have done that."*

*"You're right about that,"* she chided angrily.

*"The portal?"* he asked gently.

*"Not too far ahead. I would have been back sooner, but I thought caution would serve us better,"* she replied curtly.

*"That's good."*

*"Sir . . ."* she hesitated a moment before continuing, *"I think you need to rest as soon as possible – and I don't mean in that depressing keep of yours."*

*"Then where?"*

*"Damion's keep,"* she stated firmly.

*"But–"*

*"Don't argue with me on this. The companionship will do you good. Besides, you have to go there anyways and the refugees will be able to go where they please from there."*

Greatjon sighed mentally, both fully regretting his outburst and thankful for such an understanding companion as Lina. *"It's a good thing you're around."*

*"I know."*

Greatjon turned back to Aseria, but before he could address her, Baris arrived. Though Baris had recovered somewhat from his wounds, he still appeared weak. Seeing the stunned look on Aseria's face, he asked of Greatjon, "Is everything alright, sir?"

Greatjon nodded slowly. "It is. Would you please go back and see to it that everyone is ready to move?"

"Yes, sir." He hesitated a moment before asking, "Sir, if you don't mind me asking – where are we headed?"

Greatjon gave Baris a soft smile. "Someplace safe."

Baris nodded hesitantly before turning and making his way back to the refugees.

Turning his attention back to Aseria, Greatjon found that the shock on her face had been replaced by an angry glower. "What?" he asked, mildly surprised by her shift in attitude.

She folded her arms beneath her breasts. "I think you know."

Greatjon sighed and rolled his eyes. "Look, I'm sorry. Okay? I'm sorry. There, I said it." Aseria's face brightened and she started to open her mouth, but Greatjon held up a finger, forestalling any comment. "Don't even say it."

She gave him her most feline grin before spinning and running back to rejoin the others.

"What have I gotten myself into this time, Lina?" he muttered.

*"Don't ask me. I can't offer any advice on cats except that they make good eating."*

Greatjon could just imagine the grin that would have accompanied that comment had Deralina been able to physically smile.

Though the fresh air had infused a sense of renewed vigor in the refugees, it wasn't enough to fully overcome the emotional and physical strain of the past few weeks; as a result, it took longer than Greatjon would have liked for them to get underway. Once they were moving, Greatjon led them north at a slow pace, turning a trek of just a few minutes into an hour-long trip. While the plodding hike was irritating, Greatjon felt that the sight that greeted them at the end was worth it.

Like a welcoming light in a sea of darkness, a circular grove of perfectly healthy oaks and blossoming cherry trees stood proudly against the cold, nestled in a depression between the rise the refugees stood upon and an equally tall hill on the other. Even with everything they'd seen and been through, everyone except for Greatjon and Deralina found themselves staring in awe at the majestic sight.

Greatjon smirked as he heard someone mutter, "By Corith, how?"

"Look to your question for the answer," Greatjon stated in response before he started down the incline toward the grove. One by one, the others shook off their awe and followed.

Nearly two hundred yards in diameter, the grove was centered around a glade that spoke of spring rather than winter. Hidden from the outside by the thick canopy, the clearing once again brought people up short. Lush green grass carpeted the ground along with a sprinkling of cherry blossoms, and birdsong filled the warm air with joyous music. Though the spot of spring in this frozen land was certainly awe-inspiring, it was the structure at the center of the clearing that enraptured the beleaguered group.

Standing almost fourteen feet wide and twenty feet tall, the white marble arch occupied the center of the clearing like some sort of benevolent god. Ancient runes crawled up the faces of the arch like a maze of vines, weaving into beautiful patterns before terminating at a large blue crystal inset at the peak of the arch. Mounted on the right side of the archway, nearly chest high on an average man, was a matching marble box that was about the size of Greatjon's hand; four rows of square gems – green, blue, red and black – were fitted snuggly into the front of box.

As Greatjon approached the colossal arch, Aseria breathed in amazement, "What is it?"

"Our way out of here," Greatjon offered as he stopped before the box of gems, his eyes drawn briefly to the graceful rune etched into the top of the box, and began to tap a sequence on the jewels, each gem lighting up as he pressed on it.

"Is it magic?" Her question caused a few of the refugees to take a few tentative steps back, some making warding gestures.

Greatjon chuckled. "Magic is such an ignorant term. No offense meant – but magic was a term created by people who didn't understand the forces that surrounded them." He tapped the last gem and stood back. "Anyway, here's your *magic.*"

A gentle hum filled the air as blue-white energy began to crawl up the sides of the archway from the ends of the arch embedded in the ground, illuminating the spider web of runes as it touched each. With wide eyes, the refugees watched the progression of illuminating runes until the energy reached the peak of the arch and touch the blue crystal. The crystal then began to throb with a dull light, which grew steadily brighter until, without warning, the crystal flared and shot a beam of blue energy to the ground. The sliver of energy then began to twist and widen until it filled the entirety of the arch with a swirling blue void of light.

Aseria groped for the appropriate words as she watched the swirling energy pulse and throb with life, but could not find them. Finally, she breathed, "I don't know what to say. . . ."

Greatjon chuckled and looked back at the motley group of refugees. "Quite a sight, isn't it?" Waving toward the glowing portal as if it was nothing to be afraid of, he said, "Come on. Let's go."

As a whole, the group approached cautiously, halting just a few feet before the portal. It was apparent that everyone was exceedingly nervous about the device. Finally, though just as nervous as the others, Baris stepped forward and asked, "Where does it go?"

"To a place where you all will be safe and have a chance to rest before deciding where it is you wish to go."

Baris looked Greatjon in the eye, seeking any hint of deception. Finding none, he nodded slowly and gave one last reassuring look back at the others before stepping through the portal and vanishing. Not wanting to look weak in light of what they viewed as

Baris' bravery, the remaining soldiers plunged through one by one. By the time the soldiers were all through, the edge had been taken off of the villagers' nerves and they too vanished through the gate until only Aseria and Deralina remained with Greatjon.

"Well, I must say," Aseria quipped as a smile spread across her feline face, "things are already looking interesting. If my fate is to be around such wonders, then I look forward to it." Nodding to Greatjon, she walked through the portal with a grin on her face.

*"She's enjoying this,"* Deralina said with amusement.

Greatjon shrugged. *"Might as well enjoy it while she still can."*

*"Will you leave it active?"*

*"Not from this side. It'll cut off one more point of contact for Warrick and he won't be able to follow."*

*"Smart . . . for a human,"* she teased before loping through the arch.

Greatjon shook his head at the poke as he turned to face south. He hadn't allowed himself to look back until now, and wasn't surprised to see multiple pillars of smoke rising in the air. The distance was so great that none of the others would have seen it, but he could. A lump of anger caught in his throat and his hands balled into fists. "I do swear that I'll see you dead, Warrick," he growled into the air. "If it takes the rest of my existence to correct what you've done to me and that Vale, I will. By blood, by honor, and by deed, this I swear – you will die." Turning to face the portal, he traced the lone rune on the control crystals' box top. The rune flared blue and the simple box fell into his waiting hand.

Pausing once more before the gate, he sent his thoughts in the direction of the burning Vale and bellowed mentally, *"I'll be back for you, Warrick!"*

As he stepped through, the portal closing with a bang, he could almost swear he heard laughter on the wind.

*

I still don't see why we couldn't sail into a port closer to Merset?" It was the tenth time Mat had asked the question over the course of their two weeks at sea.

Kara sighed and answered, exasperation weighting heavily on her soothing, beautiful voice, "Because we don't *need* to go to Merset as of yet." Standing on the forecastle of the ship, her hip-length sky-blue hair blowing wildly about her warmly clothed frame, she stared listlessly at the froth peeling off to the sides of the ship as the *Blue*

*Trident* cut through the gently rocking sea. "Haltho is a much better starting point; we can easily make our way north, south or west from there. Besides, it's also closer to the front of the war, which will make whatever news we can pick up a whole lot more reliable."

Mat leaned his back casually against the gunwale, watching as the crew went about their business. The grizzled captain had made a rare appearance on deck, his large form bundled up against the cold, and was barking orders from the wheelhouse. Mat smirked as he watched the crew scurry about the deck like a colony of agitated ants. Adjusting the white bandana he had won from one of the crewmen, he settled it a bit more snuggly about his head. He'd grown sick of his purple-tinged black hair billowing about wildly, and had seriously considered shaving his head to be rid of the annoyance if the bandana hadn't worked. "I dunno, Kara," he replied in his smooth voice. "It would seem to me that making port in one of the major seats of power would ensure plenty of information and only leave us two directions in which to travel."

Kara sighed again and shook her head, her normally beautiful face marred with growing concern over events back home. "We'll be in Haltho in less than three days, Mat. I've also already arranged for supplies there. As well – any information we could pick up in Merset would be days old. Besides, journeying to Merset would cost us nearly another two weeks at sea, and the weather would likely worsen the further north we traveled. No – I'd rather get my feet on dry land and start searching."

Mat grunted his disapproval and folded his arms over his chest.

Kara gave him a sideways stare before shaking her head softly and returning her bright sky-blue eyes to the ocean ahead of them.

For the last two days, they had been trapped below deck as the *Blue Trident* was assailed by fierce storms. Rigging and sails alike had been severely damaged and the crew had suffered minor injuries. Thankfully, the afternoon had brought a break in the onslaught, allowing Mat and Kara to get a breath of fresh air and the crew to begin their frantic repairs. All three masts still stood strong, replacement sails and rigging installed before Kara and Mat had been allowed above deck. Now the crew scampered about the rest of the ship, seeking any hidden damage and making minor repairs. Through it all, the burly, grizzled captain had been barking and cursing at his crew as if he had nothing better to do; in fact, Mat was positive the man found amusement in finding creative ways to lavish his commands with a plethora of vulgarities – many of which had Mat smirking in amusement.

Through the vast majority of the journey, the crew had avoided Mat and Kara per their orders from the captain, who, in turn, had received them from Darkon. However, Mat and Kara did occasionally offer greetings in passing, and had engaged in casual conversation during meals. The captain let his passengers maintain their own schedule and roam the boat as they pleased, only imposing his authority over them if their presence affected the safety of the boat. Oddly enough, Mat and Kara had more contact with the ship's navigator than the captain. As the navigator handled most of the charts and maps, they had to go through him in order to gain access to them. In particular, they had eagerly studied the maps of Triclose to get a feel for the lay of the land along the coast. Day after day, they had studied the maps, committing them to memory. The task had helped to pass the time, but had recently served to only feed their growing anxiousness to make port. The string of storms over the last two days had only added to their growing apprehension, making mundane tasks, such as looking at the maps, difficult to focus on.

Their destination on Triclose was Haltho; nearly a four-week journey by horse south of Merset, the major port resided upon the rocky coast of Triclose. Small compared with the giant port cities that dotted Solarson's coast, it offered excellent access to the ocean and, more importantly, less official meddling than other Triclosian ports if one wanted a discrete landing or escape. It was, as far as Kara was concerned, the perfect place to make port – news of the war would be fresh, hard-to-find supplies would be easier to acquire due to the growing and lucrative black market upon Triclose, and it would be a balanced starting point for their search. As well – though she had not informed Mat of it – she had used her family contacts on Triclose to arrange for someone that knew the lay of the land to help them. While it was true that the crystals would guide them in the general direction of their new owners, neither Mat nor Kara had any idea what they might stumble into. Having been trained to be prepared and to use her head, Kara knew local knowledge would be invaluable to them. She still wished a Seeker had been sent instead of them, but orders were orders and she would see the task done. Besides, no Seeker would stand a chance against a full-blown Warden if, Corith forbid, they encounter their enemies on Triclose. More importantly – and Kara hated to admit Darkon was right – she and Mat would be better suited to protecting and training the raw recruits until they could be returned to their respective Orders.

She sighed mentally as her thoughts continued to tumble around in her head. *"One step at a time, Kara,"* she chided herself.

Though the rest of the day slipped away without incident, ominous storm clouds began to build to the west by nightfall, creating a front that was unavoidable unless one went well out of their way. Emboldened by the way his crew had handled the storms of the past few days, as well as his passengers' need to make landfall sooner rather than later, the captain set the *Blue Trident* on its course and held it true. To his relief, the morale of the crew remained jovial despite the exhaustion that had crept its way into their every muscle and his decision to hold their course into the storm. They had survived the violent storms of the past few days with little in the way of repercussions, and the storm brewing in their path look to be no worse than what they had already weathered.

So with nightfall, the crew, minus the captain and navigator, gathered for a dinner of stew, bread, fresh water and oranges. Lighthearted conversation was exchanged and jokes tossed about freely. Mat chose to join the rambunctious lot that evening, leaving Kara alone in their cramped cabin.

With the lanterns turned down low, Kara stood by the lone porthole, her gaze glazed over as she stared out to sea. The cabin was tidy and orderly as usual, their belongings packed away neatly in their packs beneath the hammocks on the far wall. A half-finished meal slid idly on the table that was anchored to the center of the room as the ship bobbed and swayed on the waves. Their weapons, which were secured to the back wall of the cabin with rope, rattled gently with the ship's movements. Kara, however, was oblivious to the grating of the plate on the table or the rattle of their weapons, nor was she aware of the noisy banter of the crew as it slipped through the bowels of the ship; her mind and focus were, literally, elsewhere. The contact had come as a surprise, and when she realized who it was, she had focused all her energy on maintaining the contact across such a vast distance.

She had been in her trance for nearly an hour when Mat walked in. He recognized Kara's state for what it was immediately and knew not to bother her. Seating himself at the table, he stripped his bracers off and tossed them, along with his bandana, on the table. He watched the boiled leather bracers roll around on the table with the sliding plate for a time, before sighing and gathering up his belongings. Moving to his pack, he stowed the items before he crawled into the top hammock and stretched out, figuring Kara would remain in her trance for a while yet.

To his surprise, she began to stir only a few minutes later. A slight tremble went through her before she shut her eyes with a deep breath, drawing Mat's attention. "Well?" he asked curiously.

A single tear escaped her shut eyes as she turned to him and opened them, sorrow dampening their normally bright and cheerful glow. "It's . . . it's not good, Mat. I. . . ." She shook her head mournfully, made her way to one of the chairs, and sat in it heavily.

Scampering down from his hammock, he sat down opposite her, his face plainly showing his anxiety over what the news was. "What is it, Kara?" he asked hesitantly.

Kara took a deep breath and wiped her eyes before looking up at him and smiling sadly. "I just spoke with Greatjon."

Mat's face screwed up in confusion. "Greatjon? I mean . . . that's great, but why not Darkon? I would have thought Greatjon would have reported to him and then him to you."

Kara shook her head. "I don't think he's talked to Darkon – at least not yet. Either way, the news is mixed at best." She took a deep breath before continuing. "Greatjon made it to Blackstone with little problem. Unfortunately, he stumbled into a hopeless situation. Cat was dead as we already knew, but Darius–" her voice caught in her throat. Swallowing she continued. "Darius was in terrible shape, Mat. Blackhearts had poisoned him."

Mat sat back heavily in his chair, eyes wide. "Dear Corith, I can . . . I can only imagine."

"I'm afraid it only gets worse. Darius died from the poison, leaving Greatjon in charge of a tired group of soldiers and refugees. With Darius' death," she shook her head, fighting back tears, "Blackstone didn't make it through the morning."

"Who?" asked a saddened Mat simply.

"There's no surprise there – Warrick was responsible."

Mat snarled and slammed his fist into the table. Granted, he wasn't even alive the last time Warrick assaulted Blackstone, but this new assault and victory was infuriating nonetheless. "Damn! How many times does that bastard have to bring ruin to those mountains?! I can only imagine the state Greatjon is in!"

Kara nodded. "I know. He sounded . . . withdrawn . . . angry," she sighed. "However, there is one bit of good news. Greatjon did escape with survivors and his mission wasn't a total failure." Mat perked up and eyed her curiously. "He secured Darius and Cat's crystals, as well as Cat's replacement."

Mat sighed and closed his eyes. "Thank Corith!" He opened them and leaned forward, asking curiously, "Who?"

Kara sat back in her chair with a small, forced smile on her face. "A darlion female."

Mat slapped his hands together and let out a laugh. "So they haven't abandoned us completely, then." The smile on his face faded quickly. "Where did they go? I'm assuming the Indigain Order."

Kara shook her head, her face blanketed with concerned puzzlement. "That's where I'm not sure. He wouldn't tell me, and I'm too far away to get a precise location on him. I can say for sure, though, that it wasn't the Indigain compound."

"What the hells is he doing?" Mat muttered, his dark eyes showing his confusion.

She looked down at the table and shrugged her shoulders, doing her best to appear dejected and unsure – which wasn't a stretch given the night's news. She knew very well where Greatjon was, in fact he'd told her as much, but he had made her promise not to reveal anything to Darkon per a request from Darius. As she trusted Darius and Greatjon more than Darkon, she consented to the request without hesitation. It pained her to withhold information from Mat, for she held him in great respect. But he was Darkon's man, and anything said this night would surely reach Darkon's ears. "I don't know, Mat," she lied. "Greatjon didn't sound like himself. And after all that . . ." she shook her head and looked up at him. "Just trust that he knows what he's doing. I'm sure he'll get around to contacting Darkon."

Mat nodded slowly and skeptically, but said nothing. Silence descended on them like a smothering cloak for a time, each one of them immersed in their own thoughts. Finally, he spoke up, his voice soft with compassion. "I'm sorry about Darius. I never knew him that well, but I know the two of you knew each other for a very long time."

Kara nodded and smiled her thanks. "We did." With a sad sigh, she stood up and brushed her blue hair from her face before heading to the door. "Get some sleep."

Mat turned around in his chair and asked, "Where you headed?"

"Up top. I feel like some fresh air and being alone for a while." She opened the door and stepped through, closing the door behind her.

Mat sat in the chair for a time, his vision set on the door. Finally, he shook his head, a small rueful smirk cracking his lips, before standing and climbing into his hammock where he stared at the ceiling for a long, long time.

On deck, the bright moon struggled to pierce the growing cloud cover. The night shift was already on duty, but paid little heed to Kara as she made her way to the forecastle and leaned against the gunwale. Shutting her eyes, she let herself feel the crisp, biting wind as she tried to relax. Her emotions were a jumble, making clarity of thought very difficult – and in her profession, that was something that could get her killed if she wasn't cautious. In all her years, she'd never known a man like Darius. Even after starting down the path that they all followed, he'd remained cheerful and lighthearted; he'd always been a bright spot everyone could turn to when things seemed their worst. When Greatjon had informed her of all that had transpired, her heart had taken a blow. Darius had been a longtime friend; so long, in fact, that they had taken to measuring their friendship by centuries, not decades. Losing him was like losing a brother or a limb. In his lifetime, people had loved him and kings had respected him, but now that was lost to the ages and the history books. With a deep sigh, she realized that only myth and the recollections of those who knew him would keep the memory of Darius alive. However, at the rate things were going. . . .

Kara pushed the dark thoughts away as her eyes tightened in frustration. Now, of the original Wardens, only Darkon, Damion, Valisiana and she remained. Greatjon, despite his prowess and power, was only a Knight in an Order with a missing Preceptor, while Mat was a fourth generation Warden and relatively inexperienced. Her hands tightened on the railing with each passing thought. As of now, according to their information, their opponents retained six first generation Wardens out of their surviving eleven, which gave them a significant advantage in skill, experience and power.

She let a soft curse escape her lips. Nothing remained for her to do but complete her mission. Greatjon had taken responsibility for the darlion, though she knew he was itching to go after Warrick. Darkon was remaining as coy as ever about how they would achieve their objectives, which came as no surprise. As for now, here on the open sea, she and Mat could only wait until landfall.

*"When that happens,"* she thought as she opened her bright sky-blue eyes, *"if even one person hinders my way, then Corith have mercy on their soul."*

"Ahum!"

Kara spun around at the guttural throat clearing, her hand reaching for her sword even though she knew it was in her cabin.

The grizzled captain took a quick step back and held his hands up in defense. "Easy now, lass! I didna mean ta scare ye!"

She took a deep breath and relaxed. "My apologies, Captain Gralan. My thoughts were elsewhere." She smiled weakly. "Is there something I can do for you?"

Gralan scratched at his scraggly salt-and-pepper beard while eyeing her with his sharp black eyes from beneath thick eyebrows. "Aye, though I do'na mean to be ask'n more of ye than I'm suppose to."

Kara nodded. "Ask away, Captain, and I'll see what I can do."

The captain nodded, but still hesitated before lowering his voice to respond. "Now – I'm not a coward 'n all that. But ye see, these storms that we been through and that one that's ah growing don't seem natural. I've done sailed these waters more than me fair share, and I ain't ever seen weather behave'n like this." He scratched at his beard. "So, I be wonder'n if'n ye wouldn't mind use'n yer abilities ta see what it's all about. Ye know . . . fer the morale of tha crew."

Kara smirked inwardly, not wanting to further embarrass the captain. She knew it must have taken a lot for him to overcome his bravado to ask for her assistance. "I think I can do that for you, Captain. After all – we cannot have the crews' morale sinking, can we?"

The captain nodded, relief flooding his eyes. "Thank ye, lass."

Smiling, she turned back to the ocean and eyed the growing storm. To her knowledge, nothing seemed amiss with the weather. However, while she doubted it was anything more than an anomaly, she also knew better than to disregard the intuition of those with more experience than she. Taking a deep breath and letting it out slowly, she opened her senses to her surroundings.

Immediately, the environment jumped into clearer focus. She could feel every bump and crack in the deck beneath her feet, the rock of the boat seemed sharper, and the weather. . . . The weather simply felt wrong. She didn't know how she'd missed it before, and that angered her. To her enhanced senses, she could feel energy not of the storm's making building up in the billowing dark clouds. There was an order to the energy that hinted at a controlling power. Narrowing her focus upon the storm, she could make out a more subtle influence skirting the edges of the storm. Like a gentle caress, it seemed to be prodding the ominous clouds gently in their direction.

Cursing to herself, she closed her senses off and turned back to the captain. "Everything seems alright," she lied smoothly. "However, it does seem like it has the potential to be as powerful as

270

the storms earlier. You might want to have your night watch keep a close eye on it."

The captain nodded hesitantly and flashed a gap-toothed grin at her. "Aye. Thank ye, lass."

"My pleasure, Captain. Now if you'll excuse me, I think I'll try and get some sleep."

The captain nodded appreciatively to her as she stepped past him.

Keeping her stride casual, Kara moved across the deck to the steep stairs that led below deck. As soon as she was below deck, she quickened her pace, making her way through the narrow corridors as quickly as possible. Once she was in her cabin, and the door secured behind her, she didn't hesitate in waking the slumbering Mat.

Yawning, he sat up in his hammock and watched as Kara snatched up her katana and tanto and belted them on. "What's up?" he asked sleepily.

"Trouble," she stated bluntly.

Recognizing the danger in her statement, his grogginess seemed to vanish as he jumped down from his hammock and accepted his matching swords from Kara. "What kind of trouble?"

"The kind that only a blind fool would miss!" she barked with self-recriminating anger. "And I was the blind fool!"

Mat furrowed his eyebrows. "What are you on about, Kara?"

She glared at him hard. "The storms, damn it – they're not natural! Someone is controlling them and aiming them at us!"

Skeptical of Kara's statement, Mat opened his senses up to the currents and focused on the storm. Immediately, he recognized what had Kara so upset. With a loud curse, he closed off his senses and buckled on his swords at his hips. "How in the hells did anyone find us all the way out here?"

"I don't know!" barked Kara as she crouched down to double-check their gear. "I never felt anyone during my contact with Darkon or Greatjon, but that doesn't mean I missed something!" She gave a violent tug on the straps of the pack in her hands before tossing it to Mat. "Corith damn it all! There's a better question to be asked – who in the hells is on Triclose with that kind of power without us knowing?"

Mat looked at the pack quizzically. "I don't know, but–"

"*Shush!*" Kara held up a hand to interrupt him and then froze, her eyes glazing over. Within moments, she was back to normal and she stood up slowly, her eyes locking with Mat's. "The storm is moving our direction – and it's moving fast," she breathed apprehensively.

"What do we do?" Mat asked as a distant boom of thunder echoed outside.

Kara grabbed her pack and slung it on her back, securing it tightly. While she and Mat easily possessed the power to counter what was brewing in the distance, the destructive potential of fending off the storm could be just as bad as the threat the storm presented . . . or worse.

Setting her mind to a course of action, she stated simply, "We make ready . . . and we pray."

# Chapter Twelve

The square room was large by any standard, and its walls, which were made of stout grayish stone, supported brass lanterns that served as the primary source of lighting for the spacious room. Fitted into the lone exterior wall, a large glass window permitted a bit of daylight to spill upon the plush, imported blue carpet that covered the floor. Bookshelves built into the far end of the right-hand wall flanked a small, elegantly carved table, each piece of furniture ladened with neatly organized books on an assortment of subjects. Five chests, neatly arranged along the exterior wall beneath the window, contained an assortment of toys and games for the lone child in the room. A thick oak door set in the center of the right-hand wall led to the child's small but comfortable bedroom, and a roaring fire burned in the hearth set opposite the door in the left-hand wall. A circular table, made to a child's proportions and surrounded by five small chairs, was set up in the center of the room and was currently serving as the play area for a child of five summers.

The child, who was currently engrossed in a game of Castle with her dolls, was Shalen Valin Merandith, daughter of Kale and Marie Merandith. Mulberry-red hair cascaded about her three-and-a-half-foot frame, accentuating her vibrant blue-gray eyes. A simple, long-sleeve blue dress provided her warmth against the growing winter. Her round face beamed with amusement, her rosy cheeks full as she smiled. Her complete attention was focused on her game, leaving the two adults in the room to talk undisturbed.

Quietly chatting and seated in two well-cushioned, high-backed chairs were two young women – Doma Marie se'Trivant Merandith and her sister-by-marriage, Doma Lalandra se'Galivantra Trivant. Doma Trivant, at the insistence of her husband, Marie's brother, had agreed to spend the winter with her very pregnant sister-by-marriage. She had never been able to spend any real time with Marie in the past, and the last month had been surprisingly enjoyable. Not only had Lalandra come to know Marie better, but she found she had a growing affection for both her and her family. However, even though she had enjoyed spending time with Marie, she still felt slighted that her husband, Lucas Trivant, had used it as an excuse to get her as far from the fighting as possible.

Lalandra was of a petite stature with a slender face and hands made for the harp that she so thoroughly enjoyed playing in her free time. Her skin was tanned from her time spent along the sea in Haltho, accenting her sparkling blue eyes and wheat-blonde hair that hung freely just below her shoulders. Thin red lips were split in a laugh as her hands smoothed out the skirt of the high-cut blue dress that clung to her figure. It might have been considered a fairly reserved dress if not for the diamond shaped cutout on her chest exposing a fair amount of her modest bosom.

Despite her delicate outward appearance, Lalandra was a very strong-willed woman. Initially, she had balked at the thought of leaving Haltho while Lucas was away fighting; however, while she was more than capable of governing Roselia on her own, she had consented to her husband's request to move to Merset in order to allow him to fight with a clear conscious. Her strong-willed personality had seen her arrive in Merset somewhat angered at her situation, which had spilt over to her treatment of the keep's staff. She had been grouchy and curt with everyone at first, but as time passed and she got to know Marie better, she had softened and begun to enjoy herself – though the keep staff still shied away from her.

Lalandra, her hands folded in her lap, glanced from Shalen to her mother and asked in her throaty voice, "Do you still think you'll have a son?"

Wearing a loose gown of green and red over her swollen belly, Doma Merandith looked every inch like a woman nearing the end of her pregnancy. Her normally slender, pale face was a bit more plump than normal, her hands and feet were swollen at times, and she ran out of energy quickly. On the other hand, she seemed to radiate a joyful glow. Her hair was a match for her daughter's in shade and vibrancy, and her blue eyes glittered with unbound joy.

In many ways, she was the opposite of Lalandra. Though she was beloved by her people and considered a competent ruler in Kale's absence, Marie was nowhere near as strong-willed as her sister-by-marriage. She was shorter and, when not pregnant, more petite than Lalandra. One might even mistake her for demure if they didn't know her better. However, like Lalandra, she was concerned for her husband; furthermore, she even had the added weight of worrying about her brother, Lucas. Given the chance, those worries might overwhelm her, but with a realm to rule, a daughter to raise and another young one on the way, she had very little time or energy for anything else. Thankfully, given her present state, she had competent and helpful people around her to ease the burden.

Marie beamed a smile at Lalandra and ran a hand over her swollen belly affectionately. "We hope so," she responded in her soft voice. "Giving Kale a son would be a blessing. Besides, Tiliea could use a male heir and Shalen a brother."

Shalen looked up expectantly from her game at the mention of her name.

Smiling at the child, Lalandra asked, "What do you think of that, Shalen? Would you like a baby brother?"

Shalen's brow immediately wrinkled up seriously and she gave a vigorous shake of her head. "No, Aunt Lalandra – boys are icky and trouble."

Marie and Lalandra both laughed sweetly before Lalandra asked, "What about a sister?"

Shalen's round face lit up at the suggestion. "I'd love a sister! We could play dress-up, have tea parties, and play Castle with our dollies!" As soon as she mentioned the game of Castle, Shalen turned her attention back to her dolls.

Laughing, Lalandra gave Marie a sideways glance. "Well, Marie, I hope you paid attention to that – Shalen wants a sister. And I do hope you don't intend on hurting my niece's feelings. A brother would do just that."

Marie laughed. "I'll do my best. After all, boys *are* icky." The two women laughed and, even though she didn't understand the joke, Shalen added her musical and infectious laughter to the joyous ruckus. Their laughter died down as Marie flinched and placed a hand on her belly where her unborn child had just kicked. "That's the hardest kick I've received yet."

With Marie's permission, Lalandra placed a hand on Marie's belly and felt another hard kick. "I'd say you've got a fighter on your hands," Lalandra quipped with a small grin.

A stern glare met her comment. "No," Marie stated adamantly. "No more fighters. Triclose has seen too much bloodshed. This child will be anything but a fighter."

Looking scolded, Lalandra sat back in her chair. "I'm sorry, Marie. I didn't mean it that way. I just meant—"

She waved the apology away and passed her hand over her eyes. "I know, I know. I'm sorry I snapped at you like that. It's just. . . it's just that I'm tired of all the fighting. I miss Kale and want him back here, not off fighting some fool war."

Shalen looked up at the mention of her father, but when it appeared nothing more was going to be said about him, she returned to her game.

Lalandra nodded sympathetically to Marie. "I know what you mean – I miss Lucas too. It's been, what now? Seven or eight months?"

Doma Merandith blushed brightly, remembering the last night she had spent with her husband. Clearing her throat she said, "Yes, well, about that. . . . Hummmm." She paused and grinned mischievously at Lalandra. "On a brighter note – when are you and my brother going to have a child?"

Lalandra blushed furiously at the turn of the tables. Keeping Shalen's presence in mind, she chose her words carefully. "Hopefully soon. Deo willing, we'll have a child of our own soon."

Cradling a stuffed rabbit like a baby in her arms, Shalen chimed in, "I think you'd make a great mommy, Auntie Lalandra." Her face turned serious and she continued, "But no one is better and prettier than my mommy! That's a fact!" she emphasized her statement with a childlike, stern nod.

Lalandra blushed and laughed at the innocent compliment and its implications. "Thank you, my dear. If you say I'd make a good mother, then it must be true."

Shalen smiled brightly and returned to her game.

Doma Merandith reached over and stroked Shalen's mulberry-red hair affectionately. "Have you heard from Oblet of late?"

Lalandra shook her head. "No. I was hoping to hear from him earlier this week. What about you? Have you heard from Kale?"

Shaking her head, Marie sighed. "No, but I really don't expect to hear from him that often. I'm sure the war keeps an iron grip on his attention."

Lalandra tapped her lightly on the shoulder. "Pashaw! That's nonsense! He loves you too much to let this Deo-awful war occupy his thoughts all the time. I'm sure he'll write you soon enough."

She smiled softly. "Thank you, Lalandra. You're right – it's silly of me to think he wouldn't write."

A gentle knock at the playroom door interrupted the conversation. Marie bade the person to enter and the door opened on silent hinges, revealing a guard posted outside the door and admitting Katan Fulorton. Second-in-command of the House Guard, Katan was of medium build and average height. His smooth features, blue eyes and short-cut brown hair were strikingly handsome and the attention of many of the keep's women. He wore a white tabard, trimmed in deep purple and embroidered with five red stars on the right breast, over a loose black shirt, brown breeches and sturdy black boots. As per his

276

duty, even when there was no known threat, he carried his broadsword at his left hip in a plain scabbard.

The look on Katan's face was one of concern. Both Lalandra and Marie read this clearly, drawing worried glances from each. Marie broke the mounting uneasiness by stating the thought on the women's minds. "By the look on your face, Katan, I'd say you have some news that doesn't agree with you."

Katan bowed slightly and then nodded. "Doma Merandith and Doma Trivant. Doma Merandith – Allanian sent me to ask if you'd be so kind as to join him in Doms Merandith's study. He has some news he thinks you should hear."

Shalen bounced up with a shrill squeal of glee at the mention of Allanian's name. She absolutely adored Allanian – probably since he reminded her of a big cat – and loved spending time with him. "Alli's back!" she squealed. "Alli's back! Can I go with you, Mommy? Please?"

Marie smiled gently. "Not right now, Dear. I'm sure, though, that Alli would love to see you later this evening when his work is done. Isn't that right, Katan?"

Katan flashed a warm, bright smile at Shalen, meeting her large, pleading eyes. "Allanian has missed you too, Shalen. He'd be more than happy to have a visit from you later."

Shalen let out a joyful squeal and gave her mother a hug. "Thank you, Mommy!"

Doma Merandith rubbed Shalen on the head affectionately. "You're welcome. Now, will you stay here and not give your Aunt Lalandra any trouble?"

Shalen removed herself from the embrace and nodded her head resolutely.

"Good," Marie said and then glanced at Lalandra. "Don't let her give you too much trouble."

She laughed and shook her head in amusement. "I won't."

With that settled, Marie turned a charming smile on Katan. "Be a dear, Katan, and help a pregnant lady to her feet."

The halls of the keep were relatively quiet that afternoon. Most of the keep's inhabitants were either eating lunch or had gone into the city to enjoy one of the few remaining days of good weather before winter fully took hold. The halls of the upper floors were ornately decorated but narrow, having been built more for defense than luxury. Tapestries of landscapes and paintings of long dead family members hung on the walls alongside brass lanterns. The few windows that dotted the exterior walls were narrow enough to prevent access from the outside. An occasional alcove contained elegant pottery or a suit of ornamental armor. The floors and roofing were bare stone, adding a somewhat cold practicality to the halls.

The short jaunt from the playroom to Kale's study on the top floor would have normally only taken a few minutes, but with Marie in her current state, it took them nearly fifteen minutes to make the trip. Her energy easily spent and her legs and lower back aching, they had to stop to rest along the way before eventually making it to their destination.

The top floor resembled all the others in its functionality-over-luxury design. The bulk of the top floor was comprised of Kale and Marie's bedroom and their individual studies, and rooms for personal servants and important guests. Kale's study, which resided just off the Merandiths' bedroom, was situated in the center of the floor plan. Doma Merandith and Katan entered the study through a set of ironwood double doors, which provided access from the hall, and found Allanian sitting patiently in the lone chair in front of Kale's large oak desk.

The study was of modest size, Kale's neatly organized desk serving as the centerpiece of the room. Made from sturdy, thick oak, it had been a gift from a foreign diplomat hoping to curry favor with Kale's father. The desk was lovingly carved with an array of mythical creatures ranging from majestic gryphons to proud dragons, each detail painstakingly etched into the polished wood. Centered on the front face of the desk was a beautifully carved star in homage to House Merandith's sigil, and seated behind the neatly organized desk was a matching high-back, padded chair.

The rest of the study, while crowded with large and sturdy furnishings, was just as clean and as organized as the desk. Bookshelves lined the wall behind the desk, filled with large volumes on subjects ranging from war to philosophy. Brass lanterns hung at even intervals on the other walls, and a matching lamp sat on the front-right corner of Kale's desk. A simple hearth occupied the right-hand wall with two chairs and a small end table arranged before it. The door to the Merandith's bedroom was on the left-hand wall, and the only other piece of furniture in the room was the simple chair that Allanian occupied.

Allanian stood to greet them even before the heavy ironwood doors shut. He was a rare sight upon Triclose as he was of a race known primarily to occupy Solarson. He was a darlion – a race of catlike humanoids possessed of long life, eerie grace and a sharp intellect. Though his height was considered average for his kind, Allanian was roughly a head taller than the tallest men of the keep. His body was muscular beneath a short layer of white fur that looked more like albino skin from a distance. Shoulder-length hair, the same color as the rest of his fur, hung from a head that was eerily reminiscent of a cat. His ice-blue eyes were almond shape and upturned sharply. Tipped with tuffs of fur, his long, pointed ears swept back from his head like the ears of a fairy from a children's tale. The hint of elongated canines peaking from beneath his thick lips, and his broad, flat nose gave the impression of a large predatory cat. Aside from his feral features, his fur, and the talons hidden in the ends of his fingers, he could easily be mistaken for a large man at a distance. He wore the same tabard over his off-white tunic, breeches and boots as Katan did. No weapon adorned him, but it was widely known that he wielded a bow more powerful than any bow produced on Triclose.

"Doma Merandith," his soft, almost haunting voice purred as he bowed at the waist. "How are you today?"

She grimaced slightly. "Good. But I'd be much better if I sat down."

"My apologies, Doma Merandith," he said as he hastily moved behind the desk and pulled out Kale's chair for her. "I felt that it would be better that we talk here than in Shalen's presence."

Katan helped Marie over to the chair, which she eased herself into. She breathed a sigh of relief as her legs and lower back were momentarily relived of their burden. "Thank you, both of you." She nodded and smiled wearily to them. "Now then, Allanian – Katan said you have some news for me."

The darlion returned to his seat, Katan moving to his side, before nodding coolly to Marie. "Indeed I do. Unfortunately, it is not good news. Two days ago, while patrolling just south of Gast, we encountered a party of about ten Jade Talons."

Marie blinked and stated wide-eyed at Allanian. "Two days ago? Deo be good, you must have ridden hard to get back here so fast. Are you sure they were Jade Talons?"

"Indeed. We had the jump on them and dispatched them quickly. They were disguised as bandits, but a quick search through their belongings found empty parchment marked with House Suldamik's seal, as well as officer badges and tabards in Suldamik colors."

She shook her head. "If that's true, then that would mean. . . ."

Allanian smiled peacefully, knowing the train of thought his doma was following. "No – Kale is still strong from what we heard. You have to remember that there are plenty of places along the border that small groups could cross uninhibited and without notice; not to mention the Contested Territories are . . . difficult to monitor. Besides that, reports have been trickling in for weeks about small, armed parties ghosting about."

She nodded, thankful for the reassurance about Kale's health. "Well then – if Kale hasn't been beaten, then what do you think it is?"

"At first, we thought it was just a rogue group; possibly even dissidents that had gotten their hands on Suldamik colors in order to make us think the Suldamiks had gained some sort of foothold in our territory. But as we made our way back here, we heard rumors of other such groups roaming the countryside. Even before that encounter, we'd met up with a few of our southern patrols who said they'd encountered and skirmished with bandits more than usual, which signifies organization and numbers beyond what common banditry is capable of. And then there's the items that easily identify their loyalties – no commander in his right mind would launch such a mission and allow them to carry items that would mark them. Putting it all together, I'd say we have raiding parties on our hands now – and they want us to know who they belong to." He shrugged casually. "As it was only me and five others, I thought it wise to return with this news and find out what you would like to do about it."

Marie sighed deeply and rubbed her temples. "It's not enough that we have to worry about a war far away from us, is it? Now we have to worry about it coming to our doorstep. What do you think Craigan is trying to accomplish with this?"

Shrugging, Allanian offered, "It could be any number of things. He could be trying to establish a foothold within our territory, disrupt our supply routes, or he could simply be trying to divide our attention."

"But," interjected Katan, "it could be nothing more than harassment tactics with no real intention of causing us significant harm."

Allanian nodded. "Point taken. But either way, I don't think we should ignore them, nor should we overreact. Personally, I'd like to head back out with a larger force and investigate the matter."

Marie nodded slowly, taking it all in. She had never had the mind for tactics and she abhorred fighting, but she didn't have Kale around to make these decisions. Instead, she knew she needed to rely on those with more experience in such matters than her. With her mind made up, she stated, "I think it would be best if we handled this as quietly as possible; although the time for that has likely passed, given what you've told me. That being said, increase the number of patrols and their size. Also, take your choice of the men and find out what we're truly up against. While they might not pose a significant threat to us, the common folk and our supply lines could very much be at risk; therefore, you have free reign to do whatever is necessary to curb or eliminate this threat." Concern displayed plainly on her face, she added, "I'll also have Lalandra write Oblet and inform him of the situation. Though I would imagine that if we're having this issue, then he's probably dealing with a similar situation given his proximity to the war. Maybe we can find a way to coordinate our efforts if this proves to be a wide-spread threat."

A satisfied, feral grin spread across Allanian's face as he stood. "Very good, Doma Merandith. I'll leave Katan here to oversee things while I do a little hunting of my own starting in the morning. Hopefully, just the thought that I may be lurking out there will discourage a few of the groups."

She nodded with a heavy sigh. "I hope so, Allanian. Also, keep Kale's edict in mind and bring back any orphans you find to the Academy. It would be wishful thinking to hope that these raiders would leave the farmers and villagers alone. I'm sure there will be more children in need before this is over."

Allanian nodded. "Yes, Doma Merandith. Is there anything else?"

Marie thought about it for a moment and then her eyes brighten as she remember Shalen's request. Smiling she said, "Just one more thing – and it's probably the most important thing you can do while you are here – Shalen would absolutely love it if her Alli would visit her before you leave."

A broad, toothy grin spread across Allanian's face and a small laugh escaped his lips. "Indeed. I'll make it my top priority. Now, if you'll excuse me, I'll see to my preparations and give the Little Lady a visit. Katan – see to it that Doma Merandith is properly attended to. I'll send for you later."

Katan, smirking at the Alli comment, nodded. "My pleasure, sir."

Allanian stood and bowed to Marie before quietly leaving the room.

Marie watched the sturdy ironwood doors shut, her heart heavy and fearful. After a moment of reflection, she looked at Katan and smiled wearily. "Alright then. I guess we should go relive Lalandra of the perils of parenthood before my daughter can cause any harm and–" she flinched as she tried to stand up. "And while I can still move."

*

Life had not been easy on Donald in the five days since his harsh reprimand at the hands of Gregor. While his bruises and cuts from the beating had started to heal, his wounded pride had not been provided a respite to mend. A variety of hard-labor tasks had been dumped upon him. Ranging from digging latrines to cleaning up after meals, or hauling large sacks of grain back and forth through camp for no other reason than being ordered to do so, he was left exhausted and reeking of sweat and the latrines by the end of each day. In fact, his bodily aches and numb mind from the day's labor even deprived him of desire to consort with the women that came to his tent at night – which had become the subject of very colorful jokes within the Sur'dathan camp.

Of Hagan's Hammer, he was the only one receiving such treatment. Word had spread throughout the unit of his verbal transgression, and the resulting responses were largely supportive or indifferent. Some of the men had been surprised that a Theirigaldian still lived, while others saw it as no big deal and felt a sort of pity for their fellow soldier. If anyone had felt the same way about the incident as Gregor and Doms Hagail, they chose to hold their tongues. Donald, however, didn't really care what the others thought; he simply wanted the punishment over with so he could return his focus to the war. He had heard that the Theirigaldian had left camp the day after the attack, which had led him to believe his penance would be over. Sadly, it had continued. However, he had been given a semblance of a reprieve when Gregor had informed him that his punishment would be over after the Merandiths left.

He started the morning with a sense of relief. The Merandiths would be leaving the following morning and he would be free of the abysmal tasks. Despite the growing cold, he dressed himself as he had for the past week – a sleeveless black tunic, sturdy breeches and boots. While such minimal attire might seem mad given the wintery conditions, he knew he would work up a sweat quickly, which would make the comfort and coolness of the sleeveless tunic a boon later in the day. Dressed for the day ahead, the cold morning began as it had for the last few days – with a bowl of what the camp cooks claimed was oatmeal, but most of the soldiers swore was two steps below six-day-old, watered-down sawdust. For the first time, Donald didn't mind. He was more like his old jovial self as he ate and socialized with his fellow soldiers. Instead of glum looks, he shared jokes and laughs, which, in turn, made the day much more bearable. While it was still annoying to have to muck the corral or clean up after the soldiers' meals, Donald was able to do it with a smile on his face for once.

As the morning progressed and Donald went about his tasks, the ground, which had frozen overnight, quickly turned to mud as it thawed and the passage of foot traffic churned the turf. To his chagrin, he soon found himself splattered with mud. However, by early afternoon, any irritation caused by the sloppy work conditions was alleviated as he turned his attention to maintenance of the horses in the corral. While it didn't take long for fresh mud to grace him, or for him to smell bad enough that he was convinced he'd never be able to wash the scent off, his jovial mood persisted. Caring for the horses was probably the only task he did enjoy, and served to sustained his high spirits. He even found himself whistling a jaunty tune as he went about grooming the thick, stocky destriders that served as the Hammer's mounts. The joy he found in the task came as no surprise, for one did not remain with Hagan's Hammer if one did not love and care for one's steed. However, despite his improved mind-set, he was still appreciative of the break that presented itself when three of his friends showed up at the corral with bowls of stew in hand.

Donald had already extracted himself from the maze of horses in the corral and was returning his tools to the stablehands' toolbox when Whistler's unique, high-pitched breathing alerted him to their arrival. Donald turned and gave the arriving trio a toothy grin, unable to hide his pleasure at their company and the food. All three of his friends served in the infantry and were from the same clan as he; while they were taller than he, their hair and eye color matching Donald's brown hair and black eyes to near perfection. As they drew closer, Donald noticed that all three looked as tired as he, and that their padded leathers were dirty and sweat stained from hard activity, which he figured was a result of them having come directly from drills.

Whistler, the tallest and oldest of Donald's three friends, offered the extra bowl of stew to Donald when they reached him, which he accepted gladly. "Eh, Whistler, get that nose o' yours fixed! I could hear ye comn' a league away," he quipped playfully as he spooned the warm stew into his mouth.

Burly and grizzled, Whistler was a giant of a man who had cut his hair short like his two friends. His most prominent feature was his nose, which was horribly crooked from numerous fights, cursing him with a permanent whistle when he breathed through his nose. Though the shrill noise had earned him the affectionate nickname of

Whistler, he had eventually come to take pride in his unique feature, using it for emphasis or to annoy his friends – the latter being his favorite use. Thus, it came as no surprise when Whistler, annoyed with Donald's jab, grunted and reciprocated with a deep exhale through his nose. The harsh noise caused the others to cringe and a few of the horses to scamper away from the corral fence with skittish steps.

Gran, the shortest of the three and sporting his fair share of scars, flashed a gap-toothed grin at Whistler, his four missing teeth making him look whimsically stupid. Pointing a full spoon at the horses, he said around a mouthful of food, "See thar! Yer even mak'n tha horses nervous with tha snout o' yers!"

Whistler grunted. "Shut yer trap for I be decidin' to squash ye flat and make bread from yer bones, ye toothless son o' a whore!"

Donald chuckled as he leaned against the wooden fence – one of the first things he'd help construct – of the corral and took in the friendly banter. Jacob, his slender build seemingly swallowed up by his padded leathers, joined Donald along the fence.

Jacob was the most unremarkable of the group. While his plain features were considered neither handsome nor ugly, the jagged scar running the length of his right cheek was prominent enough to draw the eye of any casual observer. Glancing at Donald, he asked in his dry, gruff voice, "So lad, I take it ye're glad ta be done with all this mess?"

Nodding, Donald ate a spoonful of the meaty stew before replying. "Aye. It even makes this poor attempt at food seem a wee bit better. What about ye three? They've kept me so busy I haven't ta notion to do more than sleep at night."

Jacob scowled at Whistler and Gran who were still trading verbal jabs. "Would ye two stop yer yammer'n! Yer food is gonna get cold!" he barked at the two.

They ceased their banter immediately and stared at Jacob, surprised by the harsh reprimand. Muttering halfhearted apologies, they joined Donald and Jacob along the fence, looking somewhat scolded.

"That's a wee bit better," muttered Jacob as he turned his attention back to his stew.

"Don't be so hard on tha lads. They just be poke'n a wee bit o' fun at each other," Donald tossed in.

"Bah! Ye been away from them too long, Donald. Ye've forgotten that they never seem ta be shutt'n up once they get go'n."

Whistler let out a shrill breath through his nose. "Yer an arse, Jacob."

Jacob shrugged nonchalantly. "Aye, that I am. Ye got a problem with that?"

Donald laughed and rolled his eyes. "Oh aye, it be good ta see ye all – even if ye all are obnoxious and noisy!"

The group laughed at Donald's quip, alleviating the small amount of tension that had been building.

For the rest of the meal, they exchanged friendly chatter as they took the time to simply enjoy each other's company. Donald had felt practically sequestered over the last week, and he wasn't going to pass up the opportunity to catch up on the week's events. As expected, the Houses that were withdrawing had ramped up their preparations in advance of their departure on the morning. He was, however, surprised to hear rumors that a select group of men and women had been participating in advanced training exercises in preparation for a tournament to be held to replenish Doms Merandith's bodyguards. Being a natural competitor and proud of his martial skills, Donald would have loved to have a shot at such a task. Granted, he wasn't of House Merandith and his loyalty was firmly with the Sur'dathans, but his competitive side always seemed to need scratching when he caught wind of such events.

When his friends informed him that the Sur'dathan camp was already awash in rumors of imminent action, it came as no real shock to him; an increase in drills had already led him to such a conclusion. However, he knew it wasn't in the Sur'dathan nature to just sit idly by and wait for an enemy to come to them. While the drills could be in preparation for action, per the rumors, they could simply be a way to keep idle soldiers active and out of trouble. Either way, it was better than doing nothing.

As the meal drew to a close and the conversation sputtered, it struck Donald as odd that his friends seemed to grow somewhat uncomfortable. A flittering glance shared between the three clansmen was enough to convince him that something was bothering them. Determined to find out what was gnawing at them, Donald placed his bowl on the fence and wiped his hands on his pants before turning a serious glare on the trio. "Out with it, lads – ye all have been look'n more nervous than ah polecat."

His three friends shared another nervous glance, trying to decide who should speak. Grunting, Jacob finally spoke up. "Hells, it only be a rumor, and none o' us be known' enough about tha trouble that landed ye all this extra work, but there's word go'n about that someone's look'n for ye."

Donald's eyes narrowed with suspicion. "What do ye mean, 'look'n for me'?"

Jacob rubbed his nose before continuing. "Well, word is that a beast o' a Roselian has been ask'n around about ye." He chuckled nervously. "We just assumed ye done got his sister or wife with child."

Donald's friends laughed nervously, but stopped when they saw the serious glint in Donald's eyes.

"Come on now, lad," Jacob started to ask nervously, "ye can't be meaning there's somethin' to these rumors?"

Donald nodded slowly, suddenly alert and wary. "Aye, I canna be say'n much about it, but it would na surprise me if it was true."

The others looked at one another warily before Jacob cleared his throat and said, "Well then, lad, maybe ye should be tak'n these rumors seriously."

"I'll be keep'n that in mind. So what does this Roselian be look'n like?"

Jacob paused and scratched his head. "Deo be good, I canna be recall'n. Gran!" he bellowed. "Ye and Whistler be the ones that got word o' what tha lad looks like. Tell tha lieutenant 'ere what ye heard."

Gran leaned over and spit through the gap in his teeth. "Oh, aye, we 'erd what tha lad be look'n like. A giant o' a man with tattoos cover'n him like ah second skin."

Donald glared at Gran dryly. "Covered in tattoos, eh? Hells, that's damn near every Roselian o' age! Can't ye be more specific?"

Shooting Donald an irritated glare, he said, "Aye I would, if'n ye didna interrupt me."

Donald gave him an apologetic smile. "Sorry, Gran. Continue, if'n ye would."

Gran snorted and spit again. "That's better. Now as I was say'n – he was–"

"He be look'n like that," interjected Whistler as he pointed a meaty finger toward a man who had emerged from the final row of tents and was making directly for them.

His dark-booted feet seeming to glide across the ground, the man crossing the parade grounds with a warrior's grace was certainly not the largest Roselian any of them had seen, but the confidence and power he radiated was unmistakable. He was shorter than Whistler and powerfully built, the muscles of his bronzed and serpent-tattooed arms serving as an indicator of just how strong he was. The man's tunic, which was embroidered with the five golden stars of House Merandith on his right breast, was sleeveless and dyed the same deep black as the hair that was gathered at the nape of his neck in a braided horsetail. It was his eyes, however, that caught everyone's attention and held it. Black like a deep, endless pit, his eyes stared at them with an intense determination that all four of them understood was more than just bravado.

Donald, his eyes still locked on the stranger, muttered to his friends, "Well, I guess we'll be a findn' out if what yer all say'n is true, eh?"

The others nodded without saying a word.

The Roselian stopped a few paces short of the clansmen, his dark eyes examining each man before he spoke. "Which one of you is Donald McFain?"

The Sur'dathans noted the seriousness of his tone and glanced at one another warily before Donald stepped forward, hands on his hips, and stated, "That'd be me, lad. What can I–"

He never got to finish his question as Dakan's fist connected with his face squarely, stars erupting before his eyes as he crumpled to the ground. It felt like a lifetime before his vision cleared, but even before that, he could hear cursing and the shuffling of feet as his clansmen jumped to his aid. When his vision finally cleared, he found – to his profound amazement – that his friends had been easily overcome. Whistler was flat on his back and unconscious, his nose somehow splayed even more across his right cheek than before. Jacob was on his knees gasping for breath and clutching his gut. Gran, unfortunately, was in the grips of their assailant, his arm twisted behind him in an awkward and painful angle. Oddly, Donald didn't fear for himself or his friends at that moment; instead, the first thing that crossed his mind was to wonder how he kept getting ambushed with a fist to his face.

Upon noticing that Donald was coherent, Dakan snarled and gave a sharp twist on Gran's arm, snapping it at the shoulder and ripping an anguish-filled cry from him. As Gran crumpled to the ground, grasping at his broken arm, the Roselian stepped past him, his focus narrowed on Donald.

Staring in dumbfound shock at his attacker, neither Donald nor Dakan noticed the pounding footsteps of approaching soldiers. A moment before Dakan was on Donald, a large Sur'dathan barreled into the Roselian, knocking him clear off his feet. Donald watched in shock as one after another, men piled on his assailant, fists and feet flying as they sought to subdue the tattooed man. Howls of rage erupted from the scrum as a few of Donald's rescuers stumbled back from vicious blows. Shouts from the tent line caught Donald's attention and he turned his head to see that a crowd had begun to gather about the parade grounds. More importantly, he saw Gregor and Kale's man, Jerom, sprinting towards the fight, their face masked with outrage.

Cursing and bellowing orders, the two senior officers fought their way to the center of the brawl, neither veteran afraid to land blows of their own to clear a path. It wasn't long before Jerom and Gregor had inserted themselves between the crowd of angry Sur'dathans and the Roselian. Despite the rain of blows that had left him with bleeding cuts and numerous bruises, Dakan grinned spitefully at the Sur'dathans, apparently eager to continue the melee.

Fearing that Dakan might seek to reinitiate the brawl, Jerom placed a restraining hand on Dakan's chest. Turning back to the incensed gathering, he fix a dark scowl upon everyone in his field of vision, the skin around his eyepatch an irritated red and his right brown eye glowing with an equal intensity. "That's enough!" he bellowed with authoritative rage. "Gregor – tell your men to stand down! Now!"

Gregor snarled in response, his green eyes flaring. "And ye tell that bastard beastie of yers to back off!"

Jerom turned his lone brown eye on the Roselian and barked, "Stand down, Dakan! That's an order!"

Dakan gave the others and Donald one last baleful glare before saying, "Jerom, that's the bastard that–"

Jerom reared back and backhanded Dakan across the face, splitting his bottom lip wide open. "I said stand down! I don't care if he's Craigan himself! I gave you an order! And by Deo, you will obey!"

Staring daggers at Jerom, Dakan wiped the blood away before finally consenting with a nod of his head.

Certain that he'd have no more troubles with Dakan, Jerom spun on his heel and stared down Gregor. "Get your injured to the medics, and tell the others to return to their duties! I want this place cleared now!"

Gregor scowled and gave a tug on his thick, white wool shirt, his right hand coming to rest on the hilt of his sword. "These are my men, lad – don't be putt'n yer nose where it–"

Jerom's black-and gray-bearded face turned red with rage and he took a threatening step forward, though he made no movement toward his sword. "While we're still here, I'm in command and you answer to me!" His lone eye narrowed and his voice dropped low. "Now remove your men. . . . Or do we have a problem?"

Gregor took his measure of Jerom and decided that cooler heads would better serve the situation. Removing his hand from his sword hilt, he turned to his men and ordered, "Right, lads! See that tha wounded are tended to and return to yer duties! Yer not ta breathe a word of this, or ye'll be answer'n ta me! Got that?!"

"Yes, sir!" they answered in unison before jumping to work, though it did little to keep them from shooting Dakan hate-filled, spiteful glares.

While the Sur'dathans tended to their duties, Gregor hauled Donald to his feet and made sure his subordinate was okay, and Jerom managed to maneuver Dakan away from them.

Once the grounds were cleared and the crowd had been dispersed, Jerom ordered Dakan to remain where he was while he moved over to Gregor. Running a hand through his black hair, Jerom demanded, "What in the hells is going on here?"

The white of his beard and hair standing out starkly against his flushed face, Gregor eyed Donald and then Dakan before turning his attention to Jerom. They were all very aware of the assault on Amroth, so it would do little good to lie. "Donald 'ere was the one that flapped his lips about yer lad, Amroth." He pointed an accusing finger at Dakan. "I'd venture ta guess that beastie is tha Roselian that's been snoopin' about ask'n questions."

Jerom turned to Dakan and barked, "Is that true?"

Dakan shot a stern glare in Donald's direction before stating bluntly, "Aye."

Jerom shook his head and tossed his hands in the air. "Deo be good, Dakan! You'll be the death of me! What in the hells were you thinking?"

Dakan folded his tattooed arms across his chest. "Amroth was nearly killed, and this is the one responsible. Honor demanded that I–"

"Honor?!" bellowed Jerom as he took a step forward and got in Dakan's face. "Honor?! You need to leave that blasted, twisted

289

sense of clan honor back with the Roselians! You're a Merandith now – act like one! If you can't do that, then I'll be happy to send you packing back to your clanmates! Do you understand me?"

Dakan glared back at Jerom, his jaw muscle flexing as he fought to control his temper. Finally, he managed to state simply, "Yes, sir!"

Jerom remained in Dakan's face, glaring hard into his eyes. Finally, he stepped back and turned to face Gregor and Donald. "As for you two – this could have been avoided if you'd informed me or Kale of what exactly led to Amroth's attack! Deo only knows – we don't need this kind of infighting!" He shook his head in disgust and sighed. "I'm going to overlook this because, Deo knows, the lad had it coming." The hard edge returned to his eye as he stated, "However, mark my words – while Dakan will be punished, if I catch even a whisper of this kind of petty clan violence nonsense, I will come down on the responsible parties with Deo's wrath! Do you all understand me?"

Silent, cold nods greeted his edict.

Jerom straighten and tugged on his black tabard before adding, "Good. Now I suggest we be about our business. I expect to see you and Doms Hagail at dinner per Doms Merandith's request."

Gregor, biting back his anger, replied stoically, "Aye, we'll be there. But," he glared at Dakan, "I don'na wanna see that bastard anywhere near Doms Hagail or my men, Jerom."

Jerom nodded sternly before turning and giving Dakan a shove toward the tent line.

As the two made their way toward the tents, Gregor turned back to Donald, a string of colorful curses giving voice to Gregor's frustration. "Deo be good, Donald," he muttered as he placed an arm around the beaten and bruised Sur'dathan, "I don'na know what ta do with ye. Yer bust'n me stones and causin' me no end o' trouble." With a gentle tug, he started Donald moving back to camp while continuing his lecture.

Donald paid Gregor's admonishments little heed as his attention was captured by the simple, self-pitying thought of, *"Why me?"*

# Chapter Thirteen

"**D**amn it, Dakan! What more do we have to do to drive home that this kind of behavior is unacceptable?!" Kale dropped into his chair heavily with a frustrated sigh. Bright with intensity, he kept his green-eyed gaze focused across the table on Dakan's rigid form. "No less than six separate fights in under a week! I know the clans operate differently than the rest of us, but, by Deo, you will respect me and my House and the way we function!" Kale barked, the vehemence in his tone startling Jerom, who was standing just behind Dakan.

Dakan couldn't refrain from scowling as he retorted coolly, "If you'd just let me explain, Doms Merandith. This wasn't some meaningless squabble – the man I attacked was responsible for revealing Amroth's blood."

Kale sighed again and ran his hands over his face, the roughness of two days worth of beard growth scratching at his palms. Tugging at his white shirt in frustration, he asked, "He wasn't the one who ordered the attack, now was he?"

Dakan's jaw muscles flexed in consternation. "No," he stated bluntly.

"'No'," intoned Kale, "is right. According to Doms Hagail, he's just a soldier who has a bad habit of drinking too much and flapping his lips. Apparently he'd already been dealt with." Kale shook his head in exasperation, his fingers tapping heavily on the empty table between him and the others while his eyes drifted around the room.

There were no lamps currently lit, casting the war room into shadow that seemed oddly appropriate given the situation at hand. Kale's squire and runner, Gammon, had already seen to it that most of Kale's possessions had been packed within sturdy chests, which now sat along the perimeter of the war room awaiting the army's departure in the morning.

Kale's longsword, which was hanging from the chair in its harness, rattled against the chair as he sat back hard. "What am I to do with you, Dakan? I simply cannot overlook this many indiscretions – especially this last one. You are failing in representing this House, and more importantly, you are failing yourself. I should send you back to the clans right now, but I have this feeling that the shame and dishonor that would bring you and yours would simply cause more trouble." He stared at Dakan hard. "What should I do with you?"

Dakan returned the probing gaze without flinching. "I understand what I have done. Clan honor called for it; I could and would do no less to answer that call. While I do not agree with your view point, I understand how my actions may cast a shadow on House Merandith and I am willing to pay whatever price you see fit, Doms."

The finality to Dakan's tone struck a chord with Kale. While the statement was said firmly and flatly, there was a heartfelt sincerity to it that left little doubt that Dakan meant every word. "Well now, taking responsibility for your actions even though you know it could yield less than desirable results for you – I have to respect that. However," Kale stood, his handsome face hardening to match the seriousness of his tone. "I cannot allow this to go unpunished. Harsh words or hard labor would seem trivial and invite chaos and disorder amongst the ranks." Pausing, he took a deep breath and said, "Dakan Holdreth – you are hereby sentenced to twenty lashes at sunset for your brazen actions."

Dakan met the sentence with an emotionless stare, his features seemingly carved from stone.

Jerom, however, was not so reserved. His brown eye grew wide and his jaw almost seemed to hit the floor as he blurted, "You can't be serious?! I know he's been a bit of a handful, but this is–"

"That's enough, Uncle!" Kale stated firmly, cutting his uncle off, his tone leaving no room for argument. "I cannot simply shrug this off as a mere disagreement that got out of hand. There's a bigger picture to consider, and I will not risk it all to coddle a single individual's honor! Do I make myself clear?"

Jerom pulled himself up at the admonishment, glaring hard at his nephew. "Aye. Perfectly clear," he growled.

Kale nodded. "Good. Now see to it that Dakan is escorted to his tent where he is to await his punishment. Once you've seen to that, return to me."

Jerom fought a scowl as he moved next to Dakan and took hold of his upper arm. "Aye, Doms Merandith," he answer sourly. Looking at Dakan with just a hint of pity, he said softly, "Come along, lad. Best we get this over with."

Dakan remained anchored to the spot for just for a moment, refusing to back down as he met Kale's eyes. For one very long and tense moment, it seemed like he might say or do something rash. Finally, he nodded to Kale before turning and allowing himself to be escorted from the pavilion.

As soon as they were gone, Kale sank into his chair with a heart-wrenching sigh and buried his face in his hands. He had just ordered something he and his family rarely did. Floggings, at least in their view, were a harsh and barbaric punishment that accomplished little more than to severely injure another person. But what choice did he have in the matter? Dakan had proven to be brash and strong-willed, and had also lived up to his reputation as a brawler, resulting in a flood of complaints greeting Kale nearly every morning. Kale had tried to be patient, but this fight and the surrounding circumstances had simply been too much to overlook. However, Dakan had proven to be a natural and instinctive fighter during the training that had occurred over the last week, and he was hesitant to simply toss such a gem away. In Kale's mind, Dakan was like a prized wild stallion whose will needed to be broken before he could be properly molded and trained.

A violent rustle at the pavilion's entrance interrupted his melancholy reflections as Jerom stormed into the tent, gripping his sword hilt tightly. As he stood in the entryway staring daggers at his nephew, Jerom's salt-and-pepper beard made him seem almost animal-like in his anger. Before Kale could say a word, Jerom quickly crossed the distance and slammed both hands down violently upon the table. "What in Deo's name are you thinking?! Have you gone daft?! Deo knows I did not put such a notion in your head, and your father – Deo rest his soul – would be rolling in his grave to hear such garbage come from the mouth of his own son!" Kale tried to interrupt, but Jerom's tirade wasn't about to be disrupted. "A whipping! A Deo-damn-it-to-hells whipping?! We're not some barbaric clan – and we're certainly not the Suldamiks! You start treating your troops like they're nothing but pieces of meat, and you might as well surrender – *because you'll lose your army as sure as I lost my left eye!*"

Face red and out of breath, Jerom paused, providing Kale the opening he was waiting for. "Are you finished, Uncle? Because I have to say, I'm surprised at you."

Jerom gawked at his nephew. "Surprised at me?" he blurted indignantly.

Kale nodded. "Aye, you. We have a delicate situation on our hands, and a rogue element like Dakan will only ruin things if left unchecked. We have to send a message, especially to him. Hard labor will not faze him, and his actions have been too public for a private punishment to do any good." He shook his head sternly. "No – this calls for an extreme and public measure. He's too talented to send off to waste away, but if we want to keep him around, we need that stubborn and willful personality to be broken just enough that we can train him and make him a better man. A flogging – while barbaric – will serve to show that I will not tolerate any of my men bringing dishonor to this House, nor the violent abuse of any Houses' soldiers; furthermore, it will show Dakan that he has found the line he cannot cross and – Deo willing – he will stop testing us."

Jerom simply gawked at his nephew, unsure of what to think. He detested such violent punishments and knew Kale did as well, but his nephew was – regrettably – making perfect sense. Dakan had been a handful so far, like a willful child trying to push the boundaries of authority. While he wasn't as confident as Kale was that such a punishment would work, he too was at a loss on a better way to handle it. "Fine," he conceded grudgingly with a sigh, the tension leaving his body. "But know that I do not agree with this. It may break him or it may not. Either way, I just hope your soul can handle delivering such barbarism upon another."

"I have enough blood on my hands as it is, Uncle. This is still far from the atrocities I committed early in the war. I don't think the rest of the army will react badly to a reminder that there is a line they shouldn't cross." Kale gave his own remorseful sigh and ran a hand through his short-cropped blonde hair. "Besides, Dakan *is* clan. This is probably something he's gone through before, and with the way he heals, he'll be as good as new in a few days. I'd say the price we'll pay to bring such an asset under control is small compared to the good that man could possibly do. Believe me, Jerom – I don't like this anymore than you do, but it needs to be done."

Jerom studied his nephew's eyes intensely before responding. "Alright, lad . . . I believe you. Just remember – this is a slippery slope you're on. You were there once before and saw just how quickly things can get out of hand – be mindful of that."

Kale smiled softly. "Thank you, Uncle. I will be wary, and I hope you will continue to keep me grounded as well."

"Aye, you're damn right I will! Willful, stubborn brats like you need someone around to cuff them every now and then!" He grunted at Kale whose smiled widened. "Now, if you'll excuse me, I had best see about this Deo-forsaken punishment if we're to meet with the others for dinner."

Kale arched an inquisitive eyebrow. "You're going to handle the flogging?"

Jerom scowled and scratched at the skin around his eyepatch. "Aye. If we're willing to use such an act as punishment, then at the very least one of us should be the one to swing the lash. As you can't be seen to enjoy such acts by dealing the blows yourself, it might as well be me. Besides – if we put it in someone else's hands, we'd more than likely be handing the whip to someone with a grudge against the lad."

"I see your point," Kale conceded. "Very well then. See to the arrangements."

Jerom nodded. "Aye, Doms Merandith." He turned to leave.

"Oh, and Uncle?"

Jerom stopped and turned back to face his nephew. "Aye?"

"Go easy on him. I'm not sure I could handle it if he were permanently injured." The pain this order was causing him was evident in the softness of his voice.

Jerom nodded, relief flooding his face to know that Kale took no pleasure in the punishment. "Nor could I, lad. Nor could I."


By sunset, word of the flogging had spread through the encampment like wildfire. There was a general consensus of shock and confusion at the news. Kale was known – outside of his vengeance-driven campaign when he ascended to the throne of House Merandith – as a fair, just, and kind doms. Many of the soldiers summarily dismissed the notion that he would hand down such barbaric punishment, and even a few of the men that had been so unlucky as to be a victim of Dakan's fists were hesitant to believe the news until they heard it from multiple sources. However, there were those that took immense pleasure and satisfaction in the gossip.

When word reached the medical tents that Dakan was to be flogged, Donald and his friends received the news with grins of satisfaction. Even after Gregor had explained to Donald why the attack had happened, he had still felt like his assailant deserved punishment, and the news of the flogging only served to justify his attitude toward the assault. All four of the friends were determined to attend the flogging, but their joy was cut short upon returning to the Sur'dathan camp to find themselves confined to their tents on orders from both Doms Merandith and Doms Hagail. The order was disheartening at first, but either way, they felt the assault upon themselves was being justly punished.

Across the camp, amongst House Trivant's forces, there were clan members that rejoiced at the news, seeing it as an occasion to celebrate. As far as they were concerned, it was divine justice finally being brought down by the Spirits upon an outcast that probably shouldn't have been allowed to live. A few spontaneous celebrations erupted as clan members celebrated the long-overdue punishment of the kasteri. Barrels of mead were pulled from storage and cracked open across the clan camps, and the celebrations soon devolved into drunken revelries; bawdy songs and numerous curses soon rang out – most of which were aimed at insulting Dakan and those of his blood – as inhibitions were drowned in a sea of mead.

Beliza was growing more and more irate as she made her way through camp en route to the parade grounds to bear witness to Dakan's punishment. Her sinuous, seductive strides soon lost their lustful sway in favor of an agitated and determined gait. Her toned and curved frame was tense underneath her warm deerskin leathers, the bone trinkets stitched into her tunic as decoration rattling with every movement. Her salt-and-pepper hair was pulled back from her handsome face into a braided ponytail that rested over her right shoulder, the fetishes weaved into the locks clinking together as she tugged at the braid. The only things about her that seemed fiercer than her stride were the wolf tattoos on her bare arms and the intensity and building anger in her gray eyes.

None of what had transpired since Dakan's acceptance into House Merandith's ranks was what she had wanted; in fact, she felt like Dakan was doing his best to ruin her plans. If he failed to ingratiate himself, then she would be left with little choice but to go about the difficult task of eliminating the Theirigaldian. Not that it couldn't be done, but having Dakan close to her target would make things so much easier if it came to that. In the end, no matter how it happened, the return of the Clan of the Fang to good standing was essential to both her and her master's plans. However, even though Dakan was a tool in all this, he was a tool that she loved – though her love for her master could not be surpassed, and no one said she couldn't have two lovers – and had more uses for than a means to an end; as such, she found herself growing tired of his name being slandered within the clans.

It was as she passed one such jubilant celebration that her already frayed temper finally snapped. Three members of her own clan, two men and one woman, were drunkenly dancing about a roaring fire, singing songs and toasting Dakan's punishment. It was painfully obvious to Beliza that they were drunk, which did nothing to temper her rising anger. Mead sloshed from wooden tankards as they gyrated about the fire. The firelight illuminated the wolf-tattooed, muscular

296

and hairy chests of the two men as they made a pathetic attempt to dance with a somewhat handsome woman, her wolf-tattooed left breast exposed from a sloppy and drunken attempted at fondling. Neither man was particularly handsome by Beliza's standards, scars and shaved heads making them seem more animal than human. Given the similarities in their appearance, they were probably related. She would have ignored the group if not for the words that she heard as she passed by.

"Eh! What a glorious night! The bastard o' a bastard gets tha losh," the tallest of the two men slobbered, "and we drink his mead ta tha last!"

The other two laughed and the other man bellowed, "Oh, aye! Sa tru! Mabeh that 'ore Beleeza will realize wha' a real clansman is and . . . and take a true wolf to 'er blankets!"

Beliza paused at that comment, fighting the urge to barge in. She might have continued on then, but then the woman spoke, apparently trying to imitate her. The woman cocked her hip and pouted her lips while cupping her bare breast. "Ooooh, please! I nee' a real wolf to suckle me n' show me wha' a man turly is! Years o' tha' small slippery serpent have made me forgat what it's like to have a 'eal man fill mah up!"

The three of them broke down laughing with drunken glee, unaware of Beliza's tense form beyond the firelight.

The tall man thrust his hips at the woman and grabbed his crotch. "Oh 'ere I come, Clan Elder! I show ya what it means ta be a wulf!" He then stumbled around the campfire, dropping his half-full tankard, and drunkenly kissed the giggling woman even as he fumbled at her bare breast.

By that point, Beliza had had enough. She had her own pride as well as Dakan's in mind as she turned and strode into the firelight. It was one thing for the other clans to banter and toss insults her way, but an entirely different matter for her own clan to slander her and her lover.

The shorter of the two men noticed Beliza immediately but it took him a moment to realize who was standing there. When he did, he spewed mead into the fire, the flames jumping with the addition of the alcohol, and tapped feverishly at the other man's back. "Spirits' balls! Stop it, Larn! Curse it ta all 'ells, Beleeza herself is 'ere!"

The man called Larn paused in his drunken attempts at disrobing the woman and glanced at his friend and then at Beliza before mumbling, "Wha are you on about, Vanic? That's not Beleeza, she ta pretty to be tha 'ore."

The woman took the moment to look at Beliza and seemed to sober up quickly as she took note of the violence building behind Beliza's gray eyes. The woman backed away from Larn, brushing her black hair from her round face, her blue eyes growing wide with fear. "Listen to him, Larn," she stated with fear-inspired clarity and sobriety. "He isn't lying."

Larn gave the woman a drunken, confused glance and then looked at Beliza again before letting out an annoyed breath. "PFFFFT! Yer all daft! Just another ertty that's come o'long ta bear witness ta mah ulfish manliness!" He grabbed his crotch again and thrust it at Beliza, laughing all the while.

The other two backed away from Larn even as Beliza let out an angry, wolfish snarl, and her features twisted with fury. With speed that would make her clan symbol proud, Beliza reached behind her back and drew a long-bladed dagger as she dashed forward low to the ground. Before Larn knew what had hit him, Beliza's dagger lanced out and up, the razor edge slicing deep into his groin, severing the tendons and artery and viciously removing his genitals from his body. Even as blood erupted from his groin, staining his pants as he collapsed to the ground with a howl of agonizing pain, Beliza had moved on.

A quick stride brought her to Vanic, her bloodied dagger lashing out and splitting open the inner thigh of his left leg on its way to opening his groin. As she stepped around Larn's huddled-up body, Vanic collapsed to the ground, howling in anguish even as he tried to stem the flow of blood from the deep wound. The woman, frozen in horror at the sudden and violent attack, was unaware that Beliza had slipped behind her until she felt the Wolf Elder's strong hand clamp down on her bare breast and the blood-soaked dagger come to rest just below the plump bosom.

"Now," hissed Beliza into the woman's ear, "what is all this about me being a whore? What is all this about me not knowing what a true man is? Hummm? From what I can see, these two bastards are cowards and lacking the equipment to prove it, wouldn't you say?"

The woman was shivering and whimpering as tears ran down her face. "Ye– Ye– Yes, Clan Mistress," she whimpered.

Beliza dug the dagger into the soft flesh of the exposed breast, drawing blood and a cry of pain. "Now what about you, girl? Do you think I'm a whore? Do you think it wrong of me to bed who I want? Do you know what it is to be a wolf? I see the tattoos upon you, but all I truly see is a cowardly, whimpering bitch in need of training. Do I have that right?" she hissed.

By this point, the woman was weeping with unbridled fear. "Yuu– You do, Miss– Mistress! Please! Please don't kill me!"

The woman's body shook violently in fear and horror as she watched the last breaths leave the two men's bodies as they bled out, leaving Beliza with little doubt that the statement was sincere. By this point, a crowd had gathered about the grisly scene; however, upon noticing Beliza and that all three victims were adorned with Wolf Clan tattoos, no one was in any rush to interfere with Wolf business.

Beliza glanced up at the gathering and grinned viciously. "This goes for all you goat-humping bastards – if I catch even a scent of any of you speaking ill of me or Dakan, or taking joy in what is to befall him tonight, I will hunt each and every one of you down and make sure you bleed out like these two before collecting your small stones as trophies! Do you all understand me?!"

Hard stares greeted her, but slowly she received nods from those she could see.

Grinning again, she turned her attention back to the trembling woman in her arms. "As for you – what's your name?" she whispered vehemently in her ear.

"Me– Melane, Mistress," she whispered back.

"Well, Melane," Beliza purred, "you're my bitch now – do you understand? You will serve me, clean me, pleasure me, and wipe my ass – whatever I desire, you will do. Do you understand?"

Melane whimpered through a fresh round of tears and nodded.

"Good," Beliza hissed menacingly. "And just to make sure you take this seriously, and to serve as a reminder of who is your master, I think I'll take this as a trophy."

Before Melane could even fully register the words, Beliza's grip shifted and tightened painfully on her breast, pinching and pulling hard on her nipple. With lightning speed, she slashed upward with her dagger, severing Melane's nipple from her breast. Melane crumpled in agonizing pain, her hands fighting desperately to stem the flow of blood from her mutilated breast even as she screamed for help.

Beliza quickly sheathed the bloodied dagger and held the piece of mutilated flesh up for all to see. "This bitch is mine! No one else is to touch her or give her orders until I release her and return her flesh to her!" She tucked the bloody nipple into her tunic between her own breasts. Smiling maliciously, she stepped over Melane's body and moved toward the crowd. "I have a flogging to witness, and I would be very . . . put out if my new slave were to die so soon. So, if someone would be so kind as to see to it that she doesn't bleed to death. . . . " She let the unspoken threat linger in the air as she pushed into the gawking crowd.

Horrified and angry eyes following her every move, Beliza slinked her way through the crowd with a satisfied and malicious grin splitting her face. With her gray eyes gleaming with lust and power, she noted the animosity being directed her way by those not of the Clan of the Wolf and thought to herself, *That's right, enjoy your self-righteousness while you can. Soon – oh so soon – you will all bow before me . . . or fall beneath the fangs of the Wolf.*

By the time the sun touched the eastern horizon, a large crowd had gathered about the perimeter of the parade grounds, the air abuzz with conversation and thick with tension and anticipation. At the center of the grounds, two thick and sturdy pylons had been erected, large iron nails securely affixing a pair of solidly constructed manacles to the pillars near the ground and another pair about three-fourths of the way up the poles. With as ominously as the columns seemed to loom over the parade grounds, it was debatable as to which was more terrifying – the punishment the venue promised or the venue itself.

As Beliza found a place at the front of a small group of Wolf Clan members gathered on the far side of the parade grounds, she noted with grim satisfaction that the penalty to befall Dakan wasn't being treated as merely a show for the troops. The chains of both sets of manacles were thick, sturdy, and had very little give in them; anyone restrained by the shackles would not be able to flinch away. She casually rubbed some of the dried blood from her hands – noting with pride that those of her clan that saw the blood simply ignored it – as she looked around for any sign of Dakan.

Before she could even complete her scan of the parade grounds, a voice rang out over the buzz of conversation, "Make way for the Domses Merandith, Trivant and Hagail, and the accused!"

Immediately, the din of noise died down and the crowd nearest the line of tents, which resided on the opposite side of the grounds from Beliza, parted to admit a column consisting of soldiers from all three announced Houses. The security detail quickly fanned out to form a human barrier between the crowd and the support pylons. Hands secured behind his back and still showing the results of the brawl earlier that day, Dakan and his two guards followed the column onto the grounds and immediately made their way to the supports. Dakan's face was an unreadable mask of stoicism as he took up his position between the pillars and his guards unbound his wrists.

Beliza was mildly surprised and tremendously proud of her pet when she saw that he did not resist his punishment. As his arms were raised over his head and his wrists secured in the upper iron shackles, he found Beliza in the crowd and locked eyes with her. She gave him a small nod and smile of pride even as his legs were spread apart and the lower manacles secured around his booted ankles. As the guards double-checked the shackles, Dakan acknowledged Beliza with the slightest of nods. Once assured that their charge would not escape, the guards then joined the domses who had positioned themselves a good twenty paces behind Dakan.

For some reason, Beliza found the grim posture of the three domses and their seconds somewhat comical. All six men were dressed in formal longcoats dyed in the colors of their respective Houses. Doms Trivant seemed to loom over their private huddle, his muscular bulk seeming even larger due to the bright-orange dye of his longcoat and the large golden sunburst on his right breast. He was a handsome man and just a few summers older than Kale. His brown hair was pulled back in a horsetail, and his bright-blue eyes shone as if he always knew something that you didn't. As a Clan Elder, Beliza had met Trivant on multiple occasions. Normally she held very little respect for non-clan affiliated leaders, but between the clans following House Trivant, House Trivant's claim to clan blood, and her own personal experiences, she had come to find Trivant to be bearable.

Where Trivant was the giant of the group and had a modicum of Beliza's respect, Doms Hagail was certainly his opposite. Ignoring his short stature and, as far as she was concerned, the overly vivid red and blue of his longcoat, she simply found the elder doms to be intolerable. Even his leathery skin, receding white hair, and braided beard rubbed her nerves raw. Simply put – he was a Sur'dathan clansman and, though blood might loosely tie the two realms together, that made him an affront to her way of life.

Ironically, it was Kale – flanked by a dourer Jerom and Tazrim – who perked her curiosity the most. As he stood in height between the two others, she wasn't quite sure of what to make of the man in the black longcoat. Of the domses, his longcoat was the least ostentatious; a single four-point golden star adorning each shoulder and simple brass buttons were the only sign of wealth on his coat. Where the other two domses had golden stitching and piping, his was as black as the rest of his coat, making it nearly indistinguishable from the rest of the garment. She had seen the violent side of Kale and even applauded the voracity with which he had driven his enemies before him. Yet in a contradiction that confused her to this day, she had seen him soften and relax his pursuit of what was seemingly a very successful course of action. She had little time for such weak-

301

ness, and even less respect for it. However, for a time, she had seen just a bit of her own Wolf Clan's ferocity in Kale, which held her in check when it came to passing judgment on him. She felt validated in that decision when she found herself respecting Kale for his willingness to use such a harsh punishment to remind Dakan and his men who was in charge. After all, an army without discipline was an army waiting to be slaughtered.

"Well, well. The wolf bitch herself has come out to watch her pet toy finally get the whipping he deserves," rumbled a deep voice from her left.

Beliza turned her head and cast a baleful glare upon the new arrival. "Ah, Vagain — I should have smelled your stench a league away."

The imposing, grizzled Elder of the Clan of the Bear accepted the barb with a grin, his brown eyes twinkling with amusement. "Could be that I bathed, or that blood staining your hands and chest is clogging your nose. What happened, Beliza? Did you castrate some poor soul that saw through your charms?"

Smiling sweetly, Beliza retorted, "Careful what you say Bear, or next time this blood might be yours."

Vagain scoffed, folded his arms across his chest and turned his gaze on Dakan, the fetishes in his long white hair rattling with each movement. "You know, Beliza, I'm not sure if I should pity your clan, or find it amusing that they took in a traitor's son and continue to let your family lead them. It's sad, really."

Beliza's face screwed up in anger, but before she could retort, a hush began to fall over the crowd. She turned her attention back to the center of the grounds to see Jerom, clad in the same style longcoat as Kale, standing before Dakan with his hand held high for silence. Unwilling to let Vagain have the last word, she muttered, "Another time, Bear."

Vagain simply smiled in perceived triumph.

Tapping the black whip in his right hand against his hip while he waited for the din of noise to die down, Jerom, his barely contained scowl of disgust seemingly exaggerated by his eyepatch, watched the crowd carefully for any sign that they might turn violent. While there was certainly tension in the air and, to his disgust, some of the clan soldiers appeared to have already been celebrating, there didn't appear to be any evidence that this act of punishment was going to be greeted with violence. Granted, Dakan seemed to have made enough enemies to possibly warrant such retaliatory actions, but

Jerom felt a modicum of relief that the only violent act this evening would be the whipping.

When the crowd noise finally died down, Jerom hesitated for just a moment before raising his voice to be heard about the parade grounds, declaring, "We are gathered here this evening to bear witness to this soldier's punishment for the crimes he has committed! The accused has been charged with incitement of mayhem, assault with intent to injure, and violence against his fellow soldiers! The accused has pled guilty to all charges!"

A murmur of excited conversation rippled through the ranks, and was especially energetic amongst the Roselian clan members who were all too familiar with Dakan's stubborn and violent tendencies.

Jerom let the wave of chatter continue for a moment before once again holding up his hand for silence. As the murmur died down, he lowered his hand and faced Dakan before continuing. "Corporal Dakan Holdreth – you have been accused of the aforementioned charges and have pled guilty to all of them. By order of Doms Kale Merandith, Doms of House Merandith and Doms General of the Army of Five Stars, your punishment is thus – twenty lashes to be served consecutively and to be carried out immediately!"

Beliza watched with pride as Dakan received the public statement of his crime and punishment with stoic silence. True to his clan blood, there were no pleas for mercy or cries of denial. She tried to catch his eyes to offer support and thanks for the way he was conducting himself, but her efforts were to no avail; Dakan's eyes were focused forward, his concentration turned inward as he prepared himself for the ordeal to come.

After giving the crowd a moment to absorb his words, Jerom approached Dakan. Beliza couldn't hear what was said, but she did see him hold up a leather-wrapped piece of wood. Dakan eyed the bit briefly before nodding and opening his mouth so Jerom could insert it. Once he was sure Dakan had the bit securely in his mouth, Jerom moved behind the Roselian clansman and unfurled the whip. A few quick flicks of his wrist had the whip dancing like a snake as he loosened up. Finally, he turned to Kale, awaiting the order to commence with the punishment. Doms Merandith, his jaw set and green eyes hard, gave a slight nod to his uncle. Jerom returned the nod before turning back to face Dakan. For the briefest of moments, it looked as if Jerom would hesitate or hold back, but then his arm went out and back before darting forward. The whip snaked toward Dakan, hissing as it cut through the air, and connected with his back with a loud, sharp crack.

"ONE!" barked Tazrim even as a glistening red gash opened up on Dakan's back, the serpent-tattooed clansman showing no indication of having felt the lash.

Again, Jerom's arm went back and jump forward, another red gash opening on Dakan's back to the accompaniment of Tazrim's count. Beliza noted with pride that Dakan, nor any of the clansmen around her, did not flinch. Again and again, the whip lashed out, cutting deep into Dakan's back. By the time the tenth lash cut a bloody streak across his back, there were people flinching and turning away from the gory mess that his back had become. Even the strong-willed clansman was showing signs of stress – Dakan's face was red with strain, and his jaw muscles were pulled taunt as he bit hard into the bit. Pain, anger and rage burned in his eyes with each successive lash, and the tattoos that once artfully decorated his back were now obscured by split, puckered flesh and a thin veil of blood.

By the time five more lashes landed with a wet crack, there were mutterings amongst the onlookers for pity, as well as movement amongst the rear of the ranks that suggested some were turning away from the spectacle or simply leaving. By this point, Dakan was showing blatant signs of the physical and mental strain on him – he was struggling to hold himself upright as blood flowed down his back like a twisted waterfall, and the pain wracking his dark eyes warred with his grim determination not to cry out. Even Beliza was forced to flinch as she watched the bit slip from his mouth, allowing him to bite down hard on his bottom lip, blood gushing from the vicious bite.

The next five strikes seem to take an agonizing amount of time. Jerom was breathing heavily from the exertion, and the excruciating effort Dakan was putting forth to keep himself from screaming was painted on the clansman's face for all to see. A mixture of blood and spittle dripped from his chin, combining with his pain-twisted, reddened face to make him look like a rabid cannibal; furthermore, he had finally lost the ability to hold himself anywhere close to upright, and now sagged like a rag doll in his chains. By the time Tazrim barked twenty and the last bloody gash completed the macabre latticework on Dakan's back, there was nothing but heavy, grim silence in the air. Pity had replaced rage and anger for many of them, but no matter their disposition toward Dakan, it seemed the only thing anyone could do was to silently stare at the bloody clansman that was chained up like a dangerous dog.

For Beliza, the blood-drenched sight of Dakan was a vision of clan pride. Yes, Dakan was bleeding profusely – even his lower teeth were visible where he'd bitten through his lower lip – but he had not screamed. A quick glance at Vagain showed her that even he, with his disdain for Dakan, felt pride at the way the taboo clansman had held up under the ghastly punishment. Although his jaw was set firmly, Vagain's eyes shone with the same pride that she could see in the faces of the numerous Roselian clansmen gathered about the grounds.

A gesture to the guards from Jerom drew her away from her observations as he ordered, "Take him down and see to it that he gets to the medical tents on the double."

The two men nodded their acknowledgment and quickly went about unshackling Dakan. The ankle shackles came off first followed by those on his wrists. Immediately, the ravaged clansman slumped into their waiting arms, his bloodied body as drained as his spirit was, and his mind barely holding on to consciousness. To Beliza's surprise, they carried him over to a large handcart and gently loaded him into the cart on his stomach. She was sure there hadn't been a cart on the grounds at the start of the lashings and was somewhat troubled that she'd been so focused on Dakan that she'd missed its arrival. That kind of slip of focus wasn't acceptable in her mind.

Once Jerom was sure that Dakan had been securely loaded into the cart and that it had cleared the gathering, he gave the crowd one last admonishing glance before barking, "Dismissed!"


The pavilion was dimly lit that night. The handful of House servants Kale and Jerom had brought along with them had already seen to the packing and loading of both of their belongings onto the wagon train. Only Kale's table, a trio of chairs, his cot, and his clothing for the morning remained in the pavilion. Divested of their formal longcoats, the two of them sat on opposite ends of the table with five bottles of cheep red wine – two of which were already empty – sitting between them on the cleared tabletop. Though both men were devoid of weapons and clad in plain tunics and pants, the mood in the pavilion was far from relaxed.

Where Kale's smooth-shaven face was sunken and his green eyes appeared somewhat dull behind the simple goblet he held before his lips with both hands without drinking from it, his uncle was the exact opposite. Jerom's bearded visage was grim and his lone brown eye, while somewhat glazed over from too much wine, still shone with pent-up frustration. The entire way back to Kale's tent, he had not said a single word to his nephew. Even before the public flogging had taken place, he had already been uneasy with the idea. He and Kale's father had grown up with such punishments being commonplace, and even then, he had hated how brutal it was. Sure, it drove home a point, but it left the object of the lashes weakened and, more often than not, mentally devastated. When Bordin had inherited the Merandith throne and Jerom had taken over as shi'doms, both brothers had put an end to the barbaric practice. Jerom had even gone as far as to burn all the whips on his property as a symbolic gesture to his people that he was committed to never sentencing anyone to such barbarism.

For years, under the brothers' rule, not one flogging had occurred. So when Kale had ordered Dakan put to the lash, Jerom had been taken aback. He didn't believe his nephew would go so far as to revive the act, but Kale had already shown a predilection for excessive violence in the early years of his reign, which made any step along that path a dangerous one. With that fear gnawing at the back of his mind, he had been more than happy to relieve Kale – or anyone else for that matter – of the burden of delivering the blows. As he held a strong aversion to the act, he had no fear of thirsting for it again.

While Jerom had been more than happy to accept the burden so his nephew would not have Dakan's blood staining his hands, he hadn't been prepared for how it would affect him. Before he'd even gotten halfway through the lashings, Jerom had already grown nauseous. The blood didn't bother him, but it was the act of effectively assaulting a defenseless man that turned his stomach. Even the knowledge that he went easy on Dakan did little to alleviate his conscious. When all was said and done, and he and Kale had started their silent journey back to his nephew's tent, he had tossed the whip onto the first campfire they came to, startling the group of soldiers huddled about it. His nephew had given him a sideways glance at the gesture, but had wisely said nothing.

When they had arrived at Kale's tent, Jerom had gone straight for the first of five wine bottles that had been laid out along with dinner for them. Kale was quick to follow, barely turning up the wicks on the lamps as each man sought some relief from the weight of their actions. It only took the first goblet of wine for Kale to realize that the dinner planned for the evening would be a waste of time. Therefore, he had the bread, fruits and pork taken away and given to the troops before he sent word to Doms Hagail and Doms Trivant that the dinner was canceled, remembering at the last moment to include final orders for the morning in the message. After that, they then spent the next hour in silence, each man alone with his own demons. Although the wine provided a way to dull their minds against their admonishing thoughts, Kale restrained himself, sipping slowly from his goblet; Jerom, however, threw himself into his drink, quickly draining the first bottle.

While he was inclined to let his uncle have his way with the bottles, they were starting the long march home in the morning and Kale didn't need him so inebriated as to be useless. So, when Jerom went to pour the last of the wine from a third bottle, Kale put his own half-empty goblet down and gently put a restraining hand on the bottle. "That's enough, Uncle," he said softly.

Jerom shot his nephew a harsh scowl and jerked the bottle away. "I'll tell ya when I've had enough, boy!" he growled drunkenly as he tried to pour the wine into his goblet, the red liquid splashing over the edges.

Kale sat back in his chair with an exasperated sigh, which earned him another hard glare from his uncle as he downed his wine.

Jerom slammed his empty goblet down hard, even as he continued to stare daggers at Kale. The stress of the day had finally gotten to him, and the alcohol had helped to weaken his hold on his temper. "You asked a lot of me to– today, boy! I swore that I'd . . I'd 'ever do wha I did!" He pointed an accusatory finger at Kale. "I broke mah vow for you, lad! For . . . for you! Yer hands di– didn't need any more . . ." his brow furrowed as he tried to hold his line of thought, "more blood on 'um. Yer father – my brother – would be ashamed o' us both!" He sat back heavily in his chair and looked to the roof of the pavilion, tears welling up in his eyes. "I did it for ya' son, Brother. I hope ya' understand. . . . He 'as too much blood on 'is hands already. . . ."

Kale stared at his uncle in shock. He'd never seen Jerom cry, and the only time he'd even caught wind of a vow against using lashings as a punishment had been in conversations with his father. He had no idea that his uncle took the vow so seriously – and if he had known, he would have never let Jerom administer the penalty. With concerned eyes, Kale sat forward and reached out to lay a consoling hand on his uncle's arm. "I had no idea, Uncle. I'm so sorry."

His nose red from both the tears and the wine, Jerom looked at his nephew and shook his head. "No, lad, don't . . . don't apologize. I'm tired 'n drunk. I . . . I probably don't know half of what I'm say'n, and . . . and don't mean half of what I do know I'm say'n." He patted Kale's hand with his own callused paw and sighed. "I'm an old man, lad. I . . . I should be at home 'stead 'o fightin' and gali– galiva– running around like a man half my age." He grinned drunkenly at Kale. "Don't take a drunk ol' man's ramblin's ta heart. You've got 'nough on . . . on your shoulders without worryin' 'bout a tantrum from me."

Kale smiled and laughed gently. "Uncle – the day I stop worrying and caring about family is the day I'm no longer fit to lead our

307

House. The punishment I set upon Dakan was harsh and never should have been administered, or, at the very least, someone else should have done it."

Jerom shook his head and belched. "No, no, lad. It was right thing ta do with a man as stubborn and prid– willful as Dakan. He'll know 'is limits now – that'll make 'im more mal– mallu– easy to deal with." He sighed and laughed drunkenly. "And I'm too . . . drunk ta talk straight. So, if you'll excuse your daft ol' uncle, I'm . . . I'm ah gonna stumble to my tent and pass out." Jerom started to stand and lost his balance, sitting back down hard.

Kale grinned and called out loud enough to be heard outside, "Tazrim!"

There was a moment of silence and then Tazrim, still dressed in his formal longcoat, entered. Eyeing the two men and showing mild surprise at Jerom's drunken state, he asked, "Yes, Doms?"

"Would you see to it that Jerom makes it to his tent in one piece? I'm afraid he's gone a bit heavy on the wine tonight."

Tazrim nodded, his blue eyes twinkling with mirth as he eyed the three empty bottles. "As you wish, Doms." He made his way over to Jerom and helped him stand. "Come on, old man. Your cot awaits," he jabbed sarcastically.

Jerom managed a snort but nothing more.

"Thank you, Tazrim. Once you're done, you're dismissed for the evening. Have a couple of the trainees stand watch tonight."

Adjusting Jerom's arm around his neck, Tazrim nodded. "Yes, Doms. Sleep well."

"You too," he replied as Tazrim guided Jerom from the tent.

Kale remained at the table, sipping slowly from his goblet until it was empty, his thoughts scattered to the four winds. Once the goblet was drained, he placed it on the table and made his way to his cot. Not even bothering to get undressed, he collapsed onto it and made himself comfortable. Thankfully, despite his scattered thoughts, sleep found him quickly. Morning would come early, and with it the journey home.

That night was lonelier and colder than most for Dakan. Sequestered in a small tent, he rested on his stomach upon a cot, his mind and body dulled by milk of the poppy. Not once had he passed out through the entire ordeal. Even when the medics had cleansed and bandaged his back with herbs and ointment-laced bandages, he had not even uttered a whimper. The physical pain was bearable; in fact, he had suffered far worse at the hands of vindictive clansmen. It was the mental anguish that he felt which had led to him accepting the poppy milk that so dulled his mind and body now. He knew he was a stubborn and proud man – as were the vast majority of the men and women of the clans – and had felt that it would be easy to balance the demands of House Merandith with his clan identity. He had even begun to believe that joining House Merandith was definitely the right choice and that a new home had been found. Without a second thought, he had continued on like normal, putting his all into everything he did and answering challenges to his honor and integrity like a man. Through it all, he had received no more than a minor tongue-lashing from Jerom, leading him to believe that all was more or less well.

Even though his days were filled with training, he still found time to pursue the man responsible for ordering the assault on Amroth. Dead end after dead end greeted his every inquiry until he began to firmly believe that whoever was responsible had made the cowardly decision to run away. However, his persistence paid off when rumors reached him that one of the Sur'dathans had recognized Amroth for who he was and let slip the secret of his bloodline. Honor demanded that those responsible for the attack on Amroth pay for their deeds, and Dakan viewed the loose tongue as equally responsible for the assault as the man who had given the order. Fueled by renewed vigor and the inherent dislike of Sur'dathans that was ingrained in every Roselian clansman, Dakan pursued this new lead.

It had taken him nearly three days to track down the man, and by that time he had learned his target's name was Donald McFain, a lieutenant in Hagan's Hammer. Another two days of stalking his prey from a distance went by before he was given his best opportunity to confront Donald at the corral. Even though he would have preferred to confront Donald alone, the presence of Donald's companions did little to deter him. Deciding to embrace that opportunity, he made sure to land a solid blow before giving his target a chance to respond in any fashion. Had he known the resulting lashing would be the result, he still would have gone through with it.

Though his clan was all but gone from the face of Triclose, he felt that he had to protect both his clan name and that of their allies in order to properly honor those that had come before him. Amroth was the only remaining blood relative that he knew of, and that made him family no matter how distant the relation was. Though his behavior might be viewed as shameful by non-clan, he believed the clans would whisper with pride about his actions and the way he had conducted himself during the flogging. By defending Amroth's honor and accepting the punishment, he knew he would garner at least a little more respect amongst the clans. Was it enough to reinstate his clan? Not in the least. As the Clan High Elder had told him, the only way to reinstate his clan was to serve House Merandith proudly. However, would the Clan Council judge him by his actions or by the words of House Merandith? That was a question for which he lacked a confident answer.

As he lay there in his mind-dulled state, he found himself wondering if his current path was truly enough or the right way to go about the return of his clan from shame. Though Amroth was family, Beliza had presented him with another more direct and violent means of returning honor to his clan – the head of Cravon's son, the last surviving member of Clan Theirigaldis, served up to the Elders. He knew it would demonstrate a complete separation from the events of old and remove a stain from all the clans. Spirits be good, but even the Sur'dathans might praise the action! He would be lying to himself if he believed he wasn't tempted to take the easy way out. He knew the clans would protect him from any repercussions that would result from Amroth's slaying. However, neither was he a stupid barbarian; if he killed Amroth, the act might very well tear the Five Stars apart and send Triclose spiraling into chaos. No, he would not take the easy way out . . . at least for the time being. Should the war end or prove fruitless, or his service to House Merandith end prematurely, then he would have to carefully consider Beliza's proposition again.

Slowly his thoughts grew sluggish as the poppy milk took his mind firmly in its grasp. The pain in his back lessened to the point that he began to ever so slowly drift off to sleep. However, despite the poppy milk's dulling properties, he was still a warrior to his core and he could feel the hairs on the back of his neck standing up. Suddenly his breathing changed from slow and heavy to shallow and difficult. The dullness and heaviness in his limbs spread to his entire body, making him feel like he weighed four times his normal weight. Out of the corner of his eye, he saw movement in the shadows. He tried to turn his head to better focus on it, but it was to no avail. Frustrated, and with fear starting to creep into the pit of his stomach, he could only wonder how anyone could get into the tent; there were five guards outside to prevent just such an intrusion. Yet there was no doubt in his mind that he had seen movement and someone, or something, was weighting him down.

Suddenly, the air grew thick and the shadows began to twist and writhe as they coalesced into a figure. Dakan couldn't make out any details, for the arrival seemed to be made completely of light-draining shadows, but there was little doubt in his mind that a person lingered over his exposed figure. The shadow-cloaked form shifted and moved closer before taking a knee. Frigid breath hit Dakan full in the face, causing a dreadful chill to run down his spine. Panic began to well up in him as he realized it was getting harder and harder to breathe. Time seemed to slow down as he struggled to draw breath, the lack of air feeding a terror unlike anything he had ever felt. With the way his heart was pounding, he had no idea how much longer he could handle this nightmare before it simply burst.

Then, just when it seemed like the shadowy figure would simply torture him with its frigid breath, it spoke. "Poor Dakan," it purred in a hollow, frigid voice that seemed to echo in on itself. "You lay there like a beaten dog, wondering at your fate. I bet you even have decided to tough it out like a stubborn and foolish clansman would, eh?" A cold and amused chuckle made Dakan want to flinch despite the anger he felt at the insulting statements.

What appeared to be a hand reached out and patted him on the cheek. For a moment, Dakan thought someone had set his cheek on fire, but then he realized it was burning from cold. He wanted to shout in pain even as he wondered why the guards weren't rushing in to apprehend the intruder.

As if reading his thoughts, the intruder said, "Now, now, don't worry about the guards outside. They have no idea what's going on in here. You see – I don't like unwanted guests intruding on my business. Now where was I . . .? Ah yes, your stubbornness. Quite the endearing trait when combined with your intellect and martial skills. In fact, I've been interested in you for some time now. You might say watching you has been a bit of a hobby of mine. Despite finding you clansmen to be a bit boorish and stupidly prideful, your determination has merit.

"You're right to feel wronged by all the clans for what they did to your family. After all, all they did was honor their blood ties – as they should have. It was those foolish Northmen that should have been the only ones to pay. I would like to help you, Dakan." Still struggling to breathe, Dakan could almost sense a grin on what would be the shadowy figure's face. "I applaud how you are trying to go about it. But don't you think there is an easier way? Hummm?" The man paused to let the implications set in.

Dakan had little doubt as to what the shadow was implying, and it only fed his anger. With a concerted effort, he tried once again to shake off the weight that had him thoroughly pinned down, but it was a useless gesture; he simply had no control over his body.

As if reading his thoughts again, a hollow chuckle rang out. "Not one for the easy way, eh? Well then – what if I could offer you a way to return your clan to prominence on your own? What would you say if I could offer you the power to not only restore your clan, but a way to rule all the clans? What would it be worth to you, Dakan?"

Struggling to maintain consciousness, Dakan hadn't the energy or breath to speak. It was all he could do just to understand what was being said.

After a pause in which it seemed like the shadowy figure was awaiting a response, he continued. "Tch, tch, tch. No answer for me? I'm deeply hurt." The man let out a sarcastic, echoing sigh. "I suppose that's to be expected – you clansmen are so stubborn and thickheaded. But, I'm not one to hold that against you. So here's what I'm going to do – I'm going to give you a chance to think about it." Dakan felt a frozen finger part his hair and begin to trace something on the side of his head as the intruder said, "When you decide that I'm offering you the only chance to do what is right for you and yours – and it is the only way – you will seek me out."

The finger repeatedly traced the same pattern on his scalp, the burning sensation growing more and more intense with each pass, and it was all Dakan could do not to pass out.

"Keep in mind," the voice purred, "that should you decide to reject my offer, I will be very . . . disappointed. Now sleep, Dakan, and *remember*. . . ." The last of the words came out like a growling beast, and suddenly the pattern on Dakan's scalp exploded in agonizing pain.

Dakan tried to scream, but could do little more than open his mouth wide as the pain and lack of air caused his face to turn red and his eyes to bulge. Then, just as fast as the pain had bloomed, it vanished and blissful oblivion crawled forth to claimed him.


By the time the sun broke the western horizon, casting the cloudless sky into shades of blue and gray, the encampment was already abuzz with activity. Over twenty-five percent of the Five Stars camp had been disassembled and was being loaded onto wagons, packhorses, and the backs of the soldiers. As midmorning approached, the last of the departing contingent joined the rest of their ranks, which were gathered north of camp. All that remained was for Kale to make an appearance and give the eagerly awaited order to march.

Even before the rest of the camp came to life with the dawn, Kale was already awake and attending to his duties. It came as no surprise to him that he had not slept soundly through the entire night. Between Dakan's punishment, listening to his uncle's admonishments, and his own tumultuous thoughts, Kale had more than enough on his mind to ruin his respite. Finally, after tossing and turning the latter part of the night away, he dragged himself from his cot as the gray of false dawn touched the horizon. Throwing on his clothes that had been laid out for him – a warm white cotton shirt, thick breeches, and his sturdy black boots – he emerged from his tent to find Tazrim standing watch. Garbed in full leather armor and his shaven head glistening in the new light of the day, Tazrim acknowledged his doms with a nod, which Kale returned curtly as he motioned for him to follow.

Kale made directly for Dakan's tent to check on his condition. To his relief, he was informed by the guards that the clansman was in good condition and had remained undisturbed throughout the night. After taking a quick peek at Dakan's sleeping form to confirm his health for himself, Kale then thanked the guards for their attentiveness before moving on to the rest of the camp.

With his conscious momentarily relieved of guilt, Kale was able to focus on his morning tasks. For the next three hours, he moved through the camp like a fast moving storm as he made final checks and saw to it that the remainder of the Merandith encampment came down in a quick and orderly fashion. Although Kale had his lieutenants to attend to all the details, he felt the urge to be hands-on that morning. None of the soldiers blinked at seeing their doms getting his hands dirty, for they were used to such actions from Kale, but it did leave some of them feeling uncomfortable to have the man who ordered the brutal flogging working alongside them. For Kale, it not only helped to keep his mind off the previous day, but it also served as a reminder that he wasn't a boorish beast to casually hand down violent punishments. Whether it was self-punishment or that he was enjoying himself, he eventually became so engrossed in his work that it came as a surprise when Tazrim informed him that all that remained was for his and his bodyguards' tents to come down.

Given that what remained of the Merandith camp amounted to a few stragglers and churned earth, it didn't take long for the pair to return to Kale's tent. It struck Kale as somewhat odd to see his tent and those of his bodyguards standing alone on the large stretch of empty earth – to him, the tents seemed almost lonely. Absurd notions aside, there were indications that someone either awaited them or had anticipated their return. Fully saddled, both Kale's gray destrider stallion and Jerom's destrider roan mare waited outside Kale's pavilion. As they drew closer, a quick inspection revealed that Tazrim's mount also awaited him outside his tent. Kale cracked a small smile as he realized that even after Jerom's emotional outburst, his uncle was still on top of his duties. Granting Tazrim leave to prepare for departure, Kale continued on to his own tent.

Upon entering, Kale found that his remaining personal effects had already been packed and moved to the wagon train. All that remained to greet him was his uncle and his armor. Clad in a full suit of platemail, Jerom was bent over the table where Kale's armor had been laid out, checking that all the straps were in good shape. When he heard his nephew enter, he turned to greet him. Kale noticed immediately that his uncle looked rough from the previous night. Despite his beard being neatly trimmed and his armor polished, his features looked a bit sunken and his right eye was bloodshot from the generous amount of wine he had consumed and, in all likelihood, very little sleep.

Jerom offered a grunt in greeting before turning back to the table. Grabbing Kale's padded vest, he tossed it to his doms. "You're late, lad. Nearly everyone is already gathered for the march — and they're itching to get moving."

Kale caught the vest with a smirk and put it on while he talked. "I made a last-minute check of our preparations, Uncle," he said as he secured the buckles along the center of the vest. "Besides, I didn't get much sleep and needed the exercise. From the look of you, I'd say you didn't sleep well either."

Jerom grunted and passed Kale his greaves as his nephew approached the table. "Aye, well . . . more wine than common sense will do that." He paused for a moment. "Is Dakan okay?" he asked softly.

"He is," Kale responded as he secured his right greave and moved to the left. "The guards said the night was quiet and that he slept the night away. I left orders for him to be given another hour of sleep before they moved him to the column."

Jerom nodded softly. "That's good." As Kale stood, Jerom grabbed his nephew's chainmail hauberk and passed it to him. Taking a deep breath, he said sternly, "Drunk or not, I want to reiterate what I said last night — I won't be a part of such an act again."

Kale smirked as he slid the hauberk over his head. Settling the steel garment on his shoulders, he shook his head as he began securing his bracers about his forearms. "You can be so insubordinate at times, Uncle. I'm surprised Father never had you hung or beheaded."

Jerom grunted and picked up Kale's breastplate before moving behind his nephew and helping him to lower the polished steel over his head. As soon as it was snuggly in place, Kale went back to

314

securing his left bracer while Jerom tightened the straps of the breastplate. Pulling hard on the first strap, he drew a grunt from his nephew. Ignoring his nephew's grunt of protest, Jerom cinched the next three straps just as hard and received the same results.

Kale turned a glare on his uncle as he secured the last strap. "I'm serious now – Father should have strung you up," he quipped with a sly smile tainted with a bit of irritation.

"If you recall, your mother toyed with the idea for a while. But I believe she decided that blunting an axe or wasting rope on my old neck wasn't worth it. Here, hold this." Kale laughed as Jerom handed him one of his pauldrons and then began securing the matching pauldron to Kale's right shoulder. Once that pauldron was secure, he took the other one and began attaching it. "Do you still intend to have Amroth participate in the tournament?"

Kale blinked at his uncle in surprise. "Well, that's an unexpected question. But to answer you – yes, if Mathis manages to convince Amroth of it."

With a grunt of displeasure, Jerom stepped back and slapped Kale on the pauldrons to make sure they were secure, causing them to ring out dully. "I don't like it much more than what we did to Dakan. The other candidates are either graduates of the Academy or veteran soldiers. I fear we're tossing Amroth to the wolves." He paused and looked Kale square in the eyes. "I'd hate to lose the lad because we prodded him into doing something he doesn't really want to do."

Picking up one of his cuisses, Kale paused thoughtfully. "So would I, Uncle. I would hope, though, that you will be there to make sure he's ready should he decide to participate."

Jerom scowled in disapproval and shook his head. "Aye, I'll do my damnedest to make sure he learns what he needs to stay alive." Reaching out, he took the cuisse from Kale and said, "Enough babbling. Let's get the rest of this armor on and be off. Home awaits."

The sun shone brightly upon the gathered forces, reflecting off a menagerie of metal objects. Over six-thousand soldiers stood in columns that ran thirty abreast and thirty deep, eagerly awaiting Doms Merandith's order to march. Three House banners stood out amongst the numerous pendants that flapped lazily in the breeze from atop lances and standards – House Grevorian, with its blue- and green-checkered banner; House Trivant, with its bright orange backdrop and gold sunburst; and House Merandith's black banner, with its five golden stars. While all three were prominently displayed, only House Merandith's banner stood at the head of the small army.

Gathered at the front of the column, just ahead of the Me-randith banner, were the domses of the other two major Houses that were joining in the march. Each doms sat atop a steed draped in its rider's House colors. The most prominent of the two was the muscu-lar form of Doms Trivant. Clad in gold-gilded plate armor and chainmail, a bright-orange tabard emblazoned with a large golden sunburst squarely on the center of his chest was secured over the em-bellished steel by a thick leather belt at his waist. His brown hair was in a horsetail per his usual habit, and his blue eyes shown in the morn-ing sunlight. His weapon of choice, a large lochabre axe, hung from its harness along the length of his black destrider.

His counterpart, Doms Grevorian, was the ruler of Kythir, a small Northern realm set between Sur'datha and Tiliea. Sitting astride his painted mare, Doms Grevorian was heavyset and bald. The aged doms sported a neatly trimmed gray beard, and large eyes that were just a shade lighter than his beard. He wore simple chainmail beneath his blue- and green-checkered tabard, and a plain broadsword hung from a beaten scabbard at his left leg. While he was the physical op-posite of Trivant, he shared in his colleague's concerns about the forthcoming march.

They had arrived somewhat early to the column, and for the better part of that time, they had conversed under their breath about the imminent march. Though their surrounding entourage of body-guards meant that none of the common soldiers could hear them, it didn't stop them from worrying about being overheard. Today was a day of joy, and such concerns would only dampen the spirits of the men and women gathered behind them. Let the soldiers enjoy their moment, free of the heavy burdens of war for once, and bask in this rarest of occasions. Both domses knew that the warm weather would return all too quickly, and their moment of fleeting peace would melt away like the snows.

For the rank-and-file, thoughts of war were quickly being washed away by the thrilling prospect of returning home, filling them with an abundance of energy that found a release in the nervous and anxious chatter that danced on the air like agitated birds. Throughout the morning, jealous glares had been turned their way by many of those that were remaining behind. While the homeward-bound sol-diers weren't completely oblivious to the glares, the jealousy meant nothing to them. For them, the mere thought of returning home was an unassailable bastion, making them momentarily impervious to the hardships of the world.

A sudden cheer went up from the rear of the column, draw-ing the attention of both the domses and the soldiers at the head of the column. Wheeling their horses about, Grevorian and Trivant peered over the heads of the cheering soldiers, watching stoically as Kale and Jerom galloped toward their position. The cheer swept ahead of the Merandiths like a joyful herald, engulfing both Trivant and Grevorian in a thunderous roar that reaffirmed for them how significant this day was for those returning home.

Reining in their steeds as they reached Grevorian and Trivant, Kale raised his hand in greeting. Walking his gray stallion around them, he waited for the cheers to die down so he wouldn't have to yell to be heard. Finally, the ruckus relented enough for him to state in a slightly raised voice, "Well met, Domses."

"Hail, Doms Merandith," the others replied just as loudly.

Kale pulled alongside them and nodded to them. Glancing back at the column, he smiled joyfully at the soldiers' enthusiasm even as the cheers finally diminished and relative silence returned. Returning his gaze to the domses, he asked in a normal tone of voice, "I hope the morning finds you both well?"

"Aye, Brother," answered Trivant, his deep voice seeming loud even without shouting. "We each have assembled troops as your adjusted orders asked, and left the rest under Doms Hagail."

There was a hint of worry in Trivant's voice that Kale was quick to notice. "Do I detect a hint of doubt in your voice, Lucas?"

Lucas Trivant shook his head dismissively. "Not doubt, Kale, but worry. I agree wholeheartedly that we need rest, but to take this many men with us, especially cavalry, borders on overconfidence. This is *over half* the active mobile army – *over half*, Kale. If Doms Hagail gets caught in the open this far south. . . ."

"I must agree with Trivant, Doms Merandith," rumbled Grevorian's salty voice. "To many, your actions may seem rash in light of our recent victories. I know there are many that would have you pursuing Craigan right to the gates of Chalin. And to be honest, I am one of them."

Kale nodded. "I understand your concerns, but I do not believe we have very much to fear from House Suldamik. Their forces have been decimated as of late and if we harass them through the winter, they'll have their hands too full to mount any sort of significant threat against us. Besides, the winter storms will be our greatest ally. Through all the years that these wars have been fought, House Suldamik has never adapted well to fighting in the frigid conditions." Both domses nodded reluctantly in agreement, to which Kale offered them a reassuring smile. "Good. Well, then if there isn't anything else, let us get this column moving. Jerom?"

Jerom nodded and galloped back to the column, shouting, "Attention!"

Soon, the order began echoing throughout the column as the other officers picked up on the command and echoed it, the ringing of steel alighting on the air as the soldiers snapped to attention. It didn't take long for everyone to follow the order, and soon the din of noise died down. Kale then nudged his mount to the right in order to gain a better vantage point from which he could see the column and they him. A slight smile split his lips as he suddenly felt like every pair of eyes was anxiously fixed on him, sending a tingle of excitement up his spine. Sudden movement distracted him from the giddy sensation and he shifted his vision to see twenty riders, lightly armored and armed, galloping hard toward him with Jerom at their head.

As they neared him, Jerom pulled up next to Kale and the riders continued on past them, fanning out as they sped away from the column. "Everyone is ready and, as you can see, the scouts are on their way," Jerom informed him.

Kale grinned at his uncle. "Good work. What say we go home, then?"

Jerom returned the joyful grin before turning in his saddle to face the column. Raising his hand, he waved northward while shouting, "Forward to home!"

A great cheer went up through the ranks in response as the small army lurched forward, every footstep filled with purpose, and every eye and thought focused toward home.

# Chapter Fourteen

*T*hey rode hard the first two days out of camp, mile after mile rushing by, pausing only to rest the horses and eat. Neither man said much that first morning, and what little that was said came mainly from Mathis. Somehow, despite trying to watch every direction at once with his coal-black eyes, he somehow managed to find the time to occasionally toss bits of information Amroth's way. Whether it was advice about scouting the land or odd facts about a few of the animals they saw along the way, at least it was an attempt at conversation. Amroth, however, was having nothing to do with it.

Huddled under his cloak and hunched over his reins, it was all he could do to keep himself in the saddle. The pain that wracked his body was dulled somewhat by a small amount of poppy milk, but was still intense enough to make staying in his saddle difficult. When he did manage to turn his focus from Mathis' back to the rolling and hilly plains, his dark eyes were full of pain. And on the occasions where he did respond to Mathis' inquires, misery coated every word of his short and terse responses. By the time they broke for a meal around midday of the first day, Amroth was firmly convinced that, fast healing or not, forcing him into the saddle with his injuries was tantamount to torture. Though he knew in the back of his mind that getting away from the main body of the army was the safest approach, the agony he was in convinced him that he wasn't about to let Kale live this down.

While Amroth nursed his anger and did his best to stay in his saddle, Mathis kept his attention focused on the surrounding land-scape. With the clear skies, he could see for leagues in every direction. However, it was a double-edged sword – while he could see any potential threat at a distance, he also knew any potential enemy had the same advantage. Being a veteran, he wasn't foolish enough to think that because the Five Stars had advanced this far south, there was no chance of being attacked. While the Contested Territories were distant enough to reduce the threat of bandit attacks, he felt they were just as much a threat as the rumored raiders. Either group would, in all likelihood, be moving in small, fast-moving units, which would make them difficult to identify and even harder to keep track of. If they were attacked, the identity of the instigators would matter little; dead was dead no matter who wielded the sword. Fortunately, the only things he'd seen so far were the brown grass of the plains and an assortment of the smaller animals that inhabited the sprawling prairie. Deo willing, if everything continued this way and went as he wanted, he and Amroth would be off of the open and vulnerable plains as soon as possible.

Sadly, their luck didn't hold. While Amroth's condition did improve, it was stunted by the hard pace Mathis had set; Mathis needed Amroth to heal if they wanted to move at a decent pace, so he grudgingly slowed their journey to expedite Amroth's convalescence. Day after day of tense travel was followed by night after night of fireless, exhaustion-filled camps, quickly putting them well behind schedule. By noon of the fifth day, the strain was painfully evident in Amroth. Stopping for a break in a shallow bowl that wasn't visible until they were almost upon it, Mathis dismounted and helped Amroth do the same before finding his exhausted charge a relatively comfortable place to sit down.

Once he was sure Amroth was settled, he led both mounts off to the side to allow them to graze on what they could find. Retrieving rations and two waterskins from their saddlebags, Mathis returned to Amroth and handed him one of the skins and some of the dried beef before taking a seat opposite the weary Merandith. Occupying himself with his plain meal, Mathis refrained from any attempt to converse as they ate; Amroth's hunched posture and the slow pace with which he ate were clear indicators that he was in significant pain and in no mood for idle chatter. While Mathis wanted nothing more than to slow their pace even further, or even to camp right where they were, he knew the open plain was too risky and exposed to remain there longer than they already had. Amroth would just have to endure the current pace for now.

After allowing his charge a brief rest, Mathis gathered their mounts and got them on the move again. Since early that morning, they had kept their heading east by northeast, making for a dark swath that seemed to be growing steadily on the horizon. Throughout the day, the dark line continued to grow, filling the horizon and revealing definable features. By the time the sun began to set, casting the dark mass into silhouette, they were close enough to easily identify it. From atop a small rise, they could see that the dark mass was a forest that stretched north and south for as far as the eye could see. During the spring and summer, the canopy of the sprawling forest would be dense enough to keep most of the sunlight from reaching the ground. Now, on the cusp of winter, only a few orange and brown leaves dotted the barren treetops along with a dappling of green from the evergreens.

"Alderian Forest," breathed Amroth with relief, running a trembling hand through his loose black hair. "I was beginning to think we wouldn't see it."

Mathis gave an affirmative nod as he examined Amroth's strained and pale complexion, noting the effort he was putting into remaining in the saddle. "I had wanted to make the tree line by this evening, but you look like you're about fall out of your saddle. We can make camp at the base of this hill and start out early if you wish," he offered with a hint of compassion in his voice.

Amroth glanced at him out of the corner of his eye, and it was easy for Mathis to see that the young Merandith was extremely tempted to accept the offer. "I would dearly like to take you up on that, but," he stated wistfully as his hands tighten on his reins, "I don't like the idea of spending another night in the open without a fire – Deo only knows, I'm frozen to the bone and feel like a stampede of bramhen ran over me." Amroth shook his head and set his jaw. "No, let's continue. The tree line will offer some shelter, and a fire is a luxury I don't want to pass up."

Mathis offered a crooked grin and said, "Good," as if he'd known that was what Amroth would say all along. Nudging his horse into motion, he led the way down the rise. Once on flat terrain, he set a quick and steady pace.

They made the tree line two hours after night had completely enveloped the land. To their benefit, the bright moon and nearly cloudless sky provided enough illumination so they could preserve a steady pace as they weaved their way through the maze of towering ironwoods, evergreens and leatherleafs. Mathis found them a fairly secluded spot deep enough into the forest that a small fire wouldn't be seen from outside the tree line. Surrounded on all sides by the thick and rugged trunks of ironwoods, Mathis brought them to a stop and quickly dismounted. Without a worry for his own mount, he moved swiftly to ease Amroth from the saddle.

Eyes glazed over and sitting sideways in his saddle, Amroth was past the point of being ready to collapse. Mathis easily took the reins from Amroth's limp grip before wrapping a strong arm around his waist and easing him from the saddle. Guiding him over to the base of the largest ironwood, he gently guided Amroth to the ground. With no energy to speak, Amroth smiled his gratitude weakly as he leaned back against the tree and shut his eyes. Mathis grunted to himself, impressed with the fortitude and strength Amroth had shown to ride through what must have been excruciating pain.

Returning to the horses, he removed two feedbags from their saddlebags and filled them from their stores before securing the bags over the horses' muzzles and hobbling them. With deft and practiced precision, he had their saddles and packs removed quickly before he proceeded to rub down Amroth's roan with profound thanks for the way she had carried her wounded rider. A quick rub behind the ears of his black destrider reminded her that she wasn't forgotten in all this. He spent a few more minutes attending to their mounts before retrieving Amroth's bedroll, unfurling it and carefully draping it over his charge's sleeping form, a wry smile cracking his face when Amroth appeared oblivious to the gesture. Standing back up, he double-checked that their camp was as secure as possible before making his way deeper into the woods to scavenge for wood and kindling.

With all the deadfall and discarded foliage on the ground, it didn't take him long to collect what he needed. Upon his return to camp, he found that Amroth was sleeping so deeply that he hadn't moved. With a chuckle, he deposited his findings at the center of their camp before retrieving his tinderbox. Returning to his pile of wood and kindling, he arranged them to his liking. With deft precision gained from years of being on the march, he used the flint and firesteel from his tinderbox to strike a spark onto a small amount of tinder from the same box. Once he was sure the small flame was stable, he moved it to the dry kindling and, once it caught, began feeding larger pieces to the hungry flames. Soon, he had a small, cozy fire burning, the light of which reflected warmly off the naturally polished bark of the ironwoods. Satisfied with his work, he returned to his saddle and detached his sheathed katana from it. Shadows and orange light dancing amongst the trees, he then silently seated himself against a large ironwood across the fire from Amroth.

Given Amroth's condition, it had occurred to him earlier in the day that he might not be getting much sleep that night. Seated across from the sleeping man, there was no denying that his presumption was right. However, it was simply amazing that Amroth had made it this far in his injured state. Most normal men would have collapsed or died from riding with such wounds, but not Amroth. Mathis shook his head in admonishment and corrected himself. Amroth was not normal – he was a clansman and one of the last of the old blood. Though he had fought alongside and against the clans over the years, it was still amazing how quickly they recovered. While the strength and speed of recovery varied from person to person – even amongst the same clan – it was an ability that wasn't to be taken lightly. Sitting there, watching his charge, he was reminded of just how strong the gift could be in a clansman.

Nearly a week removed from his injuries, and in spite of the pain their pace had caused him, Amroth was already showing visible signs of recovery. Despite the sweat that stained his clothes and drenched his body, his bruises were fading quickly and many of the cuts on his body were already healed. It reminded Mathis of when Amroth was young; during those adolescent years, Amroth would run about the keep with a carefree attitude that got him in trouble and injured more often than most children. Unlike most children, however, wounds and injuries didn't drive home the same message for him as they did for others. Where other children might be stuck in a splint or with a bandage for days or weeks, Amroth might heal in a few hours for a small cut or in less than a week for a broken bone. There were only two others he'd seen heal like that and both were blood relatives of the young Merandith – Amroth's father, Cravon, and Dakan. Thankfully, now that they were off the open plain, they could fully benefit from that gift, for the quicker Amroth recovered, the sooner he would feel better and the faster they would be able to travel.

Mathis adjusted his position against the tree, crossing his legs and placing his sword across his lap. Tapping his fingers lightly up and down the gentle curve of the katana's wooden scabbard, he turned his attention to the matter of Kale's orders – he was to train Amroth to fight. Normally such a task wouldn't be difficult since all those he'd trained in the past had wanted to learn. Amroth, on the other hand, essentially amounted to a pacifist. Granted, Amroth at least knew which end to hold and which end to put in an enemy, but as far as skill and his willingness to use such skill was concerned, he might as well be a scholar. Before he could even think about training him, he would have to find a way to convince him that learning to fight and being willing to fight were not always bad things. The puzzle that Amroth posed provided ample fodder for Mathis' thoughts throughout the night. As the hours crept by uneventfully, he pondered the conundrum. Then, as the gray of dawn crept into the sky and their fire burned down to embers, it occurred to him what needed to be done.

Sprawled on his side, Amroth awoke to the cold gray morning with an agonizing moan. His entire body ached worse than it had the night before, and he was slightly puzzled at the bedroll that weighed him down. Sometime during the night, he had fallen onto his side, and now both the right side of his head and his right shoulder throbbed from where he'd struck the ground. Opening his eyes, he immediately shut them again as the stinging gray light of dawn sent pain lancing through his head.

Breathing deeply, he gathered his strength to make another attempt to open his eyes and move, when he heard, "Good morning."

The simple words foiled his attempt as they rang in his skull like he had been struck with a hammer, drawing a wince from him.

"Head hurts, eh?" came the voice again. "Not surprised. You were out cold last night and never even flinched when you fell over."

Eyes still shut and grimacing in pain, Amroth leveraged himself into a sitting position, the bedroll falling from him. "Deo be good . . ." he breathed through clinched teeth. "Did you decide to let the horses stomp on me during the night? I don't think there's an inch of me that doesn't hurt." Opening his eyes a bit, he saw Mathis crouched on the other side of the remains of a fire, a waterskin in hand and munching on a trail biscuit. To his surprise, there was no indication that Mathis had slept. "Did you keep watch all-night?" he asked in embarrassment.

Mathis nodded. "Indeed," he answered simply before taking a drink from his waterskin.

Running a hand through his tousled black hair, Amroth shook his head slowly. "I'm sorry, Mathis. You should have woken me. I would have taken a watch."

A grunt from Mathis showed Amroth just how much he believed the statement. "You were in no condition to do any such thing. Besides, I've done my share of all-night watches. I'll be just fine." He finished off the last bit of his biscuit, stood up and moved to their saddles where he removed a couple of biscuits and Amroth's waterskin. Returning to Amroth, he dropped the crude excuse for breakfast in his lap. "Eat up. We need to get on the move soon."

It took Amroth a long time to finish his meal. His jaw and throat hurt, which made chewing and swallowing difficult and painful. By the time he finished, he felt somewhat exhausted from the effort. While it was tempting to sit there and continue to rest, he knew that was impossible. With what felt like monumental effort, he forced himself to his feet, groaning in pain. His grime- and sweat-laden clothes doing more to hamper him than help, he steadied himself on his sore legs before he began to walk around their campsite to get his blood flowing and to try to work the stiffness from his muscles. After about five minutes of walking, the ache in his legs began to fade, as did the cramping. Feeling a bit better, he began to stretch out his arms, shoulders and neck. Winces of pain accompanied each movement as he worked the kinks from his muscles. After nearly twenty minutes of the exercises, he finally felt like some semblance of his normal self.

By this time, not only had Mathis fed and freed the horses, but he had also saddled them and secured their belongings to their respective saddles. Rubbing the neck of his black destrider, Mathis watched as Amroth finished up. "Feeling better?"

Amroth gave Mathis a small smile, tucked his formerly white shirt into his brown pants, and walked over with only a mild limp. "I won't be running any long distances, but should be able to stay in my saddle."

"Good. I'd hate for her to do all the work again," he stated as he swung himself into the saddle, drawing a smirk from Amroth as he rubbed the roan behind her ears. Steadying himself in his saddle, Mathis added, "There's a glade I know of that will make an excellent campsite tonight. We'll join up with the Doren'thal River later today and it will lead us straight to it. So if you don't mind pulling yourself together, I'd like to get underway."

Mathis set a more casual pace for them that day. Despite the cloud cover that was starting to build, the weather was mild and plenty of sunshine made its way through the leafless canopy. With winter beginning to sink its claws into Triclose, the wildlife was sparse; however, there were signs to be seen if one knew what to look for. A few of the trees bore markings that were unmistakable signs of bears in the area, while fresh paw prints as they neared the Doren'thal River clearly indicated that wolves and smaller animals were venturing to and fro in a final dash to find a last meal or to shore up their winter stores. There was even a group of squirrels that followed the two riders for a time, jumping playfully from branch to branch, making quite a ruckus and disturbing the occasional bird that was out hunting for what was fast becoming a hard-to-find meal.

Despite the casual pace, the morning started out difficult for Amroth. His wounds still ached and his muscles still felt stiff despite the extensive stretching. Throughout the morning, the constant bouncing in the saddle did nothing but exasperate the situation. So by the time Mathis called for a break about midmorning, Amroth wanted nothing more than to lie down and die. However, he had no desire to look any weaker in front of Mathis than he had to, therefore, with a pain-filled grimace, he lowered himself from his saddle without aid. Removing his waterskin from his saddlebags, he limped over to a bed of pine needles beneath an evergreen and lowered himself ungracefully to the ground.

A slight smirk started to crawl onto Mathis' face as he watched Amroth lean his head back and close his eyes. Rubbing his horse's neck, he said, "I'm going to stretch my legs a bit and relieve my bladder. Are you going to be okay?"

Amroth nodded and replied, "Oh, just fine – I'll be ready to ride on in no time."

The sarcastic overtone did not go unnoticed by Mathis, who simply chuckled and shrugged it off. "Good to hear. Don't wander off while I'm gone," he replied in the same sarcastic manner, drawing a snort from Amroth.

Mathis' long and fluid strides carried him away from their temporary campsite and deep into the trees. While his bladder was screaming at him, he had lied about needing to stretch his legs. He had noticed something odd about some of the bear markings and needed a moment to think without worrying Amroth. After moving sufficiently far enough away from camp so that Amroth wouldn't be able to see or hear him, he unlaced his pants and began to relieve himself against a barren leatherleaf tree. Letting his eyes wander, he looked carefully for any sign that would confirm or refute his suspicions. While bears weren't uncommon in this area, he had seen a few claw marks in the ground and on the trees that, while old, seemed unusual. Finished with relieving himself, and knowing Amroth could use the extended break, Mathis laced his pants back up and began to scout the surrounding area, working his way outward from their camp in a circle. His first two passes initially alleviated his worries – he found no sign of spore, large paw prints, or claw marks in trees. After a third pass yielded similar results, he was feeling quite confident that they were safe from any potential threat. However, about a third of the way through his fourth and final pass, his heart sank as he found what he had hoped not to find.

Out of the corner of his eye, a glimmer caught his attention. Immediately upon turning to his right, the large trunk of a giant ironwood greeted him like a foreboding herald. Even from ten paces away, he recognized the marks in the tree and had a feeling he knew what the glimmering object was. With quick, determined strides that belied the anxiety that was twisting his stomach, he approached the ironwood – noting large paw prints leading to the tree and moving off to the northeast – and ran a gloved hand over the large claw marks. Despite the unnatural strength of the ironwood, it had been no match for the creature that had left its mark. Eight gashes, in pairs of four, were spread nearly to the flanks of the giant ironwood. The jagged marks started over twenty feet up the trunk and raked their way down to eye level with Mathis. Each gash was nearly two inches wide and, as he slid his forefinger in it down to the third knuckle, six inches deep. Even to the untrained eye, it was obvious that a massive creature had defaced the tree. While it was already clear to him what had made the gashes, it was what sat between the pairs of claw marks that clinched it for him.

The dark-gray bark of the ironwood had been scuffed and scarred between the pair of claw marks, revealing the near ebony-colored wood beneath it. Between the size and length of the gashes, and the scuffed bark, it was easy to imagine how large the beast was. However, it was the object gleaming in the dull sunlight that would easily put fear in a man's heart.

Carefully wrapping his hand around it, Mathis dislodged it from the tree and supported it with the palm of his hand, examining it with a practiced eye. As large as his hand and nearly half an inch thick at its center, the opalescent deep-red scale was a sight to behold. Hard, heavy and kite shaped, every edge except for the base was serrated, and its tip ended in a wicked point that was hooked slightly outward. Mathis held the scale up to the sun, carefully holding the scale by its base, and watched as the sunlight danced on its surface. The full spectrum of red seemed to float across the scale's surface, fading in and out in a hypnotic dance.

Despite the beauty and awe the scale inspired, fear was solidly rooted in his stomach. Mathis was all too familiar with the type of beast that had left the claw marks and the scale behind, and was well aware that the scale was a clear indication of how fresh the markings were. The fact that the scale still retained its color-shifting properties left no doubt that the beast had been at the tree no more than two hours ago – which meant there was a very real possibility that it was still in the area. While the mere thought of the beast was enough to inspire fear, it was the coloration that left Mathis perplexed and worried. The scale belonged to a beast that was not native to the northern lands. The animal belonged to the hot South – and the warmer it was, the better the beast thrived.

Mathis suddenly spun on his heel and took-off at an accelerated pace. Bandits and raiders were no longer the only thing they had to fear. A predator was on the loose that every man and beast capable of even a modicum of intelligence knew to fear.


It spoke volumes as to just how spooked Mathis was that he never noticed the hooded and cloaked scout that had been trailing him and Amroth soon after they had entered the forest.

Like all the other raiding parties, his was small and remaining unnoticed until the last moment was of supreme interest to their success and survival. He had spent many campaigns as a forward scout on both sides of the war. He didn't care who ruled Triclose, just so long as they let him be when it was over. Until then, he would enjoy the thrill of the stalk and the travel. So when the call came for volunteers for the raiding parties, he'd gladly signed up.

His small band had been behind enemy lines for nearly a month now, and had already done minor damage; they had intercepted a few small supply convoys and harassed a few outlying villages and hamlets, but nothing major had crossed their path until they had spotted the two riders entering the forest. Every raider had been forced to memorize the descriptions of favorable targets to eliminate should the opportunity present itself. To his commander's glee, both men appeared to match two of the descriptions. Tempering their excitement, they had kept their distance until they could confirm the travelers' identities. Up until this point, the scout had managed to keep his distance, but had risked discovery by following Mathis deep into the woods for just such an authentication. Without giving himself away, he had watched as Mathis studied the tree and the markings. While he was curious as to why his objective was so taken with bear markings, his focus was on confirming the identities of their targets.

The veteran scout got the view he had been patiently awaiting when Mathis spun and strode off. While the apprehension on Mathis' face somewhat baffled the scout, he paid little heed to it as he was afforded a solid view of the target's face. Excitement nearly overwhelmed him as he recognized the features – dark hair, dangerous dark eyes and deadly grace – and he nearly decided to attack on his own. However, they had been warned that all their important targets were to be considered extremely dangerous and not to be taken lightly. It was also preferred that targets be taken alive for public execution. In this case, seeing the danger that lurked in the man's eyes, he was absolutely sure discretion was the better part of valor.

As soon as Mathis was well out of sight, the scout broke from his cover amongst the thick underbrush surrounding a cluster of evergreens. Cowl low, he pulled his dirty-green cloak tight about him as he quickly approached the ironwood Mathis had been studying. Not bothering to look up, a cursory examination of the tracks and markings told him what he already knew – there was an exceptionally large bear in the area, but nothing to get overly excited about. It was probably just on the hunt to finish putting on weight before its long hibernation and had stopped to scratch its back on its favorite tree. With a casual and dismissive shrug, the scout vanished into the forest, making his way to the north to find his companions and inform them of just how lucrative their find truly was.

Seated where Mathis had left him, Amroth was dozing blissfully when the weight struck him in the chest, jolting him awake and drawing a cry of protest from him. Before he could fully comprehend what had happened, his eyes settled on the large red scale in his lap, driving all other thoughts from his mind. Eyes as wide as a doms' dinner plate, he gingerly picked up the scale, feeling the weight of it in his hand, and he looked up to see Mathis quickly checking their gear. "If you're trying to motivate me to move quicker, you didn't have to go to this kind of extreme," he stated nervously.

Mathis grunted. "It's no ruse – that's the real thing. Found it wedged into the trunk of an ironwood."

Amroth scrambled to his feet, made his way to his roan mare and deposited the scale in his saddlebags. As terrifying as the implications of the scale were, such a trophy couldn't be passed up. "Deo be good, what would such a beast be doing this far north? I've seen forest and crag ones from a distance before, but I'd never dreamed an ember would be seen north of the Dragonspine. I honestly didn't know if they were real."

Mathis swung himself into the saddle. "Oh they're real, alright – and they make their cousins look like a mewling mutt. I suggest we get moving. That scale is fresh, and I'd like to put as much ground between us and its owner as possible."

"Agreed," Amroth said nervously as he swung his aching body back into the saddle. "Will we stick with the same path?"

Mathis hesitated a moment, his black eyes narrowed in thought, before answering, "It will still be the quickest route. I fear the river might put us in unwarranted danger, but a more roundabout course will add time we don't really have. I can't imagine an ember would be traveling any direction but south . . . though it's beyond my imagination as to why or how an ember ended up this far north in the first place." While his feigned ignorance in regard to the beast's direction of travel was intended to somewhat alleviate Amroth's fears, it was by no means a dismissal of the danger the creature presented. With genuine concern etched on his face, Mathis nudged his destrider forward and led them further into the forest.

The next four hours passed in tense silence, both of them alert for any sign of a potential threat. Both horses could sense their riders' respective nervousness, and displayed their perceptiveness with edgy twitching of their ears, snorts, or by pawing at the ground when they paused for longer than a few tense moments. Such anxiety from both men and beasts fueled Mathis as he held them on an easterly path at a guarded, but expedited, pace. While he was intent on making up the lost time from the break, he was even more anxious to put as much distance between them and the beast. The thick underbrush wasn't helping his mood either, forcing them to go around and circle back to their chosen route more often than he would have liked. As a result, it was midafternoon by the time they finally heard the churning waters of the Doren'thal River, and another half hour of weaving their way through the forest before they found a clear path down to it.

Descending from the elevated riverbank, Mathis and Amroth reached the shores of the Doren'thal River at one of its narrowest and shallowest points. Running only about sixty feet wide and seven feet deep, the clear waters of the river rolled and tumbled over the rocky bed, serenading the forest with its bubbling melody. Mathis led them to the river's edge where he dismounted and quickly refilled both their waterskins while the horses drank their fill. He watched the surrounding area carefully as he took care of the simple chore, scanning the rocks that carpeted the shorelines and the grainy soil for any sign of the predator. Thankfully, apart from a few small game prints and fish, there was no indication that there was a large predator in the area.

Satisfied that they were actually putting distance between themselves and the ember, Mathis returned their skins to their respective saddles and mounted back up before offering to Amroth, "I think we're alright now. No signs of anything around here other than small game." Amroth, a bit pale from the pain and the ride, simply nodded, drawing a sympathetic wince from the normally stoic veteran. "Sorry, lad. Better that we moved hard than to run into that beast."

"I know," Amroth offered with a weak smile, unable to hide the ache in his black eyes, before waving Mathis on. "Let's just keep moving while I still feel like I can ride."

As he got them moving again, Mathis silently thanked Amroth for his willingness to gut it out. Knowing that they wouldn't reach his intended campsite before nightfall no matter how hard they rode, he decided on a more casual pace for the rest of the day, allowing the serenity of the forest and the lullaby of the river to sooth their frayed nerves. Remaining within sight of the river, they followed the riverbank from the shelter of the forest edge as it wound its way through the forest, doing their best to enjoy the afternoon sunlight as it cascaded through the treetops and danced along the singing waters.

As the afternoon wore on, the river dipped into a rocky part of the forest that might once have been a mountain in ages past, the treacherous terrain eventually forcing them to once again descend to the riverbank. To Mathis' chagrin, they found the shore littered with rocks and large boulders, slowing their already casual pace. As the river quickly widened to nearly a hundred yards, its waters deepening and frothing as the cold liquid tumbled over the large rocks jutting from the bottom, Mathis carefully guided them through the rocky chaos. Deep shadows, cast by the forest floor gradually rising above them, crawled across the roaring river and allied with the rocky terrain and growing moisture in the ground to make their footing dangerous. As a result, Mathis was so focused on the ground at his horse's hooves that he almost failed to notice the growing unease in his destrider. At first, he simply thought the warhorse was growing tired and agitated with the long ride and rough terrain. However, he began to see the nervous fluttering of her nostrils and ears, as well as her irritated pawing at the ground, for what it was – his horse's sharper senses were picking up on something that was making her very uneasy.

Just as Mathis was about to call for a stop so he could scout ahead on foot, Amroth gave a shout of surprise that nearly caused him to jumped from his saddle.

"Mathis!" came the shout again.

Tugging on his reins hard, which drew an angry whine of protest from the dark destrider, he turned in his saddle and was about to ask what had startled Amroth so, when he immediately noticed his young charge pointing ahead of them toward the far shore.

"What in Deo's name is that?" Amroth asked loud enough to be heard over the noise of the river.

Turning back around, already admonishing himself for relaxing his guard, he was shocked to see what Amroth was pointing at.

In the distance, the river bent hard to the left, vanishing around a rugged outcropping. However, where there should have been trees standing tall and proud, there was nothing but carnage and oddities to behold. Shattered ironwoods and evergreens were tossed about the outcropping like unwanted toys, their trunks reaching down toward the river below like men who had died of thirst with salvation just out of reach. Blackened scorch marks littered the rocky terrain as if some giant had tried to haphazardly burn warts from the land. Jutting from the walls of the rise were four man-sized, jagged spears of what appeared to be brownish stone, each one shot through with veins of emerald that seemed to pulse in the sunlight. If the pillars of earth weren't enough to bewilder the senses, then the surrounding rocks that were covered in a fine growth of moss and a cornucopia of brightly colored flowers that couldn't possibly grow in the current conditions would have been enough to make one question their sanity. The sight was simply not of this world, and had Amroth wide-eyed as he tried to comprehend what he was seeing.

Before either man could say anything, a series of loud cracks and pops violently split the air. They watched in amazement as the treetops beyond the bend in the river swayed and then fell quickly, a resounding crash erupting into the air. They flinched hard in their saddles, and their horses – both beasts normally at ease with the noises and smells of war – tried to turn to flee from the crash and whatever was the cause of the catastrophic commotion.

It was then that they heard it.

Deep and throaty, the roar blasted into the evening air like a violent and triumphant clarion call, reverberating through the air with primal power. Man and beast alike were frozen in place by the bone-rattling roar, their faculties and instincts driven into hiding by sheer terror. And while the trees and earth lacked the capacity to comprehend or react to such things, it wouldn't have been surprising if they too had cowered before the roar.

For Amroth, his mind was numb with terror and his face had turned a ghostly white. He had thought nothing could be more chilling than the haunting screams and cries of death that populated a battlefield, or his recent brush with death; however, the emotions generated by either of those could not compare to the pure terror the roar inspired. It was all he could do just to remain in his saddle. Some part of him knew he should try to react, but its voice was lost in a sea of fear.

Like Amroth, Mathis had physically felt the triumphant bellow and his face had grown a shade or two paler. However, unlike his inexperienced companion, his fear was driven by his familiarity with such beasts and their destructive capabilities. He knew that if they could hear the beast, then it was close; and if it was close, it was aware of their presence. With the forest floor both towering over them and hemming them in at this point, they were left with only forward or backward to go, but he knew running would more than likely inspire a chase that neither he nor Amroth could hope to win.

Cursing, he knew their only choice was to move forward and to hope that whatever had the beast's attention was more important than two scrawny humans. "We have to move forward, Amroth," Mathis said through clenched teeth.

Shaken from his terror-inspired stupor, Amroth gave him the befuddled look he had expected, as well as the reply. "Are you mad?! I may be hurting, but I'm not that anxious to die! That's an ember out there, Mathis!"

Mathis gave his reins a firm tug and guided his nervous horse back to his charge. "Don't you think I know that?!" he barked as he put a firm hand on Amroth's reins. "I've been around, lad. I've seen what those beasts can do, and I'm no more anxious than you to come face-to-face with it – but we've got no choice!"

"No choice?" he barked as his mare seemed to shake off her paralysis and tried to step away from Mathis' destrider. "Hells, we go back the way we came and put as much distance between us and that damnable beast!" Amroth's voice was rising in pitch as fear and his weakened state were threatening to take control.

Mathis let go of Amroth's reins and grabbed a fistful of his shirt, jerking him close. "Calm down!" he roared. "That beast will sense your fear and feed on it," Mathis added firmly but calmly. "We run and it will chase! Our only choice is to go forward and show no fear! If we're lucky, it will ignore us!"

"And if we're not?" he snapped back.

Mathis took a deep breath and let go of Amroth's shirt. "If we're not," he stated bluntly, "then we're dead either way." Without waiting for a response or to see if Amroth would follow, Mathis jerked hard on his reins, turning his agitated destrider about and departing at a steady walk.

For the briefest of moments, Mathis truly thought Amroth would turn and run. To his relief, however, he heard Amroth scampering to catch up. When the inexperienced and scared Merandith pulled along his right side, he offered his young companion a reassuring nod, doing his best to project calm and confidence in hopes of instilling it in Amroth and their mounts. Though he was pale and there was obvious fear in his eyes, Amroth's jaw was set and he sat his saddle upright and strong, accepting Mathis' challenge to move forward. They moved at a steady pace despite both their mounts' attempts to fight them every inch of the way. With their nerves on edge and breathing heavy, both men and beasts felt like time was slowing to a crawl as foot-by-foot the bend in the river slowly revealed the horror that lay beyond.

The shattered husks of ironwoods and leatherleafs that had been thrown clear across the river conspired with a pile of boulders to funnel them close to the risen embankment, temporarily cutting off their view of the river and forcing Amroth to fall in behind Mathis. By this point, Amroth's palms were sweating and his breathing was shallow. With nothing but rocks and Mathis' back to see, he was doing his best to fend off his imagination. He had only heard stories of embers, and at this point, where imaginative tales ended and the truth began made little difference to him. Shaking his head to fend off the unwanted thoughts, he was caught by surprise when Mathis came to a sudden halt.

Reining his roan mare in, he asked with a hint of trepidation in his voice, "What is it?"

Mathis sat silently, his rigid back presented to Amroth. Then, with extreme deliberateness, he urged his nervous destrider into the open and waved Amroth forward.

With a deep breath and his hands gripping the reins tightly, Amroth followed. As soon as he pulled alongside Mathis, he briefly noted that the river embankment returned to about shoulder height just ahead of them. But as his vision trailed up the swirling waters that rolled and pitched over the rocky river bottom, all thoughts about the change in terrain vanished as his eyes came to rest upon what held his companion's attention. Eyes growing wide in awe and fear, Amroth breathed, "Deo be good. . . ."

A little more than fifty yards from their position, the river began to glow a soft green as the waters swirled and mixed with the green blood that was pumping from the dead beast sprawled out in the center of the river. The dead forest drakuma would have stood nearly eight feet at the shoulders had it been upright. The opalescent green scales that armored its muscular bulk were charred black and stained with green blood. Flanking the shaggy brown mane that ran from the top of its wide, square head to the base of its short but thick tail, the large earthen spikes that ran the length of its back were either broken or shattered, and two were missing. Above its broad and armored chest, the soft flesh of its throat was completely ripped out, the surrounding scales and flesh scorched to a blackened crisp. Its powerful jaws were splayed wide in a silent howl, revealing broad teeth that were as long as a man's finger and designed to shred flesh. Its eyes, which in life would appear to glow green, were darkened specks underneath a heavy brow that was shaded by charred locks of its mane. Although it was dead, the forest drakuma was still an impressive sight. However, it was the beast that sat behind the carcass that inspired the fear that was permeating Amroth's bones.

Seated on its haunches, the male ember drakuma was easily fifteen feet tall. Opalescent red scales rippling and shifting color in the sunlight, the thickly muscled beast pawed at the jagged earthen spear jutting from the back of its massive right shoulder with a four-fingered paw that was just as dexterous as the hand it resembled and big enough to easily hold a man. Burly and wide in the chest, with a narrow waist and powerful haunches, nearly every inch of his body was clad in armored red scales. His exposed belly was composed of hardened leathery flesh that was nearly the color of a starless night. Large and heavy, the armored scales that protected its corded chest interrupted the flow of the leathery flesh on its way up to the ember's wide, angular head. The massive head was turned to the side, its glowing ember eyes focused on the spear jutting from its shoulder, granting both men a good view of the short and powerful maw from which jutted two upper canines that were thicker than a man's fist. A flowing mane of black and red fur – starting from between his armored, heavy brows – ran all the way down his back, parting at the base of his skull to flank the large, jutting scales that protected the back of his neck and spine. Two wicked horns, dotted with dull-red splotches, jutted from above the ember's brow before sweeping back and hooking around short, pointed ears that showed signs of a hard and violent life.

The ember drakuma was truly a sight to behold, and Amroth was quick to realize that no rumor or story could fully capture the marvel of such a rare creature. Yet, despite the rarity of the beast and the terrifying majesty that the drakuma presented, Amroth kept finding himself wondering what kind of creature could have caused the old scars that littered the imposing beast's exposed belly.

Before either man could make a move or utter a syllable, the ember suddenly ceased his attempt to reach the earthen spike and slowly turned his massive head to face them, revealing a jagged scar over his left eye and a host of smaller ones on the unprotected flesh around his eyes and lips. When his eyes – which seemed made of molten flame – settled on them, both men felt like they would combust from the heat and intensity in the gaze. Neither man could even fathom moving at that point; fear and awe had them firmly in its grasp. It was perfectly clear to them that if the ember wanted them dead, there was nothing either man could do to stop the beast.

With an indifference that was born of knowing he was the superior creature, the ember let out a low, rumbling growl before returning his attention to the spike jutting from his shoulder. Reaching up with his powerful paw, the drakuma finally took a firm grasp on the spike with the aid of his opposable thumb, the effort eliciting a pain-filled growl from him. Pulling hard on the spike, the ember's face contorted in obvious pain as the spike began to slide out of his shoulder. Then, with his head pitched back in a roar that reverberated around them, the ember ripped the spike out and tossed it violently to the side. The spike crashed into the forest, knocking over trees and flinging dark, viscous blood everywhere. To Amroth's amazement, steam hissed into existence where the ember's blood made contact with the water; and wherever the blood hit the ground, small flames sprouted to life and quickly winked out, leaving a series of small scorch marks as a reminder of the flames' brief existence.

The roar died off soon after the spike's removal, and the ember simply sat there, breathing heavily as he fought through the pain that was washing over him. Hidden from Amroth and Mathis' eyes, the gaping wound in the ember's armored shoulder closed and cauterized itself. While it would take time, fresh pink flesh would soon replace the cauterized wound, and eventually the protective scales would regenerate. For now, the wound was sealed and the beast could return to the business at hand. Rolling himself forward, the ember stood up on all fours – nearly twelve feet tall at his wide and powerful shoulders – flinging water about as his weight came down on his paws and his twin tails unfurled behind him. Each tail was tipped with what appeared to be ethereal flames that shifted from deep-red to a bright-white in a mesmerizing, chaotic dance. Amroth was amazed that whatever the tail touched didn't simply burst into flames.

The ember walked forward and, with terrifying power, planted a paw on the haunch of the forest drakuma, its thick, six-inch claws easily cracking through the green scales before sinking into the soft flesh underneath. For a brief moment, the ember didn't move as he stared at Mathis, further adding to Amroth's growing awe of the beast, and planting a seed of curiosity in his mind. He wasn't sure he was seeing things right, but when he pried his eyes away from the ember to look at Mathis, he saw that his companion was indeed staring intently back at the ember. Before Amroth could even begin to question what he was seeing, a small roar, that almost seemed like a bark, snapped his attention back to the ember just in time to watch the red beast give a mighty yank on the dead drakuma's haunch.

Tendons popping and muscles shredding, the back leg tore free of the drakuma's carcass in a sickening display of blood and gore. Amroth could feel bile rising in the back of his throat as green blood oozed from both the macabre wound on the dead forest drakuma, and the base of the limb that was now clutched firmly in the powerful jaws of the ember. Where the blood touched the ground, moss and flowers sprung up quickly, flowing out into the water where the color- ful display quickly faded. The ember appeared oblivious to the leak- ing blood as it continued to stare intently at the two men. Then, with what almost seemed like disdain, the ember gave one last muffled growl before turning to his right and stepping up on the slight em- bankment. As the red drakuma walked into the trees, he left not only a trail of flowers in his wake, but two men to grapple with what they had just witness.

Storm clouds began to fully engulf the sky a little more than an hour before sunset, forcing darkness to begin its crawl across the Alderian Forest earlier than expected. Amongst the growing sha- dows, Mathis and Amroth had taken a moment to rest and gather themselves. They had remained at the site of the slaughtered forest drakuma for a short while, not only to give themselves a chance to shake off the awe and fear that had gripped them upon encountering the ember drakuma, but to make sure the beast had departed for good. When they felt the beast wasn't coming back, Mathis had wasted no time in leading them upstream at a hurried pace, guiding them swiftly past the grisly carcass before diverting them back into the woods. After guiding them east for about an hour, he called for the stop they now partook of, allowing them the chance to rest their frayed nerves and collect themselves. No words were shared during that time, as each man was wrapped in an invisible cloak of solitude forged from their need to sort through the day's events.

For Mathis, the appearance of an ember drakuma had summoned up memories of his past that he had long fought to keep buried. His life before joining the Merandiths was something he discussed very little, and even then, only with a few select people. While he still maintained contact with friends from his younger days, he did his best to keep his past separate from his current life. The ember was a surprise that shook him to his very core. And while he did his best to ignore the memories the encounter had summoned forth, it left him with a host of dreadful questions that he didn't know if he was ready for the answers to.

Amroth, on the other hand, needed the time to simply try to come to terms with what he had seen. He was already stressed and troubled by the brutal assault he'd received back in camp. His pacifistic views had been called into question, and he knew that if he'd taken the time to learn more than the basics of swordsmanship, he might have been able to defend himself and avoid the miserable shape he was in. While he had believed he had all the time in the world to examine those feelings and beliefs, the encounter with the ember had shaken him to his core and banished such youthfully ignorant notions. Even with the threat of death always on the horizon while traveling with the army and being a member of House Merandith, Amroth had never felt so vulnerable and mortal as he had when he laid eyes on the drakuma. He had known immediately that neither he nor Mathis would have been able to save them should the massive predator have chosen to attack. The fact that the ember had decided to leave them alone seemed like a Deo-sent blessing, leaving Amroth feeling as if he'd been given another chance at life – and that opportunity was something he was beginning to feel he should protect.

They were back in the saddle and moving before either of them really wanted. Given their mental and emotional states, it would have been easier simply to make camp where they had stopped. However, Mathis wanted as much distance between them and the dead drakuma as possible – and that meant continuing on despite their fatigue. Granted, Mathis was sure the ember could hunt them down and kill them should the beast choose to, but at least making the token gesture of moving ever forward made both he and Amroth feel somewhat better. With those thoughts at the forefront of his mind, Mathis extended their plodding journey on through the early evening hours, pausing only to allow him to remove a hooded lantern as dusk and the building cloud cover turned the forest floor to night prematurely. Even with the lantern, the going was slow as they did their best to avoid roots or holes that could cause a devastating spill or result in one of their mount's breaking a leg.

As the minutes and then hours crept by, the fear and adrenaline from the day's events finally faded and exhaustion began to seep in. With his limbs and eyes growing heavy, Amroth began to find it difficult to remain awake; even the rocking caused by his roan beneath him seemed to be conspiring to lull him to sleep. Yet, through his increasingly bleary eyes, it seemed like Mathis remained tall in the saddle and alert. At one point, Amroth dozed off without realizing it. One moment his eyes were open, and the next they were closed as exhaustion tried to claim him, causing him to list dangerously in his saddle. The next thing he knew, he was startled awake by an arm around his waist. Bolting upright, Amroth found Mathis at his side, his strong arm keeping Amroth from falling out of his saddle. A weak and exhausted smile gracing his face, Amroth nodded his thanks and motioned for Mathis to lead on.

Somewhere along the line, he must have drifted off again because he found himself once again being dragged from the depths of a deep sleep as his mount came to a halt and he heard Mathis gently say, "Amroth? Amroth, we're here."

Amroth wearily opened his heavy eyes to the painfully bright light of Mathis' lantern, which made it difficult for his eyes adjust. When he finally felt like he could see straight, he realized there wasn't much to see. With the heavy cloud cover that had rolled in throughout the evening, it was inky black outside of the small area illuminated by the hooded lantern. He could tell that they were on the edge of a modest clearing and that the immediate area was littered with dead pine needles and leaves; beyond that, he could make out very little. "Where are we?" he asked sleepily.

"The glade I told you about," Mathis replied with a hint of an amused smile on his lips. "Come on, let's get you down from that saddle before you fall off," he added as he dismounted.

"Huh . . .? Wha . . .? Oh. . . . Right, the clearing," Amroth offered groggily as he slid from his saddle in about as ungraceful a manner as possible without falling flat on his face, drawing an amused

338

shake of the head from Mathis. With his fatigued mind and body screaming at him for sleep, Amroth immediately moved to his bedroll and, after fumbling at the straps for a moment, removed it. Without waiting to see where Mathis wanted to make camp, he found a relatively clear spot beneath the bare branches of an oak and unfurled his beadroll before lying down heavily. "Night," he muttered before quickly drifting off to sleep.

Mathis shook his head in amusement before attending to their horses and settling in for the night. Leaning both their saddles against the oak, Mathis returned his katana to his belt before moving off to gather wood for a small fire. While he was still edgy about the ember drakuma, he wasn't about to spend a cold and possibly wet night without some warmth. With all the deadfall in the both the forest proper and the glade, it didn't take him long to find what he needed. He returned to Amroth's sleeping form, cleared a spot on the ground and deposited the firewood. After building a proper firepit, he retrieved the lantern and used it to start a small fire before dousing and sealing the lantern. Gathering his saddle and his bedroll up, he sat the saddle down on the opposite side of the fire from Amroth before spreading his bedroll over it to provide some cushion. Using his saddle as a backrest, Mathis seated himself and did his best to make himself comfortable.

The day's events had brought with it a host of troubling questions that begged for answers he simply did not have. A less disciplined mind might begin to wandered down different lines of thought, needlessly searching for answers that simply were not there at that time. Mathis, however, wasn't about to get caught up in a guessing game. The answers he sought would come to him in time – of that, he was positive. A deep yawn overtook him, his jaw popping as it forced his mouth to open wide. Shaking his head, he settled back against his saddle, folded his arms across his chest and closed his eyes for a moment as he continued to reflect on events.

Drakumas and their implications aside, there was still the question of what to do with Amroth. He had intended to forcibly start training him this very night, but after the tumultuous events of the day, he wasn't so sure that would be necessary. Two life-threatening situations in a week's time would certainly be enough to make him see the folly of his ways. Still, Amroth could be very stubborn – which, depending on one's point of view, was either a tribute to his heritage or an inherent flaw with it. No, he decided, best not to take chances. Let Amroth rest a bit and then . . . and then. . . .

He must have drifted off to sleep because the next thing he knew, his years of training kicked in and he was jolted awake by a sense of danger. He immediately noticed that he had slid down onto the ground, his head and shoulders propped up by his saddle. Remaining still so he wouldn't divulge that he was awake, he cracked his eyes just enough to examine the area in his field of vision. The fire had died down to smoldering embers, a clear indication that he'd been asleep for quite some time, and Amroth remained blissfully asleep; but other than that, he couldn't make out much with as dark as it was. However, he had learned to trust his instincts, and at that moment, they told him trouble was afoot.

Maintaining his charade, Mathis rolled one way and then the other, acting like he was trying to get comfortable. In both directions, all he could make out was darkness fading into even deeper darkness within the tree line. Whoever or whatever was out there was skilled at stalking, which only further raised the hairs on the back of his neck. To his chagrin, he had no way of identifying the lurking threat, which meant he had no way to counter it; therefore, he did the only thing he could do – he waited.

Earlier that evening, as the heavy rain clouds filled the sky and the sun was just dipping below the eastern horizon, a party of twelve riders – dressed in an assortment of clothing intended to allow them to pass inconspicuously through the foreign lands – came upon the remains of the forest drakuma. While darkness had begun to make its storm-cloud-driven appearance a few hours ago, the dead moss and flowers surrounding the foul-smelling carcass like a macabre shroud were easy to see. Crows and their ground-bound, bloated mud crow cousins covered the exposed flesh of the beast like a dark blanket, picking at and fighting over the large meal. The smell of decaying flesh was strong in the air and was worse than anything any of them had ever smelt on the battlefield. Horses and men alike shied away from the sight and the stench like it was a plague, and a few of the men were even forced to lean over in the saddle to vomit.

The veteran scout responsible for leading them on the trail of their prey was mortified at the scene, and could hear the other soldiers muttering about what could inflict such wounds on a drakuma. Even with all his travel and everything he had seen in his years, the scout couldn't fathom what had done such damage to a predator of this size. He would have thought another drakuma capable of such damage, but as far as he knew, they never killed one another except in territorial disputes. The wounds on the beast had been inflicted by a creature significantly larger than any drakuma he'd ever seen, and suggested something more primal than a territory dispute. Upon further examination, the scout was forced to conclude that the primal motive behind the drakuma's death was hunger. If his conclusions were true, then this was the first evidence of a drakuma killing one of its own for sustenance that he was aware of.

Shaking his head to clear it, he turned and caught the eye of their commander. Though young, their commander had proven himself capable and practical; even presented with this unusual sight, he appeared outwardly calm and collected. When the scout caught the calm blue-eyed gaze of his commander, he received a firm nod before being ordered to continue forward via hand signals. The scout nodded, held up his hand and motioned everyone onward. Bizarre as the sight was, they still had a job to do, and their targets were well ahead of them. If they had any hope of overtaking their prey before the rough weather the clouds were promising set in, they couldn't afford to be distracted. Honor and glory awaited them all – and nothing was going to stop them.


Later that night, the scout found himself edging up against an oak tree and peaking around it into the clearing he had tracked their prey to. Like the rest of his group, his dark eyes were well adjusted to the darkness, making it easy for them to see that their targets were fast asleep around a practically dead campfire. Earlier, he had – with sincere relief – spread the word amongst the men that the campfire did indeed belong to their targets, for it had taken them longer than they wanted to catch up with them. Nightfall had made the going slow, and for a time, they thought they had lost the trail. With his frustration mounting, their commander had nearly decided to call a halt for the night, when they spotted the dull glow of a campfire in the distance. The scout had thanked whatever luck had led their quarry to set such a careless camp. Even a small fire would reflect well off the bark of an ironwood, which would provide more than enough light for even a half-wit to find. With renewed vigor, they had made their way toward the light with caution, not a single man amongst them wanting to alert their prey to their presence as they spread out around the edge of the clearing, their dark cloaks concealing and muffling their armor and weapons.

Now, they simply awaited the order to strike.

Creeping up beside the scout silently, their commander gently placed a hand on the scout's shoulder. Startled slightly, the scout turned his hooded head and, upon recognizing his commander, acknowledged his inquisitive, piercing blue eyes with a nod. Pointing to his eyes and then across clearing, the commander silently asked the scout to reaffirm that the two men in the clearing were indeed their targets. The scout nodded in the affirmative, drawing a victorious smile from his commander. Patting the scout on the shoulder, the commander tossed back his cloak and drew his sword. The scout followed suit, drawing two shortswords from his belt, before they let out a bellow and led the charge into the clearing.

The sudden war cry rang out across the small glade, startling Amroth awake and sending Mathis into motion. Springing to his feet, Mathis drew his sword in a single, fluid motion as he quickly assessed the situation. It was immediately evident that they were severely out-numbered and all avenues of retreat were cut off as, from every direc-tion, armed men came sprinting from the shadows. Before Mathis could even begin to try to figure a way out of the mess, three men appeared from behind Amroth, two of them tackling the young Me-randith before he could get his wits about him while the third contin-ued toward Mathis. As Amroth struggled against his assailants, Ma-this quickly sidestepped the man that tried to tackle him and slid his sword under his assailant's bowed torso, the keen edge of Mathis' katana gutting the man with ease as he went by. Turning to deal with the two men pinning Amroth down, a heavy weight slammed into Mathis' back, driving the breath from him and pitching him face first into the ground, his sword driven from his grip.

Mathis tried to struggle against his attacker as the man fought to pin his arms behind his back. The heavy thud of footsteps grew as more of their assailants moved in on the camp. Growling, Mathis tried to shove himself to his feet, earning him a kick to the side of his head. With his head spinning and nausea boiling in his stomach, he fell limply to the ground, which provided the man pinning him the opportunity to securely bind his hands with a leather thong. Mathis was then dragged to his feet, hauled over to Amroth and unceremo-niously dumped on the ground next to his subdued charge. Vision still swimming from the blow to his head, Mathis tried to look over to check on Amroth's condition, but was foiled by a large hand sinking its fingers into his tousled black hair and pulling him to his knees. However, a groan and curse from Mathis' right told him that not only was Amroth alive, but he was also receiving similar treatment.

From his knees, and with his vision finally back to normal, Mathis was able to attain a clear assessment of the situation they were now in. Nine armed men surrounded them while two others were busy stripping their dead companion of his gear and digging a make-shift grave. A tall man with serine blue eyes and short-cropped brown hair stood in front of he and Amroth, conferring with a short, grizzled man who carried two shortswords at the ready. Both wore heavy woodsman cloaks that hid any telling marks about their dress.

"Are these the two?" the blue-eyed man asked with a tone of authority that clearly singled him out as the group's leader.

"Aye, that's them. They match the descriptions to the letter," replied the shorter one.

"Quite the catch then, eh men?"

"Hurrah!" came the cheered reply.

The commander strode over to his captives and crouched down in front of them. "Mathis Sormantale and Amroth Merandith," he stated with confidence. "I'm curious – whatever would two such important people be doing away from the main army, eh? Care to enlighten me?"

Both Mathis and Amroth answered with silent, stony stares.

The man cocked his head to the side inquisitively. "Don't feel like talking, eh? Well that is a shame. Normally I might find it in me to use your silence as an excuse to see if I could loosen your tongues, but people more important than I would not like it if I roughed up their prize." He stood up and gestured to the shorter man. As his subordinate moved behind the prisoners, the commander said, "However, seeing as I can't have you making noise or slowing us up. . . ."

A dull thud followed by Amroth's body pitching forward was all the warning Mathis had before he felt a blow to the back of his head and stars exploded before his eyes. Pitching forward, unconsciousness claimed him before his face introduced itself to the ground.

The commander looked at all his men with a victorious smile. "Well done, men! You have my thanks! Now," he glanced at the dark sky, "be about setting up camp. It looks like it's going to rain, and there's no need for us to try to travel in this horrible darkness."

*Bing! Tink tink tink! Bing! Tink tink tink!*

*With practiced rhythm, the blacksmith rained precise blows on the glowing ingot of steel, slowly and meticulously shaping the stubborn metal. So focused on his work was he that the world about him was a foggy blur.*

*Bing! Tink tink tink! Bing! Tink tink tink!*

*Nothing in the world mattered at that moment as he hammered away at the steel. Not his family, not his friends, not even his wants and desires. His work was what was important – everything balanced on his ability to accomplish what many thought was impossible.*

*With a tired grunt of satisfaction, he returned the steel to the glowing embers of the forge and left it to reheat. Stepping outside, he was greeted by a scene of horrific design. The houses about him were covered in flames, angry-red gouts of flame spurting from the tiled, angular roofs. Charred corpses littered the ground like flower petals scattered before the feet of royalty on parade. Whether it was the corpses of children that were clutched in the death grip of their dead parents, soldiers frozen in the throes of agony, or the lone corpse balled up in a corner, it was clear that none were spared.*

*The blacksmith took a deep breath of the thick, ash-filled air and looked skyward. Soaring high in the sky, the silhouettes of giant beasts were barely discernible through the clouds of smoke and ash. "Tis' a fine day," he thought to himself even as fire rained from the sky and the screams of the dying floated on the air to his ears. "It would be a shame if all this went away should I fail."*

*Turning to return to his work, he stopped short and blinked as a drop of water hit him in the face. "Odd," he thought. "Why would it be raining on such a clear, beautiful day?"*

*Another drop pelted him, and then another. He turned his face skyward as drop after drop began to fall from the sky. Then, as he struggled to comprehend the unusual weather, the heavens relinquished their burden and the tears of the gods began to rain down upon him. . . .*

Mathis awoke from the dream with a groan of pain, his skull throbbing from the blows to his head. He was soaked through and could feel the rain drumming down on him relentlessly.

"You're finally awake," a hoarse voice stated quietly.

Leveraging himself off the wet ground into a sitting position, Mathis saw Amroth huddled just off to his right. The young Merandith looked like he was caught between being angry and being miserable in the wet weather. "Are you okay?" Mathis croaked.

Amroth, his hands secured behind his back, shrugged. "Pain and misery seem to be the new standard which I live by – so I guess I'm doing okay," he muttered in response.

Ignoring the sarcasm, Mathis nodded and began to take stock of their situation. They were still in the glade and seated on the soaked earth at the site of their original camp. Their assailants were camped along the edge of the clearing beneath canvas lean-tos. Four fires provided warmth at four different camps, their precious flames protected from the rain by the temporary shelters. A fifth fire, around which four men were huddled, burned a few paces behind Amroth. Mathis figured it was that particular group's job to watch over he and Amroth, and couldn't blame them for their lax behavior;

between the weather, their captors numbers, and their current state, Mathis surmised it would be very difficult to attempt escape.

Continuing his assessment, he saw that there was no immediate sign of their weapons or equipment, which meant it had either been discarded or, more likely, scavenged. While that was disconcerting, Mathis tucked that knowledge away and focused on possible escape options despite having already concluded escape would be exceedingly difficult. "Any idea who they are?" he asked quietly.

Amroth shook his head, his eyes staring off into nothing. "I can't be completely sure . . . but I thought I heard someone mention House Suldamik."

Mathis nodded slightly. "That makes sense. They have our descriptions and they seem well organized. I would wager they're raiders."

"Deo be good," Amroth stated without emotion, drawing a concerned look from Mathis. "I can't believe they were able to get this close to Haltho without being noticed."

Mathis didn't reply immediately as he examined Amroth for signs of shock. It could have been his imagination, but in the dim light, Amroth's eyes looked like they were burning with either anger or fever, and his skin was pale. Too much had happened to him in such a short span that it had to be taking a mighty toll upon him. "It wouldn't take much," he finally replied. "We're not that far from the front or the Contested Territories. Besides, the front is large and there are any number of places a small force could pass unnoticed. I wouldn't be surprised if—"

"Hey! Quiet you two! Bad enough we have to watch over your sorry arses! Don't need your bramhen-shite Merandith voices giving us headaches!" barked one of the men, his crass statements receiving amused, supportive laughter from his fellow guards.

Mathis responded with silence and, with a look, urged Amroth to do the same. He didn't want to give the guards any reason to harm them, nor did he wish to feed their animosity. Luckily, he needn't have worried about Amroth at that moment; with as battered and bruised as he was, Amroth simply sat with his knees drawn up under his chin and stared off into the darkness. However, that did little to put Mathis at ease as it suddenly occurred to him that Amroth might be nursing anger at everything that had happened to him of late. The last thing Mathis wanted was for his young charge to do something foolish, but there was little he could do about it at that moment. Resigning himself to remain alert and ready, Mathis settled in for what he figured would be a long night.

With silence as their brooding companion, the night slowly crept by to the accompaniment of the constant rain. Sometime during the wet night, Amroth finally drifted off to sleep, which Mathis noted with concern. Fearing for Amroth's health, he decided to keep an eye on his friend for the rest of the night; Amroth did not look good, and the wet weather would only make things worse if they didn't get dry soon.

Shortly before dawn – though the cloud cover made it impossible for the glade's inhabitants to notice dawn's approach – the steady rainfall turned into a torrential downpour. With Amroth's health foremost on his mind and his concern growing, Mathis turned his attention once again to the possibility of escape. A quick test of his bindings told him that they had shrunk due to all the rain. Their guards appeared to be professionals and, as they did now, had constantly kept at least one pair of eyes on them. Shifting his position, Mathis turned his attention to the main group soldiers. There was one man per fire standing watch while the others rested. From his vantage point, Mathis could only see nine men in total, which meant the two remaining guards were somewhere out of sight.

Suddenly, a deafening roar split the night air followed by an agonizing scream from somewhere close by. To a man, their captors sprung to their feet, weapons drawn, even as every horse in the clearing began to whine in fear or bolt for the trees. The raiders' commander began shouting orders, and the men began rushing toward their prisoners, hastily lit torches in hand, forming up defensively around them.

"What in the hells was that?" asked one of the men to no one in particular.

Amroth, who had been startled awake by the roar, caught Mathis' eye. Terror was unapologetically displayed on Amroth's pale face. Both of them recognized the roar for what it was – the ember was close at hand.

The commander caught the shared glance and motioned for two of his men to haul the prisoners to their feet. "What in the hells is out there?!" the commander barked as the prisoners were dragged to their feet and shoved before him. "I know you know what it is! Answer me!" the commander demanded with a mix of anger and trepidation.

Mathis and Amroth – though for different reasons – simply stared hard back at the man.

In frustration, the commander turned his attention to Amroth. Without warning, he clamped a hand around Amroth's throat and began to squeeze. Mathis tried to make a move to dislodge the hand, but the raider restraining him had an iron grip. "I'm going to ask again – and this time, if I don't get an answer, you'll die, and consequences be damned! I need to know what's out there, and I need to know now!" he barked even as Amroth's face turned a vibrant red.

Before Mathis could say something to intervene, the remaining perimeter guard – whose movements clearly indicated that he was wounded – came stumbling into the clearing from the north, drawing the attention of their captors. The commander released his grip on Amroth and took a few steps toward the new arrival. Struggling to draw in ragged gasps of air, Amroth sagged in the arms of the soldier restraining him.

Before the commander could address the approaching guard, horrified gasps slipped from some of his men as the wounded man entered the firelight, revealing his injuries to all. Blood gushed from where a chunk of his scalp had been torn loose, and the sleeve of his limp right arm was drenched with blood. As the wounded man passed the remaining horses, the fear-filled beasts bolted as they scented the spilt blood.

The commander, his wide eyes full of shock, caught the man before he could stumble into him. Supporting the wounded soldier by his shoulders, the commander demanded, "Deo be good man – what happened to you?!"

"A– A– de– demon, sir!" he stammered even as he continued to grow pale from the loss of blood.

"Bastion! Get over here and see to this man!" the commander barked.

The wounded guard shook his head even as the one named Bastion moved forward to tend to him. "No . . . no time. It's close. Run, sir! I b– ba– ba– beg of you!"

Before the commander could reply, one of the soldiers behind Amroth and Mathis cried, "Deo be merciful! Sir! Over there!" before pointing to the north from where the wounded soldier had arrived.

Two glowing ember eyes could be seen hovering in the air like angry wisps. Everyone around Mathis and Amroth was frozen in shock as they watched the molten eyes approach. For many, the shock turned to terror as the darkness seemed to part like a curtain to reveal the opalescent red-scaled, monstrous form of the ember drakuma. Scales glistening with rain, and his flame-tipped, twin tails waving lazily behind him, the ember paused and eyed the gathering of humans with disdain through his soaked mane.

Amongst the stunned humans, the commander was the first to shake off his shock. Stepping forward, he pointed his sword at the imposing drakuma. "What are you all afraid of? It's just a beast, not some demon! It breaths like a beast – and that means it can die like one!" He turned his head to look at the others. "What are you waiting for?! Attack!"

"Sir," one of the men said urgently as he watched the drakuma crouch down and its muscles coil.

"Come on, men! To arms!" the commander shouted.

"Sir!" the man repeated earnestly.

"What?!" the commander barked, annoyed at his men's cowardice.

"Sir, I . . ." his eyes went wide. "LOOK OUT!"

The commander turned just in time to see the drakuma come soaring through the air and land with a heavy thud, the impact knocking soldiers and prisoners alike to the ground as they attempted to flee the beast. In the blink of an eye, the drakuma clamped his massive jaws on to the commander's torso and lifted the screaming man into the air before biting down hard, silencing the screams. The two halves of the commander dropped to the ground amongst a shower of blood with a wet thud, organs and fluids spilling onto the muddy earth. For better or worse, the sight of their mauled commander seemed to wake up and inspire the others. Scrambling to their feet, the remaining soldiers charged the ember.

Most of the men never knew what hit them.

The first three soldiers were casually batted aside, the impact of the drakuma's massive, corded arm killing them instantly and launching the broken bodies into the air. By that time, Amroth and Mathis had gotten to their feet. With only the short soldier with the two shortswords in the vicinity, Mathis was ready to make their escape when one of the dead bodies careened into him, knocking him from his feet and driving his breath from him. Dazed, Mathis suddenly heard a deep, sharp intake of breath. Rolling onto his side, he saw four soldiers come to a halt on the other side of Amroth as the drakuma's massive head drew back and its chest expanded. Cursing, Mathis cried out to Amroth with as much power as he could muster, but it was to no avail. The scout, however, heard the warning and, without thinking twice, sprinted for the woods.

Frozen by the sight of the inflated chest and the ember eyes that glowed with malevolence, the four soldiers and Amroth appeared to be rooted to the ground. Suddenly, the drakuma's head dove forward, its massive, bloodied jaws parting wide even as the red splotches on his horns lit up with a ghostly red light. An enormous breath of hot air hit the soldiers before it suddenly ignited and a roaring gout of fluidic flame leapt from the drakuma's mouth, rolling over the wet ground and engulfing the soldiers. Not a single one of them was able to scream before the ferociously hot flames reduced them to cinders.

As Amroth watched the flames roll toward him, it was as if timed slowed down so death could torture him. All that had happened to him – the insults, the assaults, his tainted past – seemed so pointless at that moment. To survive it all only to die in this fashion was sadistically comical. . . . No – it was wrong.

Like a hot white light at the center of his very being, Amroth felt the anger welling in him. *"I can't die like this!"* he thought. *"Not here! Not now! I won't die!"*

A powerful, angry scream ripped through the air, and with an odd detachment, Amroth realized that it was coming from him. With strength that seemed born of desperation, his corded arms flexed and jerked on his bindings, snapping the leather as easily as if he was tearing paper. Instinctively, he raised his arms to shield himself, his angry roar of defiance echoing in his ears.

Just before the flames met his flesh, he thought – for the briefest of moments – that he could see ethereal blue tendrils of light swirling in front of him. Then the flames hit, and all he could hear was the roar of the hells come to claim him.


Horrified at the hellish fate that was rolling toward Amroth, Mathis could only hope that death was swift for the both of them as he rolled onto his side in a feeble attempt to shield himself. As the fire enveloped him, roaring and raging like the Nine Hells themselves walked Kylir, Mathis suddenly realized that not only had he heard an anger-filled scream before the flames struck Amroth, but more importantly and amazingly, he wasn't on fire. Rolling back over slowly, his eyes widened in astonishment. Bathed in the angry light of the viscous, fluidic flames, Amroth stood his ground with his head bowed and his arms raised protectively before him. As the flames continued to roll toward him, parting as if they were colliding with a barrier, small tendrils of fire licked at Amroth, but fell short of touching him.

Struggling to his feet, Mathis breathed, "Corith be good. . . ."

Without warning, the deadly flames suddenly died out, leaving small fires burning about the glade, and Amroth standing in a steaming circle of untouched land. As Mathis moved toward Amroth, he quickly scanned the clearing, noting just how lucky they truly had been. The ground, as well as the trees just a few feet from them, was charred black, thick flames dancing on the ground and trees like hellish decorations. Of the soldiers that had been standing in front of Amroth, there wasn't a single sign of their remains.

As he halted beside Amroth, he asked gently, "Amroth? Are you alright?"

Slowly, as if coming out of a trance, Amroth lowered his arms and looked up, his eyes widening in shock as he took in the sight before him. "Deo be good, Mathis," Amroth breathed. Adrenaline and whatever had happened to him had given him new life, but there was no telling how long it would last. "It's like the hells opened up and consumed them."

"I . . ." he hesitated, desperately wanting to question Amroth to confirm his suspicion. However, it appeared that the young Merandith was oblivious to what he had done, and Mathis feared the trauma it might cause Amroth if he asked the questions burning in his mind. So, instead, he said, "I know, Amroth. I had hoped to avoid you ever seeing this sight when we encountered the ember the first time."

Amroth blinked at him. "You've seen this horror before?"

"Indeed." He hesitated for a moment before admitting, "I know the beast."

"You what?!" exclaimed Amroth.

Mathis moved in front of Amroth and stared intently at him. "I need you to trust me, Amroth – I know the beast. This event just confirmed it to me. He will not harm us intentionally."

Amroth stared at Mathis like he was talking to a stranger. "You're mad," he stated bluntly.

Mathis shook his dark-haired head, dismissing the statement. "No, I'm not, Amroth. Please –for Deo's sake – trust me." He could see the confusion and turmoil raging behind Amroth's pleading black eyes, and for a moment, he feared that Amroth might do something rash. Finally, Amroth relaxed a bit and nodded.

Satisfied with the response, Mathis gave Amroth a reassuring and thankful nod before turning to face their massive, armored savior.

The scout was breathing heavily as he circled to the north just inside the tree line. They were all dead, and so was everything they had worked for! He wasn't about to let that dishonor stand! It was like his commander said – it was a beast, and it could die like one! However, it was obvious that attacking it head-on would be foolish. It would take an attack from an angle that such a deadly predator wouldn't expect. Coming to a halt just to the rear of the drakuma, he crouched down, seeking a vantage point from which to attack. To his surprise, he saw the prisoners standing unharmed in front of the beast, braving it and the deadly flames it possessed for reasons he could not fathom. Then it struck him – the beast was theirs.

If the realization had been a fist, it would have knocked him off his feet. If the Merandiths had such a creature at their beck and call, then it stood to reason that they had more. If that were true, then House Suldamik was not prepared to face such a destructive creature. As the shock of the realization wore off, anger set in. Mercenary or not, something in him felt that Doms Suldamik would have to be informed of this development. However, his loyalty to his fellow soldiers demanded that those responsible for their deaths pay dearly.

Spotting what he was looking for, he moved off silently, vengeance burning brightly in his eyes.


The ember stood amongst the flaming carnage like a triumphant lord surveying his latest conquest. Much of the viscous flames still burned, but in some areas, the downpour had managed to drown the flames. In front of him were two very wet humans that had survived his fiery blast. The first showed a healthy amount of respect and fear of him, while the second . . . the second showed no fear. Be it man or beast, there were few that did not fear him. Most of those that did not fear him were foolish and dead. However, when he first saw them at the river, he had though he recognized a friend from long ago. His master had given him orders to stay hidden, so he had not attempted to make contact. The only reason he found himself here was a stench he had caught on the wind. His hatred for the foul smell was deeply ingrained and hard to ignore, so he had followed at a distance, seeking its destruction. The death of the soldiers had cleansed the air of the disgusting odor, and now he was faced with an old friend, indecision holding him in check.

Sniffing at the air subtly, the ember probed the currents of fir'gan, seeking to satisfy his curiosity. Eyes narrowing suspiciously, the ember focused his intense gaze on the fearless man. Confidence burning in his black eyes, the man met the ember's gaze without flinching, making it clear to the ember that not only did he recognize him, but that he wanted answers.

Before anyone could make a move or say something, an agonizingly angry scream erupted from above and behind the ember an instant before the drakuma felt a weight land hard on his broad back. Positioned between two of the large spinal scales, the scout – having climbed one of the ironwoods and leapt upon the drakuma's back – drove his swords hard into the beast's back, only to have his blades slide harmlessly off the armored scales. Again and again, his blows were easily turned away, but he kept at it, working to find an opening even as the drakuma roared in irritation and started backing up. Oblivious to his surroundings, and ignoring the wicked gashes opened on his legs by the serrated scales, the scout worked frantically to wound the beast, knowing that to pause would surely mean his death.

Then, he saw it – a section of flesh on the creature's right shoulder that appeared to be weakly protected by small, translucent scales. Shifting his position to get a better angle on the seemingly vulnerable spot, he was startled when the large scales beneath him suddenly shifted and an angry roar split the air. Before he knew what was happening, the drakuma's spinal scales had flattened and he found himself falling. Landing hard on his rump, he lost his grip on his swords as he pitched to the side. Grasping desperately at the ember's mane, he somehow latched on to it and was able to steady himself before he could roll off. Adjusting his grip on the ember's mane, he managed to get his feet under him in time to look up and see the very same ironwood that he had leapt from looming before him. It was then, as the blood drained from his face and the ember reared up, that he realized his mistake.

Having fully flattened his protective spinal scales, the ember backed up to the ironwood and slammed his back into its thick trunk with a mighty roar, crushing the scout between the hard wood and his scaled, armored back. The massive weight of the beast drove the hooked ends of his spinal scales into the scout even as the pressure crushed the man as easily as a person might squash a grape. The drakuma then shook violently, shredding the scout like one might whittle wood. With a satisfied roar, the ember dropped back down to all fours and walked away from the tree. Pieces of clothing, flesh, and gore hung from the hooked ends of his spine scales like macabre trophies. What remained of the scout upon the tree amounted to an indistinguishable mush of gore and organs, globs of which were sliding down and sloughing off the tree like a thick pudding.

Sickened by the display, Amroth dropped to his knees and vomited as the drakuma approached them. Mathis, however, had watched it all coldly, never flinching or batting an eye.

Finished with his retching, Amroth slowly stood up, his throat raw and ribs aching. Giving the ember only a cursory glance, he focused on Mathis. "Let's go," he croaked. "You saw what that thing did to that man. It can't possibly be a friend of yours."

"Your friend is quite disrespectful and ungrateful, Mathis," rumbled a voice that sounded like it had burst from the depths of the earth.

Amroth, eyes wide and shock etched into his face, slowly turned to face the ember. "You . . . you can talk?" Amroth stammered hoarsely.

A throaty chuckled rumbled from the ember. "Observant as well," he quipped sarcastically before swinging his gaze to Mathis. "Greetings Mathis, from me and my master. The years appear to have treated you well."

Mathis bowed respectfully at the waist before looking up and replying, "Well met, Emberscar. You have mine and my companion's thanks for the rescue. However, if you don't mind me being presumptuous," he turned and presented his bound wrists to Emberscar, "would you mind cutting my bonds?"

With his head spinning from the shock of the day and his adrenaline wearing off, Amroth stumbled backward and fainted.

# Chapter Fifteen

*U*pon being freed of his bonds, Mathis immediately moved Amroth's limp form beneath the nearest shelter. To his chagrin, not only had the shelter's fire been scattered and doused by the brief melee, but a quick examination of the surrounding area showed a complete lack of dry timber for a fire. Normally that would have been the end of that idea, but with Emberscar around, it wouldn't matter how soaked the wood was. Moving as quickly as possible, he gathered as much wood as he could find and brought it back to the shelter where, after arranging the wood, Emberscar provided a controlled burst of flame to ignite the sodden wood. Though it was smoky to begin with, it was still a fire, and would provide the warmth Amroth needed.

His next task had him rummaging through the assortment of items that were now scattered about the clearing. He could feel the molten eyes of the drakuma – who was lounging just outside the firelight – on him the whole time, asking the question that neither of them would voice. Doing his best to ignore the prying eyes, he focused on finding their gear. While it would certainly be a boon if all their gear was intact, he was especially concerned about his belongings. Granted, he had kept the important documents on his person – and thankfully their captors hadn't taken the time to do any more than relieve them of their weapons – there were delicate and important items in his saddlebags that could not be replaced should they be destroyed. To his relief, both their saddles and gear were still intact, though their food stores had been taken.

After a couple of hasty trips, Mathis managed to gather the scavenged supplies – including their saddles, gear and weapons – beneath the shelter. Digging around in his saddlebags, he pulled out a heavy cloak that was, thankfully, dry. He then proceeded to strip Amroth of his drenched clothing and wrap him in the cloak before laying him down next to the fire. Retrieving Amroth's belt, he removed his own before tying them together and stringing them between the overhang's supports above the fire. He then draped Amroth's clothes on the makeshift clothesline before stripping himself down and doing the same with his own soaked clothing. As he crouched down to retrieve a fresh ensemble from his pack, his corded muscles danced beneath skin that was littered with scars from a lifetime of fighting. He quickly put on the simple black trousers and white woolen shirt before finally sitting down with his bare feet stretched out toward the fire. By this point, the murky gray of dawn had broken with little relief from the angry downpour or change in illumination. Mathis could see that nearly half of the clearing was a charred and muddy calamity, while the other half was a sodden swamp of deadfall. Dreary as the morning was, he knew he would have little – if any – time to sleep.

Up until this point, Mathis had ignored Emberscar's casual and inquisitive gaze, but his lack of sleep and the constant scrutinization had made him a bit more irritable than normal, so he finally asked, "Are you going to just sit there all morning staring at me, or are you going to speak what's on your mind?"

"What would you have me say?" Ember replied casually.

"An apology for nearly killing Amroth would be a start!" Mathis snapped.

Ember shrugged. "But I didn't, now did I? Besides, he was never in any real danger of being incinerated," he stated matter-of-factly.

"That still doesn't excuse your carelessness! You could have been wrong!" Mathis replied angrily.

Emberscar's gaze narrowed for a moment before he rumbled, "Testy are we? That's not like you, Mathis. You know I would never be so careless."

Mathis closed his eyes and sighed, trying to compose himself. "I know, and I apologize. It's been a few days since I've had any real sleep."

"Humph. And does that account for you not noticing those men following you, or the fact that you appeared stunned by the lad deflecting my flame? You're getting sloppy, Mathis – in the old days, you never would have missed any of this."

A muscle in Mathis' jaw flexed and he cursed silently to himself. "You're right – I should have noticed them, and the fact that I was distracted by discovering your presence here isn't an excuse. As for the boy . . ." he shook his head.

"Distracted?" Emberscar gave what could only be considered a deep, dark laugh. "I know you better than that." He paused and eyed Amroth. "Just what are you doing here, anyway?" Emberscar asked, suspicion and curiosity thick in his voice.

Mathis folded his arms across his chest defensively. "You know why I'm here – I came to serve the Merandiths after my father passed away," he stated bluntly.

Emberscar gave a snort of disbelief, which he lit on fire for extra emphasis, before retorting, "Playing that game, I see. Seems a bit silly considering the display that boy just made. He's untrained, that's for sure." His molten eyes narrowed and he asked suspiciously, "Does he even know?"

Mathis glowered at the drakuma and countered, "And what about you? Why are you so far from home?"

Eyes narrowing further, Emberscar replied with silence.

Smirking in amusement, Mathis said, "We all have our secrets to keep, don't we? Very well, when you feel like telling me why you're here, then I'll tell you why I'm here."

There was an awkward moment of silence before Emberscar said gravely, "The boy aside, I know all too well why you are here, Mathis – you have no ability to fool me like the others. As for me, I do not tell you simply to keep you in the dark; I have my orders, and should my master wish to inform you, then so be it."

Mathis shot Emberscar a dissatisfied scowl.

Emberscar thought about ending the conversation there, but the nagging feeling that he owed Mathis at least some form of explanation got the better of him. In as soft a tone as he could manage given his deep, rumbling voice, he offered, "Mathis, please consider this – do you really want to know why I am here? We both know why you are here, and if you were to continue to seek knowledge of my mission in this land, there is the possibility that it would awaken memories you do not want to revisit. Think on this carefully."

Mathis nodded slowly at Emberscar, contemplation written plainly on his face.

"Now," added the drakuma, "get some sleep. I will watch over you two while you recuperate."

Mathis blinked and scoffed at the offer. "Sleep? Nothing but nightmares await me when I do. But," Mathis laughed sarcastically as he shook his head, "as I do need it more these days, I will accept your offer. Don't let me sleep more than a few hours. We have a long way to go and no mounts to speed us along thanks to your display. This will delay us dearly."

The giant red drakuma inclined his massive head in acknowledgment. "Indeed. Now – *sleeeeep*," he breathed the last and, with an uncanny connection to the currents of fir'gan he saw flowing about them, he reached out and gently nudged Mathis to sleep before weaving fir'gan about the two slumbering humans to provide them with a deep, restful slumber. "A small gift for you . . . though you probably don't deserve it," Emberscar said quietly.

For the first time in many years, Mathis slept a deep peaceful sleep unmarred by nightmares of a past that he kept trying to escape.


His eyes opened slowly, grit from a long and deep sleep filling his eyelashes and the corners of his dark eyes. As he blinked to clear his vision and generate moisture for his dry, angry-red eyes, he became aware of a pounding in his skull that was slowly growing in intensity. It took his body a moment to fully register the pain, but when it did, he winced and hissed before moaning loudly and pressing the heels of his hands into his eyes to try to counter the pain.

"Ah, he awakens," rumbled a deep voice.

For a moment, he thought it odd that he didn't recognize the voice, but then it came flooding back to him. Black eyes widening with realization, Amroth sat upright quickly, the cloak slipping from his naked torso. Immediately, his blurry vision settled on the enormous scaled form of Emberscar and he fell back with a groan, his head striking the ground painfully. "Damn it!" he cursed as waves of pain bounced around his skull. "I thought it was a dream," he muttered through clenched teeth.

"Afraid not, Amroth," quipped the familiar voice of Mathis. "It's all real . . . for better or worse."

Taking a deep breath, Amroth sat up slowly with his eyes closed. Though his head still throbbed, he opened his eyes to once again see Emberscar's massive bulk. This time, however, there was no shock to overwhelm him and, after rubbing his eyes to clear them of grit, he was able to take in the rest of his surroundings. Mathis was crouched on the opposite side of a roaring fire over which was skewered a large side of meat. It was raining lightly beyond the shelter of the overhang and, though the cloud cover made it difficult to tell what time it was, it appeared to be either early morning or evening.

Holding a hand to his head, he asked, "How long was I out?"

Mathis stood up, his black hair hanging loose about his face, and grabbed a dagger from his saddlebags before returning to the side of meat and, using the dagger's sheath as a brace, cut a small portion from the meat. He then came over to Amroth and handed him the skewered meat. "Eat up."

Amroth took the dagger, eyeing the meat skeptically. "What is it?"

"Human," interjected Emberscar in a dead-serious tone.

Amroth blanched and looked at Mathis, his eyes pleading with him for it to not be true.

"He's joking," Mathis said, mildly irritated with Ember's ill-timed humor. "It's boar. Ember was kind enough to catch it while we slept." He turned a stern glare on Emberscar. "Isn't that right?"

Ember laid his head down on his massive paws. "You take all the fun out of it," he said with a sigh, adding dejectedly, "Yes, it's a boar."

Amroth gave the meat one last skeptical glance before nibbling on it. His eyes lit up with relief as the familiar taste of the juicy meat melted in his mouth. He then took a bigger bite, wincing as the hot meat and juices burnt his tongue a bit.

Mathis patted him on the back. "Careful," he said as he returned to his side of the fire. "We don't need you injuring yourself any further."

"You didn't answer my question," Amroth stated around a mouthful of food.

Mathis smirked. "All-day . . . as was I, apparently."

Amroth swallowed the last bite and wiped the grease from his mouth. "That long, eh?"

"You both were in need of the rest," rumbled Emberscar.

Amroth raised a questioning eyebrow at Mathis. "I'm surprised you're not fuming at the further delay."

Standing up, Mathis went back over to the scavenged supplies and collected two tin plates before returning to the fire and retrieving the dagger from Amroth. "I was at first," he answered as he began filling the plates with meat, "but as it turns out, our friend here has offered to carry us as far as the forest edge; that will make up for some of the lost time. Personally, I think he just feels guilty for scaring off all the horses . . . that, or he simply wants them for a meal."

The last drew a deep-throated chuckle from Emberscar.

Careful of his aching skull, Amroth shook his head slowly in disbelief and gathered the fallen cloak about him. "Kale will be furious for the loss of your destrider, not to mention I'll never hear the end of it for losing mine."

Mathis chuckled. "Indeed – Slate was a good friend. As much as I'd like to take the time to hunt for them," he glared at Emberscar, "Ember's display probably still has them running scared."

Running a hand through his loose, damp black hair, Amroth asked, "I agree, but carrying us or not, doesn't that still put us behind?"

Emberscar eyed Amroth. "O' ye of little faith. I can have you both there before the moon reaches its peak," he rumbled dryly.

Amroth's eyebrows furrowed, drawing a knowing and amused smirk from Mathis as he stood up and passed one of the full plates to him. "I don't think he believes you, Ember," Mathis offered in amusement as he returned to his seat and began to eat.

"Well then," Ember rumbled, "I guess I'll just have to once again stun and amaze our perpetually awed friend. . . . Once the two of you have eaten your fill, of course."

As Amroth shook his head in disbelief, Mathis smirked knowingly and added, "Indeed you will."

As soon as they finished with their meal, Mathis went about organizing their supplies while Amroth got dressed. With their mounts now lost and their saddlebags useless, Mathis redistributed their supplies and personal effects into two large packs that he had found amongst their slain captors' belongings. While Amroth had slept, he had fashioned a makeshift strap for the wooden sword case that had been concealed beneath his bedroll. Amroth gave the case a curious glance as Mathis slung it on his back, but did not ask about it. He was as keen as Mathis to get moving again and idle conversation would only slow them down.

Once he was finished donning his now dry and considerably dirty clothes, Amroth stomped his feet securely into his boots and belted on his sword before moving to assist Mathis. However, he was waved off before he was handed a thick cloak and cowl. "What's this?" he asked as he took the garment from Mathis.

"I found them amongst the belongings that survived Ember's assault. They're oiled to keep out the rain. I figured they'd be of benefit to us, seeing as the rain shows no signs of letting up."

Amroth unfurled the cloak and swung it onto his back before securing it at the neck by its clasp. "A bit heavy. But if it keeps me dry for awhile, I'll be very grateful."

"Indeed," Mathis replied as he stood up and put on his own cloak. "The last thing I need is you getting sick on top of all your injuries. I don't want to have to carry you home like a sack of grain," he added as he picked up one of the packs and handed it to Amroth. Mathis then retrieved the remaining pack and shouldered it.

Amroth secured his pack on his back, wincing a bit as he adjusted to the added weight, before shifting his attention to Emberscar and eyeing the wicked red scales nervously. There was no remaining vestige of the slaughtered man who had leapt upon Ember's back, but that did little to quell just how deadly the scales looked. Pulling his hood up, he hesitantly asked, "I don't mean to sound ungrateful, but how are we suppose to ride on you back? I can't shake the image of what happened to that man that jumped on you, and – no offense – I don't want to be skewered or shredded while riding."

Ember gave him a sideways glance and retorted, "I had not thought about it until now, but you do look like you'd make a tasty–"

"Ember!" Mathis interjected as he slid his sheathed katana under his belt. Picking up two thick saddle blankets, he moved between Amroth and Ember. "Leave him alone. Deo knows he's been through a lot in the last two weeks! He doesn't need you making morbid jokes at his expense."

Sighing dejectedly, Ember rose up into a deep crouch and offered, "Very well, Mathis. I'll leave the boy alone. However, if you're going to spoil my fun, may I suggest we get moving? The weather smells like it will worsen soon."

"That's better," Mathis said firmly as he approached Ember's front-right elbow. "As for your question, Amroth – we ride him like this." With nimbleness Amroth didn't know he possessed, Mathis leapt onto Ember's bent elbow before springing to his back. He then positioned himself just behind Ember's massive shoulders before spreading the two saddle blankets over the space between the points on Emberscar's armored spine. Pointing to the blankets, Mathis added, "There's room enough between his spinal scales to sit, the edges of his scales make good footrests, and his mane makes an adequate set of reins." Seeing Amroth's hesitation, Mathis quickly seated himself to demonstrate that it was perfectly safe. "See, nothing to it."

Amroth approached Emberscar, skepticism still painted on his face. "I don't know, Mathis. It still seems–"

With an exasperated sigh, ember stood up suddenly, forcing Mathis to scramble to keep his seat and Amroth to scuttle backward. Before either man realized what was happening, Ember turned, reached out a large paw and plucked Amroth up by his cloak.

"What in Deo's name?!" Amroth managed to shout as he was lifted out into the rain and unceremoniously dropped onto Ember's back, right behind Mathis.

Amroth let out a string of curses as he latched on to Mathis, drawing an angry growl from his guardian. "What in all the holy hells do you think you're doing?!" Mathis roared at Ember as he regained his seating and shrugged Amroth off. "You could have killed him!"

"Humph!" Ember rumbled as he glanced back over his shoulder at his passengers. "But I didn't – now did I?"

Mathis cursed loudly before asking of Amroth, "Are you okay?"

Shaken from his sudden transition from ground to the scaled and powerful back, Amroth nodded. "I . . . I– Deo be good. . . . Why me?"

Mathis shook his head in mild amusement before pulling his cowl over his head. "Well, since you're so anxious to be on our way, Ember – what say you get moving?"

"Finally," Ember tossed at Mathis sarcastically.

Both men could feel the muscles under the scales tense and coil before Emberscar sprang forward with a swiftness that seemed impossible for a creature of his size. They clung tightly to Ember's mane as the giant red drakuma weaved in and out of the trees with agility that belied his massive bulk. It felt more like they were riding atop a sleek cat than an armored giant. For Amroth, the experience started out as just another terrifying event in the long line of misfortunes that had befallen him of late. As time sped by, however, he began to relax and soon found himself enjoying the ride. Exhilaration began to course through his veins and he suddenly found himself laughing despite the bitterly cold rain that pelted his face.

Mathis adjusted himself so he could see if Amroth was alright. When he saw nothing physically wrong, he shouted to be heard about the rain and wind, "Are you alright?!"

Grinning ear to ear and laughing beneath his cowl, Amroth nodded in the affirmative, his eyes bright with excitement. "I feel great!" he answered enthusiastically, drawing an amused smirk from Mathis.

As the hours seemed to melt away, the weather began to pick up and grew colder, turning the cold drops of rain into what felt like tiny, painful daggers of ice. With his joyful mood quickly dampened by the frigid downpour, Amroth pulled his cowl tighter and bent over as much as he could to keep the rain from pelting his exposed flesh. Mathis was quick to follow suit, and as the temperature dropped and the wind strengthened to a howling pitch, both men were grateful for the warmth of Emberscar beneath them. Suddenly, Ember slid to a jolting stop, slamming Amroth into Mathis' back, and drawing a grunt from both of them.

Mathis made sure Amroth was okay before turning his attention to Emberscar. The ember drakuma's head was held low as he sniffed at the air. He was emitting a low, menacing growl that immediately put Mathis on guard. "What is it?" he shouted over the strong wind, caution etched into each word despite the volume of his voice.

Emberscar didn't immediately respond as his glowing red eyes scanned the forest, seeing what neither of his passengers could see. Like the weather about them, the currents of fir'gan had been growing more chaotic and more violent over the last few hours. At first, it had appeared to be nothing more than the natural shift in the currents that occurred with a change in the weather. Now, however, he was sure something was off – it was as if the currents were fighting something that was trying to force them to act in an unnatural way. Emberscar examined the currents repeatedly, trying to make sense of what he was seeing. It infuriated him that he couldn't quite put a paw on what was bothering him about what he was seeing. He thought about mentioning the situation to Mathis, but then thought better of it. He didn't want to cause any unnecessary panic . . . and then there was Amroth to consider. . . .

"It's nothing," he finally offered, forcing himself to relax. "Thought I smelt another drakuma on the wind," he lied easily.

Mathis gave Emberscar a glare that clearly said he didn't believe him, but he let it go, knowing that Ember would tell him what was bothering him only when and if the drakuma wanted to.

Before anything more could be said, Ember took-off at a run. This time, he was forced to slow his pace as the frigid rain had become a deluge of icy daggers, the now violent wind driving the rain that made it through the barren forest canopy at sharp angles. Where the first few hours of the trip had passed by quickly, the next three were an agonizing gauntlet of cold and misery that seemed like it would last a lifetime. Both Mathis and Amroth found themselves hunched over as far as they could without losing their balance. Even Emberscar was beginning to find the going difficult. He found himself narrowing his eyes and ducking his head as low as safely possible to cut down on the icy droplets biting into his eyes. He even began to let out heated air from his mouth to try to melt some of the rain so he could maintain some semblance of a clear line of sight.

By the time Emberscar came to a stop within sight of the forest edge, the weather had managed to grow even worse. The wind had increased and the rain was now accompanied by thunder and illuminating lightning. "We're here," he barked over the torrent of rain and howling wind.

362

Mathis nodded an acknowledgment and, after Emberscar crouched down, scrambled down from the drakuma's back. Landing on the sodden ground, he then helped Amroth followed suit just in time to avoid being thrown off as Ember shook his body to dislodge the saddle blankets. Amroth started to retrieve the blankets, but a hand on his shoulder and a shake of Mathis' head told him to leave them be. Soaked to the bone despite their oiled cloaks, both men moved in front of Ember to say their good-byes.

"Amroth – go on ahead and see where we are. I'll be along in a moment."

Amroth looked from Mathis to Ember suspiciously before finally shouting over the wind, "Well, it's been a unique experience to say the least! Thank you for your help!"

"Do try to stay out of trouble. I can't be pulling your hide out of the fire all the time," Ember joked in response.

Amroth smiled in amusement before turning and sloshing through the muck toward the tree line.

Once Ember was sure Amroth was well out of earshot, he addressed Mathis, all humor gone from his tone. "You felt it?"

Mathis nodded slightly. "Only vaguely. I'm . . . not as attuned to things as you. This storm isn't natural, is it?"

"It's not," Ember growled. "Someone is manipulating it – and they are very skilled. I can find no trace of where they are."

Mathis' brow furrowed in frustration. "That isn't good. I don't like being left in the dark."

The drakuma snorted. "Nor I." Ember paused and stared at Mathis intensely, concern etched on his features. "You cannot keep running," he stated simply.

His features growing cold, Mathis replied, "Who said I was running from anything?"

"I am. The situation is growing worse by the day, and this storm is proof of how brazen our enemies have gotten."

Mathis arched an eyebrow. "Our? You're forgetting – I left that all behind."

Emberscar barked a sarcastic laugh. "Again – I know you better. But if you insist on persisting in the lie, so be it." He hesitated a moment, then added, "I sensed one of my scales on the boy."

"I founded it lodged in an ironwood," Mathis said as he nodded. "I thought it would motivate him to keep moving. Should I get rid of it?"

The drakuma studied Mathis carefully for a moment, his molten eyes coming to rest momentarily on the katana at Mathis' left hip, before declaring, "Keep it. It might not be as good as my ancestors, but it should do the job should . . ." he grunted, "*when* you need it." Before Mathis could offer another transparent denial, Ember added, "One more thing before I go – I have a feeling this storm was aimed at my master, and I think it would behoove you to find her."

Mathis' dark eyes widened in horror. "Damn it!" he chided himself. "I had forgotten that they were arriving today! Can you sense her presence?!"

Ember shook his massive head and stared into the distance. "Only vaguely. This storm is making the currents of fir'gan too chaotic to make any sense of it. She is close though. Possibly along the coast." Ember turned his glowing red eyes on Mathis, the intensity of his gaze telling Mathis that his next comments were to be taken serious. "Find her, Mathis. I will rejoin you when you are done in the city. If she dies from this assault, no matter your game with the boy – I will hold you personally responsible," he ended with a menacing growl.

Before Mathis could respond, Ember spun and vanished back into the woods, leaving a stunned Mathis, his brow suddenly heavy with memories long ignored, to digest the foreboding words.


It didn't take him long to shake off the shock from the threat Emberscar had leveled at him. The whole experience of meeting Ember had reopened old wounds, and he knew all too well that Ember did not make threats lightly – especially when it came to his master. Fighting down the emotions that the threat, as well as Ember's criticism of his choices over the years, had summoned up, he doubled checked the straps on his pack and sword case before moving off at a trot to catch up with Amroth. Even with the bad footing presented by the soaked ground, he quickly caught up to his charge.

Crouched down just outside the tree line, Amroth was doing his best to pierce the deep darkness of the cloud- and rain-filled night. "See anything?" Mathis asked, knowing full well what the answer would be.

Startled, Amroth jumped a little before looking up at Mathis. "Deo be good! Don't startle me like that! I'm jumpy enough as it is!"

Mathis put a reassuring hand on his shoulder and offered an apologetic smile. "I'm sorry. Didn't intend to frighten you."

"To answer your question," Amroth said as he stood up, "I can't see a blasted thing in this downpour. I can smell the sea from here, so we have to be close to the coast."

Mathis nodded in agreement. "You'd probably hear the waves breaking on the rocks if the tide was in and it wasn't storming like this."

Amroth adjusted his soaked cloak. "I don't like this, Mathis. I've never seen or heard of a storm like this late in the year."

*"You have no idea,"* Mathis thought to himself. Then he said to Amroth, "Come on, let's get out of this rain. The cliffside around here is dotted with caves. We should be able to find one and get out of this Deo-forsaken rain."

Amroth nodded in enthusiastic agreement before the two of them started out at a slow trot with Mathis in the lead.

Using the chaotic flashes of lightning to gather a semblance of an idea about their surroundings, Mathis guided them north by northeast. The going was slow and rough for the pair; already soaked to the bone, their anxiousness to find someplace dry was beginning to eat at their nerves and seemed to be making everything take longer. Eventually, with the smell of salt strong in the air, the cliff edge came into view out of the inky night. Mathis angled their path to bring them alongside the cliff edge at a safe distance, using it as a visual guide to help them hold to their path as they turned north. They followed the cliff line for nearly half an hour before Mathis called for a sudden halt as lightning flashed and he caught sight of what he'd been looking for the entire journey along the cliffside.

"What is it?" Amroth shouted above the wind.

Mathis simply motioned for Amroth to wait as he kept his vision fixed on the area of the cliff where he'd spotted what he was looking for, waiting for another flash of lightning to confirm what he saw. With as violent and chaotic as the weather was, it didn't take long for lightning to illuminate the sky once again, revealing their surroundings just long enough for Mathis to get a good look at the cliff edge. Nodding to himself, he said to Amroth, "Follow me," before moving off again.

Amroth rolled his eyes and sighed before following.

It wasn't obvious to Amroth until they were right on the cliff edge as to what Mathis had seen. Another bolt of lightning lit up the sky, and Amroth could see the start of a switchback path leading all the way down to the shore. As well, they could just make out the hard-packed, sandy coast nearly a hundred feet below. "We're going down there?" inquired Amroth.

Mathis nodded. "With the tide out, it's our best option. We'll be able to see any caves better from down there. Besides, the cliffside might cut down on some of the rain drenching us."

"Why didn't you say so?" Amroth joked. "Lead on!"

The switchback path was narrow and covered in mud and loose rubble, making footing extremely treacherous. They moved carefully and deliberately, keeping one hand on the cliff face at all times. Even with their precautions, the trip down the cliff wasn't without its fair share of scares. Amroth counted at least three times where he lost his footing or balance. Only Mathis' quick reactions kept him from going over the edge on one particularly nasty slip where he had not seen a fist-sized, slick rock. Stepping on it, Amroth had twisted his ankle and nearly went over the edge. Mathis had shot back an arm, catching him and forcing him back against the cliff face. With a deep, grateful sigh of relief, Amroth had nodded his thanks and motioned for Mathis to continue on.

After nearly an hour of the treacherous descent, they finally made it down the cliff and set foot on the wet and hard-packed sandy shore with prayers of thankfulness. Unfortunately for them, the lower elevation did nothing to stem the icy rain. In Amroth's opinion, their arrival on the beach had actually made things worse. The strong wind was now blowing bitter sea spray from the surf on them, soaking them from two directions. On top of that, the roar of the surf conspired with the howling wind and the rhythmic pitter-patter of rain to fill the air with so much noise that he thought he'd been cast into a hellish torture machine.

"What now?" he yelled over the noise, irritation creeping into his voice.

Mathis pointed up the coast and yelled back, "North! Keep a watch on the cliff face for any possible shelter! Nothing on the ground, though! I don't want to drown when the tide comes in!"

Amroth nodded in agreement as they started off, his twisted ankle barking at him.

Ten rain-soaked minutes later, Amroth caught sight of what appeared to be a small red glow roughly twenty feet up the cliff face. Not sure that he believed his eyes, he blinked a couple of times to clear his vision and checked the spot again. The red glow, faint as it was, was still there. Excited that there might be warmth and shelter ahead, he moved up alongside Mathis and tapped him on the shoulder before pointing toward the glow. "Up there! It looks like fire-light!"

Mathis followed Amroth's outstretched arm and quickly spotted the red glow. "Could be!" he offered. "Let's just be careful! Given our encounters in the forest, it could just as easily be a foe as a friend!" A quick glance at Amroth told him that he had not considered the possibility. "Don't worry," he added, trying to keep Amroth's spirits up, "we'll have the advantage in this Deo-awful weather! They won't be able to see us coming!"

Amroth grimaced as he tried to swallow Mathis' reassurance. "Lead on, then!" he offered hesitantly.

They moved off at a trot, but Amroth couldn't help but notice Mathis loosening his katana in its black-lacquered scabbard. He followed suit, suddenly wishing, for the first time, that he truly knew more about using a blade than making one.

Another fifty yards up the coast and all thoughts of whom the fire belonged to were erased from their minds. Smashed crates and barrels along with shredded rigging and sails appeared out of the night, scattered along the beach like a drunken dice throw.

Amroth's eyes widened in horror as a portion of a sundered hull suddenly appeared out of the darkness, rising up from the sand like a skeletal ribcage. "What in the hells–" he started to say, when he suddenly stumbled and fell face first onto a wet, spongy object sprawled in the sand.

Lightning flashed and Amroth found himself face-to-face with the wet, bloated and pale face of a dead man. Hair plastered to his face and one of his eyes missing, the corpse's mouth was frozen in a wide, horrific scream. Shouting in horror, Amroth scrambled off the corpse.

Mathis turned around at the shout to find Amroth on his rump at the feet of a bloated corpse. "Are you alright?" he asked when he saw how pale Amroth was.

Amroth shook his head. "What in the hells happened here?!"

Mathis immediately thought of Emberscar's warning and his jaw clenched. "Shipwreck. And a recent one," he offered to Amroth, keeping Ember's threat to himself. He could see that his charge was nearing his breaking point. He'd seen plenty of death while marching with the army, so a dead body shouldn't have affect him like this. The past week's events were taking a heavy toll on Amroth, and Mathis knew he needed to get him to dry shelter and rest before he cracked under the weight of it all.

"Come on!" he barked. "Just a bit further and we can be done with this wet hell!" He walked over to Amroth and offered him a hand. Accepting the offer, Mathis hauled Amroth to his feet and gave him a reassuring clap on the back. "Let's get going! That fire is looking better than two women waiting on you naked in bed!"

The lewd joke drew a weak grin from Amroth as they started off again. Weaving their way through the scattered wreckage and bodies, they crept closer to the firelight and further from the macabre scene. A few yards before they were directly under the light, Mathis came to a halt and carefully examined the cliff face, looking for a way up. It took only a moment for him to find the start of a path, about thirty paces to the north, that appeared to wind its way to the glowing entrance of a cave.

Smiling for Amroth's sake, he pointed to the path and said, "There we go! Only a short climb and then we can rest!"

Pale, hurting, and growing tired, Amroth smiled back weakly and motioned Mathis forward.

As soon as he turned away from Amroth, Mathis' face grew grim and his left hand immediately moved to his scabbard, just below the katana's collar. As he started forward, a quick push of his thumb loosened his blade for a quick draw if necessary. If they were to be greeted by an enemy, he wasn't about to be caught off guard again.

# Chapter Sixteen

*T*he darkness cloaking her mind slowly faded as her senses began to register her surroundings. The first thing she realized was that she was cold. It was almost a foreign sensation to her, and with as long as it had been since she had last truly felt it, it took her a moment to associate the sensation with the word. The next thing she noted was that there was a roaring in her ears. At first, she was worried that her hearing was damaged, but then she realized that it was a mixture of wind, roaring surf, and falling rain that was filling her ears. It then occurred to her that her skin felt oddly slick, and she realized that she was soaked to the bone. As her vision cleared, allowing her to see that her cheek rested on waterlogged sand, she suddenly realized she was having a hard time breathing. With that revelation, her diaphragm convulsed and she began to wretch up water; violent coughing and more water followed as her body expelled the foreign substance. With her lungs and stomach aching – but cleared of water – she drew in deep, ragged gasps of life-giving air between violent coughs, her throat and lungs burning as the bitterly cold air filled her.

Finally, the coughing faded and her breathing, while still heavy, calmed down enough for her to push herself to her feet. Everything seemed to be working right and, as she peered down through her soaked sky-blue hair at what remained of her soaked and shredded clothing, there were no signs of injuries. If she had been injured, the wounds had healed while she was incapacitated.

Annoyed with the hair that was plastered to her face, she moved the sand-crusted locks out of her vision so she could see better. To her chagrin, the darkness around her was deep enough to make it difficult for her bright-blue eyes to see anything except when the chaotic flashes of lightning lit up the shore. Irritated with the intermittent glimpses, she let her vision shift, allowing the currents to illuminate her surroundings, and was not surprised by what she saw.

What remained of the ship was scattered about the cliffside beach like a child's broken toy. Splintered masts and tattered sails jutted from the sand like skeletal fingers whose flesh had been flayed from them. Shredded ropes and shattered crates littered the sandy shore along with the broken bodies of dead sailors in an unapologetic display of nature's unbiased brutality. She took it in with a calm that came from years of having seen far worse. While she would have liked to take a moment to say a prayer for the dead, she found that the fog on her thoughts had lifted and her suspicions about the cause of the shipwreck returned.

Survival and defense suddenly a priority, her left hand went to her curved right hip and found only empty air. Panic blossoming in the pit of her stomach, she began to search the chaotic currents of fir'gan franticly. The power behind the deadly storm was making it difficult for her to read the currents clearly, and for one horrifying moment, she began to believe her sword had been lost at sea. However, to her profound relief, she finally caught sight of what she had feared lost. Just a few yards down the beach, the ethereal blue currents were flowing toward and pooling around a pile of shattered hull planks as if something was drawing the currents in.

With a relieved sigh, she reached out her left hand and noticed that the tanned skin of her arm was showing. A quick glance down revealed that the damage to her clothing was worse than she had first thought, as both the upper half of her shirt and the lower portion of her pants had been completely shredded, leaving her full breasts and powerful legs bare to the world. *"Great,"* she thought, *"first the ship is wrecked, and now I look like a strung-out and desperate prostitute."* Cursing, she tossed modesty aside and focused on her sword again.

Using the currents, she pushed and tugged on the pool of fir'gan at the same time. The wreckage was flung backward and her sheathed katana and tanto leapt into the air, racing toward her outstretched hand. She caught the bound-together blades deftly and quickly tucked them through her belt. She had no need to examine the sword for damage; everything she needed to know about the katana's condition had been conveyed to her through contact with the sheathed blade. While the tanto's condition wasn't as important to her, she was so confident in the craftsmanship of the dagger that she barely spared it a thought.

With her weapons safely at her hip, she focused on regaining control of the fir'gan flowing naturally through her. Focusing inward, she found the speck of light at the core of her being and grasped it, reestablishing control of her internal fir'gan. An extremely satisfied smile crossed her face as the currents flowed through her, soothing her sore throat and aching ribs. As the currents warded her body against the cold, she formed a thin barrier between her and the rain. In an instant, she was dry and warm again, returning a modicum of normality to her. Satisfied that she wouldn't freeze, she turned her attention to finding her companion.

"Mat!" Kara shouted into the howling wind. She could feel that he was near, but with the chaos holding sway over the currents of fir'gan, she could not pinpoint him. "Mat!" she shouted again as she began to weave her way through the wreckage. Movement out of the corner of her eye caught her attention and she looked to her right to see a large crab plucking an eyeball from a dead sailor's corpse. She shuddered in revulsion and continued on. "Mat!" she screamed again, apprehension destroying her normally soothing, beautiful voice. "Damn it! Where in the hells are you?!"

"Over here!" she barely heard over the roar of the wind and surf.

Before she could move another step, a figure appeared from around the corner of the shattered hull rearing up from the sand like a broken ribcage before her. "Mat?" she asked loudly.

The figure sagged against the broken hull and rested his head on his arm before she heard, "Yeah . . . it's me."

Kara sighed with relief as she approached him. Mat appeared to be in no better shape than she. His clothes were equally shredded and his dark hair clung to his ashen face. She could only presume that he'd been knocked unconscious like her and had been injured at some point. "Are you okay?" she asked as she stopped in front of him. She noted that the rain wasn't touching his body, but he hadn't bothered to dry himself off.

"Yeah," he answered weakly. "Was knocked out, and some-where along the line, my leg was broken. The pain is what woke me up." He shook his head. "Corith be good," he began to say in his smooth voice as he looked up from where he'd been resting his head, "I'd forgotten—" the words caught in his throat as his dark eyes were immediately drawn to Kara's breasts. "Damn it, Kara!" he shouted as he blushed in embarrassment. "Have some decency!" he barked as he turned away.

Kara smirked in amusement. "It's not like you haven't seen breasts before."

"I know, but. . . . Corith be good, woman! You're more like a mother to me!"

Amused by Mat's embarrassment, she laughed and teased, "Well then, little Mat, if the sight of my breasts is so embarrassing, do you mind finding me some clothing?"

Mat gestured behind him. "I managed to find our packs after my leg healed," he muttered tersely.

Chuckling to herself, Kara walked over to where he had pointed to and collected the sodden packs, relief swelling her heart that the valuable contents hadn't been lost. However, a seed of anxiety still resided in her stomach that would only be relieved after she'd had a chance to examine the contents.

Returning to Mat, she halted just behind him and suggested, "Why don't you find us some wood for a fire while I find us some shelter."

Mat pushed away from the shattered hull and appeared to nod. "Fine, fine. Anything, if it means you making yourself decent."

Patting him on the shoulder, she smirked as she walked by him, forcing him to spin away quickly to avoid gawking at her. Given how much of a womanizer Mat was, his unabashed embarrassment caused her slightly up-tilted blue eyes to twinkle with mirth. However, as much as she would have liked to continue to tease Mat and keep the mood light, shelter was of priority. With her senses growing clearer and her control over her fir'gan growing firmer, she was beginning to make some sense of the chaotic currents about her. While there was no way she'd be able to discern the situation beyond fifty yards or so, she was able to read enough about the flow of fir'gan to find a suitable cave not too far above the beach that was easily accessed via a path a few yards up the shore. With the currents illuminating her way, Kara nimbly climbed the path to find that the cave was more of a deep recess in the cliff face than an actually cave. She shrugged. Shelter was shelter no matter its definition.

Standing just inside the rain-soaked entryway of the cave, she let her vision shift back to normal before she held up her hand at chest level and gathered a ball of air in her palm. Igniting it, a bright orange ball of fire sprung to life, casting dancing shadows on the rugged walls of a cave that was only about thirty feet deep. Focusing her attention on the small ball of fire burning just above the palm of her hand, she fed it just enough air to keep it burning for a few minutes longer before tying off the currents that sustained it and hanging it in a small crevice in the wall. The small ball of flame would last long enough to allow Mat to find her without having to battle with the currents.

She had left Mat with orders to bring wood for a natural fire because she didn't want to risk making use of a fir'gan-fed fire that might alert whoever was using the storm to assault them. While a fir'gan-fed fire made very little use of the currents, such a constant draw might serve as a beacon for someone focused on finding them. Did they need the fire for survival? Not in the slightest, for their fir'gan would keep them warm and they could easily see by the current's ethereal light. But even after all the years of not having to worry about things like a fire, there was something comforting in the act that made it worth the effort in times like this.

Satisfied that the ball of flame would suffice, she moved to the back of the cave and placed the salt-encrusted leather packs on the ground before crouching over them and opening them up, eager to crush the anxiety in the pit of her stomach. It was instantly clear that the now saltwater-darkened leather had done little to keep the seawater out as everything inside was soaked. Ignoring the other contents for the moment, she immediately opened the extra pocket she'd stitched into the inner lining of her pack and let out an emphatic sigh of relief when she saw that the small, unadorned, opalescent bone coffer was still intact – which meant its contents were safe.

With relief swelling in her, she turned her attention to their other belongings. Their small food supply was ruined, and she suspected that their water was tainted as well. Grimacing with disappointment, she pulled her spare clothes from her pack and unfolded them. Her frown deepened as she saw that the garments were not only soaked, but heavy with gritty salt. Moving to the entrance of the cave, she held each piece of clothing out in the torrential downpour until it was thoroughly drenched before wringing each piece out in an attempt to remove as much of the salt as possible. She knew there was no way she'd be able to remove it all, which meant the clothes weren't going to be the most comfortable things to wear and might likely be ruined – but it was better than parading about practically naked.

Returning to the back of the cave, she spread her clothes out before retrieving a change of clothes for Mat and repeating the process for his garments. Once she had his clothes spread out on the ground next to her outfit, she quickly created a dome of fir'gan over the soaked garments, leaving just enough of a gap in the top of the dome for heat and moisture to escape, and began to slowly build up the temperature within the barrier. She'd performed this trick many times, so she was able to reach the proper temperature quickly. Steam began to rise from the clothing as the soaked-in moisture began to evaporate and escape through the hole she had left in the dome. Holding the temperature constant for another ten minutes, she did her best to remove as much moisture as possible. Then, with the light from her fireball fading, she dissipated the barrier and released the heat and steam left within. The clothes wouldn't be completely dry, but it was better than nothing.

Removing her boots and stripping off what remained of her garments, Kara bent over to gather up her partially cleaned and dried outfit. A sudden, loud clatter caused her to jump and spin around, any thought of her nudity fleeing her mind in favor of her survival instincts. To her amusement, she found Mat standing with his back turned, hands on his hips and head hung in embarrassment, the wood he had gathered strewn across the cave entrance.

"Damn it, Kara! Give a man some warning if you're going to be walking around bare-ass naked!" Mat barked in embarrassment.

Kara let out a lilting laugh before retorting playfully, "Well then – announce yourself and ask if a lady is descent before entering a room, silly."

Mat waved a dismissive hand over his shoulder. "Just put some clothes on so I can get out of this freezing rain, please," he pleaded with a hint of grumpiness.

Despite knowing the rain was having no effect on Mat, Kara quickly dressed, sliding on her smallclothes before deftly tossing on the rest of her outfit, tucking her long-sleeve black shirt into matching black pants. She then told Mat, "There. You can turn around without worrying about searing your eyes out."

He turned around to find her with her hands on her curved hips and a playful smile on her full lips. "Thank you," he answered with relief.

Nodding, Kara added, "I've done my best to dry out some clothes for you." She walked toward him and patted him on the shoulder as she went by. "Don't worry about me peeking – you don't have anything I'd want to look at anyways," she taunted.

Mat cursed to himself. Grumbling, he marched to the back of the shallow cave and began changing while Kara gathered up the assortment of driftwood he had collected. It only took moments for Mat to dress, allowing Kara to return to the back of the cave with the wood. She began to pile the wood in an orderly fashion even as Mat fidgeted, picking at the crotch and inside thighs of his pants.

"You could have done a better job getting the salt out, you know. This is going to chafe," he stated in an irritated and accusatory tone.

"Well, Mat," she answered as she finished stacking the wood and stood up, "you're welcome to try removing it yourself, or you can simply wander about naked. . . . Or," she smirked as Mat blushed and rolled his eyes, "a simple 'thank you' will suffice."

"Thank you," he grumbled.

Kara laughed at his discomfort before saying, "Now, how about we get warm?"

Reaching out with her fir'gan, she moved what remained of the ball of fire over the soaked wood and left it hovering there. She then constructed a dome of fir'gan over the pile, as she had with their clothing, before raising the temperature rapidly within the barrier. Steam began to pour out of the hole in the dome as the temperature continued to rise, sucking the moisture from the wood at a rapid pace. Once she was satisfied that the wood was dry enough to catch fire, she reversed the flow of air, forcing fuel for the flame into the dome before releasing the fir'gan holding the small flame in the air. The fireball dropped onto the dried wood and caught immediately. Fueled by the air she was forcing into the barrier, the flames grew rapidly until she released the dome over the wood. Air poured into the fire, feeding the eager flames, and the new blaze erupted with an angry burst of heat.

Mat eyed her sideways as she grabbed their boots and placed them next to the roaring blaze. "I envy your ability to do that."

Kara shrugged as she sat down next to the fire and manipulated the currents of fir'gan to carry the smoke from the fire out of the shelter. Relaxing her control, the fir'gan warming her faded and she let herself enjoy the natural warmth of the blazing fire. "You'll get to where you've got fine control of fir'gan eventually. Remember, I've got a few centuries on you. Besides that – fire *is* my Order's specialty."

Mat grunted as he crouched down opposite Kara. He didn't bother to relax his control on his fir'gan as Kara had, but he still reached out his hands to the blaze as if it would warm them. "Point taken," he conceded. His brow furrowed in frustration and confusion, the firelight playing along his damp black hair and drawing out its purple tinge. "Speaking of power – what in the hells happened out there? I've never felt anything like it."

Kara nodded slowly in contemplation. "It's been bothering me too, Mat. I haven't seen anything of that magnitude and scale in what seems like forever. To generate a storm like that and focus it on a small area with lethal intent takes power and control that is simply beyond me. I'm not even sure Darkon or Damion . . ." she snorted, "hells, any of the elder Wardens could do that! Then again, whoever conjured up this storm doesn't know if we're dead. Otherwise, the storm would have long since been released."

"I may not have been around as long as the rest of you, but that was simply horrifying! The power behind it all actually turned the wind into scythes! It made the ship seem like it was made out of flesh and the sailors made out of parchment!" He shook his head in disbelief. "I think I have a better understanding of why the stalemate has lasted all these centuries."

Smirking grimly, Kara said, "That's more or less it, Mat. What would be left to rule if we obliterated it all in a massive cataclysm? Even the Darkness' all consuming hunger wouldn't allow it to destroy its prize."

Mat laughed darkly as he leaned against the cave wall. Adjusting his swords for comfort, he leaned his head back and looked up at the ceiling. "I sometimes wonder what it is that you all dragged me into. Power, immortality, beasts and creatures from children's stories. . . . If the stakes in it all weren't so drastic, it would make an excellent children's bedtime tale."

"I think we've all wished that at some point," Kara replied with a halfhearted smile.

"Well, look on the bright side – if we accomplish our mission here, and with Darkon's leadership, we'll win this war," he stated with firm confidence.

She couldn't find the will to agree or argue with Mat's statement. She'd been around too long and seen too much to believe it was that simple. Besides, her confidence in Darkon's ability to lead had long since eroded away to the point where she had seriously considered following Damion's lead and simply walking away. After all, their numbers had dwindled and been fractured like never before under Darkon; and compared with their enemies, their ranks were full of young and virtually untested Wardens and Knights. At best, in Kara's mind, they were at an extreme disadvantage. Her convictions, though, held her in check. There were questions she wanted answered, and the millennia had taught her that if she were patient enough, everything would be revealed to her in time. More importantly, if she gave up the fight, then the Darkness would simply be one giant leap closer to complete control. She couldn't allow that . . . even if it meant stomaching Darkon's questionable leadership. Thus she stayed – although she had certainly grown bold enough to work her own angles without Darkon's knowledge.

Very little was said after that as the toll of the shipwreck and being tossed about in the ocean like a leaf in a tornado began to catch up with them. Mat quickly fell asleep and Kara soon felt her vision growing dull and her eyes heavy. Against her better judgment, she soon slipped into a deep, dreamless sleep. It seemed like she had been asleep for a lifetime when – exhausted or not – her finely tuned instincts alerted her to movement.

Bolting awake, she saw that the fire had only burned down about halfway and that Mat was scrambling to his feet. Reading the tension in his face, she asked as she stood up, "What is it?"

"Someone's coming," he answered quickly as he drew his swords.

Kara peered at the cave entrance, noting that there was no indication that the storm had let up, but saw nothing that would signify that someone was approaching. Quickly, she looked to the currents of fir'gan, figuring that was what had alerted Mat to someone's approach. Though subtle, there was a minor disturbance that was consistent with the approach of someone in-tune with fir'gan, and they were getting close. Unfortunately, with the storm wreaking havoc with the currents, it was impossible to tell who it was and how powerful they might be. Motioning Mat to the entrance of the cave – where he took up a position along the wall where he wouldn't be seen by an arrival – Kara put the fire between her and the shelter entrance before drawing her katana and crouching down. If the approaching person was hostile, the fire would at least disguise her person long enough for Mat or her to attack while the arrival's eyes adjusted to the firelight.

It seemed like it took a lifetime before they finally heard footsteps on the rocky path outside. Mat looked back at Kara and held up two fingers to indicate there were two people approaching. Kara nodded her understanding and placed her sword across her knees, ready to strike. A moment later, a lone hooded and cloaked figure appeared in the cave entrance. For a moment, everything seemed to move in slow motion for Kara as she caught a brief glimpse of the face within the hood. Before she could call for Mat to stay his hand, time sped up and Mat lashed out with one of his swords.

Mat blinked in astonishment when his sword stopped short of connecting with flesh, and the crisp, clear ring of steel on steel sung out. The new arrival had drawn his sword straight up with astonishing speed, intercepting the attack. Mat's sword now rested below the simple collar of an elegantly curved katana.

"Call you're man off, Kara. I'd hate for someone to get hurt over a misunderstanding," rumbled a male voice Kara was all too familiar with.

Eyes wide with surprise, Kara stood up quickly and gestured with her empty hand for Mat to stand down. "Stay your sword, Mat! This is a friend!"

Eyeing her hesitantly, Mat then looked at the new arrival suspiciously before removing his sword and allowing the newcomer to sheathe his katana. Sheathing both his blades slowly, he asked of Kara, "Are you sure about this?"

Smiling broad and bright, Kara sheathed her own katana to show her confidence in the situation. "I'm quite sure." She then motioned for the newcomer to come inside the cave. "Come in out of that rain. You already looked soaked enough as it is, Mathis."

Mat gawked at her and then Mathis. Before he could say anything, Mathis gestured to someone back down the path and a second person joined him.

"Our thanks, Kara," Mathis said. "Though, I must admit," he added as he and his companion entered the cave, "from the looks of the wreck on the shore, you two have had a much rougher time of it."

"You have no idea," Kara said with a shake of her head as Mathis and Amroth discarded their cloaks, depositing their packs and a large wooden case next to the sodden garments, and came closer to the fire.

Mathis looked exactly as she remembered him – tall, athletic, dark haired and stern eyed. He was every bit his former master's student in skill and attitude. His companion, while built like a hardworking laborer – and handsome in his own right – had the awed look of someone who was trying to cope with having his world turned upside down.

"Who's your friend?" she chimed with a hint of amusement. "He looks like his head should be spinning on his shoulders."

Mathis sat down, as did Amroth, both men extending their hands toward the warm fire. "My young friend here is Amroth Merandith, brother to Doms Kale Merandith."

Amroth blinked at Mathis, confused as to why he would so carelessly reveal his identity and relations.

"Ah. . . . If I recall correctly, that's the family you and your father before you served, yes?" Kara asked smoothly, quickly recalling Mathis' back-story.

Mathis nodded. "Indeed."

"So," Mat interjected sternly, as he came back to the fire and stood over the two, "you're the famed Mathis I've heard so much about."

Eying Mat coldly, Mathis then said to Kara, "Who is your petulant friend here?"

Mat bristled at the jab, but a stern, warning glare from Kara held him in check.

"This is Matteu Halluway, Mathis," she said.

Arching an eyebrow at Mat, Mathis said, "Halluway? Ah, yes. I remember attending your Induction. You've grown quite a bit, lad."

Mat didn't know how to respond to that, so he simply nodded and leaned against the cave wall.

Turning back to Kara, Mathis smiled apologetically and said, "Well, before I forget my manners. . . . Amroth – this blue-haired beauty is Kara Yokonagito. She is a very old and good friend of mine from Solarson."

Amroth nodded. "A– A pleasure," he stammered as he caught himself staring into her blue eyes. "Any friend of Mathis' is a friend of mine."

Kara' lilting laugh echoed through the cave, catching Amroth off guard. "Oh, he is a young one, isn't he, Mathis?" Flashing a charming smile at Amroth, she said, "Well then, young Amroth, the pleasure is mine."

Amroth nodded slowly, trying to find anything other than Kara to stare at as he felt like he was blushing furiously enough to burst into flames.

Her grin growing a bit at Amroth's awkward embarrassment, Kara turned her attention to Mathis and asked, "Tell me – have you taken him on as a student, or are you two simply gallivanting about the countryside?"

Mathis shook his head with a slight smile. "Afraid not. We were on our way to Haltho to meet you two before making our way home to Merset."

Kara arched an eyebrow. "Ah, that's right. It simply slipped my mind amongst all the chaos of the past couple of days. I guess it's simple luck that we survived the shipwreck and ran into you here."

His embarrassment fading away upon hearing the declaration, Amroth stared at Kara and then at Mat incredulously. "You were in that shipwreck?! You don't even look injured, much less wet!"

Kara smiled sweetly at Amroth. "We were lucky enough to escape uninjured and most of our supplies survived. So once we found shelter, we were able to dry off and change into dry clothes." She pointed at the tattered remains of their outfits lying off to the side. "If you have any doubts about our condition when we washed up on shore, what remains of those clothes tell the tale."

Amroth eyed the tattered remains and shook his head. "Wow. Just . . . wow."

Mathis looked up at Mat and gestured to the fire. "Sit down, lad. You're making me jumpy. There's nothing to fear here . . . unless conversation scares you."

Mat scoffed, walked over next to Kara, and crouched down. "I don't fear anyone in this room, old man," Mat stated firmly, his defensive tone belying his casual posture. "I just don't feel comfortable around people of your ilk."

Amroth's eyes nearly bulged out of their sockets at the statement. He'd never once heard anyone address Mathis in such a way, and could only imagine what must be going through his friend's mind. A quick glance told him everything he needed to know – there was an amused smirk on Mathis' face, but his eyes radiated the kind of cold that only seemed to be there when he was contemplating violence. Amroth ran a hand through his soaked hair, trying to put the pieces of the puzzle together. It was obvious that there was a history between the three others in the cave, but he couldn't begin to fathom what it was.

Before Mathis could retort, be it verbally or physically, Kara slapped Mat's leg admonishingly and chided in a disarming tone, "Manners, Mat. Mathis is a friend – and a loyal one at that. You would do well to remember that."

Mat shot Kara an angry glare before standing up suddenly, saying, "I'll stand watch." He then moved off to the front of the cave, his body tense with anger.

Kara gave Mathis and Amroth a warm, apologetic smile, but before she could say anything, Mathis held up a hand to forestall her. "No apologies needed. He's young, and I'm too old to fly off the handle at ever slight."

Kara gave a short, small laugh. "Typical Mathis. It truly is good to see you again!"

He nodded with a slight smile. "And you as well."

"So, what about your friend here? Amroth was it?" Kara asked smoothly as she turned her sparkling blue eyes on Amroth. "You've been awfully quiet this whole time."

Amroth was slow to respond, his breath catching in his throat as he met Kara's blue eyes again. There was no denying her beauty, and he was finding it hard not to think lustful thoughts about her. "I . . . um . . . well," he stammered, drawing a knowing smile from her that made his cheeks warm up. Clearing his throat in embarrassment, he started over. "I'm not sure what to say. I'm certainly out of my element amongst you three. Mathis is the only one I know. Without his assurances, I wouldn't be in this cave."

"Prudent, but I think if you were still in the rain you'd have melted by now," Kara offered jokingly, doing her best to disarm the tension she sensed in him.

Chuckling, Amroth replied, "Probably so. And I apologize for my silence. I'm better with a hammer and anvil than social situations."

Kara arched an eyebrow and asked of Mathis, "A blacksmith, eh? Did you teach him?"

Amroth nearly gawked at Mathis. "You're a blacksmith as well? What else aren't you telling me and Kale?"

Mathis shot Kara a sideways glance that carried a hint of admonishment before replying to Amroth, "Only as a hobby. It was never necessary to mention it, so I didn't. None of us parade our lives around as an open book. You as well as anyone should understand that."

"I guess you're right," Amroth conceded, scratching his head partly in disbelief and partly in puzzlement. "Well, what about you two – if you don't mind me asking? How do you know each other?"

"We served together on Solarson for a few years," Kara chimed in. "Mathis was so wet behind the ears, you wouldn't have recognized him," she said smoothly.

Amroth chuckled hesitantly. "I can't imagine that. I've only ever known him as the fighter he is today." He hesitated again. "If you don't mind me saying – you hardly look old enough to have served with him before he came to Triclose."

Kara laughed joyfully. "Oh my! Why thank you!" Eyeing Mat's back, she said playfully, "You could learn a thing or two from this one on how to address a lady, Mat." When all she got was a grunt in reply, she turned her attention back to Mathis and Amroth. "Ummmm. Tis' a shame you couldn't have known him then. Mathis was so soft and kind then. Now he's just a grumpy, ill-tempered grandpa."

Mathis grunted in amusement. "Ill-tempered? I didn't have to agree to meet with you. You know that? Right?"

Kara waved a dismissive hand as Amroth asked, "About that? Did Kale know you intended to meet with someone when you agreed to this little journey?"

Mathis turned a dry stare on him. "Seriously, Amroth — there's no need for all this suspicion. I know things have been rough on you the last week or so, but there's no need for you to start jumping at shadows. I would never do anything to put House Merandith in harm's way. But to answer your question — no, he didn't. I do have a personal life, and as long as it doesn't interfere with my duties to House Merandith, I see no harm in keeping them separate."

"I guess. But still . . ." Amroth added hesitantly.

Mathis sighed and gave him a friendly smile. "Look, I can guarantee you that Kale, Jerom, or any other person or friend you know doesn't tell you every little thing. On top of that, I can't imagine you're naive enough to be totally and completely honest with everyone . . . or yourself."

Amroth leaned backward as a contemplative look crawled its way across his face. Mathis was right — he was definitely rattled by recent events, and that was provoking suspicion where it wasn't warranted. Yet, with all that had happened, and in such a short time, he wasn't ready or willing to accept it as an excuse simply to ignore things.

Before the conversation could continue further, Mat looked their way and spoke up from his position at the cave entrance, "Something has been bothering me this whole time; I find it highly unlikely that you two would be traveling in a storm like this without a good reason, and I don't see meeting with us as an urgent enough matter to brave this weather. So, my question is — how did you find us?" he asked as his eyes narrowed suspiciously.

"I must admit," added Kara, "that I'm curious about that as well. Although, unlike my suspicious friend, I don't think there is anything malicious behind your intent."

"Come now, Kara," Mat protested, "just because he's a friend doesn't mean—"

"Oh, enough with your suspicions, Mat!" Kara barked in irritation. "Judging Mathis because of his former affiliations is as frustrating and silly as my arguments with Darkon — as you like to kindly point out."

"But," he started to protest again.

"No more!" Kara barked sternly, the glint in her eyes turning hard. "Like it or not, Mathis is a friend and is here to help. If you feel like you need to complain, then feel free to cry on Darkon's shoulder! I may irritate the hells out of him, but I'm still your superior and he trusts me!"

Amroth watched the exchange with unabashed befuddlement while Mathis' gaze remained on Kara. Mat's face became a glowering mask, and he looked like he might say something else. Instead, he turned his back on the gathering and stared out into the rain.

Kara sighed deeply and the sweet smile returned to her face. "I'm sorry about that. Now then, where was I? Oh yes – the issue of how you found us. As much as Mat's question might be fueled by suspicion, he still makes a valid point. I don't believe anyone would be out in this mess without a very urgent reason."

Mathis remained quiet for a moment, eyeing Kara and gauging his response carefully before answering, "A . . . mutual friend told me where you would be."

"Mutual friend?" Kara asked quizzically, appearing baffled by the cryptic response.

"Who in the world are you talking about?" asked Amroth. "We haven't encountered . . ." he trailed off as his eyes suddenly lit up with comprehension. Staring at Mathis in disbelief, Mathis responded with a warning look of his own, imploring him to keep his mouth shut; however, either Amroth didn't catch the meaning, or his head was spinning too much from recent events and the current conversation to retain any sense of self-restraint. Either way, he continued to speak. "Oh! You can't possibly mean that ember drakuma, can you?"

Mathis closed his eyes, mentally cursing Amroth's big mouth. He had no idea how Mat would react to such a statement, nor did he know if Kara was keeping Ember's presence on Triclose a secret.

However, Mathis' fears were averted somewhat when Kara started laughing. "Oh my! That might explain why your friend's head is spinning. He's never seen an ember, has he?"

Mathis shook his head. "Embers are . . . rare here – especially one like Emberscar. Most people believe them to simply be a child's tale. Our run-in with him was . . . interesting, to say the least."

Kara's ear-to-ear grin was wiped away as Mat once again interrupted, his voice thick with annoyance and a hint of disbelief, "You sent Emberscar to Triclose? When did this happen, and does–"

"Will you relax, Mat!" Kara implored, doing her best to fight back her growing anger with him. "None of us are so far under someone else's thumb that we can't follow our own goals."

Mat folded his arms across his chest and glared at Kara, hurt that she'd been keeping secrets from him. "And when were you going to tell me?"

Kara shrugged nonchalantly. "Soon enough, I suppose. It's a bit hard to keep such a remarkable beast hidden for long." Mat's look grew more dour, causing Kara to roll her eyes. "Come now, it's not like I was–" Her eyes slid away from Mat to the cave entrance as she felt an abrupt tug on the currents of fir'gan. Suddenly, the currents seem to release from their previous servitude and began to return to their natural flow. As she stood, the others turned to see what had caught her attention. "Did the storm just stop?" she asked to cover her sudden movements as she approached the cave entrance.

As she came up beside him, Mat turned, looked outside and blinked in surprise, both the currents' sudden return to normalcy and the cessation of the storm catching him unaware as well. "It appears so," he answered, following her lead. "I wonder when–" Catching an odd sight out of the corner of his eye, he turned his head and saw blood trickling from her nose. "Kara? Are you alright?" he asked, his voice thick with concern.

Growing pale, she looked at him in befuddlement and said, "I'm fine. Why do you ask?"

Mat placed a hand on her back and stated simply, "Your nose is bleeding."

Blinking in surprise at the words, Kara raised a hand to her nose before bringing it into her line of vision. Dark, viscous blood coated her forefinger, catching her by surprise. "That's odd," she stated weakly before her eyes rolled back in her head and she started to collapse.

Reacting quickly, Mat caught her even as Amroth and Mathis moved to help. "Get back!" he snarled. "I've got her," he added in a more gentle, but no-less stern tone. Scooping her up, he carried her over to the fire and gently laid her down. "Do either of you have a dry blanket?"

"Amroth – there's one in my pack! Get it quickly!" Mathis ordered.

"What's wrong with her?" Amroth asked as he hurriedly began rummaging through their supplies. Quickly finding a modestly dry blanket, he returned to the others.

"She fainted," Mat stated simply, deftly hiding the concern rising in his mind. "She must have hit her head while we were at sea, and all this conversation took its toll on her."

"Brain fog?" Amroth asked as he handed the blanket to Mat.

Mat shook his head as he took the blanket and spread it over Kara's prone form. "I doubt it," he answered truthfully, even as he shared a short but knowing glance with Mathis.

"Is there anything we can do for her?" Amroth asked, concern evident in his voice. Confused and troubled as he was, his helpful and caring nature was showing through.

Both Mat and Mathis knew there was little that could be done, so Mathis simply gave Amroth a reassuring smile and said, "She'll be fine. She just needs some rest. Speaking of which, why don't we all try and get some sleep."

"You two sleep, I'll keep an eye on Kara," Mat stated, his tone brokering no room for argument. Mathis gave him a suspicious glare, drawing an insulted look in return. "I may not have to like you or what you once stood for, Mathis, but you are a friend of Kara and that means no harm shall come to you – you have my word of honor on that," he stated with conviction.

"Very well then. I will hold you to that – and so will Kara," he replied just as firmly before he stood up. Motioning for Amroth to lead the way to the back of the cave, he told his charge, "Let's get some sleep."

"Are you sure?" Amroth asked, his eyes jumping between Mat and Mathis.

"I'm sure," Mathis reassured him. "There's nothing to worry about. Mat has our backs and Kara just needs some sleep."

Amroth nodded hesitantly before gathering their things and moving to the rear of the cave.

Mat watched as they settled in, doing his best to contain his fury. Young as he was, he hated being left out of the loop. And to be forced to share a shelter with one of Damion's former underlings left his stomach soured and twisted in knots. That, however, was not the worst of it all. What drove the dagger into his heart was not only that Kara had suddenly fallen ill – which was nearly impossible for a Warden – but that Kara was beginning to act in the same clandestine manner that Damion, Darius and Valisiana had acted before either withdrawing from the world or having their Order practically disbanded. He knew Kara's behavior wouldn't be tolerated by Darkon, yet Kara was a friend and he didn't want to see any harm befall her. He rolled his eyes mentally. Was this how she felt about Damion? For that matter, was he setting foot on a path of emotional conflict that could compromise him?

The minutes crawled by as Mat chewed on his thoughts and waited for his guests to fall asleep. When he was finally sure that they were deep asleep, he sat down in front of the fire and crossed his legs. Breathing deeply, he began to clear his mind. If Kara was truly beginning to go down the path of betrayal, then no matter how close of a friend she was, it could not be tolerated. The Orders must remain strong if they were to have any hope of defeating their enemies for good. Darkon was the pillar of strength and knowledge that would grant them victory – of that, he was certain. Luthur must have known this to be true as well; otherwise, why would he leave the fate of Kylir in Darkon's hands? First and foremost, his loyalty lay with Darkon and that meant keeping him informed of everything, no matter how minuscule . . . or even if it meant betraying the trust of a friend.

Though he believed Kara when she said that her communication with Darkon on the boat had given whoever had attacked them their general location, he believed there was no danger of that now. Whoever had sent the storm after them had vanished quickly, causing the storm to dissipate just as fast. So with little fear of giving their position away, Mat took one last deep breath, closed his eyes and let go of his conscious self, freeing his mind to soar along the currents of fir'gan in search of his master so that he could deliver the troubling and disturbing news.

*

Throughout the entirety of his journey north, there had been hints of the scent on the wind, but it had remained fleeting until Ember had entered the forest – and at that moment, he had known something was wrong. Even without the horrors he had seen in Southern Triclose or his species' deep attunement to fir'gan, the stench on the air was unmistakable. It didn't take the primal call stirred in his fiery blood to spur him to begin the hunt, he would have set upon the path out of simple obligation to his master and the forest – for such foulness was banal, and could not be tolerated.

While those that carried the foul scent hid their tracks well, they could do nothing to hide the smell. The chances were slim that they were aware of being carriers, which meant it was just as unlikely that they knew from where or whom they had picked it up. That didn't matter – those bearing the touch of Darkness had forfeited their right to live. While the carriers lived, however, the currents of fir'gan would continue to cry out in agony beneath the sway of the Darkness' unnatural will. Yes, the miasmic presence had to be eliminated. The lifeblood of every natural creature called for such action, and more importantly – balance demanded it.

386

So it was that through his deep connection to fir'gan, and thus the creatures and plants of the forest, Emberscar had stalked the carriers with lethal intent. The trees had whispered their agony to him as the very earth they occupied was despoiled, and the spirits of the forest creatures had wailed in terror as the tainted groups passed by. Emberscar had followed their trails and, one by one, the tainted humans had died in a cleansing blaze of viscous, fluidic fire. Yet, despite killing numerous groups, the taint had remained strong. It was then that it had occurred to him that something or someone far more powerful was lurking in the forest.

While tracking the strong malignant source, he had his chance encounter with Mathis and Amroth. Knowing that his old friend had, in all likelihood, no idea what was lurking in the forest, he had elected to break off his hunt in order to shadow his friend and make sure no harm came to him. That fortunate choice had resulted in his rescue of the two from another of the tainted groups. By offering to carry them through the forest, he was able to remove his friend from harm's way so that he could return to the hunt. During their hasty trip, the storm had unleashed its full strength and the resulting effect upon the currents had provided Ember with enough information for him to conclude that the strong malignant source and the power guiding the storm were one and the same. While that was certainly worthy of concern, what had truly worried Ember was that the storm had appeared to be aimed at his master. Such concerns had spurred him to be rid of his charges as quickly as he possibly could. As soon as he had left Mathis, he had immediately turned his attention to whoever or whatever was guiding the storm.

Picking up the scent, it led him north and west, luring him deeper into the forest. He moved with an urgency that he hadn't felt in a very long time, his strides chewing up the distance with the aid of the forest. Eager to be rid of the pestilence that lurked within its borders, and seeing the drakuma as a potential savior, it was as if the trees simply moved from Emberscar's path. There were no roots to trip him up nor low-hanging branches to claw at his face. The few animals that dared to brave the torrential storm vanished into whatever shelter they could find as soon as they sensed the vibrations of Ember's powerful strides upon the earth or scented the danger that was brewing in the air. He didn't know how far he traveled that night. Five miles? Ten miles? Twenty? It didn't matter to Ember. Despite the nausea he felt at the dark presence, his blood was afire with anticipation. Very few things in Kylir could challenge Ember's strength, but whomever or whatever was directing the storm possessed such strength. Not only would he be able to find out who or what was after his master and eliminate it, but he would be able to sate his appetite for a challenge worthy of his status. However, lacking the patience of his ancient ancestors, the caution that would normally give him an advantage on the hunt was washed away by his desire to end the threat. So with a low, throaty growl, he increased his pace, eager to put an end to the hunt.

He soon found himself racing alongside the Doren'thal River, the roar of the water drowned out by the wind and rain. It made sense that the source of the violent storm would choose the river to base the attack from. The river fed the ocean and there was an unobstructed view of the sky. While the direct contact with the elements being manipulated would make the monumental task of controlling them in this fashion somewhat easier, it did nothing to reduce how terrifyingly powerful one would have to be to accomplish the task on this scale. That realization broke through his hungry anticipation, allowing him to think clearly. With haste, he slowed his pace, cursing himself for his carelessness. He had drawn too close to the source of the storm to mask his presence, and would now need to rely on the swirling currents of fir'gan to hide his approach – which he had little confidence in, given the strength of the malignant source of power.

Suddenly, his senses cried out in warning and the darkness parted like a curtain at the start of a stage play, revealing a hooded and cloaked figure standing atop a large boulder in the center of the river. Fir'gan swirled about the figure in a violent and unpredictable pool of raw power. Skidding to a halt with a spray of water, Ember was immediately on guard as he realized that, despite the massive amount of fir'gan the person was wielding, the person's sickly red aura had yet to become visible to the naked eye. However, the aura that Ember's fir'gan-sensitive eyes could already see was all that he needed to recognize who stood before him.

Crouching low, his broad, powerful face contorted into a vicious snarl. "You!" he hissed in a low, violent timber.

Without moving, the figure replied in a raspy male voice that seemed to echo in upon itself, "Ah, Ember – I was wondering when you would show yourself. You've been making quite a nuisance of yourself lately from what I've been told."

Ember could hear the smug, superior smile in the tone and it grated on his nerves. "I don't know what you're talking about, Shadowspawn," he responded with mock ignorance. "I was simply seeing the sights of this land, when you're sickening aura ruined the day."

The figure finally moved, turning to face Ember while clapping his hands slowly and mockingly. "Ah, you poor beast – all the haughty arrogance of your ancestors with none of the bite," he teased.

Grinning devilishly, Emberscar taunted, "Care to try me, Shadowspawn? I'm sure I can change your mind about that."

"As much pleasure as it would give me to eliminate your filth from Kylir, I'm afraid my *master,"* he seemed to spit the word out like poison, "would have it otherwise. You see, he wants your friends to know what's coming. He wants them to stare into the abyss and know that there is no escape this time."

That statement drew a throaty chuckle from Ember. Those sentiments were simply beyond the grasp of the Darkness, which meant that, for better or worse, someone now controlled the man before him – and that, Ember knew, had to grate on the man's nerves. "*Your* master, Garith? My how the mighty have fallen if you now answer to a pathetic mortal instead of your almighty Darkness," Ember spit. "What happened? Did you fail in an ass-kissing contest?"

Though Garith's face was obscured by the shadows of his hood, Ember knew his barb had hit home as Garith's fir'gan began to lash out chaotically. "You push your luck, beast!" Garith hissed.

"Do I?" goaded Ember. "All I see before me is the ass-kisser of an ass-kisser." Ember sighed and tossed in offhandedly, "I really don't see how you ever managed to kill Luthur. He had to have tripped and fallen on his own crusader."

"Do not mock me!" Garith roared before lashing out with a wave of fir'gan.

Grinning at Garith's reaction to the prodding, Ember easily saw the attack forming and, in a demonstration his own power, expertly reached out along the chaotic currents and pulled a barrier of earth from the riverbed to intercept the blast. The wave slammed into the barrier and shattered it, quickly expending its energy and showering the area in muddy soil.

"Come now, Garith, that cannot be the best you can manage. Hatchlings can manage more from a sneeze," Ember goaded mockingly.

Garith's fists clenched as he fought to control his rising anger. Numerous indignities had been rained upon him in the years since Luthur's death, and as a result, his temper had grown shorter than usual. In spite of this flaw, he managed to hold on to his composure as he hissed through clenched teeth, "Mark my words, beast – you will die soon! If not by my hand, then by someone else's! Until then, I have prepared a gift for you per my master's request." He noticed Ember's fiery eyes narrow in suspicion, which brought a grin to his face. "Oh yes, Ember, we knew you were skulking around in the South. And I bet you think you know what you saw." Garith took a step back, pulled a small disk with a blue crystal set in the center of it from his belt and tossed it hard on the boulder.

The currents of fir'gan began to twist and turn as a blue line slashed through the air and spiraled open into a portal that throbbed with blue energy. At the same time, the shoreline to both sides of Ember began to fill with blackhearts as they flooded from the dark woods, their sickening skin and twisted bodies making a mockery of their progenitors. It was then that two things struck Ember – the raiders had carried the scent to disguise the presence of the black-hearts, and something more sinister was approaching.

Garith saw those realizations register on Ember's face and he let out a cackling, maniacal laugh. "As I said – my master *wants* you to know what is coming." Then, with a mocking half-bow, he added, "I leave you with this parting gift. If you survive, I'll just have to kill you later. If not . . ." he shrugged nonchalantly before stepping through the portal.

As soon as Garith vanished, the portal closed with a resounding bang. With the orchestrator of the storm now gone, it began to dissipate. The currents of fir'gan, however, remained just as chaotic as the center of the disruptive force shifted to the massive form that lumbered from the shadows beyond the boulder. Rolling waves of a dark miasma heralded the beast's approach, covering the river in darkness and filling the air with the stench of death and decay. Horrified, Emberscar felt like he was staring into a twisted, macabre mirror. Though a head taller than Ember, the beast was his match in physical bulk and size. Beyond that, the features were twisted. Where Ember was a fiery red, this drakuma was the color of a moonless night, its scales glistened sickly in what little light there was. A mass of writhing tentacles composed a mane that flowed down to the four thick, barbed tails thrashing about behind the beast. Thick, milky saliva dripped from the maw of its mass head, sizzling as it hit the water, while eyes the color of cloudy milk glared at him from the shadows of its sunken sockets, their depths devoid of any sign of intelligence beyond that of a cold-blooded, bestial killer.

Emberscar took a hesitant step backward, mortified at what stood before him. Every instinct and grain of knowledge screamed at him that such an abomination could not exist. Yet his eyes, sense of smell and the chaotic currents of fir'gan told him otherwise. Despite his many years and vast experience, Ember was frozen with shock and horrified awe. He knew he had to act quickly if he wanted to survive, but he simply could not shake the mind-numbing terror that the dark beast inspired. Suddenly, his flanks bristled with pain and a sickening warmth began to spread throughout his body as a swarm of arrows, tainted with blackheart blood, cracked through his armored scales like they were made of thin parchment. The pain and spreading poison brought him to his senses even as his own fiery blood fought to counteract the dark miasma that was flowing through his veins. The situation was very real – and he was dangerously vulnerable if he didn't act fast.

Shaken from his stupor by the pain, he quickly assessed his situation and found that each riverbank was occupied by roughly sixty blackhearts raining tainted arrows on him; more importantly, the miasma cloud from the corrupted drakuma was already swirling around his legs as the beast drew closer. With his flanks quickly beginning to look like a pine-ferret, Ember let out a loud, echoing roar and violently ripped at the currents of fir'gan, forcing the riverbanks to erupt in an army of earthen spikes. Impaled blackhearts rose twenty feet in the air only to slide down the earthen barbs, their high-pitched screams of agony filling the air. Of those that managed to avoid being impaled, many were flung skyward only to land with a sickening thud or watery splash.

As the earth erupted and the carnage rained down, the dark drakuma used the slaughter as cover to pounce upon Emberscar, driving him to the riverbed and immersing his head in the water. Ember strained against the massive weight, battling to break the surface and draw in precious air. Before he could make any progress, enormous pressure built up on his neck and he felt the armored scales crack as the drakuma bit down hard. Ember's eyes and his maw opened wide in agony as sharp fangs crunched through his scales and pierced his vulnerable flesh. Crimson, fiery blood spilt forth from the ghastly wounds, sending a cloud of steam into the air and blanketing the surface of the water with dancing flames. As he felt waves of the dark miasma entering his blood through the dark beast's bite, Ember's struggles turned vehement and panic gripped his heart and mind. Thrashing about wildly, he could feel the fangs sink deeper as water began to fill his lungs.

Time seemed to slow to a crawl as Ember's vision darken and his struggles weakened. He couldn't breathe and the drakuma's fangs were sinking closer to his spine and throat. His fiery blood was doing its best to resist the poison flowing into his body, but he could feel death was fast approaching; horrifyingly, he was suddenly tempted to simply let go and embrace it.

*"No!"* he berated himself. *"Not this way! Not now! I have to warn them!"*

Mustering the last of his strength, he managed to gather a burst of air underneath him before blasting it downward while surging upward at the same time. The two drakumas shot into the air, water, blood and small flames spilling off Ember in a chaotic waterfall. Aware of the pain that was to come, Ember twisted his body in the air with feline dexterity and planted his hind paws on the dark drakuma before shoving with all his might. Horrific pain radiated from his neck as scales and flesh were torn from his body by the dark drakuma as it was dislodged and sent flying through the air. Both enormous beasts crashed to the ground violently. As Ember tumbled through the river, steam and gouts of fire erupted from where the blood flowing unhindered from the gaping wound on his neck made contact with the water. Skidding to a stop, he slowly stood up and coughed violently to expel the water and blood in his lungs. Even through the fog of pain, he knew he needed to do something fast, for he could feel the flesh and scales around the vicious bite quickly turning necrotic and slowly sloughing off as the virulent poison fought his draconic blood for dominance of his body. There was no doubt in his mind that the longer this fight took, the slimmer his chances to survive became.

Thankfully, he was quickly able to draw in much-needed air and his swimming vision settled on his opponent. The dark drakuma was already extracting itself from the rubble where it had crashed into the earthen spikes on the far shore. Crushed blackheart bodies littered the ground and one body hung limply from the spiked ends of the scales on the drakuma's back. If it hadn't been for the loss of blood, Ember would have laughed at the absurd scene. As it was, it was taking everything he had to stay upright.

A commotion from behind drew his attention and he twisted around to see five blackhearts that had treaded into the river at a shallow point to get behind him. Even as they raised their twisted bows to launch a barrage at him, Ember's instincts cried out and he swung back around to see that the dark drakuma had drawn close, its four barbed tails darting toward him. Springing to the left, the tails sailed harmlessly past Ember and impaled the blackhearts, killing them instantly.

The drakuma roared in disappointment and withdrew its tails before leaping toward Ember, intent on pinning him again. Able to see the attack coming this time, Ember rolled to his back, pain lance through him as rocks and soil were driven into the gaping wound in the back of his neck, and caught the weight of the leaping beast on all four of his massive and strong paws. Coiled muscles gave the dark drakuma a powerful shove, propelling the beast over Ember and sending it crashing into the river. Ember climbed to his feet, his whole body shaking as his strength continued to wane. A quick sweep with his tails sent three blackhearts that had snuck up behind him flying, their torsos crushed.

For once, the miasma-spewing drakuma appeared to be stunned. Unfortunately for Ember, he was too weak to try to use the advantage to escape, which left him with a simple choice – kill or be killed. Not the choice or odds he would have liked given his current condition, but it was all he had. Off balance and drained, Ember started forward, knowing that he had to end the fight now if he wanted any shot at surviving.

By that point, the drakuma had recovered and turned to face Ember. Though shaken, the beast still appeared in possession of all its faculties and its milky eyes seemed to glow with violent and malicious intent. Through his blurry vision, Ember watched the beast's chest expand as it started to inhale the miasmic cloud flowing about it. Alarmed, Ember realized what was happening and used the last of his strength to leap forward and clamp his powerful jaws down on the drakuma's maw, pinning it shut and trapping the blast that was building in the beast's chest. If Ember could have grinned at that moment, he would have. Instead, the pain and rage in his molten eyes told the story.

He had the drakuma where he wanted it.

Even as the shadow-spawned beast struggled with all its might, Ember maintained his grip, even going so far as to bash the beast alongside the head to stun it and buy some time. Inhaling as much air through his nose and obstructed mouth as possible, Ember reached out along the currents of fir'gan and enveloped himself and the dark drakuma in a cocoon of pure, rich air. Glowing brightly, the red splotches on his horns served as the only warning before he released his attack. Fluidic flames erupted from Ember's maw, spilling to the sides and back into his face. The thick, viscous flames filled the cocoon of air and quickly enveloped the two drakumas before detonating in a massive explosion. His face and upper body charred, Ember soared unceremoniously through the air only to land with a sickening thudded on the riverbank nearly two hundred paces downstream.

As for the shadow-spawned drakuma – little remained of its carcass. Both riverbanks were beset by a macabre display of brightly burning candles made of bits and pieces of sundered flesh. As for what was left of the demolished carcass, it remained in the river, crimson and black flames warring along its charred facade in a hauntingly poignant dance.

Lying prone on the riverbank, Ember could just make out the scene through his blurred vision. He couldn't help but think, as he slipped into oblivion's embrace, that the dancing flames were an omen of darker things to come.

# Chapter Seventeen

*S*lowly sleep's heavy grip peeled back from Kara's mind, allowing her to climb back to consciousness. Her heavy, swollen eyes crept open painfully to reveal a blurry gray world. She blinked a few times in an attempt to clear her vision and generate moisture for her dry eyes even as the rest of her senses slowly began to register the world around her. She was immediately aware of how damp her dark clothes were, the moisture in the air having saturated her attire throughout the night. The moist air filling her lungs and clinging to her throat carried with it the smell and taste of sea salt, which brought her around fully. With her grogginess banished, she realized that after numerous attempts to clear her vision, the cave was filled with gray fog. It then dawned on her that her head was throbbing and her body aching from sleeping on the floor, the dull, painful aches eliciting a groan of discomfort from her as her nerves screamed in protest.

"Good morning," came the warm greeting, making her wince as the noise broke the thick blanket of silence that had insulated her.

Kara sat up slowly, the blanket covering her – wet and heavy from the damp fog – falling away from her. She peered through the murkiness toward the cave entrance to see Amroth, his black hair pulled back in a horsetail, leaning against the cave entrance and looking her direction with a warm smile shining in his dark eyes and on his face. She could barely make out his simple attire in the gray shroud of fog, though it appeared to be the same from the night before.

"Morning to you as well," she managed with a slight smile of her own. She rubbed her eyes to clear them before holding a hand to her brow as her head continued to ache. Cursing to herself, she began to work on regaining her grip on her fir'gan while offering idly to Amroth, "What's with all the fog . . . Amroth, wasn't it?"

"That it is," he responded with a chuckle as he walked back and crouched down beside her. "The fog rolled in soon after the storm stopped last night. Speaking of which – are you okay? Your friend said you'd been struck in the head when your ship was wrecked and that was probably why you passed out last night."

*"Corith be good! My head hurts,"* she thought to herself before chiding, *"Get it together, Kara! Breathe, relax, regain control and it will all go away."* She then replied to Amroth, "I'll be fine. Just give me a moment."

Closing her eyes, she took a deep breath and let it out slowly before turning her concentration inward, searching for that spark of fir'gan that was so precious to them all. She found it with practiced ease and suddenly felt the warmth and exhilaration that accompanied fir'gan flooding into her. The currents coursed through every fiber of her body, banishing her headache, and alleviating the aches and pains. When she opened her sky-blue eyes, the remaining blurriness was gone and she could clearly see the currents of fir'gan flowing like ribbons of blue mist all around her. She smiled with relief and quipped, "See? All better."

Amroth gave her a skeptical look accompanied by a wry smile. "If you say so. Are you hungry? There's not a whole lot, but it's something."

With her senses fully alert, the mention of food stirred her belly. "Now that you mention it – I'm starving."

Standing up, he offered happily, "Well then, let me see what I can dig up."

Kara nodded her appreciation as he moved to their collective gear and began rummaging around. Taking the moment of freedom to stand up, she made her way to the shelter's entrance and peered out into the gray morning while stretching her muscles out. The fog was thicker than she had thought, making it next to impossible to make out much of anything. She could just make out the edge of the path leading up to their shelter, but other than that, the sound of the ocean was the only other indicator of what out there. The currents of fir'gan, however, gave her a slightly better picture of her situation. She was by no means the best at reading the currents, but she was able to get a general feel for things – the currents told her how high up she was, that it was sunny beyond her foggy shelter, and that the tide was slowly making its way in.

She was about to extend her senses further to investigate why she had passed out and to alleviate the fear that was trying to take root in the pit of her stomach, when a gentle touch on her shoulder interrupted her thoughts. Kara turned around to find Amroth smiling at her softly, three hard ration biscuits and a half-full waterskin in his proffered hands. Pushing her damp blue hair out of her face, she accepted them with a nod, adding, "Thank you."

He moved up beside her with a somewhat sheepish look on his face. "It's certainly not the way we like to feed guests, but I'm afraid it's all that managed to survive that hells-spawned storm."

"It's okay," she replied as she took a bite of the hard and bland biscuit. "I've had much worse. I'll take hard biscuits over meat with questionable origins any day."

He chuckled and shook his head. "I've heard a few soldiers say something along the same lines, and others that would beg to differ."

"What about you?" Kara asked with an arched eyebrow, then took another bite.

"Biscuits, without a doubt. Besides, I was always raised not to argue with a lady when it comes to delicacies."

Kara almost choked on her food as she fought to stop from laughing. Amroth blushed in embarrassment as she coughed a few times to clear her throat and then took a swig of the waterskin. "Oh dear," she said in a slightly hoarse tone once her throat was clear, "I don't think I've had that title applied to me in a very long time. There aren't many that would consider a fighting woman qualified for such a designation; but I thank you for the compliment, nonetheless."

An awkward silence fell on the cave after that, as thick and as heavy as the fog that filled the air. Amroth meandered to the other side of the cave entrance where he stood, arms crossed, and did his best not to look at or say anything to her for fear of further embarrassment. Kara, to her credit, restrained herself from taking advantage of the obvious opening Amroth's awkwardness had provided to tease him. Instead, she finished her biscuits in silence before taking a last drink from the skin. She stood idly by for a moment longer, then turned to face him. Arms folded beneath her breasts, she leaned her back against the cave wall and took the moment to assess her current company.

She had to admit that, despite providing awkward conversation, he was at least something pleasing to look at. Modest of height and broad at the shoulders, he had a boyish charm and handsomeness about him that was only slightly tarnished by a few days growth of a scruffy beard and travel-stained clothes. There was an air of shaky confidence about him that she'd seen in others before. Most of the time, they could be as timid as a fledgling bird on its first flight, but when they did decide something was worth standing up for, they would fight for it with all their might. Character quirks aside, he had manners and, as she caught herself staring at his butt, he had a physical appeal that was stirring thoughts in her that she'd rather not entertain at that moment.

Suddenly embarrassed, she searched quickly for something to say to keep her mind from chasing down the carnal thoughts that were racing through her head. "Sooo," she started to ask, "where are Mat and Mathis?"

Startled by her sudden words, Amroth gave her a surprised look before replying, "Those two? They took-off a few hours ago. Mathis wanted to get a better look at where we are, now that its day and the storm has passed. He thought it would be prudent to have an extra sword along in case of trouble." Amroth chuckled knowingly. "I can't say that I blame him."

Puzzled, Kara asked, "Wait a moment – you're Mathis' charge aren't you?" He nodded in confirmation, prompting her to continue in a skeptical tone, "That doesn't sound like the Mathis I know. Leaving you here with an unconscious woman in an area he deems dangerous enough to warrant someone watching his back just seems . . ." she shrugged, "sloppy and foolish of him."

Grimacing, Amroth replied, "Not really." He shifted uncomfortably, fingering the sword at his hip hesitantly before continuing. "You see – I'm not much of a fighter. In fact, you might say that I'm," he gave a self-deprecating chuckle, "quite the pacifist."

"A pacifist? An ambitious and noble path to walk. Though I must say, you don't wear that sword like someone that is totally unfamiliar with its use . . . or its purpose."

He grimaced again. "Learning to use a sword is kind of a requirement for any boy growing up on Triclose, plus that kind of knowledge makes for better swordsmithing. However," he added firmly, "I've never once drawn it for any reason other than to clean it. It might as well be ceremonial."

Smiling with gentle and pleased amusement, Kara offered, "Unabashed honesty. You're just full of admirable qualities. The number of people I've met with those kinds of aspirations are few and far between." She hesitated a moment before giving Amroth a small, warm and disarming smile, saying reverently, "If you don't mind a bit of friendly advice – I once knew a great man who held to values such as yours. He was a loving and caring man whose beliefs served him well for most of his life, but he came to learn that as noble as his values were, they could do little to protect himself and – more importantly – those that he loved and cared for. He came to learn skill with a sword doesn't necessarily mean meting out death and destruction. When he accepted that drawing one's blade in defense of the people one cares for was as noble as striving for a life and world without violence, he went from being a noble man to being a great man." Kara chuckled gently, and a sad smile crept onto her face as she looked back out into the fog, "I never once saw him draw his sword in anger."

398

Amroth could see the reverence Kara held for the man in her bright-blue eyes, as well as the deep sadness that accompanied her statement. Though the words had struck a resonating cord with him – which he took fully to heart given what the last week had been like for him – and his curiosity was perked, he avoided digging deeper and simply said, "He sounds like a great man."

Kara glanced at him and smiled softly before returning her vision to the fog, saying nothing. Amroth didn't need his time at court to see that a turmoil of emotions held sway over Kara at the moment. Feeling somewhat awkward and unsure of what he could say that would draw Kara from her emotionally driven reflections, he chose simply to remain silent. As a result, an uncomfortable and somewhat awkward silence enveloped them that dragged on for a long, agonizing moment.

When it seemed like the silence would drag on forever – and feeling like a change of subject was needed – Amroth worked up the courage to hesitantly ask, "What about you, Kara? You're from Velusyia, correct?"

"Humm? What was that?" Kara replied, startled from her reflections.

"I asked if you're from Velusyia."

"Oh. Originally, yes," she answered with a slight nod and an amused smile. "The hair and eyes gave it away, right?" she asked rhetorically.

The question drew a chuckle from Amroth. "You have to admit, the blue hair is quite the distinguishing mark."

Kara shrugged. "No more distinguishing than the orange of the desert tribes of Solarson or the green that pervades the forest dwellers around Kylir, but I understand what you mean. Velusyians aren't the most common of sights. I take it you've never met many?"

Amroth shrugged. "More than most. The coastal cities see plenty of traders and merchants, as their wine and steel is highly valued amongst both noble and commoner. But," he pointed to Kara's sword, which rested along the cave wall, "you're one of the few I've seen carrying a sword."

Kara smirked. "Lovers not fighters, right?"

"So I've been told. Children of the Sky, favored of the Gods. ... Or so the stories say. Blessed with hair and eyes the color of the sky, bringing a piece of the heavens to the darkness of Kylir."

Kara laughed at the old fables. "Oh aye, I remember the stories. The priests would hammer them into our heads to remind us of why we are who we are, and why we do not fight." She looked thoughtful for a moment as she recalled the long-faded memories of childhood. "Betrayed by those closest to our hearts, shadows and darkness were welcomed into the land and the bosom of the Light, forever stripping those that had committed the ultimate sin of the Sky's gift to us. Hair and eyes cast into darkness, those that betrayed the gods' love were cast into a sea of tears. Shalusyian they were called – Children of the Shadow Sky."

She laughed offhandedly as Amroth stared at her, enthralled by the imagery of the fable. "Quite the story – though I doubt the Shalusyian appreciate it. There's little doubt our races are related, though I cannot say why our hair and eyes are blue and theirs the color of black silk." She shrugged nonchalantly and came out of her reflection. "As for the rest of your description, it fits us for the most part. We do have our fair share of fighters and even a small army and navy, but as a culture, Velusyians have made it a goal to pursue more . . . benign habits. Art, poetry, theatre, business, diplomacy – these are the things all Velusyians are taught from birth. For some of us, though, it just doesn't fit." She smiled softly. "I respect that lifestyle, and sometimes even catch myself missing it. But it was never for me. So I left at a very young age and spent my youth traveling. Eventually, I found that I could handle a sword."

Amroth stared at her with curiosity painted across his face. "Spent your youth? You hardly look a day over twenty-five! Just how old are you?" he asked, seemingly oblivious that he'd commented on the topic from the previous night.

Kara let out a lilting laugh. "Oh my – I thought you were raised better than to ask a lady her age?"

Flustered and flush with embarrassment, Amroth could find nothing to say.

Unable to miss his discomfort, Kara smiled disarmingly and waved a dismissive hand. "Don't fret on it. I'm old enough and wise enough not to let an innocent question bother me. Besides, Velusyians tend to look younger than we are. I'll just take your statement as a lovely compliment. How does that sound?"

Scratching the back of his head, he shook it in befuddled amusement and said, "That sounds good to me."

"Good. Then where was I? Oh – Velusyia. One thing I simply don't miss is the way women were treated. They're still stuck in the past with their views on the fairer sex." She snorted. "I would be quite the sight walking around in *men's* clothing. At least the rest of the world seems to have developed a more enlightened view. It certainly made living in Solarson much easier."

"I'm kind of shocked to hear that," Amroth replied. "I've always been around women who are – depending on which part of Triclose you're in – treated with respect at worst. Hells, many of them are on equal footing with men."

"Well, young Amroth, there are even worse places than Velusyia in this world to be a woman. I've heard stories of lands where we're practically slaves or worse."

He stared at her with skepticism. "Really? That's just . . ." he shook his head in disgust.

Kara gave a shrug. "Not everyone views the world the same. If that were not the case, then maybe we could avoid senseless wars." She laughed dryly. "Hells, Triclose might actually–" She paused suddenly and stood upright, dropping the waterskin to the ground and peering intently into the fog. "Someone's coming."

Amroth tensed up at her words, wondering if he should draw his sword. "Are you sure?" he asked nervously. "I can't see or hear a thing."

Before either of them could say another word, two armed men emerged from the fog. Amroth hung his head and let out a sigh of relief when he saw that it was Mathis and Mat, both men's clothing damp from the morning fog.

Mathis caught the reaction and noticed the tension in both Kara and Amroth, prompting him to ask, "Expecting trouble?"

"Scare me to death next time!" Amroth snapped. "We can't see a thing in this Deo-forsaken fog."

Mathis walked over and gave him a consoling pat on the shoulder. "Terribly sorry. I guess we could have announced our presence. Are you alright?"

"Yeah," Amroth answered while giving Mathis a small grin to let him know everything was okay. "Just wasn't expecting you back so soon."

"What about you, Kara?" Mat interrupted as he stepped up next to her, his black eyes mirroring the concern in his voice. "Are you alright? You gave us all quite a scare last night."

"I'm just fine, Mat," she said truthfully before seamlessly lying for Amroth's benefit, "Just too much excitement yesterday. Nothing a little sleep and food couldn't cure."

Mat nodded, understanding that this was neither the time nor place to discuss what had happened.

"So," Kara added with a coy smile, "what did you two find out there other than fog?"

"More fog," Mat offered sarcastically, drawing a dry glare from Kara and Mathis.

Mat held up his hands defensively and rolled his dark eyes. "I'm kidding! Sheesh!"

Mathis shook his head before proceeding to say, "Though joking, he's partially right. There's still plenty of fog up there, but it's burning off quickly. The good news is that we ran into a patrol from Haltho and were able to get a better idea of where we are."

"And?" prodded Amroth.

"And," Mathis continued, "you should be getting our things together."

"We're close?" Amroth asked excitedly.

Mathis nodded. "Indeed. We're about two hours out, though it will probably take a bit longer in this fog."

"That's good news!" Amroth tossed in as he quickly moved to the rear of the cave and began to secure their belongings.

"That it is," Mathis responded. "They did say that Haltho took only minor damage in the storm, so we shouldn't have to worry about any storm-related delays."

Turning his attention to Kara, Mathis' tone grew serious. "I informed them of the shipwreck and ordered them to see to it that the dead are tended to."

"Thank you, Mathis," she said softly, remorse for the dead heavy on her words. "Not to be ungrateful, but how ever did you manage to order them to do it?"

Mat laugh as he walked by them to help Amroth, tossing over his shoulder, "You should have seen it, Kara. They looked at him like he was a mad pine-ferret when he started barking orders. Then he pulled out a writ with his – what was the term? Doms? That's it – with his doms seal on it. The patrol sergeant's face nearly dropped. After that, Mathis had them in the palm of his hand." He crouched down and began to secure his and Kara's belongings before adding, "Should have requisitioned some horses while he was at it."

Mathis gave him a dry glare. "They have more need of them than we. Besides, the path back down here is too narrow for horses."

"Still would have sped things up even if we'd left them at the top of the cliff," he retorted.

"Oh leave it alone, Mat!" Kara ordered in irritation. "I don't see any reason why the difference between having horses and not having them would make any more of a difference than getting there a bit faster."

Mat shrugged as he gathered up their gear and returned to the cave entrance where he handed Kara her pack and weapons. As she shouldered her pack and secured her blades to her belt, he said, "Suit yourselves. Just thought a bit of haste might be in order after last night. But seeing as we're apparently in no rush – is it too much for me to ask what the plan is?"

"Haltho is our next stop, obviously," Mathis stated as Amroth joined them and he accepted his pack and the sword case from his charge. "Beyond that, we planned on no more than a day or two layover before making for Merset. I want to be there before the winter snows begin to fully take hold. As I promised Kara, I'll make sure you have the provisions that you need and do my best to point you two in the right direction."

Puzzlement written clearly on his face, Amroth asked, "That reminds me – what are you two doing on Triclose? I don't think anyone ever mentioned it."

"No, I don't think we did mention it," Mat stated bluntly, drawing a chastising glare from Kara.

"Mat – you do realize you're speaking to a member of one of the most powerful Houses on Triclose? It would do you and I both some good if you'd watch your tongue and show some respect and courtesy," she chided.

"It's alright, Kara," Amroth said dismissively. "I hardly involve myself in House politics; honestly, all that reverent behavior makes me a bit uncomfortable."

Kara shook her head adamantly. "I appreciate the candor, but Mat should know better. You're still royalty, and that comes with a measure of respect no matter your own personal views." She fixed Mat with an admonishing glare before returning her attention to Amroth and his question. Easily recalling the cover story she and Mat had agreed upon, she continued, "Anyway, to answer your question, we're here hunting down two fugitives for our lord."

Amroth shouldered his pack and crossed his arms. "Fugitives? What are they wanted for?"

"Murder and sowing sedition amongst our lord's people," she answered bluntly.

Letting out a low whistle, Amroth replied, "Harsh charges. Even if Mathis had not already agreed to lend you a hand, I'm sure Kale would be glad to help in any way possible should you two find your way further north. With all the fighting, Triclose certainly makes for a good place for one to simply vanish."

Kara inclined her head. "Thank you for the offer. We might just have to take you up on that invitation. For now, though, I think we should concentrate on simply getting to Haltho. Don't you think so?"

Amroth chuckled and smiled with relief. "That's the best plan I've heard all week." Motioning to Mathis, he added, "If you'd do the honors and lead on?"

Mathis shouldered his pack and the case with a dry, amused grin. "Yes, Shi'doms," he added, using Amroth's title to needle him just a bit, which drew an amused shake of the head from the young Merandith.

With Mathis in the lead, they left their shelter and made their way down to the beach as quickly as the footing would allow. The fog was significantly thicker on the sandy shore, limiting visibility to a few feet in front of them. Mathis led them back south, passing within only a few feet of the wreckage from the shipwreck, though none of them could really see it, to the switchback path that he and Amroth had used to reach the beach the night before. The morning fog made ascending it as treacherous as the descent the previous night. Mathis set a deliberate and careful pace so everyone could watch their footing on the rocky, muddy and narrow path. Though the going was slow, they made it to the top of the cliff without incident. The fog was thinner at the higher elevation, but no less annoying. They could make out the sky through the dreary blanket of fog and were greeted by scattered clouds that still looked angry enough to unleash more rain. To no one's surprise, sporadic rain pelted them as they plodded northward, doing its best to ally with the fog to dampen their spirits. Thankfully, as the first hour turned into two, the fog began to burn off and with it came clearer skies and the rhythmic pounding of the surf upon the breakers at the base of the cliff.

For the majority of the journey, the number of fellow travelers that they saw were few and far between. With the war so close, that was hardly surprising, nor were the generous number of patrols they encountered. Except for one patrol that was adorned in House Merandith black – their five golden stars displayed proudly on their chests – all of the patrols displayed the orange and gold livery of

House Trivant. No matter their House affiliation, every patrol was mounted and heavily armed. Five times their group was stopped and questioned by such patrols, each successive interruption delaying them further and grating on their nerves. Thankfully, between Mathis and Amroth's presence and the writs that Mathis carried, they were able to expedite the questions and continue on their way without incident.

By the time they came within sight of Haltho proper, they had passed two small hamlets and a handful of farms. They made their way through or around the residences without incident, though they could feel curious and concerned eyes upon them every step of the way. It was a disconcerting feeling, but an understandable one; war and death were practically on the inhabitants' doorsteps, making any unfamiliar face a reason for concern. As it was easy for the quartet to sympathize with the people of the region, none of them felt offended or threatened by the lack of friendly behavior. Instead, they acknowledged the onlookers with a friendly wave or nod and continued on their way at a quick pace.

Their somewhat isolated trip officially came to an end as they closed in on Haltho, and with it, an end to their relatively swift pace. Given the lack of foot traffic earlier in the day, it came as a bit of a shock at how quickly the well-trodden road filled with both mounted and pedestrian traffic. While the slower pace was irritating, it brought with it a most welcome reprieve from the silence and emptiness the road had held for the majority of the trip. However, after the events of the last few days, it was the respite offered by the growing vista of Haltho that more than made up for any of the irritations or inconveniences the trip had put in their way.

The port city of Haltho was a sprawling mass of eclectic architecture and controlled chaos. Originally built as a symbol of unity between the Roselian clans over two centuries ago, the city amounted to little more than a large modern-day hamlet overlooking a large bay. The architecture was mainly crude timber and mud-brick construction focused around a central mortar-and-stone citadel that was intended to serve as a shining example of clan power and unity. Despite everyone's best hopes, and before the idea of establishing a port could even be conceived, the fragile peace the clans had hoped to establish with the city was shattered a mere ten years after Haltho's completion by a rift amongst rival factions in the best traditions of Triclose. By the end of the bloody feud, Haltho had been burnt to the ground by the rebels before they could be expelled from Roselia by an alliance between the ruling clans and Doms Luthur Gravit'nas.

Already well into his campaign to fully unify Triclose, Luthur decided that it was in the best interest of Roselia's stability, and for the whole of Triclose, to appoint a doms to which all the clans would answer while still allowing them the ability to govern themselves so long as it did not conflict with Roselian law. The man chosen to serve in this role was one Garivarth Trivant of a small clan called the Clan of the Claw – and thus was born House Trivant. To this very day, there are those amongst the clans that would dispute that the Clan of the Claw ever existed. Whether or not the history behind the rise of House Trivant was true, the good House Trivant did for Haltho and Roselia was undeniable.

From the start, both Doms Trivant and Doms Gravit'nas had a vision for Haltho that went beyond the current affairs of the day. While establishing an eastern base of operations was certainly important to Doms Gravit'nas, he was also eager to solidify Trivant's rule by unifying the people of Roselia behind the young House. Therefore, the two Houses embarked on a massive construction project that would not only result in a larger and better Haltho, but, more importantly, the establishment of a major port. The reconstruction of the city was the easy part of the project and was effortlessly implemented. Using stone and brick for their durability and strength, not only did they rebuild both the Citadel and the surrounding city, but they added solid defensive walls.

Despite the setbacks and difficulties the Citadel reconstruction saw, it was the establishment of a port that many had viewed as an impossible undertaking. There were only two locations that have could possibly serve as a port – land that resided a week's travel north, which would add unacceptable travel time for goods trying to make it to market, and the bay that resided below Haltho. While the decision was difficult, they decided to embark on the dangerous and ambitious task of utilizing the rocky shore of the natural harbor below Haltho. The first problem that was addressed was a method of transportation up and down the hazardous cliff face. Without a means of transporting people and supplies, the project would have been dead before it started. It was already known that there were no usable natural paths along the dangerous cliff face, so the architects were forced to engineer massive switchback ramps. However, it was evident that there was no way to safely construct ramps that were wide enough to accommodate the large cargo they were intended to support. And then there was the problem of where to begin the job. If they had started from the top of the cliff, they would have had to dream up a way to suspend hundreds of workers over the vast fall. If the work had begun bellow – like so many had clamored for – then there would have been the logistical nightmare of communication and transportation via a two week journey up and then back down the coast to deal with. In the end, after much heated debate, it was decided that they would design and construct a series of lifts first.

It was both a daring and ingenious decision that not only provided mobile platforms by which materials and manpower were transported, but also served as a place from which the workers were able to construct the ramp system. Throughout the entirety of the monumental project, a sturdy platform was anchored into the cliff face every two hundred feet of the six-hundred-foot descent. These permanent platforms initially served as bases by which the lift system was expanded, which also conveyed upon them the dual roles of rest stop and transfer point for the workers making the ascent or descent. However, as construction progressed, the platforms also took on their all-important primary role as anchor points for the ramps. In the end, it took five years to complete the ramp system; furthermore, it was decided to retain many of the lifts to handle large cargo. While the financial cost was certainly staggering for the times – at a cost of fifty-thousand talons over the five years – it was the cost in blood that soured many. Between accidents and illness, seventy-three workers were lost to the daring and dangerous project, and another ten died in the reconstruction of Haltho. In honor of the fallen, the district that developed around the cliffside was named the Tradesman's Terrace.

Because of Doms Gravit'nas' ongoing campaign, another decade would pass before construction on the port and improvements to the ramp and lift system were finished. In that time, with the influx of workers and business, the population of Haltho soared nearly to fifteen-thousand residents, which was accompanied by an explosion in the size of the city. Outside the soaring wall of the Citadel, the Commons were constructed to provide housing to the burgeoning city's residents, which was then followed by another defensive, hundred foot tall wall. Beyond that wall soon arose the Trade District. Intended to cater to all the needs of Haltho's citizens, it grew and spread like wildfire. Worried about possible incursions, a wall that was the twin of the two inside the city was soon erected.

By that time, work on the port was officially finished, providing Haltho with berths for fifty large ships along the lines of war barges and trade freighters, as well as seventy to a hundred smaller class ships and fishing vessels. The waters of the harbor were also vast enough to play host to another fifty to a hundred ships at anchor, depending on size. The result was a bustling harbor that did nothing but spur the economic and population growth of the city. The valuable land that remained within the Commons was greedily scooped up by businessmen and the wealthy alike. Where they could not build outward, they built up. Three- and even four-story homes sprung up like agitated prairie dogs, and unoccupied or unused buildings were leveled to make way for more appealing construction. Within six years, the Commons was bursting at the seams. Hungry for more room, the north and south walls were demolished and the Commons quickly expanded north and south between the remaining protective walls. Bolstered by the influx of new land, both new and old construction alike was greedily consumed by the wealthy who wished to flaunt their status and be closer to Roselia's seat of power. Those that couldn't afford to live in the Commons moved to what had become known as the Commons South, while the older and wealthy Commons was renamed Commons North.

There was no stopping the growth of the wealthy city, and soon those that couldn't afford to rent or own within the city walls began to set up outside the ramparts. Within twenty years of the port's completion, Haltho sported a burgeoning shantytown beyond its walls that quickly became a worse eyesore than gapped teeth on a prostitute. House Trivant could do little about the shantytown in the early years of the makeshift town's existence as their resources and time were consumed by the establishment of a naval fleet and the training of a full-time army in response to a rebellion against House Gravit'nas' rule over Triclose. The resulting cost of the prolonged war would mean nearly a century would pass before anyone would even think to improve on Haltho's appearance.

It would take the vision of Lucas Trivant's great, great-grandfather, Doms Silvanus de'Morvin Trivant III, to restore Haltho's shining facade. In a sweeping and bold movement, Silvanus began the systematic leveling and reconstruction of the shantytown into a new residential and business district that would become known as the Sweepers District – named so in response to the teams of officials that would sweep through the old shantytown delivering notices to the owners of the structures scheduled for demolition. While the project was by no means fully embraced by the public – in fact there were a number of violent acts and protests against the evictions – the resulting new construction was a boon to the Roselian economy.

Where Lucas Trivant's ancestors' marks on Triclose had been the construction of Haltho, his father, Doms Valarius Trivant, sought to make his mark in a more political fashion. Seeking to cement House Trivant's allegiance to House Merandith at the start of the Third Great War, he promised his daughter's hand in marriage to Doms Merandith's son and agreed to the construction of an Academy facility within the Citadel grounds. The move proved to be ingenious, as Roselia's military had suffered from a lack of attention over the years. During those years, the majority of the military duties had fallen to the clans as a result of Roselia's money being focused on both its naval fleet and on protecting its trade routes. Without House Merandith's military might, Roselia would have fallen to House Suldamik early in the war. If that had happened, House Suldamik would have acquired a significant position of power from which they could have drastically impacted House Merandith's trade and supply routes. Thankfully, that never came to be; furthermore, with time bought by House Merandith, Doms Valarius was able to begin training a permanent army with the help of the newly established Academy and the instructors sent in by House Merandith.

Upon Doms Valarius' death in battle ten years later, Lucas ascended the throne of House Trivant shortly before his sister was married off to Kale. Lucas continued to build the military and support House Merandith without question, but he also sought to make his own personal mark on Roselia. With as close as the war was to his doorstep, Lucas saw a practical way to do this and protect his people at the same time. Shortly before Doms Bordin Merandith's assassination, Lucas began the construction of a mighty fourth wall for Haltho. His advisors argued vehemently against a project they deemed wasteful, citing their proximity to the war and the drain it would put on their already strained resources. In their minds, the money would be better spent on expanding the army. However, Lucas was adamant about his wants and pushed forward with his plans. He saw the wall as a symbol that the war-weary people could rally around, and somewhere in the recesses of his mind, he felt like it would possibly make Haltho more unassailable than Chalin.

Regretfully, he would only be able to oversee the construction for a short time. With the death of Doma Merandith, Kale ascended to the head of House Merandith and put out a call to all available domses to push House Suldamik from Five Stars' territory. With House Suldamik uncomfortably close, and feeling that he owed it to his sister and brother-by-marriage, Lucas personally led his mixture of regulars and clansmen to war and left Haltho in the capable hands of the Captain of the City Guard – Doms Captain Oblet de'Trivant Torwin.


From what Mathis could make out, as they slowly approached Haltho along with the growing throng of people, Oblet had been busy attending to Lucas' pet project. The main gatehouse had been completed along with its flanking towers. Scaffolding flowed from the gatehouse like a rigid wooden spider web as masons and their crews expertly raised the walls between what was either going to be matching towers or sturdy wall platforms for wall-mounted catapults. These structures were being erected every two hundred yards as the new construction wound its way around the Sweepers District to join with the ramparts that encompassed the Trade District. In an attempt to force people to use the new gate, and to guard against unwanted intruders, squads of armored soldiers in House Trivant colors were stationed day and night wherever there was little to no construction to keep people from sneaking into the city. Given the number of men Lucas had taken to the front, it was likely that the bulk of the forces protecting the city were militia.

Mounted guards patrolled the road continuously, their eyes focused more on the surrounding land than the slow-moving column of travelers. Given what the quartet could pick out from the numerous conversations around them, the guards' presence was altogether a good thing. A portion of what they heard left no doubt that the raiding parties had been noticed; some of the people claimed to have arrived from as far north as the Roselia-Gravail border, and others from hamlets and villages less than a league away, their tales and accusations encompassing everything from rape and pillaging to killings and buildings being put to the torch. More outlandish tales came from the mouths of clansmen that were talking excitedly about how a friend of a friend swore he'd seen a fabled ember drakuma a few days ago. And then there were the more superstitious people that spoke in hushed whispers of dark creatures roaming about the Alderian Forest.

Amroth understood all too well their concern about the raiders, but he didn't know what to make of the whispers; to him, it simply sounded like they were jumping at shadows. The talk of the ember drakuma, however, did manage to draw a sly smile from him. *"If only they knew,"* he thought with amusement.

It took them nearly half an hour to finally reach the gatehouse where Mathis produced his writ for the heavily armed and armored guards. Though they appeared to be more bored than anything else, the guards showed no signs of neglecting their duties. The writ was thoroughly examined and they were questioned about their intentions in the city. Between the writ and an answer of 'official business', it was enough for the guards and they were quickly waved through. The quartet passed through the gatehouse, noting with interest the carefully placed murder holes, and were immediately caught up in the throng of humanity going about their daily business.

Sweepers District, they noted, was already alive and bustling with activity along the wide main thoroughfare that – though by no means tactically sound – ran straight through the heart of the district to the lone gate providing access to the Trade District. The street was expertly laid with tightly fitted stones that were worn down from years of constant traffic. The one- and two-story buildings flanking the bustling crowd were strictly businesses, their facades made predominantly of timber and capped by clay-tiled roofs. Of the two-story buildings, many of the second levels jutted out over the street, casting portions of the thoroughfare into shadow. Some of the businesses had signs – some with simple images and others with brightly painted text – hanging outside them, while others relied on displays of goods to indicate the types of services offered. Hawkers could just be heard over the din of noise, crying the benefits of doing business with their employer. If not for the ever-present armed soldiers, one might think the residents of Haltho had no idea that there was a war going on.

Yet, despite their evident prosperity and their apparent obliviousness to the war, there were subtle signs of war's hardships if one simply looked for them.

For Kara, she didn't have to put any effort into seeking them out; she could spot them as easily as a blacksmith could spot flaws in his metal. Amongst the crowded streets, there were those who bore horrible scars or were missing limbs; furthermore, a quick assessment of the people crowding the sides of the street and congregating in the shadows between buildings revealed to Kara haggard and dirty faces belonging to both children and adults. For Kara, no matter whom the visages belonged to, it was saddening to see the depths of despair that haunted their gaunt faces and hopeless gazes as they either begged for sustenance or wrestled with just how they were going to survive. To her chagrin – and despite the hardship she saw – Kara was positive that some of the poor were likely part of a ring of thieves looking to con folk out of their coin, and she could find little reason to pity them. However, there were those that were truly destitute, and for them, her heart wept.

Even as she took note of the victims of war and commerce, as well as a few people whose lined and concerned faces belied the rich clothing they wore, she – as well as Mat – was committing to memory the lay of the city. Years of fighting for one's life had ingrained the habit in the name of survival. Granted, any solider worth their salt would be doing the same thing, but for Mat and Kara, their attunement to fir'gan provided them with a unique perspective. Instead of merely taking note of their immediate surroundings, the flow of fir'gan helped to paint a more detailed picture of the environment beyond their field of vision. Surrounded as they were by man-made architecture, they were easily able to discern the placement of streets and buildings via the unnatural disruptions in the flow of fir'gan that the structures induced. If the city had been empty, she might have been able to get a feel for the city's layout nearly to the Citadel; however, the mass of people traversing the avenues threw the fir'gan into virtual chaos, making it impossible to read the currents clearly. As a result, she was only able to get an idea of how the streets and buildings flowed from as far away as the next street.

Focused as they were on the currents, the chaos induced by humanity's presence was nearly enough to give Mat and Kara a headache. Without question, it was worse than being in a place such as a forest where the currents remained predominantly natural. Granted, the natural currents were difficult to read in their own right, but there remained an order to the way the currents moved and adjusted to nature's tendencies. While all creatures unconsciously affected the flow of fir'gan, none were more influential than the races of Kylir. This unconscious influence was further compounded by both their propensity to congregate in large groups and, to a lesser degree, their ability to forcefully alter their surroundings. As a result, cities stood as powerful aberrations in the currents that were unreadable for an inexperienced and untrained Gifted.

As they were slowly making their way through the densely packed throng of people, movement out of the corner of her eye brought a welcome distraction to Kara. Glancing down quickly, she saw an unassuming street urchin slide in behind Mat. An average person would never have noticed the practiced and deft movements of the skilled pickpocket – which drew amused, silent praise from Kara – but for her heightened senses, the dirty boy's movements stood out like a blazing fire in the middle of the night. Just as she was about to call the urchin to Mat's attention, his hand swept back and caught the wrist of the would-be pickpocket, startling the boy. Mat turned slightly and gave the boy a knowing wink before releasing his wrist and watching the urchin slip through the crowd, fear of being turned in to the authorities driving him to vanish from sight as quickly as possible.

Kara laughed aloud, drawing curious glances from Amroth and Mathis, as well as a few of the people meandering along around them.

"What's so funny?" Amroth asked.

"Oh nothing, really," she answered with a dismissive wave of her hand. "Just like old times, eh?" she directed at Mat as Amroth turned his attention forward with a shake of his head.

Mat gave her a casual shrug. "Some things never change. Besides, in a city this size, I'd almost be insulted if someone didn't attempt to pick my pocket." Mat's answer drew curious glances from Amroth and Mathis, but neither pursued the question that was implied in their facial expressions. Mat chuckled at the looks and added, "Nothing to worry about, you two. Where I'm from, it would be

412

considered unusual for a day to go by where the denizens of the streets and alleys didn't make their presence known."

Amroth turned away, muttering, "And I thought Triclose had it bad with all the war. Imagine a city where crime roams that freely. . . ." Amroth shook his head in disbelief as they continued to slowly move forward.

Mat chuckled to himself and thought, "*Imagine being so innocently ignorant.*"

Their slow trek toward the Trade District gatehouse began to pick up momentum as they drew closer and the crowd began to thin out. Without a good reason – and more importantly, the money – to venture into the Trade District and beyond, very few of the Sweepers District's inhabitants had any motive to travel to other parts of the city. Thus, the ambling crowd around the quartet was slowly whittled down to trade wagons, merchants, a few workers, and those that certainly appeared wealthy by their dress and means of transportation. There was even the occasional luxurious carriage that rumbled by, its driver shouting for people to make way. Those that were unceremoniously shoved aside by the carriages or merchant wagons – mostly well-dressed travelers that couldn't afford something as frivolous as a carriage – were left cursing loudly at the rudeness, drawing amused, cynical laughter from the poorer onlookers.

In the end, the rush that the wagons and carriages of the wealthy were in was all for naught as they were forced to stop at the gate like everyone else. Amroth had to chuckle as he watched one carriage driver get into a heated argument with one of the gate guards – likely over how important his employer was and how the delay was intolerable – as foot traffic passed them by. By all appearances, the driver's heated words were only serving to delay his admittance, to the guard's amusement.

After another fifteen minutes of plodding up the main thoroughfare, they finally reached the main Trade District gatehouse. Once again, Mathis' writ gained them quick entry. However, this time he had to politely decline an offered escort to the Citadel; the last thing he wanted was to draw more unwanted attention to their presence than they already were by flashing the writ. While his face was known to some within the Roselian military, and Amroth's to a few within House Trivant, it was unlikely that anyone would recognize them. However, friendly territory or not, there was always the chance someone with a reason – whether it be real or not – to harm them was lurking about, and Mathis was not about to blatantly expose them to such risk without a very good reason.

Well aware that the trip to the Commons South and the districts beyond would be a bit more complicated with the arrangement of crisscrossing roads laid out in interlocking U-shapes that radiated out from the walls, Mathis pulled their group to the side as soon as they were through the gatehouse. Taking in the buildings before him, Mathis took a moment to recall what he could about the Trade District and its layout.

The Trade District was, without a doubt, the mirror image of the Sweepers District in beauty and decadence. Where the Sweepers District had been arranged in a straightforward and orderly fashion, the Trade District showed the marks of multiple architects having had a hand in both its design and renovations. The buildings were a mix of classical stone architecture, with its florid arches and carved facades, and the cleaner and more practical designs of modern times. Furthermore, where the Sweepers District was constructed of cheap but sturdy materials, the Trade District was expertly built and decorated with rich ironwoods, deep redwoods, high-quality ironwork and stone masonry, as well as vibrant limestone and a variety of colorful imported marble. There were even streets where the buildings either had been designed or renovated to share a thematic color scheme and architectural style, thus providing a more aesthetically appealing shopping experience. To the surprise of many, even the brothel on the south side of the Trade District, known as the Dirty Pillows, put forth a lavish exterior accented with their well-cared-for and beautifully presented workers.

Bereft of the unwanted smoke and smells of blacksmiths and tanneries, the Trade District was also Haltho's destination for those seeking to spend their talons on goods and pleasures ranging from the simple to the exotic. For those in need of everyday goods or fresh vegetables, then there were even a handful of small grocers that not only kept their shelves stocked with sundries, but also grew their own vegetables behind their shops. If one sought to sate their appetite, then there were delicatessens that catered to a wide variety of tastes, as well as sweetshops whose smells were enough to tempt even the stoutest of wills to part with enough coin to indulge their palette. And should one be in search of a place to rest or partake of nature without leaving the protective confines of the city, then there were gardens – which in spring and summer were overflowing with bright flowers and lush trees and grasses – scattered about the District.

However, no center of commerce was complete without a place for visitors to rest their heads. To that end, the Trade District was home to a dozen quality inns. Catering predominantly to the wealthy, they boasted luxurious rooms, full kitchens and cellars, as well as ways to indulge more exotic and risqué desires. From sexual pleasures and fetishes to exotic drugs and intoxicating brews, a variety of decadent pleasures of the mind and flesh were available for guests if they knew with whom to speak and had the talons to pay.

When Mathis finally felt confident in his recollections, he said, "Well, I don't know about you two, but Amroth and I are headed for the Citadel. If you wish, I can see to it that you are welcomed there. Between the two of us, we can also see to it that you have what supplies that you need."

"Thank you, Mathis," Kara said warmly, "but you know me – I won't impose unless I have to. Given our mission here, I wouldn't want to draw you into something that might reflect badly upon either of you."

"Are you sure? We don't mind at all," added Amroth.

"I'm sure," Kara added firmly. "Besides, we need to gather information and get our bearings. Being holed-up in a cozy room might sound nice, but would hamper our ability to do our job." She shook her head firmly. "No, we'll go where the drinks flow freely and the tongues are loose."

"I understand," said Mathis with disappointment written clearly across his face. "Then you'll be wanting to stay in the Tradesman's Terrace."

Amroth gawked at Mathis in astonishment. "Hardly the safest place in Haltho to stay, or the cleanest. I'd almost say you were treating her like an enemy if I didn't know you better."

Mathis cracked a small grin. "It's not that bad, Amroth. With all the sailors, merchants, and warehouses, it's just a bit of a rough and straightforward neighborhood."

"Definitely sounds like Solac," Mat quipped.

Before Amroth could protest further, Kara disarmed him with a smile, "It will be alright. Mat and I can more than handle ourselves."

"Then at least let us lend you some coin. Triclose's currency won't carry much weight around here," Amroth offered as he started to unshoulder his pack to retrieve his money.

"Just one moment, Amroth," Kara stated firmly before asking of Mathis, "I take it there's more than a few Velusyians that come through here?"

"Indeed," Mathis stated with a nod of his head.

"Then I'm assuming there's a Broker House here as well."

A knowing smile crept onto Mathis' face. "There's Velusyia-Ni in the Tradesman's Terrace."

Kara smiled brightly. "Good. Then I shouldn't have any problem acquiring the coin we'll need." She offered Amroth a consoling smile. "After all, I'd rather burn the money of our employer than be any further burden upon you two."

"Very well then," Amroth said with a dejected sigh. "At least let me once again extend House Merandith's aid in your search should you need it."

Catching Amroth off guard, Kara stepped forward and gave him a gentle hug and soft kiss on the cheek before stepping back. Amroth was wide-eyed and blushing furiously as she said, "I thank you for the offer, and your help. Neither Mat nor I will forget it. Should we need it, I won't hesitate to take you up on the offer."

The smile fading from her face, she turned her attention to Mathis and extended her hand. He grasped her forearm firmly and nodded slightly. "Not enough time, old friend," she said wistfully, "I would have loved to have had the time to catch-up with you."

"Don't be so quick to assume our paths won't cross again. Triclose is . . . full of surprises," he said knowingly, drawing curious looks from the others before he withdrew his hand. "The two of you will want to follow Goldcobble Street east for about four blocks before turning south onto Holy Saints Walk for another three. From there, take Wagoner's Lane east before turning south on Gateway Way. You'll finally end up on Tradesman's Approach; take it east all the way to the gate to Tradesman's Terrace. It's not the fastest way, but Commons South is not the most . . . hospitable place. Once you're settled in, send a message to me at the Citadel and I'll provide you with a list of trustworthy merchants who can get you the best goods without asking for your souls in return."

Kara adjusted her pack and offered a parting smile. "I will. Thank you again. Corith grant you safe travels."

Mathis nodded and replied, "Deo guide you well," before Kara and Mat returned to the flow of people.

As soon as Mat and Kara vanished from sight, Mathis clapped Amroth on the shoulder and started following the wall to the north, his thoughts already turning to other matters that had been troubling him. "Come along, Amroth – we have our own issues to deal with."

"Are you sure they'll be okay?" Amroth asked as he hustled to catch up with Mathis. "Turning down our aid just seems silly to me."

"Don't worry about them. They can more than take care of themselves. Besides, I've got more important things to worry about." Mathis suddenly cut to the right into a dark, narrow alley that spilled out upon a fairly empty cobbled street lined with expensive stores catering to nearly every trade need. He double-checked his location upon exiting the alley, and began following the road northeast toward the ancient, looming walls of the Commons North.

"And what might that be?" he asked in irritation as he caught up to Mathis again.

"You," Mathis stated bluntly as Amroth came up beside him.

"Me?" he asked incredulously. "Sure, I've had a bad run of luck, but you say that like it's some sort of life-altering burden."

Mathis nodded. "It is, in a way. The attempt on your life scared Kale horribly, and he doesn't want to see anything bad come to you. He wanted you to come to this decision on your own – but after everything that happened in the Forest, I'm taking the decision from you."

"And what decision would that be?" Amroth quipped angrily, drawing a glare from Mathis.

"You're going to learn to fight – and I'm going to teach you," Mathis stated bluntly, his tone brokering no argument.

"Fight?" Amroth replied in surprise, ignoring the warning in Mathis' voice. "Have you forgotten? I did learn at the Academy."

The veteran bodyguard scoffed as they move around a slow-plodding wagon filled with old scrap metal that looked destined for a blacksmith to be melted down and repurposed. "They did little more than teach you to hold a sword before you withdrew," Mathis said in disgust. "I'm going to teach you to be a weapon – deadly and precise."

Amroth rolled his eyes and sighed in exasperation. "Look, Mathis – I can understand where you and Kale are coming from, and I've even been rethinking things myself. But I abhor fighting, and the thought of taking someone's life is just–"

He was startled as Mathis suddenly stopped at the mouth of an alley between a tailor's shop and a butcher's shop. Looking around to see if anyone was watching, Mathis grabbed Amroth firmly by his arm and pulling him a few paces into the alley. With a sudden fierce growl, he grabbed Amroth by his shirt and slammed him against the wall of the butcher's shop. There was a clatter of noise from deeper in the alley as their sudden appearance startled a gangly adolescent in a bloodstained apron, causing him to drop the platter full of fresh slaughter he was carrying into the shop from a delivery cart.

"Mind your own business, pup!" Mathis growled at the boy, sending him scuttling into the shop.

"Damn it, Mathis! What in the hells is wrong with you? I'm beginning to think you would be better off spending time with your old friends!" Amroth barked, trying to break from Mathis' surprisingly strong grip.

Mathis turned his fierce glare on Amroth, the intensity in his dark eyes bringing Amroth's struggles to an end. "Now you listen, pup. I will not have Kale wasting a moment's energy worrying about your well-being! He asked me to train you, and by Deo – I will!"

"But–" Amroth tried to interrupt.

Mathis shoved him again to shut him up. "No buts this time!" he growled. "If Kale's desire to see his brother better able to protect himself isn't enough, then what you saw and experienced in the Forest should be! There are things in this world that are far more dangerous than this never-ending war for power!"

The young Merandith's dark eyes narrowed in anger, but there was a desperate plea for answers in their glint that tempered his glare. "Then explain it to me, damn it! In the span of a few days, I've seen and heard things that have flipped my world on its head! I have no idea what to make of a beast from legend coming to life before my eyes! I discover you have friends whose very demeanor screams confident lethality despite friendly outward appearances! Hells, if not for your vote of confidence, I wouldn't have shared even an hour with them in that cave! What in Deo's name am I suppose to make of that!? What am I to make of you?!" he spit.

Mathis leaned in close and growled, "The only thing you'll worry about for now is what your brother – your doms – has asked of you. You *will* learn to protect yourself so that Kale doesn't have to waste a moment fretting over you, and I will make sure you do it. Until the time comes that I deem you fit, that is all that you will worry about. Do I make myself clear?"

Amroth stared hard into Mathis' dark, violent eyes before saying, "I could simply order you to stand down."

"You know that would do you no good. I'm too stubborn, and Kale's word carries significantly more weight than yours."

Silence descended on the alley for a time, drawn painfully out by the tension in the air. The butcher's apprentice, as well as the butcher himself, peeked out from the shop at one point only to silently withdraw, seeing ignorance as the best course of action. Given that it looked like – at least to them – a well-armed and dangerous brute shaking down a worn-out man, it was no surprise that they chose to feign ignorance. The last thing they wanted was to stumble into a personal squabble or, Deo forbid, trouble within one of the city's many guilds.

The buzz of noise from the street picked up as the number of people using it increased before Amroth finally broke the silence. "Alright. I'll do it, but with one condition – you tell me everything about your time on Solarson. The events in the Forest raised too many questions to go unanswered."

Mathis gazed perceptively into Amroth's eyes, judging just how committed Amroth was to his answer. Seeing what he wanted to see, he let Amroth go and straightened his shirt. "There will be no quitting once this begins. My word will be law, and I will expect nothing less than all your effort. If – and only if – you meet my expectations will you get a word about Solarson from me. Is that understood?"

Amroth nodded firmly. "It is."

"Good. Then time is wasting. We need to check-in at the Citadel, deliver orders to Oblet and inform him of his raider problem within the Forest. After that, injured or not, you're going to learn to do more than carry that sword at your hip."

# Chapter Eighteen

They made their way along Goldcobble Street amongst a growing crowd of arrivals to the Trade District. Kara set a solid pace for the two of them, the currents of fir'gan helping to guide her accurately along Mathis' suggested route. Their quick pace and confident strides also helped to give them the appearance of locals or, at the very least, people very familiar with the city. This not only would help them blend in and present less of a target for the more unseelie denizens of the city, but it would also allow Kara to be as inconspicuous as possible for a blue-haired Velusyian. However, Mat's sheepish grin told Kara that he had another reason in mind for their pace.

After four blocks of trying to ignore the annoying grin, she let out a pensive sigh. "What?" she finally asked as they stepped on to Holy Saints Walk.

"Oh nothing," he said casually as they strode quickly along the street, his eyes taking in the surrounding clothing and trinket shops. "I was just wondering about that kiss and hug you gave the kid." He flashed her an inquisitive and mischievous grin. "What happened in the cave while Mathis and I were gone? Hummm?" He chuckled before teasing, "Did you find a love to sate that fiery heart of yours?"

Without breaking her stride, Kara quickly turned and gave Mat a firm punch to the shoulder.

Chuckling, he rubbed at his shoulder and cried in feigned pain, "Ow! That confirms it! You're more drakuma than woman! Such senseless violence!"

"Oh shut it!" Kara barked in annoyance. "You know good and well nothing happened – the kiss and hug were only friendly thanks for their assistance," she stated firmly.

"Ah, I see now – thanks for assistance that we really didn't need." He nodded with a childish smile on his face. "So . . . for everything I've done for you that actually amounts to something, my kiss and hug should be quite . . . interesting."

Kara scowled and quickened her pace. "It's going to be irritating enough to go into one of those forsaken Broker Houses – the last thing I need is your jokes and sarcasm!"

Mat laughed and ran a hand through his short-cut purple-tinted, black hair. "Come now, Kara, what's so wrong with Broker Houses? The few times you've taken me along, I quite liked them." Kara turned a murderous glare on Mat and cuffed him on the back of the head, drawing a few curious glances from passersby. "Okay, okay! I get your point," he said in surrender as he rubbed the back of his head. "I know good and well your views on Velusyia, and didn't mean anything by my comments."

*"This time it's different,"* she thought to herself worriedly. *"This time it's an actual Velusyia-Ni we're stepping into."* Then, aloud to Mat, she said, "Good. Now pick up the pace – the sooner this is over with, the better," she ordered sternly. With the currents of fir'gan as her assistant, Kara swiftly and resolutely continued onward, her face growing stoic and closed, and her bright eyes gaining a hard edge as they neared the Tradesman's Terrace. In her haste, she used the currents to find shortcuts between the lavish shops to shorten the trip.

Unlike Kara, whose attention was focused on their destination, Mat let his eyes wander and take in the sights. Being city born and raised, Mat had a love and appreciation for nearly everything a city life had to offer, and couldn't imagine living anywhere else. So whenever he visited a new city, he did his best to absorb the local color and essence. The Trade District, with its lavish shops and attention to detail, reminded him of many of the trade ports and cities he had visited across Solarson where the large influx of coin always led to lavish lifestyles and the proliferation of those willing to feed off the excess and those that were more than happy to take 'unneeded' or 'unwanted' items off their owners hands. Although there were numerous sights, sounds and smells to take in, it was the ever-looming presence of the Citadel that kept catching his eye.

Although the Citadel by no means struck Mat as a luxurious structure, it certainly was impactful as a seat of power. Thrusting nearly two hundred feet into the air, the lone spire that was the Citadel was easily seen from anywhere inside the city and for quite a distance outside the city walls. Even from the Trade District, and without fir'gan enhancing his senses, he could see that the proverbial jewel of the city was sheathed in polished marble similar to that encasing the florid and graceful buttresses that supported the spire's weight. There were no windows or balconies that he could see from their current location, but it was easy for him to conclude that they were there and provided a spectacular view of the city and the ocean. As for the interior, he could only imagine what it looked like, but he surmised that no matter how grandiose it may or may not be, such a structure would have relatively little floor space and would prove inhospitable to would-be invaders.

For the next hour, sensing the tension in Kara, Mat remained silent as they circled the Citadel to the south and east, bypassing the more direct route through Commons South and eventually coming within sight of the gatehouse to Tradesman's Terrace. The flow of traffic in and out of the Terrace was full of heavily laden carts entering the Trade District and empty carts returning to the Terrace. Most of the foot traffic appeared to be laborers and sailors, the occasional well-dressed merchant standing out like a tree amongst shrubs. It took Mat and Kara another half hour to reach the gatehouse through the milling mass of humanity. From what they could see of the ramparts and gatehouse, the construction was significantly older – there was lichen growing in cracks, some of the stone and mortar was crumbling, but for the most part, the fortifications were in good shape. In contrast to the aged defenses were a pair of sturdy, iron-banded gate doors and a relatively new portcullis, both of which stood wide open in an attempt to keep people flowing into and out of the Terrace as quickly as possible.

Yet, while maintaining a steady flow to the mass of humanity seemed important, the House Trivant guards manning the gate were diligent in their duties, questioning each person about their intentions. However, to Mat's experienced eye, it appeared that they were more concerned with whom and what was coming into the city than the flow of people into the Terrace. Mat figured that their primary goal was to stop contraband and possible criminal activity from entering the city, leave it up to their incarnation of a Harbor Patrol to handle anything or anyone attempting to flee the city. He snorted to himself at the seemingly futile nature of their actions. Corith would be the only one to know if there was a major city that existed, past or present, that didn't house its share of crime and illicit activity. No matter how diligent their efforts were, the law could only do so much, and it always came down to what those in power viewed as important to enforce.

Upon reaching the gate, the two were briefly questioned by one of the gate guards – a fairly handsome, middle-aged woman – who failed to react to Mat's charming smile. Instead, she was focused on Kara's answers to her questions, her attentiveness to her duties impressing Mat. Between Kara's distinct Velusyian features and her honest answer of their intent to visit the Broker House, they were waved on through without hassle right after the guard provided them directions to Velusyia-Ni.

Mat had to laugh as they entered the bustling Terrace. "Velusyians seem to have it so easy. I ought to change my hair color just to see how much I could get away with."

Kara scoffed at the notion. "I'm afraid you'd enjoy it too much. Corith only knows we don't need you running around pretending to be a Velusyian man – you're too much like one as it is!"

Laughing, Mat replied, "Why thank you for the compliment."

Kara rolled her eyes and continued onward.

The roads of Tradesman's Terrace were constructed according to a grid layout, brick and wooden construction flanking wide stone avenues. Ruts were cut in the middle of the roads, flowing in both directions, allowing the wagons and carts to traverse the lanes unhindered by the throng of foot traffic that was forced to walk closer to the buildings by the design. Clouds of thick smoke and a cornucopia of interesting smells filled the air – overriding any possibility of smelling the sea – originating from the numerous blacksmiths, mills and tanneries that were responsible for creating goods from raw materials and readying them for transport to their destinations. To Mat and Kara's amazement, the number of taverns and inns was staggering – they counted ten of them within a block of the gatehouse – and they could only imagine how many more were scattered about the Terrace. Neither was quite sure what they had expected to find upon entering the Terrace, but they hadn't expected to find such a thriving hub of humanity and commerce in a land that seemed engrossed in perpetual war.

Following the guard's directions, they weaved their way east through the eclectic crowd for nearly ten minutes before turning north. It wasn't long before the buildings flanking them switched from shops and businesses to predominantly warehouses. Laborers and large wagons became their traveling companions, bawdy conversations in a variety of languages filling the air. Four blocks later, they were greeted by a twelve foot tall wooden wall and an arched gate. A wooden sign – elegant symbols carved across its surface – surmounted the gate, following the curve of the arch. The gate consisted of two thick doors, painted red, that were tightly sealed. Two guards flanked the large doors, and another two stood alongside an open, smaller door built into the right gate panel.

Each guard was dressed in red-lacquered, studded ironwood armor that was secured over black silk padding by black silk ties. Each wore a helmet adorned with dragon-wing-shaped cheek guards and an elegant nose guard made of red-lacquered wood. All four carried long and graceful, yet strikingly violent polearms accented by long red tassels dangling from just below the three foot long, curved blades. Along with their matching blue hair and eyes, it was like the guards were mirror images of one another – which was altogether a bit eerie. The foreboding air about the guards was further reinforced

423

by what seemed to be an invisible line, roughly fifty yards from the gate, that no one seemed to want to cross. Thus, when Kara and Mat broke from the crowd on the street and crossed that invisible barrier, the guards' attention immediately focused on them, the two guards flanking the small door crossing their polearms before the entrance.

"Amazing what money and power can buy you," Mat muttered. "A shame, though, that they present such a damn scary front. If you don't mind me saying – you don't seem anything like the rest of your people."

"I'll take that as a lavish and very heartfelt compliment," she replied with a half-smile as they drew within ten yards of the gate. Halting, she held out a hand to restrain Mat. "Wait here a moment. It's bad enough that I'm a woman about to ask for entrance – and the last thing I need is you complicating matters."

Mat smirked, "And just how would I do that?"

Kara gave him a droll glare. "I'm not answering that. You'll get enough fuel for your jokes, puns and jabs in there as it is." Mat chuckled, drawing a dour glare from her. "In all seriousness," she stated bluntly, "wait here and keep your mouth shut. I'll signal for you once we have permission to enter."

"Yes, ma'm," he answered in a mocking fashion, trying to keep the mood light.

Rolling her eyes at him, she strode forward. When she got within a few paces of the guards at the small door, she came to a halt. Although Mat couldn't see exactly what she was doing, he had seen this routine before and knew, as her right arm moved, that she was touching her forefinger and index finger to the center of her forehead and then her heart as she bowed deeply to the guards. Even from where he stood, he could just make out their conversation, and had to admit that he always enjoyed hearing the Velusyian tongue with its lilting melody and flowing words.

"Ariomo, Samulatia deasuma," he heard Kara offer the guard in greeting.

"Karasuarta, kishanilati kasa deasuma!" the guard barked back at her.

"Seyamen et senpashi" she stated, pointing to Mat, "eterasu masikila yeto no takusa deasuma."

"Kanabishta, nosa takusa ne?" The guard asked in a none-too-friendly manner.

Mat could almost hear Kara grinding her teeth as she unslung her pack and dug around in it before producing what he knew to be a
424

blue-lacquered clay disk with an elegant and complex raised symbol, painted black, on the center of disc. Kara held up the disc for the guards to clearly see, stating firmly, "Takusa no Yokonagito Miachi."

The guards seemed dumbstruck at what she had said, and leaned in to better examine the disc. The guards eyed each other as if trying to confirm that both of them had heard her and seen what she presented correctly, before standing upright, taping their empty fist to their chest and bowing. "Tsumashita. Ikosa, Yokonagito."

Kara bowed once again before returning the disc to her pack and shouldering it. Turning to Mat, she waved him forward. Mat hustled up to her and the two of them passed through the gate, the guards' eyes staring at Kara with a mix of awe and resentment.

Once they were through the gate, Mat simply shook his head in disbelief and amazement. "One of these days, I'll have to learn Velusyian, and you'll have to tell me why nearly everyone you show that disc to starts groveling before you."

"Well, it's up to you if you want to learn Velusyian. As for the other," she shot him a firm, no-nonsense stare, "I don't have to tell you anything."

The vehemence in her statement pulled Mat up short, and he gawked at her back as she continued on without him. Very rarely did she take that tone with friends, and to hear it from her now was shocking. Shaking his head in disbelief, Mat had to run to catch up with her.

For anyone entering this part of Haltho, it was like entering an entirely different world. In effect, they would be right – the small part of Haltho Mat and Kara had entered was considered sovereign Velusyian soil, and nearly all the Velusyian inhabitants of the district referred to the area as Velusyia-Ni in tribute to their homeland. Velusyia-Ni was home to the Velusyian embassy, warehouses, a Broker House, two inns and an assortment of shops and eateries selling and serving items native to Velusyia. There were also homes for a handful of Velusyian merchants, some of whom maintained their residence in Haltho year round. However, no matter the building's purpose, they all shared a common architectural theme that was as beautiful as it was unique. Each and every structure was made exclusively from shadowashe wood imported from Velusyia – the dark, rich-red hues exclusive to that wood – and flowed with one another in a harmony of style. Sloping, curved roofs were fitted with expertly crafted clay tiles painted in shades that ran from a deep-forest-green to rich blues, their sweeping overhangs supported by red-painted, robust columns that were strung with silk streamers. Wind chimes singing their lilting melodies were suspended from a number of overhangs, and a large number of the buildings' doors were painted in rich reds and adorned with decorative handles and knockers made of brass or gold. The aesthetic themes even extended to the poles of red-painted wood that flanked the meticulously maintained cobblestone roads. Erected every thirty paces, these richly carved poles served as anchor points for lines that supported paper lanterns dyed in a variety of rich colors.

Even the people – although Kara and Mat found themselves the focus of intense scrutiny – presented themselves with grace and dignity. Women were dressed in flowery giku – a long, robe-like silken dress wrapped tightly about the waist with colorful silk. The men were clad predominantly in loose silken shirts in a rainbow of colors, and their equally loose-fitting silk pants were tucked into supple leather boots or bound by sandals similar to those that adorned the feet of the women. There were men and women in the crowd that even had their faces painted with a thick white powder that made their stunning blue eyes and hair stand out like a bolt of lightning against a pitch-black sky. It was almost shocking to see that every Velusyian man and woman wore their hair long. Ponytails, horsetails, foxtails, braids, buns – there wasn't an adult man or woman whose hair was naturally shorter than their shoulders unless, of course, they were bald. Mat was even surprised to see the variety of weapons carried by the men and soldiers, each and every piece a work of graceful, flowing craftsmanship.

Yet every beautiful thing has its flaws – and with the Velusyians, it was easy to find. Stark against the beauty of Velusyia-Ni were the bowed backs of the dark-haired and dark-eyed Shalusyian. As Mat and Kara traveled the orderly streets, it was impossible to ignore the Shalusyian in their ragged, threadbare brown woolen gis and baggy pants. Every one of them wore an uncomfortably thick leather collar around their neck and heavy leather cuffs about their ankles and wrists, each binding fitted with iron rings to which their masters could attach chains. The sullen slaves were engaged in a variety of menial tasks that ranged from transporting goods to keeping the streets clear of trash and dung. Given the extent to which the slaves were being used, it came as no surprise to Mat to see them also laboring under the weight of sedan chairs; however, the sight of the two-wheeled wagons that some of them were pulling – which apparently were intended to carry two or three people instead of cargo – was quite baffling.

There were those, however, that appeared to have accepted their lot in life, and even some that showed signs of happiness. These slaves were the lucky few that had been elevated to loftier status – by slave standards – serving their masters in an assistant capacity by running errands and attending to their personal needs. Though they still

426

wore the same shackles as the rest of the slaves, their clothing was in better shape and they appeared to be in better health. Whether it was jealousy, malice, or even a sense of betrayal that fueled it, these elevated slaves received vehement glares from their lowly brethren.

Mat finally found himself shaking his head in amused disbelief as they passed by what appeared to be an eatery of sorts. Patrons knelt at short tables, drinking tea from glazed clay cups and eating their meals with small wooden sticks held between their thumb, fore and middle fingers. Slaves, their heads bowed subserviently, waited at the customers' disposal. Though the slaves appeared to be as still as a statute, they were shockingly quick to appease any customer that wanted something, leaving Mat with little doubt that such expedient service was in fear of the punishment that would befall them should they fail to please.

"Amazing," Mat stated, trying to digest it all. "I've never seen any place quite like this. There's a familiarity to it – yet, so foreign. Honestly, I had thought the Velusyians had ceased the slave trade."

Kara, doing her best not to scowl in disgust, shook her head in the negative. "Not completely. The majority of the slaves come from defeated enemies or people who have accumulated too much debt to pay it off by conventional means. However, there is a deep-rooted hatred for Shalusyians which still fuels the occasional raid." Mat could see that she was fighting hard to control her anger. "They try to justify the raids behind grandiose claims of honor – but it's nothing more than pure hate and bigotry. There's so much beauty in my people's culture, and this horrifying practice does nothing but sully it," she said with mournful disgust.

"They're not the only people to take part in the slave trade," Mat said gently as they turned onto a wide avenue with elegant and grandiose buildings lining the streets. Lilting music from a flute, as well as a string instrument that Mat was unfamiliar with, could just be heard in the distance.

"I know, but . . ." she sighed sadly. "I find it disgusting in any culture – but to see my own people still engaged in a practice that started over one man's folly . . ." she finished with a shake her head.

*"One man's folly?"* Mat thought incredulously. He had noticed that Kara seemed to be hiding an injury or an illness since she had passed out in the cave, and he had assumed that was partially responsible for her present mood, but her reaction to her own people's culture was a wound that was deeper than anything that had happened to her when she fainted. "Dare I ask?" he asked, knowing the answer.

"No, you don't," she said in a soft, remorseful tone. "Now come along and let's get this over with. .... This is hard enough for me as it is."

The remainder of their journey to the Broker House was made in silence. Mat had no idea what kind of memories Kara was battling with, but he had no desire to further enflame the conflict. Instead, he let himself continue to absorb the beautiful and strange culture about him. Even though he had noticed it before, it suddenly struck him just how many people were staring at them. Some of the stares were inquisitive, some cold, and others full of animosity. There were even quiet exchanges between people that seemed aimed their way. It wasn't as if they were the only non-Velusyians walking the streets; after all, trade was the lifeblood of Velusyia and it couldn't exist without a partner.

He then realized that the stares were not aimed at him. Instead, the dozens of sky-blue eyes were focused mainly on Kara. Carefully examining the people around them, he was able to piece the curiosity of the citizens' together with Kara's stories. Of all the Velusyian women on the street, Kara was the only one not in Velusyian garb, and more importantly, her clothing was that associated with a man; furthermore, she was the only Velusyian female that openly carried a weapon. For the Velusyians, this was as bizarre as their culture was to Mat. Kara's appearance had to be very upsetting to their traditional values, and given how patriarchal their society appeared to be, he could only imagine the words being exchanged and the thoughts rattling around the onlookers' heads.

While Mat was hard-pressed to not tense up at the unwanted attention, he could tell that Kara seemed to be fighting a strong urge to hit someone. Knowing her the way he did, he could hardly imagine her living amongst her people and accepting their cultural practices. All those thoughts were put aside as the road they were following terminated at what appeared to be a large, ornately decorated, circular plaza. Nearly a hundred yards in diameter, the well-maintained plaza had an official and proper air about it; from the buildings' designs to the plaza's layout, everything was intended to present order and authority. While Mat couldn't be sure what kind of business was conducted in the surrounding buildings, he found that his attention was caught by a befuddling display in the exact center of the square.

Circular in shape, the small park would have been bursting with color in the spring and summer, the grass a vibrant green and the five cherry blossom trees radiant with their pink and red blooms. Now, however, the flora had already shed blossoms and color alike with the onset of winter. Central to the park was a curious sight that once again had Mat raising his eyebrows. Three curved benches surrounded a stone-enclosed circle of sand in which were place stones of various shapes and sizes. In the center of the sand circle was an artfully crafted stone fountain that resembled a fish leaping from water. Water flowing from the fish's mouth slowly filled up a green wooden cylinder that would, with perfect precision, flip down onto the rocks at the base of the fountain with an audible thud, spilling the water into the basin every minute. As for the sand circle itself, Mat was amazed to see two elderly, shaved-pate Velusyians in regal silk robes adjusting the rocks and raking the sand with white wooden rakes.

Mat shook his head in disbelief and finally decided to break the silence. "Am I seeing this right? Are they actually raking *sand?*" he question in astonishment.

Kara glanced at the park as they made their way to the left, circling around it toward the large, central building at the back of the plaza. "That they are," she said simply.

"Why?" Mat asked incredulously.

"It's called a turoigi gaia, or a 'rock garden' in—"

"A what?" he blurted, not sure he had heard her right.

"A rock garden," Kara reiterated as a slight smile cracked her dour visage. "It's used as a method of meditation and contemplation. It can be quite relaxing."

"Wha— How—" Mat huffed and shook his head in disbelief. "You know what? I don't want to know. Everything I've seen in here has been strange enough – but a garden of rocks and sand is just too much."

Kara laughed at her friend's befuddlement and frustration, some of her tension relieved by his humorous reaction. However, her good humor was short-lived as her eyes came to rest upon the Broker House. Although it wasn't the largest building in the plaza, it easily stood out from the others. It was two-stories tall with a broad, curving roof of emerald-green shingles capping its dark-red wooden exterior. Red columns, inlaid with a golden floral motif, supported an overhang that sheltered the large red double doors that provided the only visible access to the building. A dozen white marble steps ascended to the doors, a series of large bronze cats adorning them. The bronze statues were divided into rows of three that were evenly spaced up the center and flanking ends of the steps, their fierce stares comically offset by a bizarrely happy half-smile and a paw raised in greeting. Mat wasn't sure if he should be terrified or amused by the cat statues.

"Honestly, Kara – I'm beginning to wonder what's in the water in Velusyia. Are those cats supposed to ward off something, or put people into a state of hysterics?"

Kara shook her head as they started up the stairs. "They're dakon shi-nekko or 'lucky cats' if you wish. Though these are a bit more . . . twisted than the typical ones," she said, recalling the chubby, cute versions from her childhood.

"Lucky?" he stated doubtfully. "I'm not sure I'd want the luck those would bring," he quipped as they made it to the landing.

Kara quickly moved them to the side as the doors swung open to allow two elderly men, their white hair waist length and braided, in elegant silk clothing to exit the building. Neither man seemed to notice them as they shambled by deep in discussion. As soon as they were past, Mat's attention was immediately grabbed by the dainty woman holding the door open and bowing at the waist.

Like all Velusyians, her hair and eyes were a vibrant blue, but unlike the others, her outfit appeared to be an opulent version of those worn by the slaves he'd seen earlier. Made of white silk, the gi fell just short of mid-thigh on her bronze-skinned legs, and was secured by a blue silk sash low on the slender waist of her attractively delicate figure. Comfortable sandals were laced up her to her knees, and a pair of delicate gold bracelets encircled both wrists. From those bracelets, a single, equally delicate chain of gold circled up each arm to vanish beneath the short sleeves of the gi. When she straightened, he was greeted by a provocatively low-cut neckline and the exposed upper curves of her breasts. Above those gentle swells, the gold chains running up each arm were once again visible, their ends linked to a slender gold hoop that was suspended between her breasts by a gold chain originating from the gorgeous gold torque hugging her neck. Another pair of gold chains ran from the torque, up each side of her neck and behind her ears before linking with a thin circlet of gold on her brow.

As soon as she saw the two of them, her small, pouting lips parted in a practiced smile and she bowed again while motioning them inside. Kara nodded to her, offering her a soft, sad smile even though she knew the girl could not see it, before leading Mat into the Broker House. As the door swung shut behind them, Mat found himself rooted in place just inside the door. He had been prepared to see a place of practical business, as he had witnessed at other Broker Houses on Solarson, but what greeted him was totally unexpected. The center of the room was constructed of white marble recessed in three consecutively smaller squares. The bottom one was filled with clear water and flora, while the level above it supported a stone bench on each side of the pool, three of which were occupied by opulently dressed Velusyians and Triclosians. On the main level, matching red columns connected the corners of the top square with the flat wooden ceiling twenty feet above the floor.

On the far side of the pool was an ornate, three-part façade that spanned the breadth of the room. Capped by a stylized mural, its midsection was a latticework of gold-painted wood, and its base was made of unadorned wood paneling that was painted red. Three protruding kiosks, with arched openings in the latticework, were manned by young women dressed in the same fashion as the girl who had opened the door. Six other similarly dressed women, three on each flanking wall, were waiting quietly with their heads bowed and hands folded in front of them.

The mural, however, was what held Mat in awe. Painted upon a cream-colored canvas – in a simple color scheme of black, white and blue – was a Velusyian woman not unlike those standing with downcast eyes around the room. Bursting forth from the clawing grasp of a turbulent ocean's dark waves, the girl's blue hair billowed back from her head as if caught in a violent windstorm, her locks blending into the sky the further from her they flowed. The chains streaming from her collar and shackles were in the process of breaking as fierce, sinewy dragons chewed at the links while dark hands from an inky cloud grasped eagerly at the dragons. As he stared at the heavily stylized scene, Mat felt like there was something haunting about the imagery. It was almost as if the scene was trying to dig up a memory that didn't quite belong to him. Then, as he focused acutely on the girl's face, it struck him.

"Oh, Kara . . ." he breathed. "Is that . . .?"

Jaw muscles clenched, she nodded as she unslung her pack and knelt down to dig the seal out again. "Not even a word," she ordered in a low whisper that only Mat could possibly hear. "If you're nice, maybe one day I'll explain it all," she added as she removed the seal. Securing her pack, she stood back up and said to Mat, "Wait here. I should only be a moment."

He nodded as she made her way toward one of the kiosks. Still looking at the mural, and giving no indication that he was aware of the hushed whispers and prying eyes of the room's other occupants, he made his way over to the column to his right and leaned upon it. So preoccupied was he with the mural, that he failed to notice the girl from the door slide up next to him until she gently cleared her throat. Startled, Mat would have jerked away if not for the column's support.

Head down and hands folded, the girl spoke in a humble, quiet tone, "Apologies, Paisen. My paisen bids you welcome and would know how I can be of service."

Despite her grasp of the Trader's Tongue, Mat found himself still having a bit of difficulty making out her heavily accented words. "Uh. . ." he started, not sure what to say. "I . . . um . . . I'm fine, thank you. Just waiting on my friend over there."

Without looking up, she said, "Ah, you are with the Velusen, no? A great honor to be near her."

Mat's face screwed up in confusion. "Velu . . . what?"

"Velusen. It means . . ." she concentrated for a moment, " 'Princess of the Sky' in your tongue. My apologies, this one is still learning your tongue."

He couldn't help but chuckle. "Princess of the Sky, huh? What makes you say that?"

"The title is given to those that favor the great Goddess Karalisa Masumaite," without looking up, she pointed to the mural. "She who rose from lalashia to carry our people from shadow to the sky."

Mat could barely contain a smile as he checked to make sure Kara wasn't looking his way. Though he didn't know what exactly the girl meant, he was beginning to put the puzzle together. "I take it from the Goddess' dress that you are a lalashia as well?"

"You are correct. This one is one of many lalashia that serve my paisen."

"And what does a lalashia do?"

"This one and others serve all needs of my paisen. It is an honor and privilege–"

She was cut off as a gruff, aged voice from somewhere behind the façade barked, "Do misthaishna, korisan desuma! Bakasan no turishiostia!"

The girl flinched at the gruff tone and quickly said, "Forgive this one. This one has strayed too long. If you need at all, let this one or another know." The girl bowed hastily before retreating into the shadows next to the doors.

Mat chuckled to himself at the absurdity of it all. While some people might react negatively to the level of culture shock he was encountering, he coped with it by seeking amusement in the new experiences; however, in that moment, his reaction was tempered by the puzzle of Kara's past. Like all the elder Wardens, she talked very little about her past, so the opportunity to glean hints from this small sampling of her homeland was a very satisfying distraction. Firm footsteps drew him from his thoughts, and he looked around to see Kara approaching with an irritated mask firmly on her face and two heavy coin pouches in hand.

Tossing one of the pouches to him, she muttered, "Let's get out of here."

Mat caught the pouch, his eyes widening at the weight, and began tying it to his belt as he fell in behind Kara. The door girl bowed deeply to them as she opened the door to grant them passage from the building. Although he didn't know if the girl could see him, he offered her a friendly and thankful nod of the head as he passed by. As soon as they were clear of the door, it closed quickly behind them.

Kara didn't even pause to make sure Mat was with her before she started down the stairs with a frustrated sigh. "Lousy, sexist, money-mongering bastards!" she muttered angrily to Mat as he moved alongside of her at the bottom of the steps.

"That bad?"

"Oh, you have no idea! Not only did the pig try to give me a raw deal on the exchange, but he twice tried to buy me as a lalashia from you! Twice!"

Unable to hide his smirk, he said, "Not your thing, I take it?"

Kara scowled at him as they hastily weaved their way through the crowd, "I've been there once – never again!"

"So I gathered," Mat quipped.

"The mural," she stated flatly.

"Yes indeed. One of the girls was nice enough to explain the painting to me. Left me with more questions – but I have to say, it seems like they put you on a pedestal at one point."

Snorting at the comment in disdain, she reached out along the currents of fir'gan and connected with Mat's thoughts. *"Oh yes, a pedestal, but only in as much as we Wardens saved their sorry hides from annihilation. Being a woman, though, only garnered me so much respect. My appearance and family holdings are what give me power in my dealings with Velusyia – making me one of the lucky few. Those women you saw – the lalashia – are high-class slaves that were voluntarily sold to better their families."*

Mat blinked, visibly shocked that someone would volunteer to be a slave. *"I had no idea. . . . And you were one at one time?"*

*"That I was,"* she replied with just a hint of pain in her voice. *"Though in my time, it wasn't voluntary. Lalashia have it better than geashia and the Shalusyian slaves. They're treated better, clothed and fed like royalty, and can leave at any time. However, while they do serve, they are nothing but objects. They have no name, no rights, and live only to serve – no matter how baseless or profane an act their masters ask of them. Should they choose to leave before their time is up, the dishonor they would bring upon their family could destroy it for generations."*

*"Corith be good, Kara. I had no idea."*

*"There are times I wish my family had sold me as a geashia. At least then I might have had a life and a name. There were so many times I wanted to leave, but I was young and didn't understand . . . nor did I want to bring that kind of shame upon my family. By the time I understood just what I was sold for. . . ."* Mat could hear the remorseful shake of her head in her thoughts. *"If not for my ascension to a Warden . . . I . . . I don't know what I would have done,"* she explained mournfully. *"After I became a Warden and could finally have a name again, I . . . I couldn't go by my old family name – not after what had happened to me and my family, or the way the Velusyians idolized me. So, I took the name Yokonagito and . . . well, here I am."*

Mat shook his head in sadness. The excitement of finding out about his friend's ancient past was ripped from him by the cold hand of sorrow. While he knew he wasn't getting the full story, it suddenly didn't matter to him anymore. To grow up in that kind of environment and live that sort of life – he couldn't fathom it. It even galvanized his firm belief that he never should know the history of the women he slept with in the brothels. It also occurred to him that his ventures into the temples of carnal needs might be ending with this knowledge. "Well," he said aloud, "you've certainly given me a lot to think about. Might have even gotten me to clean up my act some, too." He shook his head and added sarcastically, "Thanks a lot."

"You're welcome," she answered with a weak smile. "Now let's get out of here before any more unwanted memories are conjured up."

"Where to? I certainly doubt we're staying at any of the inns in this area. Although, I'm sure it would be an experience."

"For you? You're right about that." She chuckled. "The Broker even tried to recommend one of the inns to us. Probably belongs to a relative of his, and he saw it as a way to get some of my money back."

"Then where to?"

"Back to the Tradesman's Terrace," she stated with confidence. "We should be able to find a place that doesn't ask questions and we can blend in a bit and do our work in relative peace." She rubbed her eyes tiredly. "Besides, whatever caused me to pass out last night has taken it out of me, and I could use some rest before we get started."

Mat nodded, the mention of her fainting spell drawing a concerned look from him. "Are you okay?" he asked as they continued to retrace their steps through the increasing number of people on the road. "I never got the chance to ask about that."

Kara waved a dismissive hand. "I'll be alright. Just too much stress with all that happened and how chaotic the currents were," she replied softly, knowing Mat wouldn't buy the lie.

"If you say so," he answered, his tone confirming that he didn't believe her for one moment. "Just let me know if you need anything. It's too early in the trip for things to start going wrong."

Offering Mat a warm smile that did not echo what she felt inside, she said, "I will. I promise." Increasing their pace, she added, "Enough with bad memories and reflections. Let's see about getting us some fresh supplies, clothes, food and a place to stay. I'll send word to Mathis so he can spare us the annoyance of finding a reasonably honest merchant; that way, we can deal more with our work. I want to gather as much information as possible before risking a Search. Oh, and I saw a stand when we came in that makes these snacks that you will love."

"Oh, and what's that?"

"One is called suchino – it's a meat-stuffed dough ball cooked in oil. And the other is called onigi – and that one is a ball of rice stuffed with meats or sweets and wrapped in seaweed."

Mat stared at Kara's grinning face incredulously before rolling his eyes and muttering, "Crazy Velusyians."

# Chapter Nineteen

*T*hrusting toward the sky like a lone, gleaming spear, the Citadel seemed to fill Amroth's vision as he and Mathis approached the well-maintained and heavily manned walls. This close to the spire, details were easy to identify. Every twenty feet of the first hundred feet of the marble-sheathed Citadel was ringed with reinforced battlements, of which every other merlon was surmounted by a fierce gargoyle. The ring of marble-sheathed buttresses supporting the spire's weight were composed of a mix of sweeping curves and sharp angles that were both florid and intimidating at the same time. Atop the peak of the spire, two banners snapped in the wind – House Trivant's gold sunburst on an orange field, and the gold-star-adorned black banner of the Five Stars. The few windows that dotted the Citadel were narrow and deep for defensive purposes, and likely fitted with leaded glass on the inside. Guards could be seen pacing the battlements of the Citadel and the sturdy wall that ringed the grounds.

The last time Amroth had visited the seat of House Trivant, it was for Kale's marriage to Marie. Back then, the city and Citadel alike had been blanketed in decoration, and the air had felt alive with joy and excitement. Now, however, despite the appearance of a normal flow to daily life, the Citadel and the surrounding community seemed withdrawn and on edge. There was no mirth in the eyes of the guards who watched with cautious scrutinization as Amroth and Mathis approached the gatehouse. Unlike the guards at the other gates, these men and women held themselves with the measured confidence of war veterans and moved with purpose. While their practical kits were well maintained, they showed signs of age and use – faded leather, armor that had long ago lost its sheen, patchwork to shirts or pants that the wearer refused to replace, and weapons that were simple in design but effective in use. More importantly, although the tension in the air showed on some of their faces, they didn't appear to be the least bit fearful.

"Something has them on edge," Mathis muttered as his practiced dark eyes took in the trio of guards who had moved to block the gate as soon as they were aware of Amroth and his approach.

"Whatever would give you that idea?" Amroth asked sarcastically, still bitter about being maneuvered into learning to fight by Mathis.

Glaring at Amroth out of the corner of his eye, Mathis then led them to within ten paces of the guards, two men and one woman, before coming to a halt as the woman ordered in a deep voice, "Halt there and state your business!" She raised a sunburst-orange-gloved hand out toward them for emphasis, her studded brown leather armor creaking with the movement, while her left hand remained on the hilt of one of the two short swords sheathed at her boyish hips. A black shirt with puffy sleeves, slit four times vertically to reveal sunburst orange beneath, was tucked into brown leather trousers flowing down to steel-greaved feet. Unlike her companions, who had no slits in the sleeves of their shirts, she wore a chainmail coif instead of a full visor helmet, which gave her stern gray eyes unhindered vision. It also gave Mathis and Amroth a clear look at her handsome and stern face with its high cheekbones and its narrow, slightly off-centered nose.

"Not the welcome I would have expected," Amroth muttered under his breath.

Mathis grunted in agreement before replying to the woman who awaited their answer with her full lips pressed together firmly. "Well met, Sergeant," he greeted, identifying her rank by the slits in the sleeves of her shirt. "My companion and I seek entrance to the Citadel on business from House Merandith."

Lowering her hand, the female guard moved forward, crossing half the distance and demanding, "Names and proof of mission."

Mathis unslung his pack and placed it on the ground, asking, "May I?"

The sergeant nodded, both hands on the hilts of her swords.

"Thank you," he stated. "I am Captain Mathis de'Merandith Sormantale," he informed her as he released the latches on his pack and dug out his writ. "My companion's name is not of relevance," he added as he stood up and advanced on the sergeant, offering her the writ.

The sergeant accepted the writ, giving Mathis a curious glare. "Not of relevance, eh?" Grunting in amusement, she examined the writ before looking back up at Mathis and Amroth in surprise. Glancing at the writ again for confirmation, she shook her head as she handed it back to Mathis. "Deo be goo– My apologies for the gruff greeting, Captain," she stammered in mild surprise. "With the war going on, and with a growing situation within our borders, we can't be too careful."

Turning to the men waiting behind her, she ordered, "Stand down, men. All is well."

The soldiers seemed to relax a bit before returning to their posts.

"No apologies needed, Sergeant . . .?" Mathis inquired as she turned back to face them.

"Sergeant Ilisa Korgan of the Citadel Guard," she replied as Amroth joined them and Mathis returned the writ to his pack. "A runner informed us of your arrival in the city; although, he said there would be four of you."

"Our companions had other business in the city," Amroth replied simply.

"I see," Ilisa answered with a respectful nod to Amroth as Mathis shouldered his pack. "Well then, Doms Captain Torwin has been informed of your arrival and has already made arrangements for your stay. With your permission, I would be honored to show you to your cells."

"Cells?" Amroth asked in confusion, drawing a chuckle from Ilisa.

"An affectionate term for the small rooms in the Citadel," Ilisa explained. "She's a strong and willful bastion, but was hardly designed with comfort in mind. If there is a problem, I will gladly send word to the Academy that you wish rooms there."

Mathis shook his head. "No, that won't be necessary. We won't be staying long."

"I see. Well then, if you would permit me . . .?" she asked as she stepped to the side and motioned them toward the gate.

Nodding, Mathis said, "Lead on."

Entering the inner bailey of the Citadel, they saw that it was well kept and orderly. Two sets of stables, each capable of housing fifty horses each, flanked the main gate, and the ground between the west wall and the base of the Citadel was paved with tightly set stones. Flowing around the Citadel, the stone courtyard terminated against the hard-packed dirt parade grounds that separated the Citadel and its looming buttresses from the Academy that was located at the rear of the bailey. Though unable to see behind House Trivant's seat of power, the sturdy and functional buildings of the Academy could just be seen peeking to the sides of the spire; furthermore, they could hear the ring of steel on steel and smell the smoke from the forges that shared the unseen area. And if Mathis recalled correctly, even the barracks were situated somewhere behind the Citadel.

Ilisa led them directly toward a sturdy set of stone stairs that led up to a broad landing upon which sat the steel-banded, heavy

438

ironwood double doors of the Citadel's main entrance. Flanked by orange banners bearing the golden sunburst of House Trivant, and guarded by two halberd-wielding soldiers in full plate armor, the doors were like everything else about the Citadel – function over fashion. Constructed to withstand a battering ram, their steel-banded façade certainly looked like it could withstand such an assault. As Ilisa led them up the wide stone steps, the two guards moved toward the center of the doors and grasped the doors' heavy iron ring handles. Pulling firmly on the handles, the durable doors swung open with only a mild groan of protest. Nodding to the guards, Ilisa led Mathis and Amroth through the large, arching doorway and into the Citadel proper.

The well-lit hallway that greeted them was almost exactly as Amroth remembered it; tall and narrow, the hall's arched ceiling was supported by a latticework of thick support beams, and the corridor's sturdy stone walls were free of decoration except for the brass lanterns that were evenly spaced along their surface. For anyone unfamiliar with the Citadel's layout, the hall seemed to go on forever uninterrupted. However, as they proceeded down the hall at a quick pace, they soon encountered the first of four intersecting hallways that circled the interior of the Citadel, forming a series of concentric rings about the core of the spire. Two guards were posted at each intersection they passed through, and not once did Ilisa give any indication of veering onto one of the rings.

They could see numerous doors along the rings from their vantage point, as well as a plethora of the Citadel's residents. Soldiers, servants and courtiers alike traversed the rings, attending to whatever activities or assigned duties that required their attention. Although the Citadel was designed more for function, it clearly saw its fair share of political activity – as evident by the number of well-dressed people in residence. Amroth, however, was near positive that there had not been anywhere near the number of soldiers stationed within the spire's walls when he had last visited.

All thoughts of what had the Citadel on edge were driven from him as the hall they had been following spilled into the Citadel's main chamber. Circular in shape and nearly two hundred paces in diameter, the walls of the central chamber soared upward to meet with its hardwood ceiling nearly fifty feet above them. A corridor like the one they had just traversed was built at each cardinal point of the compass, permitting entry into the central chamber from other parts of the Citadel. There were no doors along the walls of the central chamber, only Three House Trivant banners and large brass lanterns to illuminate the vast chamber. Elegant couches were set against the walls along with a series of tables and chairs to provide visitors and residents alike with a place to sit and talk. However, it was the centerpiece of the chamber that stole the breath of most people.

Merged artfully with the massive central support column that ran the length of the Citadel was a sturdy spiral staircase that disappeared through an opening in both the ceiling and the floor. At one time, the staircase had been nothing more than a simplistic, functional architectural piece. Over time, however, the domses of House Trivant had added to it. One of the earliest improvements had been the addition of steel supports – forged and twisted into artful designs – to reinforce the staircase. Later, marble sheathing had been added to the support column, and its façade was eventually engraved with graceful patterns that were reminiscent of climbing vines. The most recent addition was added just before Marie's wedding – highly polished and tediously carved ironwood railings had been installed by Marie's brother to replace the simple pine railings that had stood for decades; furthermore, he also had brass lanterns mounted on the central support column along the path of the staircase, their golden light adding to the warm glow of the room ever since their installation.

"I'd forgotten how impressive it is," Amroth said softly to Mathis.

"It is quite a sight," Ilisa tossed over her shoulder as she led them toward the staircase. "House Trivant takes more pride in that feat than many others."

"I've yet to see its like," commented Mathis.

"I doubt you ever will," Ilisa said with a nod of her head. "It's said the builders took the secrets of its construction to their graves. We have architects constantly coming here to examine it. To be honest – from what I've heard – if they want to see something truly amazing, the Utherian Valley and its gates dwarf this feat."

"That it does," Mathis said softly as they followed Ilisa onto the staircase and descended below the floor.

They descended along the twisting staircase for two floors, passing a variety of the Citadel's residents; servants made way for the trio with bowed heads, soldiers offered salutes to the sergeant, while visitors and House officials merely glanced their way with indifference. Ilisa exited the staircase at the second floor in front of an open doorway guarded by two fully armored soldiers with shields and broadswords at hand.

She led them past the guards with a friendly nod to the soldiers. "This is where we house our guests that don't have a pole up their arse," she stated as soon as they were past the guards.

"I can see why you call them cells," Amroth offered with a chuckle, laughing off the jab at royalty as he looked around at the narrow hallways with their simple wooden doors and lantern-lit pathways. "This feels more like a dungeon than anything else."

Ilisa made a right at the first intersection and led them along the gently curving hallway. "You're right – this actually served as a prison during the Citadel's early years. One of Doms Trivant's ancestors – I can't remember which – decided to convert and expand the area into rooms some time after Sea Watch was built." She laughed. "Most visitors can hardly stand staying down here, and even some of the locals simply detest the rooms."

"What about you?" Amroth asked.

"Me? I'll stick to the barracks, thank you." Stopping between two unremarkable doors, she said, "Ah, here we go. The rooms to my right and left are yours. I'll leave you two to fight about who gets which. In the meantime, if you have any needs, one of the servants will be happy to assist, or you can simply find the House steward and shake him down for what you need. The doms captain is currently out touring the city, but should be back within the next two hours. There are washbasins in the room, should you wish to clean up, and there should be something left in the kitchens if you want a meal. I'll have someone sent to find you when the doms captain returns."

"Thank you, Sergeant. You've been most helpful," Mathis replied.

"My pleasure, Captain. Now if you'll excuse me, I need to return to my duties." Ilisa nodded to them before sliding between them and returning the way they came.

"Well then, what now?" Amroth asked.

"I don't know about you – but I'd like to get cleaned up and eat."

Amroth laughed. "I second that. Something other than rations would be very nice."

"It's settled then." Mathis unslung his pack and the sword case before handing both to Amroth. "Get yourself settled in and cleaned up. I'm going to find the steward and see about getting us some fresh clothing."

"Clean clothing sounds better than a meal," Amroth said as Mathis began to backtrack their steps. "Which room do you want?" Amroth called out to him.

"Surprise me," Mathis answered with a hint of humor in his voice.

"Great," Amroth muttered before peeking his head into each room. Upon realizing that the rooms were identical, he laughed and took the room on the left side of the hall.

Lit by the warm light of two small bronze lanterns, the undersized, square room reminded Amroth of a monk's cell, which was apt given its name. A simple bed occupied the far wall with clean linens on a thick mattress that, upon pressing on it, appeared to be stuffed with feathers. In the front-right corner of the room was a simple table, flanked by two chairs, with a basin and pitcher on it. A bronze chamber pot sat in the back-left corner of the room, tucked away beside an unremarkable wardrobe closet.

"Well, isn't this quaint," he muttered sarcastically as he tossed their belongings onto the floor before unbuckling his sword belt, depositing it and his sword on top of the packs, and sitting down on the plump mattress. Stripping off his boots, he stretched his tired back as the aches and pains of the previous week caught up with him. While he desperately wanted to clean up, he could feel his dark eyes growing heavy as he suddenly yawned with exhaustion. Deciding that a quick nap wouldn't hurt, he stretched out on the bed and immediately fell asleep.

Slumbering deeply, it took a rough shake of his shoulders to awaken him. Opening his bleary eyes, he saw Mathis standing over him with a slightly amused expression on his normally stoic face. Cleaned up, shaven, and with his dark hair in a horsetail, Mathis had changed into a black long-sleeve shirt with matching pants and knee-boots.

Sitting up sleepily, Amroth yawned before asking groggily, "How long was I asleep?"

"Nearly an hour," Mathis replied. "I've got you some fresh clothes," he added, gesturing to the neatly folded stack of garments beneath a pair of boots on the foot of the bed. "Its soldier's garb, but it was all I could wrangle from the steward – stingy little man."

Amroth rubbed his eyes and then his head, yawning again. "Deo be good – I needed that."

"So it would seem." Mathis clapped him on the shoulder and said, "Hurry up. I'd like to get something warm in my stomach before we meet with Oblet."

Amroth waved Mathis off sleepily and said, "Okay, okay. Give me a moment."

Nodding, Mathis then grabbed both his pack and sword case before exiting the room, closing the door behind him.

Muttering to himself, Amroth slowly stood up, his aches and pains making him groan. Stripping off his worn and tattered clothing, he pulled a razor from his pack and shambled over to the table where he poured water from the pitcher into the basin. Dipping his hands into the cold liquid, he leaned over and splashed his face, which left him gasping as if he'd been slapped. Shaking off the shock of the cold water hitting his face, he dipped his hands back in the bitter liquid and began washing down his arms and hands, followed by his chest and legs. The water rolled down the muscles of his thick frame, washing a week's worth of dirt into the basin and onto the floor and table. Shivering from the cold, Amroth leaned his head over the basin and poured the water remaining in the pitcher over his head, soaking his black hair. Shaking his head, he rubbed his face to clear his eyes before retrieving his straight razor and beginning the tedious task of shaving the beard that had grown over the last week.

When he was finally done with the task, he used his old shirt to dry off before quickly pulling on fresh smallclothes and the outfit Mathis had left for him. The attire was a little big on him, but not uncomfortably so. Stomping his feet to settle into the new boots, he smoothed back his hair from his face and exited the room.

Pushing away from where he was leaning against the wall, Mathis asked as Amroth shut the door to his room, "Ready?"

"Ready as I can be," Amroth replied.

"Good. Then let's eat."

"Do you know where we're going?" Amroth asked as they started down the hall.

"Indeed. I had some time while the steward requisitioned us some clothes, so I used it to refresh my memory of the place. I figured we'd dine with the rest of the soldiers instead of dealing with the irritation of eating with some of the more pompous folk in the dining hall."

Amroth smiled at both the comment and the thought of warm, fresh food. "Then what are we waiting for? Lead on!"

Making their way back up to the main floor, they found the Citadel more alive with activity than when they had arrived. The increase in people flowing through the Citadel turned the already narrow corridors into a tightly packed maze of human bodies. Mathis guided them north through the corridors and found himself bestowing apologies upon the host of people that they bumped into. At the third intersection, he turned right and led Amroth around to the east for a few paces before turning left and descending a staircase that was recessed into the wall. The level below was of older construction, and reflected traditional layouts instead of the circular floor plan that dominated the rest of the Citadel. As Amroth followed Mathis along the maze of dimly lit corridors, he could see the visual evidence of the section's age – the stonework showed signs of wear and corrosion, and the thick oak supports and doors, which groaned and creaked on occasion, were darkened by moisture and time. Aside from the lanterns, there was minimal decoration on the walls, which further reinforced the Citadel's militaristic intent in Amroth's mind.

Traveling through the halls, the clothing of the people they encountered gradually shifted from civilian apparel and livery to military dress, leading Amroth to conclude that they were making their way toward the barracks. His conclusion was confirmed when they ascended an old oak staircase to find themselves in a brightly lit, broad hallway. High overhead, a wooden roof supported by robust oak beams was clearly visible despite only a handful of the lanterns hanging from the walls being lit. A surprising amount of sunlight from the narrow window slits set high along the walls was enough to brightly illuminate the spacious stone corridor for the numerous soldiers – both in armor and causal garb – traversing the hall, their conversations and footfalls filling the air with a muffled, droning clatter.

Amroth found himself nearly oblivious to the other people they passed as his attention was caught by the numerous weapons and suits of armor displayed either in recessed alcoves or mounted on the walls. The trophies of days long past were kept in pristine condition, polished and displayed with reverence. There were even full suits of leather and cloth armor from Roselia's tribal days displayed alongside the heavier plate and chain mesh armors of the present day. Enamored with the mix of armors, Amroth could only imagine the secrets and mysteries scholars could clean from comparing and studying the protective garments.

When they reached the end of the hall, Mathis didn't hesitate in turning right onto the intersecting corridor, which not only brought an abrupt end to the spell cast on Amroth by the trophies, but left him scrambling a bit to catch up. Rejoining Mathis, Amroth was greeted with a wry grin, to which he shrugged sheepishly before motioning onward.

As they wound their way through the barracks' organized hallways, it wasn't long before the aroma of food began to lace the air. Most of the soldiers barely spared the two a glance, but their unfamiliar faces did manage to draw a curious look or two. Mathis paid it

444

little heed, so Amroth took comfort in that and followed his lead. Suddenly, a chorus of chattering voices began to echo through the halls even as the smell of fresh food blanketed their nose like a thick fog. Like a hound locked-in on its prey, Mathis led them unerringly toward the succulent smells and din of noise.

A descending staircase, wide enough for four people to walk abreast, announced their arrival at the barrack's mess hall. Soldiers poured up and down the stairs like a waterfall, making the decent down the stairs feel somewhat claustrophobic. Even so, the two of them eased their way into the quickly moving line of hungry men and women with only a few cursory glances aimed their way. With the steady pace that the line was moving, it didn't take them long to reach the bottom of the stairs and pass through the gaping, arched doorway and into the very large mess hall. A wave of indistinguishable chatter washed over them, originating from the dining troops that packed the benches of the longtables that were arranged in three rows along the length of the hall. Large windows set high on the walls allowed sunlight to spill upon the masses. Six massive chandeliers hung from the solid roof, their numerous wicks ready to be lit as soon as the sun sank low enough to withdraw its light from the room.

From their vantage point at the mess hall's entrance, they could see the long line of people awaiting food. Snaking its way along the front and right-hand walls, the line terminated at a series of food-laden tables set near the back of the hall in front of an open door from which scullions scurried to and fro as they delivered fresh food to the food line or returned dishes to the kitchen to be cleaned. It was awe-inspiring and somewhat surprising to see so many soldiers in Haltho given the number of troops Trivant had led to Kale's aid. Amroth mentioned as much to Mathis, which drew a knowing nod from the veteran.

"House Trivant has the privilege, you might say, of being able to draw upon the fighting power of the clans," he informed Amroth as they moved steadily toward the setup of cauldrons and food platters on the far end of the room. "House Trivant's military is quite sizable, but most of its manpower is dedicated to their sizable fleet, and more importantly, defending Haltho and the outlying areas. Without the clans' willingness to fight under the Trivant banner, he would have been hard-pressed to bring what he did and still leave his holdings with anything resembling a proper defense."

"I see," Amroth said with a reflective nod of his head. "I never really understood how the relationship between the clans and House Trivant worked."

Mathis grunted. "It's not an easy arrangement to understand. On the surface, it has the simple appearance of the clans answering to House Trivant as all of Roselia does. Beneath that guise, however," he shrugged, "it's a lot more complicated and volatile than that."

"How so?" Amroth asked even as he noticed their conversation drawing a few curious glances.

"Well, for starters, the clans technically answer only to the Clan Elders and go where and when they please – which more or less makes them an autonomous nation running free within Roselia's borders. As long as they don't do anything to egregiously violate Roselian law, they can essentially do as they please without so much as a friendly notice to House Trivant."

Blinking in surprise as the weight of Mathis' statement set in, Amroth breathed, "Deo be good. . . . The implications of such an arrangement are—"

"Staggering?" Mathis finished, drawing a nod of agreement from Amroth. "It is. And it's been a source of tension for generations, as I understand it. If not for the clans' strong sense of honor and loyalty, House Trivant could easily be looking at a very fierce rival at its gates in the best of times." He glanced at Amroth and added admonishingly, "You really should have paid more attention to your studies."

Amroth shook his head in amazement, smiling slightly at the friendly, verbal jab. "From what I've seen in the field, and from what Dakan did to those men. . . ." He shook his head again. "I don't envy Doms Trivant, and I'm not too sure I haven't developed a whole new level of respect for him."

Mathis cracked a slight smile as they approached the food-laden tables from which the mouthwatering aromas originated. "That's good to hear. House Trivant brings a strong force to bear in the clans." He grunted. "I'm just glad they're family and not an enemy. Now," he continued as he picked up a wooden platter for himself and handed one to Amroth, "enough about politics and frightful what-ifs – let's eat."

By the time they reached the end of the food line, their platters were weighed down with tender rahken, black bread, a few berries from an early batch of snowberries, and potatoes mashed up and covered in thick gravy. Grabbing a fork and knife along with a tankard filled with goat milk each, Mathis and Amroth searched out as private a place in the packed mess hall as they could find. They eventually found two open seats along the wall in a puddle of warm sunlight. Making themselves as comfortable as they could in the cramped

446

quarters and on the hard wooden benches, they tore into their food like men who had not seen a decent meal in months. The men and women seated near them watched with mirth as the two stuffed their mouths with barely a word passing between them.

"Hells' bloody balls, lads," the slender, aged veteran in well-maintained leather armor sitting next to Amroth quipped. The leathery skin of his clean-shaven face pulled up into a smile around his small, green eyes, revealing a mouth full of chipped yellow teeth. "You'll choke eating that fast," he commented as he ran a gnarled and callused hand over his shaved head. "I'd almost think you haven't seen real food in months, cramming it down your gullet like that."

Chewing quickly, Amroth swallowed enough of his mouthful of food to speak clearly. "We haven't seen a real meal like this in a while," he said with an amused grin.

The slender solider pointed his fork at the food and stated with a snort, "You call that real food? Deo be good – you two must be daft or starving ta give it that kinda praise."

The large man, clad in armor akin to the slender man, sitting across from the grizzled solider let out a wheezing, guttural laugh in agreement.

The aged soldier motioned to the big man, whose piggish blue eyes gleamed with mirth from a full face framed by a mass of short-cut blonde hair, and added, "See! Even my friend here finds it funny! And he should know –just look at that belly! Totts here knows his food!"

Casting a small, friendly grin on the two Trivant soldiers, Mathis asked with a hint of amusement, "Well then– Totts was it?" The big man nodded. "If there's better food to be found, and the two of you are aware of it, then why are you eating in the mess?"

The aged veteran shook his head sadly and said in a bemoaning tone, "Alas, my poor friend here canna speak. Show'um, Totts."

The big man turned his head to face Mathis and Amroth and opened his thin-lipped mouth to reveal that he was lacking a tongue.

Amroth cringed at the sight and asked, "What in Deo's name happened to you?"

Totts closed his mouth as his friend spoke for him. "Afraid tha lad went and got himself caught a few years back. He was a mouthy young lad with ah wicked tongue and gave 'is captors quiet the colorful tongue-lashing. Well, they got sick of the verbal attacks and up and cut out his tongue."

"I– I– . . . My condolences," stammered Amroth.

The older man grinned broadly. "Ah don't be, lad! Without his tongue, he doesn't get into much trouble – which makes him less of a pain in tha arse for me. Between you and me though," he lowered his voice like he was about to convey an important secret, "I be think'n that what actually happened – was he went and got drunk and up and married a demon of ah woman. Once she realized what had befallen 'er, I think she up and cut 'is wicked tongue out and fed it to 'um before run'n as far away as possible." Laughing he winked at Totts and said in a normal tone of voice, "Isn't that right, Totts?"

The big man glowered at him even as Mathis and Amroth shook their heads in amusement at the tale.

The old soldier took a sip from his tankard before continuing. "Ah, where are me manners? My ma would tan my hide – Deo rest her soul – if she caught me forget'n proper behavior. They call me Leathers – Sergeant Leathers. And the big lout is Private Totts. We're with Trivant's House Guard."

"Leathers?" Mathis asked with an arched eyebrow. "How did you come by such a . . . colorful name?"

Leathers smiled broadly again before answering. "My dear ma didna grace me with such a name. Afraid the lads around here took ta calling me it around twenty years ago or so on account of what the sun done did to me flesh – turned it as dark and hard as the armor I wear. It finally got to tha point where they all joked that they couldn't tell where tha armor ended and me skin began." He chuckled. "Well the name kinda stuck, and I never saw a reason to change peoples' minds about it." He paused and eyed Mathis and Amroth in an appraising manner. "What about you two lads? I'm pretty good with faces, and don't fancy ever seeing tha two of you about. I'd say fresh meat given how wet behind tha ears this lad looks," he pointed at Amroth. "But you have tha look of a cold-blooded killer about you," he added with confidence and a nod to Mathis.

"Very observant of you," Mathis replied.

Leathers shrugged nonchalantly. "It's nothin'. But you don't go about soldiering as long as I have without ah good eye for reading people . . . and ah bit o' luck."

Mathis nodded in agreement. "Indeed. To answer your question – we're a bit of both. We just arrived in Haltho today, but we're not part of House Trivant's forces."

"Ah. . . . Then who might you two lads be then?" Leathers asked with a mix of caution and curiosity.

448

"I'm Mathis, and my young friend here is Amroth. We're with the Five Stars main army, and headed back home for some leave."

Leathers smiled broadly. "Well, isn't this ah sight ta behold – two men fresh from where all the action is! Tell us, how goes tha fighting?"

Mathis shrugged casually. "Well enough. We struck House Suldamik a harsh blow about a week back. Doms Merandith felt that with the onset of winter, along with that victory, that it would be wise to give some of the men a chance to return home and rest up."

"Deo be praised!" Leathers clapped his hands and laughed. "You hear that, Totts? They've done hurt tha Suldamiks, and now they get ta go home and sit around like tha rest of us," he said with a bit of envy in his voice, to which Totts merely shook his head sadly.

"You don't like being stationed at home?" Amroth asked in confusion, noticing a mummer at their table as the other soldiers picked up on their conversation and passed on what Mathis had said about the victory, a few of them even going so far as to raise their cups in salute to Amroth and Mathis. "I would think it would be nice not to have to worry about attacks every hour of the day," Amroth finished as he and Mathis returned a few of the salutes with acknowledging nods.

"Oh don't get me wrong, lad. I'm too old ta be running about fighting and sleeping on tha cold hard ground. But mark ma' words – if I was ten years younger, I'd be tha first ta sign up for that duty, and I'd drag this waste of space with me," he finished with a playful wink at Totts.

Even as he stuffed his tongueless mouth with food, the large man rolled his eyes and grunted back at Leathers.

Just as he was about to ask how things were around Haltho, Amroth noticed a young pageboy standing nervously behind Mathis, his blue eyes studying Amroth closely. The loose white shirt and House Trivant sunburst-crested orange doublet looked too big on the boy's lanky body, which made him seem more awkward and out of place than he already appeared to feel. "Is there something we can do for you, lad?" Amroth asked politely, startling the page and drawing the others attention to the boy.

The page looked like he wanted to leap out of his boots as Mathis turned around to catch a glimpse of who was behind him. Swallowing hard, the boy gathered his courage and stammered, "I– I– . . . . Are you Captain Mathis de'Merandith Sormantale?"

The mention of Mathis' full name stunned both Leathers and Totts, as well as drawing curious glances from the soldiers within earshot.

Amroth offered the boy a warm, friendly smile before replying, "I'm Amroth, his friend." He pointed to Mathis. "This is the man you're looking for."

The young boy blanched as he met Mathis' gaze and seemed like he wanted to, at the very least, take a step back.

Mathis softened his visage in an attempt to calm the boy. "Indeed I am, lad. What can I do for you?"

Amroth smiled inwardly, in both appreciation and amusement, as the page did his best to put on a brave face in a situation that was obviously making him very uncomfortable. "Um– I– uh–" the boy stuttered, drawing amused grins from Leathers and Totts. The boy blushed a bit in embarrassment before gathering himself and blurting in a rush of words, "Doms Captain Torwin sent me. He wishes to speak with you and your compan– compan– . . . friend. I am to show you to his study."

Amroth could hear a hint of mirth in Mathis' voice as the veteran replied, "Thank you, lad. We'll see to it right away." Mathis fished around in his coin pouch, pulled out two talons and handed it to the boy. As the boy accepted the coins nervously, Mathis added, "No need for you to lead us there. I know the way."

The boy's eyes went wide as he got a good look at the coins in his hand. With his eyes looking like they were about to pop from his head, the page bowed and stammered, "I– I– Than– Thank you, Captain!" The page bowed a second time before darting off with his prize.

Amroth couldn't help but laugh aloud as he watched the page quickly weave his way to the mess hall entrance, clutching tightly to the coins. "Well Mathis, I think you just made that boy's year. He's probably never had so much coin in his life."

"Aye," Leather's prodded jokingly. "Why'd you have ta go and do that, Captain? Now he'll expect everyone ta be hand'n out coin."

Mathis grinned as he stood up, Amroth following suit. "Not my problem," he teased dryly. "If you'll excuse us, gentlemen, it appears we've got a meeting to attend."

"Nice meeting you two," Amroth added as they started away from the table.

Leathers and Totts watched, along with the curious soldiers within earshot of the conversation, in stunned silence as Mathis and Amroth joined the flow of people leaving the mess hall. Slowly, the two Trivant soldiers looked at each other and burst out laughing.

"Well, well, Totts – we just dined with ah legend there! The women down at tha Dirty Pillows will be all over us when we walk in with that story!"

Unable to speak, and his eyes glinting with merriment, Totts gave Leathers a broad, excited grin in response.

Still chuckling from their interesting encounter with the eccentric duo in the mess hall, Mathis swiftly retraced their steps back to the main chamber of the Citadel. The composition of the people flowing through the central chamber had shifted markedly to a militaristic tone. There were soldiers leaning against the curved walls chatting, as well as at least a dozen officers ascending the central staircase. All of them looked tired and their armor and clothing was dirty and worn from time in the field. As Amroth and Mathis joined the flow of people climbing the staircase, the familiar smell of sweat, dirt and horseflesh filled their nostrils like a heady perfume. At the second floor, the majority of the officers exited the staircase and made for their quarters while the remaining few soldiers, along with Amroth and Mathis, continued upward. By the time the duo exited the central staircase on the fourth floor, the only people left on the stairs amounted to a small army of servants on their way to their duties in the living quarters on the upper floors.

Amroth wanted to groan when he noticed that the fourth floor, like the three below it, mimicked the main floor's layout. He was beginning to wonder how one could maintain sanity amongst such a monotony of design, much less avoid getting lost. Other than a shift in where doors were positioned, the only other change he could see was in the décor. Where the lower floors had been barren of frivolities, he was now seeing quality wood trim and paneling, a few paintings and tapestries, as well as elaborate and highly polished lanterns.

As Mathis led them to the outer ring, they encountered very few people. Those they did pass, were well-dressed servants and courtiers who paid little heed to the two of them in their soldiers' garb. The sight of the courtiers made Amroth wonder if the Citadel even had a throne room proper. He'd never seen one in his visit years ago, and given what he had seen up to this point, he was beginning to get the feeling that Doms Trivant ran everything from an office like a merchant would. Shrugging to himself, he followed Mathis to the floor's outer ring. Without pause, Mathis confidently turned right and moved quickly down the curved hall.

"Confident that you know where you're going, eh?"

Nodding, Mathis replied, "Indeed. The Citadel has hardly changed over the years, and Oblet is a creature of habit. I doubt the old man would have moved his quarters without serious prodding."

"And if he has moved his quarters?" Amroth asked with a smirk.

"Then I'll ask someone," Mathis replied with a casual shrug of his shoulders.

After walking nearly halfway around the outer ring, Mathis came to a stop in front of a heavy oak door with a bronze sunburst mounted on the center of it. Grunting at the status symbol, Mathis raised his hand and rapped on the solid wood with his knuckles.

The dull strikes echoed in the hall and were greeted from within the room by a rough voice barking, "Enter!"

Mathis glanced at Amroth slyly before grasping the iron handle and pushing the door open.

Upon entering the large room, they were greeted by a narrow embrasure window on the far wall that was flanked by two sturdy bookcases filled with carefully organized books and scrolls. To their right and left were two individual doors, which they assumed led to the rest of Oblet's rooms, flanked by swords and armor that Oblet had kept as trophies. An elegant but sturdy mahogany desk sat in the center of the room atop a plush red rug. Twin red-cushioned mahogany chairs were arranged before the desk, and what appeared to be a slightly larger version of the chairs sat behind the desk. An unlit brass lantern stood on each front corner of the desk like stoic sentries, while neatly stacked piles of books and scrolls were arranged along the sides of the desk. The front of the desktop was clear, except for a writing kit, providing a clear line of sight for the balding, grizzled Roselian standing behind the desk.

"I'll be drakuma fodder! I thought the steward had finally gone daft when he told me you two were here! Come in! Come in and make yourselves at home!"

Although nearly sixty-five summers old, Doms Captain Oblet de'Trivant Torwin moved with a grace that belied his average stature and muscled, heavy bulk as he strode from behind the desk. Clad in a blue-enameled breastplate with a raised golden sunburst in the center of his chest, his outfit was finished off with an off-white tunic and matching breeches, and black riding boots. The swirling patterns of golden thread that were embroidered about the edges of his clothing stood out in sharp contrast to the dirt that marred him from time in the saddle. There was nothing about his sun-darkened and lined face or his hard black eyes that said Oblet was comfortable in such lavish attire. Quite possibly the only items on his person that seemed appropriate for him were the unadorned, sturdy leather sword belt about his waist, and the equally nondescript broadsword sheathed at his left hip.

"Well met, Oblet," Mathis greeted the elder soldier as the two embraced fiercely. Pulling back from the doms captain, he added, "You're looking well."

Oblet snorted. "My bones creak more with every winter, and my arse hurts more every time I drag myself into the saddle. But if it that means I look well . . ." he let out a throaty chuckle, "then I'll take it as a compliment, coming from you." He turned his attention to Amroth, examining him with a practiced eye. "And you, young Amroth – why last I saw you, you were yay-tall," he quipped, holding his hand up at about mid-chest. "How have you been, lad?"

"Well, Doms Captain. I'm sorry I did not visit when we were marching south. A blacksmith's work is never-ending with an army that size."

"I can well imagine and, for Deo's sake, drop the titles. We're family here unless, of course, you've done developed a liking for formal decorum. In which case, I'll be more than happy to drop 'shi'domses' all about your merry head, and you can use my title till your sick of it."

Amroth grinned broadly, "Oblet it is."

"See, that's better," Oblet quipped as he led them to the desk. Seating himself behind it in the large, high-back chair, he motioned to the other chairs. "Have a seat, and tell me what brings you two away from the front lines."

They settled themselves into the chairs before Mathis spoke. "Business, mostly," he reached into his shirt and pulled out a half-dozen letters, sealed with either House Merandith or House Trivant's seal, and placed them on the desk. "We're headed for Merset."

"Merset, eh? Why there? I doubt Kale has turned tail and run." Oblet leaned forward and collected the letters. Despite the letters serving as evidence to the contrary, he grinned wickedly and said jokingly, "Don't tell me you two have deserted?"

Mathis snorted in mock disgust. "Hardly. Kale has decided to return home for the winter, and we were sent ahead to spread the word."

"Deo be praised!" Oblet said with a clap of his hands. "Does that mean Lucas is returning home as well?"

"Not quite. As I understand it, a large portion of his troops will be returning home while he heads to Merset to see his sister and reclaim his wife."

"Ah! There's the gilded dagger! I'm gonna have what? A couple hundred more hungry mouths to feed and shelter? Couldn't you have at least lied to me? I've got enough on my plate as it is."

Mathis shrugged. "Afraid I couldn't do you that injustice, my friend."

Shrugging his large shoulders, Oblet continued, "Maybe it's for the best. We could use the extra men about now."

"Raiders?" Mathis asked, already knowing the answer.

"I see someone's been flapping their lips," the doms captain replied with a snort.

"Not really," Amroth jumped in, not wanting someone to take the blame for something they did not do. "We had a run-in with House Suldamik raiders on our way here."

Mathis glared at Amroth out of the corner of his eye, but instead said, "True. Bandit raids and darker stories also seemed to be on everyone's lips as we made our way into the city. Any idea what is going on?"

"Hells, you probably know more than me if you've come face-to-face with them. We've lost twenty men to them, as well as livestock, and not gotten closer than bowshot to them. The people we've talked to have been useless as well. Can't finger them for more than bandits, but it doesn't surprise me that they'd be Suldamik's troops. Deo only knows there has been raiding since the start of the war, but this new assault seems more widespread. I've even heard rumors of attacks as far north as Tiliea." Oblet shook his head and laughed darkly. "I almost pity the poor sods if that's true. Allanian will make short, brutal work of them."

Both Amroth and Mathis cracked small grins, knowing what Oblet said about the Merandith's House Guard captain to be all too true.

"We're only going to be here a couple days, but is there anything you need us to do while we're here?" Amroth offered, trying to steer the conversation to less violent subjects.

Oblet scratched at his baldpate before saying, "Not sure, lad. If you could clear up the weather along the coast, I'd offer you a ship so you could avoid any other run-ins with raiders, but you're more likely to end up a soaked corpse if you take that route." Amroth cringed a bit, recalling the wreckage of Kara and Mat's ship. "Other than that, well . . . I kind of hesitate to mention this, being rumors and all, but– "

"But what?" Mathis prodded, leaning forward.

Oblet drummed his thick fingers on the desk for a moment before deciding to speak what was on his mind. "Well, you see, we've had rumors of darker things roaming the Alderian Forest for the past couple of weeks. Didn't think much of it at first, till the rumors persisted and even grew to include a giant drakuma – said to be clad in shadows – leaving a trail of dead forest drakuma in its wake. I sent out a squad to investigate but they never came back. At first, I simply thought that raiders had gotten them, but then I received a letter saying that a few clansmen were on their way here to talk to me about a growing shadow on the lands; they even state they have 'proof' of their claims. I was hoping you'd stick around and hear what they have to say. You've seen a hell of a lot more of the world, and even know the clans history and myths a bit better than me. I'd consider it a favor if you'd weigh in on it."

Mathis nodded slowly, his dark eyes narrowing thoughtfully. "When are they supposed to arrive?"

"Middle of next week. The weather has been foul of late, so I'm sure it's slowed them some."

Mathis cringed. A delay like that would put them even further behind schedule, which would require them to then take a faster and more risky route in order to stay well ahead of the returning troops. However, after what he and Amroth had been through in the Alderian Forest, he was keen to have answers to questions he'd rather not have to ask. Besides, an old friend asking for help was something he didn't shrug off lightly. Nodding, he answered, "I'd be happy to lend an extra ear to the story."

Wide-eyed, Amroth looked at Mathis and blurted, "What?!"

"I think it's worth the wait, Amroth. What we encountered in the Forest needs an explanation, and this looks like a very promising place to start. Besides, I don't want to rush north and miss a possible danger to Kale. We can always risk the sea route if the weather has cleared up enough . . . and there's a captain crazy enough to take us north."

Amroth stared at Mathis skeptically, but said nothing.

Relief seemed to flood through Oblet as soon as Mathis agreed to help and Amroth did not put up an argument. "That's good to hear. Oh, and one more thing before you go," he leaned forward and pulled open the large central drawer in the desk. Removing a small object neatly wrapped in thick wool cloth, he said, "We had a farmer bring this in about four days ago. Claimed his friend found it sticking out of a tree. He also said his friend nicked himself on it and immediately fell ill before dying horrifically." Unwrapping the item slowly, he presented it to Mathis and Amroth. "Said they had to burn the body quickly because the stench was so foul that they feared plague. Personally, I think he's making it all up. But with everything else that's going on, and how odd this thing looks, I thought I'd hold on to it."

Mathis' breath caught as soon as he saw the rippling black surface of what appeared to be a small, barbed arrowhead made out of obsidian. There was a flaky residue on the edges of it that had his mind screaming warnings even as he reached out and – keeping the cloth between the arrowhead and his flesh – took object in hand. "It definitely looks like it had poison of some sort on it," he said with a calmness that hid the anxiety twisting his stomach in knots. "Have you had any of the traders or smithies look at it?"

Oblet nodded in the affirmative. "Aye, with no luck. I have an appointment to meet with a Velusyian trader next week. But until then, it's nothing but a fancy rock with a powder you've confirmed as poison on it."

"Mind if I take it and show it to a few people?" Mathis asked, his eyes still focused on the shard.

"Not at all, but I have no idea who in Haltho you'd show it to that I haven't."

"I have a friend that has connections in Velusyia-Ni that might be able get me in quicker, as well as a few less than savory people that might be of help."

As Mathis folded the shard back up in the cloth, Oblet snorted and rolled his eyes. "I'd love to have the connections you and Jerom bring to House Merandith. Maybe one day you'll share with me, eh?"

Mathis secured the shard in his belt pouch before smiling slyly at Oblet. "One day . . . maybe. Now, I have a small request of you."

"Ask away. What's mine is yours."

"Kale has convinced Amroth here to fully pursue martial training, and put me in charge of him."

"Deo be good! What a day of surprises and blessings! About damn time, lad!" Oblet barked with an amused laugh.

"So I've been told," Amroth muttered dryly.

"How can I help?" Oblet asked sincerely.

"Some private time on your training grounds with no interruptions, if you would?"

Oblet nodded. "Done. Need weapons or armor?"

"No need. I have a writ that will get anything I need equipment wise, and I'm sure the practice gear at the Academy will suffice. The time is the only thing you need to concern yourself with."

"I'll see to it that you get some time tonight and every evening till you leave in the officers' training hall in the Academy. It's indoors, so you can seal yourselves in without worrying about prying eyes or the weather. Deo knows there's plenty of soldiers that would love to watch an Academy Sword Master at work."

"My thanks, Oblet." Mathis stood and signaled for Amroth to do the same. "I'll see what I can find out about your little find and let you know."

Oblet stood and said, as he walked them to the door, "Thank you. I'll send word about the training hall time as soon as possible. If there's anything else you need at all – don't hesitate to ask."

Mathis took Oblet's wrist in a handshake as Oblet opened the door. "Thank you again, Oblet. Until later then."

Oblet nodded to the both of them as they left the room before closing the heavy oak door behind them.

Mathis strode off at a casual pace with Amroth at his side. It didn't take long for Amroth to read the tension on Mathis' face and ask, "You know what that object is, don't you?"

The muscles in Mathis' jaw twitched before he said, "I have an idea – but I'd prefer not to jump to any conclusions until I've discussed it with people that might know better than me."

Recalling Mathis' remark about Velusyia, Amroth stated confidently, "You mean to ask Kara about it."

"And if I do?"

"Then you've got more questions to answer than I believed I could ever come up with."

Remaining quiet as they turned onto one of the connecting halls and made for the central staircase, Mathis was tense with apprehension. He had no intention of asking Kara about the arrowhead, as he already was well aware of what it meant, and could only think to himself, *"If things continue to go the way they are, you'll have more answers than you could ever want."*

# Chapter Twenty

*T*he dragon was huge. Not huge in the way a man would perceive a torgen or even a drakuma to be in comparison to himself – but huge in the way a mountain dwarfs everything surrounding it. Crouched as it was – the four fingers on each of its four immense feet digging shockingly large talons into the stone beneath it – the broad shoulders of its forelegs looked large enough to bear the weight of the mountain that its size drew comparisons to. Seated behind those shoulders was a second pair of mind-numbingly powerful shoulders and pectorals that were responsible for controlling the sleek and powerful wings half furled near its flanks. Like the forelegs and the primary shoulders, the extra muscle groups appeared to be coiled with enough power to propel the giant beast airborne.

As if some god had found the beast's size and apparent strength to be lacking in intimidation, every inch of the dragon's powerful bulk was also girded with armored scales that were nearly half the size of a man. Those scales, however, were dwarfed by the massive, ridged spinal scales – akin to those on a drakuma's back – protecting its spine. Spanning the length of its behemoth torso like a proud plume of feathers, the scales terminated at the base of a strong and deadly tail that was curled around its clawed feet as if ready to lash out and pummel its prey into dust.

Then there was its head; held low to the ground atop a neck as thick as a massive ironwood, it was shaped like a squared-off, angular boulder, and crowned with an array of beautiful but deadly horns jutting from the rear of its ridged skull. Smaller – but no less dangerous – protrusions were arranged along the thick-boned, heavy brow line that was furled above eyes the color of an angry green sea that sparkled in the afternoon sunlight. However, what little majestic beauty the dragon might have retained in spite of its aggressive posture was shattered by the menacing snarl that dominated its lips. Peeled back as they were, its lips revealed a powerful mouth full of serrated teeth that were as long as a man's arm and possibly more terrifying than its talons.

Even at the distance and height from which Craigan admired the massive and magnificent statue, it was impossible not to feel awe tinged with respectful fear at the behemoth piece of black-streaked, gray stone sculpture and its magnificent striations of jade. To have such an intimidating but silent guardian standing watch over the main entrance of the Utherian Valley spoke volumes about how the people of Triclose must have felt about Doms Luthur Gravit'nas. Even if Chalin Keep had been constructed next to the dragon statue, Craigan – from his perch on the sixth floor balcony of the keep – would have still had to crane his neck so his powerful blue eyes could look the beast in the eyes. No artisan, engineer or architect could begin to fathom how such a creation had been erected. So, like the Utherian Valley itself, the dragon statue's origin was credited to lost magics. While whatever or whoever had constructed it was lost to the flow of time, one fact remained undeniable – the statue's enormous size made it easy to see from any part of the city, inspiring fear in Chalin's would-be foes and strength in the city's denizens.

Bare, strong forearms resting on the balcony railing, Craigan let his eyes drift away from the entrance to the Utherian Valley and across the city, following the limestone-sheathed ramparts, and its numerous towers, as the looming structure arched its way around the city. Within the protective horseshoe-shaped barrier, Chalin flowed over the level terrain before the Utherian Valley with military precision. A carefully thought-out and constructed grid of gently curving streets and alleys divided the city into large blocks. As Craigan understood it, when Chalin was originally constructed, the city was sectioned off into districts representing the different cultures of Triclose. Towering minarets of the desert had stood side by side with the classical, soaring architecture of Central Triclose and the sturdy stone structures of the North. Velusyia had even garnered a portion of the city, contributing its organic, flowing designs to Chalin's beautifully eclectic grandeur.

After the city had nearly been razed by the end of the Second Great War, the city had been rebuilt devoid of the symbols of Triclosian unity and replaced solely with Central and Northern Triclosian architecture. This shift in perception left both the Utherian Valley main gate – over which the behemoth dragon statue stood silent vigil over – and the gardens and parks that surrounded it as the only signs of Chalin's original grandeur. In a sad way, the Valley gate stood as a remorseful reminder to the people of what was missing and what could have been.

Wispy clouds began to roll across the sun, releasing shadows to dance across the rooftops of the city below. Though he had met with resistance upon first seizing Chalin, the people of the city had grown to trust him and believe in his mission. Granted, there were dissidents, but those were rare and always dealt with in a discreet and quiet manner. While he had wanted to try to maintain a sense of distance from the war for the city's civilians, by choosing Chalin – a city far north of his actual holdings – as his seat of power, he had brought an air of militarism to the city that had not been seen since the Second Great War. The East, North and South Barracks had been renovated to house more soldiers, and the patrols within the city and on Chalin's towering ramparts had been increased significantly. Where once Chalin had been free of banners declaring the city's allegiance to anyone but itself, it now had House Suldamik banners fly from every wall tower around Chalin and from each tower of the keep. Furthermore, the Suldamik pennants were joined by other House banners in the lazy breeze – most prominent of which was House Ithikia – in accordance with Craigan's edict that each House allied with him be represented in what he viewed as his capitol.

From his vantage point, Craigan was mildly aware of the pungent scent from the tanneries and could see the numerous clouds of smoke rising from the smithies of the city. Those facilities, as well as many others, had been working nearly night and day to either repair the army's equipment or churn out new goods to replace that which was too far gone to be salvaged, and would likely do so for days to come. Beyond the wall, and mostly hidden from his view, that sense of militarism continued as a large and increasingly permanent tent city had been erected for those soldiers that couldn't be housed in the barracks or whose residences were far from Chalin. While it would hardly temper the martial aura about the city, if things went as he wanted and planned, Craigan would be sending a large portion of the mobile army home for the winter. It was a decision that had met with mild resistance, but in the end, he got his way. If Kale was taking the time to rest his forces, then he would be a fool to pass up the opportunity.

While the scene outside the ramparts was a symbol of war, the majority of activity within the city was its stark opposite. The evening of the army's return, the nobles that had remained behind to lend their aid in a more clerical and administrative capacity presented Craigan with the idea of throwing a fete in his honor. It struck him and many of the other domses and domas from the mobile army as an absurd notion given their recent defeats. Craigan had managed to avoid the subject as much as he could for nearly a week, but he was eventually cornered by his magister, who had then proceeded to argue the merits of such a celebration. According to him, even if it was only for a short time, the fete would give citizens and soldiers alike a reason to feel joy and happiness. Furthermore, his magister had been quick to point out that the celebration would be a good way for the troops to unwind in a relatively controlled environment after a long campaign.

Craigan had been hard-pressed to dispute his magister's methodical, verbal assault, and soon agreed to the event – albeit grudgingly. Now, as he gazed upon Chalin's streets, the city was now alive with the culmination of two days' worth of hastily made preparations. Banners in House Suldamik colors were being hung from buildings, cooks of all facets were busying about trying to fill more orders than they possibly could, and the cellars of shop keeps and taverns alike were being raided for any and all alcohol that could be found as final preparations were made. By tomorrow morning, the four-day event would be in full effect – and Craigan could only hope that things wouldn't get too rowdy.

A polite cough from behind him within his personal suite drew a reluctant sigh from Craigan. The wind had dried the sweat of a hard workout off his bare, scarred torso and somewhat from his black pants and white-flecked, brown hair, so his escape to the balcony had served its purpose. Turning around, he set a dour look upon his chiseled and scarred face as a reminder to his magister how much he disliked these meetings. "Continue, Tythis. I'm paying attention," Craigan drawled as he stepped back into his chambers, closing the balcony doors behind him.

The large, eight-sided chamber was walled with the same gray and black stone as the dragon statue. Weapons, most of which were spoils of war, were mounted around the room high on the wall. Landscape paintings representing environments from across the breath of Triclose provided a more artistic flavor to offset the brutality that the weapons implied. Thick, polished oak beams created a latticework across the ceiling from which hung an elegant crystal chandelier, its many oil-fed wicks burning brightly, at the center of the ceiling. A large oak table, the legs and frame of which were artfully carved to look like nude women in provocative poses, was positioned in the center of the room and surrounded by enough plush chairs for six people.

"Thank you, Doms" the short, bald magister said as he ran his meaty hands down the front of his royal-purple robes, the thick, heavily-ringed forefinger of each hand tracing the golden embroidery stitched down the center of the rich fabric. "I was beginning to think I was boring you, Doms," he added as he followed Craigan with his beady green eyes that were set astride the wide, flat nose on his aged, plump face.

"Not at all," Craigan said dryly as he strode from the balcony doors. Walking past the table to the roaring hearth expertly built into the right-hand wall, he positioned himself the opposite side of the room in an obvious attempt to put as much distance between himself and the thick stack of reports lying before Tythis on Craigan's simple ironwood desk. Lush red carpet warmed his bare feet and protected them from the cold stone floor as he paused in front of the hearth. "I wouldn't dream of missing one of your enthralling briefings," he added drolly as he sat down in one of the two high-backed leather chairs arranged before the hearth.

Though he knew Craigan could not see him, Tythis gave him a glare that quite clearly said he was not amused. "If you had been willing to attend to all these matters earlier, we wouldn't be here right now."

Craigan snorted as he reached for the crystal decanter of Velusyian Blue that, along with two crystal goblets, sat atop the small table between the two chairs. Opening the decanter, he poured himself a glass of the rich blue liquid. "Come now, Tythis, can't a man have a chance to relax upon returning home?" he asked dryly before taking a satisfying sip from the delicate goblet.

"Indeed, Doms. However, might I point out that you have been *relaxing* for three days now, and doing a good job of ignoring anything that doesn't reside beneath Doma Ithikia's gown," Tythis remarked wryly.

Craigan barked a laugh. "Why Tythis – are you jealous of me?"

"Me, Doms? Surely you jest? You know as well as I that women hold no appeal for me. Though, I must admit – I found the arrival of her people was quite the . . . welcome surprise."

Craigan scowled at the mention of the Pelasians. He had been shocked to find a thousand Pelasians – eight-hundred soldiers along with two-hundred workers and servants – had arrived three months ago. His rage had only been stoked further when everyone he questioned about it seemed to have forgotten that no one had informed him of the small army that had invaded Chalin. Even Doma Ithikia had feigned ignorance and brushed it aside with a throaty laugh. If it hadn't been for the generous assistance her people had lent to the city and his own staff, he had no idea where his rage would have led him.

Sighing, Craigan downed the rest of his wine before reluctantly standing and turning to face his magister. "I don't know which is worse about you eunuchs – the dispassionate way you look at things, women's inability to manipulate you, or just your sheer lack of stones."

Tythis cocked his head to the side and blinked at Craigan before replying dryly, "Thank you."

Craigan scowled as he crossed the room to his desk and muttered, "It was rhetorical."

Tythis shrugged and quipped, "A compliment, nonetheless."

Grabbing the top stack of reports, Craigan began to glance over them, and conceded, "Very well, Magister, you may proceed."

Inclining his head, Tythis replied, "Thank you, Doms. As I was saying before your sojourn to the balcony, we have completed our preliminary reports and counts from the mobile army. We will finish a final audit before the end of the week, but the numbers appear to be accurate. Roughly three thousand casualties during the last campaign – there were nearly two thousand fatalities, and of the roughly one thousand wounded, almost six hundred will never fight again."

"Reparations?" Craigan asked as he examined the report.

"Per your standing order, Doms, the proper requisition forms for the sixty-thousand talons is included. Those that can still serve are being reassigned to more manageable positions."

"Good. We did our best to retain the dead's belongings – see to it that the officers' families receive their possessions. The same goes for the enlisted if possible."

Tythis arched a shaved eyebrow. "If we cannot find an immediate living relative?"

Tossing the report on the desk, Craigan stated flatly, "If not, see to it that their personal goods are sold off and the funds added to the coffers."

"Very good, Doms." Craigan's magister picked up the next significantly smaller stack and passed it to him. "Next, we have a list of people being held either in the dungeon or by local magistrates and sheriffs for various crimes."

Craigan sighed as he looked over the ten-page list before casually putting it aside. "I'm positive you have it memorized, so save me the boring task of reading it."

Tythis nodded. "Very good, Doms. We have thirty-five incidences of minor crimes and violence, ten first offense robberies and or pickpockets, five grand thefts, fifty violent crimes including–"

"Fifty?" Craigan asked, incredulously.

"Yes Doms, fifty – twenty-five assaults, five assaults with intent to kill, three murders with claims of self-defense, and seventeen were murders with intent. Our informants have also reported at least ten instances of dissident assemblies. What would you have me do?"

Tythis finished as he picked up a stylus and soft clay tablet from the desk to scribe quick notes.

Craigan looked over the list and asked, "Do we have witnesses for the murders?"

"Of course, Doms," Tythis replied as if the notion of a lack of witnesses was absurd. "The sheriffs and magistrates all have sent recommendations on punishment and await your seal."

Nodding, Craigan thought it over for a moment and then ordered, "See to it that the sheriffs and magistrates deal with the minor crimes and first offence robberies at their own discretion. If their recommendations are too severe, use your best judgment, Tythis."

The eunuch scribbled on his tablet furiously. "The others?"

"For the grand thefts – a two-hundred talon fine along with three months in a cell with hard labor. I'm sure we can find a use for some extra hands. As for the violent crimes . . ." he trailed off as he thought about the decision. The laws allowed for very little wiggle room pertaining to violent crimes. If he gave in and bent the law to appear lenient, then he might encourage his detractors. No, adhering to the strictest interpretations would continue to keep him in a position of power. "For the assaults with intent – six months labor and a five-hundred talon fine. For the self-defense cases – see to it that the charged pays a one-hundred talon fine and keep an eye on them." Craigan's expression hardened. "As for the dissidents and murderers, the law brokers no quarter – public execution to be carried out immediately."

Tythis scribbled the notes on to the tablet before laying aside the writing instruments, confident in the accuracy of his transcription. Picking up the smallest and final stack, he handed it to Craigan and said, "Very good, Doms. Only two more things to cover. Firstly, those papers contain the budget and requisitions for the winter months. Tax collection was thin this summer . . . but it appears we will be fine for the next year. We are currently cataloging the large sum of metals and gems that Doma Ithikia's entourage brought with them as tribute. The gold and silver will be sent for smelting and the gems sold or used for trade."

"How much will it add to the coffers?" Craigan asked while he looked over the seemingly endless columns of numbers with feigned interest. When Tythis did not immediately respond, Craigan looked up and saw the uncertainty written on Tythis' round face. "Well?"

Tythis cleared his throat before stating hesitantly, "Between two- and two-and-a-half-million talons, Doms."

Craigan blinked at Tythis in complete and utter shock, not quite sure he had heard him right. "I'm sorry, Magister – but did I hear you right? Did you say between two- and two-and-a-half-million talons?"

Tythis nodded hesitantly before replying, "Indeed, Doms. We are currently performing a fifth audit before proceeding with the conversion. That number, however, is what we have come up with each time."

Craigan could only shake his head in disbelief. There had been hints along the way about the wealth and power of the desert-fairing Pelasians. His father had brought House Ithikia into the fold hoping such rumors would prove true, but to have that kind of wealth to simply donate to the cause was practically inconceivable. "We could easily fund the war for another three years without having to dip into our own coffers with that," Craigan said incredulously.

"Too true, Doms. The extra wealth does bring to mind one other issue. The quartermaster has asked for funds to hire rat catchers to help with an infestation problem that has been growing."

Barking a laugh, Craigan replied, "Why not?! With these extra funds, he can hire a small army if he likes!"

Tythis tapped his thick fingers on the desk as he arched an inquisitive eyebrow at his doms. "Then, 'yes', I take it?"

"Within reason, of course."

"Of course," Tythis echoed.

Putting down the final report, Craigan clapped his hands together and stated, "So, what's the final issue, Tythis? It can't possibly be more shocking than the last."

The eunuch stepped around the desk and faced Craigan, looking up firmly into his blue eyes. "One final thing, Doms – though I do hesitate to breech the subject."

Craigan folded his arms across his chest. "What is it?" he asked cautiously.

"As you know, your marital status has always been a popular topic of conversation amongst the various courts backing you, as well as amongst the common folk."

Craigan rolled his eyes and strode back toward the hearth and the bottle of Velusyian Blue, well aware of where this conversation was going. "You're well acquainted with my views on that, Magister," Craigan barked in irritation as he filled the goblet halfway.

"Indeed, Doms. With respect, though, I feel that the situation is different this time."

Rolling his eyes, Craigan turned around with a dry, sarcastic chuckle and asked, "So tell me – all-wise one – what makes now any different from before?"

Ignoring the barb, Tythis continued in his flat tone, "Again, with respect, the losses of late have shaken how many people view your success in this war. There has been talk of a possible change in leadership, which, of course, was crushed before it gained any momentum."

"Good," Craigan barked with a snort of disgust before sipping form his goblet.

Tythis strode to the middle of the room and rested a hand on the table. "I normally wouldn't bring this to your attention, but with the massive influx of coin, I don't think this can be avoided much longer. It was impossible to neither completely hide the funds nor silence where it came from, which has led to a new and, shall we say, potentially beneficial rumor."

"And that is?" Craigan prodded as he sipped on the wine, fearing he already knew the answer.

"That the jewels and metals are a gift from Doma Ithikia to celebrate your engagement to marry her," Tythis stated flatly.

Although he had an idea of where Tythis was going with the conversation, it didn't prevent him from choking on his wine upon hearing the words spoken aloud. With his face turning red as he coughed to clear his windpipe, Craigan could only hope that Tythis had developed a sense of humor. "You're joking," he finally managed to croak, putting down his goblet to prevent himself from dropping it.

"Afraid not, Doms."

Craigan shook his head again in disbelief. "Alright, seeing as you are the one bringing it to my attention – let's say I humor this silliness and hear you out." He moved around the chair to his left and sat down, "Why on Kylir would I want to do that?"

Tythis finished crossing the room and positioned himself in front of Craigan, just off to his right before continuing. "In two words – power and survival. If it has not become painfully obvious to you – Doma Ithikia is not only very powerful, but power hungry. We know very little of what goes on in the inhospitable lands below the Dragonspine, but I fear we have seen only the tip of her power. This . . . *tribute* of hers is a very brazen display of wealth and audacity."

Craigan glared at Tythis sternly. "You would have me marry her out of fear?"

"Not at all," Tythis intoned firmly. "I would, as always, have you view everything with your eyes open. I think she is like you, Doms – a powerful friend or a very deadly enemy. I would not wish to venture down a path where she would become someone we fear. That said – you could do far, far worse for a bride. We know her House controls the vast Scorchlands, and with it, the fierce Pelasians and – given her gift – vast wealth. I think honoring your father's promised union of your two Houses would entice her to come full circle on her pledged aid next spring. After all, if your vested interests become hers, she'll have no choice but to fight for it more fiercely."

Knowing that he was stating the obvious, Craigan chose to say it anyway. "But I don't love her, Tythis. At the very best, it would be a marriage of lust or a power play." He couldn't help but think of Marie and her marriage to Kale at that moment.

"Then let it be so," the eunuch replied with an expressionless face. "Plenty of royal unions are nothing more than a smart business or survival practice. If you were to marry her, not only would you bolster your power, but you would then control her holdings. House Suldamik would become the largest and most powerful House overnight, with holdings stretching from Central to Southern Triclose. I don't recall any House, other than Gravit'nas, that could claim such expansive power." Tythis could see the message strike home as Craigan's chiseled face softened thoughtfully. "Besides," Tythis continued, "you'd make a striking couple, and that would play quite well with the common folk. The powerful Doms Suldamik and beautiful Doma Suldamik crusading against the evil House Merandith. Quite the storybook tale – don't you think?" he finished dryly. Seeing that Craigan was still thinking deeply, he added, "If it makes you feel any better, you only have to share a bed as much as either of you want to – although that has never been a problem in the past."

Craigan snorted and rolled his eyes at Tythis. "You've made your point, Magister. As usual, I can find little fault with your argument other than my distaste for marriage."

Tythis bowed slightly. "Thank you, Doms. I try."

"Given everything you've told me, it wouldn't surprise me if this is exactly what she has been maneuvering for since she replaced her father." He leaned forward and stared into the fire thoughtfully. "If power is what she's after, then that puts me in an awkward position. Deny her, and risk her desires creating a war on a second front. Accept her, and possibly share control of Triclose."

"Hypothetically, she could be dealt with after solidifying your control of Triclose. Accidents do happen, after all," Tythis suggested softly.

Craigan snorted, "And risk a blood feud with a House and realm we know very little about? I would hate to make such a brash decision to find out she really has magical powers at her disposal."

"Really, Doms," Tythis stated dryly. "Though there are hints of such . . . mythical power in lore and even in the Valley, do you really think someone like that in this day and age could exist without most of Kylir knowing about it?"

"Honestly, I don't know," Craigan responded with a shrug of his shoulders. "I've seen Doms Gravit'nas' tomb and felt the energy of that place too many times to be foolish enough to believe such power never existed; and if it existed at one point, then there is nothing saying it cannot exist again. While I'm not scared of myths and shadows, her brash display of her potential power is real enough – and that's not to be taken lightly."

He sighed heavily and thoughtfully. "You've given me a lot to think about, Tythis," he said softly. "This is a burden I'm not sure I want to shoulder," he added even as he thought about his assassination of Kale's mother and the pain it had caused the Merandiths. It was that type of pain he wanted to avoid unequivocally. While it was true that he had no feelings for Alestra beyond sexual indulgence, nothing said that feelings of affection could not grow between them and bring with it the risk of such pain.

"If your shoulders are broad enough to carry the burdens of Triclose, then I'm sure they can handle the addition of a powerful woman like Doma Ithikia," Tythis encouraged. "If it makes any difference, I think your father would approve," Tythis finished with an impassive expression on his round face.

He could tell his words hit home by a slight flinch before Craigan said, "Thank you, Tythis. You've done your job well in my absence. You're dismissed."

Knowing when not to push something further was a skill that had kept Tythis gainfully employed and alive in the dangerous game of politics, so with a full bow he said, "Thank you, Doms. Send word if you have need of me," before striding to the door.

Just as he was about to open it, Craigan's voice brought him up short. "Oh, and Tythis?"

"Yes, Doms?" he replied without turning.

"I'll consider your words with great care."

"Of course, Doms," Tythis said before opening the door and exiting silently, already turning his mind to his next task for the day.

Sitting alone in front of the fire, Craigan poured another goblet of Velusyian Blue before settling himself into the chair and gazing thoughtfully into the dancing flames. He was neither a dumb nor deaf man, and had heard many rumors of the same ilk whispered since his father had brought House Ithikia into the fold just before his death. In the field, Craigan had learned to push such frivolous banter aside, for it could only be a distraction. Now that he was home, however, it was hard to ignore such talk fluttering about the keep. The news about the massive influx of coin from House Ithikia was more than enough to drive home just how serious the situation had become. With that move, Alestra had practically bought her way to power. He knew the woman all too well, and if he were simply to ignore the situation, he had no doubt it would sour very, very quickly. As much as he might be opposed to the idea of marriage, if he were to accept what he viewed as a loaded bribe, then he could manage the situation from a position of power.

Shaking his head with a chuckle of disbelief, he said to the air, "Well, Father, is this what you saw for your son when you brought them into the alliance? Was I to be the bargaining chip that bought you their full aid while Zalan ruled?" He laughed again and sipped from the goblet before adding, his voice thick with anger, "I have to say – it's a sick joke that fate plays! All your best laid plans crushed by Zalan's betrayal and your death, yet here you are still trying to control Triclose from the grave – but this will be the last time this ever happens. After this, your name will be but a memory just as fast as Zalan's detested name was struck down. I rule House Suldamik now – and it will be that way for as long as I draw breath."

Standing, he strode with purpose to his desk where he seated himself before withdrawing a fresh sheet of parchment and retrieving his writing tools. What little rest he thought he would get during this pause in fighting was over. There was work to be done to remind all who ruled the House Suldamik.

Night fell upon Chalin, draping it with a cloudless, star-filled sky. At the behest of cold temperatures, the air was bitter and somewhat uncomfortable to breathe, reminding all that winter was quickly sinking its claws into the land. Like all cities of Chalin's size, it had a robust nightlife. When businesses closed down for the evening, taverns, bars and even less reputable establishments opened their doors to the dwellers of the night. Brightly lit, smoke-filled rooms would fill with those seeking refuge from the shadows of the night, and troops bearing torches or lanterns would begin their nightly attempt to protect the citizens of Chalin from those of a less seliee nature. On this night, however, the news of the fete had compounded the guards' task by amply supplementing the typical nighttime throng with those seeking an early start to the celebrations.

While all of Chalin was a beautiful sight, it held its share of scars and blights like so many other cities – it just managed to hide it better than most. Unfortunately, that success did not extend to the blemish that was the southern portion of Chalin. Home to the city's poorer citizens, it was an amalgam of warehouses, cheap living, cheap inns, cheaper taverns and even cheaper prostitutes. During the day, it was alive with life as traders made their way to and from the warehouses, and other business owners came through to hire cheap day labor. Once the sun went down, however, those who wished to maintain a spotless or respectable reputation scurried away like rats from a cat. Once the off-duty soldiers, the destitute and the broken took to the streets alongside the cloaked and hooded, and their vices began to flow like a river, it became a place that was no longer fit for a decent person to visit.

Tythis pulled his hood lower as he watched the larger than normal amount of vermin scuttle and stumble along the street. So many tiny, useless lives squandered away in fits of drunkenness, rutting or a combination of both – it was a sight he had seen time and again, and he loathed it with a passion that was enough to make him want to vomit. However, there was one thing he did admired about the vermin – they made no attempt to dress in fancy clothing, stuff themselves with expensive food and wine and call themselves better than everyone else.

When he was young, such thoughts and passionate hate would have driven him to vent his rage on the vermin. No one ever noticed when one of them went missing, and when the violated and mauled bodies turned up, they were summarily ignored by those in power. He had seen himself as a deliverer of divine justice, cleansing the land of the parasites that infested it. Corith could not have created or loved these abominations that destroyed their own without thought and ravaged the land like a plague before moving on to another area to do the same. Tythis had known there was no way he could completely wipe humanity from Kylir, but he took satisfaction in the few he exterminated. He couldn't remember for how long he had acted in such a manner. Weeks? Months? Years? The passage of time no longer meant what it used to. However, what he did recall with clarity was when he had been shown the glorious path that would lead to the cleansing of not just humanity, but every foul, tainted existence from Kylir's beauty.

It had been a winter's night not unlike this one, he recalled. Once again, his rage had been nurtured by days of watching the human pestilence ravage themselves and others. He had visited the weekly public trials that morning and had watched as case after case was presented to the local lord. Rape, murder, theft, assault – it was a river of the vilest of the vile. The lord's justice had been swift and harsh – murderers sentenced to hanging, rapists had their genitalia removed, thieves had their hands cut off and assailants were beaten. It was violence met with horrific violence in the name of justice – and it sickened him.

Then there came the moment that angered him the most. One of the lord's magisters was brought forward to face his accuser on charges of assault and rape. Tythis couldn't remember their faces or their names, but what was burnt into his mind was the disdain and smugness of the magister as he heard the charges. To Tythis' horror, the woman wasn't even given a chance to speak. The lord quickly dismissed the charges as unfounded – despite the physical evidence painted about the woman's body – and had the woman put to the lash for spreading seditious lies about a member of his court. Outrage burned in the eyes of the citizens, but none dared to speak for fear of their lord's wrath being leveled upon them.

Tythis recalled leaving the trials with a burning rage in his gut that was so violent that he was surprised steam was not pouring forth from every opening in his body. Such injustice from vermin! Such haughty arrogance from filth! It filled him with vehement bile that stirred a hunger in him that had to be sated.

Driven by that clawing hunger, he went to the slums that night with no particular target in mind. To his emphatic joy, by midnight, five of the rats that claimed to be men and women had already fallen to his rage. He was cleaning his hooked knives over the naked, violently raped, and gutted nameless whore when he had caught sight of a hooded face. As soon as he realized that it was the magister from the trials, he knew that Corith had put him in that trash-filled alley to bring true justice to the filth in pretty clothes.

It did not take him long to get into position, and it was child's play to ambush the drunken magister and drag him to a secluded alley. Deep in the shadows, Tythis dispensed what he viewed as justice. Over the next hour, he recalled with a wicked smile, he repeatedly violated the man after having cut his tongue out and driven a dagger through his cheeks to prevent him from screaming. Through all the desecrations, cutting and dismemberment, Tythis had explained to the magister that he had been judged, and before he was sent to rot in the deepest pit of the hells, he would have met out upon him what he had delivered upon the woman.

The next day, for the first time ever, Tythis actions drew attention. For weeks, it was the talk of the city, and the story had grown in violence and stature with each telling. For the nobles, it was an embarrassing outrage. Indignant in their fury, they inflicted the citizenry with curfews, beatings and kidnappings. Tythis had watched the cannibalistic display with a grin of joy. For once, he felt he was making a difference and that Corith had finally shown him a path to a greater good.

Three weeks later, however, his life had been changed forever.

Once again in the slums, Tythis had been stalking his latest target – a man who had just killed two others in a bar fight – when he was ambushed from behind and clubbed over the head. He couldn't help but think, when he had finally awakened, that even rats could have a lucky day. He had found himself in a windowless room somewhere underground, stripped naked and secured to a pole with shackles that were too small for his wrists and ankles, and rope that bit hard into his waist and neck. There were two others in the room with him that fateful night, though he could make out very little about them. What he did remember seeing was a pair of green, piercing eyes that bored into his soul. The person with the green eyes informed him that they knew what he had done, and it was time that he paid for his crimes against them.

Tythis had laughed at them, screaming with fevered confidence that he was doing Corith's work in ridding the world of the human filth that plagued it. He then proceeded to inform them that what he had done was nothing compared to what humanity had done to Kylir, and that it was fitting punishment for the vermin.

To his surprise, his rants had brought his captors up short. The green eyes had crept close and their owner had whispered an offer to him. An offer to show him the truth. An offer to help rid the world of the vermin that ravaged it, and to start anew. The voice, sultry and seductive, had whispered promises to show him that only in blissful, complete darkness could there be true, never-ending peace.

With joyful praise, he had accepted the offer, begging and pleading to be plunged into such a euphoric existence. So fevered was his devotion that he never noticed the dagger that had flashed into the green-eyed person's hand, nor did he feel it when the steel cut his testicles from his body. A reminder, the voice later said. A reminder of what humanity had done to the world, and what he, in turn, had done to them. A reminder of what he had chosen to serve.

Tythis had laughed with joy as the words were purred to him from the darkness and as his groin was cauterized with cleansing flames. In that moment, he had seen the future in the darkness around the violent red light.

Tythis pulled his cloak closer as a cold breeze cut through the alley. After that night, his eyes were open to the greater picture and he had devoted himself wholly to it and his new master. With time, he had learned patience; and with patience, his violent out-lashings were subdued to the point where he no longer could remember the last time he had crushed a rat. After all – why crush one when they all could be razed from Kylir in one fell swoop?

Tythis eyed the tavern across the parasite-filled street with disdain. The tavern was one of the more upstanding ones in the southern part of Chalin – and by upstanding, that meant there weren't drunkards sprawled out front like a blanket of rotten flesh. The building was cheap in its construction, but fairly well maintained. Located just down the street from one of the more popular brothels, it was a fashionable destination for those going to or coming from a paid conquest. The tavern was the type of place that a much younger Tythis would have liked to burn to the ground. Time, however, had made him more patient and much wiser. Now, he simply wanted to vomit at having to go into such a place. However, as he had once heard, discretion was the better part of valor; and as he started across the street, he could not help but think that discretion was indeed preeminent this night.

With his head slightly bowed and his cloak held tightly about him, he ascended the rickety steps and shouldered open the heavy, warped door, admitting him and a blast of cold air into the tavern. A string of drunken curses from those closest to the door greeted him as he struggled to get the off-kilter door shut. Once that was done, the curses died off and he turned to find himself in a densely packed common room. The tavern was bursting at the seams with people from what seemed like every walk of life. Laughter, curses, shouts, and bawdy songs filled the air with an audible buzz that was nearly as thick as the haze of smoke from both the hearth on the right-hand wall and the numerous pipes clamped between yellowed teeth and parched lips. The sawdust and hay that was underfoot were months past replacing, adding its staleness to the cornucopia of harsh smells that wrinkled Tythis' nose. As he pressed through the throng, the aroma of burnt meat, cheap ale and cheaper beer assaulted his nose hand-in-hand with the nauseating stench of sweat mixed generously with the aroma of sex and the sickly sweet smell of deathweed.

Once he made it to the rear of the room, he caught the eye of the bartender, a disgusting man of nearly fifty summers with more boils on his face than teeth in his mouth, and gave him a slight nod. The bartender jerked his head toward the hallway to Tythis's left. The eunuch turned and strode down the narrow, dimly lit hall shivering at the foulness that had touched him as he pushed through the crowd. He hated that his master owned this disgusting nest of vermin, but understood its usefulness. One could keep an eye on the scurrying rats with holes like this, and from time-to-time, it made an excellent place to meet, for there would be no prying eyes and ears. After all – who cared what the filth of the world did at night?

A quick left, followed by a short jaunt and another right brought him to a set of stairs in serious need of repair. Tythis gave one quick look back the way he came. Seeing no one in the flickering light of the broken lantern hanging precariously on the wall, he descended the creaking stairs as quickly and as quietly as possible before opening the first door on the right. Oddly enough, given the state of disrepair the rest of the tavern was in, the door quietly swung open on oddly well-oiled hinges. Sliding into the room, he closed the door behind him before turning to find himself in a small room barren of any adornment. There was a lone lantern hanging on the wall that provided enough light to illuminate the room's entrance while leaving the rear of the room in shadow. To any person that might wander into the room, it would appear that it was a disused storage room; and for all Tythis knew, it was just that. For now, as it had so many times before, it served as a meeting place for his master.

He knew that his master was there before he saw the amber eyes peering at him from the deep shadows at the back of the room. To his chagrin, the eyes were not the vibrant emerald-green he had come to worship, but the power of their owner could not be misconstrued no matter their color. In fact, from the time he had entered the tavern, the dragon tattoo on the inside of his left arm had begun to burn as it always did when in the presence of his master's power. Furthermore, he had even felt the same power enveloping the room as he shut the door, hardening and thickening the air so anyone passing by would be unable to hear their conversation.

Oh, how he envied that power and craved it for himself! But while he could feel and sense an open display of power near to him, he wasn't a full-blooded Gifted, and therefore could not see the beautiful, glorious currents as his master did. However, something struck him as odd about the meeting this time. It was as if there was another person in the room concealing their presence from the others. Despite the foreign power, he wasn't worried. If he could sense the presence, then his master could as well; and if his master was not worried, then he would not concern himself with it.

"I hope passing through the tavern wasn't a bother for you, my dear Tythis?" purred a seductive, throaty voice from the shadows.

If he had been any other man, and still had his stones intact, that voice would have been enough to make his knees weak. As it was, he simply heard power in the sultry tones. "I am well, Mistress," he replied, dropping the Triclosian vernacular. "The vermin are . . . of little consequence."

The shadows shifted and his mistress stepped into the lamplight. Even though the dim light and her red cloak concealed her toned, trim figure, her face was enrapturing enough for any man. Slender and curving, her face was bejeweled with up-tilted amber eyes, high cheek bones and full red lips, creating a breathtaking sight nestled amongst her flowing white locks. Her red lips parted tantalizingly as she said, "I take it from your message that you were finally able to pin Craigan down and inform him of my proposal."

Tythis nodded enthusiastically. "Indeed, Mistress. I believe you have played him perfectly, and he will do more or less as you have foreseen."

"More or less?" She questioned with a raised eyebrow.

"Mistress – you cannot always count on vermin doing as you wish. Craigan is a stubborn man whose convictions and belief in his self-righteous cause are second to none. With as long as this marriage was delayed, it will likely take more than that to sway him to your desires now."

"Observant, Tythis, but I am well aware of Craigan's stubbornness and willfulness. A smart person never plays every celum they hold unless they have to," she lectured with a wicked smile. "If he can't be gently persuaded to do as we need, then I have ways to . . . sway him – forcefully if necessary."

Tythis nodded, confident that his mistress had her every possible move planned out in detail. "Very good, Mistress."

"Now," she continued, folding her arms beneath her breasts underneath the red cloak, "There is the issue of how long it will take him to propose and make the union formal. We can't have him dallying about over this, now can we? Hummm?"

"No, Mistress, we cannot – nor do I believe he will hold off on such a move. However, his honor will dictate that everything be done according to tradition," Tythis informed her gently.

476

She cocked her head to the side with a sly smile. "I'm afraid I'm not up to speed on Triclosian marital traditions. Enlighten me, please."

"Very well, Mistress. While it does vary from region to region, as you well know from your time in the Southern lands, there are three primary traditions to uphold. There is the private proposal in which he will present you with a ring; although, with royals, private tends to mean an elaborate and visible show. Then there is the official public announcement, followed by the marriage – which, in this case, will most likely consist of both a private and public ceremony during which you will both present each other with a marriage torque."

Alestra appeared bored with the description and her tone reflected as much. "And how long does this frivolousness take?"

"Traditionally . . . one year," Tythis answered with a slight hesitation.

The irritation that marred Alestra's tantalizing face was enough to tell him that she was very displeased with the answer, but it was the dry, raspy voice that stirred from the shadows that sent a terrifying chill down his spine. "That is unacceptable, Juliana!"

As Tythis felt the veiled power part, the shadows seem to fall away from the left corner of the room behind Alestra, and a crimson-cloaked man separated from the shadows. Head and shoulders taller than his mistress, Garith's black hair was wildly spiked and crowned a long, lean face that was marred with countless scars. His ears were lined with simple golden rings, and his bloodthirsty black eyes burned with mad, malicious intent from under his dark eyebrows. From the lack of pauldrons and the way his cloak draped around him, it was obvious that he wasn't wearing his armor, but the man needed nothing more than a glance to intimidate and terrify.

Tythis dropped to both knees and prostrated himself before the powerful man even as Garith, ignoring the eunuch, continued to speak. "For once, the shalarium and I are in agreement. This is taking too long," he drawled sarcastically before declaring emphatically, "We should simply slaughter every one of these royals and take the damn keys! To the hells with restraining ourselves! We have the upper hand now!" Garith growled in frustration. "Events have been set into motion, and we must push forward if we are to keep those thrice-cursed Wardens in the dark!"

Alestra turned to Garith and shot him a scowl that was a match for his angry visage in intensity. "That name is dead!" she hissed. "Don't ever use it again!"

Garith grinned darkly back at her. "What's the matter, *Juliana?* Does such a reminder make you want to cry?" He tossed in a sad, sarcastic laugh just to dig the barb in deeper.

Tythis, trembling for fear of drawing Garith's wraith, could feel the anger radiating off of his mistress along with a buildup of power as she fought to keep from lashing out at Garith. "I will not be goaded into a fight with you, Garith!" she hissed through clenched teeth.

Garith tilted his head to the side with a false frown on his face as he reached out a gloved hand, the black leather of the garment seeming to drink in the light about it, and stroked Alestra's cheek with the back of his fingers. "Poor girl – who said I was trying to pick a fight with you?"

Her eyes burning with indignant rage, Alestra lashed out with her right hand and latched on to Garith's wrist, her blue-lacquered nails digging into the leather of his glove. "Do not mock me, Garith! I will be more than happy to knock you down a few more notches if you insist on pursuing this course!"

As she shoved his hand away like discarded refuse, Garith chuckled quietly to himself and turned his attention away from Alestra to Tythis' prostrated form. "So, Eunuch, how can we solve our little problem? Hummm?"

Tythis was sweating profusely by this point, and it was all he could do to muster the strength to organize his thoughts enough to voice them. "It . . . it would help, Master, if I were better informed of our master's greater plan," he stated in a hesitant voice. Glancing up, he caught Garith's venom-filled, threatening stare. While it told him he wouldn't learn any more than he already had, the harshness of the glare was enough to force him to look back down quickly. "But," he continued hastily, "I believe we can achieve your goals by the end of winter, Master!"

"The end of winter, eh?" Garith echoed, considering the words carefully. "That would be acceptable. . . . Although the quicker the better."

"As I was telling Mistress Alestra, Craigan is very willful and stubborn. He will be very reluctant to commit any sizable force to a winter campaign, especially if it involves moving further north," he replied as meekly as he could even as his mind raced to find answers that would appease the unstable demon of a man looming over him.

Garith studied Tythis carefully, his lips pulling back to reveal his perfect teeth and overly large canines. "Well, *Alestra*, does your sweating, stoneless pig speak the truth? Will our puppet need some prodding?"

"He will," she said quickly and firmly with a nod. "It will be futile, however, to waste too much effort pushing him from our side. His position is tactically sound, and he would be remiss to forfeit it. I can only guess what House Merandith is planning . . . unless you have something to tell us? Hummm? No? Very well, then. Aside from pulling the right strings to reach our goals here, we'll need an outside influence to get him to venture forth."

Tythis wouldn't have gotten to his current position if he had not learned to carefully watch people's tendencies and to be two steps ahead of everyone else. When Craigan had returned to Chalin, Tythis was already concocting various plans based upon his mistress' possible wants and desires. Gathering himself, he pushed himself to his feet and gently cleared his throat, drawing the piercing, powerful eyes of both Alestra and Garith to him. "If I may– "

"This had better be good, pig," Garith spit.

Tythis nodded. "I think I may have the solution to your problems. Craigan will only move if something drastic happens. I think, instead of following a plan that might possibly compromise your great work here, that it would be wise to pursue Kale Merandith as a possible catalyst."

Garith's brow furrowed and he scowled. "You're treading on my territory, pig."

Alestra, on the other hand, nodded slowly, her amber eyes lighting up as she followed Tythis' line of thinking. "I think he's onto something, Garith."

"And that would be?" Garith growled, annoyance and jealousy at the silent interplay between Alestra and Tythis evident in his tone and eyes.

She let out a throaty laugh, clearly picking up on Garith's mood. "Tythis, if you would, leave us. Garith here is getting jealous of creative thinking, and I would hate for you to get hurt should an explanation anger him further."

Tythis eyed Garith warily before bowing hastily. "Yes, Mistress. Call on me should you need me," he said quickly before making for the door and exiting as quietly and discreetly as possible.

As soon as the door shut, Alestra put a hand on Garith's chest and drove him into the wall, pinning him there with her body. Intensity and lust burning in her eyes, she glared up at Garith and purred, "You may enjoy this little act and terrorizing my underlings, but I won't stand for any thoughts of harming them for your sick pleasure – nor will I tolerate jealousy in you."

Garith grinned wickedly at her. "Me? Jealous? Why would I ever be that? The number of men and women you've taken to your bed? Or maybe how you and your minions seem to know each other's thoughts?"

Another rough shove from Alestra silenced him before she retorted, "You're a mud crow's ass at times, Garith! If you thought more with your head than your muscles, you would see things clearer and wouldn't be in the position you have been for so many years!" Garith's scowl deepened and anger flared in his wild eyes, but Alestra ignored it. Instead, she trailed a long finger up Garith's chest before snaking it around the back of his neck. "As for the sex," she purred softly, "it's always just been that, and it's gained us so much. Besides," she breathed in a thick, lustful voice, "You're the only one I love, and the only one that can sate my needs." She leaned in quickly and kissed Garith full and hard on the lips.

Garith tensed up as their lips made contact. It wasn't that he didn't long for the feel of her soft, full lips on his, but he wasn't in the mood for sexual distractions. "What about–" he managed to mutter between kisses, "What about Craigan?"

Alestra pulled away slowly, her teeth pulling on Garith's lower lip, biting down hard enough to draw blood before she let go. "I think, my love," she purred as she licked at the trickle of blood seeping from his lower lip, "that if you want to acquire the keys without igniting a cataclysm before we're ready, then it's time for Bloodblade to make a trip north. Unless, of course, you'd rather continue to solely spend your time chasing blood memories that we're not even sure exist. Wouldn't you agree?"

Garith's eyes lit up with excitement as what Alestra was proposing sank in. Laughing with a mix of glee and lust, he kissed Alestra deeply before pulling them both to the ground. Events on Triclose were about to get much, much more interesting.

# Chapter Twenty-One

*T*he fete officially began shortly after dawn – although the inns and taverns had been filled to capacity since the previous night. With the tolling of the morning bells from atop the tallest spire of the soaring and majestic Great Cathedral of Deo located near the heart of Chalin, people began filing into the streets and making their way to their various destinations. The air was quickly alive with chatter and laughter as all thoughts of war and the future were blissfully forgotten that day. For a large portion of the city, their feet carried them toward the parks situated beneath the towering dragon statue.

The parks, when in full bloom, were like stepping into another world. Vibrant flowers, shady trees and lush grasses would serve as the backdrop for many of Chalin's citizenry as they took time to rest, contemplate or simply to bask in the presence of the Utherian Valley and its gigantic stone and jade guardian. Now, though, as fall and winter brought a brief interlude to the spring colors and aromas, a mass of humanity milled about on brown grass and crowded onto one of the numerous stone or wooden benches scattered about the parks. Breakfast foods were brought by many or were available for purchase from hastily setup vendors. Sweet milk, wine, bread, smoked meats and a variety of sweets draped the area in a blanket of mouthwatering aromas that lured adults and children alike into indulging in the tasty treats. A variety of entertainers – some talented and others not so much – strolled amongst the crowds both in the streets and in the parks. There were minstrels and bards to delight one's ears while jugglers, acrobats, illusionists and artists entertained one's eyes.

Inside the keep, the atmosphere was no less celebratory. True, there were nobles that came to the private celebration fully aware of the fete's purpose, but they hid their lack of enthusiasm behind false smiles as easily as they might lie to an enemy. Craigan was present in his royal finest – a fine black and jade satin doublet, and leggings accented with supple leather knee-boots, all of which had golden embroidery crawling across it like a spider web. The keep staff and those in attendance were awed by the striking figure he cut at the head of the line of domses and domas entering the massive dining hall. Doma Ithikia was nowhere to be seen – despite rumors that she would enter on Craigan's arm – but that did nothing to quell spirits or gossiping tongues. While the cavernous dining hall was packed full of chatting royals and tables filled with delicacies that most of the citizens of Chalin could only dream of tasting, none of what was transpiring within and outside of the keep would have been possible without the silent workers scurrying about the partygoers like unseen ghosts.

While the large majority of the city rejoiced in the revelry, there were those unlucky souls who labored to make it all possible. Servants, cooks, tavern keepers, shop workers and guards – each and every one of them were worked without remorse in order to keep up with the demands of the celebration. There were those kind souls that offered the workers thanks, a warm smile or greeting in return for their services, but in general, the workers were either roundly ignored or looked down upon. For so many of those working during the fete, the celebration was more of a painful curse; none of it would be possible without them, yet no one seemed to care. As a result, by evening of the first day, there was little doubt amongst the workers that someone would finally snap in anger or resentment and lash out.

In contrast to the number of people that felt downtrodden by the rest of society during such festive times, there were those who were impartial to working during such festivities. In fact, there were those that – for one reason or another – preferred it that way.

Tucked in an unremarkable part of the northern section of the city, there was a small street that the people of Chalin referred to as the Street of Dreams. To anyone laying eyes upon the street for the first time, the name would leave them scratching their heads in puzzlement, for nothing about its outward appearance even hinted at a relation to such a grandiose name. The buildings were small wooden structures – no taller than two stories – that were largely unpainted but well maintained. And while the street was well kept and clear of debris, it was made of packed gravel instead of fitted stone. As such, if one were unfamiliar with the street, it would be easy to overlook it or simply ignore it; however, those familiar with the street were well aware of the treasures it held behind its blasé façade.

Even with the fete in full swing, there were still a few people strolling along the narrow lane – many of which appeared well-to-do if their dress was any indication – hoping to find one of the stores open. Many of them had come in search of a trinket to commemorate the fete, while others simply sought to indulge a propensity to spend talons. To the chagrin of nearly all, every store was locked up tight. However, that particular hindrance wasn't enough to stop many of the potential customers from peaking through the stores' windows and becoming enraptured by the treasures that were responsible for the street's name.

Inside each of the stores was a variety of breathtaking jewelry lovingly displayed for all to see. Gold, silver and bronze had been painstakingly molded and formed into works of art ranging from the simple to the complex. Opals, jade, diamonds, jaspers, sapphires and rubies – every color of the rainbow, and then some, was represented in settings ranging from delicate and elegant to bold and sturdy. From necklaces with delicate chains, to torques with silver emboss-ments, or even rings with golden filigree, there was a plethora of jewe-lry to sate a variety of tastes and desires.

Tucked near the southern end of the lane was a small shop that appeared to be barely more than a well-maintained shack in com-parison to the larger and showier establishments that flanked it. Like the other storefronts, its façade was decorated with a sturdy door, and leaded-glass windows that were girded against break-in by wrought-iron bars. A simple, hand-painted sign – featuring a mannequin head with a gold necklace around its neck – announced the building as Ro-thumb's Royal Jewels to those on the street. The inside of the store was dominated by a showroom occupied with display cases arranged around its perimeter. Showcase pieces of jewelry were arranged with-in the displays to catch as much sunlight as possible during the day, and lamplight during the evening hours, to make them more enticing to prospective customers.

Over two decades ago, the small establishment had seen great success as the reputation of the artisan that owned the store spread throughout Central Triclose. So fine and respected was his craftsmanship, that he soon caught the eye of a young Doms Calvin Suldamik – Craigan's father. In a move to secure the rich mines of the small House Tavina, Calvin Suldamik's father, Syvian, had agreed to marry his son to the late Jilifine Tavina. Though Calvin did not know her very well, he felt it proper – and as a sign of House Sulda-mik's wealth and power – to commission the best artificer that he could find to create a ring and torque of stunning brilliance to present to his bride. Calvin found his man in the form of Chalin's noted je-weler, Togsam Rothumb.

To this day, there were still those that enjoyed reminiscing about the wild rumors that had surrounded Calvin Suldamik's visit to the small shop. Some said the haggling went on without end for three weeks; others said that the spindly jewelcrafter forced the young Sul-damik to sell his soul in exchange for his services. No matter the speculation, the truth of the month long visit to Chalin remained with Togsam and the late Calvin. The results of the bargain, however, were well known and spectacular.

For six months, Togsam's shop was closed to the public. Practically imprisoning himself within his small living quarters, workshop and forge at the back of the store, the reclusive artificer worked day and night designing, forging and fashioning the settings that Calvin Suldamik had commissioned. The ring that he eventually produced was a two-piece work of art that was hinged at the second knuckle. Made of gold and silver that had been fashioned into fine cylinders of swirling, gracefully interwoven knot work. Tiny pieces of jade tastefully encrusted the forward part of the ring, and a gleaming diamond, expertly cut into a slender oval, adorned the rear of the ring.

As for the torque, it was crafted from pure silver and adorned with skillfully molded gold flowers that flowed along the central circumference of the torque. Gold rings were evenly spaced and expertly fitted onto the raised edges of the rich neck adornment, accenting the exquisite piece. As a further embellishment, thirteen smaller jade blooms were scattered tastefully about the polished silver. Despite the lavishness of the piece, it was the large jade bloom nestled squarely in the front-center of the torque that drew one's eye. The extravagant bloom served as the origination point of the gold flowers flowing along the circumference of the torque, and was comprised of fifteen petals of faceted, light-catching jade surrounding a circular core made of a single, flawless piece of jade.

Rothumb – even in his advanced age – could clearly recall every cut, every facet and every sensual curve of the jewelry as if he held them in his aged hands before him. Such was his love for the pieces that he felt his works afterward never lived up to the quality of the doma's marriage set – though there were vehement arguments that he had created pieces before and after that were superior. When Doma Suldamik passed from a case of the Wasting, Rothumb had been devastated to hear that his beloved creations had been entombed with the doma. It came as no surprise to those that were considered close to the artificer that his sense of loss was greater for a piece of jewelry than for the doma. Rothumb had always been fairly aloof and distant; he had rarely dealt with customers in person, and had taken on only a handful of apprentices. His heart and soul had long belonged to his craft, and nothing had ever been able to change that.

As the years passed by after Doma Suldamik's death, Rothumb became more withdrawn. He produced less works himself, and turned more of the business over to his small handful of apprentices. By the time Craigan took the reins of House Suldamik, Rothumb was effectively retired and his help had dwindled to his oldest student – now a Master and part owner of the store – and a shopkeeper. Furthermore, Rothumb continued to cut back on his duties to the point that, by the time of the fete, he already had plans in place to leave Chalin before winter sank its teeth into Central Triclose, intent on spending his remaining years in the warmer southern lands.

So when Craigan showed up the night before the fete began, the sixty-five summer old Rothumb was certainly surprised, but more than happy to humor the son of his greatest patron. They exchanged brief pleasantries, as Craigan was eager to address the reason for his visit. Rothumb listened to the proposal for a set of marriage jewelry politely, even arching a bushy eyebrow in surprise at the number of talons Craigan offered as payment. However, as far as Rothumb was concerned, he was retired and fully intended to turn down the offer; he was even prepared to go so far as to recommend another jeweler.

It was then – as if he had known his offer would be refused to begin with – that Craigan brought forth a simple wooden case and opened it reverently. Inside was a padded velvet bed upon which rested Rothumb's beloved creations, looking as beautiful as the day he presented them to Craigan's father. Craigan proceeded to explain that he wanted them altered slightly to present to his bride-to-be. Initially, Rothumb was somewhat appalled to hear such a request, but when he heard the details of the changes, he could see the possibilities. The alterations Craigan was asking for were relatively simple – the addition of ruby thorns to the roses, and the inclusion of a large teardrop emerald hanging from the torque. What concerned Rothumb the most about the proposal, was that Craigan wanted it by noon of the final day of the fete. It would have been a rather easy task in his youth – and with the help of a few apprentices – but now it was an extremely tall order. However, the sight of his beloved works had lit a fire within the aged artificer, and he saw it as a final challenge put in his way by Deo before his retirement.

Never one to waste time, Rothumb asked Craigan to send someone to fetch his partner and former apprentice, a man named Gathris, which Doms Suldamik gladly did before departing. Alone for the moment, the aged artificer proceeded to shuffle his way into his small, neatly organized workshop. Placing the chest reverently on his workbench, Rothumb then lit his tiny forge and crucible before gathering the tools and materials he would need for the job ahead. The temperature in the small room quickly increased as the forge and crucible heated up, but the Master Craftsman paid it little heed. Pulling a small, secured lockbox from a hidden panel in the rear wall, he placed it next to the jewelry chest on his workbench and opened it. Inside the lockbox, sectioned off by type, was Rothumb's prized cut and uncut gems that he used only for special projects. Carefully selecting the best rubies and emeralds – along with a few pieces of jade just in case any of the old gems needed replacing – he laid out his selections on the bench.

After returning the lockbox to its hiding place, he then rummaged through his collection of ore before finding his clay jar of gold ore, as well as three other jars that held ingredients closely guarded by the Artificers and Craftsman Guilds alike. Shuffling to the roaring-hot crucible, he added a generous amount of the tiny gold nuggets to the glowing-hot pot along with a pinch of a black, dusty substance from one of the other jars before sealing the crucible so the ore could melt. Returning to the bench, he closely examined the uncut gems he had selected to make sure there were no flaws. Once he was satisfied with his choices, he put them aside for Gathris – whose younger eyes and hands were better suited for cutting the gems – before turning his attention to the torque and hinged ring. His expert eye quickly found a few age-induced flaws in the pieces that most people would never notice, but for a Master Craftsman like him, such flaws were intolerable. Picking out the tools he needed, he began to remove six of the border rings on the torque, followed by two of the jade blooms and six of the tiny jades on the ring.

Halfway through the process, a bleary-eyed Gathris arrived, protesting his removal from his home at such a late hour. Gathris – especially at this hour – hardly looked the part of an artificer. Short and rotund, his fingers were thick and his eyes appeared too small in his full, blonde-bearded face. However, despite resembling a balding barkeep more than his chosen trade, Gathris' eyes were sharp and his fingers nimble. If life had led him down a less favorable path, his quick hands and sharp eyes would have served him well as a thief.

Ignoring Gathris' indignation, Rothumb quickly put him to work designing the thorns and cutting the gems to the proper size and shape, all the while explaining the overall task at hand. As soon as Rothumb mentioned who and what the job was for, all complaints from Gathris ceased and he quickly pulled himself together before putting on his apron and jumping into his work. Throughout the night, the two jewelcrafters worked with an intensity and passion that bordered on the obsessive. By the time dawn rolled around and the fete kicked off in force, they had already made some headway – all the metals they needed either had been smelted into small ingots that could be heated and forged into any shape they wanted, or were cooling in molds; furthermore, Gathris had also begun cutting the gems into the sizes and shapes the job required. Thankfully, the only delay they encountered was an anticipated one – completion of the gems would have to wait until the new mounts were finished in case any adjustments to the gems were needed.

Three hours after dawn, Gathris noticed Rothumb slumped over his workbench. Seeing an opportunity for a break, he made sure that his master had not fallen over dead, and then quietly made his way from the workshop in search of breakfast for the two of them. The streets were already packed with people on their way to their fete destinations, making Gathris' trek quite slow and troublesome. It took him two hours to reach the nearest tavern and to return with a sack of warm meats and bread, and a small flagon of spiced wine. Waking his master upon his return, the two of them ate their meal in silence, their minds working through the numerous tasks left to do in the limited time left to them. As soon as the last crumb was eaten, they returned to their work.

For the next two days and two nights, the pair of artisans worked with a focused determination and fervor that bordered on insane. Working with only the shortest of naps and quick meals, the two men expertly molded and cut the metals and gems into the required shapes, attached the new mounts and set the gems, and replaced parts where needed. Neither of them had ever worked as hard as they did those two days; Rothumb was even forced to call in a favor from a blacksmith acquaintance to have him touch-up and assemble the links for the chain that would support the large emerald hanging from the torque. By the time they were done with the monumental task, their hands were aching and cramping, and their eyes were red and bleary. The results of their work, however, were second to none. The new ruby thorns added a sense of dangerous beauty to the elegant piece, while the addition of the large emerald – set on a chain that was just long enough so that the gem would nestle at the top of the wearer's bosom – added a risqué aura to the piece.

Craigan's messenger showed up promptly at noon on the final day of the fete. After double-checking that the pieces met Craigan's requirements, Rothumb returned the jewelry to its velvet-cushioned chest and proudly turned it over to the messenger. In return, he was given four coin purses heavy with talons and word of Doms Suldamik's everlasting thanks. As soon as the messenger was gone, Rothumb spilled the eight-sided golden coins on to his workbench and counted them. Both Gathris and Rothumb were shocked to find they had been paid six-hundred talons for the job. As surprised as they were, they counted a second and third time just to be sure. In the end, Gathris went home shaking his head at the generous amount of coin.

Remaining at the store, Rothumb secured the riches in the same hiding spot that his gem box occupied. He then penned a letter to Gathris, leaving the shop officially to him along with majority of the money, and placed it on the workbench where Gathris could not miss it. Although he was tired, the completion of the refurbished wedding set seemed a fitting way to complete his career, so he spent the next few hours gathering his things and loading them onto an old wagon he had out back. Within two hours of completing his preparations, Rothumb had passed through the main gate and was rumbling along to the south, his past behind him and his future – what little there might be left to him – ahead of him.

By noon of the final day of the fete, the air of the city was afire with excitement as rumors of a grand announcement flew about Chalin as if carried on a strong wind. Some said that Doms Suldamik was going to announce a major victory, while others prattled on about him declaring a grand new campaign that would end the war for good. However, the most popular rumor was the one that had permeated the city since the arrival of the Pelasian contingent – Doms Suldamik would be getting married. It seemed a farfetched notion given Craigan's tendency to dodge the subject, but as the day wore on, that particular rumor gained momentum as more and more signs that something of supreme importance would be revealed appeared throughout the city.

The first indication that something was afoot, appeared early that morning when messengers in House Suldamik colors arrived at the homes of some of Chalin's richest and most renown merchants and traders. Upon delivering an invitation to a party at the keep that night, those same messengers had then departed with haste, leaving the households in a frantic scramble to prepare for the event. That flurry of morning activity was followed later in the day by a host of House Suldamik runners hustling through the streets in a mad dash to both acquire a variety of provisions and sundries, and to requisition the services of some of the best musicians the city had to offer. And if those signs weren't enough for the most skeptical person to buy into the rumors, then the appearance of thirty heavily laden wagons from the Velusyian Enclave was certainly enough to finally convince the skeptics that something major was afoot. Rumbling forth from the secretive Enclave, which was located in the northeastern part of the city, a few of the covered wagons made their way to the parks, some went to the walls, and others made for the keep. Every citizen of Chalin, whether they cared about the rumors or not, understood that such wagons and their handlers only made an appearance when a great celebration was to occur. On those occasions, the secretive sect of Velusyians would appear to grace everyone with their fantastical firestars.

However, while the vast majority of the city was brimming with anticipation, there were those that listened to the rumors of marriage with apprehension. Those with the gravest concerns, both dissidents and loyalists alike, muttered their fears wherever they felt safe, dreading that the wrong word to the wrong pair of ears would draw the ire of House Suldamik. For those whose concerns were more mundane, they talked openly, debating the pros and cons of a marital alliance and which House would provide the best benefits to the cause should the dominant rumors of a union between House Suldamik and House Ithikia prove to be false. Given the general lack of knowledge about the lands south of the Dragonspine, it came as no surprise that heated debates sprung up about what House Ithikia could bring to a union other than sand and warm bodies for the war.

Then there were those people that were not only concerned about the rumors, but were so close to Craigan that their very lives would be directly affected by any union. Chief among them was Doms General Dromick de'Suldamik Leonbane. Although he had always been willing to question the doms he served if he felt his orders went too far or not far enough, he had never once in all his years of service doubted the direction that House Suldamik's leaders envisioned for both Triclose and the House. When Craigan's father had announced the marriage-alliance between House Ithikia and House Suldamik nearly nine years ago, Dromick had found the idea exciting. Granted, he had been a young officer at the time and, like most everyone else, knew very little about the mysterious lands south of the Dragonspine. In spite of the caution such ignorance should have summoned, the mystery of what House Ithikia could possibly bring to the cause was enough to fire the imagination and stifle commonsense.

The deaths of Doms Ithikia and the elder Suldamik, followed by the execution of Craigan's brother, saw an end to whatever plans the elder domses might have had. Despite the collapse of their parents' plans, Alestra and Craigan maintained their alliance without the bond of marriage – which would have given Craigan control of House Ithikia's resources – though none could say with certainty why they had done so. As a consequence of this, the rumors of marriage refused to die. However, the value of the alliance had always remained in question as House Ithikia – until recently – had barely contributed to the war. Dromick tended to agree with the perception that the missing support was because the marriage had fallen through, but a little voice in his head told him something else might be at play. What it was, he had no idea, but it was that gnawing suspicion that had grudgingly delivered him to the salon of Doms Thakian's suite in the east tower of the keep.

Dromick's strong-willed black eyes scanned the small, round salon from his position next to the hearth built into the left-hand wall of the room. Well appointed, the room was cozy almost to the point of stifling, and was centered around an opulent couch flanked by a pair of ash end-tables. The plush blue carpet that covered the entirety of the floor was accented by well-maintained, white-plastered walls that were home to polished silver lanterns whose framework had been molded to look like the glass was held within a maze of vines. Those same walls were also adorned with tapestries and paintings that were stationed above the generously cushioned benches that lined the perimeter of the room along with two serving tables.

Unable to find anything to keep his interest, he turned his attention to studying the pair of domses that were seated on the opposite side of a small table – on which rested three untouched wine-glasses – from him in thickly padded high-back chairs. Dromick's short, compact frame and military black leathers were a stark contrast to the frail and hawkish Doms Thakian, whose loose green robes seemed to be trying to swallow his long, slender frame. Doms Astica, on the other hand, appeared more soldier than royalty. Seated to Thakian's left, the short and burly doms was adorned in sturdy black trousers and a thick white shirt underneath a leather doublet. Despite their physical differences, they shared a feeling of consternation with the subject that had kept them deep in thought and conversation for the last two hours, and their faces showed it.

"Whatever anyone's opinion may be," Astica's rough voice stated, shattering the lull that had been dragging on, "there has always been something that stinks to all holy hells about this since the day Craigan's father made the deal." Running his hand through his loose, shoulder-length black and gray hair, he turned his bright-blue eyes on Dromick. "Even you have to agree – all of this is too sudden."

Dromick shifted, uncomfortable with how accurate Astica's assessment was. With the doors to the salon's balcony shut and only four of the dozen lanterns mounted on the walls lit, the salon made Dromick feel like he was taking part in a clandestine conspiracy . . . and the conversation was doing very little to alleviate that feeling. Dromick ran a hand over his baldhead as he considered how to answer Astica's assertion. Finally, with mild irritation creeping into his voice, he offered, "What do you want me to say? That I think Doms Suldamik has gone crazy? That we need new leadership?"

"What we want," Doms Thakian stated in his passive, elderly voice, "is for you to be honest with us. Neither of us have any interest in betraying Craigan – but we fear that Alestra is manipulating the situation. If she is putting herself before the greater good of this alliance, then she poses a problem."

Astica nodded in agreement. "I'll say it again – the bitch is trouble. I will be the first to admit that I thought her promises were all horse shite – and I still think most of it is – but the number of her people we found in Chalin was both a surprise and chilling. She was practically running Chalin – and we had no clue it had happened."

"But she hadn't taken over the city," Dromick pointed out, although he already knew it was a mute point.

Astica's snort of disgust told Dromick that the doms thought the same even before he retorted, "Irrelevant – it was a power play, and a damn good one at that. If the rumors are true, I'd say she's managed to scare Craigan into marrying her."

Dromick's eyes narrowed. "Craigan is not so easily deceived," he growled defensively. "The marriage-alliance between them was ended years ago. If the rumors are true and he intends to renew the contract, then he would not do so without careful consideration. I can also assure you both – it would be a political move, not one made out of dumbstruck love."

"How do you know that for sure? He's spent enough time between her legs for her to turn his brain to mush," Astica retorted with a snort.

Dromick bristled at the statement. "What my doms does in his bed is his own damn business, Doms Astica! I would remind you to remain courteous to your host while you are under his roof!"

Doms Thakian held up his bony hands, "Peace. We are not here to worry about whom is sleeping with whom, nor are we here to start a fight. I believe I have heard enough from everyone to know that, despite our differences, we are all concerned about Doms Suldamik and what the end result might be should the rumors prove true."

Astica and Dromick eyed each other sternly once more before the tension in their bodies slackened.

"Now," Thakian continued, "as I said earlier, I have it on good authority that Craigan intends their betrothal tonight. While I do not agree with this arrangement, I intend to support it unless evidence can be provided that would force Craigan to end the engagement. However, I do not intend to simply sit back and allow this unknown factor to worm its way to power."

"You two know that I am required to report all this to Doms Suldamik – so why bring me in on your little scheme?" Dromick stated bluntly, seeking not only an end to this verbal dance, but a clear declaration of what they wanted from him.

"Because he trusts you, Dromick!" Astica barked, rolling his eyes at what he felt was obvious. "If either of us were to voice our concerns to him, he would simply ignore them! Hells, he would probably do the same with you at this point! What we need is information and evidence, one way or the other."

Dromick looked at the two domses thoughtfully. "I get the feeling you two want more out of me than to simply relay your concerns to Doms Suldamik."

Doms Thakian nodded. "Indeed. We would like for you to be our eyes and ears. Find out what Alestra is up to."

Dromick folded his arms across his chest. "Just how am I supposed to do that without creating an incident? She'll notice anyone snooping around her. She's far from stupid, and certainly has eyes and ears everywhere."

Doms Thakian leaned forward. "Do the unexpected – venture into the Scorchlands and gather information on the Pelasians. Remove the veil of secrecy from House Ithikia so that we may all have a better understanding of what we are dealing with."

Dromick laughed at the absurdity of the statement. "Me? Go into the Scorchlands? Are you both daft? And just how do you two intend for me to succeed where so many others have failed? Only a Pelasian would know how to navigate the deserts beyond the Dragonspine without dying – and if you haven't noticed, there aren't exactly any of them lining up to offer their services. Not to mention, Doms Suldamik isn't about to part with me without a damn good reason."

"Don't for a moment take us for fools, General," Thakian stated firmly. "We aren't simply throwing this together at the last possible moment. Many of us have been concerned about Ithikia's involvement from the very start, and we have also contemplated sending eyes into the Scorchlands for a long while; it is with regret that we had not done so earlier. If you cannot convince Craigan that such a journey would be beneficial, then we have other ways to make it happen. With or without you, we will clear the fog of mystery around the Pelasians. With you – a man Craigan trusts – the fruits of the venture would be . . . received in a better light."

Dromick stared at the domses with consternation clearly marking his face. "What you ask is . . . difficult for me. We could be walking a path to destruction if we do this."

"We may already be on it, General!" Astica barked.

Doms Thakian nodded in agreement. "If we're already on that path – this may be the only way to stop it."

Dromick sighed and nodded slowly, realizing that what they said was true even though their motives might not be what they alleged. Without question, his loyalty was to House Suldamik; and if such a dangerous journey was needed to insure its safety, then he would do it or die trying. "Very well," he stated reluctantly. "But we do this my way, or no way at all. I will leave any mention of your involvement out when I speak to Doms Suldamik, but know this – my loyalty is to Doms Suldamik and no one else. If he says no, then that is as far as I go. You two will have to find someone else to do your dirty work. Is that understood?"

Doms Thakian offered a thin-lipped smile. "It is agreeable. Inform us of your decision quickly. You'll need to start soon, before winter firmly takes hold."

With a grunt of irritation, Dromick retorted as he stared for the door, "Don't worry. If this is going to happen, it will happen very quickly."

The two domses waited for Dromick to exit the room and the door to shut before exchanging glances.

"Are you sure this was wise, Sevarius? He is loyal to a fault. If there is nothing untold going on, there's no way we can convince him to lie," Doms Astica said with undisguised concern.

Doms Thakian shrugged his boney shoulders. "It doesn't matter. Should the truth be against our wishes, it will be easy enough to manipulate the situation. As long as we destroy any possible union between House Suldamik and Ithikia for good, our goals can be accomplished, Galen."

Doms Astica grunted. "Good. I can't wait to see those sand-crawling bastards gone! Craigan is weaker than we thought if he needs sun-baked barbarians to beat Kale!"

"Indeed so, my robust friend," Sevarius added as a grin spread across his aged face. "We will find a way to shatter Craigan's hold on the Jade Talons and remove the cancer on our power. Once we are in control, Kale will fall swiftly and every one of those demon-spawned Velusyians can follow him to the deepest pits of the Hells. Then we will turn our attention south and rid Triclose of every Pelasian. In the end, my friend, Triclose will be free of the pestilence that corrupts it – and it will be pure."

Astica could see the zeal that radiated from Thakian's eyes, and could only grin in ecstasy as he reached for his glass of warm wine. Lifting his glass from the table, he held it up in a toast, saying, "To a pure Triclose! May the Hells consume them all for all eternity!"

The rest of the evening leading up to the celebration was filled with consternation for Dromick. He had no love for Domses Thakian and Astica; in fact, he was revolted by the two. If even half the rumors about the two were true, then they were bigots of the worst kind. They hid their disgust of anyone that didn't fit their definition of perfection while in public, but Dromick had seen the contempt in their eyes in situations where anyone that wasn't from Central and, to a lesser extent, Northern Triclose addressed them. The more that a person was different from them, the greater the revulsion. While it was true that they had expelled Velusyians from their realms – as was their sovereign right – it was widely rumored that the domses were notorious for their violent treatment of foreign commoners that dared to visit. According to refugees' tales, the dark depths of the domses' biasness routinely led them to hunt down and slaughter anyone that they thought was an outsider, as well as those they deemed unclean or imperfect. While there had been discrete inquiries over the years in response to the tales, there had never been any sort of official confirmation of such acts; furthermore, House Suldamik's visits to Terial and Faridin were always carefully orchestrated, making it impossible to get a true feel for life within the realms. None of this surprised Dromick; after all, most people found it all too easy to turn a blind eye or deaf ear to such horrors, and the edge of a sword or enough talons always seemed to convince people to develop a sudden case of amnesia.

The rumors' validity aside, Dromick had been one of the few with the intestinal fortitude to voice his opposition to Doms Calvin Suldamik about the addition of the two domses to the alliance. He had even gone so far as to plead his case to Craigan and Zalan in hopes that the sons' words would be heard clearer than a mere officer. In the end, due to the Talons' lack of seagoing trade routes, the late Doms Suldamik had seen it as a necessary evil to have them as part of the alliance. During the years preceding the war – though their motives for doing so were suspect – Thakian and Astica had converted most of their sizable holdings into massive farms and crafting enclaves capable of producing large quantities of sundries and food. As a result of their pre-war actions, the inclusion of the two domses in the alliance afforded the Jade Talons a combined fighting force of nearly twenty-thousand soldiers, and more importantly, a workforce capable of working day and night on any project that either

Calvin or Craigan needed completed. Dromick had no doubt that keeping the army supplied would have been extremely difficult, if not impossible, without Doms Thakian and Astica's robust labor force; accordingly, House Suldamik would have likely fallen to the Merandiths long ago.

However, while Dromick was willing to give them the respect they deserved for providing such an invaluable service to House Suldamik, he always felt that there was something else motivating them. He only had his own hunches and suspicions to go on, but as long as Craigan chose to trust them, then he had no choice but to do the same no matter how much it disgusted him. Conflicted as he was, it didn't do his state of mind any good to find himself agreeing with Astica and Thakian about House Ithikia's motives.

Dromick descended the narrow tower staircase as quickly as he could, eager to be away from the domses. Once he was back within the main body of the keep, his powerful strides carried him through the high-arching hallways with purpose and a hint of the frustration that was plaguing his mind. So focused was Dromick on his own internal debate, that he paid little heed to the numerous workers and servants hustling about in their haste to finish preparations for the celebration that night. On more than one occasion, he brushed past someone in a manner that could have easily been construed as rude or even hostile. As for those that were lucky enough to see the frustrated and distracted general approaching, they quickly moved from his path.

The journey though the sprawling keep did little to help his mood. Between the colorful streamers hanging from the rafters, extra lanterns, fragrant perfumes, giggling servants and gaudily dressed men and women, he felt like vomiting. He was a soldier to his very core, and saw such blatant frivolities as a disgusting waste of resources and time. Celebrations could easily be had with much less, but he had long ago learned to accept that royals and the rich loved their parties and extravagances. While it might not be to his taste – and though it irritated him more than normal at that moment – he was always one to let others be themselves so long as their habits and tastes did not harm another. Besides, along with the domses proposal to him, he had his own duties to perform, which made letting such frivolities annoy him a futile endeavor.

Even as he served as doms general of Craigan's forces, Dromick also oversaw the Keep Guard, and led training exercises from time-to-time. He liked to remain busy and hands-on, uncomfortable with idleness and the thought of something important failing simply because he was too lazy to handle it himself. As a result, he had added to his demanding list of duties by volunteering to organize security for the celebration that night. For most, such tendencies – some might say obsessions – would put a devastating strain on any sort of life they had outside of their duties, and Dromick couldn't blame anyone that expressed shock when they learned he had a family life outside his work. He had seen similarly driven soldiers either lose their families or resign their commissions when the demands on them became too much. Dromick had to admit that he was quite lucky, though he often found himself wondering how and why his wife stayed with him. In the end, he tried not to reflect on it too much. She loved him for what he was and he her; that was good enough for him.

Despite the inner conflict of emotions the domses and the celebration had stirred within him, he still managed to steer his feet along a path that would allow him to check in on his other duties. He made note that the guards in their flashy, but fully functional, ceremonial garb had already begun to replace the afternoon shift. Dromick made a point to swallow his frustration and stop to chat with a few of the men and women. After exchanging a few pleasantries, he would then move on, eager to reach the keep barracks and a scheduled training session with a group of new conscripts.

Footfalls cushioned by thick rugs neatly arranged all about the main floor of the keep, Dromick continued his journey toward the rear of the complex. The thick green-dyed rugs almost made Dromick chuckle with nostalgia. He could still remember how the keep chamberlain had fought against what he viewed as a vulgar display and an affront to the keep. Oh how the chamberlain had wailed against the color choice and where the rugs were placed! In the end, he'd had no choice but to have the rugs ordered and lain down. Dromick was nearly positive he had seen the hawkish old man crying as the rugs were brought into the keep. By itself, Dromick would have to agree that the rugs were a bit painful to look at. However, Craigan had also had jade banners and curtains added to the keep's décor, turning the halls and rooms of the keep into a veritable sea of green that, for most people, made the décor more palatable – that, or people were wise enough not to speak ill of Craigan's bold choice of color. Dromick and those wise enough to read Craigan's true intent knew that the choice in décor wasn't meant to please – it was a visible and blatant reminder of just who ruled Chalin.

A growing carnival of noise toward the end of the wide, well-lit hall he was following told him he was nearing his final stop before he could turn his attention to his troops. He could see a small horde of servants pouring back and forth from around the corner at the end of the corridor. Between the frantic pace and the din of noise, Dromick couldn't help but think of a pen full of panicked rahkens – only there wasn't any blood being spilt. Although, from some of the loud curses he could hear, there certainly was enough verbal violence going on to make the toughest sergeant proud. Quickening his pace, Dromick rounded the corner, forced his way into the stream of bodies, and stepped through the massive double doors of the keep's dining hall.

Standing just inside the doors, Dromick let his gaze sweep across the hall. Like the rest of the keep, and many of the other structures scattered about Chalin, the dining hall was built to impress. Just over a hundred yards in length and sixty yards in width, the vast hall was constructed of solid stone, its vaulted, gently curve roof supported around the perimeter by a thick, fluted marble colonnade. Ten evenly spaced, twenty foot tall, arching windows lined both walls. Carefully cut, clear leaded-glass was fitted expertly in each window, permitting an abundance of light in on a sunny day and allowing those within to look out on the gardens that flanked the dining hall.

A hearth, which was large enough for six average men to stand erect and shoulder-to-shoulder in, was built into the left- and right-hand walls, the gaping maws of which were currently being piled high with timber. The twelve chandeliers, their framework composed of spiraling and twisting iron reminiscent of the organically flowing branches of a tree, currently rested on the floor while servants checked and refilled the lanterns that dotted the chandeliers like flower blooms. Thirty heavy oak longtables had been brought in for the event and were arranged around the perimeter of the room just inside the marble columns. The center of the room, once the chandeliers were raised to the ceiling, would remain clear, providing room for guests to mingle and dance.

A large stage, standing ten feet tall and made from a series of carefully fitted jade marble blocks, occupied the back of the hall. Provided access to its top were a flanking pair of staircases that were a flawless match for the platform. Beautiful white marble flowed along the top edge of the platform in elegantly carved swirls that seemed to dance their way across the shining surface. A single, richly carved and decorated ironwood High Table occupied the top of the stage along with ten matching high-back chairs, the seats already in place and awaiting the doms or doma that would occupy them.

Though satisfied with what he was seeing, Dromick couldn't help but feel his attention being drawn to the stained-glass window responsible for the myriad of colors spilling on the floor a few feet in front of the stage. The round window itself loomed over the room from its high perch in the rear wall. The colorful window was framed by silver filigree that swept its way around the circular portal, accenting the array of colored glass that made up the window's design. Comprised of green, blue, yellow and even clear glass, the expertly cut and shaped glass was mounted in a thin iron framework that was cunningly designed to present those gathered in the hall with a roaring dragon head set against a cloud-filled blue sky. At night, the window was quite a sight as soft moonlight spilled through it. But during the day, with vibrant sunlight pouring in, the window seemed to blaze with life as the stained glass cast its colors upon the floor, allowing one the chance to experience what it might be like to walk through a rainbow.

Dromick finally managed to pull his attention away from the magnificent work of art and continue on his review. Weaving his way through the crowded hall, he made sure the windows were secure, and examined niches and the underside of tables and chairs for hidden weapons. As he progressed around the hall, he even stopped to chat with a few of the guards already on hand, exchanging a few pleasantries before moving on. On one occasion, Dromick's lips almost broke into a pleased smirk as he made note of a few of his troops lending a hand with the preparations without giving the staff too much hell for pulling them into work that they might have seen as beneath them.

As he completed his inspection and reached the rear of the hall, he had to admit that he was pleased with what he had seen. Overall, despite the seemingly chaotic nature of the hall and the keep itself, it was clear that everything was coming along nicely. The troops he had assigned to guard duty had done their jobs well so far and, as he slipped out one of the side doors at the rear of the hall, he was satisfied that everything would be ready before the guests began to arrive in a few hours.

The small corridors that threaded their way through the servants' quarters and the kitchens at the rear of the keep were just as crowded with people as the rest of the lower levels. A few of the servants spared Dromick a curious glance or two, but they were used to soldiers using their isolated part of the keep as a shortcut to reach the barracks at the rear of the inner bailey. When he finally reached the unassuming servant's entrance tucked away at the rear of the keep and exited into the mild weather with its fresh air, he let out a sigh of genuine relief. While he had managed to control his frustration at his situation, he was glad to be away from the stifling crowds in the castle. Now he could let the frustration boil over without worrying about what repercussions his actions might herald.

As he crossed the inner bailey toward the three longhouses that comprised the keep's barracks, he could see that the conscripts for the training session had already gathered on the parade grounds in front of the buildings. Dromick flexed his hands, his knuckles cracking loudly, as the fresh blood noticed his approach and snapped to attention. Ahead of him, he saw not conscripts, but a vent for his anger, and none of them had any clue about the storm that was about to be unleashed upon them. Dromick had already made up his mind about his answer to the Astica and Thakian's request – and the answer sickened him.

Two hours later, after venting his anger on the recruits, Dromick found himself standing in Craigan's study and feeling very uneasy about the way his doms was glaring at him from where he sat behind his desk. The doors to the balcony were sealed shut, which would have left the study in total darkness if not for the chandelier hanging from the ceiling, the lanterns on his doms' desk, and the warm fire burning in the hearth on the far side of the room.

Half dressed for the party that night, Craigan's white shirt was loosely buttoned and his white-flecked, brown hair was tasseled. One hand played with a gold talon as his blue eyes bored into Dromick. "What am I to believe, Dromick?" Craigan asked, his tone calm, but cold with anger. "You are the most loyal man I know – yet here I am hearing that you were meeting with Doms Astica and Thakian, and that you didn't report to me. I'm not only ashamed, but furious that this news reached me through secondhand sources and not from you."

Dromick silently cursed himself for not being more attentive to who might have seen him leaving his meeting with the domses, but was more incensed that he had not done as he should and reported to Craigan immediately. "I can only offer my apologies, Doms," he stated contritely. "I should have come to you first, but the subject of conversation left me . . . irritated. I felt that I needed to vent my frustrations before coming to you. It was a mistake – I see that now."

Craigan smirked, his blue eyes twinkling. "I heard about the thrashing you met out. That's not typically you, Dromick."

The general nodded. "As I said, I was very angry."

"So it would seem. Tell me – what did our distinguished allies want with you that they felt they had to go around me to talk about it?"

A slight sneer tugged at Dromick's lips. "They wanted me to act as a spy, Doms."

"Spy?" Craigan said in shock. "No offense, Dromick – but you're hardly cut out for such a task."

"None taken, Doms." The muscles in Dromick's jaw flexed.

"Who is their target?" Craigan asked sternly.

"Doma Ithikia, Doms," Dromick answered swiftly.

Craigan's eyebrows shot up in surprise. "Oh really now? And why would that be?"

"To be honest, I'm not entirely sure. Its well-known that they have a distaste for anything they view as different – and you know I find them to be more disgusting than a mud crow – but the reason they gave me was sound enough on the surface."

"And that would be?"

Dromick met Craigan's gaze. "They are concerned about Alestra's motives and want to know more about her and her House. Honestly, whether or not this is their true intention, I have to agree with the reason they gave me, Doms. Alestra is an unknown in a war that doesn't need them. I would think, Doms, you of all people would know and respect that."

Craigan sat back in his chair and chuckled. "I'm not a fool, Dromick. I don't fully trust any of them – especially an enigma like Alestra."

Confused, Dromick asked, "Excuse me, Doms – but if that is the case, why would you now choose to honor your father's agreement and marry her?"

"I see word travels fast," Craigan said with a dry laugh. "My decision is one of practicality, General. I have come to realize that unchained, Alestra will do more harm than good. But if I marry her, I can gain a measure of control that I would not normally have. Believe me – this is truly a political union and not one of love or lust."

Dromick nodded slowly. "Then what about Astica and Thakian's plan? I'm afraid it involves more than spying."

Craigan leaned forward in his chair, curiosity written clearly on his face. "Really now? And what else did they ask of *my* general?"

Dromick hesitated and cleared his throat. "They wanted me to find a reason to travel into Pelasia to find out everything I can about her and her people."

*"Cunning bastards,"* Craigan thought. *"That should have occurred to me long ago. Kale has been too much of a distraction."* To Dromick he

500

said, "I don't know what they are really up to, but I like the idea. How would you like to take a little trip?"

Dromick relaxed a little, glad that Craigan was taking the news and plan so well. "As much as it disgusts me, Doms, I think it would be a wise thing for me to do. However, I would be remiss to not voice my concerns. Pelasia is a land we hardly know anything of, and with respect, leaving my post vacant for the winter would leave you at a disadvantage should things not go as we expect."

Craigan nodded. "Point well-taken. However, winter and Kale's retreat have just provided us with an unexpected boon. If you were to go, say . . . on the morning, you could be through the Dragonspine in less than three weeks. That would give you just over two months to conduct your search before you'd have to leave in order to return in time for the spring thaws."

Dromick nodded slowly. "I agree, Doms, but that's an ideal situation. It could take much longer than that and, Deo forbid it, there is the possibly I could be killed."

"Then what do you suggest? We haven't the spies to spare, and sending someone less skilled would simply endanger the mission."

Dromick nodded. "Agreed. I wouldn't trust it to anyone else. Might I suggest two things then?"

"Please."

"First, in my absence, I would recommend that you recall Doms Captain Jeinis Corandit to serve as my replacement. He has an exemplary record, is an excellent commander and his loyalty is second only to my own."

Craigan was familiar with his distant cousin and agreed with Dromick's choice. "Agreed. Your second request?"

"I will need a guide familiar with Pelasia and the Dragonspine."

Craigan grunted. "Not exactly an easy request to fulfill. There's plenty of Pelasians in the city now, but I would think you'd want one that is preferably loyal to us, and with no ties to House Ithikia."

"Yes, Doms. I would recommend your old axe teacher."

Wide-eyed, Craigan laughed loudly. "Shinks? Are you sure you'd want that beast leading you around?"

"We have few choices if we wish to accomplish this, Doms, and he seems the most likely and best choice," Dromick stated matter-of-factly.

Shaking his head in amusement, Craigan said, "It'll take some shifting around to make sure the border fort has a proper command structure – seeing as you're determined to strip it of valuable officers – but I'll make sure that it's done."

"Thank you, Doms," Dromick replied firmly.

Craigan shrugged his shoulders dismissively. "Think nothing of it. What you are offering to do is dangerous at best – I want you to have the best chance of success and to return to me intact. To that end, I will arrange for all your supplies and send a rider this very evening with a message to recall Jeinis, and have Shinks meet you in Shadowtown two weeks from now." Craigan's face softened with regret. "Also, I will personally visit your wife and apologize for taking you away from her so quickly."

Dromick chuckled and bowed. "Very good, Doms. I'll prepare myself to leave with the dawn – and say a prayer for your safety when you decide to deliver the news to her."

Craigan laughed at the joke as Dromick made his way to the door. Just as his general was about to leave, Craigan called out to him, "Oh, and Dromick, don't forget about the party tonight. I'll expect you to be by my side."

Turning to face Craigan, Dromick bowed again. "Of course, Doms. I wouldn't have it any other way."

# Chapter Twenty-Two

That evening, as the sun dipped below the flowing hills of the Utherian Valley, not only were the Jade Talons' medics caring for a host of battered recruits telling stories of a demon-possessed officer, but practically anyone in the city with any sort of medical training – real or not – was overwhelmed by a host of injuries as the fete exploded into a wild, riotous celebration. For the City Guard, it was the nightmare they had dreaded since the start of the fete. There were more fights and vandalism to deal with than they had manpower for, and they knew it would only get worse as the alcohol dried up and tempers flared, and as vandals and thieves used the chaos of the celebration as cover for their misdeeds. Cudgels and fists were used more often than not to break up skirmishes and other minor violence, but the temptation to draw a sword was a tantalizing option that won out on more than a few occasions. As a result, there were a handful of reported deaths at the hands of the City Guard. For most of the guards, however, such occurrences and their implications were of little relevance as they struggled to maintain a semblance of order in the joyful chaos. As for those amongst the City Guard that were concerned about the deaths, it was simply one of the many frustrating post-fete issues that would make dealing with the overzealous crowds seem easy in comparison.

Amidst the same streets that were packed with carousing celebrants and overwhelmed guards, were the carriages and sedan chairs of those attending Craigan's private party. Bogged down as the vehicles were by the masses, their retinues of guards were forced – or in some cases willingly – to use fists and cudgels to indiscriminately beat a clear path through the throng of bodies. It made for a tense journey through the chaos for the well-to-do passengers, but everyone eventually made it to the keep safely.

Upon arrival, guests found that the keep was experiencing turmoil of its own; however, the Keep Guard, along with the help of the extra soldiers Dromick had supplied for the night, were doing a fine job of maintaining order. The main gate served as a choke point for the numerous guests as the guards double-checked every invitation and thoroughly searched carriages, sedan chairs, and the rare individual horse for hidden weapons or any potential threat to the attending royals and gentry. Swords, predominantly ceremonial or dueling rapiers, were allowed in only if they were peace bonded. If the owner refused, then the weapons were confiscated for the duration of the owner's visit. While the precautions served to rankle a few of the visitors, drawing the occasional indignant threat or protest, the guards attended to their duties without hesitation. They were well aware that the insults and protests of a few angry guests were nothing compared to the punishment they might suffer should a slip in vigilance result in harm befalling anyone within the keep.

Once the guests made it through the checkpoint, a long red rug guided guests to the broad stone staircase that ascended to the wide-open, recessed main doors of the keep. Seven-foot tall iron braziers, flames glowing warmly in their basins, flanked the rug with green streamers strung between them, forming a barrier between the attendees and the rest of the inner bailey. After passing through the open doors and the watchful gaze of two more guards, guests found themselves in the keep's entry rotunda. House Suldamik banners displayed prominently upon the curved walls of the rotunda – which served as a none-too-subtle reminder of who ruled Chalin – drew the guests' eyes upward to the false ceiling of vibrant green streamers that joined the support rim of the dome to the massive chandelier suspended from the convex roof. Chairs had been arranged along the gentle curve of the white stone walls, providing a place for guests to sit and chat – of which a number of them already were. Servants in fine livery waded through the vivacious crowd with trays of wine and appetizers while others waited patiently along the walls to attend to the revelers' needs.

As the guests trickled their way through the keep, guards were strategically placed to keep visitors from wandering into places that Craigan did not want them to be. So while his guests had the freedom to roam most of the main floor of the keep, the upper and lower levels were strictly off-limits. As an added bonus, the guards' placement also served to gradually herd House Suldamik's guests to the dining hall and the festivities within. Well before the dining hall's doors were in sight, the clamor of jumbled conversations that had graced the attendee's ears since their entry to the keep was joined by uplifting music, the melodies of which inspired thoughts of revelry and graced lips with smiles.

As soon as the guests entered the dining hall, their spirits were further bolstered as the welcoming light of the fully lit chandeliers and the warmth of the roaring flames burning in the giant hearths enveloped them like a cozy blanket. Dinner had yet to be served – that would wait until Craigan arrived – but the tables were already dressed with jade-green tablecloths that were embroidered around the edges with gold filigree, and topped with tasteful, dried floral arrangements that provided a splash of complementary color. A few of the revelers were already seated at the tables, some of them toying with the expensive silver dinnerware that was neatly arranged in front of every seat along with fine, but empty, crystal goblets. Other partygoers twirled and glided their way around the dance floor as if directed by an unseen weaver that was intent on creating a tapestry of movement that was a match for the musical rhythms flowing from the minstrels stationed at the left rear of the hall. Warm light glinted off gemstones of all cuts and sizes that were attached to clothing, mounted in rings and necklaces, or weaved into hairnets. Dresses – both low and high cut, provocative and demure – made of rich fabrics were flaunted by the women that wore them. Men dressed in formal attire, ranging from simple doublets or robes to fashionable longcoats, were dancing with their partners or were already deeply engrossed in conversations with friends and colleagues.

Whether seated at the richly adorned tables or milling about the hall, guests were already partaking of the refreshments provided by the formal-liveried servants maneuvering their way through the hall. As in the rotunda, a small host of servants waited in the shadows along the walls, ready to attend to the guests and assist with the food when it was served. The servants along the perimeter of the hall also shared the shadows with armed guards who seemed to be trying to watch every direction at once from the depths of their ceremonial helms.

The festivities went on like this for another hour before the portcullis was lowered on the main gate, and the stragglers finally matriculated into the dining hall and took their seats. The hall took on a magical air as the last of the sunlight faded from the hall and soothing bluish-silver moonlight took its place, adding its own ethereal quality to the warmth of the firelight. With the appointed hour reached, and as the first of the Velusyian firestars erupted in a cornucopia of colors in the night sky over the eastern wall, the domses and domas began their procession into the hall dressed in their finest – and in some cases gaudiest – clothes.

Garbed in expertly tailored and richly adorned velvet longcoats that were dyed gray and black respectively, Domses Astica and Thakian were the first to arrive, their respective heralds announcing their presence to all in attendance. They were quickly followed by Doma Kylinis, ruler of the tiny realm of Galvat which resided to the southwest along the Dragonspine Mountains. One of the older domas, her plump figure was bathed in silks the color of wildflowers that took on a much brighter tone against her pale skin, white hair, and brown eyes. She was followed by Doms Talorn and Uthran from Western Triclose, both large, middle-aged men cutting striking figures in their respective blue and red longcoats.

In turn, they were followed by Doms and Doma Uspertain of the mountainous Southern realm of Gulthur. He in his longcoat, and she in a clingy and revealing dress, their clothing was made of silks and satin that was dyed in warm browns and deep blacks, which seemed all the more striking when set against his shaved head and her short-cut red locks. The couple was one of the few to have taken to the field together instead of one remaining behind to rule the realm. Rumor had it that not only were both husband and wife phenomenal with a rapier, but such was their love for a good fight that they often took to brawling with each other. Given the athletic builds of the young couple, how freely they flaunted numerous scars, and the way their matching blue eyes glowed with an inner fire, it wasn't hard to imagine the pair in fighter's garb or taking great joy in a good fight.

It was then that a young woman of twenty summers entered the hall and caught the undivided, lustful attention of the men and the jealous-filled glares of the women. Dressed in layers of revealing emerald- and sand-colored silk, her dress' neckline plummeted over her modest breasts and down her firm stomach to just below her navel. The rest of the fabric, which flowed over her wide hips to settle just above her knees, was bound low on her hips by a polished, delicate belt of golden disks. Black leather sandals adorned her feet, the straps of which crisscrossed their way up her toned, tanned legs before vanishing beneath her dress only to reappear on her firm abdomen, creating a black leather web as they climb her torso. Cuffs that were a match for her sandals encircled her slender wrists before separating into four straps that weaved their way up her arms, under her sleeveless dress and across her chest to connect with a solid disc of opalescent bone that served as the junction point for the all the leather straps. Crowned with a large shimmering firepearl, the disc was suspended between the swells of her breasts by a silver chain that snuggly encircled her neck before plunging down her chest.

Her fingernails and toenails were painted black to match the black lip paint that covered her upper lip and cut a stripe down the middle of her pouting lower lip. High cheekbones were sparsely dotted with subtle freckles beneath emerald eye paint that flared from the corners of up-titled sky-blue eyes that glowed with confidence tinted with a hint of sadness. Her shoulder-length bangs were gathered into two braids that flanked her face, while the rest of her mass of hair, which was the color of blue-tinged snow, was pulled back in a lush ponytail that hung to just below the curve of her hips. Four gold earrings lined each of her ears, and a lone emerald stud on the left nostril of her slender nose completed her exotic appearance.

Letting her eyes wander over the collective stares of the guests, the girl then bowed low to everyone, well aware that the normally clingy silk was drooping enough to bare her breasts to those close enough to see. As she stood back up, there was the barest hint of a frown pulling at the corner of her lips. She paused for a moment before bellowing in a seductive, throaty voice that seemed too powerful and loud for her diminutive frame, "Domses and domas of Triclose! Ladies and gentlemen of Chalin! May I present to you my mistress – Doma Alestra Ithikia of Pelasia!" Bowing low again, the girl swept to the side as Alestra entered the hall.

If it was possible, an even deeper hush settled upon the room as Alestra sauntered into the cavernous hall, her toned, curving figure stealing the breath from any man who could claim to be living. Her full breasts looking as if they were about to jump from their pitiful silk prison, Alestra's seductive figure was clad in the same revealing garments as the young woman that had proceeded her. A thick silver chain, which was strung through with gorgeous firepearls, encircled her neck before plunging down to her bosom, suspending a simple silver ring between the upper swells of her breasts. There was no web of leather crawling up her flat stomach, instead bronzed skin shone in the firelight, accented by an emerald set in her navel that gleamed provocatively in the light. Supple white leather boots climbed to just below her knees where black net stockings continued the journey up her thighs and under the dress. Matching white silk strands encircled her arms just below her strong shoulders before weaving their way down her arms to join with a forearm-length handcover, reminiscent of a Velusyian tekko, that was secured to each of her index fingers by a gold ring. Her fingernails had been painted to match the full, luminous white hair that tumbled loosely about her shoulders and down her back. She had the same designs painted around her eyes and on her lips as her herald, except Alestra's were red to accent her dangerously playful amber eyes and full, kissable lips.

For those in the hall that had never seen Alestra, they stared with unabashed awe, lust, or envy; there were even those that gawked with a combination of all three. The astute in the crowd, upon seeing Alestra and the girl side-by-side, were immediately aware that the two appeared to resemble each other. It might have just been their attire, but there was something in the cut of their features and the way they moved that seemed similar. Since the herald's arrival from Pelasia three years ago, rumors had abounded as to the relationship between the two women. Some thought distant family, others thought the girl was a gift, while still more risqué rumors suggested that the young woman was a Velusyian lalashia purchased – or gifted depending on who you listened to – to satisfy Alestra's more exotic desires. However, no one was ever able to confirm any of the rumors. Those that spent time with and around Pelasia's doma knew that asking the girl was a hopeless endeavor; she was rarely seen, and no one had ever heard her speak without Alestra's permission. As for broaching the subject to Alestra, she merely smiled broadly and laughed before changing the subject.

Pausing for a moment, Alestra rested a hand on her cocked hip, and drank-in the stares. Though she knew the girl found no enjoyment in such displays, Alestra couldn't help but find mirth in the situation and the handful of grunts and fleshy slaps that rang out as some of the women vented their frustrations on their gawking men. Once Doma Ithikia felt she had milked the moment for all it was worth, she motioned to the girl and the two of them seemed to glide their way around the perimeter of the room toward the marble stage at the rear.

With the women's first movement, the enthralling spell that seemed to have a hold of everyone was broken. That, however, didn't prevent numerous gazes from following the silk-clad pair as they sauntered around the hall and ascended the platform. Without hesitation, Alestra seated herself to the right of Craigan's chair, and the girl assumed a subservient position behind her. The confident and arrogant manner in which Doma Ithikia claimed that particular chair gave birth to hushed whispers, and confirmed the purpose of the night in many of the guests' minds. But before the speculation could gain any momentum, a crisp clear clarion call drew everyone's attention back to the hall's main doors, and those that weren't already standing rose to their feet in proper respect for the arriving doms.

House Suldamik's chamberlain, dressed in rich robes of burgundy satin, walked into the hall with an air of superiority dominating his aged gray eyes. The lighting in the room gleamed on his receding black hair as if it had been coated with boot polish. His fat lips, mashed on a pale and wrinkled face dotted with age spots, were pressed together firmly as he took in the gathering. Clearing his throat loudly, the man barked in a dry, authoritative voice, "Hear ye, hear ye! Ladies and gentlemen! Domses and domas! Citizens of Chalin and allies of the Jade Talons! I welcome you to Chalin Keep and this celebration in honor of our illustrious leader! It is my privilege and honor to present to you Doms General Dromick de'Suldamik Leonbane, and the true ruler of Triclose – Doms Craigan Murandi Suldamik!" Stepping to the side, the chamberlain pivoted and bowed as the two men entered the hall to the bows of everyone in attendance.

Paused as they were just inside the doors, both men cut striking figures in black satin longcoats that were slashed with jade silk at the shoulders and trimmed with embroidered gold filigree. Each man carried an extravagant, peacebound sword at their hip, and as a show of power, Craigan's amulet key to the Utherian Valley hung from his neck on a gold chain. With his hair combed back from his clean-shaven face, Craigan briefly examined the crowd with blue eyes that shone with unabashed confidence. Satisfied with their reception, he then, with his hands behind his back, began the trek around the room toward the platform. Dromick, his baldhead shining dully in the hall's light, followed closely while doing his best to keep his cold black stare focused on anything other than the nobles seated at the High Table.

Their trip to the High Table was delayed briefly as Craigan paused a few times along the way to shake hands and exchange plea-santries with some of the more noted guests and some of his staun-chest supporters. Upon reaching the platform – to the relief of many of the attendees that were growing tiered of standing – they ascended the steps and Craigan gave Alestra a somewhat cold stare to express his displeasure with her shameless, egotistical entrance. Unfazed, she returned his glare with a broad smile as if to say she knew full well what she had done, and had achieved the result she had wanted.

With Dromick on his left, Craigan took his place next to Ale-stra, thinking, *"And to think, she will end up my wife. . . . Deo save me from myself."*

Shifting his attention away from her, he focused on the ga-thering before him. "Greetings and well met, everyone!" he declared in a loud and clear voice. "I thank you all for joining us here this night – for it is a special night, to be sure! We are here to celebrate our victories and our foe's rash action to retreat and grant us this re-prieve. I know there have been rumors about staggering losses and defeats – but I am here to assure you all that this is not true! Our combined armies camp outside this glorious city as a testament to our strength! Our enemies bloodied our nose and think to sit and gloat! Let it be said that winter has done nothing but grant our enemies a chance to come to the inescapable conclusion that their defeat is in-evitable! Let them struggle with winter's wrath while we rest free of the frozen death they will have to battle daily! Come spring, we will unleash all the hells upon them – and Triclose will finally know peace!"

His speech was met with a roar of approval and thunderous applause. He had no illusions that the people in the room believed that they hadn't suffered demoralizing defeats; however, if there was one thing he had learn from his father, it was that you never showed weakness in front of your enemies – and especially not in front of your allies. Signaling for the crowd to quiet down, he continued once he could be heard clearly again. "That, however, is months away.

There are more immediate and joyous matters to attend to in the meantime. However, for now, let us eat!" As Craigan sat, the rest of the guests moved to find their seats and servants began to pour from the rear doors carrying trays ladened with bowls filled with a variety of fruits or steaming soup.

As servants distributed the soup and fruit bowls to those at the High Table, Alestra leaned in toward Craigan and purred, her amber eyes twinkling with mirth, "Joyous matters? Pray tell – what would such inspiring events be?"

Craigan glanced at her out of the corner of his eye and could see in her expression that she knew very well what he was to announce. However, he was not about to give her the satisfaction of a direct answer. She might be getting what she wanted, but he would leave no doubt that he was in control. With a grin, he countered, "Maybe you should take a lesson from your handmaiden and realize that patience and silence can be a virtue."

Alestra laughed and grabbed a snowgrape from the bowl of fruit set between them. "Oh yes – this is going to be fun, isn't it?" She popped the grape in her mouth to accent her point.

Craigan smirked at her reaction. He had to admit, as he turned his attention to the meal and more pleasant conversation, that no matter the reasons for the marriage, there was no doubt that boredom would be a scarce companion with her around.

The rest of the meal went smoothly, and provided plenty of activity to distract Craigan from his heavy thoughts. Throughout the evening, a seemingly endless flow of servants to and from the kitchens kept the tables clear of unused dishes and filled with a variety of food for everyone to enjoy. The soup was a thick, heady broth generously filled with vegetables and thick chunks of rahken meat that was wonderfully accented by a robust red wine from the vineyards along the Dragonspine. When the main course was finally served, it consisted of a variety of foods to cater to a plethora of palates – there was blackened sides of bramhen, filet fish cooked in red wine, and roasted rahken that was marinated in a plum sauce and stuffed with breadcrumbs. Baskets full of bread loaves sweetened with honey accompanied the meats along with pots of steamed vegetables and baskets of some of the last fresh fruit to be harvested. There were even dishes of Velusyian make – beds of rice covered with chopped rahken, bramhen, or raw fish, all of which was covered in a dark, sweet sauce. There were even vegetables that Craigan didn't recognize, and methods of preparing meat that he was unfamiliar with.

Unsurprisingly, he noted that Dromick sampled some of the more bizarre Velusyian cuisine, including what appeared to be a rock lizard skewered on a stick with roasted peppers, as well as a dish of fish and rahken bathed in the sweet sauce. The look on Dromick's face as he bit into the unusual meal was priceless. He did a good job of putting on a brave face, but Craigan knew him well enough to read the urge to vomit in his eyes. A glance down the table gave Craigan an idea as to why Dromick had chosen the way he had. Both Doms Astica and Doms Thakian had sneered in disgust at the Velusyian food and practically shoved it off the table when it was presented to them. Now, both men were watching Dromick with loathing as the general soldiered through the exotic food. Craigan did his best not to laugh at the domses discomfort, and when it appeared they hadn't notice his barely contained mirth, he figured he had more than succeeded in hiding it.

At last, what was left of the main course was cleared away before the host of servants filed into the hall again, bringing forth trays full of mouthwatering desserts. There were cakes covered in sweet white powder, and pies whose fruity aromas had many people eyeing them ravenously; other trays held sweet cakes, chocolate squares, sweetbread and sugar sticks; all of which were served with mulled wine and aromatic juices to cleanse everyone's palettes. As the sweet delicacies were distributed, some of the guests took the time to chat or dance. At one point, in an affectionate display that had Craigan blushing, Alestra fed him one of the bitter chocolate squares and then proceeded to pour some of the snowgrape juice into his mouth. She laughed with delight as more of the juice got on him than in him; caught up in the moment, Craigan, as well as those around him, couldn't help but laugh as well. Through it all, the colorful firestars cracked and burst in the night sky over Chalin, the occasional flash of multicolored light cascading through the windows.

Finally, when the desserts had been consumed and Craigan could feel the evening drawing to a close, he stood and called out to milling guests, "Attention all! May I please have your attention?!" It took a moment for everyone to quiet down, but eventually every eye was on Craigan. Certain that he had everyone's undivided attention, he continued. "Once again, I thank you all for coming and your support. Before we adjourn for the evening, I would like to take this opportunity to make an announcement."

A murmur of anticipation ran through the crowd. The rumors of a marriage announcement had been flying since Craigan's return, and the nervous excitement that now seemed to permeate the party was clear evidence of how much weight the rumors had garnered. There were some amongst the gathering that – like Dromick and Doms Thakian and Astica – remained impassive, as they were reluctant to give any indication of where their feelings on the subject rested. Those few individuals, however, were lost amongst the satisfied grins of those that had seen this night as the time when Doms Suldamik would make an official announcement.

Craigan turned to Alestra as he put his hand in the pocket of his longcoat. "Would you please stand, Doma?"

Standing, Alestra focused a wide, knowing smile on him.

"Years ago," Craigan declared, "our fathers made an agreement to bind our Houses together. To my regret and dishonor, I have shamed that agreement by not only failing to adhere to it, but by doubting you and your House's dedication to the cause. I ask that you forgive the error of my ways, and that you allow me to honor our fathers' wishes." Craigan pulled his hand from his pocket and opened the velvet case before withdrawing the hinged ring and holding it up for all to see.

There were audible gasps from those that were close enough to see the light glinting off both the numerous gemstones mounted all over the elegant ring, and along the facets of the large diamond set in its rear section. As entranced as she was by the exquisite piece of jewelry, Alestra couldn't refrain from gasping in delightful awe, nor was she aware of her handmaiden's wide eyes and sharp intake of breath – which was a display that she normally wouldn't tolerate from her handmaiden in public.

"Doma Alestra Ithikia of House Ithikia, would you do me the honor of joining me as my wife in defense of House Suldamik and the well-being of all of Triclose?"

Grinning ear-to-ear, Alestra presented her left hand to Craigan and said, "On my honor, I will."

Offering a smile that belied his heavy heart, Craigan slid the gorgeous hinged ring onto Alestra's ring finger as the hall roared with thunderous applause. Outside, a flurry of whistling and popping of firestars erupted into the night sky, a myriad of colors flowing through the windows to shower the Hall in a rainbow colors as if Deo himself was blessing the union.

Dromick watched the shameless glee wash across Alestra's face, and found his stomach twisting into tight knots. His dark eyes moved away from the sight and found the gazes of Doms Astica and Thakian fixated on the scene with barely contained disgust. The sense of foreboding he'd felt all-day suddenly took on a whole new weight at that moment.

*"Deo save us from ourselves,"* he prayed even as those around him cheered.

*The screams were painful wails of failure and death. Emanated from all around him, the horrific cries filling his ears and pounded at his skull like a blacksmith shaping steel with violent enthusiasm. Yet, with monumental effort, he managed to push the terrifying sounds into the background and concentrate on his duty. He did not know how he had arrived on the grisly battlefield, but, for the moment, the full-moon axe clutched in his blood-spattered, armored hands told him all he needed to know — kill or be killed. Confident in his purpose, he strode forth into the ranks of men clashing together like wild beasts, his axe rising and falling with powerful strokes that hewed limbs and bodies apart as if they were made of parchment. As he waded through the macabre scene, dealing death without remorse, the screams, which sounded like they were ripped from the deepest hells, continued to assail his ears and skull with wrathful exuberance. Given his current situation, he was thankful that he was able to disregard the cries . . . though he had no idea how he did so.*

*Then, through the haze of indistinguishable bodies, and the misty clouds of blood hanging in the air, his anger-filled blue eyes found a target that was free of the maddeningly fuzzy world that surrounded him. In the distance, surrounded by an army of faceless men and crowning a small mountain of ravaged bodies that writhed with mud crows, rats, and large carrion crows, was Kale. The sudden sight of his enemy caused Craigan to pull up short, and he was very nearly run through. Thank Deo, the sword somehow bounced off his armor, and he quickly responded by relieving his attacker of his head before continuing forward.*

*It then occurred to him that he could not understand why Kale was the only person on the carnage-filled battlefield that he could make out clearly. Was it merely the heat of the moment that made everyone and everything so hazy? Was he trying to block out the faces of those he butchered? He shoved the distracting thoughts aside, well aware that he had no time to dwell on such things.*

*Surging forward, his axe was a blur of dismembering death and destruction. Without warning, an all-consuming roar, like waves crashing upon breakers, filled his ears. In the blink of an eye, everything vanished and the world went black except for Kale, his army of faceless men, and himself. Before he could question the shocking change of scenery, two long and slender arms — as cold as death — snaked their way around him and pulled him into a chilling embrace. Sensual hands trailed up and down his body like a lover teasing sexual pleasures, and he could feel icy air against his cheek and neck as a pair of lips came to rest near his ear. Words that he could not understand floated past his ear, filling him with dread and tying his stomach into knots. He recognized Alestra's alluring voice, and was appalled that she could elicit such a reaction from him.*

*Then, to his horror, Kale finally saw him. His lifelong enemy raised his blood-soaked sword and pointed it at him. As Kale's mouth opened demonically wide, a wailing cry erupted from the gaping maw along with a shower of crimson blood. Signaled by the scream, the army of faceless men advanced on Craigan, fear washed over him like a tidal wave. He tried to turn and run, but to his horror, the frigid arms held fast as the incoherent words twisted into triumphant laughs. Horrified, he attempted to turn his head so he could gaze into the eyes of his betrayer, but another pair of icy hands griped his head firmly, directing his gaze at the approaching wave of steel and blood. He tried to close his eyes, but slender, deathly cold fingers pried his eyes open, forcing him to watch the unhindered onslaught of blood and angry steel that approached at an agonizingly slow pace. Terror flooded his body, urging him once again to attempt escape or even to scream, but his body refused to respond to his commands.*

*Then, as the first sword punched through his stomach and the wave of viscous blood crashed down upon him, he finally screamed.*

Craigan bolted awake, choking off the scream that had welled up in his throat. His blue eyes darted wildly around the room as he fought to comprehend his surroundings and separate himself from the dream. The sheets of his large, luxurious bed were soaked with sweat, as was the wool nightshirt that clung to his torso. He ran a hand through his white-flecked, brown hair and found it matted to his head with perspiration. Cold moonlight slipped through the shutters on the windows of his bedroom, creating an eerie glow that reminded him too much of the feel of his dream. The fire in the hearth had died down to a few smoldering embers, leaving the sparse moonlight as the only illumination in the spacious, square bedroom.

Still breathing heavily from the nightmare, he swung his legs over the side of the bed and stood up. With the nightmare and the cold stone floor urging him on, he hastily made his way across the room and entered his study through the open door. He made directly for the chairs situated in front of the study's hearth and plopped down in one of them. His hand found the glass of Velusyian Blue he had forgotten to finish before bed, and he downed its contents in one gulp before fumbling in the dark for the decanter. Refilling his glass, he emptied it without pause. Returning the goblet to the table, he dropped his head into his hands, trying desperately to get a handle on the swirling thoughts that were making it hard to think.

Why, of all nights, had such a dream invaded his sleep? Did his heart so irrevocably belong to Marie Merandith that his marriage to Alestra would conjure such dark images? Was his mind so dubious of Alestra's loyalty to him that he subconsciously thought she would hold him back or – even worse – be the death of him? He rubbed his face in anger. Even Doms Thakian and Astica's machinations were trying to intrude on his thoughts. It was beginning to feel just a bit overwhelming, especially for his current state of mind.

Frustrated, he stood up and angrily made his way back to his bedroom. Stirring the embers in the hearth enough to provide a bit of light to see by, he then shed himself of his soaked clothes before retrieving warm wool attire from the carved oak wardrobe against the left-hand wall. Once he had the green shirt and black pants on, he pulled on his black boots and a heavy green longcoat, which he buttoned up to mid-chest. Through it all, he did his best to try to organize his thoughts, but all he could manage was to remind himself that the best way to deal with things would be one issue at a time. Shaking his head, Craigan exited his room quietly, deciding that a stroll would help to clear his head more than sitting by a fire with a drink in his hands.

This late at night, the keep was eerily quiet and dark. Only one out of every five lamps was lit, and what little noise that he could hear was a result of the keep's own creaks and groans. The Guard's nightshift was on duty, and there were a handful of servants still busily cleaning up after the festivities. Craigan acknowledge the guards and servants when he did come upon them, otherwise, he kept to himself.

He wandered the keep for nearly an hour, climbing ancient stairs and exploring parts of the keep he had not been in quite some time, all the while he desperately tried to get a grip on his feelings so he could work his way through what he should do about the brewing situation. In the end, he was left baffled. There was no immediate way for him to determine what exactly was brewing in the minds of his allies. In a way, it all came down to acts of loyalty. He couldn't control every thought and action of those he counted as allies and friends, so he had to trust that they would remain loyal while he kept an eye out for acts of betrayal. From that standpoint, he wasn't sure whom he should watch more closely – his bride-to-be or the pureblood isolationists.

Where Alestra was concerned, she always seemed to be hiding or planning something no one could see coming. Her pacifistic invasion of Chalin with manpower and money had been a violent, cold slap to the face for Craigan, and had spurred him to what he normally viewed as hasty action. He did not like to be the one reacting to a situation, so if a little haste regained him control of the situation, then so be it. By consenting to the idea of marrying her, he felt it put him in a position to both temper and control her aspirations.

As for what he viewed as the lesser of two evils, he saw Astica and Thakian as less of a physical threat and more of a morale risk given their sheer distaste for outsiders and any culture that clashed with what they viewed as pure Triclosian. It wasn't a foreign problem, however. His father had managed to control the two, and up to this point, so had he. By giving in to their little witch-hunt, not only would it keep them sated for the time being, but, more importantly, it would potentially gain him information he and his father had foolishly neglected to gather on House Ithikia.

Craigan snorted in disgust at the absurdity of it all, and suddenly wondered if Kale had to deal with idiotic dilemmas like this.

Thinking about his opponent was nearly enough to drown his fears and concerns about his allies. The young doms had proven to be a staunch opponent that was very hard to predict or manipulate. To his chagrin, given the current trend of defeats, many doubted his decision to wait out the winter instead of finding a way to aggressively end House Merandith's current advantage. Craigan found that he couldn't fully disagree with his critics. While he knew the wait would benefit House Suldamik and its forces greatly, he was painfully aware that it would also rejuvenate Kale to a lesser degree. Despite what the benefits might be to House Merandith, if he was to defeat Kale for good as he and his critics desired, they would need the time to bolster their ranks and regroup. However, he was neither an idiot nor a fool, as some of his naysayers suggested. He was very conscious of the looming threat of a Merandith winter campaign and how much it could possibly hinder recuperative efforts, but he was confident that any such action by his foe was more bluster than anything else. Furthermore, even before deciding on a winter respite for the bulk of the army, he had initiated an extensive winter raiding campaign in order to keep the pressure on House Merandith and gain every advantage he could for the spring. In the end, no matter what his detractors might think of his decisions, he knew that every advantage they could gain would be vital to defeating an opponent as deceptively clever as Kale was – he had learned that the hard way.

His wanderings eventually led him from the keep and into the bitterly cold, blissfully quiet night. His feet carried him south along the well-maintained gravel paths of the grounds, guiding him through the once expertly manicured gardens that were now prepped for the winter months. Coming to a halt, he sat down on one of the cold marble benches and let his eyes drift toward the star-filled sky where the broad sliver of the moon cut a large, bright arc in the dark sky. With his mind finally clearing, he was able to think coherently.

Like his father, inaction without reason was not something he tolerated well. The fruits of his discussion with Dromick had at least made his decisions and lack of action easier to swallow. However, while it had revealed Domses Thakian and Astica goals on the surface, and spurred investigation of House Ithikia, it did little to reveal what their true intentions might be. With a grunt, it occurred to him that it wasn't much of a stretch to conclude that their thirst for power might be growing beyond their borders.

Alestra, on the other hand, was another thing entirely. She was a mystery wrapped in a mystery veiled in beguiling illusions. No amount of time spent in her bed or talking to her could have led him to believe her capable of delivering the amount of coin and manpower she had recently graced him with. He wasn't an idiot, however – he knew very well that she was power hungry and willing to go far to achieve her goals. Like Thakian and Astica, just how far she was willing to go was the question that needed answering. To a point, power hungry people were excellent tools, but beyond that invisible border, they could quickly become fatally dangerous.

Shaking his head dejectedly, he realized that the only thing he was accomplishing was to spin his mind in frustrated circles. However, with a snort of disgust, it dawned on him that he had at least come to one firm conclusion – when Dromick returned, he would have to reevaluate his alliances with all three Houses.

Suddenly, drifting on the wind from south of him, came a lilting and haunting melody. He blinked in surprise as the beautiful music tugged him from his reflections. His first thought was to question who else would be up this late other than servants and guards. His second, was that he recognized the beautifully haunting notes of a Velusyian windflute. This, in turn, perked his curiosity as to whom was skilled enough to play the breathtaking instrument in such a masterful manner. As his curiosity got the better of him and he moved off in search of the source of the melody, he found himself wondering who in Alestra's service could be playing it.

Following the paths as they wound their way south through the gardens, he eventually found himself at the gate to the Guesthouse, which Alestra had occupied to the chagrin of the other nobles. The three-story mansion was made of the same stone as the keep, the bluish-silver moonlight reflecting off the stone walls and blue-tiled roof in a ghostly fashion. Oddly enough, there were no guards at the gate, nor could he see any underneath the awning that sheltered the mansion's heavy oak door. Even the arched windows were dark, which further reinforced the notion that no one was home. He sighed to himself. Even in a situation this simplistic, Alestra was baffling. How could no one notice the soul-tugging music unless no one was home? For that matter, if no one was home, then where were they?

The music shifted at that moment, taking on a sad overtone that, for some reason, seemed to be trying to pry tears from his eyes.

His curiosity further emboldened, Craigan passed through the wrought-iron fence's gate and made his way around the mansion toward the rear-stationed gardens from whence the music seemed to be emanating from. Upon rounding the rear corner, Craigan was brought to a halt, his breath catching in his throat as his eyes landed on the source of the soul-wrenching music. The mansion's gardens were centered on a large fountain that was sculpted into the likeness of a long and curvaceous woman clad in a flowing, sleeveless dress. Head tilted back and sightless eyes cast skyward, her arms were extended before her, holding aloft a bowl from which water poured forth. Of the four curved white marble benches spaced evenly around the fountain's basin, the one closest to Craigan was occupied by the musician responsible for the tune. While the young woman had her back to Craigan, it was impossible not to recognize her blue-tinted, snow-white hair, which only further fueled his curiosity.

Dressed in a blue giku adorned with a tasteful white floral pattern, which turned blue as it crept onto the white silk wrap that encompassed her waist, the girl sat on the bench with her legs folded beside her. The baggy sleeves of her giku hung loosely from her raised arms as her delicate fingers teased the haunting notes from the windflute. With her hair hanging freely down her back, forming its own pool of white on the bench, it was hard to imagine that it was the same erotically dressed young woman from the party. In fact, her attire was a complete shocked to Craigan, and gave credence to the rumors of her Velusyian origin.

Having no desire to interrupt the lovely performance, he simply leaned against the mansion and listened. For a few more minutes, the enchanting melody continued uninterrupted. Then, suddenly, it cut off in mid-note and the girl lowered the flute, cocking her head to the side in a curious manner. Slowly she swung herself around on the bench, her white-booted feet coming to rest softly on the gravel path as her stunning sky-blue eyes alighted on Craigan. Although the giku was designed with modesty in mind, he could still see the silver necklace – which, in the moonlight, stood out like a fire in the night – around her neck that supported the opalescent bone disc hidden beneath the folds of her giku. As he drank in the mystery that was the young woman before him, he was surprised to see that there was no startlement or shock in her expression upon finding Craigan standing there. It made him a bit uneasy to realize that she had probably known he was there all along, and had simply chosen that moment to acknowledge him. Shrugging mentally, he gathered himself and approached her.

She watched his approach calmly, hands folded in her lap around the forearm-length flute that had been painted to resemble a

518

star-filled night sky. Craigan stopped a few feet short of her and bowed respectfully, keeping his eyes locked on her calm, emotionless stare. "My apologies – I could not sleep and was walking the grounds when I heard you playing. It was quite enchanting, and I couldn't help but try to find out who was responsible for such haunting music. I must say, you are quite skilled." Craigan hesitated when she didn't acknowledge his compliment. "I can leave if you wish," he offered, unsure if his presence was welcome or not.

The girl cocked her head to the side curiously, but gave no indication that she was offended by his presence.

Craigan scratched his head and laughed. "I feel like a boy trying to talk to his first love for the first time. I'm simply not sure how to talk to someone that doesn't respond." That comment drew a small, amused smile from her. "Well now," Craigan said with a smile of his own, "that's better. I'd ask your name, but I have a feeling that without Alestra's permission you wouldn't give it."

The girl nodded curtly.

"I see. Well then, if I'm going to be seeing more of you around the keep with the marriage, I simply cannot call you 'girl' all the time, now can I? What say I call you Flute? How does that sound?"

The young woman's eyes lit up with sorrow-tinged joy as she nodded enthusiastically, leaving Craigan to wonder at the treatment she received at Alestra's hands.

"Well then, Flute, I would think that your playing would wake everyone in the mansion – despite its loveliness. Is your mistress about?"

Her eyes darted to the mansion for a moment before she shrugged hesitantly.

"Odd," he thought once again of his wife-to-be. "Well," he said aloud, "either way, you have a gift there, Flute. I would be honored if you would grace me with a private performance at some point. Such skill is made to be shared with the world."

Flute smiled and nodded, drawing a grin from Craigan.

"Excellent!" he proclaimed. "Before that time, I'll have to speak to Alestra about this nonsense about you speaking when only she permits it. I won't have such abuse in my house – I assure you."

Flutes eyes widened with surprise at the proclamation, but Craigan could only fathom what thoughts and emotions he had just stirred awake in her.

Unsure of what else he could offer to a one-sided conversation, and suddenly feeling like sleep would no longer escape him that night, he said, "Well, the night has grown late and a few hours of sleep would do me good. Please, continue to play until your heart's content. Your music can only serve to inspire pleasant dreams in those that hear it." He bowed low to her as another broad smile crossed her lovely face. "Until next time, Flute."

Flute watched as Craigan disappeared into the shadows with a bounce in his step. The words he had offered her were the most gracious things she had heard in years and, even if they turned out to be hollow, made her happier than she had been in a long time. Sadly, as she turned back around on the bench, she knew she would have to fight to hold on to them when her reprieve from Alestra ended. The nights were her chance to be alone and to feel free – if only for a moment. She could feel tears welling up in her sky-blue eyes as she raised the flute to her lips and positioned her fingers over the perfectly cut holes along the instrument's length. Yes, she would hold on to the momentary joy she had just been gifted with and continue to play.

As the first note of the lilting, haunting melody rose once again into the air, a single tear slipped from her left eye and crystallized before sliding down her cheek. Leaving a streak the color of blue ice in its wake, the tear seemed to cling desperately to her jawline before falling free of her face to shatter on the bench below.

# Chapter Twenty-Three

*T*welve fully armored heavy cavalrymen thundered across the field, their armor and the sweeping blades of their saber-lances glinting in the afternoon sun. They moved with uncanny precision, maintaining their line without sacrificing speed as their powerful destriders bore their steel-girded riders as easily as a draft horse might carry a child. The wall of steel was quickly closing on twelve stuffed dummies at the end of the field. A red dot, no bigger than an average man's palm, was painted on the center of the chest of each dummy. It would be a hard target for a skilled archer to hit at range, and even harder for a mounted lancer at full speed – but for Hagan's Hammer, it was considered an easy achievement.

Saber-lances pointed skyward, and held in perfect balance despite the violence of the bumpy ride, the lancers pulled within fifty paces of the target dummies; crossing that threshold, they lowered and couched the twelve foot long weapons in perfect unison before kicking their armored steeds into a full gallop. The thunderous pounding grew louder as the large warhorses chewed up the distance. Twenty paces, fifteen, ten, five . . . and then the explosions. Twelve quad-saber-winged lance tips violently met twelve red dots – the macabre steel heads tore large, jagged holes in the dummies before ripping horrifically out the back, throwing straw and burlap into the air. As soon as the saber-lances impaled the targets, the riders released their hold on the weapons before the line split and peeled off with practiced precision. With the lancers retreat, a group of soldiers rushed forward to drag the skewered dummies from the field and replace the targets with fresh ones just before the next dozen riders began their charge.

Doms Captain Commander Gregor Netwyn of Hagan's Hammer watched the display from atop his painted destrider, his keen green eyes taking it all in from astride a crooked nose set on an aged and sun-darkened face. His rust-colored beard and hair, a strip of cloth in his blue and red clan colors tying the extra length of his hair off at the nape of his neck, showed a generous amount of white. Running from his cheekbone to his chin, a jagged scar marred the right side of his lips, which stood out starkly against his bright hair and dark skin. Despite the growing cold, he wore a sleeveless black shirt and padded riding pants, which were accented by the simple, heavy leather bracers on his thick wrists, and the sturdy knee-boots that protected his feet. His carefully maintained Sur'dathan claymore hung the length of his mount within easy reach beneath his wood-and-steel kite shield, which proudly displayed the badge of both his unit and rank – an angry kyram head with crossed warhammers behind it. He had led the emblem to significantly more victories than defeats, and was proud to be its bearer.

Glancing to his left, he was heartened to see that his lieutenant, Donald McFain, looked haler than he had in days. Clean-shaven and with his short brown hair slicked back from his long and handsome face, there was little indication of the beatings he had received the previous week. All of his cuts had healed and only the faintest of bruises remained. To Gregor's relief, Donald had refrained from drinking in public; although, the word about camp was that he certainly had not restrained himself with the women. However, he had been satisfied enough with Donald's behavior to reinstate him and get him back in the saddle.

So, it was with pride that he gazed inquisitively at the blue surcoat adorned lancer sitting proudly in the saddle of his black destrider. Like Gregor, a Sur'dathan claymore was secured to his saddle along with a similar shield that was emblazoned with a single, two-headed warhammer. There was a small grin of unabashed joy on Donald's face as he watched the other lancers practice, his black leather-gloved hands, the backs of which were adored with chainmail, flexing on his reins with pent up excitement.

The first group of lancers had returned to the starting point a few paces to the duo's left, and as they walked their mounts to give them a chance to cool down, Gregor nudged his steed a step closer to Donald and inquired, "Wha are ye grinn'n 'bout, lad?"

The young Sur'dathan shrugged nonchalantly. "Just glad ta be back in tha saddle again. Didna feel right ta be away fer so long."

Gregor chuckled. "Sorry 'bout that lad, but ye did be earn'n it," he said gently.

Donald nodded in agreement. "Aye, I canna be arguin' that. Dunna mean I liked it, though."

With a loud snort, Gregor replied, "Ye weren't suppose ta, ye thick-headed kyram! I'd be more dan happy ta send ye right back ta tha stables if'n ye prefer it."

"No, sir," Donald said quickly but firmly. "I'll be tak'n be'n in me saddle, thank ye very much."

Gregor grunted. "Well then, if'n ye like it so much in yer saddle, why don't ye be show'n me that ye can still put the right end of ah saber-lance in tha target?"

A broad smile broke out across Donald's face. "Aye! Tsst! YAH!" he shouted as he spurred his destrider toward the two groups of lancers that were resting at the start point, fresh saber-lances in hand.

A grin split Gregor's face as he watched Donald, without slowing, steal one of the twelve-foot weapons from the waiting lancers. Donald skillfully used his strong legs to keep him steady in the saddle as he adjusted his grip and set the top-heavy lance. The powerful mount beneath him grunted and snorted as she streaked forward, chewing up the distance with greater speed than the groups of fully armored lancers that had gone before. With all eyes on him, Donald reached the thirty pace mark with his lance still pointed skyward. He didn't budge at the fifteen or the ten pace mark, but as he closed in on the five pace mark, the muscles in his arm and torso exploded into motion. He deftly brought the saber-lance down and couched it neatly an instant before driving the quad-wing head of the lance through the center of the red dot on the dummy, straw and burlap bursting from the back as the quivering lance tore through the practice target. Leaving the lance where it was, Donald slowed his pace as he wheeled about and trotted his destrider back toward Gregor to the accompaniment of his fellow lancers' cheers.

Gregor met Donald's smug grin with a chuckle and grin of his own. "Well met, laddie."

"So, was I putt'n tha right end o' tha lance in tha target? Or do ye need ta show me how it's done again?" he asked sarcastically as he circled Gregor slowly and came to a halt in his original position.

Donald's playful jab drew another bark of laughter from Gregor. "Oh, aye, I'd say ye know which end be go'n where, but yer mum needed ta be teach'n ye to watch yer tone when address'n yer betters."

Smirking, Donald replied, "Aye, sir. I'll be let'n 'er know ye be disagree'n with tha way she raised 'er son."

Gregor snorted and shook his head. "Smart arse."

Donald's smirk grew into a toothy grin. "And 'ere I thought that was my most endearin' quality."

Gregor rolled his eyes and tugged on his reins, turning his mount back toward camp. "Come on, lad, let's see what Elifis is about fer I decide yer not as funny as I think ye are."

"Canna be refuse'n such a charm'n request, now can I?" he replied as he turned his mount and joined his doms captain in the short trek back to camp.

With Kale's departure a week ago, Doms Hagail had taken every opportunity to put his mark on the army. He took the responsibility Kale had put on his shoulders seriously and intended to do his job right, and if that meant making changes that Kale might disagree with, then so be it. Within moments of Kale's forces moving beyond sight, he had immediately given orders to rearrange the camp and to integrate the various House forces based upon unit type. There had been an endless stream of complaints and protests against the orders, but he had held firm; he even took the opportunity to dress down any officer or noble who came off as a bit more arrogant than he felt they had the right to be. For the rest, his reasoning was enough to, at the very least, send them back to their subordinates with a willingness to accept his orders for now.

For Hagail, there were two major flaws in the way Kale had been overseeing his army. The first of which was the division of troops by House. While he understood the logistical nightmare that integration could pose, leaving troops divided by House not only could build up resentment between troops, but also made it easier for an enemy to target Houses on an individual basis. So, despite the loud protests, he had seen to it that the entire army was integrated by troop type and that the command structure was reorganized to meet the demands of the restructured army. Secondly, he had rearranged the camp from its block layout into an elliptical arrangement, which, in his experience, would make it more difficult for an enemy to focus their forces on one particular front.

While it had taken five days for the camp to completely rearrange itself due a significant delay caused by the edge of a violent storm, the new command structure and integrated units were still a work in progress. Kale had left them with just shy of half the current active mobile army, amounting to over five-thousand able-bodied soldiers with the addition of the Sur'dathan units. Of the remaining mounted contingent, there were two-hundred heavy cavalry – of which half were Hagan's Hammer – three-hundred light cavalry and, since Kale took the Roselian clans with him, only fifty mounted archers. As for infantry and range combatants, there were one-hundred archers and nearly forty-five-hundred footmen. Except for the nobles' personal retinue of soldiers, every other man and woman of the army was left with no choice but to submit to the changes.

To no one's surprise, a large portion of the army was finding it difficult to adapt to a new chain of command and unfamiliar officers. Where the old hierarchy had seen Kale issuing orders that were then interpreted and enacted in the best manner possible by each House, the new hierarchy was comprised of a linear, rigid command structure that would see all soldiers of a particular role acting as one. Officers would report and receive orders through a chain of command that ended and started with cavalry reporting to Gregor Netwyn, infantry to the newly promoted Drake Elifis, and ranged troops to Solaria Desrosa, all of whom would, in turn, report to Hagail. It had infuriated many domses and domas that Hagail was taking even more direct control of their forces than Kale, but – as he gladly reminded them – he was not Kale, and things would be done his way until he was dead or until Kale's return.

As Gregor and Donald circled the northern edge of camp, which allowed them to check in on the other cavalry units as they went, they found themselves the target of passive-aggressive protests against the organizational changes. Some of the looks were merely out of curiosity, while others shot them baleful glares. Officers offered them curt salutes and short reports, making their dislike of the new command structure plain for all to see in the way they addressed their new superiors. Gregor had to bite his tongue on a number of occasions to keep from lashing out at the disrespectful tones addressed their way. He could tell that, in general, the attitude that had been adopted had more to do with being uncomfortable with the new situation than anything that could lead to dissention in the ranks. However, he was smart enough to keep his eyes and ears open just in case.

Though Gregor disliked the current disquiet amongst the army – and was thoroughly disgusted to find himself fearing rebellious actions by his brothers-in-arms – he and his Hagan's Hammer were used to being the target of the jealous and the disgusted. Over the years, the feared unit received more than their fair share of animosity-filled glares and heated insults because of the perceived barbarity of the saber-lances, and, depending on whom one asked, their ego-driven elitism. However, the famed heavy cavalry unit had earned its right to hold its head high. It fought in the unfriendly conditions of the Highlands and wielded the controversial saber-lance with a ruthless efficiency that left many a foe trembling in fear at the mere mention of their name. Gregor didn't hold it against any of the other cavaliers if they thought badly of the way his men carried themselves – in fact, he saw it as motivation for the offended to better themselves – but he scoffed at the notion that the saber-lances were barbarous. A heavy cavalry charge was designed to not only break an enemy, but to also inflict maximum damage in a short period of time – which the saber-lance did with an efficiency that no other handheld weapon could boast. No one survived a spearing by the weapon; the damage going in was catastrophic by itself, but if someone attempted to remove the lance by pushing it through or – Deo forbid – pulling it back out, the damage would only be amplified. In Gregor's mind, such efficiency was worthy of praise, not hypocritical disdain.

If anyone could sympathize with the passive-aggressive treatment of the Sur'dathans on any level, it was Drake Elifis. Like Gregor, the officers placed under his command had balked at his orders every chance they had. It seemed like everyone was so offended at their sudden loss of identity in the new command structure that they were willing to risk punishment – and possibly their careers – to let their distaste be known. He already had nearly a hundred troops running or doing menial labor as punishment for misplaced or belligerent remarks. He had enough to deal with without smart-mouthed officers and grunts giving him lip over orders. It had him honestly wondering what had made soldiers so soft that they thought questioning orders in the open was permissible. Regrettably, it was the least of his worries.

Under Hagail's new command structure, he was now effectively in charge of thousands of infantry. There were pikemen and spearmen to organize, a plethora of heavy and light infantry running around the practice grounds like noisy schoolchildren to coordinate, conflicts in tactics between different schools of thought to integrate, as well as a host of other small complaints or problems to deal with. Drake held no illusions that these kinds of issues did not exist before Hagail's arrival, but with the way Kale had things organized, it had always felt like Doms Merandith was the only one that had to fret over the big picture. Further compounding the maddening situation for Drake, was his difficulty in finding and placing officers to his liking. He couldn't begin to fathom how Kale had managed it all, but he had certainly developed a new respect for his doms.

Like Kale, Hagail believed in keeping idol hands busy; so with the long stretch without combat or a march, Hagail had ordered practice drills for every able-bodied person. Thus, Drake found himself saddled with thirty infantry that he was running through close-combat drills. He would have preferred to be sitting around a fire and draining tankards instead of being surrounded by sweating, grunting bodies, but someone – most likely Jerom – had let slip that he would be a valuable asset, and the result had been his new position of uninvited responsibility.

The aged and newly appointed doms captain-commander took a winding path through the paired-off combatants, a thick, sun-darkened hand rubbing at the white stubble on his chin. Dark eyes watched the practice session with a keenness that, like the way he moved and his strong build, belied his age. Despite the chill in the air, he wore a sleeveless leather tunic over loose breeches, his sturdy and comfortably broken-in black calf-boots cushioning his feet. Unadorned bracers encircled his thick wrists and a heavy broadsword hung from the hefty sword belt secured about his waist. A thick-knuckled finger tapped at the pommel of his sword as he paused to examine group after group, cursing and sometimes even going so far as to insult every fatal misstep or opening he saw. There were moments during such sessions where he found himself wishing that their swords lacked padding so the fools could weed themselves out. Not that he would ever expect such a foolish decision to come down from any doms with an inkling of sense – but still. . . .

"Come on ye lazy arses! My long-buried mother –Deo rest her soul – could fight better in her grave than the lot of you! From what I've seen here, I might as well go ahead and invite Doms Suldamik to tea so I can kiss 'is arse proper!"

A young soldier to his right pulled up short on his block upon hearing the sarcastic proposal, and caught a padded blade across the top of his head, knocking him to the ground. His partner snickered as he watched the young man, down on all fours, trying to clear his head.

Drake cuffed the shaved head of the standing man, drawing a sideways glare from him. "What's the matter, Private?! Ye think it's funny that you just bludgeoned your partner to his knees? Humm?"

Catching the intensity in Drake's black eyes, what remained of his smile vanished as he barked, "No, sir!"

Drake moved in front of the man and leaned in close enough to brush the soldier's slender nose with his own thick snout. Looking him straight in his small, pale-green eyes, Drake roared again, "I'm getting on in age, lad, and – correct me if I'm wrong – I don't seem to be hearing you. What did you say?!"

Shaking a bit both from the close proximity of Drake's anger-flushed face and the intensity in his voice, the soldier barked louder, "NO, SIR!"

Drake stood back and grinned warmly, his voice suddenly cordial as he replied, "Now, isn't that better? Collect yer friend there and escort him to the medical tents. Don't need brain fog putting someone down – especially from a damndable practice session."

Chainmail rattling and leather armor creaking, the soldier stepped around Drake and helped his practice partner to his feet before gingerly escorting him back toward camp.

As soon as the two were on their way, Drake turned his eyes on the rest of the soldiers, all of which had ceased their workout to watch the incident unfold, and barked loud and angrily, "As for the rest of ye louts – get back at it! No one gave ye all permission to stand about like a gaggle of half-wit children!"

The dull thud of padded swords filled the air again as the soldiers quickly resumed fighting to avoid becoming the object of their commander's attention. Shaking his head with a slight scowl on his face, Drake made his way back to the perimeter of his training unit and returned to his observant patrol. The next few minutes were filled with more curses, corrections and frustration before Drake noticed Gregor and Donald approaching on horseback. To both his and the soldiers' relief, Drake used the Sur'dathans' arrival as an excuse to call a halt to the training and dismiss the unit. Grateful soldiers began to slowly make their way back to camp, all of them breathing hard and moving wearily, and many of them with their shoulders slumped and heads hung in exhaustion.

Drake shot the retreating soldiers one last disgusted scowl before moving to greet the approaching Sur'dathans. "Well, aren't ye two a sight," he said as he approached them with his hands on his hips.

Gregor and Donald reined in short of him, the elder Sur'dathan acknowledging Drake with a nod of his head. "Well met, Doms Captain Commander," greeted Gregor. Ignoring the scowl Drake shot his way at being addressed by his new title, he glanced at the tired, retreating footmen and the other groups of infantry that were busy with their exercising. "Ye been work'n the grunts hard, I see."

"Oh aye, that I have," Gregor replied with a hint of disgust. "They're all needing it too. There's too many of 'um that seem like they're only good for being the first up a siege ladder."

Gregor raised an eyebrow at the demeaning observation. "That's a wee bit harsh, isn't it? None o' ye could be make'n it this far in tha war if all ye had was siege fodder," he stated with a straight face.

Thinking that Gregor was taking his exaggeration a bit too seriously, Drake snorted in annoyance before retorting, "This is why I didn't want this promotion – ye doms captain-commanders take things too straight! A man can't voice his frustrations without being taken literally!"

Matching grins broke out across Gregor and Donald's faces, drawing a string of curses from Drake as it sunk in that Gregor was joking. "And ye Lowlanders," Gregor stated with an amused chuckle, "canna see a joke when its stare'n ye in tha face."

Rolling his eyes, Drake retorted, "Oh aye, but that's because ye Highlanders' faces and brains are made of ice. No one expects ice to be able to think."

Both Sur'dathans broke out in laughter that soon had Drake chuckling. Donald finally gathered himself an offered as a final quip, "Aye, aye, but not only does it be make'n us good at gamblin', but ye got to be a wee bit frozen ta be have'n a chance ta bed our women and not get a case o' frostbite!"

Both Gregor and Drake found themselves shaking their heads at the comment. "Well, that explains a lot," Drake muttered.

"Aye," Gregor said in agreement. "Thank ye, Donald, for yer unflattering description of our women and lives. Though it does be beggin' tha question of why ye bed so many of them."

Donald shrugged nonchalantly and said with a broad grin, "What can I say, they be keep'n me hot head cool."

Drake threw up his hands with a snort and declared, "I give up! So, are you here to offer me a ride to the meeting, or are you just going to offer me glowing insights into Sur'dathan culture."

Edging his horse forward, Donald extended a hand to Drake and grinned broadly at him. "Well, see'n as I canna be convencin' ye that our women will do wonders for ye, I guess save'n yer legs from walk'n will have ta do."

Cursing under his breath, Drake accepted the outstretched hand and climbed up behind him on the broad back of the destrider.

Surrounded by tents of his officers and bodyguards, Doms Hagail's tent had taken up residency at the center of the oblong camp. The Sur'dathan tents that were made of cloth or canvas had been dyed in their respective clan colors, while those that were made of kyram hide and fur flew clan-colored pennants from their peaks. Hagail's conical tent was dyed in alternating stripes of bright red and blue, and embellished with a generous amount of golden filigree that seemed both out of place amongst the other tents and too ostentatious for the Highland doms.

Aside from the numerous men and women moving around the central part of camp, Hagail's own handpicked bodyguards were ever present. Known as Kyram's Claw, the guards were easily identified by the feathers braided into their beards, the lone black kyram claw hanging from their necks, and their golden-pommeled claymores. The closer Donald, Gregor and Drake got to the center of camp, the more of the fearsome guards they saw. Upon reaching Hagail's tent, the trio dismounted as they were greeted by three of Kyram's Claw. All three were adorned in chainmail, padded leather armor, and kilts in House Hagail's colors. One of the guards collected the reins of their horses while the other two stone-faced men stood stoically on each side of the tent's entrance. Both tent sentries appeared oblivious to what was going on around them, but Gregor and Donald knew that they were all too aware of their surroundings. As such, both Sur'dathans acknowledged the two sentries as the trio pushed aside the tent flap and ducked inside.

The interior of the tent was divided into two rooms by a thick curtain, separating the rear third from the rest of the tent. A large oak table, which served as both a desk and dining table, occupied the area of the tent that the trio now stood in. At that moment, the table was serving in both capacities. Dinnerware for five was arranged on the table along with a platter of sliced smoked bramhen, loaves of bread, a platter of mixed fruit and two pitchers of wine. Three female servants, all of them young redheads, in red dresses and blue bodices stood at the rear of the room ready to attend to Doms Hagail's needs.

The Doms of Sur'datha was seated at the head of the table, his plate already filled with hefty portions of food, perusing through reports that were stacked next to a bundle of letters sealed with House Merandith's wax sigil. Doms Loridak Hagail's short, burly figure was adorned in a gray doublet over a thin linen shirt that provided more than enough protection against the growing cold for the Highland doms. Nearly sixty summers old, the wrinkles of his leathery, wind-darkened skin told the tale of a man forged in combat. His receding hair and braided beard were white with a spattering of black that was reminiscent of his younger years. Despite his age, the green eyes that were studying the report shone with an intensity that belonged to a younger man.

Rather than waiting for his doms to notice them, Gregor cleared his throat loudly but politely. Slightly startled by the sudden noise, Doms Hagail looked up and, when he realized he had guests, smiled. "Ah, Gregor! Do come in! All of ye, come in, come in!" he offered in greeting, his deep voice authoritative even when issuing such a friendly salutation. Hagail waved them toward the chairs set around the table. "Have a seat. I had the lasses pull together something a wee bit more appetizing than dried rations. The wine don't be match'n what a good ale can provide, but it certainly won't be get'n any of ye drunk as quickly either."

As the three took their seats, Donald and Gregor with their backs to the tent entrance and Drake on the opposite side of the table next to Doms Hagail, Drake offered his thanks. "A fine spread, Doms. The smell is enough to make a full man hungry."

Donald smirked as he procured himself a hefty helping of the smoked bramhen. "Aye, or a hungry man ta think he be in tha arms of tha beautiful good spirits."

Hagail chuckled at the comment. "Aye, there's that, but it certainly covers the stink of ye three. Ye come straight from training, eh?"

"Aye, Doms," Gregor confirmed as he picked a few choice pieces of fruit to add to his meat- and bread-filled plate.

Returning the report he had in hand to the stack on the table, Hagail picked up his cup, leaned back in his chair and took a sip. "Well, might as well be telling me how things are while we wait on Solaria. I'd swear she'd be respond'n better to orders if her bow was tha one giving them," Hagail added with a frustrated shake of his head.

Drake snorted in amusement as the others chuckled. "That's a cyrian for ye. If their forest spirits aren't telling them what ta do, then it's harder than trying to wrestle a bramhen with one arm tied behind your back to order 'um around." He shoved a mouthful of the meat into his mouth to punctuate his point. "Just be glad she's not as. . . . What's the word I'm look'n for?"

"Creepy?" Donald offered with a smirk.

"Aye, that's it! Just be glad she's not as creepy as the rest of her people. Otherwise, we'd be waiting till she could find one of her holy groves before she'd do anything."

Hagail laughed. "Remind me to cross ye off tha list of possible diplomats should we ever need one, Elifis."

Drake tipped his cup in the direction of Hagail. "Gladly, Doms," he said before taking a long draw from his cup.

Gregor cleared his throat again to regain everyone's attention. "I believe, Doms, that ye want a report on tha training?"

"Aye, Aye. Go ahead before we start ramblin' about something else."

Gregor nodded. "The cavalry units be merging well, especially the lights. We still got our share of fights and disagreements with the heavies, but it be nothin' we can't be handle'n." He smirked with a bit of shameful pride. "Between our saber-lances and superior steeds, Hagan's Hammer got them other heavies grumbling night and day 'bout one thing or another. One thing is for sure, though, they've found their place and seem ta be acceptin' it."

"Well, that was ta be expected," Hagail reminded him, pride evident in his tone. He shifted his gaze to Drake. "And tha infantry?"

"Similar issues as Gregor," he stated quickly. "We got so many soldiers with their own tactics, their own weapons and their own minds, that work'n together seems almost like an insult to them." Drake grimaced and hesitated before continuing. "I hate ta be mentioning it again, but I think Doms Merandith kept everyone separate for this very reason, and to take advantage of each House's unique style and tactics."

Hagail met Drake's firm look with an even harder, authoritative glare of his own. "I'll say it again, Drake – we've all got ta be fight'n as one in tha winter. The mixed-unit tactics Kale be using is all fine in the summer, but come tha snow and ice, we'll be need'n Highland tactics – and that means everyone be learn'n ta work together in tha same fashion. Ye understand me?" he finished firmly.

Drake nodded with an audible sigh. "Aye, Doms," he acknowledge as he turned his attention back to his food.

Hagail nodded. "Good. Now–"

"Pardon me, Doms – I hope I'm not too late?" a voice that was a perplexing mix of soft and authoritative interrupted from the tent entrance, drawing the attention of all three men.

Standing just inside the tent was one of a handful of the most exotic and reclusive people in the Five Stars army – not to mention Triclose itself. Standing just over six-feet, Solaria Desrosa's lean, athletic body was composed of proportions that were longer than natural. Her skin – which eerily looked like it would feel like velvet when touched – was a natural dark tan, and her body was clad in snug leather armor that was nearly the same color. The padding on the inner thighs and crotch of her pants was dyed a deep-forest-green, as was her supple boots and the piping of the bodice-style padded armor. Her small breasts and upper torso were protected by a high-collared, padded, square-shouldered top that was secured to her strong upper arms and her bodice by buckles that had been dulled and aged so they wouldn't reflect light. A black wool shirt sheathed her arms, ending in a standard bracer on her left arm followed by a three-fingered glove, while a bracer that extended nearly to her elbow protected the inside of her right arm.

She examined each man at the table with her yellow eyes, which were eerily feral in their shape and intensity. Graceful tattoos surrounded her eyes, flaring from the corners of the yellow jewels and sweeping down the outside of her broad, somewhat flat nose in a fashion that made her appear more feral than human. Her full lips were pressed together firmly as she ran a hand over her slicked-back, short-cropped black hair, its subtle green highlights visible in the current lighting. "My apologies for being late; breaking the habits of people that shouldn't hold a bow is a . . . tedious task," Solaria said with a bit of mild disgust in her formal tone. Her eyes came to rest on Donald and a lone eyebrow raised in curiosity. "I was led to believe this meeting was for us commanders, Doms Hagail. Am I wrong?"

"Not to worry, lass," Hagail said with a warm smile. "Donald is young, brash, and a pain in our arses at times, but he's a damn good fighter with a' solid military mind. Gregor finds 'im useful ta have around – so that means I do as well." He chuckled as Solaria eyed Donald skeptically again. "Do come in and have a seat," he added as he pointed her toward the empty chair, "and stop frett'n about tha young'n. We were just discussing how the training was going."

Shrugging her shoulders dismissively, she made her way to the empty seat, her long limbs and hips swaying with a feral grace, and lowered herself into the chair before grabbing her cup and sipping politely from it. "All goes well, Doms Hagail. There are a few that would never be allowed to touch a bow if they were cyrian. . . . But for outsiders, they will suffice with a little more proper instruction."

Hagail smirked. "Well then – I'm glad we be have'n ye and yer expertise to be show'n them how to use a bow proper."

Solaria nodded and replied, "Indeed. Many of us were beginning to doubt our presence here, but our faith in the Grove and the Forest Mother was well placed. Without our guidance, your archers would be an insult to the very trees their bows are made from."

Hooded, amused glances were shared by the men at the table. Hagail smiled politely, not wishing to give voice to the thoughts running through his head. Instead, he said, "Aye. Well, it would be most generous of ye and yer people if'n ye would share those fine bows of yers."

Shaking her head firmly, she declared, "As I've explained to both you and Doms Merandith – a heartsong greatbow is not something casually made or used. We each earn the right to carve our heartsong when we come of age. If the bow is not earned, it cannot be wielded. There have been few outsiders capable of earning such a right, and the only one I ever met was Allanian – and he has already earned a right far greater than any that a cyrian could bestow upon him. Besides, we haven't the time or the resources to even make an attempt at outfitting a force this large."

"Well," Hagail said as he hung his head and shook it with a rue smile, "at least ye're straightforward and honest. That's more than I can be say'n for a lot of people."

Solaria nodded. "Thank you, Doms Hagail," she replied before helping herself to the fruit platters, a loaf of bread and a few slices of meat.

"Well now," Hagail said as he clapped his hands and motioned for one of the serving girls to refill his cup, "since we all are 'ere, let's not dally, and get right ta' business." Looking at the serving girl, Hagail offered her a smile and said, "Thank ye, lass."

The girl smiled and curtsied before returning to her post.

Turning his attention back to the gathering, Hagail said, "Now, as ye all be know'n, I'm not one ta be sittin' on me hands, so I've had scouts out gettin' a lay o' tha land. I must thank ye people for their help, Solaria. Their speed and efficiency is most appreciated."

Nodding, Solaria replied, "Thank you, Doms Hagail."

"Ta continue," Hagail rumbled, "let me say I've been in better and been in much worse situations than this one, lads and lassie. We be hav'n free and clear land to our east 'n north, but west be look'n like a' briar patch full o' irritated kyrams."

"That bad?" queried Gregor.

Hagail shook his hand. "I may be exaggerating a wee bit, but it's not good. We've got one major border fort that's been alive with activity, as well as there be'n plenty o' patrols ta make any movement of a large force impossible without bein' noticed. On top o' that, Craigan appears ta be holdup in Chalin as expected – or that was tha estimation from the scouts," Gregor finished in irritation.

"Wouldn't matter, Doms," Gregor said in a conciliatory tone. "We don't be have'n tha manpower ta lay siege, much less fight his main force."

"Aye, I know. But it don't be mak'n it any easier to accept that yer enemy is sitt'n pretty behind big walls while we're out in tha field." Hagail shrugged. "Still, pursuin' Craigan isn't what Kale brought us 'ere for."

"If ye'll pardon me for ask'n, Doms," Donald interrupted respectfully, "but I've been wonder'n tha whole time why we're so far south? I know we're take'n over 'cause tha Merandiths want a winter campaign, but if we're not pursue'n, then what are we doin'?"

Grinning, Hagail answered, "Harassment, lad. Bloody, irritatin', sleep-stealin' harassment. Kale wants us ta make sure Craigan's people don't be have'n a bit'o peace this winter."

"Oh. Well now, that's somethin'," Donald said contently. "Give'n them tha winter ta rest quietly while tha rest of tha North muddles through tha snow didn't sit right, but this . . ." he chuckled, "this is a good idea. Will give'um a winter of blood while our friends be keep'n their toes all warm by a fire."

"Doms Merandith has pursued a wise course, I would agree," Solaria added with a slight nod.

Drake snorted, "Of course he has. The man is a whole lot smarter than his age."

"Aye, he's a lot like his father . . . though I'd be prefer'n ta strike harder than glorified harassment," Gregor added.

Hagail nodded in agreement with Gregor. "As would I, lad. But orders are orders, and I intend ta be do'n me duty to tha best o' my abilities. So," he picked up the top letter from the stack that Kale had left him, "that brings us ta this – our first official orders." Hagail broke the wax seal with one of his thick thumbs, opened the letter and began reading it. As his eyes passed over the neatly written lines, Hagail's eyebrows climbed and a wry smile tugged at the corner of his mouth. "Well, he does remind me more 'n more of his father," he offered with a dry chuckle.

The other four at the table looked at Hagail curiously, but it was Drake that spoke up first. "Well, what's the word?"

Hagail put the letter down and met the eyes of the other four. "It would be seem'n that he's either left the last part of his campaign to us, or he's concerned for our safety out here." He chuckled. "We're ta be take'n tha Chalin border fort as our base of operations."

Gregor stared at Hagail with a stunned look painted on his face, and Donald grinned at the thought of a good fight. Solaria appeared so unsurprised as to almost look disinterested, while Drake shook his head in amazement.

"That's Kale for ye," Drake said. "Would also explain why he took who he did and left who he did. There was certainly nothing random about his personnel choices. No offense, but I haven't seen cavalry take a fort yet."

Hagail sat back in his chair with his thick fingers steepled before him in thought. "Aye, it makes sense now. I wouldn't normally be for attack'n a fort without siege equipment, but with Solaria's people on hand, we might be able ta make'um fidget in their boots 'nough ta make a mistake."

"I must agree," Solaria chimed in. "Doms Merandith's scouts have seen the place. The walls will be of little use against our bows. I will point out, however, that we can only do so much damage. If they decide to huddle behind their walls, our bows cannot hit them with precision, nor can your lances strike them. Nor do I think Kale left us this many men simply to break them against walls."

"Not ta be piling on tha negativity," Gregor finally said after he shook off the shock of the news, "but she's right. Heartsong bows or not, take'n a fort without siege equipment is gonna be damn near impossible.... No offense intended, Solaria," he added with a nod to her.

Solaria returned the nod respectfully. "None taken. But I think you and I are jumping to conclusions. I do not think Kale would put forth such an idea if he did not think it would work, or without a fallback plan," she stated plainly.

"Aye, she's right. Kale's not just throw'n us ta the wolves," Hagail said. "He knows winter is bearing down on us hard, and doesn't want us freezing our arses off sittin' in tha open. If'n we canna be taken it in a reasonable amount o' time, we're ta fall back here and dig in. Deo only knows we could be build'n our own fortifications with tha manpower we have, but transport'n materials from tha Alderian Forest would just be . . ." he scoffed. "Weather and numbers aside, can we be do'n it?

"It'll be take'n some luck, but aye, I think we can," Gregor answered carefully as he stared down at his plate, his mind working through the tactics and logistics of it all. "We'll be need'n a mix o' surprise and intimidation on our side ta make it work though."

Hagail nodded. "Agreed. Tha finer points can be figured out when we be take'n a look at tha maps, but if'n I give ye all of tha Hammer, around half tha infantry and Solaria's archers, could ye do it quick like?"

Gregor looked up at his doms skeptically. "Ye'd be ask'n me ta get them ta leave tha fort fer that ta work, Doms."

"Do ye see any other way for it ta be work'n in a short period o' time, or should I be start'n crews for the Alderian Forest?" Hagail asked, already knowing the answer.

536

Gregor shook his head in resignation. "No, Doms – gettin' them out from their walls be tha only way ta do it if we wish to avoid any delay."

Donald scoffed. "That and a bloody mountain o' luck, Captain."

Drake sat back in his chair, his arms folded across his chest. "Hells, I don't like the sound of any of this. But I trust Kale, and we've had Deo's luck on our side for a while. Might as well push it for all we can be getting."

Hagail looked to Solaria. "And what about ye, lass?"

Solaria met his look with a firm stare of her own. "If Kale believes it can work, then I do as well. Your heavy cavalry is famed throughout Triclose, and I've seen our infantry fight like men possessed. Kale has used my people sparingly, and most people view the stories of our skills as merely that. You will have surprise and power on your side." She shifted her gaze to Gregor. "It will be up to you to come up with a way to lure them from their walls."

Gregor grunted. "Thanks, lassie. Just what I wanted – a mountain o' trouble heaped on me shoulders."

She arched an eyebrow at him. "What good is a hammer if it can't smash a mountain?"

Hagail and Drake laughed merrily, and even Gregor and Donald eventually cracked a smile, before Hagail offered to Solaria, "Well put, lass." Then, motioning to one of the serving girls, Hagail pointed to a heavy steel-bound chest in the far corner of the tent, ordering "Lassie, fetch tha maps from the chest. The rest of ye, clear this table so we can be plan'n proper."

Springing into action, the servants quickly moved to follow his orders. As the platters and plates were removed, Hagail returned his attention to his captain-commanders. "We're gonna be find'n a way ta do this, but remember it's got ta be quick – no more than a week. I would imagine that these plains will turn into a frozen hell fast."

Focusing on Gregor, Hagail declared as the first of the maps was placed on the table and unrolled, "Ye'll have full authority over this, Gregor, and take Solaria with ye." Then, to Drake, he added, "Drake, I'll need someone here that isn't as daft as ah crazed mud crow in case things go sideways."

Drake grunted in agreement. "Fine by me. I'm too old to be bouncing around in the saddle anyways."

"When do we leave?" asked Gregor.

"Winter is coming on fast, lad. I'd say in two days – faster if'n ye can manage it," Hagail rumbled.

Gregor looked to Solaria. "When can your people be ready?"

"We are ready to go when you are. We travel light, and we have already warded our weapons and armor against the growing cold," she replied confidently.

"Well, Doms," Gregor said as he turned his attention back to Hagail, "I'll have ta check on a few things, but we might be able to be on tha trail late afternoon tomorrow; at worst, no later than dawn tha next day."

"Good," Hagail replied as he leaned over the growing tablecloth of maps. "Now, let's be find'n a way ta crack this nut, shall we?"

# Chapter Twenty-Four

*F*or three days, the six thousand-strong detachment from the Army of Five Stars lumbered its way north by northeast, every league taking them further from the fighting and closer to home. For most, that long dreamt-about day was still weeks away. However, for the Roselian contingent, that day was approaching quickly. Many of the clans still adhered to a nomadic existence and, in all likelihood, knew Roselia's terrain better than House Trivant. Therefore, on the second day of travel and well before the Alderian Forest was more than a dark swath on the horizon, it was the clans that first noticed the subtle changes in the land and the air that indicated their arrival in Roselia's firmly established borders.

Sensing a growing excitement in the youth among them that they knew would be hard to contain, the Clan Elders sought and obtained permission to send some of the more rambunctious of their numbers out on scouting trips. Kale was more than happy to grant permission; not only would it bolster his scouts with people who had intimate knowledge of the land around them, but it would improve their chances of receiving an early warning against any would-be problems. Despite the growing evidence of a violent storm brewing to the east, twenty pairs of riders fanned out to the north before sunset on the second day, riding hard into the distance with enthusiastic zeal.

By dawn of the third day, the storm broke with a ferocity that shocked the native Roselians, forcing the army to grind to a halt and secure a hasty camp. They had already suffered a handful of injured men and horses that had been unlucky enough to step in a mud crow or pine-ferret burrow, and the last thing they needed was thick sheets of rain and mud further endangering everyone. As a result, the third day and most of the following night was spent simply trying to stay dry. At its peak, the storm grew violent enough to give the impression that a wind-devil was tearing through camp. Those soldiers who were unlucky enough to find themselves standing watch did their best to stay low to the ground, and a few of them decided watching from a tent or beneath a wagon was worth whatever punishment they might incur.

Amongst the hastily erected tents of the clans, there was one person, however, who did not fear the violent storm. Beliza, Clan Elder of the Clan of the Wolf, stood in the entrance of her tent with nothing but a thick hide blanket keeping the rain off the majority of her tanned, athletic body. Her feet were protected from the damp earth by extra hide blankets that she'd managed to put down before the worst of the storm hit, but that was of as little concern as the serpent-tattooed body of Dakan resting peacefully on her blankets. Her attention, as it had been all evening, was focused on the power within the storm that had awakened a lustful hunger within her. Her defined, handsome features were twisted in a seductive smile, and her gray eyes glowed with ecstasy even as rain soaked her gray-streaked, black hair and her exposed, wolf-tattooed skin. She could feel her master's power gently guiding the storm like a lover's caress. She had never felt this kind of display of her master's strength, but instead of frightening her, she found it both comforting and arousing. To know that she served such a power. . . . She closed her eyes and shuddered with delight as she traced a finger along her scalp where her master's mark burned beneath her hair.

The emotions that her master's storm had stirred within her, as his strength always did, were strong and raw, and had demanded an outlet less they consumed her. Seeking that relief, she had come close to venting her pent up emotions on Melane – who had proven on more than one occasion to be both a competent servant, and an adequate lover in a pinch – but it would have been more of a brutal rape than the passionate sex she craved. To Beliza's great relief and pleasure, she had been saved from that option by Dakan's arrival, who had come to check on her and the clans after attending to his duties with the Merandiths. She had, with Melane's help, already erected her tent long before Dakan's arrival; therefore, upon his appearance, she had dismissed Melane before pulling him into her tent and aggressively throwing herself on her lover. Their sweat- and rain-drenched bodies had writhed with passion even as the storm vented its rage, the power behind it fueling Beliza's lust.

Even now, with the cold rain soaking her head and exposed flesh, her passion was not sated. She let the tent flap fall shut as she turned around and focused her hungry eyes on Dakan's sleeping form. Letting her blanket slip from her tattooed body, she was about to approach his prone form when the mark on her scalp suddenly went cold and the touch of her master's power on the storm vanished. She paused thoughtfully, a mix of resentment and confusion playing through her mind. The sudden withdrawal of her master's power was enough to almost make her pout, yet at the same time, she was a bit concerned about what could cause such a sudden disappearance.

Without warning, a wave of dizziness washed over her, and she put a hand to her head as she tried to steady herself. She had

540

never been exposed to so much of her master's strength for such a long time, and while it was clear to her that the sudden withdrawal was responsible for her lightheadedness, she came to the conclusion that it was also the reason for the irrational fears parading through her mind. It did little, however, to fully quench the lingering hunger she felt flowing through her.

As soon as her head cleared, she crawled under the blankets behind Dakan and pressed her breasts against his body, drawing a sleepy chuckle from him.

"More, my lovely Wolf?" he asked in a sleepy but accommodating tone.

"Wolves do have voracious appetites," she purred even as she snaked an arm around him and let her hand travel down his torso. Rolling over in response, Dakan pulled her close and flashed a grin at her, his lover's hunger reflected in his dark eyes. She laughed and grinned. "As do serpents, apparently," she said in a throaty voice before kissing him deeply.


By dawn, the storm had dispersed into sporadic pockets of rain, and the Five Stars were able to assess their situation. To the chagrin of many, it was readily apparent that they would not be going anywhere for at least a day. Not only were tents and unsecured supplies strewn about as if an angry child had rampaged through the camp, but the entire army was mired in a mud pit that a pig would envy. Thankfully, there were no fatalities, but the medics and priests found themselves overrun by a host of injured – the majority of which were minor.

As the cleanup got underway amongst complaints about the smell, a host of soldiers cursing the thick mud as it sucked their boots off their feet, and others finding amusement in using stones or arrows to pickoff mud crows stirred up by the storm, stories began to circulated about a massive fire that had violently appeared in the distant Alderian Forest before vanishing just as quickly. When someone tried to suggest an unnatural origin to the flames, it was immediately dismissed by someone else pointing out that there was more than enough lightning during the storm to start the blaze; furthermore, the heavy rain was just as responsible for the sudden end to the fire. While that explanation easily put an end to most debates, it didn't stop the more imaginative and superstitious of the army from tossing about outlandish ideas about the fire's origin simply to pass the time as they trudged through the mud performing their unceremonious tasks.

With the setting of the sun, the first groups of scouts limped back into beleaguered camp. Soaked and coated in mud, it was a miracle that they returned with only minor injuries to both men and horses. They had little to report other than catching sight of fast moving riders on the horizon before the storm made it impossible to venture any further. Kale was more than happy with the news. The last thing he needed was to hear that possible hostile forces were bearing down on his mud-shackled army – then again, it was hardly reassuring that they had made visual contact with possible raiders. The large number of scouts he had sent out before the addition of the Roselians was already in response to the reports they had received before leaving the main body of the army, but now he was wondering if he would need even more eyes afield. The plains might provide a large field of view, but there were just enough elevation changes to provide cover for an ambush by a small force.

Then there was the Alderian Forest to worry about. Their original path would have brought them within half a league of the forest, but given the damage the storm had wrought, it would be necessary to move closer to the wooded expanse to acquire materials and food to make up for what they had lost. While he didn't believe the forest was a potential danger, Kale rarely threw caution to the wind when it came to the army. The rumored raiders had him somewhat on edge, and he knew that if there was a large enough force out there that could do harm to the small army, then the forest would be the perfect place to hide them. Then again, he believed small raiding parties would have to be daft to assault a force that vastly outnumbered them.

By dawn, Kale was still struggling with the idea of venturing closer to the Alderian Forest. Even as he – accompanied by Jerom, Dakan and five other prospective bodyguards – made his rounds through the beleaguered camp, the decision weighed heavily on his brow, and his appearance showed it. He was oblivious to both the mud sucking at his black boots, and the spattering of the dark, soggy muck that dotted his black breeches and gray tunic from passing horses. His blonde hair was kempt, but he had forgotten to shave that morning. Those that caught his gaze as he made his rounds, thought his green eyes seemed distant.

Jerom had been aware of his nephew's pensive mood since the morning, and could tell that it was beginning to affect those around him. Therefore, as they trudged through the mass of soldiers that were struggling to break camp, he moved up beside his nephew and asked softly enough to only be heard by their immediate group, "What's on your mind, lad? You're looking way too thoughtful."

"Hummm?" Kale replied quietly, blinking as his uncle's words pulled him from his thoughts. "Am I?" he asked in a melancholy tone.

Scratching at the skin around the eyepatch that concealed where his left eye used to be, Jerom offered him a small, cheerful smile. "Aye, you are. Been that way since the storms rolled through."

"Oh . . ." Kale replied. "It's all this," he weakly gestured to the surrounding area. "It's not exactly what I imagined when I decided on this little break from the fighting. Everyone appears to be more miserable than before."

Picking a piece of dried mud from his salt-and-pepper beard, Jerom asked knowingly, "Was expecting things to be more cheerful?"

"Very much so," Kale answered with a nod.

"Well then, lad," his uncle said as he leaned in closer to him, "you might want to consider putting on a more cheerful expression – because that glum look of yours sure isn't helping the situation."

"He's right," Dakan said respectfully from his position behind them. "The situation is disheartening, to be sure, but if you appear weak to the others, they will pick up on it."

Jerom glanced back at the dark-haired, serpent-tattooed clansman with a stern look and thankful nod. He had wanted to keep the conversation between himself and his nephew, but Dakan's backing was welcome. Ever since the imposing clansman had recovered enough from his lashings to rejoin the other candidates, he had been practically an ideal soldier. Granted, he was hardly making friends, but he had attended to his duties admirably and managed to avoid physical confrontation. That was gaining him the respect he would need should he succeed in gaining a spot amongst Kale's bodyguards. Jerom was happy to see the serious attempt at changing his attitude and approach to life. He could only hope it was a result of maturation, and not a cold, emotionless approach as a result of pent up resentment and anger.

"The lad is right," Jerom continued, turning his lone brown eye back to his nephew. "Besides, it's just mud. Can't have word getting back to Craigan that you were brought low by sloppy weather, now can we?" he chided with a warm smile.

Kale shook his head and cracked a slight grin of his own. "No, we certainly can't have that happening – but it's not the mud that's got me worried," he said as they turned onto the main thoroughfare through camp and made for the north end.

"You're worried about the raiders," his uncle stated knowingly.

Nodding, Kale replied, "Precisely. You don't have to be Roselian to realize that the Alderian Forest is the perfect place for a force of any size to hide."

"We would certainly have numbers against any sort of raiders. It would be foolish to attack us on open ground," Dakan piped in confidently.

"Aye, lad, that would be true in a stand-up fight, but no raider is daft enough to fight fair," Jerom added in a lecturing tone.

"Ambush tactics," Dakan replied quickly, easily picking up on the train of thought. "Use the forest to hide their numbers then strike quickly. No one assault would be enough to defeat us, but enough attacks over time . . ." he trailed off and gave a snort of approval. "Thinking like clansmen. . . . But, if the forest is such a concern, why go near it? Only some of the Roselians and clans returning home would need to pass through or near it."

Kale sighed. "That's where this mess comes in, Dakan. The clans might be adept at moving lightly and swiftly, but we're lumbering along with wounded and large amounts of equipment and supplies. There are wagons, tents, cots and lost supplies to replace or repair, and the best we can do here is a quick patch job. If the rest of us are to make it home with any speed, we'll need the Forest's resources to fix the more severe damage."

Before he could say more, they were forced to step aside as a sizable group of soldiers raced by, chattering away like a bunch of housewives gossiping about the latest scandal. There was no indication of tension or danger, only curious excitement in their collective voices.

"Now where are they going in such a rush?" Kale wondered aloud.

"No idea," Jerom grumbled in confusion as they started back down the path.

They barely managed to trudge out ten paces before a mixed group of tattooed clansmen and women rushed by in as much of a hurry as the soldiers before them. Feeling a mixture of confusion and vexation, Kale was about to flag down one of the soldiers hustling by, when he saw the muscular frame of his brother-by-marriage, Doms Lucas Trivant. The large Roselian doms was trotting up the lane, seemingly oblivious to the mud he was spattering upon his leather breeches, boots and blue wool shirt. With the laces of his shirt collar and cuffs loosely synched and his brown hair hanging unrestrained about his clean-shaven face, he looked like he had just gotten out of bed.

Eyes wide with befuddlement, Kale waved at Lucas as he approached and shouted, "What in Deo's name has everyone so excited?!"

Coming to a halt in front of Kale, a grin spreading across his square-jawed face and his blue eyes twinkling with mirth, Lucas would have towered over them all comically if not for Dakan's size. "A few of the clan scouts you sent out just returned," Lucas stated, his deep voice thundering with excitement.

Kale rolled his eyes. "And?" he prodded.

"They brought a surprise! Come on! You won't want to miss this!" Lucas stated coyly before patting Kale on the back and trotting off.

"Thick headed lummox," Jerom muttered as they hustled to catch up.

Kale smiled brightly for the first time that morning. "Uncle – if he ever hears you calling him that, I won't get in his way."

Jerom rolled his brown eye. "You're devotion to family is heartwarming, lad," he muttered sarcastically, drawing another laugh from Kale and an amused twitch of the lips from Dakan and a couple of the other guards.

Catching up to Lucas, they followed him as he guided them through the northern part of camp. Even before they reached their destination, there was evidence that they were close to their goal. Aside from the growing number of people, there was a mounting commotion over which they soon heard deep-throated, rumbling braying that sounded like boulders crashing into each other. Jerom and Kale exchanged curious and somewhat baffled looks upon hearing the unfamiliar noise.

"What in the hells– " Kale started to ask, when, out of the corner of his eye, he caught Dakan grinning broadly. "What are you grinning about?" he asked, surprised to see the normally stoic clansman showing such jovial emotion.

As Dakan stepped past Kale and Jerom to walk next to Lucas, he said, "A great boon from Deo, Doms Merandith."

"A great boon, eh?" Kale asked skeptically.

"Indeed," Dakan replied before asking, "Do you know how many, Doms Trivant?"

Lucas grinned and patted the clansman on the shoulder. "Four! Can you imagine the luck?!"

Dakan nodded before looking over his shoulder and reiterating, "A tremendous boon."

"Would someone tell me – for Deo's sake – what's got you grinning, and what the hells you two are talking about?" Jerom barked in annoyance.

"You'll see, old man," Lucas said playfully.

Jerom bristled at the verbal jab. "Old man?! Lad – I'm not too old to beat you senseless or tan your hide!"

Kale laughed and put a calming hand on his uncle's shoulder. "You'll do no such thing, Uncle. Besides, I think we're almost there," he admonished with a disarming smile as he pointed toward the edge of camp.

Turning his attention to where Kale was pointing, Jerom could see that there was a large throng of people filling the spaces between the tents. He could even hear loud snorting to go along with the occasional rugged braying. Lucas led the nine of them around the crowd to the right, and as they cleared the last of the tents blocking their view, they could make out the broad, thick-furred shoulders of four enormous animals towering over the crowd. Pushing their way to the front of the gathering, both Dakan and Lucas looked back at Kale and Jerom with looks of childish excitement on their faces even as the other five bodyguards struggled to form a perimeter around the domses while gawking at the giant beasts.

Kale met their expressions with one of disbelief as he got a clear look at the torgens. "Are you telling me they brought back four torgens?"

Lucas nodded. "Four males."

"Deo be good," Jerom breathed.

Kale hung his head, hands on hips, and shook it as he chuckled. "And just what are we to do with such beasts?"

"That, Doms Merandith," Dakan said gleefully – which sounded exceptionally odd coming from him – as they began to push through the crowd, "is simple – we eat well."

Being from the North, neither Kale nor Jerom had ever seen a torgen up close. They, like most every Triclosian, were familiar with its domestic cousin, the bramhen; however, the plains-dwelling torgen were known to be overly aggressive at times and even violent when cornered, making them a dangerous beast to approach in the wild or capture without training. Throughout the clans, torgens were revered for the sustenance they provided, and nearly as respected as drakumas as a sign of strength. Kale and Jerom had seen herds of the beasts at a distance over the years and were amazed by the Roselian clans that followed the torgen migrations, relying upon what appeared to be rampaging, giant beasts for everything from clothing to food. Seeing one up-close for the first time, the two Merandiths understood why the torgen garnered the respect they did.

Nearly ten feet tall at the shoulder, the giant beasts' heads were broad and somewhat flat, and their eyes were set wide apart to better see possible predators. Their wide, wet noses seemed to swallow up a large portion of their faces, which were already difficult to distinguish amongst their shaggy black manes. Like a horrible haircut, their manes, which originated at the top of their broad noses, practically consuming their faces before enveloping their muscular shoulders and broad chests like a thick, warm coat. Strong, short legs supported their massive bulk, and powerful haunches provided a base for a thick, stubby tail that looked like it could serve as an excellent bludgeoning weapon. The thick, warm fur of all four was a mix of brown and black colorations, and their iconic ivory-colored horns were streaked with ruddy tones that were reminiscent of the stripes on a cat. All four males proudly displayed their trio of horns – two of which jutted from the top of their heads to curl around hidden ears before thrusting forward just below a chin that was crowned by a single, short but wicked horn like a well-groomed goatee.

Given how large and strong the torgens were, Kale was surprised that the clansmen's chosen method of restraining the beasts was working. To restrain the head, sturdy ropes, which were anchored to the ground with robust wooden spikes, had been securely tied to each horn. The beasts were further restrained by another series of anchored ropes that were both tightly wrapped about the torgens just behind their shoulders, and around their rear ankles. As an additional layer of security, three clansmen manned each of the ropes in case they were needed to subdue the beasts.

"How in the world are you keeping them so docile with all the noise?" Kale asked of Dakan. "Most creatures would be wild with hysterics in this situation."

Dakan nodded in the affirmative. "It's the arrows that were used. The torgen are too large to simply kill and then carry back to the villages or camps. Even if you prepared them in the field, you'd need a series of horses or pack mules just to bring the materials back to camp, and that would hinder your ability to keep pace with the herd when hunting. So we learned, a long time ago, to coat the arrows with a mild poison that would dull their wits and make them more . . . controllable. They can then be harnessed and led back to camp to be slaughtered."

Kale found himself shaking his head in disbelief. "Deo be good – what a task."

Dakan shrugged. "When your survival and the survival of your clan depends on it, then it really is very little to ask of the hunters."

Kale couldn't argue with that logic, but still, as he gazed at the intimidating beasts, it was hard to imagine what it would be like to hunt such a creature. Before he could question Dakan any further, one of the handlers noticed their group and approached them. The man was elderly despite the strong, sinewy muscles beneath skin that resembled the fur-lined leather armor he wore. The tattoos visible on his long face and bare arms marked him as a member of the Clan of the Bear. A horrific scar ran from his right cheek across his torn lips, giving him a permanent, morbid grin. His head was shaven, but part of his scalp looked like it had been ripped away at some point in his youth. He also walked with a noticeable limp that made both Kale and Jerom wonder how he managed to sit a saddle. The man's firm gray eyes answered that question for them. This was a man who had been through hells and back, and refused to let the hardships of his life weigh him down.

The clansman – who seemed to be doing his best to ignore Dakan – stopped short of the domses and bowed stiffly. "Domses – I bring greetings and the best wishes of the Clan of the Bear."

Lucas nodded respectfully, as did Kale, and offered in greeting, "Well met. I hope the storms did not hamper your group?"

"Only mildly, Doms. But as you can see," he gestured to the torgen, "we return with gifts," he finished with a mostly toothless smile.

Jerom let out a snort. "Quite the gifts. How, in Deo's name, did you come by such creatures?"

"I'd like to know that myself," Kale added.

"A stroke of luck, Domses. We were holed-up in a hollow when we were approached by outriders from the Clan of the Torgen who had got caught in the storm while pursuing the herd. We offered them shelter and bread as well as news on the war. In return, they shared some exciting news, as well as capturing and sending these torgens as tribute for each doms and the Clan High Elder."

Stunned, and with no idea of how to respond to such a gift, both Jerom and Kale stared at the man.

Dakan and Lucas, on the other hand, appeared to realize just what had been bestowed upon them. They both bowed reverently – Dakan drawing a none-too-friendly glance from the elder clansman – before Lucas said, "Our thanks to the clans for such generosity. Spirits bless the Clan of the Torgen for their gift, and the Clan of the Bear for delivering the prized resources."

Kale quickly picked up on the formality and replied, "House Merandith thanks the clans for their generosity. Spirits bless the Clan of the Torgen and Bear for sharing such prized resources."

The elder clansman bowed. "You are most kind, Domses. It would honor the clans if you would allow us to prepare the beasts for consumption and use. Do we have your permission?"

Glancing sideways at Lucas, who nodded slightly, Kale said, "Granted. . . . Just do it downwind of camp. I would hate to have a wave of sickness wash through the ranks."

The clansman smiled knowingly. "Of course, Doms Merandith. Before I take my leave, there are a few other things to tell you. First, we encountered no one other than the Torgen outriders. Second, the Torgen clansmen told us tales of a great drakuma roaming the forest and plains over the last few weeks."

Lucas' brow furrowed. "That's not uncommon. There are plenty of forest drakuma around, as well as a few crag. What's so odd about this one?"

The elder clansman's eyes seemed to light up with excitement. "It's said that the beast is a sign! They say it's a giant ember!"

Lucas, and even Kale and Jerom, stared skeptically at the man. Dakan's reaction, however, was very much unlike him. It seemed like his jaw would hit the ground as he blurted, "They must be wrong! Embers are practically a myth! There hasn't been one seen north of the Dragonspine in over two-hundred years!"

"I know and would agree that they were seeing things, but they claim to have seen the scales and marks on the trees, as well as finding the remains of a forest drakuma that had been killed and feasted on by a beast significantly larger than it," the Bear clansman declared adamantly.

"If it's true," Lucas stated hesitantly, "then how will the clans view such a sign?"

The clansman shrugged. "I cannot say. The beast is sacred. It will be up to the Council as to how to interpret this."

Lucas nodded even as he noticed that the clan members around them seemed to have overheard the news. Suddenly eager to be away from prying ears, he said politely but quickly, "Thank you for the news. Please attend to your duties and give our thanks to the Clan High Elder."

"I will. Domses." The clansman bowed and moved off.

As the clansman returned to the other handlers and began giving instructions to move the beasts, Kale and Jerom moved in front of Lucas with a mix of concern and confusion written plainly on their faces.

"What's going on here, Lucas?" Kale asked quietly as the crowd around them began to disperse, already chattering about what they had overheard.

Lucas looked at Kale with just as much concern on his face. "This isn't the place to discuss it. Shall we adjourn to your tent? I'd rather not talk about this where Roselian ears might hear." He looked at the dispersing clansmen with concern. "Word is going to spread like wildfire as it is," he muttered.

"Very well," Kale replied suspiciously.

As Kale turned to lead the way back to the Merandith's portion of the camp, and the rest of the trainees fell in behind the domses, Jerom moved alongside him and muttered, "I take it back. Things may be as bad as you were thinking they were."

Kale looked at his uncle and replied regretfully, "Sometimes . . . I hate it when I'm right."


The inside of Kale's pavilion was sparsely setup to make it easier to move each day, making the interior seem vastly larger than it was. His cot sat to the left with his chest of clothes at its foot, and his washbasin sat atop its pedestal at the head of the cot. Instead of a large table, Kale was making use of a smaller desk and three simple chairs that were set in the center of the tent. The lone lamp he had sitting on the desk was unlit, cloaking the pavilion's occupants in shadows that were barely pierced by the dim light that filtered in through both the tent's dark fabric and the crack in the entry flaps.

Dour was the mood that weighed upon the four men after hearing Trivant's explanation of the ember sighting. Kale straddled one of the chairs, his arms folded across its top, severe concern marring his face. Jerom stood next to him, arms folded and his grim visage switching between his nephew and the two Roselians that stood opposite them. Dakan, his eyes downcast, seemed to be wrestling with the emotions and memories that had been stirred within him. Lucas, for his part, seem to understand the concern his words had inspired, but his expression indicated that the full weight of what he had imparted to them escaped him.

"Is what Lucas says true?" Kale asked quietly, his question to Dakan breaking the heavy silence.

Dakan's dark eyes rose from the ground to focus on the doms he now served, his conflicted mind screaming in frustration. "To the best of my understanding – it is, Doms. It is not guaranteed that the Council will see it that way, but . . ." he trailed off, shaking his head.

"It's likely that they will," Jerom finished for him.

Dakan simply nodded.

"Okay. . . I knew my news wouldn't be taken that well, but I'm getting the feeling there's more to this than simply a possible power struggle within the clans," Lucas said, both confused and frustrated by the cryptic chatter.

"There is," Kale said simply but firmly.

His brother-by-marriage stared searchingly at Kale, his mind working to figure out what would have Kale so concerned. Suddenly, a thought occurred to him and he cursed himself inwardly for not having put the pieces together sooner. "Damn, Kale – that's why I haven't seen Amroth around. He really was attacked earlier, wasn't he?"

Kale nodded, his lips pressed firmly together.

"Was it Sur'dathans?"

Kale nodded again.

"Bloody hells! I had hunches and hints that Amroth might be someone important when your father took him under his protection, but Theirigaldis?" Lucas shook his head in amazement.

"There's more to it," Kale said coldly, eyeing both Lucas and Dakan carefully. "Seeing as you both know that much, you might as well know it all."

Lucas laughed sarcastically, "Please, I'd be happy to know how deep of a hole we're likely digging."

"He's Cravon's son," Kale stated flatly.

Stunned looks greeted the remark from both Lucas and Dakan; Lucas looked like he was torn between laughing hysterically and wanting to scream in frustration, while Dakan had the look of a man who had been stabbed in the gut.

"I–" Lucas paused, a thought suddenly striking him. "Wow," he added in bewilderment. "That makes him not only a marked man, but of your blood – doesn't it, Dakan?" he asked as he eyed the serpent tattoos on the clansman's arms.

"It does," Dakan replied quietly. "But it makes things much, much worse." He looked up at Kale, his eyes full of pain that he seemed to be struggling to control. "I wish I had not known this, Doms," he continued remorsefully, "You've put a weight upon my shoulders that I'm not sure I can bear."

"I'm sorry, Dakan," Kale replied, "but I'm not sure I understand."

Lucas suddenly cursed as it dawned on him what Dakan was hesitant to say. "Spirits old and new," he whispered the old clan curse. "I'm sorry, Kale," he said remorsefully to him, "but Amroth could be in more trouble than we can imagine."

Both Kale and Jerom shared alarmed and confused stares with each other.

"Will one of you lads spit it out? " Jerom grumbled in irritation. "Can't fight what we don't know."

Lucas looked like he was going to speak up, but it was Dakan who responded first. "Doms – should the clans confirm the appearance of an ember drakuma, there will be serious debate as to its meaning, and possibly a division of clans along the lines of their beliefs, but the odds are good that they will interpret it as a sign that Clan Drakuma should put one of their own in the seat of High Elder."

Kale's face screwed up in confusion and he looked at both Dakan and Lucas, his eyes pleading for clarification. "Clan Drakuma? I've never heard of them."

"I'm not surprised," Lucas said with a dejected sigh. "I've been thinking it through since we heard the news, and it just dawned on me while we were talking." He took a deep breath and let it out. "Clan Drakuma was the patron clan from which all others sprung. However, it was supposedly destroyed for some sort of drastic breach of Clan law."

"And?" Kale pressed.

"And, the rules were a little different back then. The two eldest sons of the Clan Elder and their followers were allowed to either join other clans or form their own." Lucas glanced at Dakan out of the corner of his eye, locking eyes with him. "The two clans born that day were what we know as the Clan of the Fang and Clan Theiri-galdis."

Kale and Jerom both looked like the wind had been knocked out of them as Dakan spoke, picking up where Lucas had left off. "You know that both our clans effectively don't exist, but . . ." he hesitated as he shifted his gaze from Lucas to Kale, "if the clans determine that Clan Drakuma is to rise and lead again, they will need to find one of the blood to lead."

"Which would be you," Lucas stated softly.

"Aye, they would not look to the Sur'dathan clans for a High Elder," Dakan confirmed with a stiff nod. "That's not the worst of it, I'm afraid. In order for any shunned clan to be welcomed back into the fold, a test of loyalty is given. It is never easy, and quite often drastic. Should they find out about Amroth's bloodline, I'm afraid that they would ask for his head."

The words brought with them a deafening silence that seemed capable of crushing a man. Kale could hardly breathe, and Jerom looked upon his nephew, unable to find the words to console him.

"Would you?" Kale struggled to ask, his eyes cast upon the ground.

"No, I wouldn't," Dakan replied quickly, but there was a quiver in his deep voice that suggested otherwise.

"What—" Jerom started to ask before having to clear his throat of the knot of anger clenching at it, "What would happen if you refused such a request?"

"They don't know and they don't have to know," Lucas interjected, drawing Jerom's stern gaze. "Ignorance is complete bliss in this case. Amroth remains safe, Dakan doesn't have to deal with a horrific choice, and we're all the merrier for it."

"Aye, there's no doubt that we're planning on keeping the clans in the dark about this – that includes you keeping your trap shut," Jerom growled at Dakan. "However, none of us are stupid enough to just pray things go right. Should they find out, we need to know what would happen if Dakan refused them." His brown eye bored into Dakan as if Deo himself were scouring his soul for the truth. "You will refuse them, lad," Jerom stated in a tone that brokered no debate.

Dakan nodded, his heart heavy with the knowledge that Beliza already knew of Amroth's bloodline. "Amroth is blood," he stated firmly. "I will not betray him."

"What will happen, then?" Kale asked dully, suddenly feeling emotionally exhausted.

"The same thing that would happen should they offer and I refuse the position. . . . Conflict," Dakan said with confidence.

"And that means?" Jerom pressed in irritation.

"It means, Jerom," Lucas interjected, "that the current High Elder will step down and a Moot will be called to decide who should lead." Lucas scoffed. "As it is, most of the Elders don't exactly get along. The High Elder is what holds the clans together and keeps them fighting for you."

"Would they listen to you?" Kale asked.

"Me? Only somewhat. Let's be honest, the clans have remained relatively autonomous since House Trivant was placed in power. My words only have weight and meaning when the Elders want them to." He shook his head. "If a Moot is called, then we can expect there to be a struggle for power."

"We could lose the clans," Kale stated knowingly.

"Worse, I'm afraid," Lucas replied darkly, drawing Kale's eyes to his.

"How much worse?" Kale asked, feeling like he already knew the answer.

Lucas' eyes softened as if they were trying to apologize for revealing this unknown burden to his brother-by-marriage. "Sorry, Kale – but if there's a power struggle, we could end up with a bloody civil war within our own ranks."

# Chapter Twenty-Five

*T*he moon's bluish-silver light bathed the area with its cool, soothing illumination as a gentle, early winter snowfall lazily made its way to the ground. Weak, cold breezes occasionally stirred the air, scattering the myriad of delicate flakes as if they were nothing more than confetti raining down on a parade. The solitary river and lake, which once ran with crystal-clear blue water, now sat still in its frozen state. All was peaceful and silent now, as it should be.

From atop the battlements of the imposing castle, he could see for leagues; open, rolling terrain flowed in every direction from the lake, providing the castle an unobstructed view from its perch at the island. During the day, the White Fang Mountains could be seen to the distant north, and the Forest of Steel to the south. Now, however, all that his brown eyes could see was the snow.

To him, the cold white flakes that seemed to rain from the twinkling stars above represented the purity of life – silent amidst a sea of darkness. Fragile as Solacian crystal, the flakes, and the light that reflected off their surfaces, could only hold back the night for so long before they fell silently to the ground. Catching a flake in his strong, dark-skinned hand, he watched as the fragile creation of the heavens melted into nothingness – vanishing into oblivion as his childhood had; destroyed as his home had been; taken over by darkness as Castle Blackstone had been. It was all the same, just on different levels. How he hated the fact that all the joyous tales of his early youth had proven false! There were days he despised the fact that he eventually had learned the undeniable and unchangeable, heart-wrenching facts about life – death and destruction reigned with vulgar intensity, while life and creation seemed to want nothing more than to crawl by without notice, their whimpering voices drowned out by their raging opposite.

In a way, though, he was better for it. But still. . . .

Turning his mind toward the south side of the island, he could sense that his longtime friend and guardian, Deralina, was fast asleep within the Ansei Grove located there, her mind enshrouded in pleasant dreams that he could only imagine. Leaving the direwolf to her respite, he directed his attention to the keep, and sorted through the myriad of Gifted to find the presence of the darlion, Aseria Mitsurea. He could tell that her focus was centered solely on all the information that had been force-fed to her over the last few days. Young for a darlion, but ancient from a human perspective, the girl was handling the plethora of life-changing knowledge in a fashion either species would respect.

Shifting his awareness to the west, he could just discern the presence of Darkon and another Gifted. The cold, fearsome darlion had been none-too-pleased with Greatjon's report and refusal to send Aseria onward to her Order, and he could only imagine what Darkon's mood would be like when they arrived.

Not wishing to dwell on their arrival, he directed his focus north, and the sensation he received on the flowing currents of fir'gan was all too strong – like a blaze of coldfire exploding in his brain. Warrick was flaunting his strength in the wake of his latest victory, his presence standing out like a cancer on the land, polluting everything around him and making him all too easy to detect. With an animal-like snarl, he slammed that part of his consciousness shut and turned his brown eyes back to the snow.

How pure and fragile it was. Like Solacian crystal – beautiful while intact, yet easily broken. How like the truth this snowy night was. . . . How utterly and frighteningly like the truth it was. . . .


Sentinel Keep, home to the Order of Stelariuos, stood solemnly at its isolated position upon the island at the center of the lake, its proud walls manned by even prouder people. For ages, the fortress had acted as the protector of the four major ancient roads that crossed the breathed of Solarson to meet at the keep's location. The Road of Iron led north, the Spice Road barreled south toward the Forest of Steel while the Kirithdal Highway led to the darlion lands in the east, and the Trader's Road led west – a bridge from the island extending in each direction. Protected by inner and outer ramparts that were fitted with towers at hundred yard intervals, the keep proper sat at the heart of the island fortress. At one time, the fortress had served as the heart of trade and commerce on Solarson, but time had taken its toll on the people, their memories, and the land, leaving the mighty roads in disrepair and their names all but forgotten outside the walls of the keep.

Designed for war, not luxury, Sentinel Keep was a reflection of harder times that resided only in the most ancient of history books. Its architecture was a fearsomely beautiful joining of ancient Velusyian and Solarian design that extended to the vast majority of its amenities. Separated by baileys that were home to a pair of barracks each and the keep's facilities, the eighty foot tall and ten foot thick stone inner and outer walls were sheathed in a rock-hard gray plaster,
556

and their battlements were girded against projectiles by angled, black-shingled roofing. Arrow slits were cunningly fitted in the ramparts to allow archers to spit death on both sides of the barrier from the protection of the corridors hidden within. Five foot thick ironwood double doors, banded vertically and horizontally with steel, protected both sides of the eight gatehouses – one gatehouse for each wall – when closed. As a double layer of protection, each gatehouse portal was fitted with forged-steel portcullises that, in conjunction with the doors, could be closed in order to trap assailants beneath the murder-holes in each gatehouse.

Nearly as devoid of blatant signs of luxury as the walls – the exception being the small, stained-glass windows that provided a bit of colorful decoration for the keep's residential rooms – the keep was a large, six-story building that faced west, with wings to the north and south that terminated at round, residential towers. Made of solid stone and sheathed in the same plaster as the ramparts, the lower reaches of the keep's walls were dotted with arrow slits and narrow, glass-protected windows. The roof of the keep slopped to a crest at its peak, and was made of the same dark-colored shingles as the battlements' roofing. Two sets of steel-banded double-doors provided primary egress to the keep at the front and rear of the main building, while smaller, mostly hidden servant entrances provided more subtle means of entrance and exit.

Like many keeps, the main building housed an audience chamber, dining hall, the usual servants' quarters and guestrooms, and a sturdy prison. Unlike most keeps, however, the interior halls were free of opulent décor; instead, the occasional subtle display of art and weapons adorned the stone walls. There were no rugs on the wooden floors of the halls, that luxury was saved for the bedrooms to comfort residents and guests alike. Such modest – and some would say excessively drab – ornamentation was prevalent throughout the keep, which not only lent itself well to the structure's militaristic and functional aura, but it made the robust library nestled below the keep seem a bit out of place. The library, however, was less of a divergence from the keep's intent than the plaza that was seated at the dour structure's heart.

Constructed to provide a place to rest and mediate in peace, the plaza brought a touch of vibrant color and beauty to the keep. Centered around a modest reflecting pool and a sizable Velusyian turoigi gaia, the grass-carpeted square was quite spacious and meticulously maintained. Year-round color was provided to the keep's centerpiece by an assortment of artfully-arranged flora that was replaced as needed in order to preserve the splash of vibrancy amongst the keep's darker overtone. Access to this unique feature of the keep was granted by wooden sliding doors – the windows of which were made of a paper-like material – that were housed beneath an elevated, covered walkway that framed the bastion of natural beauty.

Such was the aesthetic and spiritual importance of the plaza – and to a lesser extent, the library – that many would consider the keep oppressively dour without it. However, for the occupants of Sentinel Keep, it was home.

Dressed in red-trimmed black tabards underneath leather battle-harnesses, and armed predominantly with slender longswords, the men and women of Sentinel Keep could not imagine a better place to live. They were a friendly sort – which was out of line with the stereotypical perception of military behavior – and interacted with the village's residents and the keep's staff as if social status was irrelevant. In return, instead of receiving scowls when patrols made their way patiently through the streets, they received welcoming waves and even offers of free food and drink.

Indeed, like the lone, four-pointed star that adorned the black banners flying from the tops of the keep's towers, Sentinel Keep and its people were a beacon of light in the growing darkness.

Greatjon could think of no better place to be.

Upon their arrival nearly a week ago, the survivors of Castle Blackstone were greeted with open arms. Greatjon had felt the currents of fir'gan shiver with rage as word spread of Darius' death and the numerous Gifted amongst Sentinel Keep's ranks did their best to fight down the anger that the news had planted in their guts. Like their Preceptor and Warden, they pushed aside their emotions and focused their attention on the displaced residents. Under the guidance of the keep's Knight, the injured and severely wounded were rushed to healers before the other survivors were then wrapped in warm blankets and led to the dining hall. There, they were fed by the keep staff and kept warm by the hall's roaring fires until proper accommodations were arranged.

As for Greatjon, he was more than happy to allow Sentinel Keep's Knight to take control of the situation. Not only did Greatjon have Aseria to worry about, but he also had a report to make to Darkon – and he knew the Warden wouldn't take the news well.

Greatjon and Aseria had been provided adjoining rooms in the north tower at Greatjon's request, though neither of them had spent much time there after their arrival. Greatjon spent only one complete night in his room, and on that particular night, he used the seclusion to make his report. However, for some reason, he had reached out to Kara instead of Darkon. Maybe it was the trauma of the situation or simply Darius' words of warning, but Darkon was the last person he wanted to speak with. Kara had been devastated by the news, and had even gone so far as to agree with Darius' cautious warnings. The short, emotional conversation had left Greatjon feeling empty and lonely. He had no desire after that night to seek out Darkon, so it was hardly a surprise when – two days later – he had felt Darkon angrily probing for him. Knowing it wouldn't do any good to try to hide from him, Greatjon had opened himself up to the communication.

Expecting to be berated for Darius' death, Greatjon was both angered and confused when Darkon had greeted the news in an off-handed manner, as his focus was more on Aseria and the crystals. Greatjon had to choke off his anger at the slight as he finished his report. When he tried to ask Darkon's permission to train Aseria as Darius had requested, he was immediately denied, which had set Greatjon's anger to boiling. He couldn't bring himself to believe Darkon would deny the last request of a Warden, and when he had pressed the issue, he was further shocked that Darkon had chided him for such a 'foolish request'.

Greatjon felt even further slighted when Darkon had informed him that he and a contingent from the Indigain Order were coming to retrieve Aseria. As expected, Darkon had then proceeded to inquire about their location, and in that moment, Greatjon was able to claim a modicum of pleasure from the disturbing conversation. Once again realizing it would do little good to hide the facts from Darkon, Greatjon was almost giddy when he had informed Darkon of their whereabouts. The Warden's anger was practically palpable upon hearing that not only had Greatjon broken the moratorium on Portculim travel, but that they had taken up residence at Sentinel Keep. The red-hot rage that had permeated the connection had made Greatjon grin, as had the abrupt termination of the link.

Still, the manner in which Darkon had handled the report bothered Greatjon greatly, as did the idea of turning Aseria over against both Darius and Kara's wishes.

Seeking to keep his mind off both what had happened in the North and Darkon's impending arrival, he had initially thrown himself into preparing Aseria for what was to come. Sentinel Keep was the oldest of the Wardens' strongholds on Solarson, and contained a vast amount of knowledge that spanned centuries. The vast, mazelike library was built underground, and its ancient treasures were protected against the rigors of time by a fir'gan-regulated environment. Greatjon did his best to find books and scrolls that Aseria could read, but – as Aseria was kind enough to inform him – aside from a smattering of

Velusyian and a few of the tribal tongues, she only understood Tykani and the Trader's Tongue fluently. Unfortunately, this severely limited the selection, as the more informative volumes were written in languages that hadn't been spoken or written in ages. Well aware of his own scholastic shortcomings, he knew he would be of little use in her academic pursuits; therefore, he left Aseria in the capable hands of the librarian.

Suddenly in possession of an overabundance of free time, Greatjon took to visiting with the survivors and catching up with his friends amongst Sentinel Keep's ranks. For reasons unknown to Greatjon, Baris gradually joined him during his rounds. Be it from shock or simply because he had nothing to say, the young, scarred soldier had grown predominantly silent since his commanding officer had passed away. Greatjon could not think of anything to say or do that could help, so he didn't try. If the silent company helped the man cope, then so be it. Deralina had been spending most of her time in the Ansei Grove on the south side of the island, so Greatjon found the company somewhat soothing as well.

Day after day, the two of them spent a substantial amount of time with Blackstone's survivors, though they spent more of it listening rather than talking. As a result, Greatjon did his best to provide an ear for their torments. He knew he was trying to be Darius for them by providing a strong set of shoulders to bear the burdens that they could not handle; and until he could find a way to reclaim Blackstone, or until their new Preceptor and Warden could be found, it was the least he could do for the people he felt he had failed to protect.

For the rest of Sentinel Keep, the days passed in anxious anticipation. There was no love for Darkon amongst Sentinel Keep's troops; and even the keep's Knight and Greatjon's longtime friend, Quinndarius Silverhand, had expressed his distaste at having to play host to the darlion. After combining their collective dislike of the darlion with Kara and Darius' words of caution and Darkon's single-minded actions over the years, Greatjon found that he could not disagree with the mounting evidence that he had been either unwilling or unable to see.

Darkon, in recent years, had become driven and obsessed with a pursuit that he claimed would end the conflict with the Darkness once and for all, but had refused to share his knowledge with the others. In his quest to attain his goal, he had not only alienated Darius and barely retained the loyalty of Kara, but had practically brought the Bestyne Order to the edge of oblivion. In spite of his perceived missteps, the Indigain, Torthos, Osterias, Uthariyan and Velsan Orders still fell in line and gave every indication that Darkon's voice was the only voice to listen to. However, there was an important caveat to consider – the Osterias, Uthariyan and Indigain Orders lacked Preceptors, making their loyalty, in reality, an unknown factor. Even Greatjon, at one point, would have grudgingly agreed with Darkon; after all, when dealing with an ever-patient and powerful enemy, sometimes an iron fist and will were what was needed. Now though, with the fruits of Darkon's single-mindedness around him, he wasn't sure anymore. Where once he had seen strength, now he saw cracks in their ranks. By Warden's standards, he was nothing but a child, but something told him that cracks in a wall weakened it no matter what Age it existed.

By early morning of their eighth day in Sentinel Keep, there was a gentle snowfall drifting to the white-blanketed ground that belied the tension that permeated the air. Only aware that there would be important visitors this day, the village was already bustling with activity as the children played in the snow and the adults went about their daily routines. The troops of Sentinel Keep, however, began their day with nervous apprehension, well aware of the potential for the day to go very wrong. Today was the day that Darkon and the Indigain representative were due to arrive, and Greatjon was not only growing anxious about the confrontation that he and Sentinel Keep's forces knew was brewing, but he was quickly finding himself in no mood to see Aseria depart.

His small but cozy room was circular and filled with furniture that seemed a bit luxurious for the keep. Centered around a unique hearth built in the center of the room – which was more of a large brazier underneath a chimney that did a marvelous job of pulling the smoke from the room – Greatjon's accommodations were furnished with a plush bed, a modest table with a pair of chairs, and a wardrobe cabinet. Completing the room's décor were a porcelain tub and washbasin, both of which were connected to a copper tube drainage system that he had only ever seen in Sentinel Keep. Yet, for all the perks the room provided, he had spent very little time in it. That morning, however, he found himself seated, clad only in breeches, with his legs crossed before the roaring fire and his back to the door, his thoughts turned inward in meditation. His rust-orange hair, which hung loosely about his chiseled features, had grown out some, and his dark brown eyes stared blankly into the fire. Despite the heat, not a single drop of sweat adorned his muscled physic.

Deralina had returned to the keep before dawn and now rested on the plush bed – which her imposing black- and gray-furred direwolf body occupied the majority of – with her yellow eyes fixed on her master. Normally, she was privy to the majority of Greatjon's thoughts through their link, but when he was in deep meditation as he

561

was now, she could only guess what he was thinking – and that worried her. She had sensed the growing conflict within Greatjon ever since his communication with Darkon, and was having a hard time resisting the urge to offer advice. While she certainly had her own opinions on their current situation, she knew that only Greatjon could resolve his inner conflict; however, no matter his decision, she knew she would follow him to the depths of the hells if that was what it took to remain by his side.

Sighing, her gaze shifted to the untouched breakfast that sat on the table to Greatjon's right. The eggs, greasy bacon, cheese and wine smelled absolutely divine, and while she was just as irritated as Quinn was with how little Greatjon had eaten of late, she was more than happy to polish off another untouched meal if she couldn't convince the lummox to eat. After all, she'd found well-cooked spotted pigling to be much more appetizing than it was raw – although a bit of fresh blood wouldn't hurt.

A knock at the door drew only a twitch of her ears, as she recognized the scent of the person on the other side of the door. When a second, stronger knock failed to elicit a reaction from either of the room's occupants, the door creaked open and a man of moderate height and build entered, shutting the door behind him. The direwolf spared the man only a cursory glance to confirm what her sense of smell had already told her before refocusing on Greatjon. The new arrival wore the same red-trimmed black tabard, matching black tunic, breeches, and leather gloves as the rest of the troops. His gray steel pauldrons, which hung securely from his battle-harness, were trimmed in gold and sported a lone, raised gold star on the crest of each shoulder. As for the rest of his armor – chest plates, greaves, spinal guard and gauntlets – every piece was made of unadorned gray steel. In contrast to the muted colors of his raiments, blonde hair hung loosely about a slim, delicate-featured face that was adorned with a narrow, flat nose.

Knee-high black boots, made of supple leather, cushioned his footfalls as he circled around the open hearth. Placing a neatly wrapped brown package on the table, he then positioned himself on the opposite side of the hearth from Greatjon. Crouching down – which allowed the tip of the longsword resting between his shoulder blades to graze the floor – he met Greatjon's unfocused gaze with his own up-tilted sapphire-blue eyes. Both Deralina and the soldier were well aware that Greatjon knew of the man's presence despite his apparent detachment from his surroundings. To Deralina's amusement, it seemed like the two men were engaged in a staring contest.

562

This went on for a moment before, finally, Greatjon cracked a smile that seemed bizarre until he blinked, his eyes losing their glazed appearance as they refocused. "I figured you'd have shown up earlier."

The man shook his head and replied in a voice that seemed too soft for his martial appearance, "Would have, but I've had a difficult time arranging a proper reception for our guests." His face soured a bit. "There's not many here who trust Darkon, much less respect him."

Greatjon stretched his neck and rolled his powerful shoulders to clear the stiffness that had set in during his meditation. "I know, Quinn. Darius certainly didn't intend for this to happen, and I'm finding myself regretting that I even reported in."

Quinn waved a dismissive hand. "The situation would have been worse had you and Aseria simply vanished. If he's angry enough to come here himself, then I'd hate to imagine how he would have reacted to a vanishing act.'

Greatjon frowned. "I know, but still. . . ."

Quinn gave him a friendly, disarming smile and stood up. "Don't worry. I trust Darius' judgment as much as I trust Damion's. If he doesn't want Darkon to have her – then he won't have her."

Greatjon stood up slowly, shaking his head. "You're risking a lot with no Warden about. Crossing Darkon will only– "

Quinn laughed with genuine mirth. "Will only what? Anger him? Goad him into trying to disband us or wipe us out as he did with your Order?" Greatjon frowned deeply at the mention of the ugly incident – and Deralina even let out a low, displeased growl – but Quinn paid little attention to their reactions as he continued, "Darkon's displeasure – no, hate is more appropriate – hate of Damion has run deep and strong since Luthur's death. He blames him, and therefore us, for allowing it to happen." He shook his head. "As much as he is overly emotional, neither is he stupid. Even if he were to rally what's left of his own Order and the Indigain forces, he'd have a hard time defeating us. By himself?" Quinn laughed and shook his head. "He wouldn't stand a chance."

Greatjon nodded, knowing all too well the power that resided in Sentinel Keep. The number of Gifted living within its walls was staggering. Counting himself and Quinn, there were at least a dozen Gifted strong enough to stand toe-to-toe with a Warden out of the numerous Gifted that lived at Sentinel Keep. Granted, individually they'd eventually lose any sort of confrontation, but the combined power they presented would give even the most powerful Warden pause. But still, killing a Warden without another Warden would be difficult at best, and the losses would be staggering.

Greatjon finally noticed the package on the table next to the untouched meal. "What's this? I know I didn't request anything from the quartermaster."

Quinn walked over to the table and, grabbing the soft package, tossed it to Greatjon. Catching it, he raised a questioning eyebrow as Quinn answered, "It's your formal uniform."

"My– Does Damion keep a closet full of uniforms for each Order?" Greatjon asked with amused surprise.

Quinn grinned. "Something like that. You do still remember how to wear one – don't you?"

"Lina – would you get this smartass out of here?" asked Greatjon sarcastically.

Deralina perked up at the request and let out a bark as she set a playful glare on Quinn.

Holding his hands up defensively, Quinn said, "Alright, alright. I'm out of here. Meet me in the dining hall, and I'll see if we can scrounge up something that hasn't already gone cold." Without waiting for a replied, he exited the room.

Shaking his head in amusement, Greatjon grabbed the plate of cold food and placed it on the ground. Deralina hopped off the bed when she saw the gesture and padded over to the free meal. *To shoulder the burden he has since Damion left. . . . He really is amazing,"* she said to Greatjon via their fir'gan-forged link.

*"Yeah, Lina, I know,"* Greatjon replied before ripping open the package and dressing.

As he dressed, the clothing seemed gaudy to his practical sensibilities, and made him feel more uncomfortable than he ever had in battle. Slit up to his hips, the black tabard felt stifling as he secured it with a heavy belt over a loose, high-collared red tunic that was tucked into red breeches. While securing the belt and tabard, he noted the howling direwolf head etched into the gold belt buckle and stitched into the right breast of his tabard, the excessive ornamentation – at least by his standards – eliciting a deep cringe from him. After pulling on the knee-high black leather boots that went with the uniform – which seemed oddly stiff as he stomped his feet to settle them in – he pulled his hair back into a horsetail; to serve as a reminder that the uniform was not who he was, he allowed his bangs to frame his face like he always did. He chuckled at the gesture, knowing full well that the unease he was experiencing had more to do with how naked he felt without his sword. He was rarely without his claymore, but the protocol for the day forbade weapons, and with the tension that was already in the air, he wasn't about to add to it if he could avoid it.

Leaving Deralina to finish her meal, he tucked a pair of black gloves behind his belt as he exited the room, leaving the door open. Unsurprisingly, Greatjon found Baris waiting for him outside his room. Making their way through the corridors, Greatjon couldn't help but think that the young soldier was an apt, visible reminder of the cost paid by Blackstone's residents. The quartermaster had provided him with a full black uniform that was devoid of any frivolous adornments, which was fitting given what had befallen him. Baris kept the lacing of his shirt loose at the collar, and was using thick leather bracers to secure the shirt's cuffs. Like a dark, wrathful specter, the young man's amber eyes appeared haunted from astride his crooked nose. His broodingly violent – and some might say demonic – appearance was further enforced by the harsh, jagged scar that ran from where his right ear used to be, to the bridge of his nose, the macabre badge and surrounding skin an angry red.

For reasons unknown to Greatjon, the young man had shaved his head and taken to wearing a black bandana. Most likely he was trying to draw attention away from the angry scar, but there was little he could do short of wearing a mask to divert attention away from the ghastly mark. And while Baris' struggle to cope with his horrific physical misfortunes was certainly troubling, Greatjon was more concerned with his mental state. Baris had developed a troubling habit of constantly fingering the hilts of the wide-bladed shortsword and long knife he'd been issued, which, combined with the haunted look in his eyes, had led Greatjon to worry over what kinds of dark thoughts occupied the young man's mind. Greatjon had hoped that Baris' spirits might be bolstered by regaining vision in his right eye, but that hope had been crushed when Baris simply shrugged the good fortune off as if it didn't matter. To his chagrin, Greatjon understood that the best he could do would be to keep a watchful eye on Baris and hope time would heal his wounds before he did anything foolish.

After a short jaunt, they finally arrived at the dining hall. Nearly eighty yards in length and half that in width, the hall's soaring, arched ceiling was supported by fluted columns along the room's perimeter. The colonnade also served as anchor points for the ropes used to lower and raise the two rows of six massive, elegant chandeliers that hung above the three rows of longtables that spanned the length of the hall. Two large hearths – which were big enough for a man to stand upright or lay down in with room to spare – were set in each sidewall and were filled with sizable logs from the Forest of Steel to the south. When lit, the fires would provide ample warmth against the cold breath of winter.

Upon entering, Greatjon immediately noticed a lack of a High Table, which brought a small, sad smile to his face. Darius had also held the belief that leaders should never put themselves above others, and he had never once owned or sat at a High Table. Greatjon sighed inwardly as he recalled that even the Warden he served – long missing, and presumed dead by some at the hands of Darkon – had adhered to a similar belief. It suddenly occurred to him that such beliefs and the fortitude to abide by them belong to people that were part of a dying breed.

*"Have we really fallen so far instead of growing since their time?"* he thought dejectedly to himself.

His reflections were cut short by Quinn as he walked out of the kitchen doors at the rear of the Hall with two servants, each and every one of them ladened with platters of food and dishes. Taking their seats at the far end of the center row of tables – which felt odd, given that they had the open hall all to themselves – Greatjon and Baris took in the mouthwatering food that was placed before them. Upon seeing what was being served, Greatjon realized that they'd been shortchanging him with the meals that had been brought to his room. Tantalizingly arranged before them were boiled, spotted rahken eggs; exotic, baked, rainbow-colored flamestrider eggs that were larger than Greatjon's fist; and a platter of scrambled eggs that had green peppers, chunks of sausage, and a smattering of what appeared to be celery mixed into the fluffy yellow bed. There were even fluffy biscuits, sourdough bread drizzled with honey and sugar, and a few slices of pigling ham and bramhen that were glazed with honey. To wash it all down, Quinn had procured both a small bottle of red wine and a pitcher of tigram milk.

As the two servants retreated quietly to the kitchen, Greatjon grinned slyly, grabbed one of the plates and began filling it with the enticing food. "You've been holding out on me, Quinn. If you'd sent such delicacies my way, I might have eaten more of my meals."

"I know. Corith only knows the cook didn't want you eating us out of house and home, and she certainly didn't want to waste our good stuff on that mutt of yours," Quinn replied jovially.

"That's not nice," Greatjon said around a mouthful of the scrambled eggs as he grabbed a couple of the slices of sourdough bread and one of the flamestrider eggs. Picking up his fork, he gently tapped on the eggshell until he could pry off the top, releasing the aromatic and slightly sweet smell of the baked, gelatinous egg white inside. Dipping a bread slice in the baked egg, he tore off a bite with a pleased smile. "Expertly prepared as well. Lina would love to get her maw on this."

Quinn laughed. "I know." Glancing at Baris, he grimaced slightly upon seeing that the young man had put very little food on his plate and seemed in no hurry to eat. "Come on, lad," he urged gently, "you need to eat. Won't be doing anybody any good if you waste away."

Baris looked up at Quinn and shrugged his shoulders non-chalantly. "How is Aseria doing? I've seen very little of her since she barred me from assisting her."

Greatjon put a comforting hand on Baris' shoulder. "She did that for your own good," he gently reminded him. "You weren't sleeping, and are barely eating. I'm sure she'd be glad to have you around instead of the aging librarian if you'd show a little initiative in taking care of yourself."

Baris sighed. "I know, but . . ." he took a deep breath and shook his head. "Do you really think she'd accept my help again? What she's studying is fascinating, and it . . . helps to keep my mind off other things," he said softly, his eyes reflecting the hurt he felt on the inside.

"We've been trying to tell you that for days, lad," Quinn said with a friendly grin. "And if you're so interested in studying up on ancient history – literally, I might add – you're more than welcome to remain here. We could always use another talented sword arm."

Emboldened by the thought that he could return to Aseria's side if she thought his health wasn't in danger, Baris was already placing a few slices of ham, two of the spotted eggs and a biscuit on his plate. It wasn't a lot, but it was more than he had been eating. "I appreciate the offer, Quinn," he said as he scooped up some eggs and slowly began to chew on it, "but Aseria is my friend and Greatjon saved my life – I owe them too much to simply abandon them."

"You wouldn't be abandoning us," Greatjon said as he poured himself a cup of the milk. Taking a swallow, he lowered the cup and added, "You have your own life to live. And with what she and I have ahead of us, there's no telling where we may have to go, or if you'd survive it."

Baris gave Greatjon a stern stare and stated firmly, "I should be dead as it is – like so many of my friends and family. You've given me another chance, and I can think of no better way to repay that than to serve you as I did Preceptor Darius."

"You could repay me by staying safe and living a full life," Greatjon offered, already knowing the answer he would receive given how their previous short talks about the subject had gone.

"No – this is my choice," Baris replied sternly with a shake of his head.

"Give it up, Old Wolf," Quinn advised with a friendly grin. "The lad's made up his mind and there's no persuading him otherwise."

Greatjon shrugged. "I had to try," he said before stuffing another egg- and honey-coated piece of sourdough into his mouth.

"Of course you did," Quinn replied knowingly. Then, without warning, his sapphire-blue eyes suddenly grew unfocused, which caught his companions' attention. A moment later, he let out a tense sigh as his eyes refocused on the two. "Well, well – I suggest you two eat up. I just got word from Caldain that our guests will arrive shortly."

By the time the trio reached the Outer Western Gatehouse, it was already apparent to Greatjon that despite the animosity between Darkon and the members of the Order of Stelariuos, they were going to follow proper protocol. He didn't know if this would ease the tension, or if Darkon would simply see it as a tongue-in-cheek jab at him; either way, Greatjon's respect for Quinn grew. It took guts, self-control and discipline by everyone to pay homage to a leader that was practically their enemy. The entire garrison, even the off-duty troops, had turned out in full regalia for Darkon and the Indigain representative's arrival. From the troops lining the battlements, to the statuesque guards that flanked the road from the keep to deep within the village, every soldier's battle-harness armor was polished to a bright sheen and their uniforms were spotless. More importantly, a quick peek through the open gatehouse also confirmed that the front row of stone-faced soldiers lining the road and bridge were the only soldiers that were armed. Per protocol, those same men and women stood ready to present the poleaxe that each one held when the time came.

Mounting the stairs, Greatjon took note of the half-green, half-blue pennants that flew from two of the gatehouse's four towers and the midnight-purple banners that flew from the other two, signaling the arrival of the Indigain representative and the Preceptor of the Order of Valintis. Reaching the battlements of the Outer Western Wall, Greatjon's passive brown eyes saw that the same pennants, the Indigain on the left and Valintis on the right, flew at twenty pace intervals along the elegant, arching Western Bridge and onward through the village. Townsfolk peeked from windows and lined the streets behind the guards, hoping to catch a glimpse of the important visitors. Two platoons of infantry, one on each side of the bridge, were stationed on the ice, their specially spiked footwear allowing them to move and stand without falling over on the slick surface.

It was truly an orderly and proper reception, and would have been enough to ease Greatjon's apprehension about the day if they were receiving anyone other than Darkon. However, Darkon was indeed the one they had all turned out for, and as a result, Greatjon found his worried gaze drawn to the group of fifty mounted soldiers in blue and green tabards – chainmail worn beneath and longswords at their hips – that waited like unmovable statues on the far side of the bridge. At their head and on foot were two figures that would be hard to ignore for a normal person, but for the Gifted amongst the keep's forces, it was like trying to ignore a roaring wildfire outside one's home.

The smaller of the two was a woman who appeared to be in her mid-forties, but Greatjon and others knew she was actually closer to three hundred years old. Two gold circlets adorning her wrists were connected to an emerald-encrusted ring on each of her fingers by delicate silver chains. A large blue sapphire, set in a fine gold brooch, adorned the left breast of her plain, high-cut dark-green dress. Her auburn hair, which was pulled up away from her neck and held in place by a carefully designed, emerald-dotted hairnet, stood out strikingly against the green cloth garment. Hauntingly intelligent brown eyes peered from astride a slim nose at the trio of soldiers blocking their path, her rosy lips pressed together in consternation. It was difficult to ignore her commanding presence, and even harder for fir'gan-sensitive eyes to ignore both her powerful emerald aura and the manner in which the currents throbbed and flowed around her in response to her influence over them. If she had been there by herself, the display would have been considered daunting even for the most powerful Gifted amongst Sentinel Keep's ranks; however, the darlion beside her simply made her seem like a child.

Being a darlion, Darkon already stood out simply for the rarity that he was. His hair, which was neatly combed back from his face, was more akin to a long white mane, and the rest of his body was covered in short umber fur that looked more like skin from a distance. White tuffs of fur capped long, pointed ears that swept back from his sharp-featured, eerily feline head. His lean, muscled frame was clad in his traditional plain black doublet, a gray shirt, black wool stockings and knee-high leather boots. His crystalline-blue eyes were also fixed on the soldiers before him, irritation clearly written on his face. Like his Indigain companion, he too was pulsing with power, his blue-tinged black aura dancing about him like a barely controlled blaze. Given the tension that the sight of the two openly embracing their power inspired in himself and the other Gifted, Greatjon could only imagine how the common folk would react if they could see what the Gifted did.

"Well, well. . . . So he actually brought her," Greatjon breathed, even as he apprehensively noted that Darkon was unarmed; a detail he knew no one could take for granted with Gifted – especially when it came to Wardens.

Quinn glanced at him slyly and said, "He did too good of a job modeling himself after Luthur in the early days; and after what he did to your Order, he doesn't really have anyone clamoring to join his ranks." Quinn chuckled, "Well, should we let the witch and the cat across?"

Dragged from his increasingly concerned thoughts by the quip, Greatjon returned the look and, trying to keep his voice from reflecting the tension he felt in the air, replied, "Sure – that is, if you plan on greeting them armed." He then added cynically, "I'm *sure* Darkon wouldn't take that as a slight, or even a challenge." Noticing that Baris had yet to disarm, he added firmly, "You too, Baris."

"Damn it!" Quinn cursed loudly, drawing a halfhearted chuckle from Greatjon. Removing his sword-harness, he handed it and the blade it carried over to the soldier next to him. Once Baris had surrendered his weapons, Quinn sent the soldier back to the armory with the weapons.

"Good. *Now,* we can let them in," Greatjon mocked.

Quinn cursed again and jabbed Greatjon in the shoulder before they descended the steps and made their way through the gatehouse to the base of the bridge.

Like all Gifted, Greatjon could not only weave the currents of fir'gan into an insulating cocoon against the elements that would keep him free of snow or rain, but he could also harness the natural flow of fir'gan within his body to render himself immune to heat and cold. For the average Gifted, the trick required enough focus that they hardly ever attempted to manipulate the currents for anything else at the same time, which made it an invaluable luxury when inclement weather abounded. Thus, it came as no surprise to Greatjon that the vast majority of the Gifted he could see were channeling their energy into warding off the cold of the day. Yet, as the trio exited the gatehouse and ventured closer to the frozen lake, it was the mundane men and women amongst the assembled ranks that impressed Greatjon the most. All they had was their clothing, training and willpower, yet they stood tall and proud against the bitter wind that tossed about the gentle snowfall like a harsh master.

Sighing to himself, Greatjon was unsure if the display of orderly discipline from people Darkon considered traitors would rankle the darlion or not. Nevertheless, he found himself silently thanking Quinn and Damion for the discipline they had instilled in their followers; he could only hope that such conduct would not only be viewed well, but would prevent anyone from crossing Darkon in any fashion. For better or worse, Warden's memories were long – and Darkon had proven on more than one occasion that he never forgot and rarely forgave those who crossed him. Greatjon was painfully aware of this, and fully understood that – irritating or not – any slip or slight against the darlion could potentially lead to something far worse.

The trio halted at the foot of the bridge and peered across the gentle arch at the Indigain contingent as it narrowed down to two-abreast to fit comfortably on the narrow span. Right away, Greatjon's eyes settled on Darkon, and he could instantly feel the anger in the darlion's glare. It was unsettling to think about what was going through Darkon's mind, so Greatjon let his vision shift just enough to see the icy-blue, ethereal currents of fir'gan. The flowing, intertwining ribbons of ethereal light were always soothing to see, and for Greatjon, even the angry ebb and flow around the darlion was more pleasant than focusing on what Darkon would do or say.

"Where's Aseria?" he asked, trying to focus on the present instead of what may or may not happen.

Quinn unconsciously adjusted his shoulders as if his sword still hung there. "She's in the chapel, praying." He chuckled. "If I hadn't seen it before, I would be stunned to see a darlion in a church instead of an Ansei Grove."

Greatjon snorted. "I'm sure you've seen stranger."

Quinn's smooth features were ruined by a wry smile. "True." A large furry frame nudged up against his hip as Deralina padded quietly past him and sat down at Greatjon's side. "I see your pet has decided to grace us with her presence."

Greatjon rubbed the large head that rested above his waist. He had sensed the tension in Deralina even before her arrival, and he had long been worried about how she would react to seeing Darkon for the first time in a very long time. "I'd say she's more than welcome here," he replied casually, belying his concerns. "Besides – if we have to chase off a big cat, I'm sure she'd be more than happy to accommodate."

Quinn shook his head in amusement as Deralina let out a low, forceful growl of agreement. "Right then – let's get this over with," he said before taking a deep breath and letting it out. His sapphire-blue eyes slipped out of focus for a moment as he communed with his men on the other side of the bridge. As quickly as they had lost it, his eyes regained their focus and he said, "Well, here they come."

Across the bridge, they could see the tallest of Quinn's men bow to Darkon, who responded with a silent nod, before the trio of Stelariuos soldiers pivoted on their heels and led the way across the bridge. The clatter of hooves on the slightly icy bridge filled the air as the entourage began to cross behind Quinn's men. On the left of the lead group was the tallest of the three men, his hawkish features impassive and his braided, waist-length black hair gently rocking with the wind and his fluid movements. The middle soldier was nearly as tall as the first, however, not only did he appear grizzled with age, but his head was shaven and he was significantly more robust. The last of the three was the shortest and, underneath his dark attire, was a compact ball of muscle. Fiery-red hair was slicked back from a round face that was as devoid of emotion as his two compatriots.

The soldiers lining the bridge presented their poleaxes with sharp, crisp movements as the three men passed by. Greatjon cringed inwardly at the minor and intentional slight aimed at Darkon. Normally, such a salute would wait for the most important guest to pass by; so by presenting their arms to the trio first, the soldiers were showing just where Darkon stood in their eyes. The indignation burning in the darlion's eyes was unmistakable as he and the Indigain entourage stopped midway across the bridge in accordance with custom. Conversely, Quinn's men continued onward without pause until they halted four paces short of Greatjon's group and sharply saluted Quinn.

Up close, it was hard not to notice how cold the eyes of the three men were, nor miss the scars that marked them. The physical – like the trio of slashes that ran from the brow of the tallest soldier, over his right eye and down to his jaw line – were easy to see, marking their owner like a badge of honor. Others were emotional, visible only to those who were willing to brave the hauntingly troubled depths of souls that had seen and experienced more than any one person should ever have to.

The man with the waist-length braided hair and the trio of facial scars stepped forward, his gray eyes flashing, before stating for all to hear in a strong voice, "General – the General of the Indigain Order of Light, and the Preceptor of the Valintis Order of the Light," Greatjon cringed inwardly at the intentional wording that put the Indigain before Darkon, "Corith bless their souls, request permission to enter Sentinel Keep."

Quinn managed to repress an amused smile as he noted a slight flare in Darkon's aura at the minor insult. "I, Quinndarius Rulin Silverhand, General and Knight of the Stelariuos Order of the Light, grant leave for the Indigain Order of the Light and the Valintis Order of the Light, Corith bless their souls, to share shelter and bread with us until they see fit to journey onward."

The soldier bowed low, stating respectfully, "By-your-leave, General." Stepping back, all three bowed again before pivoting and returning to Darkon and the Indigain party.

*"He doesn't even deserve this much respect,"* Deralina's angry thoughts shoved into Greatjon's mind, catching him off guard.

He placed a comforting hand on her powerful neck. *"Easy now. This is no time to be cross,"* he offered hastily, the sudden anger making him uneasy. He knew all too well Deralina's feelings toward Darkon, but now was not the time for anger and primal instincts to mix.

*"My memory is longer than yours!"* came the fury-filled thoughts. *"What he did is inexcusable!"*

*"He had proof,"* Greatjon replied, knowing what the response would be.

*"Proof?!"* came the indignant cry as he felt Deralina tense up beneath his hand. *"He used a lie to sate his own wounds! You weren't there, Greatjon! I can still smell the slaughter on him!"*

Greatjon sunk his fingers into her neck forcefully. *"That's enough! What's done is done! I've said it before and I'll say it again – you are family to me, Lina, but without proof, I will not go against him in such a blatant manner! The Order was infected and had to be purged!"* Even as he finished the thought, and Lina's echoing silence greeted him, he realized that even his conviction on this wound between him and his longtime companion had faltered in the light of recent events. Was his loyalty to Darkon really beginning to crack like this?

Before the terse exchange could escalate, Darkon and the Indigains came to a halt just short of their position. Quinn's men continued forward and took up positions behind their general before all six of them bowed to Darkon and the Indigain general.

"General. Preceptor," Quinn stated formally. "Welcome to Sentinel Keep." Quinn let the slightest hint of a smile creep onto his face as he caught Darkon's eye and noted that the darlion was scowling at the numerous minor slights.

"I see the years have done little to improve your manners, Silverhand," Darkon chided with contemptuous anger dripping from his baritone-voiced words.

Quinn gave him an innocent look that he knew would further drive the burr of irritation deeper into Darkon's skin. "I'm sorry, Preceptor, if we've offended. Sentinel Keep's doors are always open to every Order, and Stelariuos always stands ready to serve." There was no doubt in anyone's mind that the willingness to serve part was true, but the undertone of Quinn's declaration left little doubt that, when it came to Darkon, he was in no way sorry for the barbs, and that the darlion's dealings with Stelariuos would always come with a cost.

"Gentlemen, if you please," the Indigain general interrupted tersely, her soft voice coming across powerfully despite its lilting tones, "the situation before us is already tense enough due to an unfortunate chain of circumstances. Let's not throw petty squabbles upon the fire, shall we?"

Quinn shot Darkon one last taunting glare before offering the woman an apologetic smile. "You're right, of course, Lady Alsa. I think we would be wise to follow your counsel."

Darkon folded his arms across his chest confidently. "I don't see any reason for squabbles at all. You know, Alsa – as well as you Greatjon –" he said forcefully, fixing Greatjon with a poignant glare, "that the quickest, most painless way for this to be handled is for them to simply hand over the girl for training. There are more important matters to attend to than this childish rebelliousness," he finished with disdain coating his words.

Alsa laid a restraining hand on Darkon's shoulder. "Peace, Preceptor. While I agree that would be the most expedient way to deal with this, I would also like to hear why Greatjon would refuse to bring her directly to us. Besides," she smiled disarmingly, "I have not had a chance to visit with these gentlemen in some time, and I think we should take advantage of Quinn's generosity before we get back to the doom and gloom of the world."

They all could see the muscles in Darkon's jaw working as he glared at Alsa and fought down his frustration. "Very well," he spit with a snort of disgust. "I know I'm not welcome here, and I honestly have no desire to be here any longer than necessary. You have one night, Alsa. I expect us to be on our way in the morning – with the girl."

Alsa inclined her head to Darkon. "Of course, Preceptor."

"As for you two," Darkon continued, focusing his glare on Quinn and Greatjon, "I would speak with our newest Gifted and have my measure of her. Bring her to me in Ansei Grove before midday."

Quinn's eyes hardened. "I won't have you trying any tricks, Darkon. She's under my protection while she's here."

Darkon snorted. "Jumping at shadows, Quinn. I merely want to speak with her and make sure that she knows just who is in charge," he stated, trying to bury his defensive tone in contempt.

This made Quinn grin. "What's the matter, Preceptor? Is your faith in your strength and position so fragile that the words of a Knight has you quaking in your boots?"

A wolfish snort entered Greatjon's thoughts. *"The bastard doesn't need anyone to shatter their faith in him,"* Deralina stated telepathically to Greatjon, and he found himself starting to agree with her.

"Oh will you two children stow your swords! This verbal fencing is pointless!" Alsa cried in exasperation, glaring at Quinn and Darkon. When both men simply continued to stared at each other, holding their tongues in check, Alsa nodded in approval and stated, "Good." She then turned a small smile, which had the feel of a mother comforting the child she had just punished, on Quinn and the others. "If you would be so kind, General, as to escort us in out of this cold?"

Quinn's scowl faded as he grinned at the small joke. "Of course, General. If you all would follow me?"

As they started back up the road to the keep, Baris settled in alongside Greatjon and said in a low, dispassionate voice, "So he is the leader of the Wardens – the man that Darius and so many effectively died for?"

"He is," Greatjon replied with a slight nod.

"I don't think I like him," Baris said in such a simple manner that the finality to words was hard to miss.

While Greatjon didn't offer a reply, he wasn't surprised to find that his amazement at agreeing with such divisive statements was quickly fading.

Her face was slender and attractive in the cat-like way of the darlions. A slender and flat nose, lightly accentuated cheekbones, and long, pointed ears that were tipped with white fur added to the feline grace and allure of her countenance. Her long yellow-blonde hair was the texture of downy fur and hung to her waist when at rest, while her blonde bangs hung just above her almond-shaped blue-lavender eyes. Fur short enough to be mistaken for skin – if not for the snowy coloration and small accent stripes of warm yellow – covered the entirety of her body. Though she appeared to be slender underneath her fur cloak, black tunic and pants of warm wool, she was athletically built with whipcord muscles that blessed her with strength that belied her slender build. However, despite her grace and allure, the nervous tension in her movements and the look in her eyes revealed how overwhelmed she was by the monstrous amount of information that had been force-fed to her during the last few days.

Aseria was informed of Darkon's impending arrival soon after Greatjon had received the news. She had been told what it would likely mean and – though brief in description – was informed of the angst between Darkon and their gracious hosts within the Stelariuos Order. It made little sense to her given the lack of details, but the tension that seemed to grow in Sentinel Keep's residents as the day approached was palpable. To distract herself, she had buried herself in the keep's library, carefully reading the ancient tomes on the Orders and the lifeblood of everything on Kylir – fir'gan. She had always had a knack for reading people or sensing things before they happened, and had always attributed it to simple intuition. However, after all that had befallen her over the last few months, that illusion had been shattered.

Greatjon had informed her that she was Gifted – one that was blessed with a natural attunement to fir'gan and, eventually, the ability to consciously manipulate the powerful essence. To that end, with her research as a guide, she had spent time meditating and trying to bring her awareness of the currents to a conscious level – with little success. However, as Darkon's arrival had drawn closer, she had found herself believing that the tension she felt in the air was more visceral than a mere sensation. On the day of Darkon's arrival, she also noted that there seemed to be a tingle in the air that raised her hackles. She had never experienced anything like it in her life and, though she could neither see the currents nor sense the number of Gifted openly embracing them, she knew that it had to be a result of her slowly emerging gift. With all these new sensations and thoughts tumbling through her mind, it came as no surprise to her that, by the time Greatjon, Quinn and Baris came to retrieve her, her stomach had managed to tie itself in nervous knots.

576

Flanked by Greatjon and Baris, and with Quinn in the lead, she was finding it difficult to keep her anxiety from growing as they followed the path that led from the Outer Southern Gatehouse to the Ansei Grove. All three men had retrieved their weapons and carried them as if they were marching to war. Their tense posture worried her, and was further compounded by the way the cold snowfall seemed to have cast the world into an ominous silence. Attempting to calm her growing anxiety, she turned her focus to the breathtaking sight of the ancient Ansei Grove they were swiftly approaching.

Measuring just shy of two hundred yards in diameter, the Ansei Grove's outer ring was comprised of trees that were unique to the ancient spiritual sites. Towering sixty feet into the air and composed of frosted blue crystal, the trees were a breathtaking sight that made most people stop and stare in awe – in fact, most people would not even consider them trees. Each of the outer ring trees, unlike those lurking further in, had been molded into the likenesses of a beautiful, long-limbed, nude woman that seemed to exude a mixture of sexual allure and maternal warmth that worked in balance with each other. The level of detail was excruciatingly precise and made the trees seem almost alive. The muscles in her full thighs – one leg positioned slightly in front of the other – were tone and supple, while her wide and curvaceous hips flowed into a long, unmistakably feminine torso. Delicate faces were tilted skyward, allowing their hair to tumble past their buttocks like a frozen waterfall, as the crystalline women thrust their chests outward as if they were proudly flaunting their full breasts. Long-fingered hands were splayed wide at the end of graceful arms that were reaching forward as if the women were welcoming visitors to their embrace.

Given the masterful level of detail and the aura of warmth and peace the trees exuded, it was easy to imagine that the trees really were giant women frozen in place. For Aseria, however, it was the way the light played on the blue, frosted crystal that always managed to enthrall her. No matter the angle of the sun, it always seemed as if vibrant-blue water flowed and danced within the structures. With what she had been learning over the last few days, it dawned on her that the crystal trees might actually be filled with the currents that she was unable to currently see in their natural state – and she didn't know how true her revelation was. The flowing and pulsing blue that danced within the crystal trees was the lifeblood of all; the energy that connected everything and fueled the Gifted's powers – fir'gan.

As they drew closer, a captivating, fluid melody graced their ears, peaking and diving as if the trees and the very world were crying and singing in joy at the same time. Such musical enchantment was always present wherever the crystalline trees grew, and only became more captivating when the wind danced through the limbs and crystal leaves like it would through a master-crafted wind chime. The melody was the source of the trees' name – kastusoul in the ancient darlion tongue, or in the Trader's Tongue, better known as crystalsong. While Aseria did not adhere to the religious beliefs and ways of her people, she normally found a visit to an Ansei Grove a soothing experience – but not today.

Today, the song sung by the crystal grove seemed more ominous than uplifting. As they passed between two of the lovely crystalsong matrons, Aseria – even without the sensitivity to fir'gan that her companions possessed – could tell that the grove was, for lack of a better term, unhappy. Ansei Groves were grown and nurtured around the ancient principles of balance and harmony; and when anything or anyone upset that dynamic, the grove's song reflected it. While Aseria knew she wasn't a paragon of spiritual harmony – and she was fairly sure her companions wouldn't make such a claim either – the fact that the song sounded a bit off before they entered the Grove told her that the balance had been upset by something or someone already within. Given that she was here to meet with Darkon, it did nothing for her nerves to associate his presence with the sadness in the Grove's melody. A quick glance at Greatjon told her that whatever she was feeling, he was feeling on a much deeper scale; and she could only conclude that Quinn was feeling the same as Greatjon from the way he kept rubbing his forehead. Baris, on the other hand, seem to be ignorant of the discordance in the song and she found herself slightly envious of him.

Once inside the Grove, they found themselves flanked by crystalsong trees in their natural form. The frosted blue crystal trees towered over them like ancient oaks, their crystalline branches and leaves, which were reminiscent of large snowflakes, weaved a web over their heads through which the sunlight filtered through, casting the area into shades of blue. Where normally the Grove's song and the soothing light would project calm, they once again found that everything seemed a bit askew.

Halfway to the center of the Grove, Quinn finally let out a growl of disgust as he brought their group to a halt. Turning to face the others, he fixed his sapphire-blue eyes on Aseria. "Well, this is as far as we'll go. Our presence will just serve to agitate Darkon – but we won't be far."

"Aye, we won't," Greatjon agreed. "Deralina is already lurking about the perimeter of the Grove's heart, and the nexus of fir'gan will obscure us from Darkon's senses unless we openly embrace the currents."

578

"Neither of you trust him very much, do you?" Aseria asked with nervous curiosity.

Greatjon held his tongue, but his visage showed his growing conflict. Quinn, however, did little to hide his disdain. "You don't know Greatjon very well, and you know even less about me and my Order. I don't know whether to commend your bravery for starting down a path you know little about, or to call you a fool."

Aseria's eyes hardened just a bit at the statement.

"However," he plowed on, preventing any possible rebuttal, "both of us can see what Darius and Cat saw in you, and we will honor their wishes to the best of our ability. So, I hope you are open-minded enough to listen to wisdom when it's offered, and to know not to blindly follow orders."

"I may be young by darlion standards, but I'm not an ignorant fool," Aseria stated with self-assured conviction.

"Good," Quinn stated firmly with a nod. "Then I hope you'll listen to me now. I'm nearing my fourth millennia," the declaration caused Aseria's eyes to widen in astonishment, "but Darkon is ancient by even our standards. He has seen and done things that none of us can fully imagine, and time has taken its toll on him. He was always somewhat a cynic, and always believed we should have a more aggressive approach to our goals. Many of the Preceptors disagreed with such an approach, and as such, peace within our ranks was maintained because our leader at the time would not hear of any infighting." Quinn's face darkened as he added, "None of us know why leadership was passed to him, and the power seems to only have made him more brazen. Disagreeing with his approach has proven to be dangerous for many."

Aseria swallowed, disturbed by what she was hearing. She had only begun to study the Orders' long history, but she had gleaned that the man that had preceded Darkon was held in the utmost esteem; because of that small bit of knowledge, she found it difficult to understand why such a man would appoint someone so drastically different to follow him. She was hesitant to voice her curiosity, but her desire to understand what she had gotten herself into got the better of her. "What do you mean?" she asked.

"My Order, the Bestyne, was . . . *disbanded* by him for reasons I'm beginning to question," Greatjon answered hesitantly.

"Disbanded?" Aseria asked, uncomfortable with the emphasis on the word.

"By himself, he slaughtered the Bestynes down to but a handful that he deemed loyal," Quinn coldly replied for Greatjon.

"Corith be good," Aseria breathed in horrified shock.

"Aye. He also more or less turned his back on Darius; otherwise, he would have sent more than Greatjon to his aid – no offense."

Greatjon shook his head. "None taken."

"I hate to ask, but what did he do to you, Quinn?" Aseria inquired in an attempt to piece together the puzzle being presented to her.

The grin that greeted her question was enough to make her shiver in fear. "Me? Not a damn thing. He believes our Preceptor betrayed the Orders long ago, and for that, he would like nothing better than to do what he did to the Bestynes to us." Quinn snorted. "The bastard was always jealous of Damion, and the traitor talk is likely his way of trying to provoke him into a fight."

Aseria's brow furrowed in confusion. "If this Damion is your Preceptor, and he's not here, then where is he and what's stopping Darkon from acting? For that matter – what in the hells are you all doing not only following, but allowing him to lead?" she demanded, her exasperation with the perplexing stories spilling over.

"To answer the first part – we don't know. All we know is that Damion received his orders and hasn't been heard from since. As to what's stopping Darkon from acting, that's a bit simpler to answer – he fears us. Preceptor or not, we have the largest number of Gifted in our ranks of any Order. Powerful as Darkon is, he is a Preceptor without an army and, while the casualties would be great, it would be extremely difficult for him to stand against us. As to why we follow him . . ." Quinn paused, growing thoughtful. "In the end, he's not a bad man – misguided and overly emotional at times, but not evil. He received leadership in the proper manner and, while his stumbles have been egregious, he has managed to keep the Orders alive through trying and tough times." He sighed and shook his head when he saw Aseria's skeptical look. "I know this doesn't make sense right now, but we've been embroiled in a war that has gone on both in public and in the shadows for longer than most people can fathom. Both our side and our enemies have done our best to avoid open conflict for fear of tearing what's left of Kylir apart."

*"What's left of Kylir?"* Aseria thought to herself. *"What does that even mean?"*

Quinn ignored the further befuddlement that crept onto Aseria's face, lost in his own thoughts. "We may not like Darkon – or even agree with him on many things – but he has managed to steer us through the years without drawing us into an open conflict."

"What conflict?!" she exclaimed, her confusion causing her head to swim and aggravating her greatly. "What kind of mad war makes use of the power I've seen on display? What, in Corith's name, justifies the destruction that I saw at Blackstone?!" Tears were beginning to well up in her eyes. "What I've read and seen is the stuff of fairytales and bedtime stories! Even seeing it and reading in the library, I'm having a hard time accepting it . . . accepting that I– I could have such power and be sucked into this– this– . . ." she growled in frustration and wiped at her eyes before looking at the others, searching their faces for answers.

Baris looked like none of this news was unexpected, but his expression was sympathetic to her. Both Quinn and Greatjon's faces had softened, but there was an air about them that screamed of a heartbroken parent punishing their child because they knew the chastisement would better the child despite the immediate pain.

"Aseria," Greatjon spoke softly, "I know you had no real idea what you were getting into, and I know you desperately want and need answers that can't be given or fully explained right now." He placed a gentle hand on her shoulder. "But the role we are asking you to play – that Darius and Cat asked you to play – is important. Without us, Kylir would be plunged into an abyssal darkness without hope, love or joy. Listen to Quinn – he knows what he is talking about."

Aseria shook her head and sighed before asking weakly, "So what do you want me to do?"

"Present yourself to Darkon," Quinn said firmly, "and show him you are worthy of the task you are to be entrusted with. Do not cower before him – he is our leader, but he is not our master. Most importantly – be your own person. Hear everyone's thoughts and counsel, but make up your own mind. Without faith and trust in yourself, you'll be nothing but a mindless sheep – and Kylir has enough of those already."

Aseria laughed dryly. "You sure know how to cheer a girl up, don't you?"

Quinn cracked a wry smile. "Sorry. My last wife passed over two-hundred years ago, so I'm a bit out of practice."

Aseria blinked at him rapidly. "Two hundred– Corith be good! I was only a babe then!"

Quinn's smile grew. "Guess you don't have anything to worry about from me, then – you're way too young for me."

Aseria blushed a bit and laughed.

"That's better. A little light in the dark is always a sign of hope," Quinn quipped supportively. "Now go on, we don't want to keep Darkon waiting."

Aseria took a deep breath and let it out. "I won't lie – I'm confused and baffled, and you've given me more questions than answers. But . . . thank you."

Quinn laughed. "Don't know why you're thanking me, but you're welcome."

Taking another deep breath, she offered them what she hoped was a confident smile before stepping past Quinn and continuing down the path.

As soon as she was out of sight, Quinn said, "Right then. Baris – you stay here. Greatjon and I will watch her from the woods."

Baris looked to Greatjon for confirmation.

"Don't worry – it'll be alright, lad." He patted Baris on the shoulder reassuringly before he and Quinn stepped off the path and vanished into the shadows.

Baris stood there for a moment, then shook his head in disgust. "I'm not being left behind anymore," he muttered. Checking that his sword and long knife were loose in their scabbards, he then trotted after Aseria.

# Chapter Twenty-Six

*A*seria was lost.

She was not lost within the Grove – the straight, well-manicured path made sure of that – but she was lost mentally and emotionally as a result of the mountain of knowledge that had been thrust upon her. Unlike humanity, however, she was not ignorant of such mythos – her childhood had been steeped in the old ways thanks to her parents and the long memory of the darlions as a whole. Yet their stories of fir'gan, powerful immortals, dragons, and battles of cataclysmic magnitude had been just that – stories. As she had grown, not only did the fairytales of her youth fade, but something within her had begun to sour when it came to her people. Their isolationist attitude irritated her. Yes, humans and their frantic lives could be annoying and their penchant for violence was appalling at times, yet she had come to find their lust for life and ability to cherish each moment to be a gift that the darlions either lacked or outgrew as they aged.

When she had come of age, she – like her father and mother before her – took her place amongst the military, as was the duty of all younglings. For thirty years, she spent her time protecting the borders of Tykandrith – the darlion lands in Western Solarson. It was a good time for her; she encountered numerous cultures and began to find that her people's growing distaste with humanity was both valid and exaggerated. Yes, humans were brash and quick to judge, as well as quick to anger and violence, but she found that their capacity for compassion and love was just as vigorous.

It was during her time patrolling the borders and mingling with the humans that she began to realize that she felt more at home amongst the short-lived beings than her own people. When she expressed this to her family, they merely laughed it off as youthful delusions, much to her chagrin. She didn't remember much of the argument that ensued other than that it was very heated and rash things were said that left all parties wounded. She moved into the barracks permanently after that, and when word reached her ears of a longterm mission beyond Tykandrith's borders, she was ready to do whatever it would take to gain the assignment.

To her amazement, she didn't have to do anything as her unit was specifically requested by, and put under the command of a human of all things! Granted, the darlions had always maintained open trade and dialogue with Darius Fultain, but for her people to so readily cede to such a request seemed completely out of character. She had no idea what could have convinced the High Council to do such a thing, but she saw it as a chance to escape her people for a time and was eager to depart. Her excitement at being away from home was short-lived, however. It took them less than two weeks to reach Castle Blackstone, but almost immediately upon arrival, her unit was ushered into use hunting down the enemy that was encroaching on Darius' holdings.

To her horror, they found themselves fighting an enemy straight out of the scary tales used to frighten younglings into obeying their parents. Silent and horrifyingly graceful, the nightmarish creatures known as blackhearts moved through the forests and mountains with a proficiency that was more than a match for Aseria's unit. It was the way they killed, however, that was truly frightening. Not only could they strike without warning, but even the slightest nick or cut was fatal. Flesh-bloating and -rotting poison, unlike anything anyone had seen or heard of, ravaged the victim and killed them within mere moments of the wound being inflicted. Yet, despite the horrors they witnessed and the loss of half their unit, she and her compatriots had remained loyal to their oaths and promise to aid Darius.

A month into their hit-and-run campaign, they were asked to meet and escort allies to Castle Blackstone. It was the easiest job they had been asked to do and, unbeknownst to Aseria, it would end up being a turning point in her life. What was left of her unit was delayed by snowfall and arrived at the rendezvous to find their new allies under attack; of the five people they'd been sent to escort, only two remained standing against thirty enemy soldiers, ten of which were the vile blackhearts. Although they all feared the death that awaited at the end of a blackheart weapon, their time in the field had quelled any action-freezing fear they might have felt upon seeing the ghastly enemies, and Aseria and her unit had rushed to their aid. Through the short battle that ensued, she found herself enamored with the grace and beauty with which the brunette woman who led the survivors fought. It wasn't just her movements or the way her longsword weaved and cut that impressed Aseria; there was an air of power about the woman that made everything she did seem unreal.

By the time the battle was over, Aseria wasn't so sure that their aid was ever needed. She could have sworn that during the melee she had seen the brunette woman somehow blast five of the assailants a good sixty feet backward, their bodies rent asunder. After the fight, she had held her tongue as they made sure the survivors, three in total, were okay. During that time, Aseria eventually learned that the skillful brunette with dark skin and vibrant yellow eyes went by the name of Catharina Durasala.

She continued to keep her thoughts to herself as they escorted the survivors back to Blackstone, but that grew increasingly difficult as she kept catching Catharina watching her with an inquisitive gaze the entire trip. Between the searching looks and her own curiosity about the fight, Aseria eventually broke down and confronted Catharina. Her questions were met with warm, sly smiles and cryptic answers that only further served to fuel her curiosity. The following two months in Blackstone gave her enough time to sate it. In fact, Catharina seemed to go out of her way to make herself available to Aseria, but not simply to chat or answer the darlion's questions; she, in turn, politely inquired about Aseria in such a roundabout way that it took the darlion a while to realize she had been interrogated. Instead of feeling angry, Aseria had laughed at the situation, for she had realized that, despite the questioning, she had made a friend in Catharina.

Two weeks before the fall of Blackstone, Catharina had fallen to one of the blackheart's arrows, shattering the budding friendship and sending Aseria's life down the path to her current situation. While grief at the lost of a friend and good person gripped those that knew Catharina, word arrived of the High Council's decision to fully isolate itself from the machinations of humanity, and that recall orders had been issued to all darlions. Her unit had immediately begun preparations to pullout, as was expected of them. Aseria had her doubts, however, and was slow in following orders.

During that time, Darius came to her and offered to make her a ward of his. Naturally, Aseria found the offer both surprising and confusing. Darius went on to tell her that he and Catharina had known she wasn't comfortable amongst her own people, and that they had seen something special in her that they had agreed shouldn't be wasted. While she was certainly confused, and oddly honored, that they had felt that way about her, she found herself accepting the offer for no other reason than to sever the last chain holding her to her people. The rest of her unit had not taken the news well, but, to her surprise, did not put up an argument.

Darius' wounding and death soon followed, as did the nightmarish fall of Blackstone. So much so fast, with so many questions left unanswered – and the answers that she did have, seemed to only sprout new questions.

It suddenly dawned on her that Darius had not requested her unit simply for their aide – he had made the request to get to her. Aseria stopped on the path and closed her eyes, shaken to her core. Taking a deep breath and letting it out slowly, she started forward again, turning her thoughts to the present and away from the heartbreaking revelation.

What she had been able to glean from the books in Sentinel Keep's library had gone a long way toward helping her to understand who and what Darius and Catharina were, but she was still having a hard time accepting that she could be part of this storybook come to life. Dragons, elves, fir'gan – legendary, fantastical entities that the books claimed had once existed, but accepting such claims would run contrary to the widely held belief that such things were nothing more that flights of fancy. While that belief now showed cracks because of her newfound, albeit basic, understanding of fir'gan's existence, she was still having a difficult time accepting that elves and dragons were ever real. . . . Then again, she had met a handful of immortals that appeared normal, but wielded godlike powers in a secret struggle against. . . . Against . . . what?

Halting, she shook and rubbed her head in frustration. She was beginning to believe that ignorance was truly bliss. However, if all these things were real – and some of it certainly appeared to be – then what, in Corith's name, could they be fighting that warranted such power? An evil god lost to even the long memories of the dar-lions? Demons from the nightmares of children? Beings like themselves? Or was it something worse?

Shaking her head again, she resumed her trek. Did it really even matter at this point? She was having enough trouble accepting her current situation, and it wasn't going to do her any good to further compound it by reaching for more things to fret about.

Suddenly, she halted and looked around in surprise, for she had entered the glade at the center of the Grove with what seemed like no warning. Had she been so lost in thought as to be oblivious to her surroundings? Her self-chastisement for her lack of attention was foiled before it could start as her attention was enthralled by the sight before her. She had been in Ansei Groves before, but never had she beheld in those what graced her eyes now. While she was aware of the pristine, soft grass flowing across the ground like a gentle sea of green – which her mind told her was impossible in winter – that oddity was overwhelmed by the centerpiece of the grove, the sight of which stole the breath from her lungs.

Crystal that was similar to what composed the crystalsong trees formed a flowing ring that was ninety feet in diameter. No . . . it wasn't just a ring, she realized. The crystal had been carved . . . no . . . had *formed* into the shape of two dragons whose limbs appeared to be grasping toward each other. Where their limbs would have met, the crystal formation twisted and spiraled upward into a majestic tree whose height should have easily towered over the rest of the Ansei Grove. Sunlight played off the frosted blue structure as it filtered down through the canopy that sheltered the clearing. It took Aseria a moment to realize that, unlike the crystalsong trees that seemed to flow with blue water, this tree and the interlocking dragons were pulsing with a cold blue light that flowed through the structures like blood pumping through a person or creature.

She was positive that such a splendid sight could not be missed from outside the Grove, yet her eyes were telling her something that her mind railed against. Once again, she was witness to another scene from legend come to life before her, and while she had no words to describe what she was seeing, she could feel it tugging at her heart – no, her very soul – in a way that made the thought of leaving such a serene and blissful place nearly impossible.

"Beautiful, isn't it?"

The softly spoken words from behind her shattered the ethereal moment so violently that Aseria jumped forward in fright. Her instincts kicking in, she spun to face the voice as she reached over her right shoulder for her sword. Grasping at empty air, she then glanced over her shoulder and cursed inwardly before focusing on the source of the voice. Tinted blue by the light of the grove, the man standing before her took her breath away even as her eyes widened and her knees went weak with genuine shock. Standing before her, his powerful and confident eyes fixed on the tree in the center of the grove, was a black-clad darlion straight from the annals of history.

"Amazing, isn't it? The power that radiates from it?" he asked casually, as if such power was commonplace.

Aseria couldn't reply as her brain raced to catch up with what she was seeing. As much as she wanted to, there was no denying what she was seeing. Every youngling was told stories of the man that had not only led their people from the edge of oblivion and into the embrace of the Light, but had sacrificed all to make a better world for all of Kylir. She had seen pictures of the revered man as a child, and knew that she was staring at the face of the last and greatest Emperor the darlions had ever known.

His crystalline-blue eyes shifted from the tree to her slowly, a sly, knowing smile spreading across his face. "What's the matter, youngling? You look as if you've seen a ghost."

Her mind clawed about her skull, franticly searching for the words to say or the actions to make. In the end, ingrained cultural tradition took over, and she found herself dropping to one knee, her forearm on her leg and her head bowed low. "Kalestia dorkithis tola de rotash, Deotorum."

The grin on Darkon's face grew broader. " 'In your name, my emperor, I live and die.' " He laughed. "I haven't heard those words in a very, very long time."

Aseria shuddered inwardly as he confirmed what she had been thinking.

"But that title," he suddenly stated seriously, "hasn't had true meaning or power in ages. While I thank you for the memories and the honorable gesture, there's no need to kneel before me." As Aseria slowly stood, he added, "I have as little attachment to our people as you do, methinks? No?" Aseria met his question with wide eyes, but she couldn't find the words to reply, which drew an amused laugh from him. "Come now, youngling, cat got your tongue? I'm no ghost or angry sprit. I'm as much flesh and bone as you are. Here – touch." He extended his hand and Aseria moved back reflexively, which earned her another amused chuckle as he withdrew his arm. "I sometimes forget the affect I have on our people. Legends stepping off the pages of history books doesn't happen every day, no?"

He cocked his head when Aseria did not reply. "Hummm . . ." he intoned as he studied her, his eyes seeming to see more than just her physical form. "No, you're not slow, and other than being a bit short, you are certainly quite healthy. Actually, your aura is quite strong. Cat and Darius certainly weren't wrong in that assessment," he said begrudgingly. "Maybe something a bit simpler and less overwhelming? What's your name, youngling?" he asked as if he were addressing a child.

His patronizing tone lit a fire in Aseria, which replaced her shock and awe with indignation. "I'm Aseria de'Tusnagi Mitsurea – and I am no youngling."

Darkon grinned. "Well, Aseria de'Tusnagi Mitsurea, I'm Darkon te'Kurashinta Velorishin, as I'm sure you already know – and to me, you are very, very much a youngling." He paused to let the implications sink in, and was pleased to see that it did. "Very good; you have spirit and fire, but you know your place – a tribute to our people." He stepped up beside her, his attention shifting to the tree again. "Do you know what this is?"

Aseria pivoted and focused on the tree, trying her best not to feel apprehensive with the living legend standing next to her. However, she felt like she was failing miserably at it, as the man seemed to radiate power in a way that was almost stifling. Doing her best to pull her thoughts from the air of power about Darkon, she said, "It looks like a Life Tree . . . but that's not possible."

Darkon arched an eyebrow at her. "It isn't possible," he echoed. "You can still manage to say that after all you already learned and seen." He sighed. "To be expected, I suppose. But you are right, it's not the Spiritlais Valariuo – not the real one anyway."

Aseria suddenly felt light-headed. "Not the real–" she started to say, staring at him wide-eyed. "Are you saying the Life Tree is real?"

Laughing, Darkon replied, "Youngling, there's so much to learn and so very little time. Yes, the Life Tree is real – or was at one point. Its location has long been lost to the Storm Sea."

Aseria's eyes bulged, but she refrained from vocally expressing her shock.

"This," Darkon pointed at the pulsing blue tree, "is Spiritlais Valariuo Nivalo."

"A seedling?" she asked incredulously.

"Aye. Every true Ansei Grove has one at the heart of it. They are nexus points of pure fir'gan." He looked at her sideways. "You do know what fir'gan is?"

Aseria folded her arms beneath her breasts, hugging herself. "I do," she said softly. "Greatjon told me of it, and I've read about it. He said . . . he said I was someone that could learn to see it – a Gifted."

"Did he now? Humph – well, he hasn't been totally useless after all."

Aseria caught the cynicism in his voice, but it hardly registered as her mind was simply trying to keep up with the seemingly implausible information being force-fed to her.

"Well, even without training, you are already seeing it. The energy you see flowing through the tree is fir'gan that has built up to the point of being visible to the naked eye. However, with the proper guidance, you'll not only be able to see it on a primal level, but you'll be able to manipulate it in ways you cannot fathom."

"I can imagine it," she answered weakly as the sounds of the battle for Blackstone came roaring back to her. "I heard the explosions and the screams when Blackstone fell."

"A tragedy we tried to avoid, to be sure – but hearing it, seeing it, and wielding it are completely different experiences," he replied solemnly.

"And why would I want any part of that?" she replied softly as she fought to fend off the tears that were trying to well up in her eyes.

"To help the world avoid what happened at Blackstone," he replied simply.

Aseria turned to face Darkon and exclaimed, "That was one man – one army! How could he unleash that on the world?"

Darkon scoffed. "That crimson devil? He's nothing but an irritant, but an irritant with powerful friends."

*"An irritant that killed two of your people and hundreds of innocents,"* Aseria thought to herself.

"His allies make him look like a newborn babe, and the power that backs them . . ." he trailed off, his face growing cold. "The power that backs them has no remorse, no pity, nor does it know forgiveness or love. The evil that it represents fuels them and pushes them for more destruction and more conquest."

"You're saying they're agents of the Nine Hells?"

Darkon laughed loudly. "Oh nothing so contrived as that." He looked her square in the eyes and declared in a tone that brokered no debate, "They are driven by the Darkness – the purest form of everything wrong with every species on Kylir. Hate, anger, rage, violence, lust, envy, sloth, power – if it's a sin and lurks in the darkest corners of your mind, then you'll find it when you stare into that abyssal darkness and it stares back."

Aseria's face screwed up in horror. "That's. . . . That's. . . ."

"Horrible?" he finished for her. "Disgusting? Unimaginable? Yes, youngling, it is all that and more. We are all that stands between that horrific fate and the light and hope that this tree represents. If we ever fail in our watch, then all is lost with no hope of redemption. You, dear Aseria," he reached out and trailed a finger along her cheek, "are now part of it – a guardian against the Darkness." Watching her emotions war within the depths of her eyes, he slipped his hand in the pouch at his side unnoticed. Pulling forth a round metal disc with a blue crystal set in its center, he said, his voice barely above a whisper, "You've got potential, youngling, and I can't risk having you trained by anyone other than me."

Intending to shatter the disc on the ground, his left arm shot up just as Aseria jumped away from his grasp, drawing a scowl from him. "Don't make this difficult, youngling! This is your–" Darkon's head shot up and they both turned as an angry scream split the air.

Baris, his sword poised to strike, came charging out of the tree line, speeding toward Darkon.

"Baris! No!" Aseria screamed to no avail.

"Fool," Darkon muttered as he turned and extended his free hand toward the young man.

Baris came to a jarring halt as if he'd slammed face first into a wall. Eyes glazed over and sword slipping from his hand, Baris was slowly lifted off the ground by a force that Aseria couldn't see.

As Darkon slowly approached the dazed man, his face cold and devoid of emotion, Aseria pleaded, tears streaming down her cheeks, "Please, don't hurt him! He's a friend and only wanted to protect me!"

"A friend, eh?" Darkon said as he stopped in front of Baris, his eyes focused on the slight green aura he saw sputtering around the man. "A noble notion, friendship; and a friend willing to lay his life on the line for you is something to cherish. However," Baris moaned as whatever was holding him in the air seemed to tighten, squeezing the breath from him, "one thing you need to learn – and learn early – is we have very little room for forgiveness, and even less for stupidity."

"No . . ." Aseria pleaded weakly, rage and terror at knowing she was powerless to stop Darkon from shredding her heart.

Though she could not see it, she could feel a sudden surge in power from Darkon as he coldly said, "Ah well, a pity. This lad had potential."

Fearing for Baris' life, she started to move forward; however, before she'd take more than two steps, an angry howl from her right brought her up short. Before she could react, a flash fur shot across her vision and slammed into Darkon with a rage-filled growl. Latching on to Darkon's extended arm, Deralina's fangs sank to the bone and her massive bulk launched the darlion from his feet, freeing Baris' unconscious form to fall unceremoniously to the ground as they tumbled to the side. Without hesitating, Aseria sprinted over to her prone friend and gathered him up, putting her body between him and the combatants.

A sudden boom rattled the air and Aseria twisted around in time to see Deralina soar through the air and hit the ground violently with a whimper. She was afraid the direwolf was dead, but was relieved to see her climbing to her feet a moment later, dazed but alive.

"Damn mutt!" Darkon roared as he climbed to his feet, the violent wound on his forearm already closing up. "I should have exterminated you with the rest of your plague-ridden kind!"

Aseria's eyes widened in terrified awe as a loud crackle and then a roaring explosion rocked the air as Darkon's blue-tinted, black aura burst to life for all to see. Although she didn't fully understand what was happening, she knew all too well that Darkon intended to kill Deralina. Petrified, Aseria watched as Darkon extended his fully healed arm toward the dazed direwolf. Immediately, ribbons of blue energy coalesced in front of his hand before shifting to the same blue-black color as Darkon's aura as the building energy quickly fashioned into a crackling ball of death.

"Die, bitch!" Darkon hissed before unleashing the pent-up power.

The ball of concentrated fir'gan shot out with a hiss toward Deralina. Aseria screamed in horror as the ball of death streaked closer and then exploded with a blinding flash and resounding bang that knocked her flat on top of Baris. When the shockwave faded and her ears stopped ringing, she slowly sat back up. Making sure that her unconscious friend was okay, she then pushed herself to her feet and turned to see the results of the mind-numbingly destructive attack. Where she had expected to see what was left of Deralina's carcass splattered about the clearing, she instead found Quinn poised defensively in front of the direwolf, his palms smoking from where it appeared he had caught the blast. His face was a mask of seething rage even as a violent-yellow aura writhed about him. Aseria desperately wanted to breathe a sigh of relief, but she could tell this was far from over.

"Out of the way, Quinn! The wolf has gone too far this time!" Darkon hissed vehemently.

"How dare you?!" Quinn roared in defiant reply. "We let you into our house and our Grove on good faith, and you not only try to kidnap Greatjon's charge, but you try to kill two others! Who in the hells do you think you are?!"

"I am your leader and master! I lead the Wardens! I see the horrors ahead! And only I can see to it that we avert the coming tragedy! Who are you to stand in my way? Your master is a traitor! That bitch of a wolf's whole order were traitors! Even Darius shunned us! And for what? Loyalty to a dead man!" He snarled and his aura flared. "Their loyalty was to me the moment Luthur died, and their refusal to work together has jeopardized everything! How dare you stand protectively over a traitor and lecture me!"

Darkon's eyes narrowed and he hissed, "Move, Quinn, and I'll forget this. Her fate was sealed a long time ago, and it's my fault for showing mercy. Don't blacken Stelariuos' reputation any more than its master already has."

Quinn, his face growing grim, stood to his full height and, with solemn intent, reached over his head and drew his longsword. "Think long and hard about who the traitor is here, Darkon – I'm not the one trying to murder one's allies."

"Traitors," Darkon hissed.

Turning to the side, Quinn raised his sword and rested it on his raised forearm, aiming the blade at Darkon. "I know in my heart that no one ever betrayed you, Darkon," he declared solemnly. "Light be good, I wish Damion was here to clear up this infernal mess, but he isn't. Corith knows I have done my best to lead in his absence, and if it means my death to stand up for my friends and against what I know to be wrong, so be it. If you believe we are traitors, Darkon – draw your crusader, and let the Light decide who is right."

Darkon, his legs spread wide, straightened up and extended his right hand to the side, an orb of blue-black energy flaring to life in his palm. Grinning maliciously, Darkon retorted, "Foolish little Knight wishes to play with the adults, eh? You're imprudent notions would do Damion proud. Shame he's not here to stop you from throwing your life away."

Quinn adjusted his grip on his sword and swallowed. "A shame, indeed."

Darkon's grin spread and his hand flexed wide around the orb. Before he could close his grip around the ball of fir'gan, a bellow from his right erupted from the woods, followed by a series of sizzling fireballs that slammed successively into Darkon. Clothes dotted with small flames and smoke streaming from his body, Darkon stumbled to the side, the ball of fir'gan in his right hand winking out of existence. Before he could recover, Greatjon shot from the woods like a bolt of lightning and slammed into him. His green aura burning brightly and violently, Greatjon wrapped Darkon in his strong arms and heaved upward with a twist before slamming the darlion violently to the ground. The earth shattered viciously from the blow, and the song of the Grove seemed to screech and soar painfully out of tune.

Angry dark eyes focused solely on Darkon, Greatjon sprang back from the crater he'd just made and readied his claymore.

Singed, but apparently unharmed, the Warden stood up with an amused laugh. "Oh you two are just a delightful joke," he mocked as he dusted himself off and turned to face Greatjon. "Two Knights think they can simply assault a Warden and get away with it?"

"No," Greatjon growled, "but we can buy enough time for the full wrath of Stelariuos to come down on you." Greatjon almost laughed as the implications registered on Darkon's face. "What do you say," he prodded, "care to push your luck? You may kill one or both of us – but what about two hundred of the finest Gifted? They already dislike you – so how do you think they'll react when they see that not only have you defiled their Ansei Grove, but killed their Knight?"

Darkon scowled and hissed at Greatjon before walking over and picking up the disc that he had dropped. Shattering it on the ground, a glowing blue portal twisted and spun into existence in the air. "You're right – I am outmanned here. And apparently my orders don't mean a damn thing to you all," he spit. "You want Kylir to burn? Then so be it. War is coming – or are you all that ignorant?"

"We're not ignorant, Darkon!" Quinn declared forcefully. "But we can't do things blindly!"

Darkon sneered at Quinn. "You want to do something about the situation and feel like you have some inkling of control over it? Fine! Train the youngling! But know that she needs to be ready, and ready fast. Our enemies are closing in on their objective."

"That's why we have to work as a team!" Greatjon barked.

"Don't you think that's what I've been trying to do?!" Darkon retorted angrily.

"No! You've been trying to be a Light-be-damned emperor again! And that's not how it works!" Quinn raged.

Darkon blinked in shock, the words striking him with a weight he did not expect them to carry. In a low, horse voice, he replied, "You want to prove yourselves to me? Prove yourselves trustworthy again? Train her and have her ready. Our enemies will not wait – and nor will I." Without waiting for a reply, Darkon stepped through the portal and it closed behind him with a bang that rang through the Grove all too ominously for the two Knights.

As soon as the portal vanished, both Quinn and Greatjon let go of the currents and their auras winked out. Both men looked long and hard at each other before Quinn asked, "Are you okay? What you just did–"

"What I just did," Greatjon interrupted as he sheathed his sword, "is protect my friends."

Quinn nodded slowly but gratefully, stating, "Indeed." He sheathed his sword with a snort and shake of his head. "I swear, that bastard probably thinks he was being gracious by giving *us* a second chance."

Greatjon agreed with Quinn, but knew there was no need to express it. Therefore, he reached along his link to his longtime companion and inquired, *"Are you okay, Lina?"*

*"I am – a bit bruised, though."*

*"That was a brave thing you did."*

He could sense the forced laugh from her. *"So you're saying I'm a fool?"*

*"Not in the least, Lina. Not in the least."*

Trotting over to Aseria, Greatjon gently grabbed her by her shoulders and wasn't surprised to feel her trembling violently. Looking down at her, he could see tears streaming down her face. "Are you okay?" he asked softly, even though he already knew the answer.

"Why?" she sorrowfully asked instead, before looking up at him. The depth of pain, fear and confusion he saw in her eyes tore at his heart in a way he never thought possible. Instinctively he pulled her in close and hugged her. The words that slipped from her trembling lips next reflected the question that was torturing his soul. "Why would you serve such a man?" she pleaded softly.

Greatjon wanted to answer; he wanted to scream his rage and confusion, but he couldn't. All he could do was stand there, hold her, and think to himself, *"I don't know."*

Across the clearing, Deralina stared intently at the two, sensing the conflict tearing at Greatjon's soul. She heard his questioning thoughts and sent her equally confused feelings across the link, *"Neither do I, Master. Neither do I."*


With all the Gifted in residence at Sentinel Keep, it wasn't long before the Ansei Grove was swarming with battle-ready troops. Auras flaring brightly, fifty Stelariuos soldiers, with Alsa and her contingent in the lead, poured into the clearing ready for a fight. Instead, they found Quinn, Greatjon and Deralina gathered around Aseria who was cradling Baris' unconscious form.

Poised to fight, Alsa looked absurd in her fine dress, which was further compounded by how quickly her brown eyes widened in shock upon seeing the destruction within the Grove. "Corith be good," she breathed, noting that others around her echoed her sentiment. Recognizing that there was no threat present, her aura winked out as she let go of her power and quickly make her way over to Quinn and Greatjon. "What in Corith's name happened here?" she demanded.

Quinn and Greatjon turned at the insistent question, realizing for the first time that they were not alone. Quinn immediately moved to intercept Alsa while barking, "Stand down, all of you! Everything is fine now! You can return to the keep."

One-by-one, the soldiers released their hold on the currents and their auras went out before they began to trickle back into the tree line.

Seeing that the Indigains had neither released their power nor shown any inclination to move, Quinn fixed Alsa with an unyielding glare and stated sternly, "Alsa. . . ."

Alsa pulled up short at Quinn's tone, taken aback by it, and glared at him before realizing what he meant by it. Turning to her men, Alsa ordered, "Stand down and return to the keep. I'll be fine." The Indigain troops hesitated, prompting Alsa to bark in irritation, "Now!"

There was only a slight hesitation at the more forceful second order before the Indigains' auras winked out and they too retreated.

Sighing in frustration, Alsa swung back to Quinn. "Now – would someone tell me what in the hells happened here?!"

"Darkon happened," Quinn stated in disgust.

"What?" Alsa asked, shock readily apparent in her voice and on her face. She looked around the clearing again and asked, "What do you mean, 'Darkon happened'? And, for that matter, where is he?"

Quinn folded his arms across his chest and stated bluntly, "Our *wise* leader decided that he'd take it upon himself to spirit Aseria away to train her himself."

Alsa's eyes widened in horror. "He did what?"

"Don't worry," Greatjon said from his place next to Aseria. "We stopped him; although we did manage to make a mess of the Grove."

Feeling somewhat overwhelmed by the news, Alsa rubbed her forehead and took a deep breath to gather herself. "So what you're telling me is that Darkon deemed it necessary to whisk the girl away without anyone's permission?" She let out a frustrated huff as Quinn nodded his confirmation. "I– I don't even know where to

596

begin! Despite your dislike of Darkon, I know you're not lying, but I just can't believe . . ." she shook her head and composed herself. "We'll deal with that later. Is Aseria – I believe you said her name was – alright?"

Greatjon snorted and glanced at Aseria who appeared to be oblivious to the conversation. "If you call alright having a revered legend step off the pages of the history books to assault and attempt to kidnap you – then yes, I'd say she's just fine."

Stepping past Quinn, Alsa shot Greatjon a cold glare as she crouched down next to Aseria. "You're sarcasm isn't needed, Greatjon." Softening her voice and forcing a smile, Alsa laid a hand gently on Aseria's shoulder. "Come, child – let's get you out of this cold and away from this mess."

Aseria looked up at Alsa with blank red eyes. "I– . . . I can't leave Baris," she said softly as she stroked his forehead.

"I'll take care of him," Greatjon assured her.

Aseria hesitated before nodding numbly to Greatjon. Gently disengaging herself from Baris, she then let Alsa help her to her feet.

Once Alsa was sure Aseria was steady on her feet, she gave both Greatjon and Quinn stern glares that would have matched the strongest stares of any Warden. "Unlike Darkon, I'm not unwilling to discuss things. We will figure out how to proceed with this girl's training this evening – and I expect both of you to attend. Do we have an accord?"

Both men nodded without hesitation.

"Good." She then placed an arm around Aseria's waist supportively. "Come along, child," she said gently before the two women started toward the path at a slow and steady pace.

Quinn shook his head at their retreating backs before turning to Greatjon. "What a damndable mess we're making. You'd think we would have learned by now to be better than all this."

Greatjon crouched down and gently picked up Baris' unconscious form in his strong arms. Striding past Quinn, he said somberly, "It's only going to get worse."

"Humph! Don't have to tell me," Quinn muttered as he followed Greatjon out of the clearing, the Grove's tearful song accompanying them as if it wept for their situation.

The rest of the day was spent under stressful conditions. Quinn had his hands full trying to calm down his officers, many of whom wanted to kick the Indigains from the keep, while others were calling for a full-fledged manhunt for Darkon. Many of the keep's Gifted could sense the occasional flash of fir'gan as tempers flared within the closed-door meeting. Although Quinn found himself repeatedly agreeing with the motions and arguments put forth, he managed to keep a cool head and did his best to reign in his subordinates. He knew now was not the time for rash and, in all likelihood, foolish actions; however, it was proving a daunting task to convince the others of this, and it took him the better part of the day to steer everyone else around to his point of view.

For Alsa, her day was spent with Aseria. She had led Aseria to the small, elegant chapel on the north side of the keep in the hopes that the sacred place would help to lift Aseria's spirits. For hours, they had sat silently on the pews, bathed in the warm sunlight that poured through the arching windows along the sidewalls, saying nothing to each other. It was anyone's guess as to what thoughts were playing out in Aseria's mind, but Alsa knew it couldn't be anything good. Alsa could barely recall the day her powers had been revealed to her and her illusions about the world had been shattered. As they sat silently in the chapel, she had to wonder if her reaction had been anywhere near as traumatic.

Aseria's beautiful eyes were red from crying and she spent most of her time doubled over, holding herself, rocking gently back-and-forth like a mother trying to sooth a child. She gave no indication that she wanted to talk, which Alsa was somewhat glad for. Not only was she sitting across from the distressed woman who would soon be her new Warden and Preceptor, but she also had her own range of emotions to sort through. Their Order had always maintained a nearly blind faith in whoever led the Wardens, but in the span of a few hours, Darkon had managed to upset that faith and she could only imagine that this was the way the Bestyne and Stelariuos orders felt. The fact that both Orders had managed to deal with their emotions for as long as they had was both admirable and mystifying. Looking at Aseria's distraught face, which desperately cried out for answers and assuagement, Alsa had little doubt that their Order would soon join the others on Darkon's bad side – and she wasn't so sure that was a bad thing.

The rest of Greatjon's day started with a hasty trip to the medics where he turned Baris over to their expert care. After a quick examination, they assured him that Baris was simply unconscious and would be just fine. Greatjon initially remained by his side, determined to be there when he awoke; however, it quickly became apparent he wouldn't do so anytime soon. Feeling somewhat irritated and impatient, he excused himself and began to wander the keep.

Alone with his somber feelings – as Deralina had chosen to remain within the comforting confines of the Ansei Grove – he wandered aimlessly for hours before finding himself in the lower levels of the keep. How or why he came to be there did not really matter to him; the fact that he came to a halt in that particular room spoke volumes about his emotional state. Located deep beneath the keep, the room remained a comfortable temperature year-round. The room was fifty paces long and fifty wide, yet it seemed so much larger than that. Black stone walls climbed upward to a vaulted ceiling lost in the shadows, while low hanging arches, which were visible in the light cast by the torches set in sconces along the walls, acted as a false ceiling. Standing just inside the room's lone ironwood door, Greatjon stared at the object that occupied the opposite end of the room.

Evenly laid stairs provided access to a six foot tall, round dais of black stone that sat within a pool of light cast by candelabras arranged around its perimeter. Atop the platform sat an inverted-horseshoe-shaped Portculim like the one he had used to escape the North, its face adorned with a beautiful spider web of creeping runes. A gem box like the one he had removed from the gate in the North was attached to its right side, the multicolored rows of gems glowing dully in the torchlight. To the untrained eye, each Portculim would seem to be identical, but to those versed in their usage, there were characteristics that made each gate unique to its location. The more subtle differences could be found in the slight variations of the runes on the face of each Portculim. But if one was seeking an obvious difference, then it was to be found in the crystal that was inset at the apex of the arch. Where the Portculim in the North was adorned with a blue crystal, this gate had a red one.

Firelight danced in the dark pools of his eyes as he stared intently at the Portculim. He very much wanted to return to his home, retrieve what was left of the Bestyne Order and lead them against Warrick in a campaign of bloody revenge. There was a sick, almost euphoric thrill that he got from engaging in combat, and he knew it was wrong to feel that way. But when it came to Warrick – the man responsible for so many tragedies in his life – it seemed that giving in to his rage and indulging that euphoric thrill was the only way to deal with him. Yet, if there was anything to take from Darius' teachings, it was the ability to push one's personal feelings aside and attend to one's duties first – and Greatjon liked to think he had learned that lesson well. So while it disgusted him to swallow his pride, he knew there were more important matters at hand. Not only did Aseria need training, but Darius' crystal needed a new owner. Those two issues needed his attention now, but when he had concluded that business. . . .

Scowling at the Portculim, Greatjon turned his back on it and left the room, closing the door gently. *"All in due time, Warrick. . . . All in due time,"* he thought as he ascended back to the main floor.

That evening, the three Knights met in one of the reading rooms in the library. Despite being tired and worn out from the day's happenings, they were ready to attend to the matters at hand. The simple room they occupied was quite cozy – a plain table with four chairs occupied the center of the room, an empty bookcase stood next to the closed door, and the small hearth built into the right-hand wall held a warm fire, though none of the occupants needed it for warmth.

Alsa, still dressed in her finery, stood facing her counterparts as she reviewed all that had happened lately with the Indigain Order, the events of the past few months as she understood it, and how Aseria was doing. She could tell that she was boring the two men – the hint of irritation in Quinn's eyes were a clear indicator of that – and as she brought her speech to an end, she fixed them with a brown-eyed, pensive stare. "Have I left anything out?" she asked in mild annoyance as she folded her hands before her at her waist.

Greatjon, seated with his back to the fire and with a stoic expression on his face, shook his head, the firelight casting his rust-orange-haired head in shadows. "No. As usual, Alsa, you have your facts straight. The problem with all this is that we do not appear to be in good shape. Our losses have been staggering over the years and, from what everyone seems to be able to tell, the Darkness appears to be growing in strength."

"Indeed," she said, biting her lower lip. "Quite frankly, I'm shocked to hear that blackhearts are loose on Kylir again. I thought them exterminated long ago."

Seated to Greatjon's left, Quinn replied, anger flashing in his eyes and adding a quiver to his voice, "We all did. I wouldn't have believed it if Darkon had been the only one to mention it, but the stories we heard from Blackstone's survivors and Greatjon's visual confirmation can't be ignored. There are nests somewhere . . . and I fear we've only seen the tip of the spear."

Alsa began to pace, the rustling of her green dress a mild, rhythmic irritation to the others. "So – we have those vermin running loose with no idea where their nests might be, we've managed to lose

600

two Wardens in a span of weeks, and we're left with a child to train. Am I correct?"

"Indeed," Quinn said, and both Alsa and Greatjon couldn't help but hear a bit of Damion in the simple remark.

"So, the crux of the situation is at hand," Alsa stated as she stopped her pacing and took a seat at the table. "The training of the child. I don't have to tell you both that she falls under the protection of the Indigain Order," she stated firmly.

Both Quinn and Greatjon looked at each other apprehensively before Greatjon answered, "No, you don't."

"Good. However, I'm not Darkon; and if you swear that Darius asked you to watch over and train her, Greatjon – I'll believe you." There was a hint of sadness in her eyes as she spoke that hinted at something deeper than merely discussing Aseria's fate.

Greatjon knew that look, and replied gently but firmly, "Aye, Alsa, he did put her in my charge. By blood, by honor and by deed – I swear it."

Alsa took a deep breath and let it out slowly to compose herself. "Very well, then. I am willing to let you join us at the Indigain compound to train her under our supervision." She didn't miss the look of hesitation that came over Greatjon at her statement. "What is it now?"

Greatjon leaned forward and rested his forearms on the table. "I don't know if that will be possible."

"Why not?" Alsa asked, a dash of suspicious anger in her voice.

Greatjon grimaced at her tone before stating, "I'll be the first to admit my faith in Darkon has been shaken greatly, but I certainly cannot deny that he is right about one thing – things are getting worse, and I get the feeling that we won't be able to simply watch from afar for much longer. Warrick and the blackhearts are proof of that."

"Get to the point, Greatjon," Alsa urged in irritation.

Sighing, he continued. "I don't think we've got the time for traditional training. I fear that we need to train her in a matter of months or – Corith forbid – weeks instead of years." He paused to let the implications sink in before adding, "We have no idea how long it will take to find replacements for our fallen Wardens, and it's damn apparent that our enemies aren't going to wait for us. The more fully trained Wardens we have, the better our chances of meeting whatever is to come."

Alsa gave a disgusted huff before replying angrily, "So you think one more Warden – a young one at that – will make a difference? We rush her training, and it's likely we'll be herding her headlong to her death. Look at how easily Blackstone fell! Their power seems to be growing while our numbers fade and we bicker amongst ourselves!"

Greatjon snarled at the mention of Blackstone, but before he could say anything, Quinn jumped in to cut off any damaging remarks. "Watch your tongue, Alsa," he warned sternly. "Blackstone was not only undermanned, but Darius was sick and the keep flooded with refugees. Greatjon did the best he could, but under those circumstances, it would have taken someone willing to see the majority of the civilians slaughtered to have a hope of keeping Blackstone from Warrick."

Alsa looked at him dubiously. "Either way, it goes without saying that the Darkness is spreading quickly and in places we cannot see. Mat and Kara should be recalled instead of out doing the job of Seekers."

Both men nodded their agreement. "I can't disagree with you on that, but we can only hope," Quinn chuckled as he shook his head in disgust, "*hope* that Darkon knows what he is doing. If he sent those two to find the crystals' new owners, then I hope he has his reasons. Besides, in that constant warzone, they're bound to encounter fighting, and Seekers are much easier to kill." He stretched his neck, the vertebrae popping loudly. "Darkon aside, I trust Kara and Mat can do the job and do it quickly."

They sat in silence for a while as the implications and repercussions of all the events settled in their minds.

Staring intently at her folded hands, Alsa finally broke the silence. "I don't like any of this one bit."

"None of us do," Quinn agreed.

Alsa looked up and met Greatjon's brown eyes. "She won't have a full comprehension of what all this is about – and Corith only knows how her powers may develop – but if you believe she needs to be trained that quickly, then we'll need to go somewhere we can push her training without fear of injuring innocents." She cocked an eyebrow at him. "I trust you've thought this out beyond this conversation?"

Greatjon nodded. "Aye, Alsa, I have. None of you may like this, and I know Darkon sure as hells won't."

Quinn grinned, "That might be the best reason to do what you have in mind."

"Where do you want to take her?" Alsa demanded.

"Gray Sky," Greatjon said bluntly.

Both Alsa and Quinn were taken aback by the statement. Quinn let out a low whistle and said, "You weren't kidding when you said it would piss Darkon off."

"Gray Sky," Alsa echoed. "Why there?"

Greatjon shrugged. "It's out of the way, for one. There's only a few people still in residence, which means there less chance of something foolish happening to bystanders."

Alsa thought on it hard, her brow furrowed in concentration. "It's not the place I would have thought of first . . . but then again, you are right – it provides what we need and," she smiled weakly, "it might just keep Darkon out of our hair. Corith knows he hates that place." She paused. "One other thing – I'll be going with you. I can't have her being trained by a Bestyne brute without someone there to add a bit of culture and proper behavior to the mix."

Greatjon nodded. "I won't fight you on that."

"Good." She turned her focus to Quinn. "Not to wish any bad luck upon you, but can you hold here if you're attacked?"

"Oh we'll hold," Quinn replied with a vicious grin. "And if we can't, then whoever is foolish enough to fight us will come away so bloodied they won't even think about a fight somewhere else."

Alsa nodded and stood up. "Well then, gentlemen, we've all had a very long day, and with longer ones to come. Sleep would be a nice thing, don't you think? If you'll excuse me." Nodding slightly to them, she quickly made her way out of the room before either man could say anything else.

"You think she'll be alright?"

"Don't know, Quinn. Darius meant a lot to her. For now, she'll have to concentrate on the tasks at hand."

"That's cold," Quinn chided.

Greatjon nodded. "I know, but that's the way it'll have to be for now."

"Ha! You're just glad to have found someone who can hate Warrick as much as you do."

Greatjon shrugged. "Is that so bad?" Rubbing his eyes, he added, "I'm gonna get some sleep now. See you in the morning."

Standing, he moved to the door where he halted and turned back to Quinn. "One more thing – I think we should get Caldain on his way tomorrow."

"Agreed. No time like the present, eh?"

Nodding in agreement, Greatjon said, "Good night," before opening the door and exiting the room, leaving Quinn alone with the fire and his own thoughts.

"Alsa! Stop for a moment," Greatjon called out as he hustled to catch up with the Indigain general and Knight.

Pausing in the empty hallway outside the library, she turned around. "What is it, Greatjon? I really must get some sleep," she replied in exasperation.

Greatjon approached her and asked, "Let me walk with you?"

Alsa nodded her consent and they continued on.

They made their way through the nearly empty halls – most of the keep's inhabitants having taken to their beds hours ago – in silence. Finally, her irritation with the day's events got the better of her, and Alsa brought them to an abrupt halt in the center of the hall. Turned to Greatjon, she demanded, "What do you want? I can't believe you just wanted to escort me to my room."

Greatjon sighed and met her eyes. "I wanted to say that I'm sorry about Darius," he apologized gently.

Alsa laughed, but he could see her emotional dam break as tears started to well up in her eyes. "Sorry, Greatjon? What do you have to be sorry about? Could you have stopped the blackheart that wounded him when you weren't even there? No, you couldn't! But you could have stopped Blackstone from being taken, Greatjon! You could have stopped that!"

Greatjon met the statement with silence, and the pity that Alsa read on Greatjon's face was the blow that broke her restraints. As the tears began to run down her cheeks, she railed at him, "Damn you! You had the strength to stop the invaders! You should have stopped them!" She accented her point with a slap to Greatjon's face, the rings on her fingers biting hard, but doing little more than leaving red welts on his cheek.

Accepting the blow stoically, he then looked around to see if anyone was about. Thankful that no one had witnessed the outburst, he leaned into Alsa and growled, "Now that that is out of your system, listen closely. There was nothing I could do – and Corith knows

I wish I could have done more than I did. It is the second time in my life that I've witnessed my home's destruction! Don't you think I wanted to do something to stop that bastard?"

Alsa's puffy eyes glared back at him defiantly, refusing to believe him. "You had Darius' men at your command! You could have stopped them!"

Pushing aside the indignation that was threatening to well up at her accusations, Greatjon placed his hands gently on Alsa's shoulders. "We were facing an army of blackhearts, and his men were tired from fighting and protecting the refugees over the months that the invaders moved in on them. Warrick was damn determined to destroy that place, and they were in no shape to oppose him. Had it just been me that I had to worry about, then maybe I could have done it; but Darius gave me a mission of far greater importance, and like him, I wasn't about to risk the lives of the innocent simply to save a castle." Greatjon knew his words were only a comforting half-truth; they both knew that without a crusader, and in those conditions, the odds of Greatjon killing Warrick were minuscule at best.

Alsa blinked a couple of times and sniffed once. "Warrick? Why would he—" she started to ask as if it was the first time she'd heard his name mention in relation to Blackstone.

"To hurt me," Greatjon explained, realizing that the day's events and Alsa's own turbulent emotions were clouding her thinking. "To hurt Darius. To sate his bloodlust. The bastard has never needed a reason to destroy things!" he growled in anger.

Alsa, her mind clearing of its sorrowful haze, saw the pain in Greatjon's eyes for the first time and felt ashamed for having been so selfish. "Oh, Greatjon, I'm so sorry. I had no idea. I was selfish to think Darius' loss didn't hurt others as much as it did me."

He shook his head. "No, Alsa, you have every right to be selfish. I know you loved him deeply. His feelings for you may never have been the same, but I know—"

Alsa held up a restraining hand. "Don't. . . . Just . . . don't. I know where his heart belonged, and that caused more pain for Darkon than it ever did for me." Fresh tears began to slide from her eyes. "I'm sorry – please excuse me." Without worrying about who might be looking or who she might run into, she gathered her skirts and fled down the hall before vanishing around the corner.

Greatjon sighed. Sleep suddenly had little appeal to him. With his thoughts turned inward, he made his way back to the main level and outside into the cold, lonely night.

Morning came too soon for many of the inhabitants of Sentinel Keep. While Alsa's contingent reluctantly assembled and departed for home on her orders, the Indigain Knight and general spent the morning in reflection within the keep's chapel. As for her troubled, soon-to-be Warden, Aseria had struggled through a night of fitful and unfulfilling sleep. So with the first light of dawn, Aseria made her way to Baris' room where she sat in silent vigil at her unconscious friend's side.

Then there was Greatjon and Quinn. Though still thoroughly disturbed by the previous day's events, they were well aware that the long road ahead of them would begin that morning with a very simple but significantly important task. So after a quiet breakfast, the two gathered in the shadow of the Portculim.

Dressed in a loose white tunic, brown breeches and black boots, Greatjon examined the Portculim with dark eyes that seemed as cold as the air about him. As he studied the gate, his thoughts turned to the North and he smiled inwardly. He now had an ally, although tentative at best, against Warrick should he need it. But as he squeezed the pouch at his waist, the crystals that resided within biting into his hand, he understood that there were more important matters to attend to at that moment.

Quinn, adorned in full armor and with his longsword firmly set between his shoulders, was just as thoughtful as his friend. Noticing Greatjon's gesture and pensive face, Quinn pushed his own concerns aside and placed a comforting hand on his friend's shoulder. "Everything alright?"

"Tell me," Greatjon asked solemnly, "do you think we'll win?" He pulled the gray crystal from the pouch at his belt and held it before his dark-brown eyes.

Quinn crossed his arms, a dry smirk on his delicate, slim face. "Should I believe otherwise?"

"I don't know," confessed Greatjon with a shrug of his shoulders. "So much has gone wrong so fast."

Quinn fixed him with a worried gaze that eerily remind Greatjon of Darius when he was about to give a lecture that was meant to be reassuring. "My friend, let me tell you this – the moment we start believing we're beaten, we lose. Period. It won't matter how many men or Wardens or tricks we have – we'll lose because men like you and me start to believe we can't win." He reached up and took the crystal from him. "We all know how much Darius meant to you and how much you want Warrick dead, but don't let that cloud your thinking. As long as we still live, we'll stand against the tide that approaches, and we will prevail because we have people like you at our side."

Greatjon smirked. "You sound like Damion."

Quinn cracked a grin. "I know – it's amazing how much you begin to talk and act like someone after years with them. As for this," he tossed the crystal in the air and caught it deftly, "we should find it a new home." He then shouted over his shoulder toward the open door, "Forsandi! Stop lurking about!"

Caldain Forsandi, Captain of the Guard and Seeker, turned out to be the tall one with the waist-length, braided black hair that had escorted the Indigains into the keep the previous morning. He was dressed nearly identical to Quinn, and had a similar longsword seated between his shoulders. A large dagger hung upside down on the right side of the breastplate of his battle-harness, and the hilts of two boot knives jutted from their sheaths along the sides of his knee-boots. Cold gray eyes watched keenly from his hawkish face, a trio of scars running from hairline to jaw over his right eye. He carried a small, travel-worn pack, and walked with a long, smooth stride that gave the impression that he thought himself lord of Sentinel Keep.

Coming to a halt in front Greatjon and Quinn, he suddenly cracked a smile and embraced Greatjon fiercely before pulling away. "It's been a long time, old friend! Sorry we hadn't gotten much of a chance to speak since you got here," the light, almost cocky undertone of his voice seeming at odds with his intimidating exterior.

"Well, well. . . . I must say that the years have been kind to you, Old Hawk," Greatjon replied with a smile he did not feel.

"The same to you, Old Wolf. Too bad about Darius; I was hoping we could share a bottle of Velusyian Blue when this whole damn mess was over with."

Greatjon nodded solemnly as Quinn presented Caldain with the crystal. He knew all too well that Caldain's light, remorseful tone reflected more regret than the way it sounded.

"Damn," Caldain breathed with a low whistle as he accepted the crystal. "I never would have thought I'd be Searching this particular crystal." He smiled and laughed softly. "I always kinda thought Darius was truly immortal." Sighing, he pulled an opalescent bone coffer, which was just large enough for the crystal, from a pouch at his hip. Opening it, he gently placed the crystal inside before securing the lid and returning the coffer to the same pouch.

Turning a sly grin on Greatjon, Caldain quipped, "Too bad you can't come with me, Old Wolf. We could drink, whore and raise hells like the old days."

Greatjon laughed and shook his head. "I went respectable a long time ago. Remember? Besides, I've got a Warden to train and a bull to gut."

Caldain shrugged his shoulders. "Just as well. You're needed here while the others play. Don't worry though – when we get the chance, we'll see Warrick hung by his toes from Blackstone's walls."

Greatjon nodded. "I'll hold you to it. So, what direction?"

Caldain closed his eyes and opened himself to the fir'gan about them before letting his senses join with the heartbeat of the crystal. "South," he said after a moment. Opening his eyes, he added, "Solac is as far as I can follow it. I should get a better look from there, though."

Greatjon nodded, turned to the Portculim and keyed a sequence into the box. Red tendrils of fir'gan began to climb up the archway, lighting up the runes as they traveled toward the red crystal set at the Portculim's apex. As soon as the energy reached the crystal, it flared brightly and shot a ribbon of power toward the ground. Upon making contact with the dais, the ribbon of energy then spiraled outward to fill the arch.

"Be careful," Greatjon warned as he turned to face Caldain. "If they sense you Searching, their people will be all over you. We're way too low on manpower to lose your experience."

Caldain clapped Greatjon on the shoulder. "Don't get all teary eyed on me. I know one or two people I can call on to watch my back."

Greatjon clasped Caldain's forearm. "Get going – we don't know how much time we've got, and the sooner you find that crystal a new home, the better. May Corith guide you well, my friend."

Caldain nodded to Greatjon and then turned and saluted Quinn. "Keep the Old Wolf out of trouble, will you? Or do I need to pull age on you?" he asked with a wry grin.

Quinn laughed and returned the salute. "I still have rank on you, Caldain, but I'll do my best to keep him from getting skinned."

Caldain nodded again, the same wry smile still on his face, and secured his pack before striding through the portal. The red energy closed quickly behind him with a loud bang, leaving Greatjon and Quinn in a pool of light surrounded by darkness.

# Chapter Twenty-Seven

*T*here were stars in the sky – which she found odd given the cold rain that threatened to soak her and her two companions despite their reed umbrellas. She looked up from where she walked between her guardians and tried to make out their faces. For some reason, their features were concealed by impenetrable shadows; however, she knew that it was her brothers that walked beside her by the large, strong hands that held her small and delicate ones. With childlike curiosity, she peered into the rainy darkness on either side of the muddy street. To her surprise, she found that she could make out very little except for the occasional paper lantern hanging from an overhang, and a few eyes that peered from between the slats of the numerous windows lining the street. The unabashed, lustful hunger she saw in the eyes made her cringe even though the implications were lost on her young mind. With fear beginning to stir in her belly, she did her best to tuck herself close to her oldest brother in a vain attempt to hide herself from the prying eyes.

A disarming laugh echoed down from the shadows that hid her brother's face. "Don't fret, it will all be okay soon," came the supposedly reassuring comment, but the coldness with which it was spoken only alarmed her even more.

She shuffled her little feet to her right, closer to her other brother. No words of comfort came from him; instead, she felt an eerie warmth emanating from him that was both frightening and soothing at the same time. As they plodded down the dark alley for what seemed like an eternity, she remained by his side, her apprehension growing with each passing moment and setting her small heart aflutter in a terrifying manner. Then, without warning, they came to a halt.

Peering into the darkness in front of them to see what had caused the sudden stop, she heard her oldest brother declare, "We're here."

As if the words were the cue, the darkness in front of them suddenly parted, revealing the two-story Lalashia House. She tried to scream as the implications of it all settled in, but it felt like someone had stuffed a rag in her mouth. To her horror, the occupants of the house began to materialize out of the shadows. They appeared to be women until she looked closer, and that only made her want to scream louder. Every one of the women was practically naked, their dry skin pulled so taunt over their skeletal frames that it appeared as if their flesh would tear at the slightest movement. Their sky-blue hair was limp and ratty, and their eyes were nothing but dark sockets over thin-lipped, drawn mouths. There was nothing alluring about any of them, yet they did their best to strike sexually provocative poses that fell far short of their mark.

*A heavy, bloated figure in a rich giku separated from the shadows and came forward, her sickly skin shinning unwholesomely in the rain. Like her brothers, the face of the woman was hidden in shadows, but she knew that the disgusting . . . thing in front of her was the Matron of the House.*

*"Katoroshi doesta, keta?" questioned the Matron.*

*The girl blinked, shocked to hear ancient Velusyian being spoken for some reason.*

*"Haisa, Nobutisha," her older brother confirmed.*

*Panic set in as the bulbous Matron leaned down to stare directly into her eyes. Although she could not see the Matron's face, she could sense the wide grin.*

*"Oh, you'll be a lovely one won't you?" the sudden shift to the Trader's Tongue shocked the girl again. "You'll have the looks of a siren, breasts that will cause men to stop and stare, and hips that will make men and women's loins ache with desire. Oh yes," the Matron purred as she tapped the girl's wrists, then her neck and forehead, each tap leaving behind golden circlets connected to each other by golden chains, "they will come and pay handsomely to ravage you and defile you – and you'll love it and beg for it, and be just as happy as all my other lovelies. And when your other gifts bloom, no woman will be your equal." The Matron stood up and motioned to the other women. "Isn't that right?"*

*She tried to scream as her brothers' hands faded away and the horrific forms of the other women began to close in on her. "Join us," they hissed with a mix of ecstasy and revulsion. "Be usssss. . . . Feeeed usss. . . ."*

*As she looked on in dumbstruck horror, she felt a thick fluid begin to flow from her eyes and nose. Reaching up, she rubbed at the substance and brought her trembling hand in front of her eyes. Thick, dark-red blood coated her tiny hand like a glove. Eyes widening in horror, she was finally able to scream. . .*

.

Nearly as pale as the sheets she was sleeping on, Kara bolted upright in bed, her chest heaving violently and her normally vibrant sky-blue eyes feverish with terror. Drenched with sweat, her smallclothes and sky-blue hair clung to her as if she had just finished a hard day's work. A sudden sensation of cold cut through the panic gripping her heart and mind like a dragon's fist just enough for her to realized that she was shivering. Pulling the threadbare blankets about her with trembling hands, she focused on her surroundings in an attempt to anchor her mind to reality.

The room she was in was very small, with just enough space for the simple bed she occupied, a chair in the middle of the room, the washstand on the far wall, and a chamber pot beneath the closed window from which cold air seeped in. As she drew in deep breaths

610

to steady her breathing, she realized that a portion of the roar filling her ears belonged to the raucous crowd that occupied the tavern on the ground floor of the inn. A few steadying breaths later, the rest of the roar gave way to the gentle rhythm of rain dancing on the roof.

*"It's okay, Kara, you're in an inn,"* she told herself as she closed her eyes and took a deep breath. *"Thank Corith, it was just a dream. . . . A damndable, horrible dream,"* she thought as she let the breath out.

Halfway through the slow exhale, a violent coughing fit overcame her and she doubled over from the force of it, her long-fingered hand darting to her mouth. As soon as the coughing fit passed, she opened her eyes and – to her horror – found her hand covered in thick, dark-red blood . . . just as it had been in the dream. Eyes wide with shock and terror, she disentangled herself from the blankets and stumbled over to the washstand. Hastily filling the ragged, cheap ceramic basin from the equally dilapidated pitcher, she washed her face with her clean hand. Then, with dark, watery blood dripping from her chin, she submerged her bloody hand in the tepid water before taking control of the currents of fir'gan and heating the liquid. Instantly, steam erupted from the basin and the water began to boil violently.

The water was quickly clouded with blood, preventing her from seeing her hand. Unaware that it was already clean, she continued to heat the water until the skin on her hand began to pinken painfully. With the horrific images from the dream assaulting her mind and making it difficult to think straight, she refused to let go of the currents and, instead, fed her fears and anxiety into the boiling water. She could feel the skin on her hand began to split and peal, pouring fresh blood into the boiling basin; yet she still pressed on, her mind telling her that she could burn away the horrid images and the nightmarish memories that had been conjured. As a torrent of heat and steam poured from the bowl, cracks began to crawl across the basin like a terrified spider hastily spinning a web. Suddenly, there was a loud crack and the basin shattered, spraying superheated, blood-soaked water everywhere.

Suppressing a cry of pain, Kara stumbled back from the shattered basin and collapsed on the floor, cradling her bloodied, flesh-deprived hand to her chest. Tears streaming down her cheeks, she held the traumatized hand before her and let out a sob of anguish as she realized the horrific pain she was feeling wasn't from her heartache, but from the exposed muscles of her bloody hand. Only through centuries of training and her connection to fir'gan was she able to avoid shock and unconsciousness from such a grievous wound. With monumental effort, she disconnected her mind from the pain and turned her thoughts inward, opening herself to both the currents about her and her inner wellspring of fir'gan. Suddenly calm from the detachment, she watched as the ethereal blue currents of fir'gan began to flow from her heart and down her arm. Reaching her wrist, her fir'gan then joined with the currents flowing about her before enveloping her mauled hand with the gentleness of a cloud settling on a field. The blood flow stopped immediately and – in a display few had ever witness – she watched as the damaged muscles and veins began to grow back, weaving their way from her wrist, over her palm and down her fingers. Virgin flesh followed, blossoming from her wrist to enshroud the regenerated tissue. Wanting no scars from the accident, she held on to the currents even after her new fingernails had hardened, allowing the currents to eradicate every trace of the self-inflected horror.

As soon as the skin on her hand had darkened to match the rest of her, she let go of the currents and simply sat in silence for a time, doing her best to organize her thoughts. She had known since her fainting spell in the cave that she was ill, and she had her fears about what it was – after all, Gifted rarely got sick, and most Wardens could not remember the last time they had fallen ill. But when things had not gotten significantly worse, she had hoped she was beginning to recover. That horrific dream, however. . . . She shuddered and hugged herself. No, the sickness was spreading and twisting her dreams. Not only that, but the symptoms were looking more and more like blackheart poisoning. She knew she hadn't been injured in the grove when she had met with Darkon and Mat, otherwise she would have fallen ill and likely died long ago; therefore, she believed the source of the miasma had to be something . . . someone else – and that thought terrified her more than the illness itself. It was one thing if she was wounded, but it was entirely another thing for it to be someone else – someone she loved – that suffered.

"Damn," she muttered, her beautiful voice weak from the strain of the dream and injury, before slowly climbing to her feet and shuffling over to the washbasin again.

Stripping herself of her soiled smallclothes, she then picked up the pitcher and dumped the remaining water over her head. She let herself feel the now tepid water, which raised chill bumps along her skin and drew a gasp from her. Though not cold, the sudden change in temperature was refreshing and seemed to help scare away some of the darker thoughts creeping about the fringes of her mind.

"One thing at a time, Kara," she admonished herself.

With her color returning somewhat to normal, she quickly raised the temperature of the air around her and dried herself and her soaked surroundings off before padding over to the foot of the bed. Crouching, she pushed aside a new pair of supple, knee-high boots – which were adorned with steel caps on the heels and toes – and reached under the bed. Grasping about blindly for a moment, she finally found what she was looking for and pulled forth a spacious, brand-new pack that was filled with provisions she had purchased for her and Mat. Opening the pack, she found herself once again grateful for Mathis' suggestions, which had been invaluable in helping them obtain quality goods without digging too deeply into their stash of talons. Inside, along with her tanto, were numerous paper-wrapped bundles that contained clothes, trail food, and items like medical supplies to keep up appearances. She pulled out the two largest packages and tossed them on the bed before retrieving her tanto from the pack. Standing, she cut the strings on the bundles and unwrapped them before laying out the items they contained.

Winter was rapidly closing its fist on Triclose, so she had purchased appropriately according to her tastes. She first removed a long-sleeved shirt – which the locals had dubbed a turtleneck – of warm black cotton, followed by a sleeveless, low-cut red tunic. She then unwrapped a decorative black bodice, which was slit vertically in numerous places for flexibility, that was secured up its front by silver buckles. Next came a pair of black breeches that were decorated with silver knotwork down the sides, and then a pair of leather bracers and matching sword belt, both of which were adorned with silver knotwork as well.

"No, Kara, you won't standout at all in this," She chided with a roll of her eyes before retrieving fresh smallclothes from the pack. "Can't just wear a dress like all the other ladies," she muttered as she began to change.

Quickly donning the new clothing, she found herself impressed with the tailor who had made the items. Only quick, minor alterations had been needed, and the result was an outfit that fit like a second skin. She flexed and stretched to make sure there was plenty of room to move and, if necessary, fight in. Satisfied, she pulled out a spool of dark-lavender silk ribbon and unwound it to the right length before cutting it with her tanto. Letting the spool and short blade drop to the bed, she then did something that she had not done in a long time. In her early, darker days as a young girl, she had employed her connection to fir'gan for the mundane purpose of styling her hair. Not only had this exercise provided a way to practice her control, but it had always served to sooth her thoughts. And after the nightmare and the bout of self-mutilation, it suddenly seemed the right thing to do.

Reaching out to the ethereal tendrils of blue light, she used them to pick up the ribbon and to remove the tangles from her hip-length hair. As soon as that was done, she let her bangs frame her face before further using the currents to gathered the rest of her thick mass of hair into three substantial strands. She then shifted the ribbon behind her and, with the grace and deftness of an expert weaver, began to weave. Kara's eyes slowly closed and a small smile parted her lips as she felt her hair pull and shift, her old habits guiding the currents of fir'gan in her task. When she was done, her hair had been interwoven with the lavender ribbon into a long, thick braid.

Suddenly feeling relaxed – though the dark thoughts were still lurking about – Kara smiled softly. "Not bad, if I do say so myself," she said into the air.

She then sighed as her eyes settled on her gently curving katana sitting in the corner of the room. There was a letter tucked into its scabbard that she had received two days ago from Mathis, and she had no doubt that the correspondence was responsible for digging up the old memories that had violently conquered her dreams. Walking over to the sword, she picked it up and gently unsheathed it a few inches so she could retrieve the neatly folded note. Returning her katana to the corner, she then unfolded the note and read it again, her face growing hard as she examined it.

*Kara,*

*I know there is more going on here than either of us think. We need to talk – and soon. I will be training Amroth two days hence at the Citadel. The room is private. Please come and ask for me. I will leave orders to have you escorted to me.*

*–Mathis*

It wasn't the content of the letter that bothered her, for she knew that Mathis might have news that she was not privy to, and in turn, Mathis would want to know why she was sneaking around behind Darkon's back by sending Emberscar to Triclose. What bothered her about the note was the handwriting. She had read many correspondences from Damion that Mathis had penned, as well as personal letters, and she knew Mathis' handwriting quite well. To her chagrin, the curves and swells of the writing in the missive weren't his. In fact, they reminded her of someone born and raised in Velusyia. The mere thought of what this could mean infuriated her. If what she believed was true, then it meant she had been lied to for a very long time . . . and she didn't like being lied to – especially by family.

Crumpling the note up, she incinerated it quickly before letting the ash fall to the ground. Snatching up her katana and tanto, she hung them from her belt at her right hip. "Well, Brother," she said aloud as she tied off the last knot, "if it is you . . . let's see what you have to say for yourself."

Pulling a brand-new forest-green cloak from the pack, she slung it over her shoulders and secured it with a simple clip. Steeling herself, she opened the door and stepped out into the hallway, slamming the door behind her.

The common room was full that rainy late afternoon. Sailors, dockworkers, laborers, and even a handful of prostitutes packed the small tavern to the bursting point. From conversations to curses and laughter, everyone contributed to the menagerie of noise that assaulted their ears, threatening to make it impossible to understand someone sitting at the same table. Smoke from the patrons' pipes conspired with the fire burning in a hearth on the far right wall – which was in desperate need of repair – to hang about their heads like a dark fog. A heady and somewhat acrid combination of aromas, some of which originated from the alcohol and greasy food that was being consumed, was nearly as thick as the smoke and battered one's nose without remorse.

As far as the spindly old innkeeper was concerned, the atmosphere was tiring but wonderful. Dressed in an apron that seemed excessively big for him, his mood was jovial as he orchestrated the madness from behind the bar. Despite how hectic it was, he shared jokes, laughter and curses as freely as his patrons, all the while ensuring that the drinks flowed as quickly and freely as the talons he pocketed.

For Mat, it was like home and he loved it. Kara had taken it upon herself to attend to their supply needs over the first few days in Haltho, which left Mat with plenty of free time on his hands. They had chosen a run-down inn – known as the Sailor's Roost – in the Tradesmen's Terrace so they could listen to the rumors and news swirling about Triclose without fear of people watching their words like they might have in one of the more upscale establishments within the city. Mat had embraced the task of immersing himself in the crowds, his pouch filled with plenty of talons for lip-loosening drink, and his ears ready to listen.

That afternoon, dressed in a loose-fitting blue shirt that was tucked into black pants which were a match in color to his boots and bracers, he sat at a small, corner table in the shadow of the staircase that led to the second floor rooms. A small pile of talons occupied the center of the table as he and his two companions were engaged in a game of Pentagris. It was similar to a game he played religiously at

615

home called Death's Deceit, but instead of the five five-sided celums he held now, there would normally be ten in a hand and a smaller stack of chance celums. Furthermore, Death's Deceit also made use of dice to determine everything from the celum one played, to multiplying the current bet. Other than that, the rules were relatively the same – each player had a hand of celums painted with images and numbers from the six Houses; during each hand, wagers are made before each player places one celum face down from their hand; players then flip the facedown celums over at the same time to reveal their play, with the highest or strongest celum wining the hand. It was an engaging game, requiring concentration and excellent bluffing skills. Though, on this afternoon Mat's thoughts were far from the game and focused more on the talk he had heard over the last few days, as well as the chatter his fir'gan-enhanced hearing was picking out of the dull roar of the common room.

For the most part, the chatter was typical banter; there was talk about the weather, cost of food and supplies, the status of the war, and even a new rumor of a House Suldamik marriage – though to which house was anyone's guess. Then there was the talk that troubled Mat the most. They had heard similar gossip while on the road from where they had shipwrecked, but the constant chatter Mat had heard while visiting the taverns – and even a quaint brothel called the Dirty Pillows that his new friends had recommended to him – was beginning to sound more and more like blackhearts were present on Triclose. Granted, he lacked first-hand experience with the creatures, but he knew enough to understand what the rumors implied.

While the thought of blackhearts on the prowl was troubling enough, Kara's health was quickly becoming of greater concern. Ever since she passed out in the shelter, she had been acting more like she was truly sick, and she had recently become oddly aloof. He didn't know how much of her withdrawal from him had to do with his displeasure at learning of Emberscar's presence on Triclose, or if it was a result of what appeared to be a growing illness. If her behavior had anything to do with his displeasure, then that was something he could handle. Illness, on the other hand. . . . He couldn't remember ever hearing of a Warden becoming sick except for blackheart poisoning; and if somehow that was the case. . . .

"Eh, lad – it's your play," an old, grizzled voice quipped.

Mat blinked his black eyes and looked at the aged, leathery-skinned old man sitting alongside a portly fellow with piggish features. Though they wore loose wool clothing akin to what most of the dock workers were wearing to ward off the cold, Mat had learned that they both served in House Trivant's House Guard, which – through care-

616

ful manipulation – had made them a wonderful source of information. Three empty bottles of such manipulation already sat on the table with an order for a fresh one still unfulfilled.

"It is? Sorry, Leathers, I must have drifted off," Mat offered the smoothly voiced, halfhearted apology with a wry smile.

Leathers ran a gnarled hand over his shaved head and snorted. "Hells' bloody balls! You'd think I'd lost me silver tongue!" He turned his small green eyes on his large companion and gave him a yellow-toothed grin. "What do you think, Totts? Am I loose'n me touch?"

The large man's beady blue eyes twinkled as he grunted a guttural reply. Mat almost winced at the noise. The large, blonde-haired soldier, who answered to the name of Totts, had lost his tongue to torture – or so Leathers said – and now responded with grunts and noises that threatened to make Mat's skin crawl.

"You see!" Leathers barked and slapped the table, "Totts doesn't think so!" Leathers turned his yellow grin on Mat. "So I'm think'n you need ta show your elders some respect, lad, and turn those young ears ta me words!"

*'Elders,'* Mat thought with a mental snort of amusement. "Well, Leathers," he said aloud, "I certainly won't apologize for being lulled to sleep, but I will raise you ten talons."

As Mat flipped the coins into the growing pile in the center of the table, Leathers laughed gleefully. "Oh, lad, that'll do for an apology!" Both Leathers and Totts matched the wager as the old soldier remarked, "I'll give ya this, lad – ye either got huge stones . . . or are dumber than ah drunken mud crow."

Mat smirked. "So, you were saying?"

Leathers looked up from his celums. "Eh? Oh, yeah. . . . Well – ye didn't hear it from me – but tha other day, a group of clansmen came into tha keep with tha body of one of their dead."

"Seems odd," Mat prodded.

"Oh aye, aye," Leathers responded as he idly shifted the celums in his hand before taking a swig from his tankard. "What was really odd, is they were hustled off, all quiet-like, ta some secluded part of tha Citadel."

Mat took a sip from his tankard to cover up his wince as he felt a surge of fir'gan coming from Kara's room. She'd been awakening from nightmares the past few days, and while it worried him, he hadn't sensed anything out of the ordinary. So, for the moment, he had chosen to ignore it. "Strange bodies? Clandestine meetings? Tell me – did you get a look at this mysterious body, or are you just trying to distract me?"

Leathers shook his head seriously. "I swear it on me dear ol' ma's grave; I'm tell'n you tha truth as I heard it from one o' tha guards stationed outside tha room."

Laughing, Mat prodded, "One of the guards, eh?"

"Ah-huh. Said he got a good look at tha body before be'n ordered ta burn it," Leathers muttered as he examined his celums. "What was it he said it looked like, Totts? Said it looked like giant black boils had been stretched over ah skeleton until they burst?" He nodded, answering his own question. "Said it didn't look like a human at all anymore."

Warning bells went off in Mat's head as he heard the description. While he was too young to remember the days of blackhearts, like everyone in every Order, he had memorized the signs of blackheart poisoning. Where Gifted were concerned, the virulent and ruthless toxin's influence was difficult to spot; however, the horrific death that the poison inflicted upon the mundane was impossible to miss.

As Leathers continued to ramble on, his words were lost on Mat as the young Warden noticed Kara at the bottom of the stairs. She showed no signs of whatever had caused her fir'gan outburst, but the look in her eyes and the pallor of her skin displayed unmistakable signs of sickness to Mat – and that tied his stomach in queasy knots. At that moment, he decided he had no choice but to report this to Darkon. While he might not have total confirmation of his fears, he felt that Kara's life was vastly more important than Darkon's ire if his suspicions turned out to be nothing.

Splitting his attention was a trick he had learned long ago, and it was a talent he'd used to great effect in gambling dens and taverns all across Solarson. Other players rarely viewed a distracted player as a serious threat, and routinely made mistakes. For Mat, however, this time it was about more than simply fooling an opponent so he could win a few coins. Relaxing his mind, he reached out along the currents of fir'gan with a portion of his consciousness and focused on Darkon's essence, hoping that the darlion wasn't masking it as he was prone to do. It took much longer than it would have had he been alone and in meditation – especially given the distance he was trying to reach across – but a few hands of pentagris later he found him.

"*Sir?*" he asked politely.

"*What?!*" came the irritated reply.

Mat winced visually, but managed to make it look like it was in response to his current hand. *"Is everything alright?"* he asked respectfully, but with a hint of trepidation.

Mat could almost see the scowl as Darkon replied, *"Nothing to concern yourself about. Now, what do you want?"*

*"It's about Kara,"* he stated hesitantly, sensing Darkon's foul mood.

*"What about her? Has she done something even worse than sending Emberscar to Triclose without my knowledge or approval?"*

*"No, sir,"* Mat replied firmly. *"It's—"* he hesitated and gathered himself. *"Well . . . I have reason to believe that she may somehow have been poisoned by a blackheart."*

There was a long, heavy and disturbing pause. *"Go on,"* Darkon said with a coldness that nearly sent shivers up Mat's spine.

*"Well, sir, it's a mix of information that has led me to this. Not only has she fainted, but there's bleeding from her nose, eyes and mouth without injury; then there's her pale skin, the occasional fever, and routine nightmares. At first I thought she might simply be . . ."* he shrugged mentally in frustration. *"I don't know. . . . It just doesn't seem right. Although she is still up and about and refuses to admit she's ill, I would say that it's been getting progressively worse for days now."*

*"Those are definitely indications,"* Darkon replied quickly. *"Have you encountered blackhearts on Triclose?"*

*"No, sir. But there are rumors abounding about violent deaths and shadowy creatures roaming the forests. I even have word from a reliable source that a victim of blackheart poisoning was brought in to the local authorities."*

*"Humph. There isn't a soul on that abysmal continent that would know what blackheart poisoning was if they were infected,"* Darkon replied with disdain, before demanding firmly, *"Are you sure?"*

*"As sure as I can be without seeing the body for myself — but they burned it soon after examining it."*

*"Prudent. But I don't like this."* There was a long, dark pause that began to make Mat every bit as nervous as Kara's condition did. *"You are positive that Kara is showing signs of poisoning?"* Darkon asked quietly but coldly.

*"I am,"* Mat responded confidently, but couldn't help but let his apprehension seep into his words.

*"I see. If you have not encountered them, then there is only one way that she could have been poisoned and the effects be advancing so slowly — Ember has*

*been attacked by blackhearts, poisoned, and, in all likelihood, is dying,"* Darkon declared as if it was nothing.

*"What?!"* Mat exclaimed in shock at both the proclamation and the casualness with which it was voiced. *"How can that be?"*

Darkon laughed, which irritated Mat greatly. *"There will always be things you don't understand, Mat. However, to answer your question – they are linked."*

*"Linked?"* Mat thought in astonishment, doing his best to keep it from seeping onto his face. *"You mean like the Bestynes?"*

*"Somewhat. Though this link is more visceral. Deep enough trauma or a violent enough injury, and the other one can feel it, suffer from it and possibly even die."*

*"That's . . . that's horrible,"* Matt replied in shock.

Darkon snorted. *"A horrible, disgusting mistake is what it is – one of many Luthur made."* Another long pause left Mat dreading what Darkon might say next. *"Mat – I need you to do something for me, and you won't like it."*

As Mat continued to play the game of Pentagris out while listening to Darkon's orders, his face slowly began to sink. He could not believe what Darkon was asking of him, yet he knew he would obey if the time came. His expression must have been horrible, for Leathers and Totts had noticed his fallen visage and were grinning broadly, thinking it had to do with his celums.

"Well, Totts, tha young'n looks like he's had a turn of luck for tha worst, judging by that expression. Guess that means we might be take'n some coin home after all!" Leathers quipped gleefully.

As Totts laughed in response, Mat couldn't help but think that Leathers had no idea just how badly his luck had truly turned.

*

"Damn it! No!" Mathis rolled his practice blade over Amroth's outstretched sword and spun in close before ramming his padded elbow into the back of Amroth's helmeted head, driving him to the ground.

Amroth still had not grown used to the thin wooden practice armor he was wearing and it showed as he awkwardly pushed himself up to one knee. Though his head was still ringing, the anger and irritation at constantly being batted around by Mathis over the last few days was clearly etched upon his normally solemn, handsome face. With a cry of frustration, Amroth sent his wooden practice sword sliding across the training room floor before tearing off his helmet and sending it after the weapon, both items rattling off the wall and coming to rest near the outer fighting circle.

Looking up, his black eyes glared in frustration at Mathis through sweat-soaked black hair that had slipped loose from his horsetail. "What in the hells are you expecting?!" Amroth barked. "I'm not a fighter!"

Mathis waved a dismissive hand at the comment and began to pace along the outer ring of the three fighting circles painted on the floor, trying his best to reign in his temper. They had spent the better part of the last four days in the training room, following a series of sporadic sessions during their first few days in Haltho, and while he understood that they'd only been training for a brief period and Amroth's instruction was limited to begin with, Mathis wasn't seeing the progression that he would have liked to have seen. The fundamentals were there, but the ability to execute was severely lacking. Not only did Amroth appear to be out of rhythm with the longsword, but he was stumbling over himself and thinking too much. To Mathis' chagrin, these were the same traits Amroth had displayed in abundance during his short time at the Academy. Mathis knew all too well that the one-handed and two-handed styles of fighting could sometimes leave an ambidextrous person uncomfortable and fighting one's self, but he also knew that the fundamentals of swordsmanship spawned from those fighting styles. Without a solid base of skills and understanding, attempting to dual-wield could be more dangerous for the wielder than an opponent. Yet, as he let his dark eyes scan the simple but functional room, Mathis wasn't so sure that tossing Amroth to the wolves – so to speak – wouldn't be such a bad thing.

The training room, roughly fifty paces by fifty paces, lacked windows and was lit by both a large chandelier hanging from the center of the ceiling, and candelabra in each corner of the room. Racks containing an assortment of real and wooden practice weapons lined the walls along with archery targets and practice dummies. There was even a row of benches, which were arranged in front of the weapon racks on the rear wall, that provided a place to sit. However, it was the weapons that interested Mathis. He had already picked out a pair of practice swords that would work well with what he intended to teach Amroth, but he was reluctant to issue them.

Halting at Amroth's discarded practiced sword and helmet, Mathis contemplated the sword for a moment. Shaking his black-haired head, his horsetail twitching with the movement, he kicked the helmet aside and decided to give it one more try. Looking at Amroth, he commanded sternly, "Get up."

Crouched down on one knee, Amroth glared at Mathis before slowly climbing to his feet. "I'm up," he said indignantly. "Now what?"

Scowling, Mathis slipped his foot underneath the discarded sword and flipped it to Amroth deftly. "Defend yourself!" Mathis barked, bringing his own practice sword to bear and charging with speed that belied the weight of the padded, wooden practice armor he was wearing.

Amroth barely managed to catch his wooden blade and ready himself before Mathis' upward arching slice was on him. He knew there'd be no time to recover, so he let his weight carry him backward, distancing himself from the series of fluid cuts that Mathis sent his way. As he reached the opposite side of the fighting circle, Amroth was finally able to get his feet under him and bring his sword into play. Solid, deep clacks resounded about the room as Amroth intercepted Mathis' attacks and turned them aside. Soon, Amroth had found a rhythm of his own – albeit a clumsy one compared to the elegant, flowing movements of his teacher.

Mathis grudgingly acknowledged to himself that Amroth was certainly putting serious effort into fending off the attacks. However, as he pressed his young charge, it became readily evident that Amroth was quickly losing his balance as he struggled to keep up with the quick attacks and sudden changes in direction. In a real fight, Mathis could have and would have easily ended Amroth's life with one of the early attacks, but these sessions were meant to teach, not kill. With his face set in a grim mask of determination, Mathis forced Amroth around the middle combat circle with a series of flowing thrusts, cuts and feints, none of which were intended to land a blow. Instead, the attacks were meant to force Amroth to learn and react.

Sadly, the ferocity with which Amroth fought them off showed not only a waste of energy, but an inability to control his temper and to calmly and quickly understand the situation. Disappointed, and confident about what would happen next, Mathis let his sword slide through a horizontal slice – which Amroth easily stepped back from – and rolled his sword back into a position at his waist for a low thrust. He could tell by the look in Amroth's eyes that the young Merandith saw the thrust coming, but Mathis went through with the attack anyway, feinting an overextension.

Amroth, as anticipated, brought his sword down in a parry that was intended to allow him to push Mathis' sword low before rolling over the parried blade for a riposte. As soon as Mathis felt the initial contact, he quickly shifted his weight to the right and spun away, leaving Amroth off balance and vulnerable. Without hesitation,

Mathis swiftly brought his sword around and down hard, ripping Amroth's sword violently from his grasp. Disgusted with the ease with which he had once again tricked Amroth, Mathis kicked the sword away just as Amroth was reaching for it. Snarling, Mathis then stalked over to the weapon rack along the right-hand wall.

Standing, Amroth spun around in irritation and threw his hands in the air as he barked at Mathis' back, "Are you going to tell me what that was about?! I thought that was better than before!"

Mathis ignored the complaints as he leaned his own weapon against the rack and picked up two practice swords that were fashioned in the vein of the short stabbing blades that spearmen and footsoldiers were known to carry for close-quarter fighting. They were not much larger than overgrown long knives – and certainly not what he would have preferred for Amroth – but they would have to do. Turning back to Amroth, he tossed the weapons one at a time to his tired charge, who caught them and proceeded to stare at them with a dumbfounded expression.

"It wasn't good enough," Mathis stated bluntly, as he retrieved his training sword.

"And just what am I suppose to do with these?" Amroth asked as he held up both swords for Mathis to see.

Mathis leveled an uncompromising, dark-eyed stare on Amroth. "You don't take well to the longsword – fine. You've proven that well enough both at the Academy and here. We both know that you're ambidextrous, so maybe if I stop trying to cram the basics with one blade down your throat and try things in a light your more familiar with, something might get through that thick skull of yours!"

Amroth gave a snort of disgust and rolled his wrists, giving each blade a twirl to get a feel for the swords' weight. He had to admit, Mathis was right. Although holding a sword still felt bizarre and somewhat wrong, the weight of a sword in each hand felt like it balanced him out. He gave each sword a practice swing, cutting through the air with authority, before glancing back at Mathis. "So, now what?"

Pointing at Amroth's left leg with his sword, he said, "You're stronger with your left hand, so I want you to step back with your left foot, toe open slightly." Amroth slid his left foot back and turned slightly to the side, which earned a nod of affirmation from Mathis. "Good. Like fencing, this position – while basic – will make you less of a target while keeping your strong arm ready to strike. Now, we won't try anything fancy, so keep your knees flexed with your right sword held before you like so." He held his longsword up before him, elbow slightly bent and wrist cocked inward so the sword angled across his body. Feeling somewhat awkward, Amroth followed suit, drawing a nod of approval from Mathis as he added, "Good. Now, with your left, you can do one of two things – you can hold it at eye level with your sword pointed toward your target, or you can hold it low and angled across your torso."

Amroth tried both positions, testing his balance and the weight of the swords. Neither stance felt very comfortable to him, but he finally settled for holding his left sword at eye level. "I guess this will work," he remarked with a lack of enthusiasm or commitment. "Still feels extremely awkward."

"Well," Mathis stated dryly before he opened his stance and slid into a slight crouch as he brought his left forearm up and rested his longsword across it, sword tip aimed squarely at Amroth, "at least you look more like you know the pointed end from the hilt now."

Rolling his eyes, Amroth replied drolly, "So now what?"

"What do you think?" Mathis asked rhetorically, his long muscles coiling before he launched himself forward.

To his surprise, Amroth held his ground with a grim and somewhat frightened look of determination on his face. Feinting a weak thrust, Mathis slid and spun to Amroth's blind side, bringing his sword around for a quick and decisive blow. This time, instead of connecting with Amroth's practice armor, a solid crack rang out as his longsword was intercepted by Amroth's right-hand blade in a sweeping parry. The parry was forced and too close to Amroth's body, but Mathis didn't have time to critique as Amroth used his strength to drive the parry wide before bringing his left-hand sword around in a sweeping cut. Mathis read the obvious move and deftly stepped back without fear of being hit.

He cracked a slight grin as Amroth recovered and reset. "Better. Still sloppy, but much better."

Instead of responding with a sarcastic remark, Amroth focused his anger and did something he had rarely done in the last few days – he attacked. Mathis was stunned to see him charge forward, and was even more amazed to feel a subtle shift in the currents of fir'gan as if they were trying to respond to a force that didn't quite know how to call to them. Amroth delivered a series of clumsily intertwined cuts and thrusts at his teacher, which were easily intercepted and turned aside. Not to be deterred, Amroth pushed onward, his speed increasing as his confidence in what he was doing grew. Mathis knew he could have ended Amroth's assault at any time, but he was both anxious to see what his student could do, and very curious to see how the swirling tendrils of fir'gan would continue to respond to Amroth's unconscious manipulations. Already, the young fighter was moving faster than most swordsmen could; in fact, his movements would have been close to a blur to normal eyes. Yet, even as Mathis gave ground and continued to easily parry or sidestep attacks, Amroth appeared oblivious to what was going on. It was as if he was in a trance and someone else was in control.

A firm knock on the training room door snapped Amroth out of his trance in mid-thrust. With a comically dumbfound expression on his face, his momentum forced him to overextend himself. Taking advantage of the gross opening, Mathis grabbed Amroth's extended arm and stepped into him, shoving his hip into his charge and flinging him through the air. Amroth landed violently on the floor, his swords knocked from his grasp and his breath driven from him.

Mathis stood over his stunned student with a wry grin on his middle-aged face, a hint of pride glinting in his dark eyes. "What say we take a break, shall we?"

Head spinning, Amroth nodded weakly.

Mathis' grin widened and he shook his head before turning toward the door and shouting, "Enter!"

The door creaked open and a guard poked his head in. "Sir, the lady you were expecting is here to see you."

"Send her in," Mathis replied, the grin on his face quickly vanishing. He had known the risk he was taking in sending the letter to Kara and knew she would be angry, but as Kara stepped into the room, he realized that he'd underestimated just how livid she would be.

Kara stopped just inside the doorway, her arms at her side, the fury that was building in her sky-blue eyes betraying her calm exterior. He noticed that she seemed unusually pale, especially in contrast to her red and black outfit, and that worried him greatly. However, his immediate concern was her brewing anger and the possible results.

Mathis took his eyes off her for a moment and nodded his thanks to the guard. "You're excused."

The guard nodded. "Thank you, sir," he replied before firmly shutting the door.

Mathis turned his gaze back to Kara and met her glare with a cold stare of his own. "Amroth," he stated firmly, "would you give us the room, please?"

Amroth groaned and climbed to his feet slowly. Upon seeing Kara, he cracked a surprised grin. "Oh! Kara! How good to see you! What brings you to my rescue?"

Kara pulled her eyes from Mathis and turned a friendly yet lukewarm smile on Amroth. "Your rescue?" she asked curiously, unable to mask her surprise as she watched ethereal tendrils of fir'gan slowing flowing away from Amroth as if they had recently been harnessed by him.

Oblivious to the real reason for her surprise and curiosity, Amroth chuckled dryly. "He's been teaching me to fight – although, I think he was simply taking pleasure in beating me like a dusty rug."

Kara looked back at Mathis and arched an eyebrow. "Oh was he now? It does seem like he takes pleasure in hurting those close to him at times, doesn't it?" Though Mathis' expression never changed, she could tell the barb hit home.

Before Amroth could respond to the curious observation, Mathis ordered firmly, "Amroth – please give us the room."

Sensing the growing tension between Mathis and Kara, Amroth looked back-and-forth at each of them before asking suspiciously, "Are you sure?"

Mathis nodded. "I'll be fine. Go get out of that armor, and I'll meet you in the dining hall for an early dinner in a bit."

Amroth suddenly felt like something was horribly wrong, and he was not altogether sure leaving was the right thing to do. However, he knew full well that Mathis could take care of himself, and was not one to be trifled with. Confident in that knowledge, he finally retrieved his swords and returned them to the weapons rack before making his way to the door. As he opened it, he hesitated a moment and looked back at Mathis only to find his teacher's scrutinizing gaze focused intensely on Kara. He spared a worried glance at Kara – who was equally focused on Mathis – before stepping out into the hall and shutting the door.

As soon as the door clicked shut, Mathis felt a surge of fir'gan as Kara not only barricaded the door, but also sealed them in a cocoon of air that would keep any sound from escaping the room. *"Not good,"* he thought.

A sudden rush in the currents, along with a brief glint of candlelight off the lavender ribbon interwoven in Kara's braided hair, was his only warning before Kara vanished in a blur and he felt a bone-jarring punch slam into the side of his jaw. The blow would have been enough to tear the lower jaw from a normal man's head, and for many Gifted, it would have been strong enough to shatter bone. Mathis, on the other hand, felt his jawbone crack as he staggered backward from the force of the blow. Recovering quickly, he righted himself and stared defiantly at Kara.

Even as his jaw began to slowly heal, he said quietly, "Hello, Sister."

Kara's jaw began to quiver and tears of rage began to well up in her eyes as the words she had feared left Mathis' lips. "Damn you," she whispered. "Damn you," she growled louder, tears running freely down her cheeks. Suddenly, her brow furrowed and her blue eyes flashed. "Damn you!" she screamed in rage before slamming a fist into Mathis' face, driving him back a step. "Damn you! Damn you! DAMN YOU!" she raged as she rained blow after blow upon Mathis, shattering armor and ribs, and breaking his nose and eye sockets. "DAMN YOU!" she wailed shrilly before hammering a blow to his chest, cracking his sternum and launching him into the weapon racks at the rear of the room, the impact scattering the practice weapons and stands.

Dazed, Mathis laid there as his fir'gan franticly repaired his body. For the moment, having vented her rage, Kara remained where she was, sobbing, her hands hanging at her sides. "Why?" she pleaded weakly through her tears. "Why didn't you tell me? So many lost. . . . So many dead . . ." she sobbed.

Mathis slowly sat up, his ribs and sternum already healed, and pushed himself to his feet. The remains of his wooden practice armor sloughed off, leaving him in his brown padded vest, black pants and boots. The skin around his eyes and nose was bruised, but that too was fading fast. Respectfully, he kept his distance, but if there was a hint of compassion in his eyes, it wasn't apparent. After a moment of consideration, he finally stated, "I swore an oath, Karalisa. Besides – it was my sacrifice to make."

Kara looked up at those words, anger flickering to life in her eyes once again. "Your sacrifice? Your sacrifice?! What in the hells do you know of sacrifice?!"

"All too much," he replied softly.

Kara laughed darkly. "The hells you do! You – who sold me into that sickening life! You – who betrayed your brother and family name in pursuit of delusions! You – who damned so many of our people to darkness! What in the hells do you know of sacrifice?!"

Mathis kept his eyes locked on Kara, but the weight of her words had hit home. "I know my failings all too well. No one needs to remind me of that," he replied in a soft, remorseful tone. "What I did . . ." he hesitated. "What I did was not easy for me – and I can only imagine what it was like for those left in the dark."

"Why not tell us?" she pleaded. "So many thought you betrayed us – leaving us to die, and the Darkness to slowly take hold." She sobbed, her fists clenching and unclenching. "Why did you betray us . . .?" She looked at him with pleading eyes. "Why did you betray me?" she breathed.

Mathis let the silence hang in the air like a thick miasma for what seemed like an eternity before offering, "There is so much to tell you, Kara – so much I *want* to tell you. However, the burden is mine – and mine alone – to carry for a while longer." He took a deep breath. "This wasn't the time or place that I wanted you to find out. But events are playing out in a way that even Luthur couldn't have foreseen, and my hand is quickly being forced." Kara's face told him just how baffled she was, prompting him to add, "I will answer what questions I can, Sister, but know that there are some answers that would put a burden upon you that you aren't ready to handle."

Kara scoffed and laughed. "A burden I'm not ready to handle? Corith be good! I'm nearly six thousand years old! What could possibly be so daunting that I can't handle it?" Mathis remained mute, drawing another disgusted scoff from Kara. "Fine! I'll play your game." She folded her arms under her breasts. "Let's start simple – where's Mathis?"

"He died in service to Luthur soon after his death," the man known as Mathis stated bluntly.

"Soon after . . .? Corith have mercy! What does that mean?"

Mathis simply stared at her.

"Fine. Then . . ." she hesitated, "how did he die?"

Mathis remained silent. This time, however, his refusal to respond told her everything she needed to know.

"Dear Corith. . . . You killed him, didn't you?" she asked breathlessly, even though she knew the answer.

"He– " Mathis started to say and stopped, picking his words carefully. "He volunteered to serve in a capacity no one else could. His death also made this," he pointed to his face, "possible."

"I'm not going to pretend to know what that means," Kara replied, referring to the original Mathis volunteering to die, "and your appearance certainly explains why no one recognized you. But," she peered closely at him, confused at how weak the currents were around him, "how are you masking your power? I didn't think it possible to

628

do such a thing in a manner that would make it nearly impossible to sense you up close without encasing your crystal in bone."

"I'm not masking it," Mathis stated bluntly.

"Not masking it? Then how, in Corith's name, are you hiding it?" Kara asked in earnest confusion.

"As I said, sacrifices had to be made."

"Sacrifices? What–" Her eyes widened in shock and her hand covered her mouth. "Oh, by the Light. . . . You didn't– "

"No," he said, cutting off the train of thought, "Not in the sense that you are thinking. Think of it more as a temporary separation."

Kara's brow furrowed. "But how are you still alive?"

Mathis tapped his chest over where his heart was. "I kept a tiny sliver – just enough to keep me alive and maintain my disguise, but very little else."

Kara suddenly felt sick as the implications of what he had done sunk in. She doubled over as the weight of it all, along with her growing illness, twisted her stomach. "This is. . . . This is just too much."

Mathis finally made a move toward her, his hands extended in an offer of help, but she waved him off. Once she had fought down the nausea, she straightened up. Though paler, her anger was finally waning. "When I came in," she began weakly, her voice gaining strength as she talked, "Amroth had fir'gan fading from him as if he'd just used it, and I also felt a foreign surge while outside. What is he that you would take special interest in him?"

"He is . . ." he hesitated again, unsure of how much of his feelings he should reveal. "He is someone of importance to us."

"Important to us? How so?"

Mathis shook his head. "I can't say – at least, not right now."

Kara wanted to laugh in frustration, but lacked the will to do so. "One of those burdens too heavy for me, right?" she asked snidely.

He nodded, but then added, "Sister, I will tell you that he has the potential to be a very powerful Warden. In fact, Triclose is thriving with unaware Gifted – many of which have the potentially to be quite strong."

"How many?" she asked, her curiosity suddenly perked.

He shrugged nonchalantly. "Hundreds, maybe thousands. Between the raw and wild way the currents seem to flow here and my current state, it's impossible to tell. Either way, the number has steadily been on the rise for the last century."

Kara blinked in amazement at the revelation. "I knew we were to Search for two crystals here, but what you're saying just seems impossible." She shook her head. "Ever since the last dragon died, the number of Gifted has dwindled over the millennia." She suddenly peered suspiciously at him. "You know why, don't you?"

He shook his head. "I can't be sure, but—"

Kara rolled her eyes and tossed her hands in the air at his tone, "You can't tell me – I know! Hells! You're frustrating no matter whose face you're wearing! And you're not even going to let anyone help you, are you?" When Mathis shook his head again in response, she sighed in frustration as her anger once again began to grow.

Sensing her growing aggravation, it suddenly occurred to him that she could be of help. "There is one thing."

She placed her hands on her hips. "And that would be . . .?"

"Amroth needs protection and training until he is ready to be told the truth. I could use your help with that," he offered.

"You seem to have forgotten – I have another task on Triclose." A sudden spasm in her chest forced a strong urge to cough on her, but she managed to hold it back.

Mathis sighed, "No, I haven't. You're task certainly takes—"

Unable to contain it, Kara coughed violently, the color draining from her face as she doubled over with her hands covering her mouth. Alarm bells went off in Mathis' head when the single cough blossomed into a series of brutal convulsions that practically had Kara on her knees. Severely concerned, Mathis started forward, but Kara waved him off.

Finally, the coughing subsided and she straightened up, her hands clenched at her sides in a poor attempt to hide the blood staining her palms. "I'm fine," she said weakly, her pale pallor and feeble voice betraying the reality of the situation.

Mathis looked at her with grave concern, oblivious to the trickle of blood seeping from one of her clenched fists. "That's a lie – there's no reason you should be sick."

She laughed darkly. "And there's no reason you should be wearing another man's face," she countered. Before Mathis could respond, she waved a tired, dismissive hand at him. "I've had enough of this. I have a Search to perform, and after that . . ." she shook her head in a mixture of confusion and frustration. "After that, I'll consider your words."

Mathis hardly heard a word of what she said, nor did he pay attention to her departure as his mind struggled to make sense of what was bothering him about Kara's apparent illness. Long after her barrier had faded and he felt her use her fir'gan to speed her away from the Citadel, Mathis remained rooted to where he stood, his mind racing. He had intended to warn her about the blackheart presence on Triclose, but in the face of Kara's anger – not to mention his shock at her unhealthy state – he had forgotten to do so. Then, like a battering ram crashing through a gate, a slight glint of red on the floor caught his attention. His breath catching in his throat, he approached with apprehension and knelt down to examine it.

The red splotch was blood.

Dark and viscous, it looked unhealthy . . . tainted. Then he noticed a subtle smell in the air, like the stench of a rotting corpse, and his eyes widened in horror. Like a death blow, he finally connected her illness to the original reason for their meeting, and knew the situation was far, far worse than he could have ever imagined.

With that revelation, he knew that any illusion he had about maintaining his charade was gone. He had failed his family too many times in the past, and knew that to do so now, would result in a tragic loss he was not prepared to accept. Oaths be damned – he would not fail them again.

*"Move,"* he thought to himself before standing and walking toward the door. *"Move!"* he thought again, and his pace quickened. *"MOVE!"* he raged at himself, and then he was through the door and running.

The halls of the Academy were a blur as he raced through the strategically narrow corridors, nimbly dodging anyone he encountered. The main door was open and Mathis barreled through, leaping the five steps to the ground and racing across the parade grounds to the rear entrance of the Citadel. Noting his frantic approach, the guards there called out to him, but he ignored them. Bewildered, the guards watched as he shouldered open the door and ran down the stairs within.

His stunningly fast pace soon had him racing through the side entrance of the dining hall. To his relief, the hall was empty except for a trio of scullions cleaning tables in preparation for the evening meal, and Amroth, who was just about to sit down with a plateful of food. Freshly adorned in a loose, comfortable white wool shirt, brown breeches, and supple black knee-boots, Amroth paused in the middle of sitting down as Mathis' echoing footsteps caught his attention.

Amroth didn't need Mathis' frantic pace, or the fact that his teacher and friend was still dressed in his armor padding, to convince him that something was wrong – all it took was the unusual and shocking sight of panic and fear in Mathis' eyes.

"What is it?" he shouted as Mathis drew near.

Not bothering to stop, Mathis shouted back, "Come on! Kara's in danger!"

"In danger?" he asked as Mathis rushed by, confused that he wasn't turning to go back to the Academy grounds. "What do you mean?!" he shouted at Mathis' retreating back, bewilderment filling his voice.

"Come on!" Mathis shouted urgently and angrily in reply, not bothering to slow down.

Left with little choice but to follow, and with his muscles still aching from the training session, Amroth started-off at a full sprint and swiftly caught up with Mathis. The pair barreled through the circular layout of the Citadel as they hurriedly made their way to the lower levels and their rooms, leaving a trail of both perplexed and angry people in their wake. By this point, Amroth was hopelessly confused. If Kara was in trouble as Mathis said, then why were they running away from the Academy? Their pace made it impossible to ask for clarification, so Amroth simply concentrated on keeping up with him.

As soon as they reached their rooms, Mathis pulled his key from under his shirt and snapped the lariat that held it around his neck. Unlocking the door, he shoved it open and made an arrow-straight shot for the bed at the back of the simple room. Pulling his pack and a long wooden case from underneath it, he tossed both on the bed.

Out of breath and leaning against the doorframe, Amroth watched as Mathis tore into his pack and remove a large, heavy leather pouch that he had never seen before. As Mathis tied the pouch to his belt, Amroth noted a lone star sigil on it that he was unfamiliar with. "What's going on?" he asked, a wellspring of suspicions and questions battling for supremacy in his mind.

"Kara's in danger," Mathis reiterated as he moved purposefully to the wardrobe cabinet in the back-left corner of the room and opened it. He immediately found what he was looking for and, turning, tossed the item to Amroth. "Put it on."

Amroth caught what he thought was a tangle of heavy leather straps, padding and a long row of steel scales. "What's this?" he asked even as it dawned on him what the leather contraption was. The long row of steel scales joined a thick leather belt to a pair of padded shoulder straps, which, in turn, could then be secured at the center of the chest by a lighter strap and buckle. Amroth raised a questioning eyebrow as he noted an odd support anchored to the left shoulder and right waist.

"It's a battle-harness of my own design," Mathis stated as he quickly unsealed the wooden case. "I'd hoped to finish it before presenting both it and these to you at a better time, but," he flipped the lid open and removed two gently sweeping, elegant bluesteel katanas from the case, "sometimes things don't go as planned."

Amroth, in the middle of securing the harness' heavy belt buckle, stared at the gleaming bluesteel blades. "They're beautiful," he breathed.

"Secure the harness," Mathis ordered. "As much as I'd like you to have the time to relish the gift you are receiving," he added as he stepped behind Amroth, "we don't have time for such an indulgence." He slid one sword and then the other into the supports on the back of the harness, which left both hilts splayed over Amroth's left shoulder.

"Are you going to tell me what's going on?" Amroth asked as he finished buckling his new harness.

Sweeping up his own katana from next to his bed, Mathis walked over and clapped Amroth on the shoulder as his student turned around and fixed him with a worried look. "If we get there in time, hopefully I won't have to," he stated cryptically before stepping into the hall and running for the stairs.

"Great," Amroth muttered as he followed Mathis out the door and shut it before breaking into a run. "More mysteries."

# Chapter Twenty-Eight

*T*he early evening rain had ceased before her hasty exit from the Academy, and slivers of red light from the setting sun were now doing their best to pierce the slowly dispersing clouds. As Kara leapt from rooftop to rooftop on her way back to the Sailor's Roost, the rush of the untainted, brisk night air felt refreshing against her fevered flesh. Her bout of illness was fading, but she could still feel the nauseating darkness lingering at the edge of her perception like a voracious predator. She knew all too well that she was growing gravely ill, and the shortlist of things that could make a Gifted or Warden ill – or even worse, kill them – was littered with horrific things. She was painfully aware that she had not encountered any of them, and that terrified her – though she would never show it. Through process of elimination, the source of her illness had become clear, and the fact that the sickness wasn't fading was ominous.

Kara came to a halt on a blue-tiled roof in the shadow of the wall protecting the Tradesman's Terrace. Crouching low, she checked to make sure that there was no one on the battlements or on the ground before leaping high into the air and over the wall. With a long, languid flip, she landed nimbly on the flat, gravel-covered roof of what appeared to be a small inn. Before she could move, a fierce coughing fit overcame her, forcing her down to one knee.

When the coughing faded, she muttered hoarsely, "Damn," before spitting out a wad of bloody phlegm. She gave herself another moment to recover before continuing her light-footed journey across the rooftops of Haltho.

Two blocks from the Sailor's Roost, she dropped down to street level, and landed in an offal-strewn alley that reeked of weeks' worth of old food, sour beer, and human waste. Steadying herself against a wave of dizziness, she made her way to the mouth of the alley and peered into the dimly lit street. There was still plenty of foot traffic this early in the evening as sailors and citizens alike finished their business for the day and sought food and entertainment for the night. Composing herself, she gathered her cloak about her and slipped into the flow of people, keeping as casual a pace as she could despite her every instinct urging her to move faster. She wanted to get her initial Search over with as fast as possible so she could seek out Ember and confirm what she did not want to believe.

As she approached the poorly maintained exterior of the Sailor's Roost – the faded sign of which was painted with a crow in sailor's garb seated in what seemed like an uncomfortable nest – she felt that she could no longer deny that blackheart poisoning was the source of her illness. Granted, she still needed to confirm it, but the symptoms were all there, and the only way she could have contracted it was via her link to Ember. While he wasn't immune to the virulent miasma, his draconic blood should have been enough to fend off the poison in large doses. So for him to have grown ill enough for her to suffer the effects. . . . She shook her head mentally. She wanted to believe that blackhearts could not be on Triclose, but after her encounter with them back on Solarson, she couldn't fight the feeling that there were darker things afoot than anyone was prepared to admit.

Ascending the rickety stairs, Kara shouldered open the warped door and was greeted by a face full of musty air and thick smoke. As she muscled her way inside, she realized that somehow there were more people packed into the common room than when she had left. Weaving her way through the throng, she occasionally caught a glimpse of Mat, who was still seated at the table beneath the stairs and fully involved in the game of Pentagris.

*"Probably draining the poor fools of every last talon,"* she thought as she reached the foot of the stairs and ascended them two at a time, anxious to reach her room.


Mat noticed Kara's arrival almost immediately, although he didn't show it. His communication with Darkon had left him with mixed feelings about his companion, but, as the evening wore on and he was able to think through it all, Darkon's orders made sense. In fact, it would be a mercy. He watched Kara carefully as she weaved through the crowd, and was acutely aware of the fact that she looked worse now than when she had left. As she ascended the stairs behind him, he realized that her increasingly sick appearance was all he'd needed to affirm his belief that Darkon's orders were indeed a mercy. No one deserved to waste away from blackheart poison. Ever.

Sighing inwardly, Mat collapsed his hand and tossed the celums onto the table face down. "Well friends, I think I'm going to have to call it a night."

Both Totts and Leathers gave him a sour look. "Ah come on, lad!" Leathers bemoaned. "You've got ta give us a chance to win back some talons! You've near cleaned us both out!"

Mat chuckled as he collected his sizable winnings. "I did warn you."

"True. But I thought you were just a' bluff'n," Leathers grumbled, earning a supportive nod from Totts.

Mat gave them a friendly smile as he stood and tossed five gold talons from his winnings on the table for each of them. "Just to show you I'm not a vulture," he added with a wink.

Leathers and Totts returned the smile. "Thank you, lad! Now we won't have ta rely solely on tha slop in tha mess!"

Mat laughed and dug into his pouch for two more talons before throwing those on the table as well. "If my friend has made our travel arrangements, I may not see you two again – so buy yourselves a nice relaxing trip to the Pillows on me."

Leathers and Totts exchanged surprised looks before Leathers exclaimed to Mat, who had just set foot on the stairs, "You're a saint, lad! Tha finest I've ever met! I swear it on me mum's grave!"

Mat shook his head and laughed at the exaggerated praise as he climbed the stairs out of the smoky common room. When he reached the second floor, the hall split to the left and right, and he immediately turned to the right. His pace was slow as he struggled with how he was going to handle things. He certainly wasn't going to rush to execute Darkon's orders, but he certainly was not going to let Kara continue to suffer through such a macabre fate. Upon reaching Kara's room, he paused for a moment to listen for any noise from within. Hearing none, he continued to the next door and entered his room.

Like Kara's room, it was small and cramped, and furnished with a single bed, a chamber pot, and a nightstand topped with a washbasin. His new supply-filled pack was stowed under the bed, and his twin, broad-bladed shortswords were resting against the foot of the bed in their scabbards. He hesitated briefly before grabbing his swords and belting them on. Settling the swords at his hips, he strode from the room and closed the door behind him before moving next-door to Kara's abode. He tested the handle to see if it was locked, and when he found it wasn't, he opened the door and slid in quickly, closing it behind him.

He found Kara kneeling in the center of the room, the simple, opalescent bone coffer that contained the crystals they'd been sent to Search for held reverently in her hands. Kara seemed oblivious to his arrival as she stared thoughtfully at the container with eyes that seemed to have grown a bit feverish.

636

"What are you doing, Kara?" Mat asked softly, concerned etched deeply into his words.

She took a moment to respond as she trailed a finger over the top of the coffer. Finally, she said weakly, "I know what you're thinking, Mat."

Mat swallowed, suddenly apprehensive. Though she had spoken softly, there was no doubting the certainty in her voice. "What do you mean?" he asked as nonchalantly as he could.

Kara looked up at him with bloodshot eyes and smiled weakly. "Neither of us are idiots – and I'm pretty sure you've already voiced your suspicions to Darkon." Mat started to protest, but Kara held up a hand to forestall him. "No need to defend yourself. You were right to do it."

Sighing, Mat asked, "How long have you known you were ill? And why didn't you tell anyone?"

Kara shrugged. "I've known something was wrong since before I passed out. As to why I didn't say anything – would it have really made a difference?"

Mat tried to find something to say that would reassure her, but instead found himself asking, "Is there anything we can do?"

Kara shook her head. "If it's as bad as I believe it is, I'm afraid there's not really anything we can do short of killing Ember and hoping it severs the link and the symptoms fade."

"But there's no guarantee that it would work?" Mat asked, already confident of the dreadful answer.

"No guarantee," Kara echoed.

Mat felt his heart sink. "I know Ember means a lot to you, but isn't it worth a shot?" Mat pleaded.

"Worth a shot? Probably – but I can't and won't do it." She fixed Mat with a firm stare. "And neither will I allow anyone to try."

Mat knew it would be useless to argue when she got this way, so he nodded and said, "As you wish." He then eyed the coffer again. "Are you planning on Searching now, then?"

"I am."

Mat let out a dry, cynical laugh. "I guess I don't need to mention that opening yourself to the currents like that could seriously speed up whatever is feeding through the link?"

Kara's solemn nod told him that she understood the possible repercussions all too well and had made peace with it.

Sighing and shaking his head, Mat said, "Fine. I see there's no changing your mind. At least do me the favor of moving this outside the city. Corith only knows what this could do to you, and the last thing we need is to chance that hellish plague getting loose in a city of this size."

Kara remained on the floor, gazing into Mat's eyes as if she was searching for something. Finally, she stood up slowly and said, "You're right – it would be safer. The forest isn't far away, and it should buffer us from civilization." Stepping toward Mat, she placed a hand on his shoulder and gazed resolutely into his eyes. "If anything fatal happens to me, burn my body to prevent any possible infection spreading."

Mat swallowed hard; he felt like he was hearing Darkon's speech all over again. "I understand. If . . . if it comes to that, I'll make sure your crystal is returned to your Order."

Kara shook her head, surprising Mat. "No. If it does come to that – I want you to find Mathis and give him my crystal."

"What?!" Mat blurted in astonishment.

"Trust me on this, Mat. Give him my crystal, and tell him . . ." she suddenly looked like she was going to cry, "tell him I'm sorry and I forgive him. Okay?"

With his heart breaking, Mat couldn't find the words to express his befuddlement, so he simply nodded.

Kara offered him a sympathetic smile before stepping around him and opening her door. "Good. Then let's get this done."

Mat followed her out the door and shut it behind him before they proceeded down the stairs and out the inn's front door. As soon as they found a deserted ally, they took to the roofs where they could speed their way out of the city.

As they deftly leapt across the cityscape, all he could think of was, *"I'm sorry, Kara. I'm so very, very sorry."*

*

The speed with which they rode through the streets of Haltho bordered on insane. Not only did Mathis and Amroth's frantic ride draw its share of concerned and suspicious looks, but it also drew a litany of curses from the pedestrians that were nearly trampled by the mad dash. While Amroth could find no reason to blame them for their reactions, he was more concerned about the possibility of their mounts slipping on the cobblestone streets, which would easily be enough to break one of their mounts' legs and send both men careening into the street with enough force to kill them. If it had been anyone other than Mathis, he would question such recklessness; however, he had faith enough in the man to know he wouldn't push so hard without a very good reason.

Just as they turned onto the main thoroughfare that would take them to the Tradesman's Terrace, Mathis reined in his horse violently, causing the tired beast to rear fiercely. Struggling to rein in his own mount, Amroth just managed to avoid crashing into Mathis. Onlookers eyed the two with naked suspicion as they walked past the tired animals, but kept anything they might have said to themselves.

"What is it?" Amroth asked with apprehension as he swung his mount around and came up beside Mathis, who was, oddly enough, looking to the quickly darkening sky. Following his line-of-sight, Amroth could distinguish nothing but a sky rapidly filling with stars. "Ah, Mathis . . . I don't think this is the time to be stargazing," he quipped dryly.

Mathis appeared oblivious to his words, and upon looking around them, it was becoming clear to Amroth that both Mathis' violent halt to their proceedings and his statue-stiff gaze toward the sky were beginning to garner unwanted attention. Unease welling in him, Amroth reached over and placed a concerned hand on Mathis' shoulder. "Mathis," he said softly, "What's wrong? It's beginning to feel awkward with all these eyes on us."

When Mathis didn't respond immediately, Amroth's concern grew greatly. Then, as if awakened from a nightmare, Mathis' head snapped down and worried, angry eyes settled on Amroth. "Damn it! They're on the move!" he growled.

Amroth blinked in surprise and only managed to blurt out, "What?" before Mathis violently turned his mount about and started backtracking their route at a full gallop.

Sighing and shaking his head, Amroth spared one last glance and an apologetic shrug for the small crowd of gawkers that had gathered, and then nudged his mount into motion.

Moments later, he caught up to Mathis as he turned onto a side street that would take them west through the city. "Where are we going?" Amroth asked in vexation as he pulled up alongside him.

"They've moved outside the city," Mathis stated as if it were a simple, easy to understand fact.

"What?" Amroth asked incredulously. "I didn't see anyone! So how in the hells would you know that?"

Mathis responded by leaning further over his horse and urging it to faster speeds, leaving Amroth to catch up and deal with his growing frustration over a mounting pile of unanswered questions.

*

The wind felt refreshing as it bathed her fevered face in cool air. Even with her growing illness, she managed to set a pace that Mat was having difficulty matching. Racing to the west, they quickly made their way across the rooftops of Haltho, their footfalls so brief and gentle as to leave only the occasional wood groan or rattling tiles as evidence of their passing. Upon reaching the outer wall, they showed neither hesitation nor fear of being noticed by the Watch as they leapt skyward and soared over the towering wall to land gracefully on the other side. Kara had planned their route to put them well south of the main road leading into Haltho, so she hesitated just long enough to confirm both their location and that no one was watching before racing off into the distance with Mat in tow. Thankfully, there was no evidence of other travelers as they sped toward the Alderian Forest. However, if anyone had noticed their passing, they would have witnessed nothing more than a streak across their vision or a sudden breeze.

The journey to the edge of the Alderian Forest took only a matter of minutes, and they soon found themselves weaving amongst the trees as they moved deeper into the woods. In a swirl of dirt and dead leaves, Kara came to a sudden halt in a small clearing that was barely large enough to warrant the name. Mat appeared next to her a split second later, his dark eyes fixed on her increasingly pale complexion with concern. He wasn't sure if it was a trick of the sparse moonlight or not, but he could have sworn that he could see black veins throbbing near the surface of her skin at her temples and the corner of her eyes; furthermore, it even seemed like her sky-blue hair had lost its luster. However, he held his tongue, for he knew that once Kara had set her mind to something, convincing her otherwise was next to impossible.

"This'll do," Kara commented weakly as she moved to the base of a large ironwood and eased herself to the ground. Putting her back against the tree, she crossed her legs and settled in. Mat watched with concern as she closed her eyes and took a few steadying deep breaths. When she opened them, there was a sad, knowing glint to them that tore at Mat's heart.

She cracked a weak smile as she read Mat's expression. "No, Mat, this is for me to do," she stated firmly, knowing what was going through her friend's mind. "Should my Search attract unwarranted attention, you're the only one strong enough to defend me . . . or strong enough to make a run for it."

His face sinking, Mat started to say, "Kara, I– "

She shook her head weakly. "You've got a kind heart, Mat. Don't lose that as the years roll on."

The words were like a dagger in his heart, both from the finality of the statement and the suddenly devastating burden of Darkon's orders. He wanted to say something . . . do something . . . anything to avoid what was quickly becoming unavoidable. Instead, he found himself simply standing there, painfully aware that there was nothing he could do to change the fate that had befallen her . . . or his grim task.

Seeing the heart-wrenching conflict written on Mat's face, Kara smiled weakly and held up the coffer before her. "Let's get this done, shall we?"

Mat nodded slowly as he took up a position across from Kara, his hands settling heavily on the hilts of his swords.

Placing the opalescent bone coffer on the ground before her, Kara reverently unlocked the latch and lifted the lid, allowing vibrant-blue and dark-red light to spill forth from the container. The gently pulsing lights filled the small clearing and bathed Kara in a mix of colors that made her pale skin – now riddled with dark, spider web-like veins – and fevered eyes seem even worse than they already were. Mat's grip tightened on the hilts of his swords as he watched her lift out a dark-red crystal that was nearly the size of a man's fist. He could see the pain in her eyes and movements, and he desperately wanted to end the suffering that she was valiantly fighting to hide. Yet, he knew she was right – given her condition, she was the only one to do the Search, and he was the only one that could guard her and continue the mission. As much as he didn't want to admit it, Kara was choosing to make the ultimate sacrifice for the good of them all. He would honor that, but only to a certain point. No one deserved to suffer a death at the hands of blackheart poisoning – and he would make sure she didn't suffer any more than what was necessary.

Kara held the gently throbbing crystal before her eyes, examining the beauty of the red crystal as if she would never see such a thing in her life again. Finally, she cupped the crystal in both hands and held it in her lap before offering Mat one last sad, apologetic smile. She then took a deep breath and closed her eyes, turning her focus to the crystal and the job at hand. Mat watched as the ethereal blue ribbons of fir'gan that were drifting aimlessly about them suddenly shuddered and began to flow toward Kara. For a moment, the currents simply pooled about her. Then, a sudden pulse rippled through the currents before the tendrils swirled into the air and engulfed her in a cocoon of breathtaking blue light. The pulsing light of the red crystal then began to shift its rhythmic dance as Kara slowly synchronized the pulsing of the crystal to her heartbeat.

Suddenly, the light wavered and Kara's brow furrowed as the poison in her threatened to interfere with the process. Mat could see sweat beginning to bead up on her face despite the cold temperature, and he found himself wondering if she was truly capable of the task.

His concerns were answered, for the moment, when the spasmodic light finally settled into a normal rhythm and Kara's face relaxed. *"You can do it,"* he silently urged her on.

Yet even as he offered his silent encouragement, he could see wisps of darkness about the edges of her body that seemed to be eating away at the ethereal blue currents. Mat swallowed hard and his grip on his swords tightened even further. He'd never borne witness to anything like this, but it was evident that – as he had feared – drawing this deeply on the currents was increasing the flow of poison through the link, which could only serve to expedite her fall into death's embrace.

To his chagrin, Mat could do nothing but watch, wait, and grow more and more concerned with each passing minute. Then, without warning, Kara's body began to twitch and the cocoon of fir'gan around her began to waver. More of the dark, spidery veins began to creep across her face and hands as sickly black blood began to seep from her nose and the corners of her eyes and mouth. Suddenly the currents fell away from her like an avalanche and she pitched forward, the crystal tumbling from her hands as she collapsed on the ground, her body convulsing uncontrollably.

"Kara!" he shouted in alarm as he bolted to her side. Wrapping her in his strong arms, he did is best to stop the convulsing, but it was to no avail. Thinking that fir'gan might succeed where brute strength failed, he released her and stood back before he tried binding her in a cocoon of air. To his horror, the fir'gan sloughed off of her like water on a well-oiled cloak.

Then, without warning, black blood spurted from her mouth as a violent convulsion tore through her body. Even though none of the blood came anywhere close to touching him, he took an instinctive step back as he whispered in alarm, "Oh, dear Corith. . . ."

Hopelessly lost as to what he could do, he simply stood there, unable to tear his wide-eyed vision away from the ghastly sight of Kara's spasming body; granted, it was only for a moment, but it seemed like an unbearable lifetime to his anguish-riddled mind. When he finally did move, rubbing his face in an attempt to settle his nerves, he realized that, like it or not, there was no time or chance now to find Emberscar and potentially end this without killing Kara.

Heart sinking, he knew what he had to do.

Steadying himself, he drew both his swords and turned his thoughts inward, searching for the fir'gan that was buried deep within his own essence. Finding it, he latched on to it and drew it forth with practiced ease before channeling it into his weapons. With the infusion of catalytic power, the swords began to shimmer and lose their mass, dissolving into tiny balls of blue light that rose into the air and faded away. When the blades had fully vanished, he held his hand before him, palm up, and in it coalesced an orb of bright blue energy.

With his eyes full of anguish, he whispered, "I'm sorry, Kara," as he clasped his hand around the orb of energy.

The orb gave way beneath his grip and expanded outward from both ends of his hand. As the energy reached its limits, each end curled gently backward before the entire mass solidified with a flare of blue light. When the light faded, Mat was left holding the red-leather-wrapped, two-handed grip of a ten foot long bluesteel glaive. Simple, round collars separated the grip from the two foot wide, sweeping blades that seemed to shimmer as the blue runes etched down the center of each wing throbbed with power. Giving the glaive a twirl, the weapon cut through the air with a mournful cry that seemed to echo Mat's inner turmoil before he settled the giant weapon at his side. Moving closer to Kara, he looked down on her shaking form and felt his heart clench with a mix of fear, sadness and regret.

"I'm so sorry," he whispered before taking a two-handed grip on his glaive and raising it high in the air. Poised to strike, he hesitated for only a moment before, with a frustrated cry of anguish, he thrust down with all his might.

\*

Blood and froth dotted the noses and mouths of their exhausted horses as Mathis pushed the beasts beyond their limits. Amroth had no doubt that if they continued at this pace, then their mounts would die out from under them. They had raced through the streets of Haltho with a reckless pace and had somehow maintained it well beyond the new outer wall construction. It quickly became apparent that their destination was the Alderian Forest, and the reason for it was beyond Amroth. There was no way that he knew of, other than the surreal ride on Ember that he had experienced, that someone could travel that far in such a short span of time. However, other concerns occupied him at that moment. With night now firmly holding sway over the sky, their pace had gone from being extremely risky to downright suicidal. He could barely make out Mathis in front of him, let alone the night-covered ground. At this pace, they were more likely to step in a hole than to live through the night.

"*Damn it! You stupid child!*" Mathis suddenly roared as he jerked his mount to a stop, causing Amroth to pull on his reins violently.

As his horse reared in protest, Amroth fought to stay in the saddle and calm his ride. When he had managed to bring his horse under control, he looked around to see if Mathis was alright. Thankfully, he saw him only a few paces away, already dismounted and stalking back toward Amroth. Stunned to see the intensity burning in Mathis' dark eyes, Amroth remained in the saddle, unsure of what to do.

"I'm not going to fail this time! I won't be late!" Amroth heard Mathis mutter as he strode up to him. Taking the reins from Amroth's hands, he barked, "Out of the saddle! Now!"

"What?" Amroth asked in complete, unabashed confusion.

"Down, now!" Mathis barked again, and this time the anger and urgency in his voice had Amroth scrambling from his saddle.

"Look, do you want to explain what we're doing all the way out here?" Amroth asked as his feet touched the ground and he started to turn to face his teacher. "I thought that we were– Hey! What are you– !?" He didn't get to finish as Mathis leaned a shoulder into his midsection and, with strength that he couldn't possibly possess, lifted him upon his shoulder as if he was nothing.

"Hold on!" Mathis barked.

Head hanging toward the ground, and with only one of Mathis' strong arms to hold him in place, Amroth had only a passing moment of confusion to wonder how, why, or what he should hold on to before he felt his stomach try to jump into his throat as they suddenly lunged forward. Though he couldn't see much more than Mathis' back and the ground, the blur beneath his black-haired head told him something that he knew he should find impossible. They were flying.

"*No,*" he thought as his brow furrowed in concentration, "*that's not right. We're . . . we're– Deo be good! We're running?!*" The sensation reminded him of riding on Ember – terrifyingly fast, but exhilarating at the same time. However, the undignified manner in which he was currently being carried served to destroy any enjoyment he might have taken from the experience. Still, even with blood rushing to his head, he couldn't help but conclude that his list of unanswered question had just grown considerably.

Although it was difficult to make out the ground beneath his head, Amroth did notice a change from grass to deadfall that indicated they had entered the Alderian Forest. It suddenly occurred to him that, at the speed they were traveling, even the slightest bump against a tree or a stray branch could inflict harsh and possibly deadly damage on either of them. He unexpectedly found himself praying that Mathis was in control of whatever was allowing them to move as fast as they were.

A moment later, everything around him began to glow a dull red, and he felt his stomach lurch as they slowed down just a bit and Mathis cried in anger, "No!" before he felt himself suddenly falling.

With a violent thud, he crashed into the ground, his breath driven from him, and found himself rolling until he smashed into the trunk of a tree, further dazing him. Groaning, he rolled over and, through swimming vision, he saw Mathis had a man pinned against a tree by the throat while, with his other hand, he struggled for control of what appeared to be a giant glaive that had glowing-blue etchings down the center of each wing. After all he had seen, and with his head swimming like it was, he could not find the wherewithal to question the absurdity of the sight.

"Let me go!" he heard the pinned man shout hoarsely. It slowly dawned on Amroth that the voice belonged to Mat, and with that realization, Amroth pushed himself into a crouch and looked around the clearing.

Bathed in pulsing red light that was emanating from what appeared to be a crystal as big as his fist, Amroth found the setting to be somewhat macabre. His eyes quickly settled on the prone and shaking form of Kara, not three feet from him. If not for her blue hair, he might have been unable to identify her. Her pale skin was littered with black veins and spatters of what appeared to be black blood. Amroth abruptly cringed as a rancid smell – which reminded him too much of a dead body left out in the sun for too long – assaulted his senses. Whatever the smell was, he realized that Kara was unquestionably in need of help.

Climbing to his feet, he stumbled toward her vulnerable form, but was brought up short by a loud grunt. Looking back at the struggling pair, he saw that Mathis was doubled over, apparently from a knee to the stomach. Mat, his face contorted in anger, walked over to Mathis and stood him up before landing a bone-shattering punch to his face that launched the veteran bodyguard across the clearing with the force of a trebuchet flinging its deadly ammunition. Mathis hit the ground with a resounding thud, then bounced and skidded to a halt.

Horrified, Amroth watched as Mathis, whose face was a bloody mask, somehow pushed himself slowly to his feet. The strength of the blow Mat had landed struck Amroth as comically absurd. He knew no one should have been able to survive it, yet, given everything he'd seen this night, seeing his bloodied teacher still standing suddenly seemed perfectly logical.

"Don't interfere, boy!" Mat called out to Amroth, drawing his attention. Turning, Amroth saw Mat approaching, the absurdly large glaive at the ready, and his purple-tinged, dark hair hanging wildly about his face. "This has to be done," Mat continued. "For her sake and ours – this has to be done!"

Initially, Amroth had no idea what Mat was going on about; but as the giant glaive was raised into the air, it dawned on him that Mat intended to kill Kara. Amroth wasn't sure what snapped in him at that moment, but he suddenly knew he could not allow Kara to die. He was well aware that he wasn't good with a sword, and it was obvious that Mat was an experienced fighter, which made his chances of stopping him slim even in normal conditions. But this was far, far from normal, and Deo only knew what he could do against that giant weapon. So Amroth did the only thing he could think to do – he charged.

With a growl, Amroth launched himself over Kara and drove his shoulder into Mat's stomach. Given what had occurred so far, he didn't know why he fully expect to feel Mat give beneath the force of the blow; therefore, he found himself not only confused, but dazed when he felt like he had just charged headfirst into a brick wall.

"Foolish boy!" Amroth heard a split second before a burning, tearing pain ripped through his body.

Amroth's eyes widened in horror as warm red liquid spurted from his mouth. As a spreading warmth crawled across his right shoulder and down both his torso and legs, his legs abruptly felt weak. Suddenly, the wall that was Mat was gone, and Amroth collapsed to the ground with a thud, though he could barely feel it. He wasn't aware of his hands clutching at his torn chest and shoulder, nor was he aware of the effort he put into rolling over so he could see Kara. He wanted to move. He wanted to help her. But for some reason, his body seemed distant and refused to function.

"Stupid, stupid kid," he heard in the distance as someone stepped over him, blocking his view of Kara.

"*Damn you, you bastard!*" Amroth heard someone roar. Then, like a bolder crashing into a wall, he felt the concussion of what seemed like a giant fist slamming into the man standing in front of him.

Slightly puzzled as to why his blow had glanced off of the katanas on Amroth's back, Mat looked up and spun in surprise when Mathis let out his angry curse. Caught completely off guard, Mat found himself amazed at the force of the blow as it lifted him from his feet and tore his glaive from his grasp. Shaking off his shock, he managed to right himself and land on his feet before he could collide with the wall of trees behind him. He quickly spotted his glaive off to the left of the dying duo and sprinted for it. To his chagrin, he was forced to pull up short as a booted foot slammed down on the glaive, pinning it there. Before he could react, Mathis' other foot came up and connected solidly with Mat's chin, flipping him through the air. Though nothing was broken, the force of the blow was enough to stun Mat as he landed hard on his stomach. Groaning, he pushed himself to his feet just in time for a charging Mathis to clamp an iron grip about his throat and drive him up against the solid trunk of an ironwood.

"What in the hells have you done?" Mathis growled, trying to restrain himself from attempting to kill Mat, though he knew that was impossible in his current condition.

Mat stared down at him with bloodshot, angry eyes. "My job! I have my orders!" he shouted hoarsely.

Mathis scowled deeply. "Your orders?! What bastard orders someone to kill a friend?!"

Mat clawed at the hands around his throat. "Dar– Darkon's orders!" he rasped.

Darkon's name only served to deepen Mathis' scowl. "Why?!" he roared and slammed Mat against the tree again, the strong wood cracking under the blow, to cut short his pawing.

Mat blinked rapidly to clear his vision. "She's got blackheart sickness," he gasped. "It can't . . . it can't be allowed to spread."

Mathis knew that to be true. Allowing blackheart poison to spread would be catastrophic. Yet, only a fool would think there was only one way to solve a problem. With a growl, he let go of Mat and stepped back, already pulling at the ties on his pouch.

Bent over and gasping for air, Mat's angry gaze focused on Mathis. "Who in the hells are you?" he croaked. "No Knight is that strong."

"I'm not a *Knight*," Mathis said bluntly, as he reached into his pouch and pulled forth a golden disc, its center set with a blue crystal.

Mat's eyes widened in surprise. "Where in the hells did you get a portculim disc?" he asked as his face screwed up in confusion. "Just what are you going to do with that?" he rasped.

Mathis threw the disc violently against the ground, shattering the crystal. A streak of blue energy shot about chest high into the air before it began to twist and spiral outward, opening into a glowing, swirling blue portal. "Unlike your master," he spit, "I won't simply sacrifice Kara. Nor will I let Amroth die."

"There's no helping either of them," Mat stated firmly, still rubbing at his bruised throat.

Mathis turned his back on Mat, stating, "Perhaps. But I learned long ago that not trying is as good as surrendering to one's enemy." Mathis then stepped to the portal and paused. Looking back at the slowly dying forms of Amroth and Kara, he declared bluntly to Mat, "When I come back, if you're not here guarding these two with your life – or if they are dead – there won't be a corner of Kylir where you can hide. By blood, by honor and by deed, this I swear." Not waiting for an answer, Mathis stepped through the portal and vanished.

Mat was stunned by not only the use of such a rarely used and strong oath, but by the fact that the portal did not dissipate as they were designed to do. Part of him was tempted to follow Mathis to see where he had gone, while another part of him screamed for him to flee. He even – albeit briefly – considered retrieving his glaive and putting an end to the dying duo, but the veracity of the oath held him in check. There wasn't a single part of him that believed the oath was simply bluster and, after the strength Mathis had exhibited, that terrified him.

Stumbling over to his glaive, his shocked and confused eyes focused on the dying pair, he sat down beside it to wait.

*

The cavern was vast. So large, in fact, that even the light of the torches, which were mounted on stands that were arranged around a marble disk at the center of the cavern, were unable to reach the ceiling. Two towering steel doors at the rear of the cavern loomed over the circle of light like an ominous deity preparing to pass judgment. Standing as tall as five average men stacked on each other's shoulders, the gate was snuggly recessed within a relief-carved marble archway. Torchlight poured over the doors and danced over the archway's carvings, casting the portal and its housing into hues of red and orange. At the peak of the arch was the roaring dragon sigil of House Gravit'nas, which served as the origination point for the finely carved and amazingly detailed dragons that twisted and turned their way down the archway. Some of the dragons appeared to be at play, while others appeared to be locked in combat. It would have been a beautiful sight to behold if not for the unnerving way the eyes of the dragons seemed to follow anyone that happened to be in the cavern.

The torches at the center of the room began to waver as if a sudden gust of wind had originated at the center of the circle they created. The pure-blue crystal that surmounted the center of the disk began to pulse slowly before quickly gaining in strength. Suddenly, a bolt of blue light jumped from it, cutting a vertical slash through the air before spiraling outward to form a glowing blue portal just above the crystal. A moment later, Mathis stepped through the portal, his determined black gaze focused on the gate. Making no attempt to move, he stood his ground as if he was expecting something.

It took only a moment before he saw what he was waiting for. At the center of the double doors was a pair of concentric rings that surrounded a central carving. The inner ring was composed of circular recessions, fourteen in all, that surrounded a carving of two dragons circling one another, their taloned feet locked together and their eyes gazing out upon the world. The outer ring, however, was where his gaze was focused. Consisting of carved script in a language that was ancient beyond anyone's wildest dreams, the words began to glow with a cold blue light that swiftly spread to the ring of circular recessions. Once each of the recessions was filled, the eyes of every dragon along the archway began to glow the same cold blue light.

"It's been a long time, my friend," a voice seemed to echo from the doors.

"Too long," Mathis conceded.

"I have done my job well – no one tainted by the Darkness has breached the Valley."

"That is good to hear, but I am afraid I'm in a hurry and cannot chat."

"You know as well as I do, time is a matter of perception," the male voice echoed.

Mathis did his best to fight down his frustration. "I do indeed. But lives depend upon me retrieving what has been sealed in here."

"Ah – then it is finally time, then?"

"Earlier than I would have liked, and more urgent than I could have ever imagined," Mathis admitted, quickly losing patience with the Valley's gate.

"If you retrieve what you have come for, then I will not be able to protect Luthur," the voice stated with what seemed like sadness.

"Only his body will remain," Mathis answered bluntly.

"Ah, I see then. What will my purpose be then?"

Mathis sighed. "You will be a decoy then – a trap for our enemies. The power remaining in the Valley will be enough to keep their focus here for a while longer."

"Ah," said the voice with a hint of joy. "That will suit me just fine." Suddenly, the seal at the center of the doors flared with light, and a line of energy crept up the seam between the doors. "Enter and retrieve what you have come for, then. I will remain and guard my brother's body until it is time for me to rest," the gate intoned solemnly as the doors swung open.

"Thank you, Mathis," the man known as Mathis offered as he started through the gate.

"Master?" the voice echoed.

"Yes?" the man asked.

"There are powerful agents of the Darkness on Triclose, and some of them very close at hand. They will know that you have returned."

The man laughed, the dark and malicious sound echoing in the cavern. "Good," he stated simply. Then, with a flare of fir'gan, he sped off into the depths of the Valley.


The Utherian Valley – final resting place of Luthur Gravit'nas – was a land of perpetual spring and life. Vibrant plants and abundant animals occupied the small, perfect world without fear of the dangers lurking outside the Valley's impassable hills. Normally, every night and day in the Valley was one of peace and tranquility whether it be spent in the lush forests, by one of the crystal blue rivers, or – should one chose – within the heart of the Valley at the tomb of Luthur. However, on this night, there was a sense of suspense and tension that was notable to all the Valley's inhabitants – for the Valley knew its creator had come home. Through the currents of fir'gan, the Valley informed its denizens of this, and urged them to provide a clear and unhindered path.

As glowing wisps darted about in agitation and animals huddled in the shadows, the man sped through the forest like a man possessed. He had very little time to do what he had come to do, and as much as he might have wanted to stop and enjoy the splendor of the Valley, he knew he couldn't spare the time. So he ran like the warm wind that flowed about him, his journey aided by the Valley adjusting the normally winding path so that it ran straight and true to the center of the vale.

In a flash, he cleared the forest and came to a stop at the edge of the giant lake that occupied the center of the Valley. Bluish-silver moonlight slid across the mirrored surface of the large, pristine lake, whose waters lapped gently at the shore. On this night, a host of wisps danced and darted over the surface of the lake in nervous anticipation to the accompaniment of the roaring waterfall that emptied into the lake in the distance. Before him, an elegantly crafted stone bridge arched from his side of the shore to the island in the center of the lake, the white stone of the bridge seemingly aglow with moonlight. All that was enough to enrapture a person no matter their status; however, as the man strode forward, it was the object floating over the island that managed to make him pause.

The Sky Tomb – the final resting place of Doms Luthur Gravit'nas. To most, it was just a legend that they would only know of in word, but never see. Majestic in all aspects, no other creation on Triclose came close to matching its haunting beauty. Suspended in the air a few feet off the ground, it was inclined slightly to face the bridge. A frame of solid gold, which glowed softly in the moonlight, supported the six-sided coffin's clear crystal panels. The panels caught the myriad of light from both the heavens and the wisps before casting it about in a cornucopia of color. As he crossed the bridge quickly, his footsteps echoing off the stonework, he could see the runes that were etched into the crystal radiating a soft light. There also seemed to be a gentle, warm hum emanating from the casket.

Halting a few paces from the casket, the man bowed quickly, but reverently, to the man entombed within. Preserved by the magic of the Tomb, Doms Luthur Gravit'nas' body was clearly visible through the panels. Though long dead, he looked as he had before he had passed on – his skin and blonde hair untouched by the ravages of time. Adding to the grandeur of the Tomb, Luthur's body was encased in finely crafted, gold-plated platemail that had been meticulously etched with filigree by the finest of craftsmen. The gem-studded hilt of a ceremonial longsword was clutched in his hands over his heart, the polished blade of which extended just past his feet. It was a sight the man had not seen since Luthur's burial, yet it still managed to leave him speechless.

'*Focus,*' he chided himself before turning his attention to the waist-high marble plaque that had been erected before the casket. Runes were carved around the edges of the top face of the plaque, framing two phrases –

'*By blood, by honor and by deed, this I swear. . .*'

'*Hope*'

He could only hope that the second, simple phrase would hold true on this night. "Sorry, old friend, but I have to reclaim what is mine now. Events have unfolded in ways we foresaw so long ago – and many things have gone horribly wrong. I can only hope I'm not too late this time," he stated remorsefully.

Resting a hand on the plaque, the man fed a tendril of fir'gan into it and watched as the runes lit up one-by-one. When the final rune ignited, there was a momentary pause, and then a rumble in the distance. Then, suddenly, he could no longer hear the waterfall. Approaching the beautiful casket, he place a respectful and reverent hand on it for a brief moment before he departed at a run across the surface of the water as if the bottom of the lake was just below the surface.

In a spray of water, he came to a halt at the base of where the waterfall had once flowed, and was confronted by a wall of solid, wet stone. Examining the wall closely, he quickly found the mark he was looking for. Carved nearly at eye level, a lone four-pointed star was barely visible in the moonlight. Taking a deep breath, he steadied himself and drew on as much fir'gan as he could before driving his fist into the stone with enough force to send chunks of granite flying through the air and cracks racing across the water-worn cliff face. Tirelessly, he slammed his fists repeatedly into the hole he had created, each blow digging deeper into the rocky surface and raining shards of stone about him. As the stone fell away, a wall of opalescent bone began to shine through in the moonlight.

Spurred on by the sight, his blows intensified. A moment later, having sundered the majority of the stone from the bone, and with his objective drawing painfully near, he forced himself to draw deeper on the currents than his weakened body should. Channeling the extra power into his blows, he pounded away at the bone wall.

Even as he felt the skin of his knuckles tear away and the knuckles fracture from the repeated blows, cracks began to show in the extremely hard surface. Finally, he broke through the thick wall and stale air rushed out to greet him. The hole he had created was big enough for both his arms, so he reached in and grabbed the back edge of the rim on both sides of him and pulled. Veins bulging against his skin, his face quickly turned red as he focused everything he had on dislodging the shimmering bone. Then with a loud crack, the thick bone gave way and Mathis fell backward as he flung clear two wall-size chunks of the opalescent structure.

Water and sweat dripping from him, he gathered himself and pushed to his feet before moving back to the gaping hole. Ducking, he stepped through the enlarged entry and into a small alcove. His eyes quickly adjusted to the dim lighting, and he found himself standing before a stone altar of unremarkable design. Upon it, rested three items that made his breath catch in his throat. On the left side of the altar laid the remains of a gently curving katana that was fitted with an artfully carved bone handle. The bluesteel blade was shattered into three pieces, each piece arranged as they would have been had the blade been whole. To the broken sword's right was a large, silver-clawed paw protruding from the altar. In its taloned fingers was clutched a silver crystal the size of a man's fist – which was missing three sliver-sized pieces – that throbbed with a dull light. On the right side of the altar was a simple opalescent bone coffer that was large enough to easily hold the crystal next to it.

The man knew the horror and pain that was to come, but he had no time to second-guess himself. Reaching out, he touched the taloned paw softly and it opened, freeing the crystal to fall gently into his waiting hand. Upon contact with him, the light of the crystal became tainted by a subtle, cold blue glow as it grew brighter and pulsed more fervently. Sensing a moan of bereavement from the Valley, he offered a silent apology to it.

It had been a long time since he had held the crystal and sensed the power that resided in it, and it almost made him light-headed. Shaking his head to clear it, he used a sliver of hardened air to cut through his armor padding and shirt, revealing his bare, heaving chest. He tried to steady his breathing, but it was no use. There was no way to get through this calmly, so with a final deep breath, he took a firm grip on the crystal and wrapped his hand in a gantlet of air that was made to cut. Then, with all the force he could bring to bear, he rammed the hand holding the crystal into his chest. His eyes went wide as agonizing pain ripped through his body. He tried to scream, but nothing came out of his painfully wide mouth except a trickle of blood. He wanted nothing more than to collapse and pass out – but he knew he could not. Instead, he forced his hand deeper into his chest even as blood continued to pump from the ghastly wound. To his relief, he quickly found what he was searching for as his hand connected with a solid, faceted surface where his heart should have been. Twisting his hand, he touched the crystal he held to the surface of the shard. There was a sudden, powerful lurch in his chest and his body convulsed violently, forcing him to withdraw his hand as he stumbled back toward the entrance and collapsed to his knees.

The currents of fir'gan began to swirl about him as they flowed into the gaping hole in his chest and bathed him in a cloud of ethereal blue power. He managed to close his eyes in dreaded antici-pation as he felt his flesh tingle from the infusion of fir'gan into every fiber of his being. Without warning, the tingling grew from a mild irritation to feeling like his flesh was on fire. He fought the urge to scream as he felt his skin melt, his muscles tear and snap, and his bones break, grow and realign over and over. Collapsing into a pile of smoking flesh and spasming limbs, the pain finally tore powerful, an-guish-filled screams repeatedly from his raw and bleeding throat.

Suddenly, from the core of his being, he felt a surge of fir'gan explode forth, shattering the bone and stone of the entry and burying him under a pile of scream-silencing rubble. The abrupt hush that descended on the Valley was deafening, and even put an end to the wisps' chaotic flight. Nervous with anticipation, the wisps merely hovered in place as the minutes crept by.

A flare of blue-tinged, silver light from the pile of rubble was the only warning given before the heap exploded outward, showering the lake and the alcove with stone, and freeing the wisps to dance about in excitement once again. Slowly, as if he were a child first dis-covering how to stand, the man stood up. Where once he had been shorter and bulkier, he was now tall and lean, his body defined by wiry muscles. There were no hints of scars or injuries on his lean frame, nor on his long, hawkish face. Slightly up-tilted coal-black eyes peered out at the lake from beneath a heavy brow on a face framed by long white hair. He took one deep, steadying breath after another as he felt the power of his crystal heart pumping through his veins.

*"So very long,"* he thought, exhilaration coursing through is veins.

As his senses returned to him, he remembered his purpose for being there. With a gentle tug on the currents, he cleared the alter of rubble to find that the remaining objects were unscathed – as he knew they would be. Swiftly, he gathered up the shattered sword, storing the smallest blade fragment in his pouch before tucking the hilt and the large fragments into his belt. With similar haste, he then collected the coffer and added it to his pouch. Turning away from the altar, he let his senses reach out in a way that they had not in close to two centuries, and the world came into sharper focus.

*"Oh yes,"* he thought, *"it is good to be back."*

Setting a grim, determined mask on his face, he gathered the currents of fir'gan to him and, with an explosion of water, vanished into the night air.

*

Mat didn't know what to do. Mathis had been gone for what felt like an eternity, and both Kara and Amroth were fading fast. If not for the tendrils of fir'gan that raced franticly through their bodies, both would have long been dead. Kara had ceased to convulse, but there was little doubt in Mat's mind that she was in horrific pain. Amroth, on the other hand, was as still as a corpse, his arms wrapped tightly about the gaping hole in his torso.

*"Probably already dead,"* Mat thought with a snort of disgust, even though the currents told him otherwise.

He was still having a hard time sorting out events, but how Amroth was clinging to life baffled him more than the enigma that was Mathis. Crusaders had been forged with the express purpose of killing both dragons and Wardens – or at least that is what he'd been taught – and such a devastating blow should have easily kill a normal person. Granted, somehow the swords on Amroth's back had deflected the blow enough so that it missed his heart – which would have severed any connection to fir'gan Amroth had – but the gaping wound should have been enough to kill him anyway. He snorted again and focused on the twin katanas strapped to the dying man's back. There was nothing unusual about the blades that he could see. Other than excellent bluesteel craftsmanship, they gave no hint of being fir'gan influenced; yet, he'd clearly seen and felt the slender blades deflect his crusader.

A tingling at the edge of his senses suddenly drew his attention to the glowing blue portal that hung in the air like a ghostly lantern. He could feel a surge of power coming from the other side of the portal, which he knew he should not have been able to feel. "Corith be good. . . . What in the hells is causing that?" he asked into the air as the surge vanished as suddenly as it had appeared. He couldn't imagine what had caused it, but he was glad he was nowhere near the origin of the surge.

A few more minutes ticked by before he felt another surge of power from the portal. It wasn't like last time, he realized. Something was coming through the portal. Scooping up his glaive, Mat sprung to his feet and prepared to defend himself.

A booted foot suddenly appeared from the portal and planted itself firmly on the ground. Mat recognized the boot and pants as those Mathis had been wearing, though they now appeared torn and shredded. As the rest of the man emerged from the portal, Mat's breath caught in his throat. It clearly was not Mathis. In fact, as the portal closed with a bang, Mat recognized the features from pictures Darkon had shown him. And in that instant, words Darkon had spoken to him long ago came flooding back.

*'You see this picture, Mat? This is the bastard that betrayed us and left us to rot. If you ever encounter him, capture him if you can, but his death will more than suffice.'*

The man's coal-black eyes immediately settled on Mat and – feeling both the power in the stare and that which was flowing from the man like a never-ending river – the young Warden knew true fear for the first time. The man standing before him was walking death.

Finding his voice, Mat managed to breathe, "Damion."

Damion nodded. "So you recognize your elders, boy," he stated in his deep, authoritative voice. "That's good because I'm going to give you an order – and I expect you to follow it."

Mat had never liked being patronized, and the anger Damion's tone had awakened was enough to cut through his fear. "Wait just a moment! Who are you to give orders? You're a damn traitor!" he retorted.

Damion gave him a dark grin. "That's Darkon talking. However, there's no time to argue. Once I've saved their lives," he motioned to Kara and Amroth, "then if you want to follow Darkon's orders and try to take me into custody – you're more than welcome to try." His eyes hardened on Mat. "Try to stop me before then, and I'll use your own crusader to gut you. Understand?"

Fear welling up in him again, Mat couldn't keep his eyes from widening as he nodded.

With another nod, Damion walked over to Amroth and crouched down. Rolling him to his back, he examined the gaping wound in the upper-right portion of Amroth's chest with an expert eye. A normal man would have been long dead by now, but the Theirigaldian blood was strong in Amroth – and with it came a strong connection to fir'gan that was deeper than any human could possibly have. The mere fact that the crusader-inflicted blow had not done its job spoke volumes about just how deep his connection to the ethereal lifeblood of Kylir was.

"Stupid, selfless fool," Damion muttered as he reached into his pouch and pulled out the coffer. Setting it down, he opened the lid and an emerald-green light spilt forth, pulsing like a strong, healthy heart. Damion then lifted the crystal from its resting place with reverence and turned back to Amroth.

"Dear Corith!" Mat breathed as his dark eyes came to rest on the crystal, the weight of what he was witnessing hammering into him like a Warden's punch. "That's Luthur's crystal! Darkon has been searching for that for years!"

"I know," Damion said succinctly as he tore open Amroth's shirt with a cutting slice of fir'gan.

Mat's eyes widened as he realized what Damion was about to do. "Wait! You don't know if– " He never got to finish his statement as, with a speed he'd never seen before, Damion weaved a protective barrier over Amroth's body, leaving an opening for him to escape, before plunging the hand holding the crystal into the young man's chest.

As the crystal settled into its new host, the currents of fir'gan responded by bathing Amroth in raw power. Suddenly, Amroth's eyes popped open and his mouth widened in a silent scream as the currents invaded him. As fir'gan rushed into the holes in Amroth's chest, Damion realized it was time to move. Withdrawing his hand, he then quickly stepped through his barrier and sealed it. A moment later, Amroth's wounds closed shut just before an explosion of emerald-colored fir'gan filled the interior of the barrier, obscuring Amroth's form from the others.

Watching the barrier expand and flex as it fought to contain the outpouring of power, Mat was astounded to see that Damion's barrier could withstand the force of a Joining – and that left him feeling like a mere mortal for the first time in a long time.

Ever so slowly, the pulsing emerald light began to fade and the barrier began to contract. Once he was sure it was safe, Damion carefully unraveled the barrier, allowing the excess power to bleed away in a controlled manner. Finally, the light within vanished and the last of the barrier dissolved, leaving a peacefully sleeping and totally unscathed Amroth lying on the ground.

Mat looked from Amroth to Damion and back, his mouth agape. "How did–" he started to ask.

"How did I know?" Damion finished for him. Mat nodded. "That would take longer than we have to explain," he added as he scooped up Amroth gently and stood up. Turning to Mat he ordered, "Pick up Kara. We have to move."

Mat nodded and moved over to Kara. With a thought, he released his crusader, the blue runes on the glaive flaring before the giant weapon dissipated in a wave of fir'gan wisps. When his twin shortswords reappeared in his hands, he quickly sheathed them before gingerly picking up Kara's unconscious form. She was extremely feverish and, as if she was wasting away from the inside, felt light as a feather.

Turning to Mathis, he asked, "Where are we going?"

"To Ember – I can't save her without him."

"You know where he is?" Mat blurted in surprise.

Damion arched an eyebrow at him. "You can't feel him? He's like a cancerous blot on the currents." When Mat shook his head in the negative, Damion scoffed. "Pathetic. But then again, I wouldn't expect any less from Darkon's tutelage." Turning his back on Mat before he could retort, Damion ordered, "Let's go. I sincerely hope you can keep up." Without waiting for a response, Damion seemed to simply vanish as he started running north.

Mat shook his head in sincere befuddlement before he too began running north. It was soon obvious that there was no way he could keep pace with Damion, but he was easily able to follow the trail of power the elder Warden left behind. He ran for nearly a half hour before he emerged onto the banks of the Doren'thal River and halted beside Damion.

The white-haired Warden glanced his way and said, "You see, there he is."

Mat was astounded to see that Damion was right. Before them – collapsed in the middle of the river – was Ember's massive form. Yet, despite his amazement at having found the dying drakuma, it was the sight of the other bodies scattered about the river that caught his attention and turned his stomach.

At least two dozen broken and bloated blackheart corpses were visible from where they stood, the rotting stench of the sullied corpses filling the air, and the ground around the bodies desecrated by their blood. His eyes then settled on the remains of a darker and larger form that was sprawled behind Ember.

"What in Corith's name is that?" he breathed with a mix of horror and revulsion.

"An abomination," Damion said as he started forward. "One I had thought wiped from Kylir long ago."

"Is it a drakuma?" Mat asked as he scrambled to catch up.

Damion snorted. "A perverse, twisted shadow of one."

"Corith be good," Mat said as he shook his head.

"Indeed," Damion responded darkly.

When they got close enough to make out Ember's details, it became apparent that he was in worse shape than Kara. His opalescent dark-red scales had lost their luster and most of them had fallen off, exposing flesh that had turned a sickly black. Most of his talons had fallen out, and dark blood had pooled beneath his broad head. The smell of death and decay was thick about him, and Mat was ready to believe that Ember was long dead.

Damion stopped in front of Embers head and – of all things – laughed. "Quite the situation you've gotten yourself into."

Ember's massive form suddenly shifted and his eyes opened, their molten depths lacking their usual fiery luster. "Ha!" he barked hoarsely, "I knew you couldn't stay away."

"Yes – well you and our sister managed to find a way to get me to give up my quiet life," Damion stated drolly.

Ember tried to laugh, but only ended up coughing up a chunk of gooey black blood. "Sorry to ruin your fun," he replied dryly as his molten eyes shifted to Amroth's limp form. "Well now, seeing him was worth holding on this long. I guess I won't be able to call him a boy after a few centuries."

Damion moved to the riverbank and placed Amroth on an untainted patch of ground before returning to Ember. "First thing's first – you've got to live if you ever want to see that day."

Ember gave a weak snort. "I'm not going anywhere. So do your worst."

Damion looked over his shoulder at Mat. "Bring her over here and lean her against his chest."

Mat nodded, dumbfounded by what he had heard, and moved over to Ember. Kara, Damion and Ember were siblings? He simply could not get his head around it, but it certainly explained Kara's fierce loyalty to them both. It also left his emotions concerning Darkon's order even more convoluted, which raised further questions that he wasn't sure he wanted answered any time soon.

Crouching down, Mat gently laid Kara against the blackened flesh of Emberscar's chest and backed away. "What are you going to do?" he asked, fearful of the answer.

"Try to save them both," Damion stated bluntly, his eyes fixed on Ember's.

Ember tried to snort again. "Corith knows I never thought I'd have to go through this again. You'll probably enjoy this – you cold-hearted bastard."

Damion shook his head sincerely. "No, I won't. I swore I'd never do either of you harm again – remember?"

Ember merely snorted.

Keeping his gaze locked on Ember, Damion ordered, "Mat – I want you to join Amroth and shield the both of you from what is about to happen. I can't spare the energy this time."

The graveness of Damion's voice brokered no room for argument, so Mat trotted over to Amroth's prone form and quickly erected a shimmering barrier of fir'gan around the two of them. "Will this do?" he asked, genuinely wanting Damion's opinion.

Without looking, Damion replied, "That'll do. But first. . . ."

There was a sudden surge in the currents as gouts of raw, angry fire erupted from every one of the blackheart corpses, the ravenous flames eagerly consuming the tainted flesh and land. A loud roar soon followed, announcing the arrival of a billowing blaze that quickly enveloped the shadow drakuma's massive carcass. Mat watched in awe as Damion not only ignited each fire, but also controlled and maintained them all at once without straining. Then, as one, Damion smothered the flames, casting them back into darkness.

"There, that's better. No more taint to disrupt the currents here," Damion declared before looking to Mat and nodding to let him know he was about to begin whatever it is he had planned. Then, returning his gaze to Ember, he said remorsefully, "I'm sorry."

Ember snorted. "Get it over with."

Mat had no idea what was about to happen, but he could feel a nervous anticipation flowing through the currents that gave him the impression that the forest knew what was coming and was somehow fearful of it and excited about it at the same time. Wide-eyed, he watched as Damion took a deep breath and opened himself up to a massive amount of fir'gan. He'd never seen anyone take control of such a large amount of power, and as he watch Damion weave a barrier between himself and his dying siblings that was unlike any he had ever seen, he suddenly felt like his paltry shield was going to be of little use against what was to come.

As Mat started to reinforce his protective shield, the ground around them began to rumble and shake. Then, one-by-one, ten foot thick pillars of stone erupted from the ground around Ember and Kara, their tips climbing twenty feet into the air. When the last of the pillars slid into place, entombing the drakuma and Warden, Mat watched in awe as Damion reached out along the currents and tore an equally thick slab from the ground. Elevating it to the top of the improvised cairn, he then lowered it into place with an ominous thud. As the slab settled into place, Mat had no idea what was about to happen, but his apprehension had his stomach twisted in knots.

Then Mat saw something he'd never seen before. Despite his years of practice, he could hardly follow the intricate weaving of the currents Damion had begun. The elder Warden deftly picked individual elements out of the currents as a chef might measure ingredients with a practiced eye. Accented by pure fir'gan that was tinged with Damion's own inner silvery power, Air was mixed with a generous portion of Fire, a bit of Earth, and even some Water before being fed in an unceasing flow into the cairn.

Suddenly, as the power built, Damion's aura flared into the visible spectrum, bathing the river in silver light. Mat watched in awe as the power grew and Damion underwent a change he had only heard about. The elder Warden's irises and pupils faded away, leaving his eyes a silver-flecked, solid white. At the same time, the skin around his eye sockets, running from just above his eyebrows to the corners of his mouth, began to darken. Then, almost as if his face was bleeding, the edges of the blackened flesh flowed to red, leaving Damion's face marked with matching red-trimmed fangs.

"Corith . . .! He bears the mark of the Death Bringer!" Mat breathed in shock.

There was another flare of power and Damion's aura expanded, a cold-blue glow tinting his aura. Suddenly, Mat felt like what warmth there was in the air was being drained from it. With a growing sense of dread, he watched as Damion extended his hand toward the cairn and the elements he had been weaving ceased their flow into the structure and altered their composition before building over his palm. As the temperature continued to drop, Mat wasn't surprised to see the river beginning to freeze over. And just when he thought it couldn't get any colder, it became so frigid that, if he'd been a normal human, his flesh would have started burning. A moment later, there was a small, powerful flare at the nexus of power above Damion's hand and a small, cold-blue flame burst to life.

"Coldfire," Mat breathed in awe. "By Corith — what has returned to this world?"

As he watched, the small, bluish-white flame floated away from Damion's hand and slipped into the cairn through a crack between the pillars. Damion then began to feed the same composition of power that had spawned the flame into the cairn, fanning the painfully cold flames with a never-ending flow of power. As Mat watched Damion feed the coldfire the fuel it so hungrily craved, the icy blue flames grew and eventually sprouted wildly from the cracks in the cairn, leaving the stone blackened and frosted wherever they touched.

Overwhelmed with awe and dread, Mat simply could not believe what he was seeing.

A sudden roar from Damion startled Mat and he turned his attention to him. His silvery aura had doubled in size, and the amount of fir'gan he was drawing on — at least as far as Mat was concerned — was beginning to grow dangerous. The ground around Damion began to crack, the virgin fissures draining the unfrozen water like a dog that hadn't drunk in months. With terrifying speed, the cracks spread, shattering the earth like one might snap a twig.

Watching the building power, fear gripped Mat's heart. "Oh Corith . . ." he managed to utter before the cairn exploded — violent, cold flames raging into the air as they spread to engulf Damion.

Mat stared in horror as the icy-blue flames rolled toward him in what felt like slow motion. Then, the flames hit his barrier and exploded as the two powers met. The last thing Mat remembered as he was flung from his feet, was the searing-cold arms of death embracing him before darkness consumed him.

\*

Far to the southwest, in the city of Chalin, two women were awakened from their slumber.

Silk sheets sliding from her naked body, Alestra bolted up in bed as the wave of power washed over her like a lover's caress. Her amber eyes shone as she recognized the source of the powerful outburst. Grinning, she laid back down, her mind racing with all the juicy implications of what had just been revealed.

Deep in the mansion's cellar, Flute looked up from where she had been huddled in the corner of the closet that served as her room, her eyes red as frozen tears slid down her cheeks. She pushed her snow-blue hair from her face as she recognized the source of the power. She had not felt its touch in so long that it almost felt too good to be true — but it was there, and it was real.

Then, for the first time in a long time, she smiled a genuinely warm, joyous smile.

*

Far to the north, where the mountains ended and an endless sea of snow and ice began, a small party of travelers had stopped to rest for the night in the shelter of a cave. They were known as the Ice Walkers – a group of Northerners viewed with a mix of fear and awe. They dressed in the furs of giant white bears and the skins of seals that inhabited the frozen lands they called home. Each and every one of them wore a mask made of bronze that was fashioned into a wailing face. It was a disturbing sight to behold in any situation, and made people very uncomfortable around them – which many suspected was exactly what the Ice Walkers wanted.

While the main body of the party took shelter in the cave, one man had made his way to an icy outcropping overlooking the cave. One leg couched and the other hanging over the deadly drop to the frozen earth below, he sat there idly tossing a dagger into the air. Sensing the wave of power, he sat forward and caught the dagger deftly. Recognizing the source of the power, his lips twitched behind his mask.

Suddenly he began to laugh – full-throated and full of maniacal glee. Then, with his dark eyes ablaze with anticipation and delight, he whispered into the wind, "Let the games begin, old friend."

# About the Author

Born and raised in the Southeastern United States, J.M. Williamson has always been an avid fan of fantasy in its many forms. He developed a love for writing, myths and fantasy lore at an early age; as a result, he wrote and fleshed out many stories to hone his skills throughout the years. His training mainly came from observation of other authors and entertainment media, as well as formal training in the development of video games and their plotlines. The Dracus Saga combines Williamson's love of fantasy and history with some of the more outlandish features of comics and manga to create a style of writing and fantasy storytelling unique to him.

www.ingramcontent.com/pod-product-compliance
Lightning Source LLC
Chambersburg PA
CBHW070147120726
47909CB00001B/12